P9-CNI-897

POOR
RICHARD'S
LAMENT

"A tour de force"

Poor Richard's Lament

A most timely tale

Tom Fitzgerald

HOBBLEBUSH BOOKS
Brookline, New Hampshire

Copyright © 2012 by Tom Fitzgerald

All rights reserved. *Reasonable* excerpts from this book may be photocopied or reproduced without explicit permission from the publisher, provided these excerpts are to be used in conjunction with published reviews of the complete work, or for sharing a specific idea or concept with someone who may benefit from exposure to it. *Reasonable* in this context is meant to constitute no more material than *you* would want copied or reproduced free of charge if you were the author. For further information, please contact the publisher:

Hobblebush Books
17-A OLD MILFORD ROAD
BROOKLINE, NH 03033

Cover art by Steve Lindsay
Book design by Sidney Hall, Jr.
Composed at Hobblebush Books in Kepler Std with Cronos Pro display. Both typefaces are by Robert Slimbach. Body text is set 10.7/13.3.

First Hobblebush edition published January 17, 2012
Printed in the United States of America

Author's website: www.PoorRichardsLament.com

Publisher's Cataloging-In-Publication Data
(Prepared by The Donohue Group, Inc.)

Fitzgerald, Tom.
  Poor Richard's lament : a most timely tale / Tom Fitzgerald. — 1st ed.
  p. ; cm.
  "A tour de force."
  ISBN: 978-0-9845921-3-5
  1. Franklin, Benjamin, 1706-1790—Fiction. 2. Franklin, Benjamin, 1706–1790—Influence—Fiction. 3. United States—21st century— Fiction. 4. Fantasy fiction. I. Title.
PS3556.I848 P66 2012
813/.54   2011932158

Publisher's Note

TOM FITZGERALD, in the plentiful pages of *Poor Richard's Lament*, manages to violate all of our editorial standards here at Hobblebush. We are strong adherents of a Strunk-and-White terseness and take Polonius at his word:

> brevity is the soul of wit,
> tediousness the limbs and outward flourishes . . .

If there is a short way to say something, Tom chooses the longest way. If the limbs and outward flourishes could be done without, Tom creates a forest of them. But there is a reason for all this, just as there is a difference between Polonius and Shakespeare, and what at first might seem a little daunting to a contemporary reader ends up as brilliant and inevitable.

Poor Richard's Lament is narrated primarily from the point of view of Benjamin Franklin, and therefore includes all the "colorations" of Franklin's 18th-century America. Switching your modern sensibilities to this new (or, rather, old) language, and cultural and linguistic milieu is like switching from one vintage of wine to another. It requires open-mindedness, but the effort pays off handsomely and soon you will not want it any other way.

The potential benefit is an intellectual and spiritual experience that could well change not only individual lives but (and here comes a big claim) the national ethos as a whole, much as *Common Sense* and *Uncle Tom's Cabin* did in their tumultuous times. We don't pose this possibility lightly. *Poor Richard's Lament* is anything but "business as usual."

We do not normally publish works of fiction, and a book of this size tends to scare us. But after reading Michael Zuckerman's Foreword (brilliant in its own right) we couldn't resist launching into the manuscript, and it soon became clear that *Poor Richard's Lament* is no ordinary work of fiction, that the central character is no ordinary protagonist, and that Hobblebush was very lucky to be able to bring this "most timely tale" to as wide an audience as possible. By the time you reach the "Last Word" in this extraordinary offering (nine years in the making), we expect that you will fully appreciate why we found this to be the case.

SIDNEY HALL JR., PUBLISHER
Hobblebush Books

I wish it were possible ... to invent a method of embalming drowned persons in such a manner that they be recalled to life at any period, however distant; for, having a very ardent desire to see and observe the state of America a hundred years hence, I should prefer to any ordinary death the being immersed in a cask of Madeira wine, with a few friends, till the time, to be then recalled to life by the solar warmth of my dear country.

BENJAMIN FRANKLIN, 1754

In honor of…

Sarah Franklin Bache

Deborah Read Franklin

Elizabeth Downes Franklin

In memory of…

| William E. Ada | C. William Snyder |
| 1920–2004 | 1943–2011 |

| Terry J. Fitzgerald | James E. O'Neill |
| 1942–2010 | 1873–1959 |

| Marston La France | J. Donald Youmans |
| 1927–1975 | 1903–1982 |

In appreciation of…

Helen Evans Ada

Helena Spafford Bentley

Dorothy Kingsley Sandeman

All men would be tyrants if they could.

ABIGAIL ADAMS TO JOHN ADAMS
March 31, 1776

The wisest of men allows his wisdom to be perpetually broken against the rocks of femininity.

MADAME BRILLON TO BEN FRANKLIN
December 20, 1778

Contents

Foreword

Michael W. Zuckerman

Poor Richard's Lament is not only a grand and gorgeous novel; it is also, as Fitzgerald's Franklin might put it, a most timely one. At a time when a host of economic and social ills is causing many of us to contemplate a world beyond materialism and narcissism, *Poor Richard's Lament* juices up the process with an ever-building sense of moral urgency. Toward this end, this hugely ambitious imagination (nine years in the making) moves seamlessly from savage diagnosis to prophecy; from lush inventiveness to inspiration; from damning indictment to redemption.

Where to begin to sing the praises of this singular work? Perhaps by confessing that, as an historian who has devoted a goodly portion of his professional life to studying the life and times of Benjamin Franklin, I was not far into the first half of Fitzgerald's delicious invention when I found myself marveling at the depth of the author's understanding of America's greatest Founding Father as well as the long-ago world in which this great man moved. Fitzgerald had clearly done his homework.

I did wonder, though, whether—despite the dynamism of the court-room histrionics that dominate the first half of the book—others might be so taken. Indeed, at first blush, these early pages seemed to me they might hold far more fascination for those steeped in the sensibilities of 18th-century America than for those who were largely innocent of such. And as much as I found myself fascinated by Fitzgerald's devastating case for the prosecution, in the fanciful celestial court before which Franklin stands trial, I also found myself wishing to get back to Fitzgerald's interwoven tales of the present, and of the skullduggerous ethic of "a little conveniency of expediency" that Fitzgerald's Franklin would, bit by painful bit, learn to lament.

Little did I reckon with Fitzgerald's audacity! Little did I anticipate that, with a little patience, I would soon enough have Ben in the very midst of the sordid Machiavellians of our own time! Little did I appreciate that Fitzgerald would have the brilliance to sustain two distinct dictions—almost two distinct languages—as 18th-century Ben engaged 21st-century America!

There is, in fact, sheer genius in Fitzgerald's imagination of Ben Franklin in the twenty-first century. *Poor Richard's Lament* sees our world as Ben would have encountered it in all its manifold strangeness and, at the same time, makes completely plausible Ben's deciphering of it. Fitzgerald accomplishes this astonishing feat over and over and over again, versus just making one Herculean effort in that direction, for effect, then giving himself a pass on the rest. Fitzgerald dares to put Ben into our world *literally*—diction, clothes, bifocals, cane, gout, and all.

There is genius also in the way in which Fitzgerald draws a most telling indictment of our mutual alienation from one another and our common indifference toward each other. He shows us to ourselves, terrifyingly, through the ways in which our barbaric isolation from one another strikes Ben's 18th-century sensibility. And he does all this with sly comedic wit and dazzling verbal virtuosity, multiplying, and multiplying again, the deft ways in which Ben deflects the occasional strays who do actually notice his oddness, fending off their curiosity without ever descending into dishonesty.

Fitzgerald's wizardry with words comes through most breathtakingly in the daring way he pitches his tent right on Franklin's aphoristic turf. From start to finish, he propounds Poor Richardisms all his own, many of them so good that Franklin would have envied them and, as was his wont, stolen them. Better still, Fitzgerald uses those succulent nuggets exactly as paradoxically as Franklin did, affirming the power of the past at every turn, even as he insists we can set that power at naught.

For all that Fitzgerald gives us a reformed Franklin, he also catches exquisitely the old one, in all the equipoise of intense seriousness and incorrigible playfulness of which he was such a rare master. If there is any way at all in which *Poor Richard's Lament* misses Ben, it may be that it renders him intelligible in the urgency of his desperation to make amends, whereas the historical Franklin coiled himself in impenetrable ironies that we will never quite penetrate.

If I have any other historian's pedantic criticism of this remarkable historical fiction, it is that the displacement of egoistic isolation by way of a compassionate concern for others that Fitzgerald imagines in Ben's second chance was, to my mind, already evident in Ben in his first time round. Maybe not with his wife and children, but with virtually everyone else (including slaves).

Nonetheless, I like Fitzgerald's imagined Ben better than I like my "historical" one. And not just because redemption makes a better story, but also because Ben's desperate repentance, in the one day that the novel grants him to come back to life in the twenty-first century, makes him endearingly reckless as he never was for long in life. I adored watching Fitzgerald make Ben's every outlandish gambit and suicidally foolhardy gamble seem somehow plausible, even verisimilitudinous, in a veritably Enlightened magic realism. I adored the connections and coincidences that strain credulity yet unfold so naturally that I began waiting avidly for what would unfold next and how it would work in the gleefully convoluted plot line that itself asserts so exuberantly the kindredness of all humankind across the centuries.

There are a hundred hits here, maybe a hundred hundred. The pleasures of Fitzgerald's prose, passion, and intelligence pervade every page. There is not only a brilliant weaving of race and gender inequality but also a still more brilliant weaving of Ben's unforgivingness toward his son William and the unforgivableness of Ben's capitulation on slavery and the three-fifths clause, all entwined with consummate artistry by way of a single metaphor: "for want of a nail."

There is also the gorgeous turning of Ben's own words and best principles against him throughout the prosecution, and the excruciating detail of Ben's heartlessness toward his wife, his children, and even his grandson, on and on, now one, now the other, now the one again, the probing going ever deeper and the pain growing ever more palpable, the more because Fitzgerald understands and evokes the plight and the heroism of those forgotten members of Franklin's family so keenly. Even I, an ardent Franklin admirer, felt a sympathy for them, and a horror toward Franklin, I had never felt before.

Fitzgerald can coin fabulous phrases, as in "the miracle of compound disinterest." He has a pitch-perfect ear, as in the succession of news clips that he concocts so convincingly that I was through the first ten of them, thinking he'd just found them and cobbled them together here before it began to dawn on me that he'd made them all up. He has an extraordinary way with words, as in the prophetic Poor Richardism, *When the grease of commerce is falsehood, how long before the wheels fall off the wagon?* He can catch vast implications in a few clauses, as in the pithy Poor Richardism that for people to give a shit, they must first be led to the privy, a veritable if vulgar epigram for the whole book.

But the beauty of this book is not just in its verbal pyrotechnics, ravishing though they are. It is, still more, in the constant breath of humane inspiration that guides a steady succession of searing, soaring triumphs of communion and caritas. Fitzgerald is that rarest of birds: a great writer and a great soul. He has summoned from unfathomable depths of despair an imagining of the greatest of Americans that is not only better than the original but also worthy of his own remarkable spirit.

MICHAEL W. ZUCKERMAN
University of Pennsylvania
Philadelphia, PA

We have what we give. We make ourselves rich
by spending ourselves.

ISABEL ALLENDE
This I Believe, NPR
April 4, 2005

The want of most men [is] knowledge of a sort which
brings wisdom rather than affluence.

THOMAS HARDY
The Return of the Native

[Our primate relatives] show us that compassion is not a
recent weakness going against the grain of nature but a
formidable power that is as much a part of who and what
we are as [are] the competitive tendencies it
seeks to overcome.

FRANS DE WALL
Our Inner Ape

When I was a Child of seven Years old, my Friends on a Holiday filled my little Pocket with Halfpence. I went directly to a Shop where they sold Toys for Children; and being charmed with the Sound of a Whistle that I met by the way, in the hands of another Boy, I voluntarily offered and gave all my Money for it. When I came home, whistling all over the House, much pleased with my Whistle, but disturbing all the Family, my Brothers, Sisters & Cousins, understanding the Bargain I had made, told me I had given four times as much for it as it was worth, put me in mind what good Things I might have bought with the rest of the Money, & laught at me so much for my Folly that I cry'd with Vexation; and the Reflection gave me more Chagrin than the Whistle gave me Pleasure.

I conceived that [a] great Part of the Miseries of Mankind, were brought upon them by the false Estimates they had made of the Value of Things, and by their giving too much for the Whistle.

BENJAMIN FRANKLIN TO MADAME BRILLON

November 10, 1778

How great must be the condemnation of poor creatures, at the great day of account, when they shall be asked what uses they made of the opportunities put into their hands; and are only able to say, "We have lived but to ourselves; we have circumscribed all the power thou hast given us into one narrow selfish compass; we have heaped up treasures for those who came after us, though we know not whether they would not make a still worse use of them than we ourselves did."

SAMUEL RICHARDSON, 1751

From *Pamela*, Volume One

Milestones in the Life of Benjamin Franklin

1706   Born on Milk Street, Boston, on January 17, a Sunday, to Josiah, a candle and soap maker, and his second wife Abiah Folger; fourteenth of seventeen children by Josiah.

1714   Attends Boston Grammar School and Bownwell's English School.

1716   Josiah removes BF from school and indentures him in his shop to become a chandler.

1718   Josiah gives up on making BF a chandler and indentures him to BF's older half-brother James to learn the printing trade.

1721   James launches *The New England Courant* and publishes fourteen "tongue-in-cheek" essays by Silence Dogood, unaware BF is the author. BF becomes "a thorough Deist."

1723   Flees Boston and James's harsh treatment for New York. Unable to find work, BF is directed by William Bradford to Philadelphia, where he finds work at Samuel Keimer's print shop. Boards with John Read, father of Deborah Read.

1724   Returns to Boston to borrow money from his father to open a print shop; is denied. Returns to Philadelphia and courts Deborah Read. Sails for London under assurances from William Keith, governor of PA, that he will be able to buy equipment on credit for opening a print shop. Betrayed by Keith, BF spends eighteen months working at London printing houses to earn passage home. Hangs out in coffee shops.

1725   Deborah Read, feeling abandoned by BF, marries John Rogers, who four months later steals a slave and disappears. Deborah returns home to live with her parents. BF publishes first pamphlet, *A Dissertation upon Liberty and Necessity, Pleasure and Pain*.

1726   Returns to Philadelphia and goes to work in Thomas Denham's
        clothing/hardware store.

1727   Returns to work for Samuel Keimer; founds the Junto, a
        Friday-night club for "self-improvement, study, mutual aid, and
        conviviality."

1728   Opens a printing business in partnership with Hugh Meredith,
        a ne'er do well. Composes *Articles of Belief and Acts of Religion*.

1729   Buys a failing newspaper from Keimer; relaunches it as *The
        Pennsylvania Gazette*.

1730   BF's son William is born out of wedlock. BF enters into a
        common-law marriage with Deborah Read Rogers; buys out his
        alcoholic business partner.

1731   Initiates the Library Company of Philadelphia; joins St. John's
        Free Mason Lodge.

1732   Publishes first edition of *Poor Richard's Almanack* (twenty-four
        editions were to follow). BF's second son, Francis Folger, is born.

1733   Divines a regimen for arriving at "moral perfection."

1734   Elected Grand Master of the Masons of Pennsylvania; bribes
        post riders to carry his newspaper.

1735   Helps establish volunteer fire-fighting societies; proposes a
        night watch.

1736   Francis Folger Franklin dies of smallpox at age four. BF is
        appointed clerk of the Pennsylvania Assembly. Organizes the
        Union Fire Company.

1737   Appointed postmaster of Philadelphia (serves sixteen years in
        this capacity).

1740   Hears evangelist George Whitefield preach; begins to publish
        Whitefield's sermons.

1741   Invents the Pennsylvania fireplace (Franklin stove); refuses to
        patent it.

1742   Organizes a project to fund plant-collecting expeditions by
        naturalist John Bartram, who later names a new flora after Ben:
        the *Franklinia alatamaha* (now extinct in the wild).

1743   BF's only daughter, Sarah (Sally), is born. BF publishes *A
        Proposal for Promoting Useful Knowledge*, which leads to the
        founding of the American Philosophical Society. Begins long
        relationship with London printer/publisher William Strahan.

1744   Reprints Samuel Richardson's *Pamela*, the first novel to be published in America.

1745   Begins electrical experiments; initiates a correspondence on the topic with Peter Collinson in England. Josiah Franklin dies in Boston at age eighty-seven.

1747   Reports his theories on electricity to Collinson, who presents them to the British Royal Society. Collinson sends BF an electric tube.

1748   Retires from active business a wealthy man, at age forty-two. Buys first of several Negro slaves. Elected to Philadelphia City Council.

1749   Invents lightning rod; refuses to patent it. Writes and publishes *Proposals Relating to the Youth of Pennsylvania*, which leads to the founding of an academy (to become UPenn).

1750   Conducts electrical experiments on turkey fowl. Lightning rods proliferate.

1751   Elected to Pennsylvania Assembly. His electrical experiments are published by Peter Collinson in London as *Experiments and Observations of Electricity*.

1752   Abiah Franklin dies in Boston at age eighty-four. BF conducts his famous kite experiment, and invents first flexible catheter for his brother John (a soap maker). Receives Royal Society's Copley Medal for his experiments in electricity.

1753   Appointed Joint Deputy Postmaster General of North America.

1754   Composes a plan (Albany Plan) for unifying the seven colonies. Publishes first political cartoon, "Join or Die," a snake divided into sections.

1757   Sails for England with son William to serve as agent for Pennsylvania (later also for Massachusetts, Georgia, and New Jersey); composes *The Way to Wealth* en route. Takes rooms at 7 Craven Street with Margaret Stevenson, a widow whose daughter, Mary (Polly), BF comes to view as his own. (Ben is attendant at Polly's wedding; Polly is attendant at Ben's deathbed.)

1758   Hobnobs with Boswell, Priestly, Hume, others; travels to Northamptonshire (with William) to locate his father's relatives near Ecton; invents chimney damper.

1759   Receives honorary doctorate from St. Andrews University; is thereafter known as Dr. Franklin. Tours Scotland and meets Adam Smith, Lord Kames, others.

1760   Attends the coronation of George III.

1762   Returns home after five years in London. William remains behind and marries Elizabeth Downes; five days later, William is named Royal Governor of New Jersey. BF invents the glass armonica, for which Mozart subsequently composes an adagio.

1764   Elected Speaker of Pennsylvania Assembly; denounces the "Paxton Boys" for massacring friendly Indians in Lancaster County; returns to London as agent for the Pennsylvania Assembly; resides again with the Stevensons.

1765   The Stamp Act becomes law.

1766   Argues for repeal of the Stamp Act before the House of Commons; Act is repealed.

1767   Travels to Paris with Dr. John Pringle, the Queen's physician; is presented to King Louis XV at Versailles. Sally Franklin marries Richard Bach in Philadelphia.

1769   Deborah suffers a stroke that leaves her partially incapacitated. BF and others found the Ohio Land Company in an effort to obtain land grants in American wilderness for speculation. Grandson Benjamin Franklin Bache (Benny) is born.

1771   Visits Bishop Jonathan Shipley and daughters at Twyford; subsequently begins writing his *Autobiography* there. Tours Ireland and witnesses opening of Irish parliament. Visits Lord Kames in Scotland and promises to write *The Art of Virtue*.

1772   Obtains letters written by Thomas Hutchinson, royal governor of Massachusetts, that call for colonial repression; sends these to Thomas Cushing in Massachusetts.

1773   Is suspected of stealing the Hutchinson letters; files a petition calling for Hutchinson's removal. Conducts experiments on the use of oil to calm rough waters.

1774   Boston Tea Party. BF is denounced before the King's Privy Council by Solicitor General Alexander Wedderburn; loses his position as Deputy Postmaster General for North America. Deborah Franklin dies of a stroke in Philadelphia at age 66.

1775   Returns to Philadelphia; drafts the Articles of Confederation;

is elected Postmaster General for the Colonies. Confers with General Washington in Boston.

1776   Serves on committee to draft Declaration of Independence. Attempts to negotiate an alliance with French Canada (returns with his famous marten cap). William Franklin, choosing to remain a Tory, is imprisoned in Connecticut. BF sails for Paris (with grandsons Benny and Temple) to serve, with two others, as Commissioners of Congress to the French Court. Meets French Foreign Minister Comte de Vergennes.

1777   Appoints Temple his personal secretary; sends Benny to school in Geneva. Establishes complex relationship (both paternal and flirtatious) with Madame Brillon, wife of a French bureaucrat. Obtains secret loan from the French.

1778   Negotiates the Treaty of Alliance with France; is made Minister Plenipotentiary by Congress; joins the Masonic Lodge in Paris; helps initiate Voltaire. John Adams replaces Silas Dean as Commissioner. BF negotiates additional loans. France declares war on England.

1779   Obtains another loan from the French; installs a printing press at Passy; befriends Madame Helvetius, widow of a French intellectual. Spain declares war on England.

1780   Obtains another loan from the French. Proposes marriage to Madame Helvetius; is refused. Vergennes is offended by Adams and refuses to deal with him.

1781   Appointed by Congress to peace commission. Cornwallis surrenders at Yorktown. BF tries to resign from the commission, due to age and health; is refused.

1782   Helps frame the terms of a peace treaty with England; obtains another loan from the French; is much afflicted with the gout.

1783   Signs Preliminary Articles of Peace with England, France, and Spain.

1784   At request of Louis XVI, helps discredit Mesmer's theory of "Animal Magnetism."

1785   Invents bifocal lens. En route to America, briefly visits his estranged son William. Elected president of the Supreme Executive Council of Pennsylvania.

1786   Designs the "long arm" for lifting books from high shelves. Adds a library to his Market Street house to accommodate his 4,000 volumes, the most in any library in America.

1787   As eldest delegate, helps frame the articles of the U.S. Constitution; signs the final document; becomes president of the Pennsylvania Society for the Abolition of Slavery.

1788   Revises his will to give his daughter Sally most of his property and grandson Temple most of his books and papers; gives virtually nothing to his son William.

1789   Sends a petition against slavery to the U.S. Congress. Sends copies of his *Autobiography* to friends in America and Europe.

1790   Dies on April 17 of pleurisy. His funeral, attended by 20,000, is the largest recorded event in 18th-century America. Buried at corner of 5th and Arch, Philadelphia.

Book I

Great Expectations

Though the hour is late, yet still there is time.

Celestial Chamber of B. Franklin

17 January 1706–17 April 1790

B en could not recall having been quite so ebullient in the 200-odd years of his confinement. The closest likely he had come in this regard had occurred on the occasion of his completing the thirteenth and final volume of his *Autobiography*, near a century ago now, or so it did seem.

He had been particularly ebullient on that occasion, he now recalled, for having resolved a most vexing dilemma—whether to close his personal history with the ratification of the Constitution, 17 September 1787, or to extend it by another thirty months, precisely, such as to include the occasion of his very last breath upon Earth, 17 April 1790.

Felicitously, he had chosen the ratification event, firstly because it was climactic in and of itself, and secondly because it had allowed him to crown his personal history with perhaps the finest oratory of his eighty-four years on earth—which oratory he had managed to capture in full, every word of it, not by recollecting it, which he could not do, but by returning himself to the actual event, by no greater than thinking upon it, as one thinks upon a thumb such as to frolic it, and witnessing thereby Mr. Wilson, his more-than-adequate surrogate that day, put flesh and blood upon every syllable, as only that gentleman could do.

Mister President:

I confess that there are several parts of this constitution which I do not at present approve, but I am not sure I shall never approve them; for having lived long, I have experienced many instances of being obliged by better information, or fuller consideration, to change opinions even on important subjects, which I once thought right, but found to be otherwise. It is therefore that the older I grow, the more apt I am to doubt my own judgment, and to pay more respect to the judgment of others.

Most men indeed as well as most sects in religion think themselves in possession of all truth, and that wherever others differ from them it is so far error. Steele a Protestant in a dedication tells the Pope that the only difference between our churches in their opinions of the certainty of their doctrines is the Church of Rome is infallible and the Church of England is never in the wrong.

Though never an orator of the esteem of an Adams or a Whitefield, Ben adjudged his oratory of that occasion, although delivered by a surrogate, the most momentous of his efforts in that category of persuasion, more so even than his argument before Commons against the Stamp Act, and therefore the perfect instrument by which to bring to close an accounting of a long and not altogether undistinguished tenure upon earth.

And there's an end on it!

Ben chuckled to visitation now, before mind's eye, of a dainty apparition. Dipping pen to ink, he committed his visitor unto an enduring preservation before she might withdraw into the very aether from whence she had only just emerged, as all such were wont to do.

> We are the slaves of our biology
> and of our ideology
> But the clowns of our theology.

He read the rhyme twice more, and upon issuing a last chuckle, pinned a label on her, 706, such as to mark her sequence in an accumulation of kindred other such, they to be put to press one day as *A Compendium of Lit'l Ditties and Doodles, for the General Amusement of the Irredeemably Idle* by Philomena Micklewick.

Feeling farther encroachment now of a fatigue most agreeable, Ben snuffed the candles at either side of his writing desk, the tallow of the one being ruby red, that of the other being sapphire blue. Rising then, he hobbled to the chessboard adjacent to his reading chair, whereat a drooling candle, emerald green, yet burned, and smiled upon the sheaf of scribblings, only recently reviewed by him, on which his formal petition had, he trusted, been expertly wrought.

He would peruse these sheets again on the morrow, he allowed, such that he might not wait too closely upon a certain Intermediary likely to be irksomely tardy, and also, as icing upon cake, such that he might kindle an agreeable smolder of anticipation concerning the effect the major credits of his life would have upon—

Precisely *whom?* Precisely *what?*

Reasonableness, surely!

Entering into his bed chamber, Ben avoided taking notice of the furnishments marking the very chamber in which he had breathed his last. Although he had attempted several times over to supplant this chamber with another—that at 7 Craven; that at Passy; even that at Fort Hamilton—he had, for no cause ever communicated to him, been restricted all these scores of years to this unhappy chamber, by way of being denied all efficacy toward imagining another into its place.

Shedding himself of his old brown suit, the very one in which he had been buried, Ben caught glimpse of a most comical image in a looking glass attached upon the wall to rightward, this instrument being neither expected by him there nor added by him. The glass, in being near floor to ceiling in extension, and ornamented in rococo, tended to render the image presently within it—this being a close likeness to (dare he confess it?) a puffball—all the more comical.

Have we here the beauty, Dr. Franklin, or have we the beast?

Dr. Franklin chuckled, and pulling on his nightshirt, crawled under the coverlet on his four-poster, this badly in need of a tightening, and had little sooner snuffed out the fleece-white candle upon the nightstand than was visited by another apparition before mind's eye. Well knowing he would be tortured the night through over retaining memory upon morning of a visitation but nary a notion of the visitor, he crawled from his bed, and feeling his way into his study, rekindled the wicks at either side of his writing desk. He thereupon scribbled, with swift strokes, a dainty little ditty upon the same sheet on which he had preserved the previous such:

> If puffballs were to choose
>   the most beautiful puffball of all
> Would they choose one round and fat
>   or one lean and tall?

Issuing more a giggle than a chuckle, Ben affixed a label to this newest foundling, this being the number 707.

Such a generosity of mischief in one evening, Ben allowed, had truly to be an omen! Indeed, he would sleep this night through as if upon a cloud of contentment, or he would toss about as if upon a sea of anticipation—it mattered not.

The morrow was nowise to be just another day.

The White House

September 16th, 6:07 a.m.

Gilbert felt a flutter of anticipation as he relinquished his tote to the willing servitude of his chair. He smiled.

He'd *never* top it. It was the *perfect* gift.

He triggered the latch on his tote.

No one would ever know, of course, except the President—and Tom—but that didn't matter in the least. The true pleasure of influence—the only form of power worth the bother—was not in having it noticed, but in having it. Notice was for the irredeemably puerile—the Bill Clintons and Paul Kenyons of the world—those who seemed driven as if by force of addiction to organize their lives around being forever the center of attention.

Gilbert's smile deepened on a seventyish face that, although puffed and shadowed around the eyes, exuded the dignity and confidence of a man who knew exactly who he was and precisely how much he was worth.

Dr. Gilbert Henry Bahr had long since inventoried the particulars of his genius and found them lacking in no significant regard.

Which, for the President, was a damn good thing.

Opening his tote, Gilbert pulled a book-size package from the only compartment that wasn't stuffed with folders showing a red, blue, or green tab. The package itself was wrapped in glazed white paper, perfectly squared at the corners, and was bound with red, white, and blue ribbons culminating in, at one end, offset to one side, an elegant tricolor blossom.

Gilbert glanced at his watch, and pressing a button on a desk console, received an almost instantaneous response. "Good morning, sir. Costa Rican Excelsior today. Shall I bring you a cup?"

"Oh, good, great—yes—in a sec. I've got to step out for a minute. I'll stop by on my way back. Any calls?"

"Director Fiske left a message on your voice mail. He'd like you to call him at your earliest convenience—on his private number."

"When did he call?"

"His message was stamped 5:43 a.m."

"OK, thanks."

"I'll have your coffee waiting for you."

"Excelsior, right?"

"Yes sir."

"Perfect. I'll be right back."

Gilbert slipped the gift package—the bloomless end—under his belt, against a stomach as flat as it had been half a century earlier, and buttoning his suitcoat, made certain nothing of the package showed. Exiting his office then, through his private entrance, he bore right and headed down the crimson-carpeted corridor toward the southwest corner of the wing. Walking briskly, he responded to eye contacts with perfunctory grunts and nods. At Morrie Stern's office, he turned left and headed toward the southeast corner of the wing.

Entering the open door to Teresa Gutierrez's office, Gilbert glanced toward Stephanie Blanchard's desk—Stephanie usually didn't get in until around 7:00—then slipped the package from under his belt, and keeping his back toward the doorway, held the package close in, such that only someone in the direction of Teresa's desk could see it.

By Morrie Stern's decree, absolutely no personal gifts, of any kind, no exceptions, were to be given to the President by individual staff members. In each of the previous three years, however, Gilbert and Teresa had conspired—Gilbert had suggested, Teresa had acquiesced—to supplement their own modest contributions to the group gift with "a little something extra," because of "our unique relationship with the President."

Teresa looked up without interrupting a dance of flawlessly choreographed fingers over her keyboard. Gilbert beheld this miracle, as he usually did, with deep reverence. His own fingers knew where the keys were, but only for as long as his eyes remained fixed generally on the keyboard. The moment he would divert his eyes, as Teresa had just done, his memory map would go blank, as if by wave of wand, and he would type gibberish.

He had noticed this same affliction, and similar, in other males of the species, and some decades ago, the nascent psychologist in him had formed a theory. Because males tended to be more averse than females were to making mistakes, as a function likely of a Y-mediated fear of appearing weak, males instinctively tended to play it safer than females did when learning new tricks, so to say. Hence, instead of willfully engaging in error until rote competence should emerge, males tended to keep their eyes on the keyboard in order to *prevent* error, to the unfortunate end of denying themselves any possibility of inscribing upon their prideful psyches an indelible memory map.

So completely were males suffused with this kind of innate stupidity, Gilbert had posited, that in most cases it couldn't be excised without gutting the entire corpus.

After first formulating this theory, back in his third year at Andover, Gilbert had begun to look for patterns of male behavior that would tend to support it, and had no sooner begun his search than was reminded, one late-spring afternoon at Fenway, of his father's only paternal counsel to him, delivered several years earlier when his father, a fervent Red Sox fan, was trying to teach his only son how to hit a baseball: "Keep your eyes on the ball! See? This thing! Keep your eyes on *it*—not me. You can't hit what you're not looking at!"

In that epiphanous moment at Fenway, Gilbert had grasped his father's true message: "Do not strike out. Do not embarrass me. Do not *shame* me."

Indeed, when it came to human behavior, Gilbert had discovered, all Gaul was divided into not three parts but only two—*innate* instinct on the one hand; *instilled* instinct (a.k.a. belief) on the other. And it was knowledge of this simple truth that was the source of all political efficacy. Want to control the voting behavior of women? Identify the individual strands of innate female instinct—Yin-stinct, Gilbert had called it in one of his books—the female's reflexive deference toward male authority, for example—and manipulate these as if strings on a marionette. Want to control the voting behavior of religious wing-nuts? Identify the individual tenets of their instilled beliefs—Americans are exceptional in the eyes of God, for example—and manipulate these as if strings on a marionette.

It was just *that* simple.

Pompous pretenders like John Adams, hopelessly pinched and pruned as they were with Puritanism, or some other desiccating astringency of mind, never understood this. True geniuses like Benjamin Franklin, ol' twinkle and a nod himself, did.

Teresa, eyeing the package Gilbert was holding, smiled. "A little something for the birthday boy?" A distinctive accent betrayed an extra-national origin.

In fact, Teresa had spent the first eighteen years of her life in Mexico, mostly in Juarez, but had been living in the United States for over twenty-seven years now, mostly in El Monte, east of Los Angeles, where she had resided, with the youngest of her three children, when President-elect James Michael Kinney phoned her out of the blue one early-November morning—in fact, at 5:33 a.m.—to ask her to serve as his private secretary.

Little did Teresa suspect—or give any indication of suspecting, anyway—that the man standing in front of her at that moment had been the chief architect of her Cinderella-like transformation from obscure legal secretary in a five-person ethnic law firm in L.A., into the private secretary of the President of the United States of America.

Gilbert had first taken notice of Teresa during a visit he had made to LA over four years ago now, to make arrangements for a crucially important primary rally for then-candidate Kinney. Teresa was one of the worker bees that Roger Hornby, California state chair of the Kinney campaign, had recommended to the rally committee to help plan the event. Gilbert had found Teresa an interesting anomaly—a Chicano woman working for Republican causes—but had sensed more, and in making discreet inquires, had discovered Teresa to be, in fact, a poster mother of self-reliance and personal responsibility. Abandoned by a faithless husband, she had raised three children single-handedly, first by earning a college degree at night while holding down two cleaning jobs, and then by running her own home-based transcription service, until it began to detract from her motherhood duties, and finally by becoming a high-paid (relatively) legal secretary.

Put a worker bee of a certain complexion into a position of real versus symbolic responsibility, Gilbert had counseled the President-elect in the early morning following the President's razor-thin victory, and one or two other worker bees of a certain complexion were certain to take notice—and well before the next election.

In the dog-eat-dog world of politics, Gilbert had further counseled the President-elect, *any* advantage could be, and increasingly was, tantamount to *every* advantage.

Smiling knowingly, Teresa motioned with her head. "Go on in."

Gilbert entered the chamber in which he had been meeting with the President every morning now for the past three years. Instead of bearing right, however, as usual, toward the facing two-seat couches,

Gilbert steered toward the President's desk, the same one that John Kennedy Jr. had made famous by peeking through the knee hole, before it was paneled over. The golden drapes framing the three floor-to-ceiling windows behind the desk seemed almost incandescent, like autumn aspens at forest's edge.

Gilbert took special notice of the two alabaster figurines symmetrically positioned on the desktop. The closer one, "Industry," depicted a man, eyes cast downward, wielding a scythe; the farther one, "Frugality," depicted a woman, eyes cast downward, trundling a loom. Gilbert had given these pieces of Franklinia to the President exactly three years ago, to great effect, but in so doing had left himself little room in which to trump them—

Until today, of course!

Moving behind the desk, Gilbert noticed that Teresa's gift package, resting on the seat of the President's chair, appeared to be precisely the size of his own.

O God!

Gilbert grinned.

O happiness! It didn't matter!

Hearing Teresa's phone ring, Gilbert checked his watch. It was a bit early. Ten minutes, in fact. The President, Gilbert surmised, had seen the latest poll numbers.

Perfect.

Placing his package next to the other, Gilbert hurried back into Teresa's office and found Teresa just rising from her chair.

"The President's on his way down," Teresa said, smiling. "You might as well stay and save me the call."

Gilbert hesitated just long enough for Teresa to make the decision. "This is not going to be an ordinary day."

Gilbert followed Teresa back into the Oval, and Teresa disappearing into the President's dining room, sat down in the further of the two facing couches. These stood perpendicular to the massive Resolute desk, and in so doing often reminded Gilbert, as they did now, of the chapel at Bowdoin, where the pews were arranged in like fashion relative to the altar.

Gilbert enjoyed these little happenstances of similarity, and the private, often amusing symbologies they often elicited, even if they were not fresh out of the oven.

Taking a deep breath, Gilbert looked toward the open door to Teresa's office and entertained the notion of making a dash for it. He loathed utterly the awkwardness that rituals such as a witnessed opening of gifts seemed specifically designed to inflict.

Desperate for an upside to staying put, Gilbert assured himself that at least this way, by grinning and bearing it, like a good sport, he'd be able to witness the look on the birthday boy's face the moment he realized what was actually being given to him on this most momentous of occasions—the day he learned he was six points behind in the latest *New York Times*/CBS poll with fewer than fifty days to go until election day!

Teresa reappeared carrying a silver tray holding the usual carafe, linens, and condiments, but two maroon mugs instead of the usual china cups. The mugs, Gilbert immediately recognized, were from the set of twelve UMass mugs that he had given to the President on the occasion of the President's fifty-ninth birthday. Each mug in the set showed a radiant grin on the face of one of Jimmy Kinney's "Minutemen," the band of college mates who had helped Jimmy build a part-time real-estate development business into a multi-billion-dollar enterprise.

Teresa was followed by Roy Peoples, the morning steward, who was carrying, Gilbert well knew, a platter of assorted donut holes—"fat pills," the President called them. There would be twice as many chocolate, Gilbert also knew, as Boston cream and honey dipped combined.

While Roy waited for Teresa to place her tray down on the table between the two couches, he and Gilbert exchanged their usual greeting: "Good morning, Dr. Bahr." "Good morning, Roy."

Roy Peoples was a smallish, dark-skinned black man, mid to late fifties, whose pole-thin limbs and only slightly larger neck seemed to dictate the pencil-thin mustache he wore.

While Teresa filled the Bob Driscoll mug with coffee, Gilbert exchanged the usual banter with Roy, which, over the baseball months, centered on the Red Sox and the Phillies; over the football months, on the Patriots and the Eagles; or, as now, in the fall time frame, on all four teams. Roy had grown up in West Philadelphia, hence his allegiance to the Philly teams; Gilbert had grown up in Brookline, Massachusetts, hence his allegiance to the Boston teams.

As Gilbert leaned toward the steaming mug in front of him, Roy, with a small bow, took his leave.

Gilbert squinted through the middle tier of his trifocals toward the college-age face of Bob Driscoll. Driscoll had become CFO of Jimmy's development company, JMK Enterprises, and later had served as "the money man" for Jimmy's first senatorial campaign.

Gilbert smiled. The puckish baby face well cloaked the jackal the man had become.

That the President likely hadn't used any of these mugs over the past year did not bother Gilbert one bit. Actual use had never been the intention. The intention had been simply to remind the President of his average-Joe, working-class origins, which, for Jimmy's first senatorial campaign, Gilbert had distilled down to a bumper-sticker-sized sound bite, "Southie's Homeboy," to become, ten years later, "One of US."

Jimmy Kinney, Gilbert wanted everyone to know—and Jimmy himself to be reminded—was no privileged, power-suited, know-it-all elitist, but a self-made, all-American boy who had graduated from UMass on his own nickel, not from Hahvid on his daddy's dime.

When people attained power, Gilbert well knew, there was always a real-and-present danger of their forgetting who they were, or at least who they needed to appear to be. This could be especially true, obviously, when one was ensconced in a Palladian Great House hosting twenty-eight fireplaces and thirty-five toilets.

Thirty-five toilets!

Holy shit!

Teresa set the second mug, this one showing Lew Grady's "mug"— Gilbert wasn't sure the President had ever gotten the pun—on a glass coaster opposite Gilbert. She smiled. "Aren't these the mugs you gave the President last year?"

"They are indeed."

"I thought we should use them this morning."

Gilbert chuckled. "The *only* morning."

Teresa held the platter of munchkins toward Gilbert, perfunctorily, as if expecting a refusal, which she got. "You give very thoughtful gifts, Dr. Bahr. I'm sure they're very much appreciated." Teresa set the platter down on the table, biased toward the opposing couch.

"As, I'm sure, are yours. Those indestructible little spheroids you gave the President last year were an absolute stroke of genius."

Teresa smiled. "Thank you, sir. I try."

Gilbert shrugged. "That's all any of us can do."

Teresa excused herself—her phone was ringing—and hurried back to her office.

Gilbert, leaning forward, took a cautious sip from his steaming mug, and settling back into his seat, looked up at his "old friend" hanging over the fireplace. He smiled.

This particular portrait, by Duplessis, showing a serenely confident elder statesman attired in a rust jacket lined at the collar with fur, was by far both Gilbert's and the President's favorite rendering of Franklin. A subsequent version, better known because of its iconic centrality on the $100 bill, showed Franklin in a silver-gray jacket sans fur collar.

The frame on the present rendering—entirely fitting to it, Gilbert felt, but hardly to the subsequent version—was an ornate golden oval showing a raised crown of laurel at the pinnacle; a golden serpent beneath this, interwoven into sprays of filigree; and a single Latin word, *VIR*, boldly imprinted at the bottom.

An earlier portrait, by Martin, showing Franklin in ruffles and curls, his right hand delicately poised, was traditional in the White House, but both Gilbert and the President considered this rendering inappropriately effeminate, in contrast to Duplessis' red-jacket rendering, which, they both felt, captured the full *VIR* of the man who arguably had been the most important force in shaping America's exceptional, can-do character.

So strong was the President's feeling for the Duplessis rendering of Franklin, and so intent had he been that it should hang in the Oval during his tenure, that when on the day after inauguration the President had been informed by Morrie Stern that the Metropolitan Museum of Art in New York had refused his request for a loan of the portrait, due to "insurmountable obstacles," Jimmy Kinney had done what he had always done when confronted with "insurmountable obstacles." He had turned the matter over to his chief political counsel, who had, within the hour, dispatched a cohort of "linebackers" to New York to "sip a little tea."

Two days later, a Brinks truck had arrived at the White House carrying two guards, a curator, and a robustly crated artifact.

Gilbert grinned up at Franklin. *VIR indeed.*

Catching a glimpse of peripheral movement, Gilbert looked toward Teresa's office. Ken Rankin, the President's physical twin, was standing in the open doorway. Ken was one of a special security unit, formed since the recent attack on the White House, whose job it was to lure to themselves whatever lethality might be directed toward the President.

"Morning, Ken."

"Morning, sir."

Ken finished scanning the room, then stood to one side. A trim, less-than-sixty-looking man, rendered perhaps a little taller than he actually was by a closely tailored, dark-blue suit, strode into the room, his gait that of a man who breathes gasoline fumes instead of oxygen. Lily, the President's retriever, trotted in directly behind, carrying a red "spheroid" in her mouth. Following Lily, a young man appeared, mid 30's, freckle-faced, wearing a smile as waggly in unabashed friendliness as Lily's plume-like tail. He was dressed in a medium-brown, pinstriped suit that served to accentuate a well-coiffed mane of carrot-colored hair.

Gilbert placed his mug on a crystalline coaster and rose to his feet. "Tim!"

"Cratchit!"

Gilbert and Kevin had been greeting each other in this fashion since the day Kevin, then fourteen, badly sprained an ankle on a family outing at Attitash. Gilbert, a guest of the Kinneys on that occasion, had carried Kevin off the mountain on his back, until the ski patrol could take over. This event had occurred just a few days before Christmas, hence the inevitable Dickensian association, rendered indelible now by way of several years of affectionate repetition.

Some things, Gilbert often quipped, were worth repeating.

Gilbert smiled toward the President. "Happy Birthday, sir." The President responded by wagging a folded newspaper at him. Holding back a grin, Gilbert navigated out of the sitting area and greeted Kevin with a hardy handshake, while the President continued on toward his desk, to call, Gilbert knew, Norbert Chambers, his campaign manager. Lily, as was her wont, began to circle the room in the manner of a lioness entering center ring.

"Down for the big event?" Gilbert asked, giving Kevin's firm grip a little extra squeeze.

"Came down last night—as a surprise, as it turned out. I didn't think I was going to be able to make it down until tomorrow." Kevin glanced toward his father, who was punching a number into one of his color-coded consoles. "Then I got late word that some mysterious benefactor had arranged for special transportation." Kevin winked, then glanced at his watch, the face of which glowed with a greenish phosphorescence. "I've got to be back by 10:00, but, of course I couldn't leave without saying hello. Annie sends her love."

"Give Annie my best."

"I will."

They started moving toward the open doorway to Teresa's office.

"How's everything at the firm?"

"Couldn't be better."

"Any invitations for a glass of sherry in the partners' lounge?"

Kevin grinned. "Not yet, but I've logged more billable hours so far this year than there are billable hours."

Gilbert laughed. "Excellent—excellent."

Kevin patted Gilbert's back. "Any chance of you coming up for the big showdown next weekend?"

"I can't think of anything I'd rather do, frankly, but a certain someone, whose name will go unmentioned, seems to think he can't get along without me, even for a day."

Kevin leaned closer. "He can't."

Gilbert grinned.

Kevin glanced furtively toward his father, then spoke in a low voice. "Mum's the word on this, Cratchit, but Annie and I just might have a little announcement to make by next weekend. If you came up, you'd be the first to hear it." He winked.

Gilbert smiled. "Been spending a few of those billable hours at home, have you?"

Kevin grinned. "On call, you might say. Annie's been wearing this monitor thing that alerts her whenever she's—as she'd put it—'in heat.'" Kevin grinned. "She calls it her 'tryst kit.'" Gilbert chortled. "She thinks it's already done the trick, so to say, but she wants us to stay on the program for a bit longer, until we know for sure." Kevin grinned. "Who ya gonna call?"

Looking suddenly distracted, as if by a whisper privately received, Kevin reached inside his suit coat, and, grinning—"Speaking of which"— produced a vibrating cell phone. Flipping it open, Kevin pushed a button and looked at Gilbert. "I'll reserve three seats in the company box for next weekend, just in case." He winked. "Grandpa Cratchit—huh?"

Gilbert smiled.

Kevin turned away and speaking into his phone, in a hushed voice, moved to face the near wall, just to the right of the Houdon bust of Franklin.

Gilbert looked toward the President, who was speaking animatedly toward the Rose Garden, then returned to his couch seat. About to pick up his mug of no-longer-steaming Maxwell House Classic, he felt an insistent tickle against his chest and, pulling his own cell phone from its marsupial pouch, flipped it open and checked the screen: Tom Fiske. He answered in the discreet manner of a commentator at a golf match. "Just a sec—I'm in the Oval." Getting to his feet, Gilbert moved to the wall opposite the one Kevin was facing. "OK," he whispered, "what's up?"

"Did you get my call?" The director's voice was freighted with pique and fatigue in about equal measure.

"Five forty-three a.m.—very impressive. The President's down early, Tom. I haven't had a chance to get back to you. He's apparently seen the poll numbers. Good timing, eh."

Tom chortled. "You, of course, had nothing to do with that."

"You hold me in much too high an estimation, my friend."

"Is that possible? There seems to be a page missing from chapter seven, book three. I trust you have it."

"Oh, sorry. Yes, I have it."

The director audibly exhaled. "You can understand my concern. When a goldfish is missing from the bowl, one might reasonably infer a cat."

"Yes, sorry. I should have mentioned it. I wanted the President to have something to hold in his hand. You know the old saying: A goldfish in hand—"

"No copies, though, right?"

"No copies."

"Good. Well, I hope everything goes well."

"Thanks, Tom. And thanks again for all your help on this."

"It was fun, actually—a chance to strut our stuff over here."

"The President will be more than pleased." Gilbert checked his watch. "And I'm sure he'll find an opportunity to express exactly that sentiment to you in person. Are you en route?"

"Yes, but at the moment we're stuck in traffic. More goddamn protesters. They always seem to know exactly what route we're going to be taking—which is a little unnerving, actually."

"Stop by after your briefing."

"OK, but I've got to be back at Langley by no later than 9:15."

"Not a problem. I just want to make sure our little goldfish finds its way back into the bowl."

"Oh gosh, yes, of course. I'll see you in a bit then—I hope."

"You could always run over a couple o' those retards, you know."

"Yeah, right. Just before the election. Great idea: 'U.S. spy chief runs over pesky soccer moms—two dead, four critical. Film at 11:00.'"

Gilbert lapsed into talking-head speech: "'Director Fiske's driver, sensing an immediate threat from a group of anarchists, tried to remove him from harm's way.'"

"Do what those jerks believe you'd *never* do, then put out a credible explanation for why it was done, and repeat this until it becomes an answer without a question—and that, as America's first spinmeister might put it, 'would be an end on it.'"

"See you in a bit, Gil."

"Drive carefully."

When Gilbert turned around, Kevin was gone. The President was still talking on his white phone, still facing the Rose Garden. Apparently he had not yet taken notice of the two packages awaiting him on his chair.

As Gilbert returned to the couch, it became apparent the President was talking to Fiona Bartlett, his press secretary, about the speech the President's Democratic opponent, Paul Kenyon, had made the previous day in Boston.

Clearly the President was agitated.

Gilbert smiled. This was truly going to be a wonderful day!

Lily, lying on the embroidered Seal on the floor, her red ball abandoned, lifted her head and looked wistfully up at Gilbert, who responded with a frown. Lily whimpered, looked in the direction of her master's voice, and lowered her chin back onto one paw.

Gilbert took a sip of tepid coffee, grimaced, and continued to listen in on the President's conversation with Fiona. He considered indulging himself with a donut hole, but decided against it—a foolhardy *in*consistency becoming too easily a foolhardy consistency.

By the time the President finished his conversation with Fiona, Gilbert was concerned that the President might have become too agitated to take notice of the packages resting on his chair. Gilbert's concern, however, was short lived.

"Looks like the Tooth Fairy's been up to her old tricks." The President grinned toward Gilbert, then called toward the open doorway to Teresa's office: "T'rese, can you come in here for a sec, please?"

Gilbert placed his mug on the glass coaster and rose from his seat.

The sudden surge in activity apparently signaled "playtime" to Lily, who, rising to all fours, retrieved her red ball and, carrying this to Gilbert, nudged it, and a seeping muzzle, against Gilbert's left pant leg.

Gilbert responded to Lily's overture by ignoring it—refusing even to make eye contact with her—having long ago learned that the best technique to use against nuisance canines (as well as insufferable children), without offending their adoring masters (or parents), was to refuse to acknowledge them in any way. Too much of this technique could establish a pattern of "negative disengagement," however, and patterns can be dangerous, vulnerable as they were to being discovered and thereupon judged. On occasion, therefore, Gilbert would latch onto Lily's drool-slimed "indestructible spheroid" and pull on it as if he were having the time of his life, disengaging from his ecstasy only when the President intervened, as he did now.

"Hey, Lily!"

Lily looked to her master and cocked her ears.

"Go get the green one, girl. The green one!"

Had Gilbert had any inkling when he had suggested to the President, in the presence of the Grand Ayatollah of the Glorious Union of Islam, a lover of all things obedient, that *Canis familiaris* was very likely able to differentiate shades of gray down to a very fine level of nuance—had he known then that this little mustard seed of reasoned speculation might take root in the President's mind and eventually blossom into Lily's insufferable "Get the Colored Ball from the Matching Room" routine, he would never have mentioned it. The point he had been trying to make at the time was simply that the world of experience was a vast kaleidoscope of shades of gray, that the human ability to perceive vividly contrasting colors could, and often did, contribute to an unfortunate impoverishment of perception, not to mention an unfortunate tendency to emphasize appearance over substance, as in the case of modern cinema, where relentless streams of flash and dash had long since drowned out such quaint notions as plot and character, not to mention such superfluous notions as nuance and indirection.

One only needed to contrast *Citizen Kane* with *Spiderman*, *Casablanca* with *Ironman*, to grasp the enormity of what had been likely irretrievably lost.

Lily dropped her red ball onto the Great Seal and lurching through the open doorway to Teresa's office, caused Teresa, just entering, to step deftly to one side.

The President lifted Gilbert's neatly wrapped package from the seat of his desk chair and looked toward Teresa. "This one yours?"

Teresa, looking girlishly shy, shook her head.

The President grinned toward Gilbert. "Wrap this yourself?"

"Ever tireless are the minions of your court, sir."

"Wonderful. I'll know just who to call when Maggie turns sixty."

"1-800-NO-SLEEP."

Teresa chortled.

The President, both Gilbert and Teresa well knew, required no more than four or five hours of sleep per night. Given this unfortunate "pathology" (Gilbert's term), and the fact the President used the telephone (never e-mail, never snail-mail) as if it were a fifth appendage,

Gilbert had been doomed from day one of his service to Jimmy Kinney, accumulating now to over 20 years, to receive phone calls in the middle of the night: "Hey, Gil, sorry to disturb you [at 4:37 a.m.], but I was wondering if you could . . . what you thought about . . . how we should respond to . . ." Teresa had received many such calls also, over the almost four-year span of her own service to the President, and so was much appreciative of Gilbert's quip.

Setting Gilbert's package on top of his desk, the President lifted Teresa's from the seat of his chair.

"Would you like your coffee now, Mr. President?"

The President kept his eyes fixed on Teresa's package. "In a minute, thanks. Great paper."

The wrap on Teresa's package showed a tattered American flag flying over the World Trade Center memorial, juxtaposed to a similarly tattered flag flying over Fort McHenry.

"Thank you, sir."

Lily appeared, tail wagging, a green ball clutched firmly in her drooling muzzle, and trotted directly to her master, who was opening Teresa's package. Receiving a "Good girl" but no eye contact, Lily took her ball to Teresa, who, although terrified of dogs, having once been attacked by a Rottweiler in L.A., managed, as she always did, to give Lily a couple of tentative pats on the head. Lily moved over to Gilbert, who, sticking to plan, ignored her.

"Oh Lily, look!" The President held toward Lily a photograph framed in an oval of repeating ceramic balls—red, green, and blue. The photo itself showed Lily sitting in her master's chair, front paws resting on the famous Resolute desk, her green ball clutched firmly in her jaws.

"Come 'ere, girl."

Lily moved behind the desk and cocked her head to one side as the President held the photograph directly in front of her.

"I hope you don't mind, sir," Teresa said.

The President grinned. "Not at all. It's no secret who's really in charge around here."

Gilbert smiled at a scuff mark on the toe of his left shoe. About to respond then to the President holding the photograph toward him, Gilbert deferred to Teresa, who served as intermediary. Gilbert took the photo from Teresa.

"The blue one, girl! Go get the blue one!"

As Gilbert smiled at the photo, Lily trotted from behind the desk and, dropping the green ball onto the Great Seal, hurried from the room.

Gilbert directed a wink, along with the photograph, toward Teresa. "Very thoughtful," he said.

Teresa smiled—"Thank you"—and passed the photo on to the President, who, pulling the standard from the back, stood the photo on the credenza behind his desk. The immediately adjacent photo showed his freckle-faced wife Maggie, daughters Tess and Tonya, and freckle-faced son Kevin, posing on the deck of the family sloop, *High C.* The President thanked Teresa lavishly for her thoughtfulness, causing Teresa to appear about to succumb to a fatal antagonism between self-conscious flattery and self-conscious embarrassment.

Taking Gilbert's gift package into hand, the President hefted it a few times, then gave it a firm shake.

Lily appeared, a blue ball clutched in her mouth, and trotted, tail wagging, directly to her master. The President stroked one of her ears— "Good girl"—then tried to pull the ribbons on Gilbert's package over a corner without doing injury to the bow. Becoming frustrated, he tried to pull the ribbons over a different corner. Becoming even more frustrated, he tried to pull the ribbons over a third corner. "Jesus H. Christ, Gilbert!"

Gilbert stepped forward and held a pocket version of the Swiss Army knife toward the President.

"1-800-BE-PREPARED."

Teresa chortled.

Taking the offered instrument into hand, the President made a show of scrutinizing the topside of the knife, and then the underside. "What? No scissors?"

Gilbert looked dead-pan toward Teresa. "It's never enough."

Teresa giggled.

The President opened the knife blade, and using this to sever the pesky lacings, pulled heavy, stark-white wrap from a cardboard box. Returning the knife to Gilbert, the President opened the box at one end and slipped out a crimson leather-bound volume trimmed in gilt.

From the President's expression, Gilbert knew he had scored a bull's eye.

The President read aloud: "*The Autobiography of Benjamin Franklin,* Tercentenary Edition."

"Oh perfect!" Teresa exclaimed.

Gilbert smiled.

Opening the front cover of the volume, the President stared blank-faced a moment, then lifted his eyes toward the ceiling. He shook his head, then handed the book, still open, over to Teresa.

Teresa looked to the flyleaf, as if for an expected inscription there, then to the inside cover. "Number 1 of 1500," she read. "Oh my goodness. What a wonderful gift." Smiling toward Gilbert, Gilbert smiling in return, Teresa returned the book to the President, who began to riffle gently through the gilt-edged pages.

"I don't know what to say. I'm—"

The President snatched into hand an envelope about to fall to the floor from between pages, and holding this toward Gilbert, grinned. "The bill?"

Gilbert grinned in return. This was going to be a very good day indeed!

The President set the book down on his desk, and orienting the envelope, read the familiar scrawl on the front of it. "Eyes Only." He peered toward Gilbert. "Let me guess. A picture of our friend taking an air bath, on the morning of his sixtieth birthday."

"How'd you know?"

"I know you."

"These eyes were just leaving," Teresa interjected.

The President smiled toward Teresa, glanced toward the new addition on his credenza, and smiled again toward Teresa. "Thank you again for your *very* thoughtful gift."

Teresa beamed. "You're most welcome, sir."

As Teresa stepped briskly toward her office, the President glanced at his watch, and looked toward Gilbert. "Shall we sit? I think I see a mound o' fat pills over there. You haven't eaten all the chocolate ones already, have you?"

Teresa called back from the doorway to her office. "Oh, sir—excuse me. Director Fiske called to say he'd be late. He's stuck in traffic."

The President nodded; Teresa closed the door.

The President stepped around shoals of chair and table, Lily following him, and took his usual seat on the couch opposite Gilbert's usual seat. Lily flopped down on the carpeted floor, just outside the embroidered Seal, and began to chew on the green ball.

Before Teresa had had these "indestructible spheroids," as Gilbert referred to them, specially made by NASA—from the same "miracle material" used to make seals for fuel-line couplings—Lily had been chewing to pieces two to three dozen colored tennis balls a week.

The President set the greeting-card-sized envelope on the table and selected a chocolate donut hole from the platter Roy Peoples had delivered. Popping the whole of the munchkin into his mouth, the President offered the platter over to Gilbert, who, as usual, begged off, claiming, as usual, a continuing need to forestall any unfortunate reenactment of the battle of the bulge.

Gilbert had long prided himself in being able to maintain the same degree of trim he had established for himself during his four-year stint in the Marine Corps. Since becoming the President's chief counsel, however, what had been a relatively painless regimen of physical maintenance, oriented far more toward exercise—running, squash, swimming, weights—than toward dietary restraint, had become almost entirely reversed. Presently, the only exercise Gilbert was able to get on a regular basis consisted of a few quick sets of push-ups and sit-ups each week, usually in his office.

Gilbert had every intention, however, just as soon as this election was over—or it should become clear the President had become a shoo-in, by way of some fortuitous confluence of events—of getting back to at least his daily pool workouts.

Gilbert filled the President's mug—Teresa having forgotten this part of her regimen of morning service—and expecting to hear something about the latest poll numbers, or Paul Kenyon's Boston press conference last night, was surprised, but not really, to hear the President's view on the prospects of the Red Sox making it to the Series this year. The President was concerned that, although the Sox had won again last night, taking two out of three from the Orioles, at Baltimore, they were still four games behind the Yankees, and there were only a dozen or so games left in the season. This circumstance seemed, in the moment, an insurmountable obstacle, especially with four games against the Yankees coming up next week *in* New York.

Gilbert beamed reassurance toward the man he had spent the past two decades carefully shaping and molding into a winner. "For one breed of jockey," he offered, "the very worst position you can be in when you turn into the home stretch is four lengths behind the front runner. For another breed of jockey, however, the very *best* position you can be in when you're turning into the home stretch is four lengths behind the front runner."

The President grinned.

Concerned that the President might have forgotten the envelope resting next to the platter of donut holes, Gilbert held his eyes on it for a moment, then watched, awe and envy intertwining like the serpents of a caduceus, as the President popped a chocolate donut hole into his mouth, whole. Not only could this man get away with only four hours of sleep a night, suffering not a single spontaneous nod during the course of an ensuing 18- to 20-hour day, week after week; he could eat junk food with abandon, week after week, and not gain a single ounce. To Gilbert, these anomalies were somehow linked, part of the same metabolic equation.

As the President chewed, Lily continued to chew on her green ball. When the President wiped his mouth with a linen napkin, Lily paused a moment, and then allowed the green ball to drop from her mouth.

The President took a cautious sip of coffee, and another, and picking up the "Eyes Only" envelope, settled back into his seat.

If the President had made any connection between the Minutemen mugs and present circumstance, he did not let on. "Shall I open this now?"

"The occasion could not be more fitting, sir."

"I was afraid of that."

Leaning forward, the President extended a hand toward Gilbert, palm up.

Smiling in a triumphant sort of way, Gilbert slipped his pocket knife from his pocket and placed it on the President's palm.

"1-800-SEMPER-FI."

"You're a man of many numbers."

"But only one caller."

The President slit the envelope along the top and returned the knife to Gilbert, who worked it back into his pocket.

"I assume you read the *Post* this morning."

"I did indeed."

"You saw the latest numbers."

"I did."

The President shook his head. "And you saw the 'Robbin' Hood' thing."

"I did."

The President was referring to a pair of front-page articles in the morning *Post*, the pair serving as sort of bookends to a follow-on story about the oil spill off Santa Cruz. The "latest numbers" article, on the right, gave the results of the latest *New York Times*/CBS poll, which showed Paul Kenyon steadily increasing his lead over the President. Kenyon had gained two percentage points over the past two weeks alone.

The "Robbin' Hood" article, on the left, concerned a speech that Kenyon had delivered the previous evening in South Boston, the President's home turf, in which Kenyon had accused the President of being a modern-day "Robbin' Hood" who had employed "a band of law-yers" to steal from the poor to make "Jimmy Kinney and his Merry Men" ever richer. To put flesh on this bone, Kenyon had paraded in front of a throng of eager cameras several "victims" who claimed to have been made homeless at the hands of "Southie's own Mr. Potter."

The latter quip had caused Gilbert to audibly wince when he first saw it, not so much from an undeniable truth finally being laid bare as from the likely effectiveness of a play on the "Southie's own Homeboy" slogan Gilbert had so successfully used to brand his then-senatorial candidate ten years ago. Indeed, invoking the vile Mr. Potter from *It's a Wonderful Life* in the cause of re-branding Jimmy Kinney, Gilbert had to admit, was nothing short of brilliant. If his man were politically vulnerable in any particular regard, it was exactly where His Holiness the reverend Kenyon had been aiming his poison darts from the get-go.

In truth, Jimmy Kinney had been creating this Achilles heel for him-self since the summer before he entered UMass-Amherst—beginning with his father, according to some, being able to get several substan-dard triple-deckers (the "Hood" part of "Robbin' Hood") condemned as fire hazards. Jimmy's father, "Iron Joe" McKinney (Jimmy had subse-quently "dropped the Mick," as he put it), was a fire inspector in South Boston at the time.

Using 100-percent financing, backed by unit presales, most of which were bogus, according to some, Jimmy had purchased the condemned apartments for "next to nothing," according to some, and had then refurbished them into upscale condos.

By the time Jimmy graduated from UMass, with a degree in finance, he had grown his business, JMK Enterprises, into five full-time employ-ees, including himself, squeezed into a two-room office on Tremont Street, and a professionally designed, four-color business card shared by all five. Over the next twenty-one years, Jimmy had grown JMK into a major real-estate development powerhouse, focused on financing and constructing apartment and condo complexes, shopping malls, and suburban office campuses throughout the Northeast and down the Atlantic Coast.

At age forty-two, at the very height of his success, Jimmy had sold the entirety of his business to a transnational corporation, Argo Enterprises Ltd., and a year later had run for the U.S. Senate. Bankrolling his cam-paign entirely out of his own pocket, he had, as a moderate Republican in a state overwhelmingly Democratic and liberal, won the race by a single percentage point, at a personal cost of $17.51 million.

It was Jimmy Kinney's early years in the real-estate-development business, however, that had been the focus of Paul Kenyon's speech in Boston, strategically held in front of one of the condo units Jimmy had converted, decades earlier, from a triple-decker condemned—with a wink and a nod from "Iron Joe," some would say—as a fire hazard.

To Gilbert, Paul Kenyon—"that silver-piped sonuvabitch"—had represented a real threat to the President's reelection chances from the very day of the reverend's announcement for the Democratic nomination. This assessment owed in part to the oratorical wizardry Kenyon had displayed on that occasion, but mostly it owed to something Gilbert had found far more ominous—a level of moral authority that Gilbert had not seen in any public figure since the turbulent '60s, when Martin Luther King had, on many memorable occasions, stood in solemn silence before a great throng, as if upon Sinai itself, until the heavens veritably began to rumble, the sea to part. By the time the man actually spoke, it more or less didn't matter what he said. The man had become the message.

Kenyon's moral authority derived in part, certainly, as also for King, simply from his status as an ordained minister. Mostly, however, it derived from a brilliantly constructed reputation as an intrepid crusader against public and private corruption.

After a remarkably modest beginning—serving for over fifteen years as pastor at a relatively small UCC congregation in Oregon— Kenyon had been named executive director of the Charles and Marion Pickering Foundation, an Oregon-based NGO dedicated to promoting ethics in society by "emulating the child in the crowd who dared point out that the Emperor had no clothes." In his capacity as executive director, Kenyon had won over to the Foundation's core mission, in just five years, the loyalty and avid support of a vast legion of "Knights in the Cause" (or KIC, as in "KIC ass"), the make-up of which cut across sectarian as well as ideological lines. Over the ensuing five years, Kenyon had parlayed his "canonization into sainthood," as Gilbert had once put it, and the ecumenical organization he had so "ingeniously built," Gilbert had once admitted, into a Nader-like campaign to "expose and root out unethical behavior in all organizations and individuals charged with honoring and upholding the public trust, not excepting those standing in a religious or educational capacity."

As a result of this campaign, which certain elements had attempted to smear as McCarthyesque, ineptly in Gilbert's opinion, Kenyon had become widely credited with causing the downfalls of the CEOs of five major corporations, nine congressmen and two senators, three university presidents, and thirty-eight clergymen and women, including a coterie of Italian and Irish priests running an international pornography ring.

Kenyon had first aimed his poison darts at the President's Achilles heel during his prime time acceptance speech in August, at the DNC in San Francisco. In this address—"a masterful piece of tar work," Gilbert had generously granted it—Kenyon had referred to Jimmy Kinney as "Lord Jim" early on in his remarks and had repeated this label, chant like, over and over again, in the manner of a fulling machine. The intent, of course, was to tar Jimmy Kinney as a Dickensian villain (the "Lord" part), while at the same time associating him with the Conrad character who had, in an act of craven selfishness, condemned an entire boatload of hapless victims to a watery death while saving himself.

The label had stuck, catching on especially well with certain "frothy-mouthed commentators." To keep this monster alive in the public consciousness, "Dr. Frankenstein" had subsequently used every possible opportunity to conjure it as if from a moorish mist, even convincing a major network to run the 1965 *Lord Jim* film immediately following a preseason football game. Last evening, in Boston, Kenyon had once again played the conjurer, this time by parading thirteen "documented victims" who had been turned out of their homes at the hands of one of the most monstrously selfish, abjectly craven characters in all of British literature, Lord Jim, in the guise of one of the most monstrously selfish, abjectly avaricious characters in all of American pop culture, Mr. Henry Potter.

There was no doubt in Gilbert's mind—or in the President's, Gilbert well knew—that Kenyon's campaign to insinuate Jimmy Kinney as, in effect, the only man to escape the Titanic in a lifeboat, was the reason for the President's steady erosion in the polls. The brilliant transformation now of Lord Jim into Mr. Potter, thereby into Ebenezer Scrooge, could only, if left unaddressed—indeed un-neutralized—continue the erosion.

"How do we get to that bastard?" the President wanted to know, holding "the bill" envelope off to one side.

"Live by the dart, die by the dagger," Gilbert offered, allowing a knowing sort of smile to insinuate itself into the subdermal tissues of a remarkably unwrinkled seventyish face.

The President regarded Gilbert a moment, as if to read the specials from the chalkboard, and grinned. "You have something in mind; I can tell."

"As indeed you have something in hand."

The President lifted the envelope and, pulling from it a single folded sheet, unfolded the latter and began to read the typescript.

Gilbert watched the President's eyes grow wider.

The President looked toward Gilbert with eyes like griddling eggs. "Jesus Christ, Gilbert! Is this legit?"

Lily lifted her head from the floor and stared at her master, her amber eyes as if laden with concern.

Gilbert smiled. "It depends on what the meaning of 'legit' is."

The President read aloud:

Dr. Shaara: Was that the only time he asked you to do that to him?

Ms. Ramos: No.

Dr. Shaara: There were other times?"

Ms. Ramos: Yes.

Dr. Shaara: How many?

Ms. Ramos: Every session.

Dr. Shaara: How many sessions?

Ms. Ramos: I don't remember exactly. We started out just once a week, then increased to two or three times a week.

Dr. Shaara: So how did he explain this to you, as your pastoral counselor? What did he tell you the purpose of this was?

Ms. Ramos: He told me it would liberate me. He told me the Catholic Church had taught me to think of sex as something to be ashamed of, and because of this I had developed many unhealthy associations with it. He told me the only way I could get rid of all those bad associations was to engage in the kind of therapy he was willing to offer me.

Dr. Shaara: And by "therapy," you mean sex.

Ms. Ramos: Yes.

Dr. Shaara: Now, this is very important. You are absolutely certain, beyond any doubt whatsoever, that these sexual encounters actually happened—that you did not imagine them, or come to believe them at someone's suggestion.

Ms. Ramos: [nods, tearing up].

Dr. Shaara: And you are absolutely certain, beyond any doubt whatsoever, that these encounters involved Dr. Paul Kenyon, then rector of First Congregational United Church of Christ in Eugene, Oregon, in his capacity as your pastoral counselor.

Ms. Ramos: [nods, breaks down].

A hoot from the President and Lily was on all fours. She stared at her master a moment, as if for a cue, then picked up the red ball from the Great Seal and, approaching her master, lifted the ball toward him. The President held the sheet from which he had been reading directly in front of her. "See this, girl? Know what this is? Four more years—in the bag!" He hooted again, with even more exuberance, bringing two Secret Service agents, one uniformed, the other Ken Rankin, through the door leading to the Roosevelt Room.

"Four more years!" the President sang out to them, holding up both arms.

The two agents apologized and quickly withdrew.

The President grinned at Gilbert, ignoring Lily, who was still offering the red ball toward him. "This is incredible, Gilbert—too, too good!"

The President postured as if to continue reading, but then looked again at Gilbert. "Who's this Shaara guy anyway?"

"All in due course. Please—enjoy."

Lily flopped down onto the floor between the green ball (resting on the clutch of arrows), and the blue ball (resting on the olive branch). She continued to hold the red ball in her mouth.

Her master continued:

Dr. Shaara: Why didn't you recall these incidents, do you think, until you were placed under hypnosis?

Ms. Ramos: I—[begins to cry again].

Dr. Shaara: You don't have to answer. This is not a court-room. If you can, however, I'd like you to describe the room, including any furnishings you can remember, in which these encounters occurred. Could do you do that for me?

"Yes!" the President exclaimed, sending Lily again to her feet. "I assume that's what she said, yes? I mean, she said 'yes,' yes?"

"Yes."

"Yes!" the President exclaimed again, punching the air. "Holy shit!"

The President popped another chocolate donut hole into his mouth and offered the plate to Gilbert, who selected a honey-glazed one.

The President tried to talk through a mouthful of donut, paused, and swallowed. "This is absolute dynamite," he finally managed. "And this is just a sample, right? I mean, there's more, right?—a whole platterful of little yeses—yes?"

"We have three transcripts taken from three different recordings involving three different women and three different therapists. Dr. Shaara, of course, is one of the therapists."

The President smiled, shook his head, took a sip from his mug, grimaced. Pouring fresh coffee into his mug, he gestured toward Gilbert's cup with the carafe.

Gilbert looked at his watch. "Time's about up."

The President looked at his own watch and then settled against the back of his seat. "This is all legit, right? I mean, you're not out to bust the birthday boy's balls on his Big Day, are you?"

Gilbert wiped his fingers on a linen napkin, then gestured with his head toward the portrait of Franklin hanging over the mantel. "Remember the account our friend wrote about a massacre of women and children by a band of Indians, savages, working with the Red Coats?"

The President grinned.

"More than one way there is, our friend well knew, to win a war."

The President sniffed at the envelope. "Am I beginning to smell a rat, Dr. Bahr?"

"'A cat with gloves catches no mice.'"

The President hooted.

Lily lifted her chin.

Gilbert settled against the back of his couch. "As I mentioned, we have three separate tapes from three different therapy sessions, involving three different women and their therapists. What you just read, as you surmised, is an excerpt from one of the transcripts. The voices on the tapes are the voices of real women who were actual members of Paul Kenyon's UCC congregation in Eugene, and the other voices are the voices of actual therapists. However—"

The President clapped his hands over his ears.

Gilbert raised his voice. "*However*"—the President lowered his hands—"the specific statements recorded on these tapes never happened, although we strongly suspect they, or something strongly akin to them, *could* have happened, Kenyon being the slime ball he most certainly is."

"How is that even possible?"

"You know those hypnotic voice-overs you hear everywhere these days, by a guy named Bob?" The President nodded. "Well, there is no Bob. Well, there is, and there isn't. All those sonorous 'sweet nothings' you hear from this guy are in fact sweet nothings. They're all computer-generated—all from a database of actual words spoken by an anonymous donor, you might say, and then broken down into little bits of speech called phonemes, which are then reconstituted into new words by means of a highly sophisticated algorithm. In other words, the real Bob drops his load into a database, and is no longer needed, so off with his head. Thereafter you just tell a computer program what you want Bob to say, and he says it."

The President shook his head; Lily whimpered.

"However," Gilbert continued, "and this is where it gets really interesting, the speech algorithms used to do this are not very good at replicating the kind of high emotion one would expect to be exhibited in a therapist's office. In fact, they're terrible at it. Which is why Melodious Bob is actually a rather dull fellow indeed. To address this problem, our good friend over at Langley had a couple of his nerds try their hand at an algorithm that could infuse appropriate emotional content into any given base level of semantic content." Gilbert smiled. "Guess what?"

"They failed utterly."

Gilbert grinned. "Utterly. When Fiske demonstrated what they'd come up with, using me as a guinea pig—he got me all exercised about The Standard Model; his little joke—I absolutely could not tell that what I was hearing had been generated by a computer program instead of by me. Absolutely could *not* tell. Of course, Fiske had benefit of a rich sampling of my speech—and that's the other part of the equation. For this thing to work to the level required, the database for each speaker has to be rich enough in both phonemes and what Fiske calls 'monemes' that you can replicate not only all possible speech for a particular speaker, but a full range of emotional content as well. There's no way around this. So what Fiske & Company did is they bugged all six subjects—the three women, and the three therapists—over a period of several weeks." Gilbert shook his head. "You don't want to know the details. Suffice it to say that they managed to get a very rich sampling of each subject, in a variety of venues, in a remarkably short period of time."

The President grinned. "What great big teeth you have, Grandma."

Gilbert grinned. "It gets better."

"What—no 'however?'"

"*However*, it gets better. All three female subjects were, at one time, actual patients of the therapists involved in the interviews. Each therapist kept records, of course, and in each case these records included tapes of actual therapy sessions. Of course, these tapes have been replaced with substitutes, except for one in each case, which, as they say these days, has 'gone missing.'"

The President threw both arms up over his head and hooted, again alarming Lily, who again rose to all fours. "Gilbert, you are a certified fucking genius—but then you already knew that."

"1-800-NO-SLEEP."

Lily approached her master and again nudged his leg with the red ball. As the President fondled one of Lily's ears, his face seemed to dim a bit, as if from a rogue cloud passing over the sun on an otherwise cloudless day. "OK, so what happens when these three women start appearing on television with teary-eyed denials?"

"Which is more likely to hold more weight in the court of public opinion: The up-close and personal denials of three keening females with documented histories of emotional problems, or the actual voices of these same women as recorded by their therapists?"

The President threw back his head, hooted at the relief on the ceiling, then looked again toward Gilbert. "What great big balls you have, Grandma."

Gilbert grinned.

The President popped a Boston cream into his mouth, chewed a moment, then settled back into his seat and narrowed his eyes. "OK, so where's the weak spot? There's always a weak spot."

Gilbert nodded. "The human factor—people in the know—of which, in this case, there are three, not including present company. There's Fiske and two of his wunderkinds."

"Fiske is certainly safe. What about the nerds?"

"They have a direct link only to Fiske. They could certainly surmise a link from Fiske to us, but there's no way they could ever substantiate one. As far as assurances of personal discretion go, they're both under the Code, so they both know what would happen to them, and their grandmothers, if they were ever to, shall we say, become infused with the Holy Spirit."

The President grinned.

"That's the stick part. The carrot part consists of two numbered accounts, of generous proportion, at a certain bank in the Cayman Islands, and two routine Social Security disability retirements, presently in the pipeline."

"What about the missing tapes? How're you accounting for those?"

"Ransom notes demanding cash payments in exchange for their

return to the recorded subjects have already been prepared. All three notes were constructed by the same hand, and, in each case, salted with the fingerprints of the same secondary party who had obviously served as an amateur thief in behalf of the extortionist. After a series of events, these fingerprints will be traced, in each case, to someone, an office worker or the like, who had access to the relevant case files, and, until recently, had a significant burden of credit-card debt."

The President lifted his eyes to the graven Seal on the ceiling, and shook his head.

Gilbert continued. "Now, as to the targets of these extortions, these were very carefully selected. From all appearances, each of the families involved could be construed as being comfortably well off. In actuality, however, each family is anything but, owing to"—Gilbert smiled—"a history of *in*frugality."

The President threw his head back, threw up his arms, waved these wildly about, and looked toward Gilbert. "I'm in awe."

"1-800-NO-SLEEP."

Springing to his feet, the President extended a hand across the table toward Gilbert, who rose to clasp it. "Dr. Bahr, sir, this is absolutely the best birthday I've *ever* had in my entire life, bar none."

"So to say."

"So to say. When I read those stories in the *Post* this morning, I thought this was going to be absolutely the *worst* day of my life, never mind the worst *birth*day of my life. You are truly a miracle worker. You have single-handedly given me this election, and I thank you."

"We do what we have to, sir—what is best."

"We do."

Sitting back down, followed by Gilbert, the President popped a chocolate donut hole into his mouth.

Lily flopped onto the floor just outside the Great Seal, and releasing the red ball from her mouth, rested her muzzle on one paw. She shifted her honey-amber eyes between the two men as they spoke, then closed them.

Book II

Trials

To patience goeth glimpse of fawn and doe
To else, what regret doth spawn and sow.

—Philomena M.

Celestial Chamber of B. Franklin

17 January 1706–17 April 1790

Ben awakened to the notion—nay, the hope—that what he had just witnessed as if from the vantage of a fly upon the wall was no greater than a contrivance of that dark spirit which, in advantaging itself of one's slumber, imposes all manner of mischief upon one's imagination.

He noticed then, with a start, that he was not in the chamber to which he had retired, but instead was as if returned to his former bed-chamber at 7 Craven Street.

Indeed, the chestnut bed in which he presently resided appeared to be the very same. The cherry-wood wardrobe in the corner askance appeared to be the very same. The Spartan chair in front of the only window appeared to be the very same, as did the window. And the commode upon the floor appeared to be the very same indeed that had toppled him one moonless night to such a clamor as to rouse Mrs. Stevenson unto discovering him prostrate in a puddle.

Removing himself from the bed, to a pinch of stone, Ben made his way to the wardrobe, and opening the doors on this, to a familiar plaint, discovered hanging from the rod within—O happiness!—the very suit of Manchester velvet he had worn on two previous occasions of high moment, the first being his appearance before the king's Privy Council, whereat, at the hands of one Alexander Wedderburn, he had been malevolently abused in the stead of Samuel Adams & Company; the second being his appearance at the signing of the Treaty of Alliance, under terms of which the colonies had gained sufficient means by which to render unto those blue-blooded nincompoops at Whitehall precisely what they had accumulated in just deserts.

His eyes wetting of bosom's dew, Ben reached forth and touched—nay, caressed—the swaddling fabric of his beloved suit. He had first

petitioned for the comfort of this at the urging of Clarence, his current Intermediary, after expressing to Clarence, during a particularly
strenuous chess match, that he wished not to appear before the court
of his judgment in the same raiment in which he had been buried. His
petition had thereupon gone unanswered for weeks become months,
as had a succession of inquiries, to effect ultimately of bringing Ben
unto such despondency of spirit as to cause him to contrive a last, bold
attempt in the form of a satire, titled *The Virtue of Efficiency*, under the
good name of Fanny Frugal, widow.

In giving Mrs. Frugal free rein, Ben had imagined a Directorate of
Residential Affairs become so encumbered of ineptitude that its victims had resorted to invoking the Statute of Celestial Limitations, to
end of vast numbers of souls being returned to Earth to resume their
mortal existence at the very point of their departure, and being granted
just recompense to boot, in the form of current specie, as compounded
over the entire period of their involuntary absence.

The simple reply, which had come within days, had brought Ben up
short: "Two loaves for thee," it had read, as rendered from the Greek.

What, pray tell, Ben had wondered, was to be made of so unexpected
a response, biblical not only in its diction but also in its obfuscation?
Firstly, he had no utility, in his present situation, for two loaves of anything; secondly, he had no idea how this cryptic message related to the
aim of his bagatelle. If, as he was inclined to suspicion, the Advocate
General, the principal to whom he had directed his satire, was none
other than his old nemesis Lord Hillsborough himself, then a scatological interpretation of "two loaves" might properly be imagined.

Short of such, however, the only speculation toward sense that Ben
had been able to contrive at the time was the possibility of some kind
of association betwixt the loaf-sized rolls to which he had given some
notoriety in his *Autobiography*—they being mentioned by him there
in relation to his arrival at Philadelphia, at age seventeen, close unto
starvation—and the loaves of this strange reply. There had, however,
been three loaves involved on the occasion of his Philadelphia arrival,
not two.

Unable at the time to solve the mystery at hand, Ben had lapsed into
recollecting, toward his amusement, the particulars of his Philadelphia
arrival, including walking up High Street with one fat roll levered under
each arm, a third held to mouth, but then had broken off his reverie
before mere recollections might materialize into an intimate reality, as

had been their power to do, of some mysterious efficacy, over the entire span of his two-centuries tenure at the Plantation of the Unconfessed.

To the positive, Ben had been able to employ this singular ability toward completing his *Autobiography*, which now totaled to thirteen volumes. To the negative, he had many times been transported by way of careless musings to venues he did not wish to revisit, and indeed chose not to revisit for any longer than it should take him to alter the present course of his thoughts.

Looking now to the shelf overtop the rod holding his velvet suit, Ben discovered a fine silk shirt, a pair of white silk stockings, and—O happiness!—the very cap he had worn in lieu of powder and wig over the entirety of his tenure as Commissioner in Paris. Looking to the floor then, Ben discovered a pair of silver-buckle shoes, and standing close upon these, the very crab-tree cane—O happiness!—that had been given him by Madame de Forbach, the "rival" toward whom the ever-mischievous Madame Helvetius had pretended a wicked jealousy.

Discarding his nightshirt onto the chair, Ben dressed himself in his beloved suit and, upon donning his fur cap, smiled as the image in the looking glass attached upon the inside of one of the wardrobe doors transformed from a portly old gentleman costumed in a suit of blue velvet and a cap of marten fur into a statuesque knight resplendent in silver plate and plumed helmet.

He grinned then as the image in the looking glass corrupted into a rabid old knight crowned not of a plumed helmet but of a dimpled old barber pan.

He winked then as the image in the glass returned to the portly old gentleman costumed in a suit of blue velvet and a cap of marten fur—the latter pulled close unto the top of his spectacles.

He was true! He was ready!

Entering into his study, one half filled with books and papers, the other half with electrical apparatus, the whole being in a state of disorder most agreeable, Ben sat down in his reading chair and removed from the checkerboard table, adjacent, a copy of the notes he had given to Clarence several months previous to deliver unto the advocates he had named to plead his case.

As he perused the familiar words, he felt an agreeable warming within, as if indeed old embers, long in dormancy, had been revived by a generous chop of half-breaths from a bellows.

Finally, he was going to have his day in court.

Finally! Finally! Finally!

Grimacing now, Ben shifted his bulk in his chair, to end of rendering himself at least a temporary respite from an unrelenting—eternal, one might feel compelled to speculate—colic of stone. Reading onward then, he continued to be well pleased with his notes. There was no ornament here, no powder and wig, only the barest of facts, each one attired in no greater fashion than what would be welcomed at a meetinghouse.

Of course, there had been a few errata along the way, but what mortal had escaped his earthly tenure without such? Of far greater import, certainly, were the credits one had accumulated in relation to his debits—a notion his petitioners would make much of, he did trust, by making little of.

Not *too* little, however.

Ben smiled to recollection now of his petitioners as last he had seen them, each one.

It would be so very good to see them again! Three more agreeable friends and colleagues no soul could wish to have held to bosom.

Animated by a tease of anticipation, Ben looked to the ebony doorway through which he had not passed in over two centuries, but would now, soon—very soon.

Just as soon indeed as dear Clarence should show himself.

Anticipation corrupting unto impatience, Ben plumbed the watch pocket in his vest for feel of a tenant but encountered naught.

Alas, he had not thought to include a timepiece in his petition.

No matter, he assured. Little was to be gained from so habituating an instrument in any event, beyond encouraging small vexations unto larger.

Ben looked again to the ebony door, which had not, of an apparent immunity native unto it, been altered in either substance or coloration during the entirety of his tenure in his apartment. All else had been transmuted from one thing unto another a myriad of times, simply by force of his historical reminiscences.

Sensible now of impatience corrupting unto resentment, Ben of a sudden discovered himself sitting at levee in Thomas Penn's parlour at Spring Gardens, waiting to be beckoned for an interview concerning the refusal of the Penn heirs to contribute funds, any funds soever, toward the common defense of the Pennsylvania colony.

Waiting, and waiting, and waiting—

Clarence, where *are* you?

A sharp report at the door—startling even though expected—was followed by two others in close succession.

Rising from his chair in simultaneity to a pretentious parlour transforming unto a practical study, Ben hobbled his way to the doorway, wincing the while to sharp twinges of gout. Upon the door opening, Ben was surprised to discover Clarence standing in company not with himself alone but with a taller second.

Of course!

B. Franklin, Petitioner, was to be accompanied unto judgment not only by the very last of his Intermediaries, but also by the very first.

Ben embraced Bartholomew as if to peril of fracturing him unto a pile of bones, and shook his hand as if to peril of wresting the poor man's arm from its attachment. He greeted Clarence with, although less animation, no less the affection.

In both instances, Ben's enthusiasms were returned in kind.

Clarence and Bartholomew were attired in costumes the likes of which Ben had never before witnessed. Each Intermediary was draped in a robe of two halves, the one half being of white satin, the other of black. Upon Clarence, the seam betwixt halves was extended from the right shoulder unto the left hip, and downward to the ankle. The whole of the gown was girded at the waist by a braid of two silks, one black, one white; and tethered by way of this braid, upon Clarence's right hip, he being left favouring, was a sword sheathed in a scabbard ornamented of rubies, emeralds, and sapphires.

On Bartholomew, all of these aspects were the same, but in opposing arrangement, such as to suggest a looking-glass image. The only exceptions owed to the individuals themselves, Bartholomew's eyes being blue, Clarence's brown; Bartholomew's stature being perhaps six feet and two, Clarence's being perhaps five feet and seven.

Cocked upon the head of each Intermediary was a rakish hat, black as jet, ornamented not of feather or plume, as might be expected, but of a single instance—O happiness!—of the lush bloom of the very flora John Bartram, dear friend and able botanist, had named the *Franklinia alatamaha*. On Clarence's hat, five creamy-white petals, radiant around a golden core, were biased to leftward; on Bartholomew's, the very same to rightward.

No more salutary symbol could these two fine gentlemen have chosen for this, the most momentous occasion of B. Franklin, Printer's entire existence.

The two Intermediaries stiffened unto a martial posture, and bowing then, stepped one to side such as to invite Ben to precede them over the transom. Doing as bidden, Ben discovered himself standing close upon a skiff easy upon a stream the luster of quicksilver. The stream itself was little broader than a post road, and in coursing straight ahead, in even undulations, served to cleave a garden of rose shrubs into looking-glass images. Overtopping the whole of the garden was a dome of seven rings, from deepest red at center unto deepest violet at perimeter.

Clarence took station close upon the prow, such as to face forward, whilst Bartholomew settled Ben close upon the stern. Placing himself amidships, upright, Bartholomew took hold of the oar and stroked the skiff smoothly forward. As they progressed, Ben was surprised to glimpse of furtive movements to side, in likeness indeed to the cautions of feral cats.

Coming upon a curtain of mist, they entered into this without caution, and emerged into a second garden, this one as lush in verdance as the previous was in bloom. Here also an overarching dome showed seven concentric circles, but with deepest green at center. And here also Ben caught glimpses of furtive movements to side, these giving impression now of the vacillations of something being pushed forward by one impulse, held back by another.

Sensing a condensation upon his lip, Ben wetted his tongue of it, and tasting of it, flinched to a sensation he had not experienced in over two centuries—the sour of fetid milk.

Coming upon another curtain of mist, they entered into this without abatement, and emerged into yet a third garden, this one resplendent of the azure of the hydrangea. Here also an overhead dome showed seven concentric circles, but with deepest blue at center. And here also Ben caught glimpses of furtive movements to side, these become most unnerving.

Sensing a fresh wetness upon his lip, Ben dared wet his tongue of it, and tasting of it, relished a sensation he had not experienced in over two centuries—the sweet of honey.

They arriving finally as if at the same doorway just departed, Clarence and Bartholomew assisted Ben in disembarking the skiff, and led him thereupon unto the ebony door. Ben hearing a low moaning, he turned half-circle around, and was startled to discover, showing overtop every shrub, for as far as his eyes would allow, the face of a child.

The moaning growing ever more plaintive, Ben looked to Bartholomew.

"There is naught to be done here, good sir," Bartholomew assured. "Your business is within."

His guides gesturing thereupon for him to precede them, Ben passed through the doorway and in the instant, as if by flick of a conjuror's wand, was rendered unseeing. No little affrighted, Ben held stopped until such time he felt a gentle grasp upon either arm. Even so, as he progressed in measured steps, he used his walking stick to query ahead after any treacheries that might lurk there, such indeed as a chamber pot half filled.

~

Catching hint, or so he thought, of a low sound, of indistinct origin, Ben adjudged himself yet hearing even if unseeing, and was reminded, to taste of bitter in equal measure with sweet, of playing blind man's buff with Jane and Lydia.

Poor Jane. Whatever had become of her? Would he *ever* know—ever be *allowed* to know?

Not knowing, not knowing—this had, by far, been the worst of his deprivations. Nary a book or newspaper to read; nary a parlour or coffeehouse to visit; nary a crier or gossip to hear—nary even a preacher or sophist to suffer! Indeed, what he wouldn't have given over all these decades, endlessly accumulating, to hear the bay and howl of some itinerant prophet reeking of sulphur and rum.

Catching hint now of low sounds, these reminding of an assemblage grown animated of expectation, Ben strained toward discerning merest image or movement—straight ahead, to side—but was unable to capture physical evidence even of his two close-upon guides.

Feeling a gentle tug upon both arms, as a horse must feel its reins, Ben stopped in place, and had no sooner done so than was restored to sight, and was no sooner restored to sight than was struck near insensible.

He was in the Cockpit!

Indeed, he was as if returned unto the very venue in which he had appeared before the King's Council, ostensibly to advance a petition for the recall of Governor Hutchinson from Massachusetts, but in fact to stand as whipping boy in the stead of Samuel Adams et al., with the cat o' nine being the viper tongue of one Alexander Wedderburn, pettifogger for hire.

For one terrible moment, Ben was uncertain as to whether he should be able to remain upstanding, so enfeebled had his knees been rendered of shock, the latter emanant not so much from what he was beholding as from what such might portend.

Perhaps all those howling doomsayers of his youth had been right after all.

Ben closed his eyes and pictured himself at Versailles, in one of the receiving rooms, waiting on being summoned unto the signing room. He was comfortable in his suit of Manchester velvet, though naked of the customary wig and sword, two instruments of pretense with which he refused to have any relation soever.

He strained to recollect every detail: what Deane and Lee were wearing; where they stood; what Vergennes said upon entering the room—the entire tone and texture of the occasion.

When he opened his eyes, he was crestfallen to discover himself yet standing in the Cockpit. It would seem that, in abandoning his apartment, he had abandoned all facility toward rendering a few fibers of memory unto a whole cloth of materiality.

Capturing his attention now was a curious difference betwixt the Cockpit of 29 January 1774 and the one presently at witness. In place of the table at which Lord Gower had sat to center, his lesser colleagues to side by rank, stood a high bench of variegated marble, black and white; and to either side of this, oblique to it by forty-five degrees, stood an ivory seat elevated upon a round ebony pedestal. Each seat showed a splayed back in likeness to a scallop shell, and providing access to each seat was a spiral of steps twining counterclockwise in the one case, clockwise in the other. The steps themselves alternated betwixt ebony and ivory.

Outside these articles of difference, several held familiarity, including the balcony that circumvented the whole of the room, and the swags of crimson tapestry that hung from the underside of this to front. Also familiar were the pillars of the Doric style, and the Royal Seal framed by these, at center behind the high bench, and, too, a distempering ambience of dank air scented of musk and soot.

These aspects of familiarity served now to excite an ancient resentment unto a fresh burn, they having been the sole objects of Ben's attention for over an hour's duration such that he might not give Solicitor General Wedderburn even one moment's countenance during the course of this unprincipled mountebank's outrageous defamation of Ben's very character.

"You *had* your opportunity, Dr. Franklin, sir; Silence Dogood, madam;

Miss Polly Baker, madam; Poor Richard, sir; Father Abraham, sir—but you would not profit of it."

The booming voice was unmistakable. By force of nativity, it should be indelibly tinctured of Scottish brogue, as in the example indeed of William Strahan, but instead was largely, though not wholly, absent such. Alexander Wedderburn, born to disadvantage outside the bastion walls of the British aristocracy, had long ago discovered the lessons to be learned from that slippery, dragon-like chimera known as the chameleon.

Ben looked to source.

Draped in a black robe, stiffly Tory in a wig coiffed unto longish curls, Solicitor General Wedderburn was standing behind a table poised perpendicular to the high bench of variegated marble, hence half-perpendicular to the intervening perch. He was flanked to his left by the Reverend William Smith, seated, and to his right by old owl face himself, John Adams, also seated. All three men were smiling toward him in the manner of schoolboy bullies anticipating a wanton infliction of torment upon a hapless victim at earliest opportunity.

"You were given every opportunity to render a full accounting of your—as you might confess it, sir—errata, but you steadfastly chose not to do so. In fact, sir, you were given far more latitude in this regard than was your due. To present, you have accumulated the service of thirteen Intermediaries, close upon a celestial record, and each one of these, sir, including those two standing at your side, has lodged at least one petition of extension in your behalf, unbeknownst to yourself. The last of these extensions has now run its course, with no better outcome than any other." Wedderburn looked to Smith, and to Adams. "Are we struck insensible of surprise, gentlemen?"

Adams and Smith shook their heads with downcast solemnity, Adams's jowls quivering to the effort.

Wedderburn looked again to Ben: "There is an old saying, sir—'One can lead a horse to water but cannot make him drink'—to which I must presume you have some familiarity, given your long history of promulgating the like of it."

Ben held to silence. To approach upon any bait held forth by the likes of an Alexander Wedderburn was to be drawn into the jaws of a trap.

Wedderburn continued. "The wonder is, sir, that some Poor Dick did not take advantage whilst opportunity availed to derive from this old saw its corollary, to wit, sir: 'A horse so stubborn must surely be an ass.'"

Adams and Smith erupted into guffaws, and slapping the tabletop to front, were joined in their cackle by an assemblage, previously sensed, gathered behind whereat Ben presently stood.

Ben steeled himself by stiffening his spine, as he had on that previous occasion. Indeed, he would not allow himself to be affected, either demonstrably or privately, by any insult, however egregious. He would be no supplicant here, no sycophant. He would be as he had always been, so to say, a man of perhaps too many errata, but also a man who had consigned unto the public larder far more than ever he had claimed of it.

He had no apologies to make—not in this venue nor in any other.

The facts were as they could not otherwise be, and naught else in all eternity could be more eloquent in the cause of establishing, beyond all pettifoggery, what truth might be made of them.

Reminded now of the agency by which the truth as regards B. Franklin was to be established beyond all pettifoggery, Ben looked to leftward, and—O happiness!—discovered at table there, opposing directly his three examiners, to a burst of euphoria such as might be attributed to a generous indulgence of a well-traveled Madeira, his dearest of dear friends—Peter Collinson, William Strahan, and Bishop Shipley—smiling as if three become one ever so warmly upon him.

He was in good hands! He was in good, good hands!

Each man appeared in both years and manner of dress as Ben had last seen him, which event, Ben realized with a start, had occurred just previous to Ben's return to America, in 1775, to, in effect, wage war against him.

Could the stew of any life benefit from a better spice than irony?

Ben nodded to his petitioners, who nodded in return.

The opposing tables, Ben now noticed, in league with the high bench at front and the two elevated seats at the oblique, formed the better part of an oval, with this geometry being completed, Ben surmised, by an arc of spectators behind.

At center of this oval, a few paces forward of where Ben presently stood, a vitreous circle, perhaps six feet in diameter, was inscribed into the wood floor. Ben could not recollect any such circle in the Cockpit of 1774. He could recollect, however, the parquet floor into which the circle was inscribed, especially as regards a particular stain, located close upon the high bench. It had resulted, so legend held, from an affliction of gastric intolerance owing to a dotty lord having ingested a leaf of American tobacco thinking it a wafer of Dutch chocolate. How that leaf of tobacco had gotten itself into that particular lord's tin had ever remained a mystery.

Ben noticed now, by glimpse of peripheral movement, a gowned gentleman reposed upon the elevated seat betwixt the marble bench and the examiners' table. The man was strikingly angular of countenance, and reedy of limb, and appeared to be wearing a wig too small. Curiously, the other elevated seat, betwixt the bench and the petitioners' table, stood empty.

Ben was struck by how strongly the present setting was suggesting of an altar and chancel of the High Anglican taste. Indeed, the only ornament lacking in this regard was the Archbishop himself, attended by a troop—troupe?—of bowing and cooing supplicants.

Of a sudden, the perched gentlemen sprang to upstanding, in likeness indeed to a jack released from its box. "Dr. Franklin, sir, be it your wish to be seated or to remain upstanding?"

Ben stiffened. "I shall remain upstanding, if it please the court."

"Errata," Clarence whispered, from rightward.

"To sit would be to suggest weakness," Ben whispered in return. "And it is errat*um*, dear man, not errat*a*. Let us not needlessly compound a humble singular unto a needless extravagance."

"Weakness, sir?" Bartholomew whispered, from leftward. "Or absence of a foolish pride?"

"Are you gentlemen here to lend me assistance or to see me griddled?"

"We are here, good sir," this in two-part harmony, "that you should not stand alone."

"Would the gentleman," the clerk instructed, by way of inquiry, "be so kind as to remove his head dressing—unless, of course, the gentleman should regard the unfortunate creature presently sheathed over the temple of his soul, a wig."

Feeling a burn of cheek, Ben doffed his marten cap, and executing a bow toward the clerk, gave "the unfortunate creature" over to Bartholomew, in the manner of a schoolchild passing a forbidden communication to a schoolmate.

"Auspicious beginning," Bartholomew whispered.

"Why did you not alert me?" Ben whispered.

"You colonials are forever doing things your own way," Clarence whispered.

"Instead of 'Do unto others as you would have them do unto you,'" Bartholomew added, "it's 'Do as you like, whenever you like, for whatever reason you like.'"

"Seeing your manner of dress," Clarence continued, "in light of our intimate knowledge of you, we judged the hat to be a piece with the suit; the suit to be a piece with the man; the man to be a piece with his pride."

The ambient light, emanant from no apparent source, as in the case of the domed gardens, began now to diminish. When it had waned near unto total eclipse, the clerk sang forth, in striking falsetto, "All rise," giving particular height to the latter syllable, and holding it.

Hearing a rolling rumble, as if in counterpoint to the yet-lingering falsetto, Ben cast his eyes upward and discovered not the ceiling of heroic panels expected, but a firmament of roiling clouds, these of strikingly purplish, greenish, and blackish casts.

Feeling a hint of vertigo, Ben recollected the recent counsel of his Intermediaries concerning his choice of repose, and thereupon suffered a pang of regret for having embraced "a foolish pride." To his good fortune, however, his endangerment was apparently detected by his Intermediaries, by some auxiliary sense, for each grasped him by the arm, and firmly so, to end of instilling a common assurance against a humiliating, not to mention debilitating, collapse.

His comfort was short-lived, however, for a bolt of brilliant light, reddish in cast, stabbed through the ambient pall and struck upon the marble bench with such thunderous violence as to cause a quaking underfoot. A second bolt followed, this one greenish in cast, and a third, bluish. Sizzling fluxations thereupon erupted over the surface of the bench until the whole of it was consumed of a frenzied turbulence of ever-changing colorations.

Of a sudden all went still and in place of the high bench of variegated marble stood now a crystalline monolith glinting of the glow of a luminous object descending toward it.

As this curious object grew ever closer, its body grew ever more elongated, until it had grown unto likeness indeed of a tongue of fire.

If in the beginning was the "Word," Ben allowed, there must needs have been a tongue by which to give it voice.

Catching hint of what sounded like a chiming of silver bells, Ben noted that the volume of this sensation seemed to increase in proportion to the nearness of the descending luminescence. Then—O happiness!—he realized that this sweetness of sound was emanant not from silver bells, but from the crystalline bowls of a glass armonica, and that the music being excited therefrom, by fingers obviously well practiced, was no other than the *Adagio* young Mozart had composed for it.

Ah, but was this unexpected recital a salutation of a kind, for deeds to which his gift of the armonica unto the world at large was emblematic, or was it but a sly baiting of a vanity too willing toward an abiding indulgence?

The tongue of fire came to rest now close upon the top of the crystalline bench, to effect of the latter becoming equally as luminous, in suggestion indeed to an infant suckling its fill without diminishing the stock of its nurse. The *Adagio* abating, it had no sooner quit than the tongue of fire swelled unto such an expansion of brilliance, as compounded by the body of the bench, as to absorb unto itself everything it bathed in a balm of purist light.

Shutting his eyes of reflex, Ben opened them soon thereafter to discover suspended over the bench not a single tongue of fire, but three separate tongues—one red, one green, one blue—they dancing over the top of the bench, whilst also pulsating and undulating, to end of rendering the body of the bench into a sort of kaleidoscope of three dimensions.

Within this singular chamber now, a wondrous infinitude of colorations began to coalesce into intricate symmetries, these suggesting of snow crystals tinctured of more colorations than were imaginable, and thereupon to dissolve back into the very formlessness from which they had only just emerged—the one state, being Order, seeming indeed to be the very cause of the other state, being Disorder, and vice versa.

The ceiling having restored itself, the ambient light returned, and with it came a sweetness of air reminding of that which follows an electrical storm.

The clerk, yet upstanding upon his perch, as if indeed nothing soever had just occurred, sang forth in striking falsetto, "Hear ye! Hear ye! Hear ye! The Supreme Celestial Court of Petitions is now in session. Petition of B. Franklin, 17 January 1706 unto 17 April 1790, to be considered. Petitioners, here present, kindly state your case, or forever hold your peace."

The clerk sat down, in the manner indeed of a jack returned to his box by reflex of the very spring that had launched it, and was followed into repose near in simultaneity by every other witness in the chamber, except, of course, for Ben and his two Intermediators.

William Strahan rose, at center of the table to leftward, and cleared his throat. "May it please the court," he began, in a brogue long since become tempered toward the English sensibility. "Benjamin Franklin, Petitioner here present, born at Boston, Massachusetts, on 17 January 1706, a Sabbath Day, unto Josiah Franklin and Abiah Folger Franklin, the tenth issue unto this union, the fifteenth of seventeen issued unto Josiah, an industrious"—giggles—"and frugal chandler, does hereby petition the court's favour, for cause."

Adjudging Strahan's volume a little restrained for circumstance, Ben leaned discreetly toward Clarence and ventured a whisper: "Might we encourage our good friend toward a bit more push on the bellows? Have you a signal?"

"What truth spoken plainly, sir, is not volume sufficient?"

Ben startled as if to a pinch, and staring upon his Intermediary of thirteen years as if upon a stranger, ventured another whisper: "From what quarry, pray tell, did you mine that little nugget?"

"I but picked it from the leavings of another, sir, he having claimed to himself all the gemstones."

Ben stared upon Clarence as if upon a cock yodeling matins.

Strahan continued. "In his youth, the Petitioner did become proficient in the printing trade, by way of a providential yet infelicitous apprenticeship to an elder brother, James, and whilst learning this trade, the Petitioner did educate himself, by way of considerable Industry and Frugality, in the essential arts—to include letters, mathematics, discourse, and natural philosophy—toward gaining a general understanding upon which to layer the specific."

A most auspicious beginning, Ben allowed. Most auspicious indeed!

Strahan continued. "In the year 1727, having heretofore removed himself to the nascent city of Philadelphia, the Petitioner, in his twenty-second year, did enlist several other tradesmen into an intimate fellowship, named by him the Junto, to be dedicated toward advancing the character and condition of each member, thereby the community at large, which organization henceforth did serve as a model for innumerable others of like service."

Strahan paused such as to look upon his notes, held a bit unsteadily in hand, then resumed: "In the year there following, the Petitioner, in his twenty-third year, did establish himself as a commercial printer, against very great odds, owing to the Petitioner's youth, and a grievous want of pecuniary resources, but no want of competition, and did ultimately attain, by way of much Industry and Frugality, a level of flourishment heretofore unknown amongst practitioners of his chosen trade."

Ben was gratified to be upstanding.

"In the year 1729, the Petitioner, in his twenty-fourth year, did acquire, and become the principal functionary of, a heretofore ineffectual newspaper, the *Pennsylvania Gazette*, and did transform this article—so to say—by way of much Industry and Frugality, into a practical instrument in service to the two primary necessities of civil society: Truth and Reason. And in this same year, the Petitioner did open a stationer's shop, thereafter to be ministered by his loyal helpmeet, Deborah Read Franklin, whose Industry and Frugality exceeded even that of her husband in several noteworthy regards, and did publish in this year, he being a man of much Industry, a prescient pamphlet, titled *Nature and Necessity of Paper Currency*, toward advancing the wealth and well-being of every citizen, hence the colonies at large, as a flood tide floats all boats, and did set this pamphlet to type under a name not his own, that the merits of the message might not be lost in speculations over the motives of the messenger."

Well said, Strahan! Well said!

Strahan continued. "In the year 1731, in his twenty-sixth year, the Petitioner did advocate and establish the Library Company of Philadelphia, it being the first subscription library in America, toward advancing the general education and improvement of every citizen; and in the year following, did publish the first number of *Poor Richard's Almanack*—of the twenty-five thereof in total number—under the name of Richard Saunders, beleaguered husband to Bridget, toward end of offering a modest diet of agreeable wit and worldly wisdom to a public well appreciative of gaining a little practical guidance on the one hand and a little relief from the unrelenting vicissitudes of life on the other."

Ben looked sharply toward Clarence. "Vicissitudes?"

Clarence made an accusatory gesture of head toward Bartholomew.

Ben looked sharply toward Bartholomew.

Bartholomew shrugged.

Strahan continued. "In the year 1736, the Petitioner, being in his thirty-first year, did commence a lengthy tenure of service to the Pennsylvania Assembly, by assuming in that body the office of clerk, and did organize in this same year, he being a man of much Industry and Frugality, the Union Fire Company of Philadelphia, to end of one hundred buckets being brought to bear upon the accidental conflagration for each one bucket previously brought thereon."

Ben stole a glance toward Wedderburn, who, presently seated, was holding his head in both hands.

"In the year 1737, the Petitioner, in his thirty-second year, was appointed postmaster of Philadelphia, and did effect many innovations and improvements to the local postal system, to end indeed of causing an initial, and thereafter a sustained, profitability. Also in this year, the Petitioner did conceive of and advance the notion of a constabulary toward keeping the general peace, to include those neighborhoods that could ill afford their own protection."

Hearing a halting staccato, rudely guttural, reminding indeed of a grievously distempered bowel, Ben looked to the examiners' table to discover Adams, closest of the examiners to the clerk's station, to be in a slumber, his head rested against the back of his chair, his mouth agape. Smith was similarly postured, at the opposing end of the table, whilst Wedderburn, at center, yet held his head in both hands.

In the moment, Wedderburn's head slipped from its props, as if grown too heavy for these, and struck upon the table with such a report as to excite Smith into joining Adams in a raucous harmony of horn, basso, and treble.

To a burn of bile now, Ben recollected Adams's envy-fueled attempts to impugn Ben's character and reputation, whilst supposedly supporting Ben's efforts at winning the favor of the French court, by way of insinuations of sloth and moral turpitude, and thereafter, when that ink made no stain, by way of insinuations of disloyalty and treason.

Strahan continued. "In the year 1740, the Petitioner, in his thirty-fifth year, being ever a willing slave unto his own curiosity, was instrumental in the founding of a nonsectarian temple wherein itinerant partisans of any philosophy might air their doctrines without fear of censure or reprisal. By natural progression, this same space thereafter came to house an academy of higher learning, to come, by invitation of the Petitioner, here present, under the tutelage of the Reverend William Smith, here present." To Ben's delight, Strahan paused here such as to scowl upon the slumbering Smith, and thereby direct a renewal of attention upon his continued rudeness.

Straightening his back, Ben allowed himself a moment of gratitude for having refused the repose of a chair. Indeed, whilst he yet stood upright in dignity, his examiners slumbered away in shame.

Strahan continued. "In the year 1743, the Petitioner, in his thirty-eighth year, did propose and advocate the founding of a learned society, thereafter to be known as the American Philosophical Society, for the purpose of collecting and disseminating knowledge toward the advancement of general learnedness and understanding.

"In the year 1747, in response to a growing threat of ravage or worse at the hands of foreign privateers, these advancing ever more brazenly upon the waters of the Delaware, the Petitioner did establish, in his forty-second year, a general militia for the common defense of all concerned, by way of encouraging formation of local Associator companies.

"In the year 1748, the Petitioner, in his forty-third year, was elected to the Philadelphia Common Council; the year hence, was appointed Justice of the Peace; two years hence, was named City Alderman."

Ben smiled to resemblance of Strahan's litany unto the cadence of a dripping water spigot—one drip following upon another unto a bucket overflowing.

"It must here be noted, however," Strahan interjected, "that, concerning the second of these offices, to wit, Justice of the Peace, the Petitioner did, in adjudging himself too little schooled in the articles of practical law, voluntarily withdraw from it."

A most excellent footnote! Most excellent indeed!

"In the year 1749, the Petitioner, in his forty-fourth year, did pen and promulgate a pamphlet, *Proposals Relating to the Education of Youth in Pensilvania*, which, in addressing an unattended need to educate middling youth in the practical arts—to include Accounts, Numbers, and, I quote, 'the Advantages of Temperance, Order, Frugality, Industry, Perseverance, et cetera'—did result in the founding of the Philadelphia Academy, heretofore mentioned in relation to its tutelage under Reverend Smith, thereafter to become the University of Pennsylvania."

Collinson and Shipley smiling upon him, such as to show pride, Ben took it, as well as an ever building confidence, Ben beamed, though not quite, he did hope, unto a glow.

Strahan continued. "In the year 1751, the Petitioner, interrupting inquiries into the mysteries of the electrical fluid, these most agreeable unto him, that he might contribute yet another service to the public good, did agree to stand for election to the Pennsylvania Assembly, and did subsequently serve in this capacity, with distinction, until the year 1757, whereupon the Petitioner commenced a long and effectual tenure of service in the role, ultimately perilous, of agent for the Pennsylvania Assembly in London.

"In the year 1752, the Petitioner, in his forty-seventh year, did cause to be founded in his beloved city of Philadelphia, a Contributionship for the Insurance of Houses from Loss by Fire, toward protecting each subscriber, at a modest fee, against ruinous loss to accidental conflagration, by way of distributing the cost of restoration amongst all subscribers in common."

Drip—drip—drip—

"In the year 1758, the Petitioner, in his fifty-third year, did cause the Pennsylvania Assembly to reform the watch system employed in the city of Philadelphia, to end of all neighborhoods being watched over, instead of those alone that could afford such; and did cause the Assembly to provide general street lighting throughout the city, toward the same end, and the same justice."

Strahan lowered his notes, and straightening himself, directed his attention toward the lights ever moving atop the high bench. "In summary, the Petitioner did, by way of uncommon Industry of Mind, Magnanimity of Spirit, and Dedication of Person, make many contributions to the civic good, those here given voice, and others left to silence, at no expected or calculated advantage to himself."

Strahan bowed toward the high bench, toward the three slumbering examiners, and toward Ben, who returned the favor in kind. Upon Strahan resuming the repose of his chair, Collinson upstood from his, thereupon presenting an even more imposing figure, Ben adjudged, than had Strahan, Collinson being taller than the relatively squat Scotsman, and even more noble in natural aspect of countenance.

It had been Collinson—Quaker by character, scientist by inclination, merchant by necessity—who had encouraged Ben in his electrical experiments, and who had brought Ben's subsequent insights and discoveries concerning the electrical fluid to the attention of the Royal Society. It had been Collinson also who had helped Ben secure his appointment as Deputy Postmaster General for the colonies—a fact, it now occurred, that Strahan had not included in his litany, he mentioning only Ben's tenure as postmaster of Philadelphia, thereby opting, it would appear, to privilege modesty over boast.

Even during the war years, Ben recollected, to an upwelling of warmish brine, Peter Collinson—friend first, gentleman second, citizen third—had remained a loyal and dear friend.

"In addition to being a man of tireless and exemplary Civic and Domestic Service," Collinson began, "the Petitioner here present did also, during a long and uncommonly productive life, make contributions of considerable merit to Invention and Philosophy."

Collinson looked to the slumbering examiners, then to the lights ever moving atop the bench. "So as not to burden the court with a recounting overly long, I shall make a partial mention as being representative to the whole. To wit:

"In the year 1740, the Petitioner did invent a stove of novel and rational design, toward improving the comfort and ease of the general public, and did refuse offer of a patent, thereby an opportunity to secure unto himself and his family a level of financial ease enjoyed by few tradesmen of his time and circumstance.

"In the year 1743, the Petitioner did study the great storms of the eastern seaboard of colonial America, and did deduce from his observations a rational explanation for their movement from southeast to northwest, as opposed to their heretofore-presumed movement from northeast to southeast—which explanation did allow for the possibility of prediction, and thereby, of preparation.

"In the year 1746, the Petitioner did conduct imaginative and oft perilous experimentations into the nature and peculiarities of the electrical fluid, and in the year 1751 did propose, on the basis of deductions made by him, a general employment of metal rods atop steeples, chimneys, roof peaks, and other such elevations, as protection from the unpredictable and dangerous effects of lightning; and in this same year, the Petitioner did devise and execute an experiment proving an equivalency betwixt said lightning and the electrical fire of common experience."

Drip—drip—drip—

"In the year 1753, in honor of his bold adventurings into the realm of the unknown, and the contributions to understanding that were derived therefrom, the Petitioner did receive the Copley Medal of the Royal Society, the first of many honoraria to be awarded to the Petitioner, not only for his contributions concerning the peculiarities of the electrical fluid, but for his many other contributions to natural philosophy as well.

"Subsequent honoraria did include: Masters degrees awarded to him by Harvard College, Yale College, the College of William & Mary, and Cambridge University; a Doctor of Laws degree awarded to him by the University of St. Andrews—this despite his resignation from the office of Justice of the Peace several years previous"—titters—"and a Doctor of Civil Laws degree awarded to him by Oxford University. In addition, the Petitioner was elected a fellow of the Royal Society of London, and was made a foreign member of the French Royal Academy of science."

A rude sound rent a halting but robust tear through Collinson's seamless delivery.

Looking up from his papers, Collinson frowned upon the examiners' table, whereat John Adams was yet reposed with his head against the back of his chair, his mouth agape. Adams issuing forth another halting snore, in deepest basso, he was joined by his colleagues, they reposed in similar postures, the one in treble, the other in baritone. The cavernous chamber seemed to amplify this harmony unto suggestions of a full bellows of flatulence from all the gods of Olympus.

As if sprung loose of this thunder, the clerk jumped to his feet, and reaching forth with his left arm, this spontaneously extending in length, grasped upon Adams's nose with thumb and forefinger.

Adams began to flail of arm and leg, the latter striking upon the underside of the table, to end of awakening himself and his colleagues, and eliciting from the assembly an explosion of guffaws, joined by a thunderous stomping of feet.

Whilst Adams, become aware of a grievous injury to his pride, made attempt to stanch the wound, the clerk turned to Collinson and nodded. Taking the cue, Collinson continued his litany, although in a more deliberate—and more effective, Ben adjudged—cadence.

Collinson mentioned the Petitioner's invention of the bifocal lens, in service to those afflicted with attenuations to their sight both near and far; his invention of shelf grippers, in service to those with high shelves in their libraries; and his invention of the glass armonica, in service to those with an appreciation for the sweetest of notes.

At this point Collinson broke from his papers, and looking to the dancing lights atop the high bench, suggested that the Petitioner's glass armonica had become so well regarded as "to have become a source of auditory bliss even within the celestial realm." He bowed.

Buoyed almost unto levitation by this aside, Ben found himself recollecting that day when, having recently assumed proprietorship of a printing business he could afford by no rational accountancy, he had received his first order, in the amount of five shillings, and with it, knowledge certain that his endeavors were all but assured to compound unto satisfaction.

Collinson made mention of a few more points, each of modest import, then looked again to the high bench. "In summary," he declared, in bold voice, "the Petitioner did, through uncommon Industry of Mind, Magnanimity of Spirit, and Dedication of Person, make many contributions to Invention and Philosophy, those here given voice, and others left to silence, at no expected or calculated advantage to himself."

Collinson bowed toward the high bench; toward the examiners, they again reposed as previous; and toward Ben, who returned the favour in kind. As he thereupon reclaimed his chair, Shipley abandoned his.

In gazing upon a countenance of untempered kindliness, Ben recollected the many occasions the good bishop had generously hosted him at Twyford, the good bishop's country home near Winchester, whereat Ben had become particularly enamored of Shipley's youngest daughter, Kitty, who had become to him, over the years, as if a third daughter, after Sally, his own, and Polly, Mrs. Stevenson's.

It was at this very home indeed that Ben had begun to scribe his *Autobiography*, spending many delightful days in the good bishop's study exercising his memory, and many delightful evenings in the good bishop's parlour reading the day's scribblings to the family, toward their general amusement and, in the spirit of the kindliness ever aglow in the bishop's solicitous eyes, their considerable approval.

"In addition to contributing notably to Invention and Natural Philosophy," Shipley began, his voice showing a careful grooming toward an efficacious delivery, "the Petitioner here present did also contribute mightily to Statesmanship and Diplomacy, most especially in this regard toward the founding and flourishment of a novel and progressive nation, his many contributions toward this end earning him the esteemed title amongst many, to include even certain of his detractors"—Ben looked to Adams, discovering him yet postured with his head rested against the back of his chair—"of *Pater Patriae*."

"To wit: In the year 1754, the Petitioner did conceive, and propose in convention, a plan for a union of the colonies then extant, which plan, prescient in vision, came to be known as the Albany Plan of Union. Many a subsequent statesman did credit the articles of this plan with having laid the foundation for a federated union to be conceived and implemented several years hence, thereafter to be known as the United States of America.

"In the year 1757, as previously mentioned, the Petitioner was appointed agent for the Pennsylvania Assembly, to represent that body regarding all interests before the British government, and did serve honorably and tirelessly in this capacity, at cost to himself of a five-year separation from his wife and daughter, until the year 1762. In the year 1764, the Petitioner was again appointed agent for the Pennsylvania Assembly, and did thereupon serve in this capacity until the year 1775, and did devote himself during these eleven years—toward the end of which his dear wife, Deborah, passed on to her eternal reward—to the noble cause of keeping the colonies and their progenitor bound together in a felicitous union, toward the general betterment of all concerned. During the course of this extended service, by virtue of his ever-growing stature as statesman, the Petitioner was appointed by the assemblies of New Jersey, Massachusetts, and Georgia to serve also as their agents before the British government.

"In the year 1766, the Petitioner was examined before the House of Commons on the issue of the Stamp Act, and thereby became, by force of the arguments presented by him to this body, instrumental in the repeal of this regrettable action, to the greater, if but temporary, happiness of his countrymen."

Ben smiled unto himself in private. The crescendo of his petition, as deftly wrought and rendered by his most able advocators, was building even more agreeably toward an efficacious climax than he had allowed himself to hope for.

"In the year 1775, upon returning to Philadelphia from London, the Petitioner was appointed to the Second Continental Congress, and did serve in that body with uncommon vigor and distinction, despite an advanced age, until directed, by acclamation of his fellow members, to sail to France with utmost haste, there to serve as agent and commissioner to the court of King Louis XVI, in company with two others, they being messieurs Silas Deane and Arthur Lee."

Ben felt gooseflesh rise upon his arms. The grand finale was at hand—a fusillade as if of a dozen cannons a-booming.

"As commissioner to France, the Petitioner, despite untoward intrigues against both his patriotic conduct and his personal character, at the hands not of declared adversaries but of presumed friends, did seek out and establish a strategic relationship with the French foreign minister, the Comte de Vergennes, and did expeditiously render this eminent 'Voice Unto the King's Ear' into both an admirer and a personal friend.

"The Petitioner did thereupon secure from the French Crown, by way of his intimate relationship with Messieur Vergennes, the essential funds and munitions necessary for the American colonies to wage a successful rebellion against a master who would not be swayed by any other means. In addition, the Petitioner did actively aid, support, and abet American privateers in interdicting British shipping on the high seas; the Petitioner did enlist into the American revolutionary cause the Marquis de la Fayette, son of a Frankish nobleman, who, in subsequent service to said cause, would prove instrumental in helping General Washington defeat General Cornwallis at Yorktown; the

Petitioner did enlist also in the colonial cause one John Paul Jones, son of a Scottish gardener, who, in subsequent service to said cause, would humble the entire British Navy by means of a fleet of one ship, the *Bonhomme Richard*, named in honor of the clever scrivener of the *Almanacks*. The Petitioner did also represent the overseas interests of the nascent American Navy; did negotiate with British counterparts for the humane treatment of American prisoners of war; did finance, often from his own accounts, numerous Americans escaped to France from Britain; did arrange for the purchase and transport of arms and other critical materiel for General Washington's chronically impoverished Continental Army; did author and disseminate propaganda toward swaying both English and French sentiment toward the American cause."

So rapt had Ben become in the mounting crescendo of Shipley's litany that he had taken no notice of a mounting undertone, suggestive indeed of a chorus of bullfrogs, that had presently reached such volume as to near drown out all else. Indeed, not only were Wedderburn, Adams, and Smith blowing their nasal horns at remarkable volume, so was, it would appear, every other denizen in the great hall, save for the clerk.

Springing unto his feet, in the celeritous manner previous, the clerk raised his arms as if to command a great throng unto silence. The ambient light dimmed; a great wind began to swirl through the hall; and a boil of dark clouds, glowing of an eerie inner light, began to encroach ominously from overhead. A blinding flash then was followed, in near simultaneity, by a thunderclap so shocking as to leave Ben feeling boxed upon both ears. Looking to the examiners' table, Ben witnessed Adams, startled awake by the thunderclap, topple over backwards in his chair and impact upon the floor behind, his stubby legs thereupon flailing overhead as if to make a froth of naught but air scented of soot and musk.

As if bounced from their own chairs, Wedderburn and Smith lifted their dazed and disheveled colleague to his feet and thereupon helped him regain his chair if not quite his honor.

All but giddy with excitement, Ben felt as if levitated into a Parisian dawn by way of a Montgolfier balloon. Never could he have predicted such a finish!

Taking cue from the clerk, Shipley continued his remarks—he needing to do no greater now, Ben adjudged, than put a goodly froth upon a hardy ale a'ready poured. The good bishop mentioned the crucial service the Petitioner had rendered unto the cause of the Constitutional Convention of 1787, bringing forth his Great Compromise at a moment most opportune, such as to save the proceedings from certain dissolution; and thereupon finished by mentioning, in terms most modest, the Petitioner's efforts, despite an accumulation of tormenting infirmities, toward a total abolition of slavery in his "dear country," a true *Pater Patriae* being obliged to do no less.

"In summary," Shipley concluded, in resolute voice, "the Petitioner did, through uncommon Industry of Mind, Magnanimity of Spirit, and Dedication of Person, make many contributions to Diplomacy and Statesmanship, those here given voice, and others left to silence, at no expected or calculated advantage to himself."

Shipley bowed unto the dancing lights, unto the examiners, unto Ben, who returned the favor in kind. As he thereupon reclaimed his chair, Strahan again abandoned his.

"May it please the court," Strahan began, his voice stronger, reflecting perhaps, Ben allowed, a raised sanguinity on the part of the speaker. "We have recounted this day, inadequately of necessity, we being unworthy to the task, a life of uncommon personal achievement and public service. As no summary from this table could serve to advantage that which has a'ready been but summed, I would like in lieu of such to offer one fact as representing the full body of the others, to wit: that the Petitioner did choose, at age forty-two, to retire from private commerce, that he might place himself fully in service to the public good, and that he did accept in this regard, over a tenure spanning also forty-two years, little recompense, of any kind, in return.

"Indeed, whilst many a contemporary to the Petitioner was devoting his facilities of mind and body toward filling his larder of spice, his lockbox of specie—or chasing after offices bearing exulting titles—the Petitioner was devoting himself to a virtuous improvement of his character and his prospects, that he might thereupon devote himself to Civic and Domestic Service, to Invention and Natural Philosophy, and to Diplomacy and Statesmanship, to the common good."

Strahan looked to Collinson on the one side, to Shipley on the other, and again to the high bench: "On behalf of my fellow petitioners, I thank the court for its indulgence." He bowed to all parties, and reclaiming his chair, exchanged collegial nods with his fellow petitioners, whilst manifesting upon his countenance, Ben adjudged, the same level of raised confidence Ben had sensed in the man's voice.

⌒γ℀⌒

Feeling yet levitated overtop Paris at dawn, Ben allowed himself a measure of ease, such that he might enjoy whatever theater might follow—all the greater, he had to confess, had he condescended to the repose of a chair.

A foolish pride indeed!

Wedderburn rose at center of the examiners' table, and stretching his robed arms overtop his curls, yawned without restraint, as if mistaking himself in the privacy of his toilet, and shook his head in the manner, Ben adjudged, of a cur attempting to rid itself of an infestation of fleas. Emerging thereupon from behind the table, Wedderburn stationed himself to front of Ben, all but obscuring the ever-changing colorations within the high bench. Placing his hands upon his hips, he looked hard upon Ben.

"Dr. Franklin, sir—why are you here?"

Ben stiffened such as to bring himself to fullest possible height. "I am here, sir, as Petitioner."

Wedderburn elevated his chin, to effect of assuming a haughty poise, and looking upon the assembly, raised his arms at either side, elbows partially bent, palms upward, and lifted his shoulders into a shrug. "He thinks he is here as *Petitioner*."

A roar of guffaws.

When this had subsided, Wedderburn again looked hard upon Ben. "What private illusion, sir, is not the conjure of a private need? You are here, sir, for the reason I heretofore attempted to bring unto confession—to no lasting credit, it would appear." Wedderburn again looked to the assembly and shrugged. "Are we *surprised*?"

More guffaws.

Wedderburn narrowed his eyes. "You are here, sir, to see of necessity what you would not see of conscience. You are here, sir, to bear witness, and bear witness, sir, you shall."

Spinning away, Wedderburn marched to the examiners' table, and accepting a small object into hand from Smith, the latter showing a mischievous comportment of countenance, returned to his previous station. "Do you recall, sir, when you were a lad of seven years, making purchase of a pennywhistle, and giving up for this instrument several halfpence recently given to you?"

"I do."

"And do you recall, sir, your elder siblings bringing to your attention, as you were entertaining them with unpracticed notes from your fife, that you had paid four times too much for it?"

"I do."

"In hindsight, sir, was this assessment accurate in substance even if punitive in intention?"

"It was."

"And was the reason you paid four times too much for your whistle, sir, that you had four times too much desired the pleasure of it?"

"Exactly so, as I have freely, and frequently, acknowledged."

Spinning away, Wedderburn returned to the examiners' table, and snatching into hand one of several sheaves of papers arranged afront his chair, returned to stand afront Ben, although in not so intrusive a proximity as previous. "Indeed, sir," he continued, "not only did you freely acknowledge this erratum, you generalized it for application to the errata of others, did you not?" Wedderburn looked to his papers. "'In short, I conceived that [the] great part of the miseries of mankind were brought upon them by the false estimates they had made of the value of things, and by their giving too much for the whistle.'"

The excerpt, Ben well recognized, was from a bagatelle he had contrived for the amusement of Madame Brillon—in 1779, if memory served—and had subsequently included in one of the volumes he had, during his unbounded confinement, added to his *Autobiography*. "I did indeed, being ever loath to confine public lessons to private eyes."

Wedderburn slipped the top sheet of his papers to bottom, peered a moment upon the sheet newly exposed, and looked again to Ben. "Now, sir, in your *Autobiography*, as confined at the time to but a single volume, that one unfinished, you identified thirteen cardinal virtues as being 'necessary or desirable,' am I correct?"

"You are."

"'Necessary or desirable' toward what, sir, if we might inquire?"

"Moral rectitude."

"And by 'moral rectitude,' sir, do you intend Christian piety—making one's self acceptable in the eyes of an exacting deity—or do you intend something else?"

"Making one's self acceptable in one's *own* eyes firstly; making one's self acceptable in the eyes of *others* foremostly."

"Would you be so kind, sir, as to recite your 'necessary or desirable' virtues to the court, all thirteen?"

Ben bowed unto Wedderburn, then looked to the high bench.

"Industry," he began—flinching in the instant to a brilliant flash and a loud whoosh.

A serpentine stream of multicolored light, having emerged from the body of the high bench, now undulated through the space betwixt Ben and the bench. Reaching in close proximity to the petitioners' table, it coiled itself into a column of swirling threads of light, which thereupon swirled themselves into the form of a small boy, of about seven years. The lad was wearing a blouse and breeches patterned in small squares, black alternating with white, and was wearing across his breast, right shoulder unto left hip, a crimson sash bearing upon it, in an elegant calligraphy, the label *Industry*, and was holding at one side, in his right hand, a compass arrow, also crimson, pointing to rearward. Upon the lad's head rested a crown of scarlet blooms.

"Are there no others?"

Looking again to the high bench, Ben resumed his recitation: Frugality—Resolution—Order—Cleanliness—Silence—Chastity—Sincerity—Temperance—Justice—Tranquility—Moderation—Humility. Each time he gave voice to a virtue, another small boy coalesced from a serpentine stream of kaleidoscopic light emanant from the high bench. Each boy was costumed in a blouse and breeches patterned in small squares, black alternating with white, and each was wearing across his breast, right shoulder unto left hip, a silken sash of distinctive hue, and upon this sash was writ the name of a virtue. Held at one side of each boy, in his right hand, was a compass arrow of the coloration of his sash, pointing to rearward, and upon the head of each boy rested a crown of blooms of the same coloration as his sash and arrow.

Upon thirteen lads accumulating in a file, Wedderburn took station behind the lad bearing *Industry* and laid a hand upon the boy's right shoulder. "Kindly show us, dear lad, the natural tendency of your aim. Are you a virtue that tends to aim outward, toward other, or are you a virtue that tends to aim inward, toward self?"

"I am Industry," the boy replied, moving his compass arrow such as to aim it toward the temple of one's appetite. "I am *The Way to Wealth*."

Wedderburn stepped briskly sidelong.

"I am Frugality," the next lad announced, moving his compass arrow such as to aim it also toward his stomach. "I am *The Way to Wealth*."

"I am Resolution," the next boy declared, moving his compass arrow such as to aim it toward his stomach. "I am *The Way to Wealth*."

And so it went, through Order, Cleanliness, Silence, Chastity,

Sincerity, Temperance, Justice, Tranquility, Moderation, and Humility until all thirteen lads were pointing their compass arrows, each of the coloration of his sash and crown, toward their stomachs.

Wedderburn resumed his station afront Ben, and uplifting his chin one click, struck a pose inclined toward haughty. "Being a man of science, Dr. Franklin, and therefore necessarily a man of keen observation, would you agree that we have something of a consensus here, as to the aim of these young lads?"

"I would agree, sir, that *you* have something of an aim here, accomplished sorcerer that you are. If by this demonstration you intend to impugn the virtues that guided my life to many a worthy accomplishment, and in so doing taint my character such as to match the accumulated stain of your own, much as you attempted to do in this very chamber on a previous occasion, I must protest—at the very least as regards Sincerity and Justice. In point of fact, sir, do not these two noble virtues compel, prima facie, that their compass arrows be aimed outward—by means of *their* hands, sir, as opposed to, by sly artifice, yours?"

Wedderburn elevated his chin one click farther. "True enough, sir, Sincerity standing by itself, or Justice by itself, would indeed seem deserving to have its arrow of concern aimed outward, or at least at some oblique compromise. Standing in company with these particular virtues, however, in contrast to certain other virtues you might have chosen, does the same truth hold forth? Alas, is a canine in company with a pack of wolves ravaging upon a herd of sheep yet a dog, sir? Or is it, in such company, a dog in name only?"

Spinning away, Wedderburn took station to rear of the file of boys, betwixt Industry wearing a crimson crown and Frugality wearing a green crown, and continued. "In addition to promoting these cardinal virtues in your *Autobiography*, sir, as 'necessary or desirable,' did you not promote them also, with Industry and Frugality held to fore, as you have them here, in the scripture you contrived as a celebration of the long success of your *Almanacks*, which scripture—dare we tell it?—you titled *The Way to Wealth*, and attributed to one Father Abraham?"

Wedderburn grinned. "Father—Abraham. New Testament—Old Testament. Most clever of you, sir. Most clever indeed."

Ben gazed hard upon Wedderburn's haughty pose. "I intended, sir, what you name 'scripture' to be naught other than a small parody on that pretense toward virtue that was necessarily incidental to advancing the little pieties I included in the *Almanacks*."

"Or did you intend, sir, to bathe sour berries in cream, such as to make them palatable to the greatest number?"

Ben dropped his eyes as if to study a pattern of loops, suggesting of bow wakes, ingrained upon a parquet square close upon the vitreous circle.

Wedderburn approached. "Now, sir, as to the thirteen virtues of your *Autobiography*, here represented, being 'necessary or desirable,' would I be correct to take your meaning to be that whilst some of the thirteen are *vital* to cause, therefore *necessary*, the others are but *salutary* to it, therefore *desirable*?"

"You would."

Wedderburn pursed his mouth, and furrowed his brow, as if in reflection of a great burden of consternation. "Now, sir, you tell us *here* that the aim of your thirteen virtues is toward 'moral rectitude,' and that by 'moral rectitude' you intend, if memory serves, 'Making one's self acceptable in one's own eyes firstly; making one's self acceptable in the eyes of others foremostly.' Am I correct?"

"Does a wolf have teeth?"

"Only under a certain age, I suspect, sir. Above such, they, like us, are likely to have no greater than what might amuse their looking glass."

Titters.

"Now, sir, if you are so willing to confess the aim of your thirteen cardinal virtues in this forum, why did you not do the same in your *Autobiography*? Why is there no mention of 'moral rectitude' or of 'firstly' and 'foremostly?' Are we to infer, sir, that the author of the *Autobiography*, the same conjuror who thought to attribute his *Way to Wealth* to 'Father Abraham,' such as to invoke, ever so subtly, the moral imprimaturs of the Christian and Hebrew traditions, that this same clever fellow simply did not think to carry 'necessary or desirable' to its fullness of meaning in his *Autobiography*? Or are we to infer, sir, that our clever fellow did, in fact, think to carry this beggar phrase to fullness, but calculated it expedient *not* to do so?"

Wedderburn looked to the assembly. "Indeed, sir, might the truth of the matter be that you chose *not* to attach an explicit purpose to your 'necessary or desirable' virtues because you did not wish thereby to place them under the shadow such a fullness of confession might cast?

"Could it be, sir, that your intention—not simply within the context of your *Autobiography*, but within the larger context as well—was to project a certain image of yourself, by giving coloration, and thereby visibility, only to certain aspects of the truth of yourself, such as to fashion thereby a sort of patchwork of colorations—a mosaic, indeed, of 'moral rectitude?'"

Wedderburn looked to his papers. "Your words, sir: 'In order to secure my credit and character as a tradesman, I took care not only to be in reality Industrious and Frugal, but to avoid all appearances to the contrary. I dressed plainly; I was seen at no places of idle diversion. I never went out a'fishing or shooting; a book, indeed, sometimes debauched me from my work, but that was seldom, snug, and gave no scandal; and, to show that I was not above my business, I sometimes brought home the paper I purchased at the stores through the streets on a wheelbarrow. Thus being esteemed an industrious, thriving young man, and paying duly for what I bought, the merchants who imported stationery solicited my custom; others proposed supplying me with books, and I went on swimmingly.'"

Wedderburn looked to Ben. "'Swimmingly' being synonymous with 'virtuously,' sir? 'Virtuously' being synonymous with 'expediently,' sir? 'Expediently' being synonymous with 'profitably,' sir?"

Ben admonished himself that in his previous encounter with Wedderburn, he had remained steadfast to his policy never to allow himself to be drawn into a public argument. His adversary was an oratorical magician, a clever pettifogger born to the trade, while he was himself anything but. That which agile orators like Wedderburn could contrive upon air by instrument of a forked tongue, he could only himself contrive upon paper by instrument of a quill, and indeed on the leftward folio such that he might use the rightward for emendations.

He would see the present repartee to completion and allow himself to be drawn into no others.

"My life served as template for what I intended of these virtues. In the first half of my life, I toiled with Industry and Frugality that I might thereafter devote the second half to Charity and Service. But for the one, not the other."

Wedderburn elevated a little his chin. "So then—as long as one ends up in Charity and Service, sir, it matters not how one should arrive there? If a dog fills its stomach in the manner of the wolf, does it then become a dog again simply by force of its own declaration: I am dog? There are no ravaged sheep to atone for? No orphaned lambs?"

Ben felt as if he were stroking against a waxing tide. He was, however, he reminded himself, a strong swimmer—had *always* been a strong swimmer.

"Swimmingly" indeed!

"If a man does not inherit wealth," Ben continued, "necessity requires that he, by one means or another, acquire it. And such is the intimacy betwixt honest toil and good character that, as a man toils of necessity in honest labor, he must necessarily amass, not only the wealth he requires to sufficiently provision his family, but also the character, the Temperance and Humility, he requires to properly comport himself."

Wedderburn rolled his eyes whilst Adams and Smith, at the examiners' table, shook their heads. "And by 'honest toil,' sir, what do you intend exactly? The labor commanded of the African servants kept by you and others of your station? The labor commanded of the mud-hutted peasants you witnessed in Ireland betwixt stays in the great houses of their masters? The labor of those necessitated into trades for which they had no natural inclination or competence? The labor of those coerced by circumstance unto toils that fill the swamp by draining the pond? Would you be so kind, sir, as to elaborate on the point?"

A steady stroke was all that was required—lose no ground, advantage every slacking. "Swimmingly" indeed!

"Examined under sufficient magnification, by an eye practiced for such, even the most glittering of diamonds will confess an imperfection or two."

Wedderburn turned to face upon the file of boys. "If you lads would be so kind as to give us your name, the name of your own person as against that for which you are symbol, and in good voice, the court, I am certain, would be most obliged."

The first boy, Industry, took a step forward. "My name is Andrew Carnegie." In the very instant, the boy was transmuted, to a flash of crimson light, into a large black wolf, its eyes as if rubies fired of menace. Crouching now, its head held low, the wolf snarled after Ben, strings of drool oozing from its muzzle.

Ben cringed whilst yet—taking comfort in Bartholomew and Clarence standing close upon his flanks—holding his ground.

The boy labeled Frugality stepped forward and upon proclaiming himself John Pierpont Morgan, was transmuted, in a flash of bright-green light, into a snarling black wolf, its eyes as if emeralds fired of disdain. Thereupon came, in rapid succession, John D. Rockefeller, Jay Gould, and Cornelius Vanderbilt; thereupon Charles Keating, Michael Milken, and Bernard Madoff; thereupon Enron, Bank of America, AIG, and General Motors. Finally, the boy labeled Humility stepped forward and upon proclaiming himself dot.com, was transmuted into a snarling black wolf, its violet eyes as if amethysts fired of avarice.

The wolves beginning to circle upon Ben, in the clockwise direction, Ben looked to Wedderburn. "I do not know these names, nor why they should be threatening upon me. I have done nothing in relation to them."

"*Nothing*, sir? You have done *nothing* in relation to the snarl of predation; nothing in relation to the drool of greed? That is your apprehension of the matter, sir, after two centuries of reflection? You have done *nothing*?"

In the instant, the wolves leapt after Ben, sending him cowering onto the floor, whilst almost in simultaneity a fusillade of pulses of colorated light shot out from the high bench, and each striking upon a wolf, transmuted it back into the youth from which it had emanated.

Bartholomew and Clarence helped Ben onto his feet, Ben thereupon shaking off any farther charity. "Where were you when I *most* needed you? Where were your mighty swords?" Weakening precariously in knee, Ben yet refused any farther assistance. "I understood you to be steadfastly declared to me, that I should not stand alone."

"As others thought of you," Wedderburn boomed, from outside the circle of lads. "Indeed, sir, what say you on the matter: Can any injury be more affecting to a man than being abandoned by those closest to him in his hour of greatest need?"

Ben lifted his eyes until they rested upon the Royal Seal.

He was being toyed with—provoked such as to warrant yet farther abuse, just as had been the case on the occasion of his previous examination in this infamous pit, so aptly named. Wedderburn was naught but a cock for hire, and he but fodder to peck upon, to the amusement of a host of slavering patrons: "O, tut tut, 'tis a pity—look at the beady orb hanging from that poor creature's socket—here's a wager—he won't last the hour."

Wedderburn insinuated himself betwixt Humility and Industry, and entering into the ring of boys, began to circumnavigate the inward perimeter, in the clockwise direction. As he proceeded, each boy he passed spun half-circle around, in the counterclockwise direction, to the effect of showing, whereat should be his backside, the front side of a girl of no greater than seven years. Strangely, the countenance of each girl held no discernible feature or aspect, as if the artist in each instance had been distracted from his project before he might finish.

Each girl wore a starched gown sprinkled of polka dots, black dots upon white to one side, white dots upon black to the other, the whole divided at the diagonal by a silken sash the same coloration as that of her male counterpart, but at the opposing bias. Each girl was holding to side a compass arrow of the same coloration as that of her male counterpart, but in her left hand as against her right, to the effect of it pointing to forward as against to rearward.

The girl whereat the boy Industry had stood bore the label Trust; the girl whereat the boy Frugality had stood bore the label Tolerance; then came Loyalty, Fairness, Nurturance, Contrition, Forbearance, Generosity, Reverence, Sacrifice, Forgiveness, Empathy, and Compassion.

"Dear lasses," Wedderburn continued, "if you would be so kind as to show us the natural tendency of your aim, the court would, I am certain, be most obliged. Are you a virtue that tends to aim inward, toward self, or are you a virtue that tends to aim outward, toward other?"

The girl bearing Compassion upon her sash moved her arrow such as to aim it from her breast unto Ben. Thereupon each girl in the ring followed suit, in the counterclockwise direction, until all thirteen— Compassion, Empathy, Forgiveness, Sacrifice, Reverence, Generosity, Forbearance, Contrition, Nurturance, Fairness, Loyalty, Tolerance, and Trust—were pointing their compass arrows toward Ben, full circle around.

Insinuating himself betwixt Compassion and Trust, Wedderburn entered again into the circle, and moving from girl to girl, in the counterclockwise direction, requested of each one her name. The girl bearing the label Compassion upon her sash curtsied; the girl bearing the label Empathy did likewise, as did the others, in succession, full circle around.

"O my goodness!" Wedderburn boomed. "Not one of our fair lasses has a voice! How can this be?" Wedderburn showed unto Ben now a countenance mockingly forlorn. "How can this be, Dr. Franklin? How could one half of these inseparable wholes have a voice so very strong, whilst the other half has no voice soever?"

Launching forth before any reply might be made, or ignored, Wedderburn circumnavigated the inward perimeter of the circle of lasses, in the clockwise direction, and as he swept past each girl, each one began to rotate in place, in the counterclockwise direction, showing alternating images—boy-girl, boy-girl—until these were merged into a whirling vortex of a color, red to violet. Thereupon the separate vortexes began to merge, in the counterclockwise direction, until these were wholly commingled, Compassion unto Trust, into a single vortex of purist white.

Feeling Bartholomew and Clarence grasp him just above the elbow, their grip firm, Ben offered no resistance.

As the whirling vortex began to slow, a shadow began to form within it, in likeness to a fetus, and to mature then, it did seem, in proportion to a diminishment in radiance. Of a sudden, to a brilliant flash, the fetus bloomed into the likeness of a small boy, more diminutive in stature than the lads previous.

Ben staggered as if to a blow to the head, and would likely have tumbled backward had Bartholomew and Clarence not been holding him as if in bondage.

"Papa!" the boy exclaimed, his countenance radiant, innocent of all travail.

Wedderburn stepped close upon Ben and looked to his papers. "'I always thought he would have been the best of my children.'" Wedderburn looked to Ben. "And that he might have been, sir, had the virtuous shopkeeper who was his protector not been too much preoccupied with parading his wheelbarrow upon Market Street to carry his son to the office of inoculation."

Ben shook his head. "No! He was too frail! The cure would have too much advanced the risk."

"And the neglect, sir—it did no such?" Wedderburn looked to his papers. "'Francis Folger Franklin, October 20, 1732—November 21, 1736. The DELIGHT of all that knew him.'"

A rhythmic squeal soon proved harbinger to a wheelbarrow pushed by Adams, who navigated it counterclockwise around the vitreous circle, the boy yet standing upon this, and rested it close upon Wedderburn.

Wedderburn mounted onto the wheelbarrow, Adams holding it steady, and looked to the assembly. "*Early to bed, and early to rise, makes a man healthy, wealthy and wise—God gives all things to industry—Plough deep, while sluggards sleep, and you shall have corn to sell, and to keep—Be ashamed to catch yourself idle—Sloth, like rust, consumes faster than labor wears—He that by the plough would thrive, himself must either hold or drive.*"

Wedderburn stepped down, and as Adams pushed the wheelbarrow toward the examiners' table, Frankie, standing atop the vitreous circle, began to show a diminishment in countenance, which diminishment progressed until no discernible countenance remained.

Of a sudden wresting himself from the grip of his Intermediaries, Ben rushed forward—"Frankie! Frankie!"—but before he might advance more than three steps, absent his walking stick, Frankie's form became enveloped in a clockwise swirl of brightening light, which thereupon, as Ben gasped after it, flashed into a blinding pulse, and was gone, leaving in residue a faint glow upon the surface of the vitreous circle.

Ben moaned in the manner of a cow after a calf taken for veal, and collapsing onto his knees, lowered his head onto the circle, as if to absorb the faint glow of this unto himself.

Upon a respectful interim, Bartholomew and Clarence aided Ben to his feet, and upon restoring him of his walking stick, returned him to his station.

The clerk rose to upstanding upon his perch. "Might the Petitioner be disposed toward reconsidering the repose of a chair?"

Ben bowed, and upon being turned half-circle around, was led—O happiness!—unto the very chair, or a close likeness thereof, that General Washington had occupied during the whole of the Convention. Most distinctive of this article was the representation upon the back, at the very pinnacle, of a sun rising or setting.

Two centuries previous, it might be rising one day, setting the next. Presently, it would be construed ever rising!

Giving his walking stick over to Bartholomew, Ben collapsed into Washington's throne, wincing to a pinch of stone.

"Unfortunately," Wedderburn continued, his voice uncharacteristically restrained, "these proceedings have only just begun. This would not be the case, however, I feel compelled to remind you, sir, yet again, had you employed your time in your apartment in service to opening *all* the closets and cupboards of your history as against only those known by you to hold confections of honey or treacle. There can now be no alternative." Lifting a bit his chin, Wedderburn gazed upon the assembly. "Full witness must now ye bear!" he boomed. "Full measure must now ye abide!" Spinning away, Wedderburn strode unto the examiners' table as if to precede all others from a building newly discovered aflame, and thereat reclaimed his chair.

⁓

The only sound being now a sometimes rhythmic, sometimes arrhythmic hum from the three lights dancing atop the high bench, Reverend Smith rose unto a diminutive stature, and moving out from behind the table, took station atop the vitreous circle, this yet showing a residual glow. In hand, he held a sheaf of papers noticeably greater in heft than those of his predecessor.

Feeling his spirit slump, Ben reminded himself of the sun ever rising close upon to rearward.

"Kindly bear with me, sir," Smith began, "that I might bring to proper close the line of inquiry begun by my esteemed colleague." Smith's thin voice seemed overly coiffed in the powder and wig of a High Anglican sensibility such as to cloak the embarrassment of a humble origin.

Ben allowed to his credit that he had included amongst his public confessions the egregious erratum of having recommended the Reverend Smith to the position of provost of the Pennsylvania College. Alas, what greater error could any man commit than to hand to the hangman the very noose with which to hang his benefactor?

"My intention is to inconvenience you no farther in matters pertaining to virtue than holds essential to the purposes of these proceedings." Smith looked to his papers through the lower panes, alas, of a pair of bifocal lenses.

Although the irony of this circumstance was not lost upon him, Ben surmised it lost upon the assemblage at large, and most especially upon the Reverend Smith himself, who would not recognize a subtlety of this category, Ben was certain, even if this self-declared "man of God" should encounter it on the very road to Damascus taken by another pretender after "truth."

Indeed, one of the traits of character held in common, so to say, by the hereditarily privileged and those pretending after them, Ben had come to apprehend, was an almost total inability to perceive, much less appreciate, any wit spawned of happenstance.

"In September of 1757, sir," Smith continued, looking again upon Ben, "the London *Citizen* carried an article over the name of your son, William, titled 'A Defense of the Quakers and the Pennsylvania Assembly.' Do you recall this article, sir?"

Ben bowed.

"Given the nature of this court, sir, might you be willing to confess to being not only the wielder of the will behind this article but also the wielder of the pen that writ it?"

Ben bowed.

Smith looked to his papers. "I quote, sir: 'It is indeed a matter of equal astonishment and concern that in this time of danger and distress, when the utmost unanimity and dispatch is necessary to the preservation of *life, liberty, and estate*, a governor should be sent to our colonies with such instructions as must inevitably produce endless dispute and delay'—et cetera, et cetera." Smith looked to Ben. "Your words, sir?—versus indeed those of your son?"

Ben bowed.

"Now, sir, the phrase to which I gave special emphasis—'life, liberty, and estate'—was not original with you, but was in fact coined by John Locke, the late physician and philosopher of Somerset; am I correct as to this point, sir?"

"You are."

"And by the term 'estate,' sir, what likely was the intention concerning this term under Locke's pen: tangible property only—such as chattel and coin—or those items plus such intangible possessions as title and station?"

Ben pondered upon holding to silence, but decided against seeming needlessly obstructive. "One might reasonably include title and station," he offered, "considering the longstanding English tradition of a title being regarded as a birthright."

"Very good. Now, sir, did you have occasion, at a subsequent date, to participate in the authoring of a public document in America to known unto perpetuity as the *Declaration of Independence*?"

"I did."

"And did this document contain a phrase in close likeness to the preceding phrase, this being 'life, liberty and the pursuit of happiness'"

"It did."

"Given the degree of similitude, sir, and the weight of Locke's original rendering upon the educated mind of the time, might one, a neutral party, sir, reasonably be led to view the phrase 'pursuit of happiness' as being cognate with the phrase 'pursuit of estate?'"

"The relation would seem a reasonable one, arithmetically in the first place, logically in the second, semantically in the third."

"In fact, sir, might one view 'happiness' as used in the *Declaration* as the American form of the British original, 'estate,' the only difference being that in England property tended to be acquired by birthright, largely within the aristocracy, whereas in America property could be attained by any class, simply by exercise of Industry and Frugality?"

"I cannot fault the logic."

"In fact, sir, was it not your personal philosophy, both when you authored 'A Defense of the Quakers' and when you participated in authoring the *Declaration of Independence*, that 'happiness' is in relation to 'estate' essentially as laughter is in relation to wit; heat in relation to ember? And was it not an abiding investment by you in this philosophy, sir, that caused so many of your public counsels concerning happiness, as exemplified in your *Almanacks* and your *Way to Wealth*, to be invocations toward acquiring and keeping material property?"

Ben stared hard upon the man he had made his enemy by no greater injury than "doing him too much kindness." "My personal philosophy, sir, ever was, and ever remains, that happiness derives of virtue, as I have declared in several public testaments, one of these being *Articles of Belief and Acts of Religion,* which testament, sir, it would appear, you have chosen to exclude from your close accountancy, with perhaps some measure of profit anticipated toward your private purposes in this chamber."

Smith composed a wry smile by way of coercing a modest asymmetry of cheek and mouth to either side. "Ah yes, we do seem to keep circling back upon virtue, don't we, sir—as if indeed under spell of that nettlesome old gadfly of Athens. Our question in the moment, however, sir, is not 'What is virtue?'—as it was for Socrates—but 'Which?' Which virtues in particular, sir, should we embrace such as to ensure ourselves of happiness. Indeed, not all of virtue is of equal stripe, just as not all of Madeira is of equal stripe, nor all of humanity; would you not be inclined to agree, sir? Indeed, how else to explain how one man can harness a Negro servant in the manner of a horse or an ox whilst another man can steadfastly refuse to follow suit at considerable cost to him of his material prospects?"

Ben looked to the same parquet square previously regarded.

"Ah, but I step onto ground to be overturned by another plow, pulled indeed by another ox. Let us hold upon the ground at hand." Smith riffled through his papers, and pulling a few sheets to top, looked to Ben. "As regards the issue, sir, concerning which virtues are most delivering of happiness, allow me to speak a few verses from the testament to which you recently alluded, this being the Epistle of B. Franklin unto the Quakers, also known as *Articles of Belief and Acts of Religion."* Smith looked to his papers. "I quote: 'I conceive for many reasons that he'"— Smith looked up—"*he* being the Christian god, God the Father; correct, sir?" Ben, yet gazing upon the parquet square, made no reply.

Smith continued, "'—that *he* is a good Being, and as I should be happy to have so wise, good and powerful a Being my friend, let me consider in what manner I shall make myself most acceptable to him. Next to the praise due to his wisdom, I believe he is pleased and delights in the happiness of those he has created; and since'—emphasis mine—'and since *without virtue man can have no happiness in this world, I firmly believe he delights to see me virtuous, because he is pleased when he sees me happy.'"

Smith looked to Ben. "Ergo, happiness is derived of virtue, as indeed only recently declared by you, your precise words to this effect being, if memory serves: 'My personal philosophy ever was, and ever remains, that happiness derives of virtue.' Quite so?"

Ben making no response, Smith looked to his papers. "I continue: 'Let me then not fail to praise my God continually, for it is his due, and it is all I can return for his many favours and great goodness to me'—emphasis mine—'*and let me resolve to be virtuous, that I may be happy*, that I may please Him, who is delighted to see me happy. Amen.'"

Smith looked to Ben. "Ergo—echo—happiness is indeed derived of virtue. Quite so?"

Ben yet making no reply, Smith lowered his papers to side and looked to the high bench. "The court shall construe the Petitioner's silence to the affirmative"—Smith looked to Ben—"unless the Petitioner should presently raise objection to the contrary."

Ben held to silence.

"Very good. And so, sir, with cause and effect betwixt virtue and happiness established beyond all doubt, by way of consultation to scripture—the horse's mouth, one might say—versus the oracle upon the opposing end"—titters—"the question now becomes, rather, remains: *Which* virtues in particular, sir, are tributary to that subterranean garden of peace and repose, ever bathed of a warming sun, which we name happiness? Shall we lay upon oar that we might pull ourselves unto a full discovery?"

Ben looked hard upon Smith. "You shall, presumably, indenture this prisoner to whatever servitude fits your purpose."

"Ah, yes, but only because the 'prisoner' would not, I must remind him, indenture himself toward a full discovery, despite being granted every opportunity to do so. Indeed, although given full power to witness all there was to witness, to confess all there was to confess, our 'prisoner' used his powers of reification and insight instead to bring to fore only those articles of experience and memory that might serve to increase the volumes of a virtuous vanity, by count of a dozen of such, to a total of thirteen, to be exacting."

Smith looked to the examiners' table, whereat Adams and

Wedderburn had stacked into a crimson-and-gilt tower the twelve volumes Ben had added to his *Autobiography* during his confinement, together with the relatively slim original volume rested atop. Smith thereupon looked to the assembly, his chin uplifted as if in mimic of Wedderburn: "Are we surprised?" Cackles and hoots erupting from the assembly, Smith pulled to fore a sheet from the several in hand, waited for the din to subside, then continued. "'I wish the out-of-fashion practice of praising ourselves would, like other old fashions, come round into fashion again. But this I fear will not be in our time, so we must even be contented with what little praise we can get from one another.'"

Lowering his papers to side, Smith peered overtop his bifocal lens toward Ben. "May I offer you the comfort of assurance, good sire, dear *Pater Patriae*, that your plea toward the future of vanity, undressed of the gossamer wit with which you veiled it, has been very well honored by the several generations succeeding you, very well honored indeed."

Smith paced to leftward, turned half-circle around, was pensive a moment, then looked again to Ben: "We have now been reminded, sir, of the thirteen virtues you espoused as being 'necessary or desirable.' Likewise, we have been reminded that you espoused these virtues in your *Almanacks*, under guise of Poor Richard; and in your *The Way to Wealth*, under guise of Father Abraham; and most especially within the pages of your *Autobiography*, which volume you long struggled to bring to term, against much adversity, in lieu of, we should here mention, the volume you had promised several times over to your friend Lord Kames, as well as others, to be called *The Art of Virtue*; quite so?"

Ben held fast upon Smith's eyes, but made no reply.

"Our standing question, then, sir, as regards *which* virtues are necessary to happiness—happiness being the natural harvest of virtue, as declared by you—would seem to find answer in these same thirteen virtues; would you be inclined to agree, sir?"

Ben held such heat of eye upon Smith now as if to melt the object of his attention into its constituent oils.

"In effect, our standing question has, by virtue of remaining in the foreground, allowed answer to come unto it, instead of the other way around; would you be inclined to agree, sir?"

Ben held to silence.

"Cat got your tongue, sir?"

The clerk jumped to his feet. "Whereat truth is held mute by a spiteful tongue, only ill might proceed." He sat down.

Ben looked to a parquet square close to foot, then again to Smith. "I find no error in your deductions, within the boundaries allowed."

"How kind of you to say so, sir." Smith leaned into a small bow, then continued. "Might we declare as truth then, sir, that the very virtues you espouse in the *Autobiography* as being 'necessary or desirable,' toward an end not explicitly declared by you, are the very same virtues you allude to in *Articles of Belief and Acts of Religion* as being instrumental toward achieving happiness?"

"What *seems* under limelight is not necessarily what *is* under daylight. Indeed, if you would back-paddle a few strokes from your eager row, I believe you would discover at the source of your embarkation that I give explicit mention within the *Articles of Belief and Acts of Religion* to a score or more of virtues I *explicitly* intend to be construed as necessary to a virtuous life, hence to happiness."

"O indeed," Smith sniffed, chin slightly uplifted. "Let us do precisely as you recommend. Would you be so good, sir, as to paddle to one side whilst I paddle to the other, that our aim might be true?" Turning away, Smith stepped to the examiners' table, exchanged his sheaf of papers for another, and returning to stand atop the vitreous circle, this yet showing a faint glow, began to read from the topmost sheet:

> *In as much as by reason of our ignorance we cannot be certain that many things which we often hear mentioned in the petitions of men to the Deity would prove REAL GOODS if they were in our possession, and as I have reason to hope and believe that the goodness of my Heavenly Father will not withhold from me a suitable share of temporal blessings if, by a VIRTUOUS and HOLY life, I merit his favour and kindness; therefore, I presume not to ask such things, but rather humbly, and with a sincere heart, express my earnest desires that he would graciously assist my continual endeavours and resolutions of eschewing vice and embracing virtue; which kind of supplications will at least be thus far beneficial, as they remind me in a solemn manner of my extensive DUTY.*
>
> *That I may be preserved from atheism and infidelity, impiety and profaneness, and in my addresses to thee carefully avoid irreverence and ostentation, formality and odious hypocrisy,*
> *Help me, O Father.*
>
> *That I may be loyal to my prince, and faithful to my country, careful for its good, valiant in its defence, and obedient to its laws, abhorring treason as much as tyranny,*

Help me, O Father.

That I may to those above me be dutiful, humble, and submissive, avoiding pride, disrespect and contumacy,
    Help me, O Father.

That I may to those below me, be gracious, condescending and forgiving, using clemency, protecting [the] innocent [from] distress, avoiding cruelty, harshness and oppression, insolence and unreasonable severity,
    Help me, O Father.

That I may refrain from calumny and detraction; that I may avoid and abhor deceit and envy, fraud, flattery and hatred, malice, lying and ingratitude,
    Help me, O Father—

"Et cetera, et cetera, et cetera," the reverend ended, to likeness indeed of three strokes of scissors. "Your words, sir?"

Feeling again his spirit slump, Ben again reminded himself of the sun ever rising close upon the back of his head. "They are," he could not but confess.

"Taken from the same scripture as previous, this being *Articles of Belief and Acts of Religion*?"

Ben nodded.

"And the virtues mentioned therein—'*to those above me be dutiful, humble, and submissive, avoiding pride, disrespect and contumacy; to those below me, be gracious, condescending and forgiving*'; et cetera, et cetera—these are the virtues you 'explicitly intend to be construed as necessary to a virtuous life, hence to happiness?'"

"They are."

"We being now returned, by aid of your paddle with mine, to the point of recent embarkation, shall we aim toward discovery of the true object of these virtues, sir; and return thereby, yet again, to the original issue at hand?"

"When a horse is led, does he have a choice as to which pasture to graze?"

"As with the trough, sir, might he choose to graze of no pasture?"

Ben looked to the floor square of recent interest.

Smith looked to his papers. "I repeat, in part, the excerpt previous: 'I have reason to hope and believe that the goodness of my Heavenly Father will not withhold from me a suitable share of temporal blessings if, by a VIRTUOUS and HOLY life, I merit his favour and kindness.'"

Smith looked to Ben. "In the stead of 'temporal blessings,' sir, as used by you herein, might we place, as rightful cognate, the term 'HARD GOODS'—or even the term 'estate'—or even the term 'property?' In fact, sir, is not the very object of the virtues you espouse in your various scripture no greater than what might yield a temporal glow of material comfort? And do we not see, sir, most clearly now, that by Justice in your pantheon of thirteen virtues you intend justice to one's patrons, that they might be inclined to revisit one's shop, and not Justice to such as the Negro race?"

Ben could not help but notice in the moment that absent the softening effect of the nested loops in the parquet squares on the floor, that the squares themselves, the sharp angles of these, ever compounding, would be too harsh.

"Cat got your tongue, sir?"

Ben held to silence.

Smith continued. "Now, sir, in turning over one dung heap have we not inadvertently loosened its neighbor? Do you not smell the odor, sir—of flattery? Of falsity? Of expediency? *Help me, O Father!—O Help me!—*

"Alas, do we find any such religiosity as this, sir, even distantly akin to it, in the *Autobiography*?"

Ben held to silence.

"Do we find any such in *The Way to Wealth*, sir?"

Ben held yet to silence.

"Do we find any such in the twenty-five *Almanacks*, sir?"

Ben held yet to silence.

"Do we find any such in any other volume, broadside, article, or bagatelle ever previously or subsequently writ by you?"

Ben held yet to silence.

"Kindly apprise me, if you would, O, good sir, of the age you had attained when you contrived your epistle unto the Quakers?"

Ben held yet to silence.

The clerk jumped to his feet.

"I had only recently, if memory serves, celebrated my twenty-second birthday."

"And what was your circumstance at this time, sir, as regards a livelihood?"

"I was engaged in the print trade."

"You were, in fact, newly the proprietor of a print shop, were you not?"

"A dear friend and I had recently joined in a partnership."

"And who of the citizenry of Philadelphia at this time, sir, might I farther inquire, were most likely to become your patrons?"

"Any widow in need of an advertisement."

Chuckles.

"No other?"

"Any tradesman, shopkeeper, artisan, or farmer in need of same or similar."

"Many of whom, not to except the widows, were Quakers, were they not?"

"They were."

"And would it be accurate, sir, to assume that these same Quakers were rather inclined toward piety?"

"I could not argue the point."

"In fact, sir, it was just such a Quaker who had urged upon you that you add Humility to your list of 'necessary or desirable' virtues, heretofore confined to twelve, was it not?"

"It was."

"And when, sir, you published *Articles of Belief and Acts of Religion*, on November 20, 1728, only a few months following your entering into the printing trade—in partnership, it must be said, with a man too dissipated of drink to make any meaningful contribution toward the success of your business—was it not toward these same pious Quakers, toward in fact the opinion of these same pious Quakers, to whom you intended your scripture—for whose sensibilities in fact you specifically composed it?"

Ben lifted his gaze such as to regard the Royal Seal.

"In truth, sir, were you not, by way of this scripture, by way of the 'score or more of virtues' you included therein, by way indeed of a shameless pretense toward Quaker piety, presenting yourself in the silks of a certain allure, as might a London harlot, such as to attract patrons of a certain sensibility, not to mention of a certain means, unto your shop?"

Ben held to silence.

Smith continued. "If in this very moment, sir, we were to look in full upon the venue of our inquiry, might not something of a pattern emerge? Indeed, sir, might not your pretense toward piety by way of your epistle unto the Quakers be seen as of a piece with your pretense toward humility by way of parading your wheelbarrow full of paper before your fellow merchants?"

Ben slumped of head and shoulder.

Hesitating not for a reply, Smith turned away, and stepping to the examiners' table, exchanged his present sheaf of papers for another.

Adams and Wedderburn, Ben noticed, were each peering upon a volume taken from the tower of his *Autobiography*, their heads alternately drooping and lifting.

Taking station atop the vitreous circle, it yet showing a residual glow, Smith assumed a demeanor less haughty. "I have but a few more queries to make of you, sir. I beg your toleration. Firstly, if I may, I would like to inquire as to your opinion concerning happiness, whether this term includes a multitude of species, as in the case of love, or but one, as in the case of lust."

Ben gazed upon the crystalline bench, wherein random colorations were forming into remarkable symmetries and reverse. "I would hold there to be one such, experienced in degree, as in the analogue of heat."

"And what of pleasure?"

"Pleasure I would hold to be the experience of happiness—that radiation indeed which is felt in degree."

"But not happiness in or of itself."

"Nor separable from it, as ember and its heat."

"And you hold that happiness derives of virtue; that is, of one conducting a virtuous life; correct?"

"That is my opinion, as I have declared."

"And have attested to, not least unto the Quakers of Philadelphia. Now, sir, taking these declarations by you as fact, might one reasonably conclude that the virtuous life is also a pleasurable one—pleasure being the experience of happiness, and happiness deriving of virtue?"

"The logic underlying your deduction would appear to be self-evident."

"Very good. Now, sir, as to the debauched life, a life dedicated to self-indulgence and personal dissipation, such as that of your partner in the print business, Mister Meredith. Is such a life not also a life of pleasure?"

"Yes, but pleasure of a different species."

"So, whilst there is but one species of happiness, there are at least two of pleasure?"

"Exactly so."

"Each one experienced by degree?"

"Exactly so."

Smith looked to his papers. "'Natural or sensual pleasure continues no longer than the action itself, but this divine or moral pleasure continues when the action is over, and swells and grows upon your hand by reflection. The one is inconstant, unsatisfying, of short duration, and attended with numberless ills; the other is constant, yields full satisfactions, is durable, and no evils preceding, accompanying, or following it.' Are these words familiar to you, sir?"

"They are."

"Their source, sir?"

"If memory serves, they are taken from a dialogue betwixt Philocles and Horatio."

"Which dialogue appeared in your *Pennsylvania Gazette*; am I correct?"

"You are."

"Were you the author of it, sir?"

"I was not."

"In fact, you discovered this dialogue already printed in the esteemed *London Journal* over two issues; am I correct, sir?"

"You are."

"And thereupon you reprinted it in your *Gazette*, but without attribution as to source; did you not, sir?"

Ben glared. "Worthy authors were not of a vanity, sir, that required any such immodesty."

"Nor of a vanity, sir, that required protection of their good names against attributions being made by credulous readers provided no correction?"

"As you wish."

"I wish naught, sir, other than that the truth, convenient or no, become known in this forum. And such that we might move a little farther toward this end, allow me to inquire, sir, if you would, as to whether it is within the realm of logical inference that a young tradesman in his twenty-fourth year, much burdened of debt from purchase of a newspaper representing no guarantee of success, this coming close upon purchase of the aforementioned print shop, that he might look upon attributions made innocently to his name for literary contrivances wrought by clever minds elsewhere, as a most fortuitous accident—manna indeed from heaven—especially if he were not entirely undeserving of the reputation being attributed unto him?"

Ben glared the harder. "And under what circumstance, sir, should one look upon the insinuating speculations of a hypocritical, treasonous, back-stabbing scoundrel as anything even approximating a noble search after the truth, convenient or no?"

Smith looked upon Ben as if through eyes become besotted of

maternal affection. "You would appear, sir, by flush of cheek, to have become overly warmed. I am certain the court would allow the Petitioner to remove his jacket, if such would allow him more comfort. One might speculate, on the basis of the available evidence, and its likely farther accumulation, that he might have little farther need of it in any event."

Chortles from the assembly.

Ben took pains to affix every button upon his coat, starting at the bottommost of these.

Smith contrived his thin face into a wry smile. "As you wish."

Titters.

Upon Ben affixing the topmost button upon his coat, Smith continued. "Now, sir, as to the first pleasure described in the dialogue just quoted you, being the 'natural or sensual pleasure,' should we assume this pleasure to owe to pursuing a life of virtue, or to else?"

"'Tis the pleasure owing to the Lower Instincts, one might say."

"Would it be accurate, then, sir, to suggest that, even though the words from the dialogue just quoted you were not your own, the sentiments carried by them concerning pleasure and virtue were consonant with your own sentiments at the time you stole them—forgive me— *borrowed* them—into your *Gazette*?"

"It would . . . with the correction."

Smith bowed. "Now, sir, into which category would you place the pleasure or satisfaction of a fine Madeira—into that owing to the Lower Instincts, or into that owing to—how shall we say?—the Higher Instincts?"

"The former."

"And the pleasure or satisfaction, sir, owing to a generous slice partaken from a golden loaf newly removed from a kitchen oven—into which category?"

"The same."

"And the pleasure or satisfaction, sir, owing to a mother who endangers her own life such as to bear another into the world? Of a father, sir, who plows deep into the evening so that his son might spend his mornings at school? Of a traveler, sir, who bears the load of a hobbled stranger? Of a soldier, sir, who takes the bayonet in the stead of his comrade? Of a minister, sir, who leaves the warmth of his hearth to render comfort unto a bereaved widow? Of the man, sir, who treats ill words with kind? Of the man, sir, who returns a blow to his right cheek with presentation of his left? Of a father, sir, who forgives a despairing son all his shortcomings? Of a husband, sir, who returns from important business afar to hold a dying wife in his arms? Into which category, sir?"

Ben averted his eyes unto the loops engrained into a parquet square to front.

"Have I fed too many faggots into the fire, sir, such as to smother it?"

Ben lifted his eyes. "The opposing category, as you well apprehend."

"And by 'opposing category,' sir, may we assume you refer to that species of pleasure or satisfaction owing to the Higher Instincts?"

"As you wish."

"And when you stated in your *Articles of Belief and Acts of Religion*, sir"—Smith looked to his papers—"'I have reason to hope and believe that . . . my Heavenly Father will not withhold from me a suitable share of temporal blessings if, by a VIRTUOUS and HOLY life, I merit his favour and kindness,' were you likewise referring, specifically by way of the term 'temporal blessings,' sir, to that species of pleasure or satisfaction owing to the Higher Instincts?"

"When a discourse is navigated by sleights of hand and feints of steerage, how might it arrive at any destination other than the one contrived aforehand?"

"Should we assume by your avoidance, sir, a reply to the negative?—and that we might therefore spare these proceedings any farther mention of an equation betwixt 'temporal blessings' and 'HARD GOODS?'"

Ben bowed. "As you wish."

Smith bowed in return. "Thank you, sir. Now, sir, as regards the young lads who bore upon their sashes the names of the virtues you espoused in your *Autobiography*—toward what object, sir, was each lad directing his compass arrow?"

"Upon first appearance, each lad generally to rearward. Upon an interrogative by you, each lad specifically toward his belly."

"And this interrogative, sir, do you recollect it?"

Ben assumed a nasally intonation overly colored of a High Anglican sensibility: "'Are you a virtue that tends to aim inward, toward self, or are you a virtue that tends to aim outward, toward other?'"

Laughter.

"Most excellent, sir. You are indeed a man of many talents. And one cannot other than marvel at your powers of recollection." Smith bowed, Ben thereupon returning the gesture in kind. Smith continued. "Now, sir, might a reasonable man, in your learned opinion, stand the term

'Lower Instincts' in the stead of, or as cognate to, the term belly, or stomach, as used in the figurative sense?"

"If an object pulled from a hat bears strong resemblance to a hare, it is entirely reasonable to construe that the object in hand is, in fact, a hare."

"Might we construe this response, sir, as bearing toward the affirmative?"

"As you wish."

"Now, sir, as regards the young lasses who circled around you, each bearing upon her sash the name of a virtue not included amongst the thirteen mentioned in your *Autobiography*. From what article of self, sir, was each lass pointing her compass arrow of concern?"

"From her breast, it would appear."

"The heart being included within that cavity?"

"And the spleen."

"Hers, sir, or yours?"

The clerk banged his gavel upon his bench to effect of startling examiner and petitioner alike. Turning half-circle around, Smith bowed toward the high bench. "My apologies."

Ben, yet seated, bowed to equal measure.

Smith continued. "Now, sir, might a reasonable man, in your opinion, stand the term 'Higher Instincts' in the stead of, or as cognate to, the term breast, or heart, as used in the figurative sense?"

"If an object pulled from a hat bears strong resemblance to a goose, it is entirely reasonable to construe that the object in hand is, in fact, a goose."

"And if an object brought forth from darkness into light, sir, is not in and of itself false, nor illusory unto others, does it matter by what means it is brought forth?"

"If the means are illegitimate, can the ends be other than suspect?"

Smith's eyes widened as if to a happenstance wholly unexpected. "Are you suggesting, sir, that the virtuousness of an end gained is, in some measure, the virtuousness of the means employed by which to attain it—as if the one is indeed simmered in the broth of the other?"

"I am."

"Are we to infer then, sir, that expediency in service to gain is subject to some measure of constraint—or at least it ought to be?"

"A fair inference."

"Thank you, sir. I shall keep this valuable insight very much in mind.

Now, sir, to pursue our previous line of inquiry to conclusion: If our logic should hold—and should it not, sir, I invite you to discover the flaw to me, that I might not bring an embarrassment upon myself—it would appear that we have an equation by which the sum of one set of virtues results in satisfaction to one set of instincts—to wit, the Lower Instincts—by way of rendering gain unto one's self; and a second equation by which the sum of another set of virtues results in satisfaction to a second set of instincts—to wit, the Higher Instincts—by way of rendering gain unto one's neighbors. Is this a reasonable conclusion, sir?"

"It cannot be otherwise, as you have contrived it."

"Very good. Now, sir, let us at this juncture, in the interest of clarity, construct a modest demonstration of these two species of satisfaction. Let us suppose that two good men of your acquaintance, let us name them Monsieurs Horatio and Philocles, each bakes three loaves of bread. Let us suppose farther that Monsieur Horatio sits down immediately upon removing his golden loaves from the oven and has for himself, and himself alone, a small feast, consuming a majority of what he has baked, together with a majority of a bottle of fine Madeira, leaving the remains of each item for the morrow. Does Monsieur Horatio experience some measure of satisfaction, sir?"

"Indeed. As regards the bread, the pleasures of taste, texture, and satiation; as regards the wine, the pleasures of bouquet, body, and euphoria."

"All owing to the Lower Instincts, sir?"

"The term 'Lower' being here, it would seem, both deliberately and unjustly pejorative."

"Perhaps so, sir, but how does one make comparison without making distinction?"

"Where might one discover the comparison, the 'er,' sir, in the distinction betwixt male and female?

"You have not heard or used the term 'weak-*er* sex,' sir?"

Ben glanced upon Bartholomew, who shrugged.

Smith continued. "Returning to our demonstration, sir—might we also expect Monsieur Horatio to derive a certain measure of pleasure from the accomplishment of baking three fine loaves of bread?"

"We might."

"Owing also to the Lower Instincts?"

"If the action be in service to himself alone, it would seem so."

"Now, let us suppose farther, sir, that Monsieur Philocles, upon removing his own golden loaves from the oven, happens to espy, through an unshuttered window, a beggar woman hobbling upon the near road. Without pausing to cipher a moral calculus, he hurries to the window and summons the old woman. Although suspicious at first, from disappointments past, the old woman hobbles to the window, her fear overwhelmed by her need, and Monsieur Philocles gives over to her two of his loaves, in company with his very best bottle of Madeira. 'Two loaves for thee,' he says unto her."

Ben looked to Clarence, the very agent who had first borne this strange message unto him. Clarence shrugged. Smith continued. "Now, sir, how far into the future might endure the pleasure gained by Monsieur Horatio? Of industry, he has produced three fine loaves of bread, better in quality perhaps than those of Monsieur Philocles. Of appetite—of desire, perhaps we should say—he has consumed his loaves and his wine unto satiation. Of frugality, he has saved the remains of each article for the morrow."

Ben discovered himself salivating to memory of golden loaves resting upon his mother's baking hearth.

"Likewise, sir, how far into the future might endure the pleasure gained by Monsieur Philocles? Of industry, he has produced also three fine loaves of bread. Of compassion—of love, perhaps we should say— he has given over two of his loaves to one in greater need than himself, leaving himself open thereby to deprivation and hunger."

Allowing but a brief pause, such as to render his interrogative rhetorical, Smith continued. "Let us farther suppose, sir, that Monsieur Horatio, sated of bread and warmed of wine, removes himself to his library chair, and he being suffused now of that species of satisfaction that quiets the Lower Instincts—the appetites, sir, if you like—he does likely what, sir?"

"Reads a page or two of Defoe or Bunyan and slips into a very pleasant slumber."

"From experience, sir?"

"From observing those false scholars unto whom you are sycophant, sir, and who speak in the very affectations of diction you presently mimic."

Before Smith, his eyes flashing of fire distinctly, and strangely, bluish, could joust a retort, the clerk hammered his bench a sharp blow with his gavel.

Ben rose from his seat, as if by buoyancy of an ocean swell, and bowed. "My apologies." He resumed his repose.

Smith continued. "And Monsieur Philocles, sir, removing himself to his own chair, within his own library—he likely does what, sir, relative to your supposition regarding Monsieur Horatio?"

"Relative to my supposition regarding Monsieur Horatio, I would be inclined to speculate that Monsieur Philocles, given his name, removes not Defoe from his shelf, but Socrates, and reads perhaps the greater part of a dialogue."

"And thereupon slips into a pleasant slumber?"

"Slumber being inevitable in either case."

"And when each man awakens, sir, which one is likely to have the greater satisfaction yet lingering?"

Ben gripped his chin of thumb and finger, stared upon Smith's shoes for three counts, and looked then upon Smith's countenance, indeed as he might, at age nine, look upon Master Brownell's. "Might it be the one who has dined sparest, slumbered least?"

"I am the preacher here present, not the philosopher."

"Were you indeed both, sir, one might rejoice at prospect of your having something of merit about which to preach."

The clerk hammered his bench with such a blow now as to cause Ben, upstanding in the moment from his seat, and Smith, spinning upon his heels, to issue apologies toward the high bench in near simultaneity.

Returning again to his repose, Ben felt a touch upon his shoulder, from Bartholomew, and, taking the message, resolved to put his temper into harness—or, better, to return it there, he having allowed it, of a lack of vigilance, to unfetter itself.

Smith continued. "Let us attempt now, sir, to relate the current demonstration, involving Monsieurs Horatio and Philocles, to my esteemed colleague's recent demonstration involving the two groups of children—the first of these, the thirteen lads, being, as you will recollect, well formed of countenance; the second of these, the thirteen lasses, being wholly unformed of countenance.

"In the case of Monsieur Horatio, sir, the face upon his Industry would seem very well formed. To be sure, a notable level of skill, derived of dedication and experience, had gone into the manufacture and baking of his three loaves. Can we say the same, however, of the face upon Monsieur Horatio's Compassion? Alas, was there means by which it might see beyond an unshuttered window? Was there means by which it might summon a hobbling old woman in obvious need?"

Hearing sounds as if from table at an inn, Ben discovered Adams and Wedderburn chewing upon morsels of bread pulled from golden loaves, whilst intermittently slurping a darkish red humour from goblets of cut crystal.

Smith continued. "Now, as regards Monsieur Philocles, sir, we perceive a well-formed face not only upon his Industry, but also upon his Compassion, do we not?—to effect indeed that his Compassion has eyes by which to see beyond an unshuttered window; voice by which to summon a hobbling old woman in need?"

Smith seemed wholly unaware of the bacchanalian repast taking place at his back, Ben noticed, whilst his petitioners, staring from their table, seemed only too aware.

Smith continued. "We must be wary, however, must we not, sir, that we not cast aspersion upon our friend Horatio? He did not, after all, in keeping three loaves to his own purposes, commit any deliberate act of injury toward any other party. Or might it be the case, sir, that one can transgress as egregiously by acts of omission as by acts of commission? Have you opinion on the point, sir?"

"The only point serving as rod to my opinion in the moment, sir, is whether or no you are yet arranging the stage to advantage for a comedy in which I am ever to be made the fool." Ben stared upon Smith for three counts. "I must construe my silence on the matter to the affirmative."

Titters.

"One would hope, then, sir, that you have sufficiently committed your lines to memory that you might not be made the fool by no greater than ill preparation."

"I have yet to be delivered the script."

"The script, sir, has been available to you all these many years. You had only to deliver it unto yourself. And had you done so, Dr. Franklin, sir, you would not now be in the embarrassment of having to be confronted, by way of these proceedings, with a point of philosophy most fundamental. In truth, sir, had you included in your *Autobiography* the thirteen virtues heretofore demonstrated unto you, the thirteen virtues of the Higher Instincts, sir, in counterpoint to the thirteen virtues you chose as 'necessary or desirable,' the thirteen virtues of the Lower Instincts, sir; indeed, had you formed of line and hue the faces upon the lasses with the same attention and ardor with which you formed the faces upon the lads, ask yourself, dear sir, whether the animus giving rise to those predatory forms you recently witnessed, to your horror, would have been able to avail itself so completely, so tragically, sir, toward the ends it has over the several generations succeeding your own, over the same multitude of decades indeed that you have been reposed within your chamber, your castle unto yourself, sir, adding to the tower of your vanity."

Smith gestured an arm toward the examiners' table, upon which yet stood the tower of red-and-gilt volumes, less two. "Whether it be a disparity of electrical charge betwixt poles, a disparity of sovereignty betwixt peoples, a disparity of justice betwixt races, a disparity of voice betwixt genders, such a state is amongst the most pernicious to be avoided by mortal kind, would you not agree, sir? Indeed, when one polarity bears too much charge, the other too little in relation, what is the only result possible betwixt them?"

Of a sudden a bolt of electrical fire shot forth from the high bench, and striking upon the tower of volumes atop the examiners' table, disintegrated the lot, save the two recently perused by Adams and Wedderburn, into a blizzard of dust and debris, and caused in the moment such a concussion as to send Adams and Wedderburn fleeing to the underside of the examiners' table, and Ben, in simultaneity, to flinch against the unyielding back of his chair.

As Adams and Wedderburn thereupon reclaimed their seats, Smith looked to the assembly, and raising an arm in the manner of a Roman tribune, sang forth: "Hail Industry! Toileth thee unto profit! Hail Frugality! Holdeth thee unto wealth!" Thereupon a most remarkable image coalesced of the colorations within the crystalline bench, of a landscape witnessed from a great height, framed to one side by what appeared to be a river, tinctured not of azure but as if of barnyard effluvia; to the other side, by a second river, narrower than the first, more serpentine, tinctured to an even darker hue of brown. Something about these two tributaries, in juxtaposition, one almost standing in mirror image to the other, began to bear some familiarity. Of a sudden Ben realized he was looking upon no other than his beloved Philadelphia!

O what unspeakable horror had been visited upon his dear child? Had the vile minions of some deranged monarch finally overpowered her? Ravaged her of all innocence? Indeed, the enormity of the injury suggested a wounding of biblical wantonness, rendering field and forest alike barren of all but a few remnants of vegetation, these largely in proximity to the two rivers.

"Hail Industry!" Smith sang forth. "Hail Frugality!"

A flash of coloration now and the scene was changed as if to a burying ground in which the stumps of trees stood as memorials to that part of themselves that had been removed—which interpretation indeed, as the eye of view moved closer upon the stark landscape, proved to be the very truth. Indeed, acre upon acre of trees—they being, by inference of girth, ancient in origin—appeared to have been felled by the scythes of titans, leaving not a stick upstanding.

The eye of view closed now upon an ungainly Goliathan, other-worldly in aspect and proportion, which, in embracing upon a hapless pine, caused it to shudder and tremor, in the manner of a soldier being ripped of bowel by bayonet, as a large blade, circular, sliced through its lower trunk. The Goliathan thereupon dismembered the tree of its limbs, and cast the residual stalk upon a pyre of other such, these accumulated upon the carriage of a large-wheeled wagon showing a cabin but no horses. As the great reaper embraced another hapless victim, the eye of view retreated to reveal yet another such monster, and another, and another, all engaged in, at various stages, the same ritual slaughter.

"Hail Industry! Hail Resolution!"

Another flash now and the scene was changed to a bosomy moun-tain being eaten away, it appeared, by a wanton cancer. As the eye of view closed upon a lesion of hideous scale and aspect, the agents of decay, a horde of mechanical vermin, came into view. These strange creatures bore to front a large maw affixed to a levering neck, and were scooping into this great swaths of the essential substance of the mountain, and dumping it then into a box covering the whole of a great wagon, the latter being as massive in scale as the tree-holding wagons, but much stouter.

"Hail Industry! Hail Order!"

Another flash and the scene was changed to what appeared to be a massive carbuncle, black as coal, discharging its fester in the sub-stance of an inky sublimation, reminding in cast of the choking mists of London in February. As the eye of view drew closer, what resembled a massive pustule became in fact a smoldering pyre of wheel-like objects similar in aspect to, but smaller in diameter than, the wheels on the two species of wagons recently witnessed. The source of the smolder itself seemed so deeply embedded within the pyre as to include the embers of hell itself, whilst the overall expanse of land consumed by the pyre seemed to include sufficient acres as to have been able, if under plow and till instead of flame and fume, to feed the whole of General Washington's army over a year's duration.

Surrounding this hideous mound of smolder and smoke was the apparent source of its tinder, an accumulation of the metallic carcasses of innumerable carriages, denuded of their black wheels, all showing symptoms of having suffered ill treatment previous to their abandonment.

"Hail Industry! Hail Temperance!"

Another flash and the scene was changed to what appeared to be a vast deposit of offal being scavenged by a swarm of seagulls in likeness to flies upon carrion. Large horseless wagons were dumping yet more effluvia upon this great deposit, whilst great mechanical rams, crawling upon circulating tracks, were leveling previous dumpings by way of a rectangular blunt at front, the rude intrusions of these sending hordes of seagulls into an ascending spiral of complaint.

"Hail Industry! Hail Justice!"

Another flash and the scene was changed to a multitude of barn-like structures—metallic in aspect, low in profile, remarkably long in length—arranged in paralleling files. The eye of view swooped low now, and entering into one end of the nearmost of these structures, passed row-upon-row, tier-upon-tier of heavy-mesh cages, each congested of fowl reminding in head and comb of that noble bird Ben had advanced to become the National Symbol.

Ben was shocked now to discover each bird maimed of beak to effect of disarming it of all agency by which to defend a sacred sovereignty.

"Hail Industry! Hail Humility!"

Another flash and the scene was changed to a garish cacophony. To center, a roadway bore in either direction two files of self-ambulating carriages, these creeping head to tail, in fits and starts. To either side of this, for as far as the eye could see, various venues of commerce, of no common aesthetic or architecture, seemed veritably to shout out for attention by way of a profligacy of garish ostentation and tawdry aspect. Along one side of the roadway, unsightly spans of filaments, pole to pole, seemed to constitute a net by which to foul any bird so foolish as to intrude upon so forbidding a nightscape. Barely a leaf or blade was to be discovered, nor a single perambulator upon a single walking path.

Hail Industry! Hail Tranquility!

Another flash and the scene was changed to several files of self-ambulating carriages, many of these being in likeness to those previously witnessed; others being much larger, with a cabin at front and a closed box to rear. All were moving at remarkable speed—three files in one direction, three in the opposing—upon a roadway wholly free of ruts or potholes. And whilst most of these vehicles remained regimented in separate lanes, delimited by intermittent striping upon the roadway, some of the smaller ones were interloping from file to file, seemingly in an effort to gain some measure of advantage. The eye of view moving closer upon one such, Ben could see a woman steering with one hand whilst holding a small device to ear with the other. Of a sudden the woman bore leftward causing thereby her vehicle to strike upon the side of a smaller vehicle. The offending vehicle thereupon tumbled onto its side, and rolling over and over, erupted into a violent conflagration, whilst the smaller vehicle shot across a narrow median and struck, head upon head, a large cabin-and-box vehicle moving in the opposing direction, launching thereby, through a shattering pane, the form of a small child, in similitude to a cannonball being propelled toward a distant redoubt.

As if by wave of wand, the vehicles vanished, and the eye of view drew closer unto the surface of the roadway itself, thereby revealing, as it moved forward, the carcasses, some well desiccated, others yet robust of flesh and bowel, of a menagerie of unfortunate creatures, accumulated sometimes one atop another.

Another flash and the scene changed again, showing a different roadway, this one comprising but two lanes in parallel. A self-ambulating wagon, cabin at front, open box to rear, was moving in the rightmost lane, and seemed to take deliberate aim upon a squirrel stopped just previous to the pavement, tail fluttering in staccato. The right front wheel of the wagon thereupon struck upon this hapless creature, popping its eyes from its tiny skull and disgorging its bowels through a gaping maw. As the carriage sped on, a hand protruded from a window to side and released an amber bottle onto the perimeter of the roadway, joining there a generous accumulation of kindred such.

Ben shook his head. "No more! I beg of you! No more!"

"No more, Father Abraham, sir? No more, *Pater Patriae*, sir?" Smith looked to his papers. "'I wish it were possible . . . to invent a method of embalming drowned persons in such a manner that they be recalled to life at any period, however distant; for, having a very ardent desire to see and observe the state of America a hundred years hence, I should prefer to any ordinary death the being immersed in a cask of Madeira wine, with a few friends, till the time, to be then recalled to life by the solar warmth of my dear country.'"

Smith looked to Ben.

Ben looked to Strahan, who, taking up his pen, scribbled earnestly upon a sheet to front, as if indeed to capture a thought before, like a butterfly, it might flitter away.

"Hail, Industry!" Smith boomed unto the assembly, extending upward his right arm.

"Hail Industry!" returned the assembly.

"Hail Frugality!" Smith boomed.

"Hail Frugality!" returned the assembly.

"Hail Property!" Smith boomed.

"Hail Property!" returned the assembly.

"Three loaves for Me!" Smith boomed.

"Me! Me! Me!" returned the assembly.

Turning away, Smith returned to his place at table, whereat a golden loaf and a goblet of dark-red wine lay in wait. Reclaiming his chair, Smith pulled a generous tuft from the steaming loaf, and upon masticating this in the manner of a child unpracticed in the restraints of etiquette, washed it unto the arms of contentment with a generous draw of wine.

Arising from his chair, Adams stretched as if to escape the cocoon of a night's slumber, and moving then from behind the examiners' table, with aid of a walking stick, posted himself atop the vitreous circle, this showing a residual glow become dim.

Ben peered hard upon a strikingly owlish face. "I trust you found your fame, sir, presuming no loss in appetite for such following my departure."

"I found my peace, my friend, as you are here to find yours."

"I shall find no peace here, sir, as your presence in this infamous pit, in company with two fellow copperheads, does so extravagantly attest."

"And your presence 'in this infamous pit' attests to what, sir? *Surely* not to a disposition toward vanity yourself. Surely—O silly me; already I seem to have forgotten. 'Tis a disposition toward *virtue* that your presence here 'does so extravagantly attest.'"

"A bird flies in consonance with having been given wings. Would you prefer that I had crawled upon my belly, sir, in company with yourself?"

Laughter.

Adams took rude notice of the strained seam upon Ben's coat. "One might suspicion, sir, on basis of a leviathan girth given emphasis by way of a stubborn buttoning, that one too many visits to one too many Frankish salons has long since rendered it inadvisable for you to assume the posture of a lithesome serpent."

Guffaws.

Adams returned to the examiners' table, and lifting into hand a sheaf of papers from proximate one of the residual volumes of Ben's *Autobiography*, posted himself a step forward of the vitreous circle. The din abating, he continued. "Now, sir, if I may, I would like to remind you of a letter you wrote to the Abbés Chalut and Arnaud, they residing in Passy, you having returned from there to Philadelphia following the colonial struggle for independence."

Ben smiled upon mention of two of his dearest interlocutors.

"In this letter, sir, you include an exemplary instance of the 'moral sentences, prudent maxims, and wise sayings' you invented, or purloined and improved upon, for spicing a little the hardy stew of your *Almanacks*." Adams looked to his papers. "'Dear Friends, your reflections on our situation compared with that of many nations of Europe are very sensible and just. Let me add that, only a virtuous people are capable of freedom.'" Adams looked to Ben. "'Only a virtuous people are capable of freedom.'" He bowed. "Most eloquent of you, sir, despite—or perhaps because of?—an economy of words most severe."

"There are perhaps as many examples of long-windedness amounting to eloquence as there are of intemperance amounting to sobriety."

Adams smiled. "Very good, sir. Yet another little pinch of sagacity to hold dear in our snuffbox. There is, however, sir, a cost to employing frugality in service to eloquence, is there not? Indeed, in the present case, does not brevity leave us to ask: *Which* virtues in particular had you in mind to be associated with the term 'virtuous?' Had you in mind the virtues you promote in your *Articles of Belief and Acts of Religion*, or had you in mind the virtues you promote in your *Autobiography* and *The Way to Wealth*?"

"I had in mind those aspects of character required of a people, exhausted by eight years of war and deprivation, to be able to build a nation fully reflective of those same principles for which they had only recently been disposed to sacrifice their very lives."

"Might it be fair, then, sir, to include under 'virtuous' *both* sets of virtues, there being in fact some overlap betwixt them, not to mention some complementing—call it complementarity?"

"It might."

"Now, in your opinion, sir, does a man who takes it upon himself to promulgate such 'moral sentences, prudent maxims, and wise sayings' as the one just quoted you; does this person have a perhaps special obligation to exemplify the very comportments of mind and behavior that he, by way of his various promulgations, advocates in others?"

"He does."

"And in this regard, sir, should such a man be concerned more with the actuality of being virtuous or with an abiding appearance of same?"

"What costume fashioned of silk can long cloak the bristles of a swine?"

Adams uplifted his arms. "I stand in awe, sir. Yet another little pinch for our snuffbox! Now, as to the point at hand, sir, I must burden you with a little repetition." Adams looked to his papers. "'In order to secure my credit and character as a tradesman, I took care not only to be in *reality* Industrious and Frugal, but to avoid all *appearances* to the contrary. I dressed plainly; I was seen at no places of idle diversion. I never went out a'fishing or shooting; a book, indeed, sometimes debauched me from my work, but that was seldom, snug, and gave no scandal; and, to show that I was not above my business, I sometimes brought home the paper I purchased at the stores through the streets on a wheelbarrow.'" Adams looked to Ben. "Do you recollect these words, sir, only recently recited in this chamber?"

"And likely to be recited again, it would appear, unto madness."

"The emphasis placed upon the terms 'reality' and 'appearances,' sir; yours?"

"If you discovered it to be so, so it must be." Ben watched a remarkable mosaic emerge from the void within the high bench only to dissolve back into it.

"Now, sir, at the time you were parading your wheelbarrow up High Street in demonstration of your Industry and Frugality, not to mention your Humility, you were consorting with—let us use your own term on the matter—'low women'—indeed to ultimate consequence of producing a bastard son; am I correct on this point, sir?"

Ben glared of sufficient heat as to, it might seem, melt a little lead. "As I have fully and freely confessed."

Adams looked to the assembly. "Correct me if I err, sir, but was not Chastity one of the thirteen cardinal virtues advanced by you in your scripture as being 'necessary or desirable?'"

Titters.

Discovering the clerk poised to bang his gavel, Ben held to silence.

Adams continued. "Now, sir, just previous to fathering this child of lust, presumably whilst your wheelbarrow was stopped elsewhere than at the mother's door"—titters—"did you serve as landlord to the Godfrey family, they occupying the rooms directly overtop your print shop?"

"I did."

"And over the course of your lordship, sir"—more titters—"did you, with Mrs. Godfrey's encouragement, become romantically entwined with Mrs. Godfrey's niece?"

"I did."

"And did you, sir, after winning the heart of this young lady, offer to take her to wife for the tidy sum of £100, which sum would retire the debt you had recently incurred in purchasing the aforementioned print business, and which represented a wolf at the door?"

"In response to an enquiry made by the young lady's family, with Mrs. Godfrey serving as intermediary, I made representations as to a proper dowry."

"Proper for which party, sir? The young lady's family made clear to you that they had no such sum to offer; did they not?"

"They made remonstrations to that effect."

"And in response to those remonstrations, sir, you counseled the family to mortgage their home such as to assume unto themselves the whole of the risk you heretofore had been yourself carrying"—Adams struck the floor a sharp blow with his walking stick—"am I correct, sir?"

"They held no legitimate claim to innocence. Had I softened my terms, they would have acceded to them, as thereafter became clear. They but wanted to unload a burden without taking on the equal."

"Are we to conclude then, sir, that this unfortunate young lady meant nothing to you of herself—that she was naught to you but an expediency toward a certain conveniency, one not quite attainable by exercise of virtue alone, or even by *appearance* of same?"

Ben looked to his petitioners, they each returning but a shrug.

"And so, sir, spurned at that door, what does our virtuous trades-man do? Alas, in the manner of a stray denied a bone at one door, only to seek charity at the next, he shows himself at the doorstep of one Deborah Read Rogers, she not quite widowed, though Mr. Rogers had long since decamped unto mystery. Deborah, it seems, had taken Mr. Rogers to husband during the protracted and altogether silent absence of her previous suitor, none other than our virtuous tradesman, whilst the latter was distracted in London with 'low women.' Before embarking to that city, however, in search of means by which to set up a print business, our virtuous tradesman had given Miss Read every indication he would take her to wife upon return. Am I correct, sir?"

"The 'virtuous tradesman' of whom you speak, sir, would have taken Miss Read to wife *previous* to his departure had her mother not been overly meddlesome in that particular regard."

"And that snorting, rearing steed that was your ardor for this young innocent, sir, had you harnessed it to the wagon of your inestimable powers of persuasion, might not you have been able to leap over this obstacle, sir, if not upon a first run, upon a second?"

Ben looked again to his petitioners, they each again showing him a small shrug.

"During the entirety"—Adams struck the floor with his walking stick—"of your absence from Miss Read, sir, to length of one and a half years, you were moved to write to the object of your ardor how many times in service to reaffirming that ardor?"

"One might suspect the interrogator to have already in hand the very facts he would appear so urgently to seek."

Adams struck the floor with his stick. "Once, sir. And then only to apprise your dearly beloved that you would not be returning anytime soon." Adams grinned. "A familiar refrain, sir?"

Smith jumped to his feet. "In the fall!"

Wedderburn jumped to his feet. "In the spring!"

Ben affixed his eyes upon the grain of loops eternally incarcerated within a parquet square.

Adams continued. "In any event, Miss Read—become Mrs. Rogers—was returned to her mother's house on Market Street, having been abandoned by Mr. Rogers, and was thereby subject to petitions from other parties. Indeed, the situation was as if the hands of the clock had been run backward, and there you were, once again sniffing at the poor woman's door, the aim of your attentions being now, however, a bone of a different sort. In truth, instead of a dowry with which to service a debt that might sink you, you now sought a wet nurse— and perhaps, dare we suggest, an appearance of legitimacy unto your Quaker congregation—for a bastard son about to be burdened unto you. Do I err as regards any of these points of fact, Mr. Chastity Himself, sir?"

"Childish ridicule would hardly seem to befit a man of the stature the present inquisitor so ardently esteems of himself."

"As indeed, sir, would willful hypocrisy"—Adams struck the floor with his stick—"false declaration"—he struck it again—"and crass expediency"—again—"hardly seem to befit a moral philosopher of the stature the present petitioner so ardently esteems of *him*self."

A sharp report from the clerk's gavel elicited an apology and a bow from Adams; a bow only from Ben.

Adams consulted his papers, then continued. "Elliot Benger, of Virginia. Do you recollect this gentleman, sir, and the circumstance of your knowledge of him?"

"I do. Mr. Benger was Deputy Postmaster General previous to my accession to that office."

"And do you recollect the circumstances under which you succeeded to that office, sir?"

"I made application."

"In fact, sir, did you not, whilst Mr. Benger lay gravely ill in his bed chamber, deliver to your friend here present, Mr. Collinson, in his capacity as MP, a correspondence requesting he make overtures in your behalf toward gaining the favor of Mr. Benger's position should Mr. Benger's affliction prove, in your words, 'irreversible?'"

"I had adjudged it prudent to make my interests known."

"Prudent, sir?—as in '*prudent* maxim'? The man is not yet tepid in a bereaved wife's arms and already we have a vulture—*turkey* vulture, sir?—circling overhead, such as to be the early bird unto the carrion." Adams looked to his papers. "Your words, sir: 'I would only add that as I have a respect for Mister Benger, I should be glad the application were so managed as not to give him any offense, if he should recover.'"

Ben stiffened. "You show the hue of one part such as to color the whole. If I had not made application, sir, some dim-witted powder-wig three thousand miles distant would have delivered the office unto some simpering sycophant to carry into ruin."

"Might we infer then, sir, firstly that all such offices should be awarded of merit as opposed to relation; and secondly, that you were most deserving of this particular office because you were most meritorious of it?"

"As borne out by the improvements I made subsequent to my appointment, the most notable being a significant and sustained solvency."

"And so, sir, when you were elected to the Pennsylvania Assembly, necessitating thereby that you vacate the office of clerk to that body, to which office you had been appointed several years previous, was the vacancy of that office given public notice such as to deliver unto its seat the most meritorious and deserving replacement?"

"It was delivered unto my son William, as you well know."

"Ah, yes, but delivered to your son, we must presume, not because—as might appear to some scurvy-afflicted outlander—your son was deserving merely by accident of birth, so to say"—titters—"but because, being the issue of the eminently deserving Benjamin Franklin, he was ipso facto most deserving, sons being, as anciently decreed, constructed in the very image of the father. A fair assessment, sir?"

Ben looked to Collinson, whose smile showed little more radiance than a new moon.

"And likewise, sir, in regard to your son's subsequent appointment to the office of Postmaster of Philadelphia, to the office of Continental Comptroller, to the office of Royal Governor of New Jersey—meritorious father ipso facto meritorious son? Most deserving father ipso facto most deserving son? Do I capture correctly your calculus of merit, sir?"

Ben watched a remarkable symmetry take form within the high bench and dissolve almost in the same moment unto the very disorder from which it had only just emerged.

Adams glanced upon his papers, and then continued. "Now, sir, subsequent to your entering the print business, you and your partner, Hugh Meredith, aforementioned, purchased the property rights to a weekly newspaper being published at the time by your former employer, Samuel Keimer, which instrument was titled *The Universal Instructor in All Arts and Sciences; and the Pennsylvania Gazette*, which title you thereupon truncated to *The Pennsylvania Gazette*. Am I correct, sir?"

"I believe the major facts regarding my history in the print business have already been established."

"Let us add then, if we might, sir, a few *minor* facts regarding this history, and thereby a few pastels to our mosaic. At the time of your purchase, sir, your Gazette had a rival in the name of *The Mercury*, a weekly instrument being published by Andrew Bradford, son of William Bradford, the same printer who had sent you to Philadelphia from New York when you could find no employment in the latter; am I correct, sir?"

"You are."

"And Mr. Bradford, by virtue of being Postmaster of Philadelphia at the time, had an unjust advantage over you, in that he could distribute his newspapers by way of postal carriers whilst denying you access to the same means of distribution; am I correct?"

"You are."

"And your response to this injustice, sir, was what?"

"I struck a private arrangement with the carriers."

"Such arrangement consisting of fattening a little the wallets of Bradford's carriers in exchange for including your *Gazette* in the same pouch with *The Mercury*, in direct violation of the terms of their employment, and thereby at risk of that employment; am I correct, sir?"

"I met thrust with counter thrust."

"Eye for an eye? Tooth for a tooth? This is the example all of posterity should emulate, sir?"

"I but bettered a little the lot of the carriers and their oft deprived families."

"And had the cuckolded employer, sir, been sufficiently alert as to unmask the betrayal of his trusted carriers, what then? Would he not have struck each one from his book of accounts? Would he not have scarred each one with the mark of Cain, such as to deny him future prospect, whilst you continued to give appearance of a virtuous rectitude at the helm of your wheelbarrow?"

"All commerce might rightly be likened to war, with each tactic provoking a counter tactic, to end of the cleverest winning the day. Ever has it been so."

"And to what ultimate end, sir?" Adams struck the floor with his stick. "To end of the virtuous life?" Bang! "To end of general well being?" Bang! "To end of happiness?" Bang.

Ben glared. "Even the road to virtue must have its potholes, the wagoner thereby a splintered spoke or two."

"Is that what we have here, sir, a pothole; the occasional splintered spoke? Or is what we have here, sir, a little expediency in service to conveniency, leading unto yet another little expediency in service to conveniency, leading unto yet another little expediency in service to conveniency, leading unto—unto what, sir? A conscience wormed through with holes perhaps? A soul pustuled over with carbuncles?"

"He who must repair the wheels upon his own wagon knows well where lays the line that separates a wanton indulgence from a deliberate responsibility."

"And he who is *not* required to repair his own wagon, sir?" Adams held his eyes hard upon Ben, Ben returning in kind. They both seeming at the same time then to come into an expectation of the clerk's gavel, Adams turned to his papers, Ben to his thumbs. "In the spring of 1782, sir," Adams continued, showing no heat, "when you were resident at Passy, did you publish, upon your private press, a broadside titled *A Supplement to the Boston 'Independent Chronicle?'"*

"I did indeed."

"And did you include in this broadside, sir, a letter written by one Captain Gerrish of the Albany militia?"

"I did."

"And did the content of this letter, sir, include an inventory of scalps harvested from women and children by savages serving the interests of the Crown?"

"It did indeed."

Adams looked to his papers. "I quote: '43 scalps of Congress soldiers'"—Adams tapped the floor with his walking stick—"'98 of farmers killed in their homes'"—tap—"'88 scalps of women, hair long'"—tap—"'211 girls' scalps, big and little'"—tap—"et cetera"—tap—"et cetera"—tap—"et cetera"—tap. "Were these facts, sir, as carried from Albany to Passy, in all ways accurate?"

"They were accurate as regarding the reality to which they stood in representation."

"In other words, sir, they were contrivances—expedients—as was indeed the very episode producing them. Your confession on the matter, sir, as whispered, so to say, to one of your conspirators." Adams looked to his papers. "'The *form* may not perhaps be genuine, but the *substance* is truth.'" Adams looked to Ben. "Your words, sir? Your emphasis?"

Ben nodded.

"Now, sir, what virtue worth the teaching of it might we distill from this sentence were we to apply the proper heat? I repeat it: 'The *form* may not perhaps be genuine, but the *substance* is truth.' With which house of spirits, sir, should we thereupon place our order?"

Ben glared hard upon Adams. "Is it upon the bony backs of facts that the nursery rhyme carries its moral sentiment to summit, or is it upon the gossamer wings of fancy?"

Adams took a step forward. "Does the nursery rhyme pretend fanciful fact to be literal truth, sir? Does a man of great influence have no obligation soever to notify his audience when his accounts are but an expedient contrivance as opposed to a body of historical facts? In the absence of such, sir, how is there to be any distinction betwixt truth and falsehood, rationality and superstition, order and chaos? Consider, sir, the ultimate destination of expedient contrivance in the service to private purpose. What, sir, would be left of public trust? And in the absence of public trust, sir, what would be left of civil society itself?"

Ben glanced to the petitioners' table, and finding Strahan scribbling a note, affixed his eyes upon the nesting of loops within a parquet square.

Adams continued. "Now, sir, you once had occasion to visit a school in Philadelphia overseen by the Reverend William Sturgeon, rector of Christ Church, which parish counted amongst its congregants your good wife; am I correct?"

Ben glanced to the clerk, and discovering this party staring close upon him, in the manner of a mother determined to forestall any farther misbehavior, nodded unto Adams.

"And this school was dedicated at the time to the general education of children of the Negro race, was it not?"

"It was."

"Now, sir, in response to this visit, you confessed to John Waring, who had been instrumental in the establishment of this school, as follows." Adams looked to his papers. "'I have visited the Negro school here in company with the Reverend Mister Sturgeon and some others, and had the children thoroughly examined. They appeared all to have made considerable progress in reading for the time they had respectively been in the school, and most of them answered readily and well the questions of the catechism; they behaved very orderly, showed a proper respect and ready obedience to the mistress, and seemed very attentive to, and a good deal affected by, a serious exhortation with which Mister Sturgeon concluded our visit. I was on the whole much pleased, and from what I then saw, have conceived a higher opinion of the natural capacities of the black race, than I had ever before entertained. Their apprehension seems as quick, their memory as strong, and their docility in every respect equal to that of white children.' Are these your words, sir, hence your sentiments at the time?"

"The *substance* of your reading would *appear* to be a faithful representation as to the truth."

Titters.

"In sum then, sir, might we say that you came away from your empirical visit holding Negro children to be generally on the same intellectual plane with white children, whereas, previous to your visit, you had held certain prejudices that would place Negro children, Negroes in general, on a somewhat lesser intellectual plane?"

"I had long considered the Negro race to be less naturally clever in the arts of apprehension and invention."

"In fact, you confessed as much to Mr. Waring in the same correspondence just quoted, did you not, sir?" Adams looked to his papers. "'You will wonder perhaps that I should ever doubt it, and I will not undertake to justify all my prejudices, nor to account for them.'" Adams looked to Ben. "Very noble of you, sir."

About to sound a note of gratitude, Ben withheld it.

Adams continued. "Now, sir, as a result of this change in sentiment, confessed privately by you to a man a'ready in sympathy with your amended opinion, what public confessions did you undertake toward swaying other white people from their own prejudices concerning the Negro race, in particular those others who held you in high esteem?"

"I have no specific recollection of making any such confessions—at the time."

"And yet, sir, when you made novel discoveries concerning the electrical fluid at about this same time, did you not take steps to broadcast these discoveries to anyone who might hear them, using as instrument toward this end, in fact, your petitioner here present, Mr. Collinson?"

Ben looked to Collinson, who nodded just perceptibly.

"How might we explain the apparent difference in urgency here, sir, betwixt these two discoveries, other than to hold the discovery of an essential equality betwixt African and European children to be of a lesser import than the discovery of an essential equality betwixt lightning and the electrical fluid?"

Ben glared. "I did not deliberately undertake to weigh either discovery over the other."

Adams glared in kind. "You would have us believe, sir"—tap—"that the preeminent moral philosopher of his time did not, upon discovery of a moral equivalence betwixt Black and White children, hence betwixt Black and White people in general, also discover, in simultaneity, a great moral error in a continued exploitation of Negro children, in company with their mothers and fathers, in the manner of oxes and asses? You would have us believe, sir"—tap—"that in removing all essential differentials betwixt Black and White, save for the accidental pigmentation of their skin, you did not also remove all justification for their continued exploitation and abuse? You would have us believe, sir"—tap—"that in remaining silent about your discovery, you did not search amongst your pantheon of virtues for justification to sustain such a silence, and indeed find it, not in company with these others, but lurking in the shadows just beyond whereat they stood?"

Glancing to the petitioners' table, Ben discovered Strahan slouched, eyes downcast, as if weighted of news too heavy upon the spirit to bear.

"Shortly following your visit to Reverend Sturgeon's school, sir, did you make a public response to an atrocity committed by certain of your countrymen against native peoples supposedly under the protection of certain others of your countrymen? I speak specifically, sir, of the massacre of twenty unarmed Conestoga Indians in Lancaster County at the hands of the infamous Paxton Boys. Do you recollect this incident, sir, and your response to it?"

"I do."

"And the instrument of your response, sir, was this not a pamphlet titled *A Narrative of the Late Massacres in Lancaster County*, writ of your hand and printed upon your press?"

"It was."

Adams looked to his papers. "'The guilt will lie on the whole land till justice is done on the murders. THE BLOOD OF THE INNOCENT WILL CRY TO HEAVEN FOR VENGEANCE.'" Adams looked to Ben. "Might not these same words have been applied, and by the same pen, sir, to the aforementioned enormity, to wit, the continued exploitation and abuse of the Negro race? And might the reason they were not, sir, have been a matter of expediency? Indeed, did you not at this time own as property, and exploit as such, two Negro slaves, named Peter and King? And did not one in five other households in the colonies at this time also own and exploit at least one Negro slave? And did not a kindred expediency, sir, lead you to contrive, but a few years hence, in a pamphlet titled *A Conversation between an Englishman, a Scotchman, and an American, on the Subject of Slavery*, the sentiments I now quote?" Adams looked to his papers. "'Perhaps you imagine the Negroes to be a mild-tempered, tractable kind of people. Some of them are so. But the majority [are] of a plotting disposition, dark, sullen, malicious, revengeful, and cruel in the highest degree.'"

Striking the floor a heavy blow with his walking stick, Adams looked hard upon Ben. "Might we have something of a pattern here, sir, as regards the employment of certain expediencies unto the gain of certain conveniencies?"

Discovering himself slouched a little in his chair, Ben made attempt to straighten himself.

Adams, returning to the examiners' table, consulted a few papers there, and upon taking station atop the vitreous circle, this showing now no glow, continued his inquiry: "One last item, sir—but a trifle. Upon your escape to New York, sir, from Boston, in your eighteenth year, you attempted to find work in the printing trade, and were directed to the shop of William Bradford, as previously established; am I correct?"

"No less so now, I can assure, than previous."

"Very good. And William Bradford, having insufficient work, referred you to his son Andrew, who was in the print trade in Philadelphia, and had, by coincidence, only recently lost the services of his assistant, one Aquila Rose, to an untimely demise; am I correct?"

"You are, it being difficult to imagine how you could be otherwise."

"Most gracious of you. Now, sir, this act of kindness on the part of the elder Bradford, he being under no obligation to assist you in any regard was the central circumstance that brought you to Philadelphia, which event spawned the many others that were to conspire and accumulate into a truly momentous life; a fair statement, sir?"

"One would be hard pressed to fault it."

"Now, sir, when finally you arrived at Philadelphia, and found your way to Andrew Bradford's print shop, you discovered therein the elder Bradford in company with his son, the elder having traveled from New York by way of horseback and ferry, versus foot and oar; am I correct as to this point, sir?"

"Unerringly so."

"To your grave disappointment, you being close upon starvation, you learned that Andrew had only recently taken on a new assistant in replacement to Mr. Rose. Instead of turning you out, however, good luck to ye, Andrew gave you breakfast, referred to a second printer in town, one Samuel Keimer, and told you that should Keimer not be able to accommodate you with steady employment, he, Andrew, would give you room and board and such employment as to keep you solvent until better prospects should avail; am I correct, sir?"

"Perfectly so."

"And the elder Bradford, sir, extending upon the grace of his son, thereupon accompanied you unto the Keimer shop such that he might lend you support; am I correct, sir?"

"And, in his son's interests, to conduct a little reconnoiter."

"Be that as it may, sir, William and Andrew Bradford, by way of their acts of generosity and kindness, did rescue you that day from a pauper's peril, did they not?"

"They were most forthcoming as regards both generosity and hospitality."

"And, had this not been the case, sir, had William and Andrew Bradford not taken you unto their hospitality and generosity, what might have been the course of your life? How different might this course have been, sir, from the one ultimately navigated?" Adams looked to his papers. "'For want of a nail the shoe was lost; for want of a shoe the horse was lost; for want of a horse the rider was lost.'" Adams looked to Ben. "In fact, sir, in the absence of William Bradford's generosity toward you in New York—this single act being the 'nail' that provided the 'shoe' that provided the 'horse' that you thereupon rode unto greatness, sir—circumstance could well have compelled you to return unto Boston, there to complete your indenture to your brother James, there to be reimmersed into the stifle and stupor of Puritanism.

"In other words, sir, but for a single act of kindness, by a man making no expectation as to recompense, you might well have had to sow your seeds of genius in the same soil you had but recently escaped for its want of fertility—to likely effect, sir, of your riding a very different horse unto a very different destination. Do I propound a fair speculation, sir?"

"The hand holding the helm of one's life is only in appearance the one upon the wheel."

"Our snuffbox spilleth over!"

Ben glared.

Adams continued. "Now, sir, in return for this fateful act of kindness, did you not, several years hence, enter into an agreement with one James Parker to set Parker up in the print business in New York, in direct competition to the very same William Bradford who had steered you to Philadelphia, and unto rescue? And did you not thereupon, sir, by manipulating certain advantages of capital, connection, and expertise, push William Bradford into a despairing retirement, to effect indeed of pushing him into his grave?"

"No cock goes unrivaled."

"And that was your guiding principle, sir?—the law of the barnyard?—wherein betrayal, being expedient to the conveniency of triumph, constitutes virtue? You could not, sir, instead of lurking in shadow like a highwayman, have exercised the decency of informing Mr. Bradford of your intentions?—of inquiring after his sentiments concerning such? You could not, sir, have forgone an unneeded profit altogether, that you might hold to honor a fateful charity? You could not, sir, have chosen to demonstrate unto a pliant posterity, by way of example, the necessity and virtue of favoring Loyalty over Opportunity, Restraint over Return, Generosity over Expediency, in all circumstances affecting interests beyond one's own?"

Turning half-circle around, Adams wagged his walking stick toward the high bench, wherein in the instant a scene formed in which an old man, of about eighty years, was slumped in a chair afront a scrivener's desk. The man's red-rimmed eyes were brimmed near to overflowing.

"No cock goes unrivaled!" Adams boomed.

No sooner did Ben recognize William Bradford than he felt himself being drawn from his chair as if by force of a fierce magnetism.

Of a sudden he was sitting afront the scrivener's desk, upon which lay an envelope, seal broken.

Upon his lap lay a single sheet, unfolded.

Honorable Father,

Nothing has ever hurt me so much—Ben wailed—*as to discover you betrayed in your old age by a man, although a rival of a kind, you ever had cause to hold in highest esteem. Recent intelligence has confirmed indeed that it is with the militia and means of Dr. Franklin that Mr. Parker has taken up arms against you. I find I am too much affected by this injury to pray for the man's soul. As in the case of a loose tooth which must be wriggled, I find myself recollecting that day when a ragamuffin well short of his majority entered my shop, you present, to beg for work that he might fill his belly and see the morrow. Fortunately there is salve in remembrance of that paternal affection you demonstrated unto so brave and determined a spirit, not only in your own example, but also in mine in imitation of yours—*

A flash—Ben was returned to his chair.

"Probity be damned!" Adams boomed, striking the floor with his stick. "Long live Property!

"Loyalty be damned!"—bang!—"Long live Rivalry!

"Generosity be damned!"—bang!—"Long live Expediency!

"Expediency! Expediency! Expediency!"

Of a sudden, Adams snapped his walking stick overtop a lifted knee and looking straight upon Ben, flung the pieces close upon Ben's head, prompting Clarence and Bartholomew to duck theirs to side. Two pulses of light shot forth from the high bench, and striking upon the two missiles, incinerated these unto a London mist. Simultaneous cannon-like reports sent Ben lunging headlong from his chair—and peering as if through a spying glass upon a most remarkable bumble bee buzzing overtop a watery landscape.

New York City

September 16th, 9:43 a.m.

Kevin lifted his headphones from his ears and slipping his cell phone from inside his suitcoat, checked caller ID. He grinned—Annie. Holding his phone and one hand against one ear, he pressed his free hand against the other ear.

"Louder!" he shouted.

"I'm in heat!"

"Woo-hoo!"

"Don't be late—or the doorman gets the duty!"

About to make a meretricious quip, Kevin met the eyes of the two crewmen sitting opposite, not more than six feet away, and thought better of it.

"I'll be there!"

Slipping his "joey" back into its marsupial pouch, Kevin smiled.

It was all beginning to get a bit real.

Annie's OB/GYN had given them a year to get pregnant "the old-fashioned way," with a little help from LH monitoring to "maximize the moment." Give it a good go, she had counseled them, and if that didn't work, there were others measures they could try.

Meanwhile—lots of sex! And for god's sake, relax! Make a game of it!

Pulling his headphones back on, Kevin edged forward on his seat, and looking through the windshield, could see the Pier 6 heliport coming up dead ahead, and behind it, the Lower Manhattan towers. Among these, he could make out his destination. He smiled. Or was it his destiny?

It was all beginning to get a bit real.

The moment the chopper touched down, the two crewmembers moved quickly to open the door and deploy the steps. Kevin waited for a thumbs up and then quickly disembarked into a glare that, almost three months off its peak, triggered an immediate squint.

A white limo with "373" showing on one of the windows was standing only yards from the chopper. Russ, conspicuous in blue sunglasses and a buzz cut, was holding a door open at the rear; Travis, equally conspicuous, was approaching at a brisk pace.

Taking Kevin by the arm, Travis hurried him to the open door at the rear of the limo and all but pushed him inside. The door slammed, the lock clicked. Another door slammed, and another. CNN was playing on one of the TVs; Fox on the other. Kevin turned them off.

The world was a goddamn mess.

His father was no help. His father was part of the problem.

As the limo moved up the access road, Kevin slipped his phone from its pouch and speed-dialed a number.

"I'm on the ground."

"Everybody's here." There was a tone of relief in Callie's voice.

"Ten minutes."

The limo turned onto FDR, left onto Old Slip, becoming William, left onto Exchange, and right onto Broad. After passing over the retracted barriers on Broad, it entered into as if a time warp, with the flag-draped Stock Exchange resembling the Reichstag; the darkly uniformed police, the SS.

It had been a long time since Kevin had heard his father quote Franklin on "essential liberty."

As they passed the Exchange, Kevin peered through the tinted window at a flock of Japanese tourists, each of whom was either clutching or wearing a camera. Intending to snap a shot of a likely very surprised Japanese tourist, Kevin found his cell phone on the seat beside him, but then remembered he wasn't able to open the window. He slumped.

The limo turned right under the steady gaze of George Washington and stopped a little over a block up Wall Street. The door opened almost immediately. All but pulling Kevin from his seat, Travis escorted him to a swing door between matching sets of revolving doors, and then into a polished-marble lobby, gold and gray, where large gold letters on the wall behind the reception desk allowed no ambiguity: THE TROMPE BUILDING.

About to mount a short set of steps to the left of the reception desk, Kevin turned to the sound of his code name, BT, being shouted from behind. Russ handed Kevin his cell phone.

Kevin smiled a sheepish thank-you—this was not the first time this had happened—then climbed the steps, and pressing a thumb on a paten held by a security guard, walked to the further of two elevators. Entering the empty chamber, Kevin inserted a key into a slot below the floor buttons and turned it a half-circle clockwise. The door closed.

As the elevator ascended, none of the floor lights flashed. When the elevator stopped, a chime sounded. Kevin turned his key a half-circle counterclockwise; the doors opened.

Callie was waiting in the alcove. After a quick thermometer check— "How'd it go?"—she hurried Kevin through a maze of empty corridors and into a dimly lit room with upholstered walls.

Kevin nodded toward his guests, all of whom—three women, nine men—he knew by face and reputation, but not by personal acquaintance. They were strangers.

But not for long.

"Good morning." His voice seemed so dead as to carry no further than his own ears. He was all but surprised when he received several good mornings in return.

Five of the guests were standing by a small table arranged in the far corner of the room, to Kevin's right. The other seven were sitting at or standing near an oval table centered in the room. Charlie, Kevin's IT guy, was standing at the end of the table to Kevin's left, fussing with a laptop. A projector, attached to the ceiling directly above the table, was displaying a test pattern on a screen drawn from the ceiling at the other end of the room.

Kevin glanced at the greenish face of his watch. "Sorry to keep you all waiting."

"Not a problem," one of the women standing by the small table said, smiling. "The food's excellent." Several of the other guests concurred with nods.

Kevin recognized the speaker: Mary Hunley, executive director of the American League of Concerned Women. "Excellent," he said, returning Mary's smile. "We're off to a good start—and it's only going to get better!"

Moving now to the end of the table where Charlie had stopped fussing, Kevin laid a hand on Charlie's shoulder. "All set?"

"Good to go."

Stationing himself then just to the left of the laptop, Kevin looked to his guests. Those still standing, taking the cue, sat down.

Kevin introduced himself as "Kevin Kinney, private citizen," and invited introductions from around the table. Christopher Dawes, executive director of The American Way, being closest to Kevin, began; Jacob

Wurlitzer, Executive director of the american Preservation Society, sitting to Dawes' left, followed; and then—

Carl Forbusher, ED of the American Heritage Institute.

Paul Brinkley, ED of the American Enterprise Foundation.

Priscilla Conyers, ED of the American Council on Family Values.

Ruth Ann Galleon, ED of the American Family Institute.

And so on around the other side of the table.

When Edward Beasley had finished introducing himself, Kevin welcomed his guests with a promise of good things to come, and then reminded them that they were in a lead-lined, sound-proofed, peek-proofed room that could be compromised only by "the human factor," hence the need for the agreement they had all signed, "in blood"—smiles—and by which they had promised to abide by the rules, these being: No notes, no briefcases, no pocketbooks, no wallets, no glasses cases, no cell phones, no writing instruments, no watches, no jewelry, no pads, pods, or PDAs—in other words, "no nothing." Everything they would need over the next thirty minutes would be provided to them. In case of an emergency, a porta potty would be brought in.

More smiles.

Kevin slipped a thumb drive from his suit coat and placed it near the laptop. Apologizing then, he asked his guests to submit to a personal search, which, he promised, would be no more intrusive than what they had likely endured at their respective airport of embarkation. If anyone wished to decline, there was still time to leave. Once the door was locked, however, there would be no opportunity for anyone either to leave or to enter, as the door would be under the control of a robotic timer preset for thirty minutes.

After a pause, Kevin directed the women to Callie, the men to Charlie. When Charlie had finished searching the men, his search taking longer than Callie's, there being three times as many men as women, Callie tagged and issued receipts for the several items of contraband found, which included a silver money clip holding seven $100 bills, and a diamond-studded crucifix. Callie and Charlie removed these items by removing themselves.

Kevin locked the door behind his two assistants, drew a heavy curtain across it, and returning to his station at the end of the table, inserted the thumb drive into the laptop, and pressed a key. A bright-green banner appeared on the screen at the opposite end of the room: *One Penny More*, with the "O" in "One" and the "o" in "more" being shiny Lincoln-head pennies instead of letters.

"Thank you all for agreeing to be here," Kevin began, "and, once again, I apologize for the body search. It was both necessary and prudent, as you will soon appreciate. And, of course, the necessity for this kind of thing on the larger scale is part of the reason we're here this morning. By the way, there will be no record of this meeting, of any kind. Both this presentation and this computer will be destroyed immediately following this meeting.

"You all have a general idea of why you are here—why you were *chosen* to be here. We'll now get down to the specifics." Kevin pressed a key and a series of images and video clips played on the screen: Two men grinding against each other while riding on a pink and magenta parade float, three men attending to separate body orifices on a woman groaning in ecstasy, a suggestively undulating throng of naked-midriff nightclub dancers, a pounding rap video populated with near-naked bodies emblazoned with garish tattoos, a slow-mo disembowelment scene from a "Saw" movie, and so on, and so on. "One of the many threads binding you together," Kevin went on, "is a deep concern over what is happening in our world, *to* our world—the direction it's headed in—the cliff toward which it seems to be headed."

Kevin triggered another set of images: A clip of the Columbine school shooting, a clip of the Red Lake school shooting, a clip of the Nickel Mines school shooting, a clip of the Bethesda school shooting, a black-and-white clip of three boys beating a homeless man with baseball bats, and so on, and so on. "Another common thread is a deep sense of frustration and powerlessness in the face of your concern. What can *you* possibly do? You are but one—even collectively, but a few—and they, the sources of your concern—the liberal elite, the far left, the New Agies, the postmodernists, the deconstructionists, the radical feminists, the anarchists, the aristocrats of 'feel good' relativism—are many and ever increasing. Like a cancer metastasizing into every vital organ of a human body, these agents of moral decay have become entrenched in positions of power and influence in almost every sector of our society— in our media, in our schools, in our academies, in our corporations, in our arts, in our entertainments, even in our public charities—and it would appear there is no power on earth that can dislodge them before it becomes too late to do so. The juggernaut is in motion, is ever gaining momentum, and we are *all*, in the moment, directly in its path. The ultimate fate of our world would appear already to have been determined—by others. A global cataclysm of social and economic chaos would appear already to have been made inevitable—by others."

Kevin triggered another series of images: A dead baby being recovered from a dumpster in a garbage-strewn back alley, a father being arraigned for murdering his estranged wife and their three young children, and so on, and so on. "In the world you and I live in, visibility has become the ultimate source of power, for only in visibility, in gaining and keeping people's attention, is there any possibility of influence. But how to gain such visibility in a world of sound bites and pandemic ADHD? The means would appear to be twofold—by creating a cult of personality, as in the case of the celebrity talk-show host, the celebrity actor, the celebrity rapper, the celebrity politician, the celebrity guru; or by buying it outright, with hard, cold cash. Indeed, there is not a vendor of a product or service today, not a politician in pursuit of office today, not an interest in pursuit of a strategic advantage today that is not intimately acquainted with this inescapable truth."

Kevin triggered another set of images: A view of Times Square at night, a view of Las Vegas at night, a view of an anywhere-in-America "miracle mile" at night, a view of a "starter castle" decorated top-to-bottom, end-to-end with Christmas lights, and so on. "The equation, then, for us—those of us holding out little hope of attaining celebrity status—is simply this: He with the most money buys the most visibility, hence the most influence, hence the most control over the course of human events. In other words, friends, he with the most money seizes the day. For the rest, a lament. But for one penny more, the nail was lost; but for one nail more, the shoe was lost; but for one shoe more, the horse was lost; but for one horse more, the battle was lost."

Kevin triggered an image of a shiny penny radiating golden rays of light. "So, the issue becomes, quite simply, how do we ensure, how do *you* ensure, that you always have in your pocket one penny more?"

Kevin triggered an image of a bowman, dressed entirely in green, his mask included, aiming a plumed arrow from atop a magnificent white horse. "Enter the Beneficent Archer of Sherwood." After a moment, Kevin pressed another key and the green banner, *One Penny More*, returned.

"Now, before we get to the heart of the matter, I must remind you that, before coming to this meeting, you gave your oral consent to an oral agreement, of which there is no paper or electronic copy, under which you vowed to disclose absolutely nothing of what transpires here today to anyone, ever, for as long as you shall live. I now remind you of this agreement." Kevin looked around the table, at each face in turn, for any sign that the threat just issued had not been fully received. He pressed another key, triggering an image depicting a virus invading the body of a cell much larger than itself.

"As of four days ago, a computer virus, code-named Robin Hood, was introduced into the computer system of the United States Treasury. This virus, wholly invisible and undetectable, performs three key functions." Kevin triggered a color-coded flowchart. "On a preprogrammed, scheduled basis, Robin Hood creates official purchase orders, originated by the Central Intelligence Agency, for certain highly classified services, to be provided by various offshore entities. Subsequent to this, it matches corresponding invoices, which it also creates, against these purchase orders, and then issues payment, in the form of electronic transfers, to designated accounts in certain offshore banks. Once the internal audits are complete, the records of all the transactions are expunged from the system. In effect, they never existed. Although the amounts of money involved are modest, they are cumulative—cumulative, that is, into perpetuity."

Kevin triggered an image of a world map. Several points were marked with red dots; many more with blue dots; a few with green dots.

"Robin Hood has already enlisted a band of Merry Men and assigned these to duty in hundreds of banks around the world. These banks include those receiving direct electronic transfers from the Treasury, the red dots, but also many other banks around the world as well, the blue dots."

Kevin triggered an image showing Merry Men, all in red, marching from Washington, DC, to several points around the world, each of these becoming red upon contact; blue Merry Men marching forth from these red points to hundreds of other points around the globe, each of these points becoming blue upon contact. "Now, what these Merry Men do, both the red ones and the blue ones, is they transfer funds, without any human intervention whatsoever, first from the red banks to the blue banks, then between blue banks. What happens overall is this: An electronic payment is made from the Treasury to one of the red banks. The funds in this bank are then dispersed, at random, to several of the blue banks. These blue banks, in turn, disperse their funds to several other blue banks, and so on, and so on—to the ultimate effect of making traceability completely and utterly impossible." The map showed a web of lines becoming increasingly dense until no individual lines were distinguishable. "The amount of any one transfer is always some random fraction of the whole amount in any one account at any one time."

Kevin pressed a key that showed a world map dotted with red and blue points, along with a few, clustered in Europe, in green. "Now, why go to such lengths to prevent even the remotest possibility of traceability? Because, my friends, there are twelve additional accounts, not yet mentioned. I refer you to the green dots. These accounts are, in fact, the ultimate destination of all the transfers." Kevin triggered an image of twelve large honey pots, each pot a different color, being filled by worker bees dumping little pots of honey into them. He then triggered an image of a billiard table with twelve pockets, six to a side. Each pocket was marked by a different color. Green balls were being shot like pinballs onto the tabletop from the near end of the table. The individual balls were then bouncing from bank to bank until ultimately they dropped into one of the pockets. "You might liken the overall dynamic just described to you to what you see in this video. The individual balls are being banked—little pun there—and banked again, until ultimately they end up in one of the colored pockets."

Kevin triggered an image of twelve bankbooks arranged in an oval, each one a different color, each showing a different number at top. "Now, is there anyone here who doesn't have a pretty good idea at this point where all this is going?"

Carl Forbusher, smiling, lifted a hand. "You're making sure our organizations will always have enough money—one penny more, as you put it—to carry on the good fight."

Kevin smiled.

"This is stunning," Ben Beasley interjected. "Absolutely stunning." He grinned. "Does your father know about this?"

Kevin smiled. "The only people on earth who know about this are the twelve of you, myself, and one other person, who must remain forever anonymous for reasons you can well imagine."

"The wizard behind the screen?"

Kevin smiled.

"Well, whoever that person is," Ben added, "he . . . she . . . *it* . . . should get the Nobel Prize as far as I'm concerned . . . in . . . what?"

"Billiards," Mary Hunley quipped.

Ridge Proctor grinned. "As in balls?"

"Precisely."

Everyone laughed.

Kevin fetched a shopping bag from under the refreshments table and setting this on the table, at the near end, removed several packages from it, each one wrapped in paper of a different color. "Now, presumably," Kevin said, "when each of you arrived here today, you were given a small piece of colored paper by my assistant." All twelve nodded.

"If you would, please place this slip of paper in front of you."

Kevin distributed the wrapped packages, and when everyone had the package matching the color of his or her slip of paper, he said, simply, "Go!"

The excitement became palpable then as each guest removed the wrapping paper from his or her package to find a small, hinged box inside, and opened the box to find a watch with a face tinted the same color as the associated slip of paper.

"If you will look at the back plate on your watch," Kevin continued, "you will find a number at the bottom. This is the serial number of your individual watch. It also happens to be the number of a bank account. A little above it, you will find an acronym consisting of two to four letters. Reverse the first and last letters and you will have the acronym of the bank holding your account. CPBT, for example, is The People's Bank of China."

Kevin paused while his guests examined the back plates on their watches, then continued. "Each of you has complete control over the bank account assigned to you. From this point on, you can use the funds accumulating there toward whatever ends you deem appropriate. In this regard, it is hoped, but in no way mandatory, that you will contribute to candidacies for higher office who are likely to help you achieve your goals.

"The initial password to your account consists of the last seven digits of your account number. You will want to change this number at your earliest opportunity. Any questions?

"Anyone who wants to decline their watch, please speak now or forever hold your peace—little pun there."

Ben Beasley began to applaud, and standing up, was quickly joined by all eleven of the other guests.

Kevin bowed. "Thank you." He bowed again.

⚬

As the limo moved slowly eastward on Wall Street, Kevin pulled his cell phone from his suitcoat pocket and dialed a number from memory.

"Timmy!"

"Cratchit!"

"How'd it go?"

"God bless us everyone."

Supreme Celestial Court of Petitions

Clarence and Bartholomew helped Ben to his feet and, restoring him to his chair, reassumed their stations at either side. Solicitor General Wedderburn, upon quitting the examiners' table, held a magazine, its facing page tinctured as if of spilt tea, in front of Ben. "Would this instrument be of any familiarity to you, sir?"

Ben peered overtop his bifocals. "'Tis, as the masthead attests, the 15 April 1747 number of the *Gentleman's Quarterly*."

"Is there known to you, sir, a particular significance to this magazine?"

"'Twas the very first, if memory serves, to call itself such."

"A magazine?"

"Correct."

"And is there a particular significance concerning this particular number?"

"I presume you refer to the inclusion therein of the *Speech of Miss Polly Baker*."

"That item numbered *VII*, sir?"

Ben examined the cover sheet. "Indeed."

Wedderburn stepped briskly to the examiners' table and exchanging there the magazine for a sheet, returned and held the sheet close upon Ben. "And this item, sir—would it be of any familiarity to you?"

Ben studied the sheet. "'Tis a favour by hand of my nephew, Benjamin Mecom, to my good wife."

Wedderburn withdrew the sheet. "Posted from St. John, Antigua, sir, whilst Master Mecom was serving there at your behest?"

"It was."

"His charge, sir?"

"I bid him to serve as overseer of a print shop owned by me and abandoned by its previous overseer, Thomas Smith, by way of an untimely death."

"Although not addressed to you, this letter was made available to you, by your good wife, that you might be privy to its contents; am I correct, sir?"

"My good wife and I withheld nothing one from the other."

"Nothing, sir?"

"Nothing."

"Most touching."

Wedderburn returned to the examiners' table, and exchanging the sheet for a larger such, presented this also to Ben. "And this item, sir, would this be of any familiarity to you?"

Ben nodded. "'Tis a fair copy of the *Memorial of the Pennsylvania Abolition Society 3 February 1790*."

"Which memorial was, in fact, a petition addressed to Congress, over your good name, beseeching that body to"—Wedderburn looked to the sheet—"I quote, sir, 'promote mercy and justice towards this distressed race' unquote, by way of, I quote, sir, 'discouraging every species of traffick in the persons of our fellow men,' unquote." Wedderburn looked to Ben. "'This distressed race,' and 'persons of our fellow men,' being references to the Negro race, sir?"

"Correct."

"Now, sir, is this petition substantially different from, or substantially the same as, the petition your friend Benjamin Rush, and other members of the Pennsylvania Society for Promoting the Abolition of Slavery, had implored you to submit to the Constitutional Convention during the course of its proceedings two and one half years previous?"

"It is in substance and intent generally the same."

"And did you agree to present that earlier petition to the Convention, sir?"

"I did not."

Wedderburn stepped briskly to the examiners' table and depositing thereon the memorial, strolled empty-handed toward the vitreous circle, hands clasped behind his back. Stopping close upon the circle, he looked to Ben. "Now, sir, as a man intimate in the mechanical arts, pray tell, if I were to fashion a three-legged stool such that one leg was four inches shorter than the others, what likely would be the condition of my patron's repose?"

"Precarious."

"Indeed. Now, if I were to erect a domicile such that one half laid upon a bed of rock, the other half upon a crust of bog, what likely would be the condition of my patron's repose?"

"Precarious."

"Indeed. Now, if I were knowingly to fashion stools or domiciles in the manner described, what deserts might fairly be delivered unto me as decreed, let us say, by a court of justice?"

"To be denied the very comfort of repose that you, in your folly, denied your patrons."

"Eye for an eye?"

"Some eyes are more deserving than others."

Wedderburn smiled. "Aye, that they are." Wedderburn paced a few steps, stroking his chin, then looked again to Ben: "Now, sir, as a natural philosopher, has it been your experience that Nature tends naturally toward a state of equilibrium—call it 'balance'—or toward the opposite?"

"Toward equilibrium."

"How so?"

"No seed takes root in shifting sand. As balance begets tranquility, so tranquility begets life. That there is life, ever continuous, would imply a natural and general tendency toward tranquility, hence toward equilibrium."

Wedderburn looked to the assembly as if upon Atlantis newly arisen from the sea, then looked again to Ben. "Are these your words, sir, your sentiments, sir, or are you but playing mime here to those posy-adorned dandies aside you?"

Ben stiffened. "No whisperings from aside, sir, could be sufficient to counterpoint the odious trumpeting continually emanant from your brass horn."

The assembly erupted.

The clerk, springing to his feet, pounded his bench with his gavel. "Odor! Odor! There will be odor—*order!*—*order* in this court!"

Wedderburn leaned closer, eyes flashing of greenish fire, such that Ben could not but notice, to no little alarm, that Wedderburn's ears seemed to have grown larger, toward a point atop, and that his countenance seemed to have taken on a chthonic cast—purple and green.

Pulling a pennywhistle from his robe, Wedderburn blew a shrill note upon this, and another, causing Ben to press his head against the rising sun to rear.

The assembly erupted.

The clerk pounded his gavel. "Odor!—Order! Order!"

Spinning half-circle around, Wedderburn retreated a few steps, paused, spun half-circle around, and continued his inquiry as if there had been no parting of it: "Would you be inclined to agree, sir, that equilibrium is a form of equality—that state whereat one thing or force, including a force of wind, sir"—titters—"is in precise opposition or counterpoint to a like thing or force?"

"I would."

"The natural state of Nature then, being ever toward equilibrium, is ever toward equality?"

"It is, allowing, of course, for the occasional disruption, equilibrium being ever subject to transitory disorderings of one sort or other, as in the case of a tumult of lightning disrupting a summer picnic."

"In fact, a tumult of lightning is itself consequent to a transitory inequality betwixt like forces, is it not?"

"It is."

"Might it be apt, then, sir, to liken a tumult of lightning in restoring electrical equality to a tumult of sword in restoring political equality, as indeed in the case of the American Revolution?"

"A most felicitous analogue."

Wedderburn bowed. "So very kind of you to say so, sir." Ben bowed in return; Wedderburn continued. "Now, sir, if an inequality of any particular sort should become too long frustrated from relief, what might we expect in way of consequence? Might the bolt of lightning, when finally it comes, as surely it must, be so severe as to destroy the very objects it intends to bring unto balance?"

"Well it might, as many a burnt barn does attest."

"And might the same be said, sir, of a kettle left too long unvented by way of a valve?"

"Well it might."

"And might the same be said, sir, of a nation tardy in delivering equality unto all its members, they being confessed by public preachment to be equally deserving?"

Ben stirred to a chill of dread, as if to realization that his queen had been lured into false advantage.

Wedderburn reclaimed the *Gentleman's Quarterly* from the examiners' table and held it toward Ben. "I call your attention, sir, to item *VII*, aforementioned, being titled 'Speech of Polly Baker.' You are the author of this article, albeit anonymously, at the time, are you not?"

"I am."

"Given your familiarity with this item, sir, might we prevail upon you to grant the court a brief summary? Or would you prefer, sir, that I pass the sweet breeze of it through my brass horn?"

Guffaws.

The clerk sprang to his feet and banged his gavel upon his bench. "*Or*der! *Or*der in this court! *Or*der!"

Ben peered upon Wedderburn. "The sweet breeze to which you allude, sir, is a defense attributed to one Miss Polly Baker, a young unwedded mother who, having four times given birth to a child out of wedlock, and having four times been brought to justice for transgressing the fornication laws of the colony of Connecticut, is presently being prosecuted on a fifth count, before a panel of men well steeped—or should one say, steepled?"—titters—"in the moral strictures of Puritanism."

Ben noticed, to a bit of a start, that Smith and Adams were undergoing transformations in appearance strikingly similar to that yet progressing upon Wedderburn. Looking to his petitioners, Ben was relieved to discover them yet innocent of any such change. He continued. "In her oration, Miss Polly points out to her judges the absurdity of the situation. Here she is being prosecuted with fines and stripes for obeying the foremost commandment of the God of Creation—to be fruitful and multiply—and adding thereby usefully to the number of the king's subjects in the spare colonies—whilst the man who plucked the flower of her innocence, amidst a shower of promises, and took flight then from all responsibility, was being rewarded for his trouble with all the blessings owing to the innocent."

Wedderburn raised a hand more purple than pink. "That is well sufficient, sir. I thank you. Now, was this defense an accounting of facts collected by you, or was it a compilation of imaginings conjured by you?"

"A good huntsman is never absent his trap."

Wedderburn stared for a moment, then smiled. "I am such a huntsman?—that is your implication, sir?"

"Does the shoe fit?"

"Phrase the query to your own safety then, sir, or give it no reply, as you wish."

Ben glanced to the clerk, who showed ever so slight a nod. "The speech," Ben owned, "was a winding of ribbons of various colorations around the pole of a particular cause."

"O, such a pretty picture, sir. We thank you for the grace of it. And the cause, sir, to which you allude? Was this perhaps the endeavor by you to bring attention unto the folly of laying down laws grounded other than upon a bedrock of justice, in particular those laws that were, at the time, being coerced upon the colonies by the English Parliament, in particular those that absolved the Pennsylvania Proprietaries of any tax liability soever upon their holdings?"

"It was."

"Now, sir, even though it was well within custom at the time to publish criticisms and satires under false names, or under no name at all,
yet even after you finally confessed authorship of Miss Polly's speech,
some thirty years hence of its first appearance, you held the audience
of your confession to but a few intimates and acquaintances; am I
correct?"

"You are."

"Of course, we must allow here, as to cause for so steadfast an anonymity, the possibility of an abiding modesty on the part of the progenitor. Even so, are we not obliged to inquire, sir, as to what greater good
might have been achieved, over those three decades and beyond, had
you made a general confession as to your paternity of Miss Polly Baker?"
Titters. "Indeed, sir, as a man of keen observational facility, what, in
your opinion, was the general condition of the female sex at the time of
Miss Polly's speech, as compared to the general condition of the male
sex? I inquire in particular, sir, as regards the issue of intrinsic worth—
of equality, sir."

Ben held to caution, as if any step not well considered might trigger
a snare.

"Whilst yet you stir the pot, sir, allow me to add a little beef to the broth."
Wedderburn stepped briskly to the examiners' table and exchanging
there the magazine for the sheet held earlier, returned to his previous
station. He studied upon the sheet a moment, then looked to Ben. "Now,
sir, in the letter shown you earlier, from your nephew Benjamin to his
aunt, your wife—your 'Country Joan,' sir." Wedderburn shook his head.
"I shudder to speculate upon the consequence to my own person had I
ever been so dangerous as to refer to Mrs. Wedderburn, even in private
chambers, as my 'Country Joan.'" He smiled. "You are a man of exceptional courage, sir—aye—but I stray from course. Forgive me."

Wedderburn raised a little the sheet in hand. "In his letter, sir, your
nephew, in the role of the journalist you would have him be, describes
the ravages of an exotic storm that had recently struck upon Antigua.
Many an innocent had perished. Your nephew makes mention of the
novel means by which notice of each new death was generally communicated on the island—this being nine tolls of bell for a man; six tolls
for a woman; three tolls for a boy; and two tolls for a girl."

Wedderburn furrowed a purplish brow unto green also. "Now,
sir, does anything regarding this ritual strike you as discordant or

unnatural? More to the point, sir, did anything strike you as such at the time you became privy to your nephew's letter?"

"I recollect neither the ritual, as you call it, nor my impressions of it."

"Most interesting." Wedderburn returned Benjamin's letter to the examiners' table with alacrity, and as swiftly resumed his station afront Ben. "Now, sir, in light of your intimate knowledge of your nephew, might it have been the case that in describing this novel ritual in some detail, that is, in making more than mere mention of it, your nephew was, albeit by indirection, demonstrating some degree of discomfort with an equation that implied an intrinsic value to women and girls that was but two-thirds that implied to men and boys?"

Ben lowered his eyes as if to study the path close to foot for hint of any discontinuity or aberration in the lie of the leaves. He looked to Wedderburn. "I cannot know my nephew's intention and therefore will not speculate on it."

"Pray tell us then, sir, if you would, if this equation is reminding to you of any other such?"

"You refer, I suspicion, to the Three-Fifth's Compromise by which the Constitutional Convention was saved from certain failure."

"I do indeed. Under terms of this so-called compromise, each Negro in the several states was to be counted as three-fifths a person for the purpose of apportioning representation in the lower chamber of the central legislature, correct, sir?"

Ben glanced upon the clerk. The latter nodding, ever so slightly, Ben nodded unto Wedderburn.

"Now, sir, whilst yet you were mortal, did you ever hold it to mind that three-fifths the worth of a White man was the proper valuation of a Black man?"

"I did, in general if not in particular. However, I corrected that erratum, as previously noted in this chamber."

"Privately corrected long before publically corrected; quite so?"

"As you wish."

"Whilst yet you were mortal, sir, did you ever hold it to mind that two-thirds the worth of a man was the proper valuation of a woman?"

"I did not."

An explosion of guffaws.

Adams howled unto leaking eyes.

Smith buried his face in his arms.

Wedderburn looked to the assembly and raised both hands.

Upon quiet, Wedderburn continued. "Granting you exception, sir, in honor of your reputation for truth telling, many of your sex did so hold, or worse; did they not?"

"They did."

"As evidenced indeed by the tolling of knells on Antigua? As evidenced indeed by the withholding of suffrage from females of every station? As evidenced indeed by the travails and injustices inflicted upon untold numbers of Miss Pollys?"

"True enough."

"Would it be fair to hold in general, sir, that at the time of your anonymous engenderment of Miss Polly's speech, the general condition of women in society, with respect to that of men, was not one of equality—not as regards intrinsic worth; not as regards practical worth; not as regards social worth; not as regards moral worth; not as regards intellectual worth; not as regards any other species of worth worth mentioning? Or do I draw too much inference from too little cause?"

"It would be difficult to enlist a worthy body of evidence to the contrary."

"I thank you, sir, for your candor. Now, in your opinion, Dr. Franklin, does an abiding inequality in intrinsic worth betwixt the sexes—or, for that matter, betwixt the opposing parts of any category of human difference—gender, race, age, religion, ethnicity, class, trade, native cleverness, what have you—generally serve or generally hinder the progression of well-being and happiness in any society in which such an inequality is suffered to persist?"

"It generally hinders."

"How so?"

"A cancer to one organ needs by natural communication to become a cancer to all others."

"As Poor Richard would say?"

"If you like."

"Must we not inquire then, sir, as to the boon you might have delivered unto the general happiness and well-being of society at large had you freely confessed your authorship of Miss Polly Baker's speech at the time of first publication?—had you lent your considerable moral and philosophic stature to the cause of gender equality? Indeed, sir, considering the female sensibility in contrast to the male, how many subsequent contests for power and dominion, how many instances of war, sir, might have been avoided had the forces of amelioration and collaboration been given license to oppose unto equal weight the forces of competition and conquest?" Wedderburn leaned closer. "Do I make too much of too little, sir, or did Poor Richard have it right when he lamented, 'A little neglect may breed great mischief?'"

Ben lowered his eyes and was surprised by apparition of a pair of diminutive hands, white as alabaster, poised as if in a gesture of invitation. Wedderburn continuing, the hands disappeared: "Consider, if you would, sir, a duet of voices, one basso, one soprano. Should the basso voice be privileged to sing forth at full throat, the soprano restricted to sing at but two-thirds her own throat, what, sir, would likely be the effect upon the music sung?"

Wedderburn parted his robe a little, and slipping something from his vest pocket, held toward Ben a closed fist. "Lend me your hand, sir, if you would be so kind."

Ben complying, Wedderburn dropped into Ben's hand a three-penny nail. "For want of a public confession, sir, the message lost? For want of the message, sir, the opportunity lost? For want of the opportunity, sir—"

Spinning away, Wedderburn marched unto the examiners' table and snatching a sheaf of papers into hand, took station upon the vitreous circle.

Feeling a tickle upon his palm, Ben beheld thereon, to a bit of a start, not the three-penny nail dropped there, but a silvery serpent, which, melting in the moment as if into quicksilver, sundered into several globules, these pooling to center such as to congeal into a coin so reflective as to imitate a looking glass. Peering upon this now, Ben beheld not an image "as well-known as that of the moon," but a hideous apparition of demonic aspect. Before he might withdraw, he was surprised to witness a most remarkable transformation: Two counterpoised shapes, one in likeness to the numeral 6, the other in likeness to the numeral 9, began to emerge from the perimeter of the coin itself. Whilst closing upon each other to center, each rotated in the counterclockwise direction such that each numeral, when rotated half-circle around, became the other, indeed the value of the other. They came to rest finally such that the head of the one was nestled against the tail of the other, thereby covering in sum the whole of the surface.

Ben closed his hand upon this strange apparition, his eyes in simultaneity, and when again he opened both, the nail was restored.

Wedderburn continued. "Now, sir, in your considered opinion, are there species of evil of such enormity that any countenancing of them, to any measure, for any reason, would not only be highly deleterious toward all persons and events in the present, but would, in effect, be a form of complicity toward perpetrating a most deleterious effect upon all future persons and events as well?"

"A particular mass execution, indiscriminate as to the weight of guilt of any particular party, springs eminently to mind."

"Your reference, sir?"

"Genesis 7."

The clerk sprung to his feet. "Verse 17 through 23: 'And the flood was forty days upon the earth; and the waters increased, and bare up the ark, and it was lift up above the earth.

"'And the waters prevailed, and were increased greatly upon the earth; and the ark went upon the face of the waters.

"'And the waters prevailed exceedingly upon the earth; and all the high hills, that were under the whole heaven, were covered.

'Fifteen cubits upward did the waters prevail; and the mountains were covered.

"'And all flesh died that moved upon the earth, both of fowl, and of cattle, and of beast, and of every creeping thing that creepeth upon the earth, and every man:

"'All in whose nostrils was the breath of life, of all that was in the dry land, died.

"'And every living substance was destroyed which was upon the face of the ground, both man, and cattle, and the creeping things, and the fowl of the heaven; and they were destroyed from the earth: and Noah only remained alive, and they that were with him in the ark.'"

The clerk sat down.

Wedderburn smiled. "A most apt example. Might another such, sir, be an unrelenting abuse of person perpetrated by one group, the stronger, against another, the weaker?"

"Most certainly."

"Might another such example, sir, be a tyrannous dominion over the essential means of production by one group, the stronger, over a second group, the weaker, to end of the utter impoverishment and dependence of the second?"

"It would."

"And thievery, sir—in the form of a license granted to one group, the stronger, to steal at whim from a second group, the weaker—might this be yet another such evil?"

"Most certainly."

"And the reason for your judgment, sir? What in the character of these particular evils forbids even merest toleration of them?"

Ben noticed that a hideous wart had sprouted from Wedderburn's purpled and bloated nose. "I can but recount what I offered previous: A cancer rotting one organ, if not excised, shall ultimately rot all others, by an insidious communication of an infectious agent, to ultimate effect of destroying the corpus at large."

"By way of analogy, then, sir, might we posit that a burning roof left unredressed must necessarily become a city ruined?"

Ben smiled. "A most apt analogy."

Wedderburn bowed: "And by way of yet farther analogy, sir, might we liken any toleration of the evils aforementioned to shortening a leg upon an instrument of repose, a chair, sir—such a corruption, although local, serving to destroy, by general communication, the utility of the whole?"

"I am in awe."

Titters.

"And the aforementioned evils themselves, sir—abuse of person, impoverishment of prospect, thievery of property—might these enormities rightly be likened to the evils inflicted upon the American colonies by the English government prior to the American Revolution?"

"Indeed they might."

"And was it not your arriving at the opinion, sir, that there should be no farther countenancing of these same enormities by the English government, or by anyone who might call himself a moral man, that became the wedge that sundered you from a felicitous union with your son William, whilst he held fast to his appointment as Royal Governor of New Jersey?"

Ben lowered his eyes.

"In fact, sir, did you not come to view William as having willfully made a pact with the very devil himself such as to farther his own interests, at the cost indeed of all decency, not to mention the lives of countless innocents?"

Ben looked to his feet as if to take measure of the seawater rising in the bilge.

"Consider now, sir, if you would be so kind, the institution of slavery as generally extant within the colonies at the time of the crafting of the American Declaration. In your opinion, sir, is there any similarity to be noted betwixt the way a tyrannous Parliament regarded three millions of its subjects previous to the Declaration and the way a good many of these same three millions regarded their own several thousands of subjects, both previous to and following the penning of that most memorable preachment: 'All men are created equal?'"

"I could but ill argue to the contrary."

"In fact, sir, does not human bondage represent an evil of such enormity that any amount of countenancing of it would be to threaten, in likeness to a festering wound, sir, loss of not only the limb infected, but also, ultimately, the corpus in a whole?"

"It does." Glancing upon the three-penny nail in hand, Ben felt no little relief to discover it yet a nail.

Wedderburn continued. "Your own words on the matter, sir, as read by you to an assembly of abolitionists on November 9, 1789, five months preceding your death." Wedderburn looked to his papers. "'Slavery is such an atrocious debasement of human nature that its very extirpation, if not performed with solicitous care, may sometimes open a source of serious evils.'" Wedderburn looked to Ben. "In other words, sir, there is a species of ink of such stain as to corrupt all it should touch, or should touch it, even that which might wash it away; am I correct?"

"You are."

"And yet, sir, but a few years previous to this noble declaration, did you not tolerate a compromise concerning 'this atrocious debasement of human nature' of such magnitude as to allow the corpus at large to become ever more corrupted? In fact, sir, when requested by the principal members of the Pennsylvania Abolition Society to submit to the Constitutional Convention, then in session, this very petition"— Wedderburn held up the *Memorial* previously presented—"toward including into the American Constitution a clause forbidding human bondage in all the states to be united, for all time, did you not decline to do so, sir, for fear such a proposal might serve to sour the milk for the representatives from South Carolina and Georgia, the two colonies then most vested in 'this atrocious debasement of human nature?'"

Looking to the nail yet held in hand, Ben discovered the piercing end of this to bear a reddish stain. He shivered.

Wedderburn continued. "Previous to this fateful refusal, sir, you had condemned your son for accommodating an evil of such enormity that no redemption from it might ever be gained, this being your son's choice to remain loyal to his king versus following you into the Revolution. And for this unpardonable transgression, sir, you banished your son from the temple of paternal affections for all time. Yet, is it not true, sir, that whereas your son made accommodation to an enormity regarded as such by you but not by him, you on the other hand made accommodation to an enormity that you yourself regarded to be 'an atrocious debasement of human nature?' For what extraordinary reason then, sir, we must inquire, should you not yourself be banished from the temple of Paternal affections for all time?"

Ben noticed that a second wart had sprouted upon Wedderburn's ever darkening and distending nose, this become now more a proboscis than the native article.

Whirling half-circle around, Wedderburn gestured, to a flourish of festooned robe, toward the crystalline bench. "Behold, sir, what species of mischief a little toleration of 'an atrocious debasement of human nature' might beget!"

In the moment, a scene formed within the bench and thereupon expanded well beyond this, in which perhaps several hundred Negroes— men, women, and children—were hoeing upon sodden earth betwixt row upon row of what appeared to be grass shoots grown to a height of four or five inches, but which Ben surmised to be rice plants.

In the foreground, to leftward, one of the Negro women straightened, and unburdening herself of her hoe, began to step unsteadily across the rows of rice, toward an earthen levee. A pair of wetted spots coincident with the woman's breasts suggested a party not present in urgent need.

A white man, mounted upon a mottled mare, issued commands toward the errant woman, in a tone most harsh. When the woman showed no obedience, the man charged down the slope of the levee, and dismounting, began to flog the woman with his whip. The woman, her eyes wide and uncomprehending, as those of a child awakened from one darkness to discover herself in another, tried to shield herself with her hands. Her desperate attempts toward preservation seemed, however, only to inflame her tormentor. As the woman crumpled unto her knees, head bowed, body ripped and bleeding, a boy of no greater than nine or ten years sped from a nearby row, and leaping upon the beleaguered woman, knocked her to the sodden ground, face down, and making of himself then a shield, began taking onto head and body the lashes of whip and bludgeons of boot that would otherwise have accumulated unto the woman, these blows delivered not by the one overseer now but by two others as well.

A second boy, smaller than the first, now launched forth toward the horrific scene, but was intercepted by a Negro man, and quickly returned, by force of an iron grip upon a tender nape, to a submissive, if whimpering, apprenticeship.

The eye of view closed now upon the visage of the Negro man, revealing thereby bold disfigurations of pock and scar, until naught but a pair of stricken eyes might be witnessed.

Ben startled to a tug loosing him from his seat. This violence repeated, Ben discovered himself peering through the eyes just witnessed, whilst a torment in his breast exceeded even that owing to the death of Frankie—even that owing to the betrayal of William.

Nothing has ever hurt me so much.

Ben held fast to his namesake as one of the white men dragged Delmyra back to her station, and reacquainting her there with her hoe, whipped her into an acceptable cadence of service. The other two men heaved Jacob's broken body into a wagon pulled by a mule.

Looking to Justus, upon more of contempt and rage than any child of seven should ever be caused to show, Ben felt some delicate little thing, of no substance soever, pop deep within his breast, in the manner of a soap bubble, which, so expiring, leaves naught of its wondrous iridescence behind.

A flash and Ben was returned to his chair, witnessing now another horrific scene, in which two Negroes were hanging by the neck from a robust limb extended near horizontal from an ancient oak, whilst several white men, eerily illuminated in the agitated light of a pyre, prepared a third Negro for the same fate as the two—binding his hands behind his back, drawing a noose tight around his neck.

The eye of view closing upon the Negro's face, this bruised and swollen to hideous effect, Ben saw that he was no more than a boy.

Startled again by a violent loosing from his seat, Ben attempted to cover his eyes with his hands, that he might not bear any farther witness, but soon discovered himself close upon the crackling pyre, hands bound behind, mind hot with rage, stomach cold with terror. Of a sudden, he felt his chin snap upward, a crushing pressure bear upon his throat.

Another flash and he was returned to his seat, gasping—bearing witness to yet another scene, in which a Negro woman was leading a

Negro girl through a moonless night toward the backside of a red-brick mansion. They passed through a doorway into a large kitchen, through the kitchen to a narrow stairwell, up a flight of stairs, a few steps up a dark hallway to a door framed of a faint flicker. The woman tapped upon the door with more hesitation, it seemed, than intention. Upon a command from within, she led the girl inside, where a young white man, short of his majority, lay atop a four-poster. The glow of a drooling candle was the only light.

The young man, upon lowering his feet unto the floor, commanded the woman to pull the nightdress from the girl, and thereupon commanded the girl to pull the nightshirt from himself.

Feeling himself being again loosed from his chair, Ben squealed for mercy—only to discover himself standing in the dimly lit room, his breast near upon bursting of grief and shame. Absent all facility to do else, he held mute as the young man wrestled himself atop the girl, and penetrating her of an eager manhood, thrashed and grunted as if become mad of a rabid bite. As the young girl winced and wept, the young man thrust and grunted the harder—howling then in the manner of a coyote after the bloodless desolation of the moon—

A flash and Ben was returned to his chair. "Enough!" he screamed. "I can bear no more! I beg of you!"

"Enough of what, sir? Enough of 'this atrocious debasement of human nature?' Enough of 'mischief begot of a little neglect?' Enough of 'a little expediency in service to a little conveniency?'"

Slumping his head, Ben shut his eyes as if to deny them farther offense, but sensing then a near presence, opened them to discover, close upon, the same apparition of hands, white as alabaster, as recently glimpsed. Following these unto source, slowly, so as not to provoke flight, Ben discovered standing before him one of the young lasses witnessed earlier, showing no face. A silken sash, emerald green, bore the word *Empathy* in finest calligraphy.

Acquiescing to a gesture of invitation, Ben took the girl's hands into his own, and in the instant the girl's face jeweled of eye, bloomed of mouth, and ruddied of cheek.

Smiling now, the girl curtsied. "With my first speech, sir, I give thee my gratitude, for bearing me a face with which to smile, a voice with which to speak. I am sorry it was at the cost of so much discomfort to thee."

Ben bowed.

The girl's eyes sparkled like beads of dew upon a spider web. "With my second speech, sir, I must burden thee with a grave mystery. Although the male sex is equipped with the capacity to practice the virtue for which I am named, the heart of all hearts, it is not likewise equipped with the inclination. The latter it must be taught. But who is to teach them, sir?

"The industrious? The frugal? The resolute?

"The ambitious? The acquisitive? The egoistic?

"And if they are not to be taught, sir, who shall stand against them?"

The girl slumped of such extremity in the moment that her hands slipped from Ben's.

Reaching forth as if of reflex, Ben recovered the girl's hands into his own, and discovering these not the diminutive articles of purist white intended, but two as if putrefied paws, green and purple, he uttered a cry not unlike that of an animal newly trapped.

Recoiling against General Washington's chair, Ben shook his head as if to rid it of something foul stuck upon it, and continued until, feeling a touch upon either shoulder, he was able to still himself. Taking into hand then a pocket linen from Bartholomew, Ben wiped his eyes and cheeks with this, and thereupon returned it, folded, to its owner, with a nod.

The Reverend Smith, eyes flashing as if of fired sapphires, was regarding Ben in the moment as if with a fair measure of sympathy. "Are you able to continue, sir, or do you require a respite with which to restore yourself?"

Ben stiffened. "As Captain Jones required no respite whilst his *Bonhomme* was being condemned unto the deep, nor shall I as regards mine."

Smith lifted a little his chin, and projecting an arm overhead, looked to the assembly. "He has not yet begun to fight!"

Guffaws.

The din continuing, Smith stepped—strutted, one might be inclined to say—unto the examiners' table.

Become aware in the moment of the nail yet held in hand, Ben slipped this article into pocket, and looking to Smith returning from the examiners' table, could not but notice a progression of hideousness exceeding even that of Wedderburn's.

Smith took station upon the vitreous circle and looked to Ben. "You had a younger sister, sir, Jane—Mecom by marriage; mother of the aforementioned nephew, Benny—with whom you carried on a most agreeable correspondence; am I correct, sir?"

Poor Jane. An unfortunate husband and twelve children scourged of every ill known to afflict mankind had brought her naught but heartache. Never once, though, through it all, had she issued one word of complaint, at least not unto the ears of her brother.

"You are correct."

"In fact, sir, although afflicted of that species of religious sentimentality that tends to view curiosity as a weed to be pulled and withered, she was the only one of your sixteen siblings whom you regarded as an equal; was she not?"

"She was."

"Equal in judgment, sir?"

"Better."

"In the year 1757, sir, just prior to your embarkation for London to take up residence there, such as to represent the interests of the Pennsylvania Assembly, you received a letter from Jane in which she begged your intercession in a certain family matter, a feud, over of all things, soap. Do you recollect the matter, sir?"

Ben smiled. "I do."

"According to Jane, her son Peter and Peter's Aunt Elizabeth were at loggerheads over some trifling injury grown into a grave calamity. The base facts are these: Aunt Elizabeth's deceased husband, your brother John, had been in the tallow trade for many years. John had been successful in this endeavor at least in part by way of exploiting the Franklin recipe for crown soap. At the time of his death, John had been employing the assistance of his nephew, Peter, Jane's son. Is this a fair summary, sir?"

"It is."

Smith bowed. "Now, according to Jane, Peter, continuing in his uncle's stead, had had a falling out with his aunt over some petty matter, and in the heat of this, had taken himself, and the family recipe for crown soap, into the employ of a rival. Aunt Elizabeth, taking great offense to what she adjudged an act of betrayal, had recently sought charges against Peter for thievery."

Ben smiled.

"In response to Jane's plea for intercession, sir, you wrote as follows." Smith looked to his papers. "'Above all things, I dislike family quarrels,

and when they happen among my relations, nothing gives me more
pain . . . What can I say between you but that I wish you were reconciled, and that I will love that side best that is most ready to forgive
and oblige the other." Smith looked to Ben. "Do I read your artful hand
correctly, sir?"

"You do."

"Allow me to repeat, sir: 'I will love that side best that is most ready
to forgive and oblige the other.' Might one infer from this declaration,
sir, that you placed a high value, at the time of the penning of it, upon
Forbearance and Toleration?"

"One might."

"Upon Magnanimity, sir?"

Ben nodded.

"Might one infer then, sir, by way of symmetry, that you placed a pro-
portionally low value upon Intoleness and Vengefulness?"

"One might."

"Upon Hypocrisy, sir?—that loathsome practice of declaring allegiance unto one master whilst serving its rival."

"Reasonably so."

"Now, sir, over the autumn of 1766, and into the spring of 1767, you
were made aware, by way of favours from your wife—your Country Joan,
sir"—Smith rolled his eyes—titters from the assembly—"as well as from
your daughter, Sarah, called Sally, that a gentleman by the name of
Richard Bache, proprietor at the time of a dry goods shop on Chestnut
Street, had become suitor for your daughter's hand?"

Ben nodded. "I was."

"Your response upon gaining this intelligence, sir—may we have it?"

"I was disapproving."

"And the reason of your disapproval, sir?"

"Upon inquiry, Mister Bache's prospects—thereby his motivations—
thereby his character—were discovered to be of questionable merit."

"Discovered, sir, or suspicioned?"

"Both."

"By whom?"

"My son."

"He being of intimate acquaintance with Mister Bache?"

"He being in a position to make discreet inquires. One need not be
bit by a snake to become acquainted of its intentions."

Adams jumped to his feet. "When it comes t' snuff, it ain't never 'nough!"

Wedderburn jumped to his feet. "One pinch o' mine's worth nine of thine!"

The clerk jumped to his feet. "Make ill fun, be undone!"

Adams and Wedderburn sat down.

Smith continued. "And your daughter's judgment on the man's character, sir; it was commensurate with your son's?'"

"It was not, nor could it be expected to be, she being under spell of an infatuation."

"And your wife's judgment on the man's character, sir; it was commensurate with your son's?'"

"It was not."

"She being likewise under a spell of infatuation, sir?"

"She being much solicitous toward her daughter's declarations."

"And your sister Jane's judgment on the man's character, sir; it was commensurate with your son's?'"

"I do not recollect her having offered an opinion on the matter."

Smith raised a little his papers. "Your sister had recently visited Philadelphia, sir, where she had met Mr. Bache, and even more recently had lost yet another child to an untimely death—she would lose eleven of twelve, sir, in her lifetime—and so, when she sat down to write to you, her heart was heavy with grief; and yet, sir, she rose above all such to give you cause for celebration." Smith looked to his papers. "'But why should I entertain you with this melancholy subject when you are called to rejoice at the settling in marriage of your beloved daughter to a worthy gentleman whom she loves and [is] the only one that can make her happy. I congratulate you on it and wish it may give you a lasting pleasure.'" Smith looked to Ben. "Have you recollection now, sir?"

"I do."

Smith took a step closer. "One must presume, therefore, sir, that you have recollection now of having allowed your sister's opinion regarding Mr. Bache, coming as it did from your equal or better in judgment, to influence your own opinion regarding this 'worthy gentleman,' 'the only one that might make her happy.' Quite so?"

Ben couldn't help but fix his eyes upon a riot of knots erupted upon Smith's nose, this become, as in the case of Wedderburn's, more a proboscis.

"In fact, sir, you continued to make it quite clear, especially to Mr.

Bache himself, that you did not approve of"—Smith looked to his papers—"'a proceeding that may be attended with ruinous consequences to you both.' Quite so?"

"Where there is gold, or perceived to be such, there will be no want of diggers."

"As in the example, sir, of the suitor of Mrs. Godfrey's niece?"

Ben cast a glance toward his petitioners, and upon discovering each one as if wincing to a pinch of stone, winced to a pinch of dread.

Smith continued. "Ultimately, sir, you begrudged to your wife license sufficient to permit the marriage of your daughter to Mr. Bache, and assume unto herself thereby, of course, full culpability should your cautions on the matter prove superior." Smith looked to his papers. "'I would not occasion to delay her happiness if you thought the match a proper one.'" Smith looked to Ben. "And so, sir, by sanction of your good wife, and in your absence"—Smith looked to his papers—"'Mister Richard Bache, of this city, merchant, was married to Miss Sally Franklin, the only daughter of the celebrated Doctor Franklin, a young lady of distinguished merit.'"

Smith looked to Ben. "And that 'lasting pleasure' wished unto you by your sister, sir, you thereafter manifested in what manner?"

Ben looked to his hands, these clasped upon his lap, and held to silence.

"In fact, sir, for more than a year following the occasion of your daughter gaining 'her happiness,' did you not engage in a campaign of silence most keen, thereby to communicate a disapproval most keen? Indeed, sir, did you not refuse to respond to overtures made directly unto you by your son-in-law? Did you not, sir, refuse even to acknowledge your son-in-law's existence, not unto him, not unto your 'beloved daughter,' not even unto your Country Joan?"

Smith took a step closer, his eyes as if sapphires became incandescent. "Is this Forbearance I see before me, sir? Toleration? Magnanimity?" Smith looked to his papers. "'Above all things I dislike family quarrels, and when they happen among my relatives, nothing gives me more pain'—'I will love that side best that is most ready to forgive and oblige the other.'"

Smith uplifted a little his chin, this become greenish and purple, and forcibly sniffed. "What is this odor most foul, sir, bringing insult upon this hallowed chamber? Have you no sense of it; or have you, sir, to your advantage, that immunity peculiar to the barnyard wallower?"

Titters.

"When finally you judged your family sufficiently punished, sir, for—for exactly what, sir? For being of their own mind? For exercising their own best judgment on the knowledge directly available to them?"

Ben held to silence.

"When finally you loosed the cord upon a girded heart, sir, you closed a note of greeting to Mr. Bache with the following declaration." Smith looked to his papers. "'I can only add at present that my best wishes attend you, and that if you prove a good husband and son, you will find me an affectionate father.'"

Smith took a step closer. "*If,* sir? *If* Mr. Bache is 'a good husband and son,' *then* you will regard him worthy of your affection? Is this your apprehension of Forbearance, sir; of Toleration; of Magnanimity; of being the party 'most ready to oblige?' Or is this something else altogether, sir?" Smith uplifted a little his chin and sniffed. "Indeed, have we not here, sir, odor of a little conditionality in service to a little conveniency?" Leaning of a sudden forward, Smith near struck his head upon Ben's. "Must all of affection be gained or given by barter, sir? My affection for your obedience? Your obedience for my affection? Is the heart naught but a marketplace for advantage, sir; felicity naught but a wheelbarrow for show?"

Smith peered hard upon Ben, then turned away, and returning to the vitreous circle, continued. "A single erratum, being singular, is oft of little consequence; 'tis a plural of such that commands the attention; true enough, sir?"

Ben held to silence.

"Cat got your tongue, sir?"

Ben stole a fleeting glance upon the clerk, who showed barest hint of a nod.

"Your declaration would appear to be true enough."

"Thank you, sir. I will take 'true enough' as good enough. Now, sir, in December of 1776, you removed from Philadelphia to France, specifically to Passy, threat to represent American interests to the Court of King Louis XVI, and took with you on this occasion, such as to assure their protection and better their prospects, two of your three grandsons at the time—your bastard son William's own bastard son, Temple, then seventeen years of age, and your daughter Sally's elder son, Benny, then seven years of age. Have I the base facts correct, sir?"

Ben stared hard upon Smith. "What of the marriage ceremony, sir, so sanctimoniously valued by you, is not utterly arbitrary, and but 'a little expediency in service to a little conveniency?'"

Smith smiled. "Have I perchance pinched upon a nerve, sir?"

Espying by peripheral sense movement upon the clerk's station, Ben held to silence.

Smith continued. "Now, sir, explain to the court, if you would, kindly, why it was that Benny's mother—Mrs. Richard Bache—well following your arrival in France, having heard naught from you in seventeen weeks, felt it necessary to ingratiate from you a declaration of assurance that her young son was comporting himself—in her words"—Smith looked to his papers—"'so as to make you love him?'"

Smith held his eyes affixed upon Ben a moment, as if in anticipation of a reply, then looked again to his papers. "'I have refused dining at Mister Clymer's today that I might have the pleasure of writing to you and my dear boy, who I hope behaves so as to make you love him. We used to think he gave little trouble at home, but that was perhaps a mother's partiality.'"

Smith looked to Ben. "The obedience of the grandson in exchange for the affection of the grandfather? Is this not the barter being represented here, sir? And is it not a remarkable likeliness to the barter represented by you to your son-in-law?" Smith looked to his papers. "'If you prove a good husband and son, you will find me an affectionate father.'" Smith elevated a little his chin and sniffed with robust exaggeration. "Indeed, have we not yet more odor here, sir, of a little conditionality in service to a little conveniency?"

Ben held to silence.

Smith continued. "In the year 1774, sir, shortly following your examination before the King's Council, this conducted by my able colleague here present, the Honorable Alexander Wedderburn, First Earl of Rosslyn—" Smith bowed toward Wedderburn, who, upon rising, returned the favor. Wedderburn sat. Smith continued. "Following this event, sir, you posted to your son, then Royal Governor of New Jersey, a letter urging him to remain in office despite the abuse delivered to his father before the Privy Council, until such time he should be forcibly removed." Smith looked to his papers. "'One may make something of an injury, nothing of a resignation.'" Smith looked to Ben. "Quite so, sir?"

"Quite."

"And no tardier than might an 'amen' follow upon a 'hallelujah,' sir, than you posted to your son a second communication, in which you urged him to resign the very office you had only just counseled him to hold fast upon." Smith looked to his papers. "'I don't understand it as any favour to me or to you, the being continued in an office, by which with all your prudence, you cannot avoid running behind hand, if you live suitably to your station.'"

Smith looked to Ben, "Quite so?"

"Quite."

"Now, sir, what are we to make of such a muddle of meddling? Should we regard it a reflection of the author's own ambiguity on the matter; or should we regard it as no muddle at all, but instead an artifice by which you might educate your son, by way of example, as regards the alacrity with which a man of principle might accomplish a change in sentiment, hence in loyalty?"

Ben looked to the muddles of coloration within the high bench, these becoming unmuddled seemingly of their very muddledness, thereupon becoming muddled again seemingly of their very unmuddledness.

Smith continued. "In fact, sir, up until your examination before the Privy Council, you and your son had held equally fast to the notion of preserving the fledgling chicks unto a felicitous union with the mother hen, quite so? Indeed, sir, whilst you labored fervently toward this end from your apartments in London, to peril, eventually, of your own safety, your son labored with equal fervor toward the same end from his offices in New Jersey, to peril, eventually, of his own safety; quite so?

"There arrived then, however, occasion of your public humiliation, and of a sudden the partnership with your son became altered by way of your changing your sentiments regarding preservation to the negative, and expecting your son to do likewise, indeed with alacrity; quite so?

"Ay, but your son, yet holding fast unto hope, and choosing to honor the oath he had sworn unto God and king, kept his own sentiments on preservation to the positive—as did also, sir, I feel obliged to mention, several of your long-standing friends, including Mr. Galloway, with whom you had entrusted for safekeeping the entirety of your personal papers, including the only extant copy of your *Autobiography*; and as also did, sir, fully one-third of the population of the colonies of the time, this fraction amounting to near one million English souls.

"In fact, sir, as we have previously touched upon, what for your son was an expression of loyalty to duty and king, by way of conviction and conscience, became now for you, peering through eyes narrowed of grievance, an expression of *dis*loyalty, by way of spite and defiance;

quite so? Indeed, whereas you had long encouraged your son to be thoroughly English in mind, manner, and allegiance, and to aspire toward station and stature within the English system of patronage—in truth, had long encouraged for your son exactly what you had sought for yourself—you now all but command your son to respond to *your* public humiliation precisely as you had committed yourself to respond to it, indeed such as 'to give it a little revenge.'"

Ben noticed, to a bit of start, that Smith's hands had transformed such as to bear now, in place of fingernails, those lethal accoutrements distinctive to mammalian predators.

Smith smiled. "'To give *it* a little revenge'—a most felicitous use of the neuter pronoun, sir. Most felicitous indeed. Dare we count the ways?" Smith stepped closer. "Coincident, sir, with your encouragement in your son of all things English, you entertained notion he would one day take an English bride, specifically in the person of one Polly Stevenson, daughter of your landlady; did you not? But what does this bastard progeny of yours do in the face of your magnanimous aspirations toward him? He becomes enamored *not* of his father's dear Polly, but of his own dear Betsy! Even worse, he makes public announcement of his betrothal before such time his father might conspire against it. And your response to this untoward course of events, sir? Did you not, in fact, but a fortnight previous to your son's wedding, pack your trunks and sail for home—this in juxtaposition, sir, to having previously delayed a return to Philadelphia several times over, on merest pretext?" Smith looked to the assembly. "Did you perhaps give *it* a little revenge, sir?"

Smith stepped closer. "When first it hatched upon your imagination, sir, to take your son William's only son, William Temple, to Paris with you, for an interim likely to comprise several years, did you solicit the approbation of the boy's father on the matter? Did you solicit the opinion of the boy's stepmother on the matter? In fact, sir, did you not, by artful stratagem, lure the boy from his stepmother, whilst the boy's father languished in a Connecticut jail, and issuing then no announcement, steal him to France with you, thereby leaving the boy's father and mother bereft of all familial society with their only child?" Smith looked to the assembly. "Did you perhaps give *it* a little revenge, sir?"

Smith stepped closer. "Eight years following, sir, in July of 1784, whilst you and Temple were yet residing in France, your son William, estranged from you now these eight years, having learned of your

imminent departure for America, posted to you from England an emis-
sary of some length. I recount, sir, if I might, the first and last verses of
such, they representing, I beg your agreement, the whole." Smith looked
to his papers. "'Dear and Honoured Father: Ever since the termination
of the unhappy contest between Great Britain and America, I have been
anxious to write to you, and to endeavour to revive that affectionate
intercourse and connexion which till the commencement of the late
troubles had been the pride and happiness of my life.'" Smith looked
to Ben. "Now the last verse, sir." Smith looked to his papers. "'I shall
therefore, if you are not likely to be soon in England, be happy to have
your approbation to wait on you at Paris. In the meantime I beg you to
be assured of my constant prayers for your health and happiness, and
that I am, as ever, your very dutiful and affectionate Son.'" Smith looked
to Ben. "Do you recollect these verses, sir, chanted to you, so to say, in
the cause of reconciliation?"

Ben nodded.

"And do you recollect your response, sir?"

Ben lowered his eyes.

"Allow me, sir, to recount two excerpts from the reply posted by you,
August 16, 1784, these representing, I beg your agreement, the whole."
Smith looked to his papers. "'Nothing has ever hurt me so much and
affected me with such keen sensations as to find myself deserted in my
old age by my only son; and not only deserted, but to find him taking
up arms against me, in a cause wherein my good fame, fortune, and
life were all at stake.'" Smith looked to Ben. "Now the second." Smith
looked again to his papers. "'Your situation was such that few would
have censured your remaining neuter, *tho' there are natural duties which
precede political ones, and cannot be extinguish'd by them.*'" Smith looked
to Ben. "The emphasis given by me by way of intonation, sir, was in fact,
you may recall, your own, by way of underlining." Smith looked to the
assembly. "Did you perhaps give *it* a little revenge, sir?"

Ben glanced to the clerk, and finding him slumped, glanced upon his
petitioners, and finding them slumped, looked to Smith, who, holding
a sheet separate from the others, read from this now unto the assembly,
in a fine soprano: "'What can I say between you but that I wish you
were reconciled, and that I will love that side best that is most ready to
forgive and oblige the other.'"

Hoots. Guffaws. Foot-stomps.

Adams jumped to his feet. "How spelleth thee, hypocrisy?"

Adams sat. Ben slumped.

Turning half-circle around, Smith returned to the vitreous circle, and turning thereon half-circle around, faced again upon Ben. The din quieting, he continued. "In the same moment your son extended toward you, sir, a most ardent overture toward reconciliation, had he not lost his own 'good fame,' sir; his own 'fortune?' Had he not lost his very livelihood, sir, and all prospect? Had he not lost his beloved wife, sir, and his only child—the latter to you, by way of your theft of him? And yet, sir—or so it would appear—all you could see of your son, as you peered through eyes narrowed of an aggrieved pride, was but an insensible and disloyal son who had sacrificed everything of his own *not* of principle, *not* of conviction, *not* of duty, but simply of an inexplicable desire to deprive his father, for whom he had always held and displayed the greatest respect and affection, of his 'good fame, fortune, and life.' Is this not indeed the very conviction, devoid of all logic, from which flowed the poison of your hypocrisy, sir?"

Ben felt a sharp constriction at the back of his throat.

"Of all people, sir—*you*, who had himself once rebelled from a controlling and domineering elder, your brother James, sir—*you* could not see in your own son the very likeness of yourself struggling to be his own man, aspiring toward his own vision, sacrificing with manifest courage and conviction toward realizing his own vision? It never occurred to you, sir—a polymath indeed of remarkable grasp and insight—that independence of thought and action were as central and necessary unto your son, in the face of a controlling and overbearing father, as they had been to you, in the face of a controlling and overbearing brother; in the face of a controlling and overbearing Proprietary; in the face of a controlling and overbearing Parliament; in the face of a controlling and overbearing king? Is *this* what you would have us believe, sir?"

Smith stepped closer. "And even had your son's offense constituted a blow upon the cheek of Lady Justice herself, sir, as opposed to a pique of discomfiture upon a father's pride, was it an offense of such enormity it might never—*never*, sir—be acquitted? Was it indeed greater in evil, sir, than Monsieur Brillon de Jouy's betrayal of his wife? Do you recollect the counsel you offered Madame Brillon, sir, upon the occasion of her husband's confession to bold couplings with the governess of their daughters, in the very domicile they five shared?"

Smith looked to his papers. "'If you exact a vengeance by punishing them'—*them* being here inclusive of a host of gossipers as well as Madame Brillon's husband himself—'you restore them to the state of equality that they had lost. But if you were to forgive them, without any punishment, you would fix them in the low state into which they have fallen, and from which they can never emerge, without true repentance and full reparation. Follow then, my very dear and always amiable daughter, the good resolution that you have so wisely taken, to continue to fulfill all your duties as good mother, good wife, good friend, good neighbor, good Christian, etc., (without forgetting to be a good daughter to your papa), and to neglect and forget, if you can, the wrongs you may be suffering at present.'" Smith looked to Ben. "Do you recollect this noble sentiment, sir, and the good intention toward which it was offered?"

Smith stepped closer. "Might you recollect also, sir, the original rendering of this same wisdom, as included by you in one of your *Almanacks*, of three decades previous?" Smith looked to his papers. "'Doing an injury puts you below your enemy; revenging one makes you but even with him; forgiving it sets you above him.'" Smith looked to Ben: "Now, sir, should we turn this very counsel, the one version or the other, half-circle round, such as to direct it toward yourself, what might be your response?" Smith looked upon the assembly. "Or have you such immunity, sir, as to be able to abstain from practicing what you preach and feel not a pang of shame for it?"

Smith swept an arm toward the crystalline bench. "Behold, sir, the profit owing to a heart darkened of an aggrieved pride, a soul eclipsed of shameless hypocrisy." In the moment, a scene formed within the bench in which a man of middle age, sartorially resplendent in blue coat and gold buttons, was sitting in a room dimmed by lowered swags and drawn draperies. The man's wig was fastidiously coiffed and braided aback.

The eye of view drew closer upon a countenance most somber, until Ben, with a start, recognized the distinctive features, though disfigured as if of a burden long borne, of William Franklin, sitting close upon a Chippendale desk. Ben gasped now as his dear Billy reached forth, and taking a pistol into hand, placed the barrel against his temple.

Launching forth from his seat, as if by force of a coiled spring, Ben charged forth, through an agony of gout and infirmity, toward his dear Billy, exclaiming a most desperate plaint: "No! Please! I'm sorry! I'm so very sorry!" Impacting then upon the face of the crystalline bench, in

the manner of a bird upon a pane, Ben recoiled from this, and staggering backward, toppled to the floor. Restoring himself to upright, Ben
hurled himself sidelong against the monolith, as if to shatter it by sheer
force of will, and pounding upon it then, with clenched fists, continued
to plead toward the unhearing man within, he yet holding the pistol to
temple: "O, Billy! Billy! No! No!"

Sinking unto his knees, Ben continued his petition by no greater
than holding his hands in supplication, whilst uttering a low moan,
until such time the horrific scene within the bench dispersed into an
infinitude of colorated sparkles, these in likeness to a swarm of fireflies.

Raising himself unto hands and knees, Ben propelled himself in this
posture to where Smith stood, and grasping the reverend by the ankles,
bowing his head, issued forth a most pathetic plaint: "Tell me he did
not do it, sir! Tell me! I beg of you!"

There coming no answer, no sound soever beyond a low hum from
the undulating lights atop the bench, Ben slumped farther to forward,
until his head rested upon the reverend's shoes. The entirety of his body
began to quake.

Become sensible after a moment of a gentle encouragement upon
his arms, Ben submitted to the will of his Intermediaries, who aided
him to his feet, and slowly then to his chair. About to turn half-circle
around, such that he might reclaim his seat, Ben heard—nay, felt—a
distinctive sound, the discharge of a small firearm, and slumping as
if of a mortal wounding to himself, near upon collapsed to the floor,
being saved from this peril by a redoubling of the sustaining grip of
his Intermediaries, who thereupon maneuvered him, by a felicitous
collaboration, into his seat.

Returned to his previous view, Ben discovered, to no small sensation of relief, that Smith, and no other, was in possession of the pistol
recently discharged. This instrument yet issuing fumes, Smith tossed
it toward Ben, who, reacting of reflex, managed to take it into hand, to
end thereby, as in case of the three-penny nail, of making it his own.

"Pray tell us, sir, by weight of your philosophy, who pulls the trigger that brings mercy unto unrelenting despair: the one tormented,
sir, or the one at cause of the torment?" Awaiting no reply, Smith
removed himself from the vitreous circle, and stepping briskly—nay,
triumphantly—to the farther side of the examiners' table, reclaimed
his seat with a flourish, and nodded then toward Wedderburn, who
returned the gesture in kind, and then toward Adams, who did likewise,

showing the same fullness of transformation that had alike afflicted his colleagues.

To an unnerving sound now, a loud whoosh, a serpentine beam of bluish light emerged from the high bench, and undulating its way unto the vitreous circle, by circuitous route, coiled itself thereon into a spiral, which thereupon, slowing, coalesced into the form of a girl of no greater than thirteen years, she bearing upon her face no aspect of countenance. The girl was wearing the same gown as the thirteen lasses—black dots upon white to one side, white dots upon black to the other, the whole divided at the diagonal by a silken sash, this being, in the present case, blue, and bearing *Forgiveness* in an elegant calligraphy. In all appearances, except stature, the girl appeared to be the very one who had borne the same label previous.

Approaching upon Ben, the girl extended her hands toward him, palms poised upward. Ben grasping these, the girl grasped his in simultaneity, to end of forming betwixt them, of the angle of their arms, likeness of a cradle, and in the instant of their touch, features of countenance began to appear upon the girl's face.

Ben stood transfixed as the girl's complexion darkened unto ebony, and her features assumed the distinctive aspect of her race. Of a sudden, as if to a jolt of electrical fire, Ben recognized the countenance of the Negro girl he had witnessed violated by a white boy in the ineffably tortured presence of the girl's mother.

His eyes flooding of warmish brine, such as to near wash away all vision, Ben squeezed the girl's fingers, as if even so mild a gesture might bring unto her some measure of solace.

The girl squeezed upon Ben's fingers in return, to equal the firmness, and showed in her eyes equal the wetness. "My tears are yours, sir, as yours are mine. We are two hearts; one pulse. Thank you, good sir, for bearing me the gift of a countenance with which I might smile, a voice with which I might speak. I am so very sorry it was at the cost of so much discomfort to thee. Please rest assured, good sir, that your beloved son did not succumb to his despair, though he were long at risk in this regard. He did in fact, sir, live past his eightieth year."

Ben wept. The girl wept.

The girl continued. "Your son restored himself to happiness, sir, by devoting himself to the care of a granddaughter, named Ellen, born to his only son, your grandson, sir, William Temple, who, I am sorry to acquaint you, had abandoned her." The girl smiled. "Your son said of his granddaughter, sir, when she was in her ninth year, that she was—his words, sir—'very like my father, and has every promise of making a fine, sensible woman.' Which she came to demonstrate, sir, in nursing your son in his infirmity, indeed unto his last breath."

Ben held his eyes shut a moment, advancing thereby a wash of warmish brine onto his cheeks, then looked again to the girl. "I thank you for this kindness."

Accepting offer of Bartholomew's pocket linen, Ben wiped his eyes and cheeks, and returning the linen then unto Bartholomew, with a bow, took the girl's hands again into his own. "I am so very sorry for the violence done unto thee. So very sorry."

The girl bowed. "Thank you, sir—as I am for your own suffering in this chamber." The girl's eyes gleamed. "It is necessary."

Bowing again, the girl released her grip upon Ben's hands, and upon returning to the vitreous circle, smiled upon Ben of such radiance that her countenance—nay, the entirety of her being—seemed aglow of a robust luminescence within.

"You must endure, sir."

Turning in place now, in the counterclockwise direction, the girl was soon transformed into a whirlwind tinctured of sapphire, which thereupon disappeared, to a brilliant flash, leaving behind a bluish glow within the vitreous circle.

No sooner was Ben restored to his repose by aid of his Intermediaries, than Adams was standing before him, his ears enlarged and pointed, his nose flared and warted, his countenance greened and purpled.

A most appropriate costume, Ben confided unto himself alone.

"If you would, sir," Adams began, "kindly apprise us of your notion of cruelty. Might it include indeed the manner in which you were just now treated, not by the young lady, of course, but by my colleague here sitting?" Adams nodded toward Smith, Smith nodding in return.

Adams's voice, previously a booming basso, seemed to have progressed so much farther in that register as to become near upon a growl.

"It would."

"Pray apprise us farther, sir, if you would, if ever there might be circumstance in which you would engage in such an act yourself, indeed as regards either man or beast?"

"There might not."

"And your passion as regards your affirmation in this regard, sir; would it include offering your neck unto *les* Hangman, or your head unto *le* Guillotine, in preference to causing man or beast a torture of any kind?"

"I would dine with the very devil himself in preference thereto, as would appear to be my lot in any event."

Adams smiled, indeed unto sinister effect. Stepping to the examiners' table then, he lifted into hand a sheaf of papers from near whereat lay a surviving volume of Ben's biography, and taking station upon the vitreous circle, this yet showing a bluish glow, looked to his papers. "'Help me, O Father, that I may to those above me be dutiful, humble, and submissive, avoiding pride, disrespect, and contumacy. Help me, O Father, that I may to those below me be gracious, condescending, and forgiving, using clemency; *protecting* [the] *innocent* [from] *distress*; avoiding cruelty, harshness, and oppression.'" Adams looked to Ben. "Are these words of some familiarity to you, sir—including the emphasis I placed upon the *innocent* and their *distress* by way of intonation?"

"You repeat what your artful colleague previously removed from venue for calculated effect."

"And by 'venue,' sir, do you refer to the *Articles of Belief and Acts of Religion* in its entirety?"

"I do."

"And by 'artful colleague,' sir, do you refer to the inestimable Reverend Doctor Smith?"

"I refer to William Smith, provost near unto ruin of the College of Pennsylvania."

Adams smiled, and upon nodding unto the inestimable Reverend Doctor Smith, the inestimable Reverend Doctor Smith returning the gesture, he looked again to Ben. "Now, sir, did the prayer just read you reflect sincere sentiments held by you at the time, or did it but constitute more pulp for your wheelbarrow?"

"It was however you would have it to your purposes."

Adams bowed. "Be that as it may, sir, would you condescend to agree that 'protecting the innocent from distress; and avoiding cruelty, harshness, and oppression' were in fact virtues embraced by you at the time, whether deliberately or otherwise?"

"I would."

"They are consonant, then, with your declaration against engaging in acts of cruelty in likeness to that just suffered by you at the hands of the inestimable Reverend Doctor Smith."

"They are."

"Now, sir, just previous to the departure of you and your son William for England in 1757, did the child to be left behind, your fair Sally, sir, then thirteen years of age, confess to you an interest in learning the French language?"

"She did."

"And did she thereupon persuade you, sir, by fervor of an earnest petition, into granting license to engage in private lessons?"

"She did."

"Now, sir, you were removing to England, not to France; hence, there would seem little practical advantage for Sally to correspond with you— or anyone to become acquainted with you—in the French language. For what reason then, sir, in your opinion, might Sally have made such a request of you?"

"For no greater reason than to better herself. The English language, she knew; the French language, she did not."

"To better herself in relation to what, sir?"

"My daughter was not unacquainted of the advantages to be credited to those who become fluent in the language of Voltaire and Rabelais."

"Ah, so your daughter's request related more to a noble aspiration toward high culture than to any inflammation of the spirit she might have been suffering over prospect of an extended abandonment by you. She was not, in other words, sir, seeking means by which to earn an occasional wink and nod from you during a prolonged absence; nothing so tediously prosaic as that."

The clerk showing no threat of censure in the moment, Ben held to silence.

Adams continued. "Now, sir, a few weeks following commencement of your daughter's lessons, you received at your Craven Street apartment, London—whereat you, your son, and your servants, Peter and King, had taken up residence—a letter writ entirely in French in Sally's hand; did you not?"

Ben nodded.

"And do you recollect your response, sir, as given not directly unto your daughter, but through her mother, such that you might swat two flies with one blow?"

"I recollect the favour sent, of its novelty; I do not specifically recollect my response."

"Allow me, sir, if I might, to 'joggy' a bit your memory." Adams leered, to hideous effect, then looked to his papers. "'I should have read Sally's French letter with more pleasure but that I thought the French rather too good to be all her own composing. I suppose her master must have corrected it.'" Adams looked to Ben. "One could hardly imagine a sharper reproof, sir, were one not privy to a second such delivered close upon the first. Might you have recollection of *it*, sir?"

Affixing his eyes upon a floor square close to front, Ben noticed that each loop of grain therein seemed as if gestating the previous, to end, by natural extrapolation, of an infinitude of gestations extending in either direction, toward the ever larger, toward the ever smaller.

"In company with your favour to your wife, sir, you included 'a French *Pamela*,' and strong implication thereby that your linguistically equestrian daughter should be able to take to saddle and, given the horsemanship demonstrated by her letter, ride the French text unto Richardson's original English, and thereupon deliver unto you, by next packet, confirmation of Sally's genius. Have you recollection now, sir?"

Ben held his eyes affixed upon the same floor square.

Adams continued. "The adoring daughter desperately solicits a reassurance of approval and affection from her oft-absented, oft-distracted father; the oft-absented, oft-distracted father responds with rebuke and humiliation." Adams shook his head. "One struggles to gather sufficient breath with which to replenish that escaped to a heavy blow of astonishment."

Holding his eyes affixed yet upon the floor square, Ben was visited by a notion most remarkable: Indeed, it would seem that any infinitude involving a material article repeating toward the ever larger was necessarily limited to that point in its repetition at which the universe held no farther material with which to contrive yet another instance of that article; whilst any infinitude of a material article repeating in the opposing direction, toward the ever smaller, was limited to that point in its repetition at which the material contriving that article could no longer be even minimally physical. Every true infinitude, therefore, it would seem, was necessarily non-material and confined to the realm of the purely mathematical. Most remarkable indeed.

Adams continued. "Sixteen years hence, sir, in the year 1773, your daughter, now twenty-nine, a wife and mother, confessed to you, by favour delivered unto your 7 Craven Street apartments, a frustration over not being able to assist her mother in the economy of *your* household to full measure of *your* urgings she do so. Of course, Sally bore this frustration not of any infirmity on her part, but wholly at cause of her mother's hostility toward any assistance regarding the care and maintenance of her home, from any party. In response to this confession, sir, you issued a most remarkable counsel. Have you a recollection of it?"

"I recollect an abiding inhospitality in my wife toward any form of meddling, as she would name it, in any chamber or corner of domesticity that she considered of pride to be her own. I do not recollect my daughter's expression of frustration in the face of such."

"Allow me then, sir, to reacquaint you of the details." Adams looked to his papers. "To your daughter, sir: 'It will be of use to you if you get a *habit*'—your emphasis, sir; here and following—'of keeping exact accounts; and it will be some satisfaction to me to see them. Remember, for your encouragement in good economy, that whatever a child saves of its parent's money, *will be its own another day*. Study Poor Richard a little, and you may find some benefit from his instructions.'" Adams looked to Ben as if stricken. "'Study Poor Richard a little,' sir? 'What a *child* saves,' sir? 'You may find some benefit from *his* instructions,' sir? This to a 29-year-old woman—a wife and mother, sir—who might well have schooled Poor Richard to 'some benefit' in several of the practical arts, had ever the opportunity been allowed?" Adams shook his head. "One struggles to regain one's breath."

Hearing a pathetic sniffling, Ben discovered Wedderburn and Smith wiping their eyes and cheeks with pocket linens, one of these green, the other blue.

Adams dried his own eyes with a crimson linen, then continued. "Now, sir, as regards your notable investigations into the nature of the electrical fluid, did you, during the course of these, come to entertain a curiosity concerning the effect of electrical strokes at various strengths upon the health and well-being of living organisms?"

"I did."

"And did this curiosity lead you, sir, to deliver measured strokes of the electrical fluid unto chickens and turkeys standing in the stead of yourself and your own kind—one jar of shock, then two, then three, then four, and so forth?"

"I did."

"To end of a compassionate use of these creatures, sir, they being deserving, by virtue of their being sentient, of a certain measure of respect?"

Ben affixed his eyes upon the silver pistol yet held in hand.

Adams looked to his papers. "'The turkeys, though thrown into violent convulsions, and then lying as dead for some minutes, would recover in less than a quarter of an hour.'" Adams looked to Ben. "Whereupon you would deliver them yet a greater stroke, sir, and a greater, and a greater, until such time your hapless specimens could endure the scale of your torture no longer and took flight, so to say, unto a blessed death; am I correct, sir?"

Ben held his eyes affixed upon the pistol in hand.

"And your regard toward this torture, sir? Was it in likeness to the regard you demonstrated toward the torture suffered by twenty savages at the hands of the Paxton Boys?" Adams looked to his papers. "'I conceit that the birds killed in this manner eat uncommonly tender.'"

A flash from the crystalline bench now, and a scene appeared within, expanding without, in which herds of cattle were compressed into adjoining corrals. The eye of view closed upon one of these, upon an individual animal at front, it prostrate upon a ramp inclined unto the box upon a large wagon. The animal, apparently too weak to stand, was being jabbed by a mechanism having two fangs to front, whilst several men pulled upon a tether tied around the animal's neck. The animal emitting a most plaintive cry, a man stepped forth and began to kick it in the vaginal area, over and over.

Another flash and the scene changed to show three white rodents, red of eye, lying atop a metal table, quivering, each diminutive head bearing three wires of differing coloration.

Another flash and the scene changed to show acre upon acre of calves, each confined to a cage little larger than twice itself, each absented its mother.

Another flash and the scene changed to show a litter on which a chimpanzee lay upon its back, limbs flayed and tethered, the top of its head removed such as to expose its brain.

Another flash and the scene changed to show a great ape staring from behind heavy bars, no discernible luminosity showing in its eyes.

Another flash and the scene changed to show a swarm of men severing from a felled elephant its tusks and penis.

Another flash and the scene changed to a circle of men shouting and gesticulating as two bloodied dogs tore the flesh one from the other.

Ben covered his eyes with his hands and shook his head. "No more! Please! No more!"

"'As we must account for every idle word, so we must account for every idle silence.' Is this sentiment perchance of some familiarity to you, sir?"

Ben shook his head yet holding his hands over his eyes.

"You included it in one of your *Almanacks*, sir, specifically in the number for 1738."

Ben removed his hands from his eyes. "'Tis consonant with the purposes of that instrument."

"In choosing to include this 'moral sentence' in your *Almanack*, sir, might it have been the case at the time that you were embracing of it unto yourself with a fervor at least approaching that with which you were recommending of it unto others?"

"I recommended naught unto others, in the *Almanacks* or elsewhere, that I did not recommend unto myself."

Adams looked to the assembly. "'I recommended naught unto others, in the *Almanacks* or elsewhere, that I did not recommend unto myself.'"

Guffaws.

Adams held silent a moment, then sang forth in a mocking tone: "'O Father, that I may to those below me be gracious, condescending, and forgiving, using clemency; *protecting* [the] *innocent* [from] *distress*; [and] avoiding cruelty, harshness, and oppression.'"

Hoots—catcalls.

Upon Adams taking on a comportment of countenance now of one anticipating moving his rook unto 'check and mate,' Ben suffered a keen chill of dread.

"Might the name Daniel Rees be of some familiarity to you, sir?"

Ben slumped.

"The essential facts, I believe, are these. Feel free to correct me, sir, should I err." Adams consulted his papers a moment, then continued. "In June 1737, sir—the year previous to the one in which you included in your *Almanack* the moral sentence regarding 'every idle silence'— Messieurs Benjamin Franklin, John Darby, and Harmanus Alrihs were appointed auditors by the Court of Common Pleas to settle a dispute betwixt Dr. Evan Jones and Mr. Armstrong Smith. One Saturday morning, our named auditors gathered at the Indian King tavern on Market Street, in company with Dr. Jones and Dr. Jones's attorney, Mr. John Remington, such that the issue betwixt Mr. Smith and Dr. Jones might be mediated unto a settlement. Do I err in any regard thus far, sir?"

Ben shook his head.

"Mr. Smith being tardy, Dr. Jones took it upon himself to provide entertainment to the others by recounting the details of a ceremony, recently held in which Dr. Jones and his attorney, Mr. Remington, in company with two other gentlemen, not present, pretended to initiate young Daniel Rees, a clerk-apprentice to Dr. Jones, Jones being the proprietor of an apothecary, into the fraternity of Freemasonry. In truth, neither Dr. Jones nor Mr. Remington, nor either of the other gentlemen present at the ceremony, was an active Freemason at the time. Do I remain straight upon the path unto truth, sir?"

Ben held to silence.

Adams continued. "As part of this spurious rite, sir, the Rees lad was taught, according to your own account of Dr. Jones's narrative, 'several ridiculous signs, words, and ceremonies,' which arts you found so irresistibly humorous as to cause you to laugh out loud, and most heartily so 'as'—in your words—'my manner is.' Amongst these irresistibly humorous arts, sir, was, according to your own accounting, a ritual bussing of Mr. Jones's bared posteriors; a recitation of an oath unto Satan himself; and a ritual purging by an administered physic, this no doubt procured from Mr. Jones's apothecary, the basement of which was the site of this holy rite. Do I so far state the facts fairly, sir, as originally accounted by Dr. Jones, and subsequently accounted by yourself?"

Ben held to silence.

Adams continued. "At about this time, according to your accounting, sir, the Rees lad appeared at the tavern, such that he might consult with his master, Dr. Jones, who thereupon introduced him to you, saying, 'Daniel, *that* gentleman is a Freemason; make a sign to him.' You will notice, sir, that Dr. Jones did not say, 'Daniel, this is Benjamin Franklin, a *fellow* Freemason,' or *another* Freemason. He said, 'Daniel, *that* gentlemen is a Freemason'—implying thereby, by word and by intonation, that no one present other than '*that* gentleman,' was a Freemason, despite representations to the contrary made by Dr. Jones and his attorney to the Rees boy at his initiation. However, as you well knew, Master Rees could not have been expected to perceive, much less parse, such subtleties of tongue and tone, because Daniel Rees was infirm in all the facilities of mind required for such. He was, in fact, a simpleton. Am I correct as regards this point, sir?"

Ben affixed his eyes upon a parquet square.

Adams continued. "After the Rees lad had departed the tavern, his business with his master satisfied, Dr. Jones and his attorney confessed their intention to hold a second ceremony in pretense to elevating the boy unto a higher rank, this rite to transpire in the near future, and extended to you an invitation to attend, that you might farther your amusement. You declined this offer, to your credit, but thereupon requested—toward mitigating, it might be inferred, the awkwardness of refusing the gentlemen's invitation—you requested loan of the very oath that had been administered by Mr. Remington unto the Rees boy, that you might show it to friends and acquaintances—patrons of your shop, sir?—toward their amusement, and thereby, it might be inferred, toward farthering your standing amongst them. Do I venture off course by cause of a faulty compass, sir, or do I maintain straight and true?"

Ben held to silence.

Adams continued. "Now, sir, pray tell us, in failing to condemn the first ceremony, did you not, both as a Freemason of rank and as a stalwart of moral principle, give implicit license to the second? And did you not thereupon, sir, by way of requesting loan of the specious oath, imply approbation of its ministrations to a guileless simpleton, and by this approbation, imply a condoning toward the greater abuse to come?"

Adams intruding his purpled and pocked countenance toward Ben, Ben cringed in reflex, as much to an odor reminding of burnt sulphur as to an intrusion upon his sovereignty.

Adams continued. "Indeed, were you not complicit in the death of this innocent, sir, he being tortured to death during the course of the second ceremony? Is this not the inescapable truth of the matter, sir, despite all the protestations and indignations subsequently made by you in cause of preserving your reputation amongst your Quaker patrons? In fact, sir, did this tragedy not occur—was it not *allowed* to occur, sir—because you chose *not* to challenge its perpetrators when opportunity for such was laid at your feet. And was not the reason for your choice to the negative, sir, that you feared offending these gentlemen of standing and influence and losing thereby favour, not only of their commerce, but of their letters of credit?"

Turning half-circle clockwise, Adams swept an arm toward the crystalline bench. "Behold, sir, the wages of 'an idle silence.'" In the moment, a scene formed within the bench in which a boy of about ten years was sitting in a room that, by virtue of its stone walls and hewn beams, was obviously foundational. The chair in which the boy was seated was, of its high back, robust arms, and crimson upholstery, in likeness to a throne. Toward either extremity of the room, the boy occupying its center, were two large pots, atop tables or pedestals, emitting eerie blue flames from open mouths. Four figures, draped in black robes and hoods, were crouched behind the flaming pots, two at front the boy, two at back.

The figures to front raised their heads slowly above the flaming pots, uttering guttural moans, and thereupon, moving slowly out from behind the pots, began to stalk toward the boy, who, upon sight of these apparitions, began to chafe against the tethers binding his arms to his throne. Afront the robe of one figure was emblazoned a likeness of a skull and crossbones, stark white, it seeming to glow of the eerie ambience. The two figures behind the boy encroached upon him in likewise fashion, whilst also uttering guttural moans.

The boy, thrashing and chafing with ever increasing violence, of a sudden lunged forward, screaming, and in a desperate attempt to gain purchase on the wood-plank floor with his feet, stumbled awkwardly forward, yet tethered to his chair, and thereupon lunged headlong into one of the votive pedestals, thereby spilling upon self, throne, and floor alike, the contents of the flaming pot. To an ominous whoosh, the flames erupted over the whole of the boy, and these brightening with celerity unto a lurid orange, the boy began to scream and thrash the harder—

A flash and Adams intruded himself directly to front of Ben. "I quote once again, sir, from the scripture aforementioned, *Articles of Belief and Acts of Religion*." Adams looked to his papers. "'O Father, that I may to those below me be gracious, condescending, and forgiving, using clemency; protecting the innocent from distress; and avoiding cruelty, harshness, and oppression.'"

Adams looked to the assembly. "As we must account for every idle word, so we must account for every idle silence.'"

Turning half-circle around, Adams marched to the farther side of the examiners' table, and climbing boldly onto his chair and onto the table, held forth a sheet, of both hands. He recited then in the elevated voice of a crier: "'A likely Negro wench, about fifteen years old, has had smallpox, been in the country a year, and talks English. Enquire of the printer thereof.'"

Adams looked to Ben. "'Enquire of the printer,' sir." He held forth a second sheet: "'To be sold: A likely Negro girl, about fourteen years of age, bred in the country, but fit for either town or country business. Enquire of the printer.'"

Adams looked to Ben. "'Enquire of the printer,' sir." Adams held forth a third sheet: "'A very likely Negro woman, aged about thirty years, who has lived in this city from her childhood and can wash and iron very well, cook victuals, sew, spin on the linen wheel, milk cows, and do all sorts of housework very well. She has a boy of about two years old, which is to go with her. Also a very likely boy, aged about six years, who is the son of the abovesaid woman. He will be sold with his mother, or by himself, as the buyer pleases.'"

Adams looked to Ben, his eyes flashing in likeness to fired rubies. "'As the buyer pleases,' sir." Adams held forth a fourth sheet: "Also a breeding Negro woman about twenty years of age. Can do any housework."

Adams looked to Ben. "'A breeding Negro,' sir."

Descending from the table, Adams resumed his previous station at front of Ben, his features of countenance become so transformed in aspect and coloration now as to leave little likeness of the man so remarkably altered.

Adams tossed upon Ben's lap the notices just read. "Pray tell us, sir, if the odor yet emanating from these notices is of any familiarity to you?"

Ben studied upon each advertisement in turn, then looked to Adams. "I do not, in truth, recall any particular one of these, specifically."

"The *odor*, sir; not the medium. Is the *odor* of any familiarity to you?"

The clerk jumped to his feet. "Odor! Odor in this court!" He sat down.

Ben wrinkled his nose. "There being such stench from another quarter in the moment that no other might be sampled, pray tell, sir, how is one to give proper satisfaction to your request?"

Adams turned away, and retreating unto the vitreous circle, this no longer showing a bluish tint, faced again upon Ben. "Be so kind, sir, as to hold your notices, as printed by you in your *Gazette*, toward a more intimate relation to your nose, in single or en masse, as you should have the courage, and draw from them, or it, what you might."

Showing no hesitation, Ben held the sheets close upon his nose, en masse, and drawing in an unmeasured breath, suffered in the instant so violent an affliction upon the tender tissues of his olfactory as to trigger spasms of violent retching. There being, however, no substance in his stomach with which to bring satisfaction, he could naught else than gag and cough toward ultimate effect, it would seem, of inverting himself inside out.

When finally he was able to quiet himself, Ben accepted from Bartholomew the pocket linen previously lent, wiped his eyes and cheeks with this, and returned it to its keeper, with a nod.

Adams continued. "In fact, sir, these notices just read to you are but a representation. You included many other such in the pages of the *Gazette*, over many a year, did you not?"

Ben became aware of an anxiety centered amidships that, although well familiar, he had not suffered in over two centuries. He was hungry. "I published notices of many sorts, as there could be no prosperity absent such."

"No prosperity absent publishing such; and no prosperity absent serving as agent unto the merchants ordering them; am I correct, sir?"

Ben's stomach rumbled of such notice in the moment as to elicit looks of wonderment from both Intermediaries. Ben pretended unto innocence. "'Tis the prosperous barber who shears his patron's tresses the one day, pulls his teeth the next."

"And in fact, sir, you were the very 'barber' as regards the first notice recollected unto you, ending 'Enquire of the printer thereof,' by way of serving as barker the one day, broker the next; am I correct?"

Ben affixed his eyes upon Adams as if to burn a hole into him.

"And likewise as regards the second, sir, ending 'Enquire of the printer?'"

Ben narrowed his eyes yet farther as if to yet farther concentrate an augering heat.

Adams smiled. "Consider, sir, a looking glass held such as to face upon a concentrating glass. What might be the consequence, sir?"

Ben averted his eyes of such haste in the moment as to suggest a pubescent caught peeping where naught he should.

Adams continued. "Now, sir, were we to carry your analogue to fullness, might we include among the services of the barber, in addition to trimming tresses and extracting teeth, that of bleeding patrons of their distempers. And if we might do so, sir, might we likewise include among the services of the printer, in addition to serving as barker and broker for such notices as those just recollected to you, that of serving as the compositor of these—the very smithy who chooses the articles of language with which to advance their purpose?"

Adams held mute a moment, as if in hospitality to a reply, then, upon a glance to his papers, continued. "Dr. Benjamin Rush, sir. A name familiar to you?"

Ben glanced upon the clerk, then looked to Adams. "Well familiar, as you well know."

"In fact, sir, Dr. Rush was a most agreeable friend and correspondent, and a fellow expositor, in company with your present examiner"—Adams bowed—"toward swaying the timid and the reluctant toward the necessity of the Declaration; am I correct, sir?"

"You are."

"And although Dr. Rush was well learned in the medical arts, sir, by the necessities owing to his profession, he was also well learned in many other arts, by encouragement owing to curiosity and interest; would you be inclined to agree, sir?"

"I would."

"And would you be inclined to agree also, sir, that this most learned of men, in company with yourself, was a man of bold imagination?"

"I would."

"In fact, sir, in one of his many discourses with you, Dr. Rush advanced the notion that the articles of one's character might well become known by way of scrutinizing the articles of one's dreams. Do you recollect such, sir?"

"I do."

"'Tis interesting, is it not, sir, the articles one tends to recollect as opposed to the articles one tends *not* to recollect." Adams leered. Ben averted his eyes.

Adams continued. "In any event, sir, if we were to take as truth Dr. Rush's notion concerning the articles appearing in one's dreams, might it be reasonable to apply this same notion, by way of analogy, to the articles appearing in one's compositions? In other words, sir, might the articles of language one chooses to compose one's notices be as if players upon a stage which comport themselves such as to reveal truths heretofore gone unnoticed?"

"I must confess little understanding upon which to base an opinion."

"Allow me then, good sir, to call your attention to the third notice recently recollected to you—the one in which you ascribe upon the two-year-old Negro boy the status of mere object, by way of assigning unto him the neuter pronoun *which*, whilst you imply upon the older Negro boy, he being six years of age, the status of mortal being, by way of assigning unto him the personal pronoun *who*. Might not one infer from the choice of these articles, sir, that in the eye of the compositor, the two-year-old Negro boy, in having not yet attained an economic value of significance, is to be regarded as a mere *which*, as in the case of a field stone, whereas a six-year-old Negro boy, in having attained a notable level of economic value, in the form of exploitable facilities of mind and body, is to be accorded the dignity of a *who*?"

Ben looked to the crystalline bench, and regarding therein the trans-formations of order and disorder, one unto the other, was visited by a most curious notion, to wit, that Disorder, the idea of Disorder, could not have preceded Order, the idea of Order, in a chain of creation, nor the reverse, anymore than Up, the idea of Up, could have preceded Down, the idea of Down. Indeed, each of these states would seem the very progenitor of the other, in simultaneity, unto all eternity.

Remarkable.

Adams beginning now to encroach, Ben cast upon him a wary eye. Adams continued. "Although the subtlety we mark here might seem much ado about very little, sir, might not such a subtlety be as if a her-ald, in the manner indeed of a scent, to the presence of something far more substantial? Indeed, were we to follow the odor presently sham-ing all others in this chamber unto its source"—Wedderburn and Smith commenced in the moment a great commotion of sniffing—"would we not discover, well close by, sir, a master of hypocrisy, he embracing with one hand the notion that '*all* men are created equal,' whilst with the other assigning exception to certain of these as being no greater than field stones? Would we not discover, sir, a master of expediency who, whilst broadcasting 'life, liberty, and the pursuit of happiness' unto those of his patrons who might lift him unto Influence, broadcasts 'A likely Negro wench, about fifteen years old' unto those of his patrons who might lift him unto Wealth? Do we not discover, sir, a master of conveniency who is able, by way of acts of *o*mission as well as acts of *co*mmission, to condone the enormity of a six-year-old boy—a six-year-old child, sir—being ripped from his mother's bosom, 'as the buyer pleases,' never again to be embraced by her, never again to be smiled upon by her, never again to be lullabied to by her?"

Adams leaned forward. "Would we not discover, sir, the same master of sly invention who, cloaked in the guise of a hen-pecked alter ego, composed for us such warming sentiments as 'Nothing but money is sweeter than honey?'"

Turning half-circle around, to clockwise, Adams swept an arm toward the high bench. "'As the buyer pleases!'"

In the instant, a scene formed within the bench in which a burly man, unkempt of hair, hooked of nose, was attempting to pull a Negro boy, no greater than six years, from the arms of a Negro woman much aggrieved. A second man, bulged of eye, pocked of countenance, was in simultaneity attempting to unlatch the boy's arms from around the woman's neck, the boy wailing, the mother screeching. A third man, portly in girth, pinked of cheek, was standing to one side, a pipe clenched in teeth glinting of gold. The second man, wielding a truncheon, began to strike upon the boy's head and shoulders, the boy and his mother shrieking the harder for it.

A tugging sort of pull began to separate Ben from his chair. Desperate to affix himself to his seat, Ben clutched upon the arms of his chair and in simultaneity pushed his heels against the floor, the latter effort being as if toward ensnaring his heels into the nested loops engrained upon the parquet squares.

A flash and Ben felt an affliction of agony beyond toleration.

If he held fast upon his child, the man would beat him to death.

If he let go, he would never see his baby again.

Ben faced upon the man pinked of cheek, and addressed him without benefit of subservience. "I beg of you, sir! Have mercy!"

The man chuckled, piping a puff of smoke, jowls quivering, and thereupon chastened his men, in a jocular fashion, for their womanly weakness.

Another flash and Ben was kneeling upon the vitreous circle, clutching to breast his little Frankie, in counter to a hooded specter pulling in opposition.

Desperate for advantage, Ben glimpsed a silver pistol no farther than an arm's reach, and upon a moment's calculation, loosed his embrace of Frankie such that he might take the pistol into hand. In the instant, an intruding foot nudged the pistol an inch beyond Ben's reach, whilst, in simultaneity, the hooded specter wrested Frankie from Ben's loosened grip.

A flash and Ben was restored to his chair, Adams standing close upon, leaning forward. "Consider, sir, what benefit might have availed unto all posterity had Benjamin Franklin, virtuous wheeler of his own barrow, refused, openly and forthrightly, to broadcast unto his patrons such notices as recently recollected to him; had the gentleman refused, sir, openly and forthrightly, to serve as agent unto any merchant ordering such; had the gentleman foregone, sir, openly and forthrightly, all profit deriving of such?"

Adams leaned yet closer, broadcasting thereby an odor of such acridity as to burn Ben's eyes unto tears. "Consider, sir, what benefit might have availed unto all posterity, sir, had Benjamin Franklin, esteemed gentleman and exemplar, chosen to risk monetary ruin in preference to bearing an 'idle silence' in the face of an evil of such enormity that no man, of any moral sensibility soever, might fail to recognize it as such."

Wedderburn rose. "For want of a nail, the shoe was lost." Smith rose. "For want of a shoe, the horse was lost." Wedderburn rose. "For want of a horse, the rider was lost." Smith rose. "For want of a rider—"

A flash and the colorations within the crystalline bench precipitated into a scene in which a Negro boy, about ten years, was entering into what appeared to be a common area for the exercise of children. The nearer part of this, into which the boy was entering, was circumscribed by a tall, heavy-mesh fence, the surface on which was as if well tainted of tobacco juice carelessly spat. At the farther end, a vertical board, rounded atop, was attached upon a standard vestigially blue. A hoop, vestigially red, was attached unto the board at a height of nine or ten feet. A nearer board, also attached upon a standard vestigially blue, showed four grievous wounds whereat a matching hoop would, of symmetry, be expected to be attached. Drifts of litter were accumulated along the bottom of the fence, amidst tufts and snarls of weeds.

The farther part of the common area was unfenced and contained apparati, fashioned largely of piping, it would appear, that seemed intended for children to climb upon, and, in two instances, to slide upon. One distinctive arrangement of piping seemed intended to bear several swings, in the stead of a sturdy limb, but bore naught of these, nor aught else.

Across a narrow street, several juxtaposed domiciles, their doors and windows shuttered, their stoops and grounds prodigiously littered of leavings, had fallen into such a state of dissolution as to preclude, it would seem, all possibility of redemption.

The boy bounced a large ball upon ground showing glints of what appeared to be granules of glass, and approaching the farther board, heaved the ball in the direction of the hoop, in an earnest effort, it would seem, to direct the ball into the hoop. The ball ricocheted off the board and thereupon bounced, in a decrescendo of amplitude, to the heavy-mesh fence, and from there, being redirected by Newtonian imperative, rolled toward the opposing standard.

Whilst the boy was in desultory pursuit, two larger Negro boys, having entered upon the play area, took possession of the ball and began to pass and bounce it betwixt them. When the smaller boy attempted to exercise a rightful ownership, one of the larger boys pulled a slender object from a pair of breeches overly slack, and with a flick of wrist, triggered appearance of a long blade with which he made menacing gestures toward the smaller boy. The smaller boy turned and fled a few steps. There being, however, only one escape, this denied him, the boy pulled a pistol from a harness strapped above one ankle and shot the boy with the knife in the forehead, thereupon the other boy in the back, he taking flight. Moving closer upon the second boy, he writhing upon the barren ground—"Mama! Mama!"—the smaller boy shot him in the back of the head—again—and again.

A flash and Ben discovered himself standing close upon the vitreous circle, holding in hand the very pistol denied him but moments previous. At his feet lay a wigged figure, face down, unmoving, his royal blue coat boldly stained.

Uttering a lament most pathetic, Ben fell upon the prostate figure— and discovered himself lying atop the vitreous circle, peering upon, in the perspective of a hovering bird, a bearded man standing at an easel. A rendering upon the easel showed a vestigially red hoop bearing a pert netted skirt, purist white, against a backdrop of deepest gloom.

N. 37th and Mt. Vernon, W. Philadelphia

September 16th, 12:51 p.m.

P rescott glanced at his watch and noticing a yellow jacket pulsating atop his barely touched sandwich, encouraged the interloper into flight with a wave of his left foot. Noticing then a large reddish ant brazenly feeding on grease congealed on the wrapper, he stowed his brush and palette into his pack, and squatting onto his haunches, his right knee cracking ominously, nudged the ant from its ecstasy. Prescott smiled. Bacchus interruptus. Rewrapping his sandwich, he stuffed it into a side pocket on his pack.

The chances of him getting to finish it were slim to none, he well knew, but, what the hell—there was always hope!

Rising slowly, remembering to, Prescott scrutinized his opus-in-progress, looking between it and the backstop at the end of the far court, and then, pursing his lips, shook his head.

It still had a ways to go.

He smiled, recalling the many times Delmyra had chided him for not being able to declare any of his pieces "finished," much less "finished-finished."

He'd "finish" this one maybe tomorrow—maybe even "finish-finish" it—weather, and his car, permitting.

Prescott made a mental note to ask Barry Popkin to have a listen to that ominous grinding noise coming from the left front every time he turned left.

Prescott clipped the cover over the wet side of his canvas, carefully inserted the canvas into his tote, and laying the tote on the ground, collapsed the easel into its box. Inserting the box then into his pack, Prescott slung the pack over his left shoulder, picked up the tote, and walked to where his "Green Hornet" was parked, just beyond the sole entrance to the court.

About to reach for the passenger-side door handle, Prescott hesitated, thinking he might have heard the plaintive cry of another stray in search of what a certain scrawny, ankle-rubbing, orange-and-white stray, now named Rosie, had found last Friday.

Hearing no repeat, Prescott found himself staring at the mural across the 37th and Mt. Vernon intersection that had first captured his attention on one of his scouting missions. It covered the entire side of an abandoned three-story tenement, and showed a black boy, ten or eleven, dressed in mauve and magenta, reaching toward a star just within his grasp. To the boy's left, recessed a little into the background, was a cozy nest of modest but tidy row houses, all their windows aglow with amber light.

Prescott wedged his tote between the passenger seat and the dash to protect it from jostling, but also to serve as a reminder *not* to leave it in the car. He stowed his pack in the trunk, and was just opening the driver-side door—"squeeeek"—when a plum-colored Cadillac, showing a large spider-web fracture on the windshield, and no caps on its wheel hubs, stopped mid-street. The driver, wearing a UPenn baseball cap, red with blue lettering, flashed a set of piano keys through an open window. Prescott recognized the face immediately, the grin actually, despite an unexpected, shocking even, degree of facial emaciation.

Tom Mayback, or Uncle Tom as he was known on the street, had been Prescott's "main man" during the entire span of Prescott's five-plus-year "crack up." The face of this particular man, therefore, the fundamental physiognomy of it, had become as indelibly imprinted on Prescott's brain as had its association with a blessed, albeit temporary liberation from an agony against which a match held to the scrotum would be but a needle prick. Since getting himself straight, however, Prescott had seen Tom only a few times, the first of these being deliberate, to explain to a man he had come, however perversely, to respect, why he would be avoiding him forever more; the others being purely accidental, although probably inevitable, their "separate" worlds being fated, it would seem, forever to intersect.

Tom extended a massive pink palm though the open window.

Grasping this, Prescott felt a familiar stir, but also, in near simultaneity, a palpable sense of power. The old snake was still there, would always be there, coiled in its lair, flicking its tongue on occasion, slithering on occasion, but *he*—not it—was now in charge.

The snake quieted.

"You lookin' good, m'man," Tom's voice was raspy, phlegmy, as if from breathing coal dust for twenty-five years instead of hawking blue-tip vials for thirty years.

"Feeling good, thanks. Yourself?"

"Feelin' fine. Real fine."

Prescott leaned forward and stared hard at two blood-shot eyes. "I'm looking at two Bloody Marys here, Tom."

Tom chuckled, sniffled. "Little red roses m'man. Little red roses." He shifted his eyes toward the empty basketball court. "Doin' a l'il paint'n', is ya?"

Prescott nodded. "A bit. How'd you know?"

"Seen ya around." Tom gestured with his chin toward the court. "Not zakly a daisies in the field kinda guy, is ya?"

Prescott smiled. "Daisies of a different sort maybe."

Tom nodded. "I'll be able to say I know'd ya when."

"When I was piping three a day?"

Tom grinned, sniffling, wetness showing beneath his nose.

"What about you, Tom? When do I get to say I knew *you* when?"

Tom chuckled, lapsing into a fit of coughing.

Prescott stepped to one side.

Tom spat out the window and wiped his chin with a swipe of one hand. "Sorry 'bout that."

"You sound like shit."

"Am shit."

"Shit being as shit does, if I remember correctly." Slipping his wallet from his back pocket—big mistake, he realized—Prescott slipped a card out and wrote on the back with a pen pulled from his shirt pocket. He handed the card to Tom. "The number on the back's my cell."

Prescott slipped his wallet back into his pocket. "I can get you into a program in a heartbeat, Tom. All you gotta do is call."

"Lotta water over the dam, m'man."

"Lotta water left in the pond, though, isn't there?"

Tom rolled his eyes. "What this world do' need, Brother Bahr, is 'notha goddamn preacher man."

"Not to mention another goddamn crackhead."

Tom grinned, shaking his head.

If Tom Mayback had gotten himself into any other line of work, Prescott had long believed, he would have ended up in *Who's Who*. The key to success, Tom obviously understood, was customer loyalty, and the key to customer loyalty, Tom obviously understood, was quality of service. Tom always had the best stuff, always had it available, and never took unfair advantage. Of course, this level of service came at a premium. For a crackhead, however, getting that next fix, being *assured* of getting that next fix, was more than worth Tom's "l'il axtra."

Unfortunately, the level of success consequent to Tom's model came to the attention of a rival named Cool Hand, who, instead of learning from Tom's example, had chosen to view Tom as a threat and had dealt with him accordingly, specifically by having Tom's left knee shattered with a baseball bat.

The next time Prescott had seen Tom, over a year later, Tom was working a corner near the 40th Street Station as a common tout, hobbling from car to car on a stiffened leg. Rumor had it Tom was working for Cool Hand, the very dealer who had put him out of business.

A freefall into crack addiction, Prescott well knew, was a plunge ever deeper into humiliation. And the only way out, Prescott well knew, was to hit some kind of bottom beyond which it was physically, psychologically, and spiritually impossible to plunge any further.

Tom removed his cap, exposing a bald spot that gleamed like a polished shoe, and slipped Prescott's card under the sweatband. "Where I keeps all the port'n stuff," he chuckled, returning the cap to his head, pulling it tight.

Tom took on the look now of a puppy in the window of a pet store. "Hey, man, hate t' ax ya, but be all right t' hold twenty for ya? Was jus' on m' way t' pick up a loaf 'n some fixins."

Even though Prescott knew this was coming—not only had he flashed his wallet, for god's sake, he had demonstrated a willingness to help—still he felt a pique of resentment.

No anger, though. No anger for Uncle Tom.

Prescott pulled two tens from his wallet and handed one to Tom. "You hold ten for me"—he held up the other bill—"and I'll hold ten for you. Whenever you want your ten back, you know where to find me. Whenever I want mine back, I know where to find *you*."

Tom grinned. "Full-time job tryin' t' keep up with the likes o' you, m'man." Tom tucked the ten under the sweatband in his hat, at about the same place he had tucked Prescott's card, and returning his cap to his head, pulled it tight. "Do I get t' see it?"

Prescott stared.

Tom glanced in the direction of the empty court. "What you been paint'n'."

Prescott glanced at this watch. "A quick peek, then I've gotta get going. Somebody has to work the day shift, y'know, Tom."

Tom grinned.

Prescott retrieved his tote and barely touched sandwich from his car, and hurrying to the passenger side of Tom's Caddy, tossed the sandwich onto a seat cluttered with, among other things, several empty cans of Coke (life was nothing if not ironic), the sports section from the *Inquirer*, a tattered copy of *On the Road*, and an even more-tattered copy of *Zen and the Art of Motorcycle Maintenance*. The cover on *Zen* showed a boy sitting on the rear of a motorcycle, back toward the reader, with his arms wrapped around a driver facing a featureless horizon.

Prescott carefully slipped the canvas from the tote, unclipped the cover, and held the canvas at chest level, being careful not to touch the wet oils.

"Should I keep my day job, you think?"

Tom nodded. "In m' mind, tha' real good, *real* good. But you knows the deal—a man gotta make a livin'."

"A man's gotta do what a man's gotta do."

"Ah, right you is, m'man. Right you is." As Tom continued to study the painting, his eyes seemed to grow brighter, like window drapes to a deepening sunrise. He nodded. "Sorta like Rembrandt—all dark n' gloomy 'cept the midda, where they's like canda light but no canda."

Prescott recoiled as if to a punch to the head. "Jesus Christ, Tom— Rembrandt? What in hell's a guy like you doing in a place like this?"

Tom grinned. "Might ax the same o' you, m'man."

Lapsing into another fit of coughing, Tom spat out his window, then looked at Prescott with Rembrandts no longer aglow "in the midda." "Well, I bes' not be keepin' ya"—he grinned—"you bein' on the day shift 'n all. You take care now."

"Who ya gonna call, Tom?" Prescott pointed at his own head in counterpart to the approximate location of the 'port'n stuff in Tom's hat.

Tom flipped a hand dismissively toward Prescott and, shaking his head, drove off, bluish fumes issuing from a sagging tailpipe.

Prescott watched Tom's car until it was in momentary counterpoint to the mural of the black boy reaching for a star.

He had just emerged from the bookstore at the corner of Walnut and 36th and was standing at the crosswalk close behind three coeds headed in his direction. To a bit of a start, he recognized a well-dressed, dark-skinned black man standing to the right of the coeds. Several gold chains and bangles seemed to require the purple silk shirt and the black leather high-tops. The yellow bag Tom was holding suggested he had just emerged from the bookstore.

It soon became obvious that the coeds were having a discussion on the meaning of *Phaedrus* in *Zen and the Art of Motorcycle Maintenance*.

Just before the light turned, he heard Tom's soft but commanding baritone: "All the man's gotta do t' find what he lookin' for is jus' turn 'round and give 'is boy a hug. All he gotta do. He do' see what right there behind 'im, 'cause he all caught up with 'is own self and all that *Phaedrus* shit. Not the onliest one either, is he?"

⤳

Prescott glanced at his watch.

He was going to be late.

Hurrying to the passenger side of his car, Prescott stowed his tote, then rushed to the driver's side, and climbing in, feeling suddenly weak all over, was about to turn the key in the ignition when he cringed to a dread sensation resembling a pressure change deep inside his brain.

Too much up-and-downing; too much hurrying.

Only four weeks ago, Prescott would have likened this sensation to those tonal shifts one experiences now and then in the inner ear—little anomalies in brain state that amounted to no more than a moment of strangeness. Since then, however, what had been a little anomaly deep inside his brain had become harbinger to something much worse.

Prescott squinted against a noontime glare that seemed to have greatly worsened.

He clutched his head.

Tears welled.

⤳

The pain had subsided to a dull ache by the time Prescott reached the Treatment Research Center, tote in hand. He paused at the top of the steps to gather strength.

He wiped wetness from his cheeks.

His one-fifteen was waiting.

The process of elimination was not difficult. Only three people were sitting in the blue-and-plum chairs arranged along the interior wall, and although all three were black, only two were male, and only one of those two was radiating an aura of self-pride.

The other male, sitting off by himself, was obviously a walk-in.

Rodney grinned the moment Prescott's eyes met his, the process of elimination having apparently worked equally well in both directions. Upon Rodney standing, to a height at least three inches over Prescott's, Prescott introduced himself.

Rodney shook Prescott's hand with an enthusiasm befitting the reunion of old friends.

Prescott smiled. "A week?"

Rodney beamed. "Whole week, man."

"Congratulations. You look great."

"Feelin' great, man. Never better."

Rosie, one of the attendants behind the reception desk, caught Prescott's attention and notified him that a Mr. Frank Peoples had stopped by to inquire about a program.

Prescott excused himself to Rodney, parked his tote on an empty chair, and introduced himself to the walk-in, who looked too feeble to stand. Sitting down next to him, Prescott caught a whiff of a familiar sweet-smoky odor, and explained to Frank that he would speak with him in a few minutes, that he had a scheduled appointment he needed to attend to first.

"Can I get you anything?"

Frank, avoiding eye contact, seemingly at all cost, shook his head.

"Had lunch?"

Frank hesitated.

Prescott glanced toward the reception desk. "Laura will order you something—on us. Just tell her what you want. If it gets here before I'm done, you can eat it over there." Prescott pointed to a table to the right of the reception desk. "Otherwise, you can eat it in my office. Hang in and I'll be with you just as soon as I can. Don't go away, OK?"

Frank nodded.

"So, you going to order something?"

Frank shrugged.

"You like cheesesteaks?"

Frank grinned.

Prescott looked toward Laura, who was on the phone, then stood and caught the attention of Rosie, after whom he had named his cat. "Please order a cheesesteak"—he looked to Frank—"Cheez Whiz?" Frank nodded. "Extra?" Frank grinned. "Extra Cheez Whiz, for Mr. Peoples!" Prescott looked to Frank. "One enough?" Frank nodded. "You sure?" Frank nodded. "OK, I'll be with you in just a few minutes. Don't go away. OK?" Frank nodded.

Retrieving his tote, Prescott led Rodney into a corridor perpendicular to the reception area and almost immediately right into a small office, which, with all four walls holding paintings, looked more like a gallery. Prescott offered Rodney the only visitor's chair, this squeezed between a bookcase and a desktop, and setting his tote on the floor, at the near end of a small metal desk, sat down in a swivel chair.

The main desk area, L-shaped, extended from where Rodney was sitting to the near corner, and along the end wall to the opposite corner. A large painting hanging on the end wall featured a white wicker rocking chair.

A middle-aged woman appeared in the doorway and apologized for interrupting. She was holding a very pregnant tote. Prescott introduced the woman to Rodney as Dr. Lewis, one of the research directors—director, in fact, of the program Rodney was presently enrolled in—and introduced Rodney to Dr. Lewis as a very brave man who was celebrating his first full week on the clean cart. Rodney started to get up, but Dr. Lewis—"Please call me Mary Ellen"—stepped forward and shook his hand before he could unseat himself.

"I owe it all to this good man," Rodney said, smiling toward Prescott. "He made me believe I could do it." Rodney shook his head. "Never thought I could. Never."

"He has that way about him. We're lucky to have him. He knows the territory like none of the rest of us ever could, as I'm sure you're aware." She smiled. "We intend to keep him here a good long time."

Prescott flushed.

Mary Ellen glanced at her watch. "I'm on my way down to NIDA, Prescott, but wanted to ask you if you thought Delmyra might be interested in participating in a little research project I just learned about at lunch. A friend of mine over in the sosh department has a grad student who's going to be running a study to see if she can tease out the effect skin tone has on the socioeconomic fortunes of African-Americans. She's looking for a few volunteers to do a sort of a trial run on. Delmyra came immediately to mind." Mary Ellen smiled. "At a minimum, she'd get to find out if she's related to Thomas Jefferson."

"Geez, I thought we all was," Rodney quipped, a twinkle in his eye. "My ho' name's actually Rodney Jefferson Scheetz. When I was a little Scheetz"—he chuckled—"my grandmamma call me Jeffry 'stead o' Roddy. She like it better. She was the onliest one, though."

Prescott smiled. "Would you like *us* to call you Jeffry, even though you're no longer a little Scheetz?"

Rodney chuckled. "Roddy's good."

"I like Roddy," Mary Ellen offered, smiling, looking then to Prescott: "I've got the researcher's contact info, if you think Delmyra would be interested."

"I can't imagine she wouldn't be."

"Me neither." Mary Ellen pulled a paper napkin from her tote and handed it to Prescott. "Sorry, that was all I had to write on. Can you read my writing?"

Prescott nodded as he checked the legibility of the print in front of the "at" symbol. He refolded the napkin then and standing up slipped it into his pocket. "Thanks."

Mary Ellen congratulated Roddy again on his achievement, then took her leave, closing the door behind.

Roddy nodded toward the tote Prescott had rested upright on the floor. "You got 'nother one in there, right?"

Prescott smiled.

Roddy scanned the paintings on the wall behind Prescott. "All these yours? You done 'em?"

"We ran out of room on the fridge."

Roddy chuckled. "I don't know nothin' 'bout art 'n all wise like that but in my mind these is real good," he nodded. "I like 'em."

"Make me an offer."

Roddy stared.

Prescott smiled. "They're not for sale. The Delmyra that Mary Ellen was just referring to told me if I didn't hang them up in here, where they belonged, she said, she'd do it herself. So here they are." Prescott swiveled and peered up at the painting hanging over his desk. "That one up there started it all. That's the chair Dee was rocked in when she was a baby, and her mother before her, and her mother before that. We hope one day to rock our baby in it."

Roddy peered up at a white rocking chair—freshly painted, it seemed—that stood in striking contrast to several chairs to either side of it that seemed broken beyond repair. "Shine like an angel," he said. Shifting his eyes left, Roddy peered up at a teddy bear, intensely white, that sat in striking contrast to several drab and threadbare kindred creatures, most of which were missing an eye or an ear or more. He looked back to the white rocking chair. "Got sumthin' t' say, too, don't it?"

Prescott smiled. "Such as?"

Roddy scanned more paintings—a Christmas-tree globe, intensely white, hanging on a "Charlie Brown" tree; a pigeon, intensely white, sitting on a broken fountain; and so on around, until he was once again peering up at the white rocking chair.

"They's always hope."

"And is that true, you think?"

Roddy exhaled. "T'day I do. Sittin' here with you, I do. Dunno 'bout t'marra, tho'. Dunno 'bout a 'nour from now." He sagged.

Prescott scooched closer. "I've been clean and sober now for five years, three months, and seventeen days, Roddy, and I can't allow myself to even think about tomorrow, not even for a second, even after all this time. Today, this moment—keeping myself clean from this moment to the next—that's all I can handle. And I couldn't do that much if I didn't have a good reason to—beyond just staying clean for clean's sake." He paused. "As I mentioned when you and I talked on the phone, I'm not a shrink or a drug counselor or anything like that. I'm just an intake tech for the research programs conducted here. I recruit and screen addicts to serve as research subjects. So I can't offer you anything clinical. I hope to start a program in counseling next fall, after Dee finishes her program. But"—he smiled—"one step at a time."

Prescott pulled at his beard. "If I may, though, I'd like to tell you a little story."

Roddy brightened.

"I take that as a 'yes.'"

Roddy nodded once, grinning.

"I presume you've been attending NA meetings."

"Ever day—mornin' 'n night. Coupla times, mornin', *noon* 'n night."

"Good job!"

Roddy beamed.

Prescott patted Roddy on the knee. "That's why you're here today."

Roddy beamed.

Prescott sat back. "OK, this story concerns two dudes who, like you, attended NA meetings every day in their first week on the clean cart. Unlike you, though, one of them attended only morning meetings; the other only evening meetings. On the seventh day for each, the first dude, let's call him Ed, attended his usual morning meeting, and after being congratulated by his meeting mates, he set out for home with a bright blue ribbon pinned to his chest, feeling pretty good about himself. After walking about a block or so, he was approached by a little girl dressed in rags who held a daffodil in one hand and a crisp one-hundred-dollar bill in the other. 'Take one,' she said to Ed, 'and leave the other behind.'

"Now, being a wily, street-savvy dude, Ed was a little suspicious at first, but a quick look around for obvious signs of a setup put his mind at ease, and so he took the hundred-dollar bill from the little girl, examined it for signs of counterfeiting, and stuffed it in his pocket. He walked on feeling like he had just won the lottery, and soon came to a corner where a tout named Tom was slinging his wares."

Roddy grinned. "This must be a true story, 'cause I knows ol' Tom *real* well."

Prescott smiled. "Ed knew ol' Tom real well too, and ol' Tom knew Ed, and in no time at all, good ol' Tom had good ol' Ed all fixed up with the best rock money can buy. What the hell, Ed told himself. He deserved it. He'd gotten himself through a whole week clean and sober, and he had just won the lottery! It was time to party! So Ed continued on, in a party mood, and after sauntering a block or so further on, came upon an old derelict druggie named Fat Annie, for her swollen arms and legs, who had tried to go straight more times than she could begin to remember. Ed greeted Annie by showing her his blue-tipped vials, invited her to his party, and needless to say, was never seen at morning meeting again."

Roddy shook his head.

"OK, now, the other dude in our story, let's call him Henry, also attended a meeting on the seventh day, in the evening; was also praised by his mates for making it through a whole week; and was also given a bright blue ribbon to wear on his chest. And after walking about a block or so after his meeting, he too was approached by a little ragamuffin holding a single daffodil in one hand and a crisp one-hundred-dollar bill in the other. 'Take one,' she said to Henry, 'and leave the other behind.'

"Noticing the girl's rags and unwashed hair, Henry removed the ribbon from his nice clean shirt, pinned it to the little girl's grimy blouse, and left her with the hundred-dollar bill. Continuing on, he soon came to the corner where ol' Tom was slinging his wares. Recognizing Henry, Tom offered him the best rock money can buy, and, just for him, at a special price. To which offer, Henry held up the daffodil and said, 'How many hits for this lovely flower, Tom?' To which query, ol' Tom turned his attention to a more promising prospect, and Henry continued on his way, soon happening upon an old derelict druggie named Fat Annie. Smiling into Annie's blood-shot eyes, Henry offered her the daffodil and said, 'For you, Annie. For all the times you tried.' Taking the flower into a trembling hand, Annie wept, and said back, 'No one's ever given me a flower before.' To which lament, Henry replied, 'The error was theirs, dear Annie, not yours,' and then, with a nod, he walked on.

"The following day, when Henry arrived at evening meeting, he noticed a new person in attendance, sitting in the back row, and sat down beside her. Saying not a word, he reached over and, taking hold of Fat Annie's swollen hand, gave it a squeeze."

Roddy's eyes filled.

"Ed is the person I used to be, Roddy, and could be again"—Prescott snapped his fingers—"just like that. Henry is the person I had to become in order to keep Ed from rearing his ugly head every time some little thing went wrong. Ed I can become without any effort at all. Ed is always willing. Henry I can become, or be, only by choice. Moment to moment. Step by step."

"There's a man out there in the waiting room right now, Roddy—with grease running down his chin, I suspect—who's going to need someone to take him to meetings, and make him feel that he's not alone." Prescott smiled. "And that's the end of the story."

Roddy swiped at his cheeks. "Sound like the beginnin' o' one t' me."

"In which case"—Prescott stuck a pen into Roddy's shirt pocket—"you might need this." He opened a desk drawer, pulled out a small notebook, and tossed it onto Roddy's lap. "And this. Keep a journal."

Roddy shook his head. "I ain't no Henry." He swallowed.

Prescott tossed a box of tissues on top of the notebook. "Well then, we've got a problem, because Ed doesn't cry. He can't. He doesn't give a shit."

Roddy wiped his eyes with a tissue. "You don't see everthin'."

"No, I don't. May I tell you what I do see?"

Roddy shrugged.

"I see a crackhead who's been clean a whole week now, because he wanted to be; because he had the strength and the guts to get the job done. I see a man who regrets things, choices he's made, because he cares. He gives a shit. I see a man who's struggling like bloody hell to be Henry because he's sick and goddamn tired of not being in charge of his own life."

Roddy blew his nose, cleared his throat, exhaled deeply.

Reaching behind, to his right, without looking, Prescott picked up a wastebasket from the floor and held it toward Roddy. Roddy tossed the tissue into it.

Roddy looked at Prescott. "How'd ol' Ed get 'is hooks into the likes o' you, enaway?"

"As compared to the likes of you, Roddy?"

Roddy dropped his eyes.

"OK, I know a little bit of your story, so I guess it's only fair that you know a little bit of mine. In a word: failure. I managed to fail at everything my father ever wanted—expected—me to succeed at, from the time I was born until about five years ago." Prescott gestured toward the painting over his desk. "One of the reasons that painting is up there, why Dee wanted it to be up there, is to remind me of what success is in my own eyes. We all tend to see ourselves as others see us, especially the important others in our lives. Year after year of failure upon failure and I became in my own eyes the worthless piece o' shit I saw in my father's eyes every time he looked at me."

Roddy shook his head.

"The only escape"—Prescott smiled—"the easiest escape—was to blast off in a rocket ship for a view of the world, and one's self in it, that wasn't real, of course, but sure did feel like it, at least for a couple of wonderful hours."

Roddy smiled, nodded.

"I started blasting when I was a sophomore in prep school, right after I failed to make even water boy on the football team." Prescott grinned. "Literally true. I got beat out by a girl named Sylvia Weston, who, I found out later, was banging the coach." Prescott grinned. "There's a lesson there somewhere."

Roddy chuckled.

"At Bowdoin, my father's alma mater, instead of trying to measure up to my father's legacy there, I went completely in the other direction. When I got here, at Wharton, and it became glaringly apparent to me that I had once again allowed myself to be made a fish out of water—I had only gotten into the place because my father had pulled every string at his disposal—well, anyway, let's just say I went off the deep end."

"Your daddy must be real 'portan' t' be pullin' all them stings like that."

"'Important' being a relative term. Ever heard of 'ironic altruism?'"

Roddy shook his head.

"It's a theory that holds that Good Samaritanism, or Do-Goodedness, practiced on a large scale, will always end up doing more harm than good. Saving thousands of African children from starvation, for example, will eventually lead to overpopulation and therefore to even more starvation. My father wrote a book about it. The *real* irony, though, is that both the term and the theory originated with my mother, when she was one of my father's grad students. She wanted to do her dissertation on it, but my father discouraged her, and then knocked her up, with me, to make sure he had complete control. Then, after dumping her, he wrote a book called *Ironic Altruism*, which was on the *New York Times* Best Seller List for over three years."

"Wha' happen t' yer mama?"

Prescott cleared his throat. "Three years after my father dumped her, she swallowed nineteen 50-mg tabs of Trazodone, washed them down with half a fifth of vodka, and slipped into a nice warm bath."

Roddy's eyes watered. He pursed his lips. He wiped his eyes with a tissue. "Had ya enabody left then? A sista maybe, or an auntie?"

"I had me"—he smiled—"through the eyes of my father."

Roddy shook his head. "So whadya do, if it all right t' ax?"

"What any self-loathing son of Dr. Gilbert Henry Bahr would do. I blasted myself about as deep into failure as any human being could possibly get, then one stifling August night, I mainlined some of Uncle Tom's best stuff, swallowed nineteen 50-mg tabs of Trazodone, and washed them down with half a bottle of vodka." Prescott smiled. "As irony would have it, though, a Good Samaritan happened along, as I was drowning in my own vomit, and tossed me a life line."

Roddy wiped his eyes. Prescott held the basket toward him.

"That same Samaritan helped get me into a program here, where I eventually got a job as night janitor, which, at the time, was all I could handle. Then one day, after about a year, Mary Ellen called me into her office and asked me if I'd be interested in becoming their intake tech. The current tech was leaving for a job on the West Coast, and they wanted to replace her, if they could, with someone who knew the territory firsthand. This same aspiration also applied, she said, to their counseling staff, in case I needed something to shoot for over the longer term. No sooner had Mary Ellen made this suggestion than I knew I was going to become a drug counselor and use art as part of my shtick. Why I hadn't thought of this earlier, when I was still trying to pound square pegs into round holes, I'll never understand. Anyway, I'll get a combined degree in counseling and art therapy in about three years, after Dee finishes her program. She's getting a degree in family therapy. I'm hoping to become a counselor here, if there's an opening, but, to tell you the truth, I'd go anywhere they'd have me." Prescott smiled. "All said and done, one way or another, I'll have a real job with real purpose. I'll have my personal art on the side. I'll be going home every night to a woman and a kitty, and, hopefully, a child, who're very glad to see me. All in all, not a bad life—for me. For who *I* am."

Roddy grinned. "They's always hope."

Prescott pulled at his beard. "I'm beginning to think you should be sitting where I am, and I should be sitting where you are."

"Whadabout yer daddy?"

"See what I mean?"

Roddy chuckled.

"About a month after I got kicked out of Wharton, I got a copy of my father's will in the mail. No note, just the document. Heavy black lines had been drawn through all mentions of my name. I had been expunged. I no longer existed. I haven't heard from him since. I've been sending him birthday and Christmas cards every year, although not entirely magnanimously." Prescott smiled. "I make the cards myself, out of original artwork. I doubt my father ever sees them, or even opens the envelopes, but the message is really for me: I can't be expunged. I exist. I am here! I am here!"

Roddy peered up at Prescott's paintings and rested his eyes on the white rocking chair. "A daddy should be proud o' the likes o' you, man. Real proud."

"Thank you. And the same applies to the likes of you, Mr. Scheetz. The path you're on now takes an enormous amount of courage, and an even greater amount of strength." Prescott smiled. "You're on your way, dude!"

Roddy beamed.

Prescott looked at his watch. "Which is a good thing, because Mr. Peoples has probably finished his cheesesteak by now."

Roddy set the box of tissues on the near desktop, and taking the notebook into hand, sat forward. "I 'preciate yer time, an' everthin' you done fer me."

"You're entirely welcome, Roddy, and you're always welcome here, no matter what. Catch my drift?"

Roddy nodded, then looked toward the tote Prescott had rested upright on the floor. "Jus' curious—tha' one like the others? They's always hope?"

Prescott smiled. "Would you like to have a peek?"

Roddy animated. "Hey, love ta, man—if ya got the time."

Prescott removed the painting from the tote, avoiding contact between it and the wet oils, then removed the cover. Turning around then, he held the painting in front of Roddy, still seated, whose eyes, at first studious, suddenly flooded. Clutching his head, as if to stop it from exploding, he moaned, and sprang from his chair.

"Don't do it!"

Roddy stopped, his hand on the doorknob.

"Run, Roddy, and Ed wins! You'll lose everything you've gained!"

Roddy slumped, hand still on the doorknob.

Prescott set the painting down, buzzed Rosie and asked her to tell Mr. Peoples he'd be a few more minutes, to please wait. He turned toward Roddy. "Sit down, Roddy. Talk to me. Tell me what you saw. I think I know, but I need you to tell me. Tell me."

Roddy returned to his chair.

Prescott scooched closer.

Roddy trembled. "I kilt my boy." He wept.

"He was one of the boys murdered on that court."

Roddy nodded.

"I'm sorry, Roddy." Prescott pulled two tissues from the box and placed them in Roddy's hand. "You feel responsible because you were too busy being Ed to look after your boy."

Roddy nodded, wept.

"But you're not Ed anymore, Roddy. You're Henry. You're looking through Henry's eyes now, and it hurts. Because you see everything, Roddy. You see it all. You feel it all. It hurts. I know. It hurts like hell, Roddy. It is hell. Keep talking to me."

Roddy wiped his eyes with the tissues, then blew his nose. Prescott held the wastebasket toward Roddy, then placed two more tissues in Roddy's hand.

"I see m' boy gettin' tight with them gangbangers, this one dude in particula, full o' swagger, but I don't do nothin' 'bout it. I got other shit I gotta take care o'. His mother should be lookin' after 'im, I tell m'self, instead o' whorin' herself around."

"The boy your son was tight with, Roddy; was he the other boy killed that day?"

Roddy nodded. "Jinxy Broaddus. He was a couple o' years older 'n Paulie, 'n full o' hisself. Paulie looked up to him like he shoulda been lookin' up t' me, had I give 'im a reason."

Roddy wiped his cheeks, blew his nose, wadded the tissues into a ball.

Prescott lifted the wastebasket from the floor and held it for a shot from the paint. Roddy hit for two.

Prescott scooched closer. "Instead of playing round ball with your boy, out on that court"—Prescott gestured toward the painting—"in the place of Jinxy, you were either stoned or trying like hell to get that way, and now, as Henry, you're full of regret." Prescott patted Roddy on the knee. "All to the good, Roddy, all to the good, 'cause ol' Ed doesn't feel any regret. Ol' Ed only feels what he wants to feel, which isn't much of anything. For him, being numb, being stoned, is the best of all possible worlds. Only Henry feels what you're feeling now. And that's part of the deal. A *big* part of the deal. No pain, no gain. You with me?"

Roddy nodded.

"I'd like to suggest something, Roddy, if I may." Prescott touched the top of the painting. "I'd like you to take this painting home with you, as a gift. It's yours."

Roddy held up his hands. "Oh no, man, I can't be doin' nothin' like that. That yer paintin', man. That belong here, like Miss Dee say."

"It belongs where it can do the most good, Roddy. That was Dee's message to me—put it where it will do the most good—and I'm thinking it'll do the most good in your possession, not mine. Will you accept it or not?"

Roddy looked as if torn between the hundred-dollar bill and the daffodil.

Prescott looked at his watch. "Ed or Henry?"

Roddy nodded. "OK—but if ya ever needs t' have it back, all ya gotta do is jus' give a shout, OK?"

"Will you take it, Roddy, to own, or will you not?"

Roddy nodded.

"OK, here's what I suggest. Put it where you'll see it several times a day, and let it remind you, every time you look at it, of everything—all the Ed stuff—that's making you feel responsible for your son's death. Do this for as long as it takes to be able to forgive yourself—however many days, weeks, months it takes; it doesn't matter. When that day comes, stand in front of a mirror and say to yourself, out loud: 'Roddy, you really fucked up, didn't you? But you're not a bad person, and certainly not the person you were the day your son was killed. Back then, you were Ed. Today, in this moment, you're not Ed; you're Henry. You chose the daffodil, not the hundred-dollar bill. And even though Paulie is no longer around to look up to you for getting yourself clean, and staying clean, there's another Paulie out there somewhere, right now, in desperate need of someone like you—a Henry, the real deal—to look up to, to model himself after. Roddy, I forgive you.'"

Prescott stood.

Roddy rose, and allowing himself to be embraced, wept.

Sobbed.

When finally Roddy had quieted, Prescott fortified him with several tissues, slipped the painting back into the tote and warned Roddy about the wet paint. "Bring it back next time you're in—the tote, I mean. No hurry, though—OK?"

"Y' sure 'bout this? I—"

Prescott scowled.

"OK, thanks, man—for everthin'."

Prescott opened the door. "You're going to make it, Roddy. It isn't going to be pretty—it never is—but you're going to make it. Most don't." He looked to the tote. "Look at it every day, Roddy. Feel the pain."

Roddy nodded, and starting out the door, tote in hand, turned back. "Ed and Henry—them's real people or just made up?"

Prescott smiled. "Henry Jekyll and Edward Hyde, from *The Strange Case of Dr. Jekyll and Mr. Hyde.* It's a quick read; or there's a decent movie. You might want to check it out."

"Man, y'sure give out a lot o' homework."

"No pain, no gain."

Roddy chuckled.

Prescott led Roddy into the foyer, shook hands with him at the door, and found Frank Peoples sitting at the table beyond the reception desk. "How's the sandwich?"

Frank smiled, chin glistening with grease.

Prescott laid a hand on a cadaverous shoulder. "Go ahead and finish up. Just let Laura or Rosie at the desk know when you're finished. Take your time."

Frank nodded.

Prescott slipped Laura the ten-dollar bill he was holding for Uncle Tom, indicating that it was for the "sandwich fund," and asked her to buzz him when Frank was finished. Returning to his office, he dialed his voice mail, putting his phone on speaker, and logged onto his computer. He had gotten seventeen e-mails since last check.

The first voice mail was from Avery Thompson over at the 47th Street Shelter: He had an opening—he'd just had to boot someone for a rules violation—and Prescott had first dibs.

Prescott hooted. If Frank Peoples didn't already have an address of record—most likely the case—Prescott would be able to get him one immediately, and at the same time get him under the same roof with Rodney.

The best way of staying on track, Prescott well knew, especially during the early days, was to have a buddy in the same boat with you.

The next message came on: "This is Dr. Rosen's office. Please call at your earliest convenience."

Supreme Celestial Court of Petitions

Upon Ben being restored to his chair, Wedderburn, his countenance grown hideously ghoulish, rose from the examiners' table, and treading across the vitreous circle, climbed to the top of the clerk station that stood betwixt the crystalline bench and the petitioners' table. Thereupon extending his arms, in the manner of a preacher about to address an assembly of eager penitents, he struck a haughty pose.

"Little strokes fell great oaks."

Cheers. Whistles.

"The rotten apple spoils his companion."

Cheers. Whistles.

"Great affairs sometimes take their rise from small circumstances."

Cheers. Whistles.

Wedderburn bowed—leftward, rightward, to middle. Upon descending then, he took station at front of Ben, his eyes glowing in the manner of fired emeralds. "Grand words—such as to arouse indeed a ready mind as well as an eager spirit. And they are your own; are they not, sir?"

"They—" Ben cleared his throat of encumbrance to a hardy voice. "They are."

"Now, sir, I assume no pretense toward knowing the intimacies of your mind, but I have myself long been fascinated by the number of goslings that one mother goose might accommodate under her bosom. Case in point. Although you very likely had a particular event in mind, or category of such, when you scribed the third maxim just read to you, to wit, 'Great affairs sometimes take their rise from small circumstances,' the goslings it might gather under wing would seem sufficiently numerous as to include even the case of a vast conflagration emanating from a single spark flown from a flint; would you tend to agree, sir?"

"If a 'vast conflagration' might rightly be interpreted a 'great affair.'"

"Assuming to the positive sir, for the moment, would it be reasonable to interpret the term 'great' in your moral sentence to mean 'large in enormity' as well as 'large in felicity?'"

The clerk gesturing toward a more erect posture, Ben straightened himself. "Semantical logic would seem to require to the affirmative, 'great' not being defined in the particular."

"Likewise, sir, might it be reasonable to include amongst 'small circumstances' certain local conditions and factors contrived of the will of men?"

"Likely so, 'circumstance' being as broad in the beam at one end as 'affair' is in the other."

"Might it be reasonable, then, sir, to amend your moral sentence to read: 'Great enormities might rise from small afflictions?'"

"Had you started here, we might be farther toward tea."

"My apologies, sir. I will attempt to be more direct. Now, sir, toward that end—ay or nay. Did you, at the time of your first posting to London, hold in your possession—by way of legal bondage—two servants, one named Peter, the other named King, neither named aught else, they being denied that felicity of heritage that is carried upon the wheels of a proud surname, such as indeed Washington, Adams, or Franklin?"

Ben averted his eyes.

"Ay or nay, sir."

"Ay!—as you well know."

"Ay! And were these 'servants' in fact slaves, sir, human chattel, they being clothed in twills of euphemism such as to redress piques of guilt before such might even arise?"

Ben looked to his hands.

"We will interpret your silence to the affirmative, sir. And did you, sir, whilst serving in your posting to London, take one of these servants in company with you on a sojourn to Ecton, there to acquaint your son William, as well as yourself, with the Franklin ancestral home, it being yet known as 'the Franklin house,' and to visit the gravesites whereat your grandfather, his father before him, and his father before him, were alike interred—in other words, sir, to enjoy the felicities of lineage and legacy?"

Ben stole a glance toward the clerk, and nodded.

"And was this slave who accompanied you, sir, the one named Peter and naught else?"

Ben held to silence.

"And whilst visiting the family gravesites, sir, did you instruct Peter to remove, by instrument of a wetted brush, obstructions of moss and lichen from the stones, such that you and William might parse the inscriptions engraved thereon?"

Ben nodded.

"And did you, sir, well prior to this event, include in one of your *Almanacks*, as universal truth, the solemn declaration: 'All blood is alike ancient?'"

Ben nodded.

"And by this declaration, sir, did you intend to convey that you and every other man on this earth, past and present, were brothers under Eve, that is, were of the same fundamental essence and worth and deserving thereby of the same deference and respect commonly afforded one kindred by another?"

Ben held to silence.

"In fact, sir, is not the declaration 'All blood is alike ancient' simply another way of saying 'All men are created equal?'"

"A reasonable equation."

"And did you, sir, include also in one of your *Almanacks* the declaration: 'Nothing dries sooner than a tear?'"

Ben nodded.

"*Which* species of tear did you have in mind, sir—the one welled in the eye of the master afflicted of a little pique of sentimentality at the grave of his grandfather or the one welled in the eye of the 'servant' denied all heritage?"

Ben held to silence.

Wedderburn leaned forward. "*Which*, sir?" Of a sudden spinning away, Wedderburn marched to the examiners' table, snatched up a sheaf of papers, and once again ascended to the clerk's box adjacent to the petitioners' table.

Holding his papers in the manner of a scroll, Wedderburn began to read in the manner of a town crier: "'The small-pox had now quite left this city. The number of those that died here of that distemper is exactly 288 and no more. Sixty-four of the number were negroes; if these may be valued one with another at £30 per head, the loss to the city in that article is near £2000.'" Wedderburn looked to Ben, his eyes flashing green fire. "Does this notice toll the bell of familiarity, sir?"

Ben held a steady gaze upon Wedderburn; himself to silence.

"In fact, sir, are these not the words of the very compositor who offered up 'A likely negro wench, about fifteen years old?'"

By no greater in the moment than fleeting glance, Ben discovered his petitioners sitting slouched with their eyes cast downward, as if to frolic thumbs by no greater than thinking on them.

Wedderburn descended from his perch and took station upon the vitreous circle. "Not 'Negroes' uppercase but 'negroes' lowercase?' '£30 per head?' 'In that *article*?' Pray tell us, sir, how are we to reconcile such debasements as these with such pronouncements as 'All blood is alike ancient?' Must we perhaps correct the compositor, sir, such as to communicate the whole of the truth, to wit: 'All blood is alike ancient, except when an expediency should require otherwise?' Or must we debit our esteemed compositor's account, sir, in an amount owing to a shameless act of hypocrisy?"

Ben affixed his eyes upon his hands, these clasped upon his lap, and frolicked his thumbs by no greater than thinking on them.

Wedderburn continued. "Or make we too much of too little, sir? What is a small *expediency*, after all, in the grand scheme of things?" Wedderburn waved a hand dismissively. "Little ado about nothing. And what is a little *hypocrisy* in the grand scheme of things?" Wedderburn waved a hand dismissively. "But a trifle."

Smug assurance gave way of a sudden as if to a surprise epiphany. "Ah, but 'Small strokes fell great oaks,' do they not, sir? 'The rotten apple spoils his companion,' does it not? 'Great affairs sometimes take their rise from small circumstances,' do they not? Indeed, what forest does not compound from a single sapling? What conflagration does not compound from a single spark?" Wedderburn lifted his eyes and began to speak as if to an apparition visible to him alone. "Alas, what is this I see before me? Is this yet another coin of expediency being compounded unto a trove of hypocrisy? Come, let me clutch thee, that I might credit thee!"

Breaking of a sudden from his histrionics, Wedderburn looked to Ben. "Now, sir, if I were one of your advocates here present"—Wedderburn bowed toward the panel of petitioners, they gazing yet upon the majesty of their opposable thumbs—"I would attempt at this juncture to present mitigations in the name of Common Practice. Indeed, I would present argument, with demonstration, that you were only practicing, in regard to your participation in the small debasements and trifling afflictions aforementioned, your trade in the etiquette of the times. Of course, such an argument would be devoid of any moral content, as must generally be the case regarding any argument in service to expediency. However, were I indeed an advocate in service to your cause, sir, the aforementioned is the course of defense I would pursue. And in anticipation of such, within the courtroom of your own mind, sir, I now draw your attention to one Christopher Sauer, Printer. Do you recall the gentleman, sir?"

Ben nodded.

"In fact, Mr. Sauer, whose print shop was located in nearby Germantown, procured most of his paper from you, taking advantage of your ever-adequate stores of such, though not your ever-filled wheelbarrow, did he not, sir?"

Ben held to silence.

"And do you likewise recall, sir, the etiquette by which Mr. Sauer practiced his trade, with reference to the etiquette by which you practiced yours? I speak specifically, sir, of the categories of advertisement this gentleman accepted in relation to those he refused."

Ben averted his eyes.

"You recall the man's commerce, sir, but not his etiquette?"

Ben held to silence.

"Must we infer, sir, a memory rendered, at least for the conveniency of a moment, in likeness to a wedge of Swiss-made cheese?"

Ben yet held to silence.

"Let me pour then a bit of whey into the wormholes. At the time you were including in your *Gazette*, sir, that lucrative species of notice recently reminded to you—'He will be sold with his mother, or by himself—enquire of the printer'—Mr. Sauer was refusing to do likewise in his own newspaper, called the *Collection of News*. Not passively avoiding such notices, sir, in the manner of a moral ditherer, but steadfastly refusing them. In fact, sir, the measure of the gentleman's inconvenience in this regard was well reflected in your own book of accounts, wherein Mr. Sauer was forever in arrears; am I correct as to this trifling point, sir?"

Wedderburn paused as if to accentuate silence, then continued. "What I find of novelty here, sir, is not so much Mr. Sauer's refusal to participate in 'this atrocious debasement of human nature'—to quote a renowned moralist of the time—but that such a noble stand as his seems not to have been brought to the attention of the public at large, for the recognition it deserved, certainly, but foremostly for the example it offered. Imagine, sir, an American tradesman, daily indulging in the same heady liquors of Industry, Order, and Resolution as his contemporaries, but refusing to succumb to the heady lures of Madam Expediency! Indeed, one would have thought that some keen-eyed freethinker of the time, some alert and clever scripturist, would have redressed such an egregious oversight with a public comment or two; quite so?"

Wedderburn stepped forward to effect of positioning himself directly afront Ben.

"Abiah Folger Franklin, sir, Wife and Mother. Do you recall also this person?"

Ben lurched to his feet of such force of resolution that his roundish girth nearly impacted upon Wedderburn's flattish counterpart. "You will not disrespect my dear mother, sir, neither in name nor in character, in service to your nefarious ends in this chamber. I will not have it!"

Wedderburn, three inches greater in stature than Ben, six inches less in girth, lifted his purple-green chin, and, wry amusement compounding the demonic disfigurement of his countenance, looked to the assembly. "He will not have it!"

A thunderous roar.

Ben looked sternly upon his petitioners, who responded by no greater than a small shrug each. Urged strongly then by Clarence and Bartholomew, Ben resumed his repose.

When the pandemonium had sufficiently subsided, Wedderburn continued. "Be assured, sir, that your good mother will suffer no disrespect in these proceedings. Now, one of the practices of your good mother, public and private, was to advocate for the welfare of all God's children, was it not?"

"It was."

"And was it this same practice that led your good mother, upon learning of her youngest son's possible involvement in the torture-death of one Daniel Rees, a child simpleton, to express apprehension as regards his keeping company with a congregation of men, I refer to the Freemasons, sir, which, all evidence availing to her would suggest, did not regard all of God's children equally; am I correct as to this point, sir?"

Ben held to silence.

"And on the occasion of your receiving these sentiments from your mother, instead of standing tall before the measure of your good mother and, in the first place, expressing genuine sorrow as regards the reprehensible mistreatment of this simple child, and, in the second place, accepting at least some measure of culpability in his horrific demise, by acts of omission if indeed not by acts of commission, you exculpated yourself from any responsibility soever, not by forthright denial, but by way of reminding your mother of her ignorance concerning the character of the Freemasons." Wedderburn looked to his papers. "I quote, sir, from the letter you posted to your father on the matter, you being disinclined to address your mother directly: 'As to the Freemasons, unless she will believe me when I assure her that they are in general a very harmless sort of people; and have no principles or practices that are inconsistent with religion or good manners, I know no way of giving my mother a better opinion of them than she seems to have at present (since it is not allowed that women should be admitted into that secret society). She has, I must confess, on that account, some reason to be displeased with it; but for any thing else, I must entreat her to suspend her judgment till she is better informed, and in the mean time exercise her charity.'" Wedderburn glared upon Ben, his eyes flashing as if of green fire. "In other words, dear mother, mind your own business!"

Thinking but a vague command upon his thumbs, Ben watched in wonderment as the one moved in the clockwise direction, the other in the counterclockwise direction, absent any specific instructions given unto each muscle involved, in proper sequence.

"In fact, sir, who is the only party here present to have delivered toward your dear mother a disrespect?"

Ben comported his clasped hands into likeness of a beaver hovel, aperture to front, which he thereupon closed with his thumbs.

Wedderburn continued. "On a similar occasion, sir, you gave answer to your mother concerning an inquiry made by her into the status of your 'servants.' In your reply, dated April 12, 1750, and addressed directly to her, your father being unavailable by way of being deceased, you wrote as follows." Wedderburn looked to his papers. "'I shall keep those servants; but the man not in my own house. I have hired him out to the man that takes care of my Dutch printing office, who agrees to keep him in victuals and clothes and pay me a dollar a week for his work. His wife, since that affair, behaves exceeding well; but we conclude to sell them both the first good opportunity, for we do not like Negro servants.'"

Spinning away, Wedderburn marched to the examiners' table, disposed of his papers, and taking station on the vitreous circle, looked again to Ben. "'Servants,' sir? 'I shall keep those *servants*?'—'we do not like Negro *servants*?'" Wedderburn lifted a little his chin, and forcibly sniffed. "Do I detect odor of yet another little expediency, sir, as regards in the present case your choice of terms? Indeed, would I be correct, sir, to adjudge that you are *not* making reference in your letter to 'servants' in the literal sense—functionaries such as cooks and maids hired into service; but are, in fact, making reference to *slaves*, sir; indeed those suffering an 'atrocious debasement of human nature?'"

Ben held to silence.

Wedderburn continued. "At this point in your life, sir, two years following your retirement from the printing business, could you not have well afforded to give your 'servants' their freedom as opposed to selling them 'the first good opportunity?' Could you not have well afforded, sir, to exercise toward your 'servants' the very charity commanded by you of another?"

Ben frolicked his thumbs such that they alternately opened and closed the aperture on the beaver mound. Or were his thumbs frolicking him?

"Instead, in a fit of pique, sir, over some trifling disobedience, you sunder husband from wife; you speak of the couple as if in reference to a yoke of oxen; and you declare your intention to continue to hold your beasts of burden to bondage until such time as you might make a profit on their sale—to wit: 'the first good opportunity.'"

Wedderburn looked to the assembly. "Hail, ancient blood!"

The assembly: "Hail, ancient blood!"

Wedderburn: "Hail, expediency!"

The assembly: "Hail, expediency!"

Ben extended his fingers into likeness of a steeple.

Wedderburn continued. "And when you, in fact, were able to realize a fine profit on your recalcitrant cattle, rhymes with chattel, what thereupon did you do? Did you honor the declaration implicitly made to your good mother to hold slaves no more—'for we do not like Negro servants?'" Wedderburn shook his head. "In fact, you did not, sir. In fact, you replaced them 'the first opportunity' with Peter and Jemima, the very Peter you subsequently took to England with you, sundering thereby yet another union of husband and wife. And when eventually you grew weary of this brace of oxen, sir, you replaced them with yet another such, compounding thereby expediency upon expediency, hypocrisy upon hypocrisy. Do I speak the truth on the matter, sir, or do I smithy fact such as to fit the mold of a little expediency?"

Ben comported his thumbs and fingers into likeness of a heart.

Or was it a spade?

"Twice over, sir, your good mother delivered opportunity unto you to stand tall before her, indeed before all posterity, in company with the likes of Mr. Sauer, and twice over, what did you do, sir? Have we a name for it?"

Spinning quarter-circle around, Wedderburn stepped to the examiners' table, and snatching up another sheaf of papers, took station again upon the vitreous circle.

Ben took notice now of what appeared to be a trail of footsteps leading from the circle unto the examiners' table, and returning. To a start then, he noticed that Wedderburn appeared to be standing in a puddle atop the vitreous circle, the latter having become tinctured of a reddish glow.

Wedderburn continued, oblivious, it would appear, to the apparent thawing underfoot. "In the year 1747, sir, you made it your cause to incite your fellow Philadelphians into providing for a common defense against privateers increasingly encroaching upon the Delaware, am I correct?"

Ben looked up from his thumbs. "Unerringly."

"And in prosecution of this cause, sir, you wrote, and yourself published, a pamphlet titled *Plain Truth; Or, Serious Considerations on the Present State of the City of Philadelphia and Province of Pennsylvania*; correct?"

"Unerringly."

"I quote therefrom." Wedderburn looked to his papers. "'Confined to your houses, you will have nothing to trust to but the enemy's mercy. Your best fortune will be to fall under the power of commanders of king's ships, able to control the mariners, and not into the hands of *licentious privateers*'—your emphasis, sir—'who can, without the utmost horror, conceive the miseries of the latter—when your persons, fortunes, wives, and daughters shall be subject to the wanton and unbridled rage, rapine, and lust of *Negroes, Molattoes*'—again, *your* emphasis, sir—'and others, the vilest and most abandoned of mankind.'"

Wedderburn looked to Ben. "Do I quote without prejudice, sir?"

Ben held to silence.

Wedderburn held his eyes cast downward a moment, whilst shaking his head, then looked again to Ben. "Now, sir, I know not the effect of this lurid tableau on others, but the images most vividly left to torment my own mind are of sweat-soured, frothing-at-the-mouth Negro and Mulatto beasts, seven feet tall, violating the sanctity of virgin daughters and innocent wives with pustuled pikes of manhood twelve inches in length. And, in fact, sir, such a nightmare was precisely your intention, was it not? You contrived your broadcast of such triggers unto fear as might motivate husbands and fathers to action by way of gravest alarm, did you not? And indeed what better way to accomplish such an end than to paint images of *Negroes* and *Molattoes* of such extremities of prejudice as to conjure feral beasts rabid with insatiable vexations of appetite. Not *Frenchmen* and *Spaniards*, mind you—who were, in fact, the true enemy at the gate—but *Negroes* and *Molattoes*. Need to procure a cannon? Serve up a 'wanton' *Molatto*! Need to enlist a regiment? Serve up a 'licentious' *Negro*!"

Wedderburn stiffened himself unto martial posture and bowed unto Ben. "My congratulations, sir. You accomplished by a truly remarkable economy of inflammations precisely as you had designed. Indeed, upon general dissemination of your bowel-knotting portrait of 'the vilest and most abandoned of mankind,' the good men of Pennsylvania enlisted into local militias by the legion. But at what cost, sir? In exploiting a debasing prejudice, did you not serve to magnify it? In protecting a few innocents of one complexion, did you not commit legions of others of another complexion unto a living hell? In placing a corrupt apple next to a good companion, sir, did you not thereby corrupt also the companion?" Whirling to clockwise, Wedderburn swept an arm toward the high bench. "Need a cannon, malign a *Molatto*! Need a regiment, demonize a *Negro*! Hail ancient blood!"

The assembly: "Hail ancient blood!"

Wedderburn: "Hail expediency!"

The assembly: "Hail expediency!"

The orderings and disorderings within the high bench of a sudden transformed into a rural scene in which several Negro children were standing afront a ramshackle domicile little larger than a coop. The eye of view closed upon one set of eyes and the next, capturing in each instance a hardness of ground upon which little more than thistle might be expected to root.

A flash and the scene was changed to an urban setting in which several Negro children were standing afront a corrupted domicile juxtaposed to the like, side to side. The eye of view closed upon one set of eyes and the next, capturing in each instance a hardness of ground upon which little more than thistle might be expected to root.

A flash and the scene was changed to another rural setting; to another urban setting; to another rural setting; to another urban setting—back and forth, over and over, faster and faster.

A flash and Ben was returned to his seat, Wedderburn standing to leftward. A column of reddish mist shone now above the vitreous circle, whilst a fresh trail of footsteps led from the circle to whereat Wedderburn presently stood.

"In fairness, sir," Wedderburn boomed, showing a set of sallow fangs whereat but modest canines had only recently dwelled, "we must confess that you did indeed come, over time, to correct yourself regarding certain prejudices, both as to the exercise of these and as to the furtherance of them, in particular by way of coming to oppose not only the commerce of servitude but also its institution."

Wedderburn stepped closer.

Ben flinched to a sulfurous scalding of his olfactory.

Wedderburn continued. "And you did indeed make public mention of your evolving sentiments, at least in some instances. Your public characterization of slavery as 'an atrocious debasement of human nature' comes to mind."

Wedderburn stepped closer.

Ben retreated as far as Washington's rising sun would allow.

"Now, sir, a small curiosity. Would you judge the evolution of your sentiments as regards these prejudices as being reflective of a changed heart, a changed mind, or both? In other words, sir, did you come to oppose the institution of slavery as a result of a moral calculus, whereby you deduced human bondage a *moral* evil, or did you come to oppose slavery as a result of a prudent algebra, whereby you came to hold slavery a *practical* evil?"

Ben looked to the papers Wedderburn presently held in hand, whilst squinting against another insult of noxious exhale. "One suspects you hold in hand the very satisfaction you seek."

"I hold in hand, sir, but a trail leading unto—indeed, sir, let us discover whence." Wedderburn looked to his papers. "I quote from *Observations on the Increase of Mankind, Peopling of Countries, etc.*, writ by you in the year 1751. 'The whites who have slaves, not labouring, are enfeebled and therefore [are] not so generally prolific; the slaves being worked too hard, and ill-fed, their constitutions are broken.'" Wedderburn looked to Ben. "Not their spirits, only their backs; correct, sir?" He continued. "'And the deaths among them are more than the births, so that a continual supply is needed from Africa. . . . Slaves also pejorate the families that use them; the white children become proud, disgusted with Labour, and being educated in idleness, are rendered unfit to get a living by industry.'"

Wedderburn lowered his papers. "In other words, sir, if allowed to continue unabated, slavery would, over time, leave the white race generally unschooled in the lessons of Industry and Frugality, to end of their becoming dangerously dependent and enfeebled. In addition, a continuation of slavery would make daily commerce increasingly

dependent on the African ox, hence on a steady supply of this species, which supply would unavoidably be vulnerable to all manner of
marauders and malingerers; is this a fair interpretation of your sentiments on the evil of slavery, sir?"

Ben flinched to another acrid blast from Wedderburn's bellows.

Wedderburn grinned unto ghoulish effect. "I will take your reflex to
the affirmative. Now sir, would you adjudge these sentiments the result
of a moral calculus, or of a prudent algebra?"

Ben held his eyes squinted, his nose wrinkled.

Wedderburn looked to his papers. "I quote, sir, from a letter you composed to Mr. Richard Jackson, MP, concerning the Sugar Act of 1764:
'The duty on Negroes I could wish large enough to obstruct their impor-
tation, as they everywhere prevent the increase of whites.'" Wedderburn
looked to Ben. "Moral calculus, sir, or prudent algebra?"

Ben held squinted his eyes, wrinkled his nose.

"I quote farther from your *Increase* essay of 1751." Wedderburn looked
to his papers. "'The number of purely white people in the world is pro-
portionably very small. All Africa is black or tawny. Asia chiefly tawny.
America (exclusive of the new comers)'—the Europeans—'wholly so.
And in Europe, the Spaniards, Italians, French, Russians, and Swedes
are generally of what we call a swarthy complexion; as are the Germans
also, the Saxons only excepted, who, with the English, make the principal body of white people on the face of the earth. I could wish their
numbers were increased. And while we are, as I may call it, scouring
our planet, by clearing America of woods, and so making this side of
our globe reflect a brighter light to the eyes of inhabitants in Mars or
Venus, why should we in the sight of superior beings, darken its people?
Why increase the sons of Africa by planting them in America, where
we have so fair an opportunity, by excluding all Blacks and Tawneys, of
increasing the lovely White and Red?'"

Wedderburn looked to Ben. "In other words, sir, the best Negro is
not indeed the dead Negro, nor the Negro conjured to the imagination
such as to fever the public mind unto a fervor of action, but the Negro
denied any opportunity soever by which to contaminate the purity of
the Anglo-Saxon race; is this a fair interpretation, sir?"

Looking to the unceasing transformations transpiring within the
crystalline bench, Ben wondered whereat in the process of disorder
blossoming into order, order corrupting into disorder, did the one state
leave off, of a boundary absolute, and the other begin.

Or was such a curiosity reflective of an ignorance never to be satisfied?

Wedderburn spun half-circle around, and striding several measured steps toward the high bench, hands and papers clasped behind his back, head extended forward, took station upon the vitreous circle, becoming thereby illumed of reddish glow unto hellish effect, and spun half-circle around such as to face again upon Ben.

"What have we now before us, sir, in sequence and in sum? Have we that species of example, sir, that might serve to mold a callow youth unto a harmless, even beneficent, citizen? Have we that species of moral testament and scripture, sir, that might serve to guide a susceptible youth against the pied pipers of prejudice and faction? Have we that species of virtue, sir, that might serve to encourage an unformed youth toward compassion and wisdom? Or have we instead, sir, a sequence of little strokes felling, in sum, a great oak?"

Ben frolicked a thumb by no greater than thinking on it.

Wedderburn approached a step closer. "In the latter days of your tenure as Minister Plenipotentiary to the Court of Louis XVI, sir—close upon your subsequent acclamation into the Pennsylvania Abolition Society—a Negro servant named Abbe, property of one John Jay, a fellow commissioner, escaped her shackles and sought asylum within the very bosom of the Enlightenment itself. Do you recall the incident, sir?"

Ben glanced upon the clerk, then nodded by no greater than thinking upon it.

"And do you recall your response, sir, upon hearing Commissioner Jay's woeful plaint of deprivation and misery?" Wedderburn here feigned a weepy voice. "Alas, who now will scrub my granddaddy's stone?"

Chortles.

"Did our great moral philosopher celebrate the courage of this atrociously debased woman? Did he openly, or even secretly, abet her? Did he posture himself toward this servitude-escaping woman as he had long labored to sway Enlightened France into posturing herself toward the servitude-escaping colonies? Did he place principle atop pedestal, sir, that it might serve as beacon unto succeeding generations navigating the shoals and narrows of a complex life?"

Wedderburn stared hard upon Ben, his eyes flashing as if of fired emeralds. "Nay, in lieu of such, our great moral philosopher hastened his carriage to the local constabulary, as if called to a conflagration by clamorous alarm, there to make urgent petition for swift apprehension of the errant property, which application was readily honored, despite its flagrant illegality."

Wedderburn looked to his papers. "'Scriptures assure me that at the last day we shall not be examined what we thought but what we did; and our recommendation will not be that we said *Lord! Lord!* but that we did good to our fellow-creatures.'" Wedderburn leaned closer. "*Your words, sir!*"

Ben flinched to a near-asphyxiating inhalation of sulphurous effluvia.

Wedderburn continued. "We are left then with something of a conundrum, are we not, sir? Indeed, how are we to reconcile such a lofty sentiment on the primacy of good deeds over public piety with your complicity in the 'atrocious debasement' of a woman escaped from bondage in a realm in which she held the legal right, not to mention the moral right, to do so?"

Ben looked to his thumbs.

"In fact, sir, is not what we have here yet another rotten apple in service to spoiling the barrel, yet another cancer of organ in service to corrupting the corpus, yet another little whack of axe in service to felling the oak?"

The floor quaking now, to a ponderous rumble, the mist atop the vitreous circle deepened unto a pillar of hellish red light, which thereupon began to swirl in the counterclockwise direction, and to sculpt then, in the manner of clay to a potter's touch, unto the form of a great oak.

Upon leathery leaves touching upon the high ceiling, the quaking ceased, and Adams and Smith, each bearing an ax upon his shoulder, took station at either side of this arborous apparition, such as to face one upon the other. Standing well to rightward, Wedderburn nodded toward Adams, who cocked his axe over his left shoulder, showing all the aplomb of a veteran to the task. Smith followed suit, raising his own axe over his right shoulder, manifesting not quite the poise that experience teaches. Upon a second nod from Wedderburn, Adams swung his axe such as to make an upward cut afront the great oak.

"*A likely Negro wench!*" Wedderburn boomed unto the assembly, as if in reflex to the report of the axe blow.

Smith struck the trunk at a downward angle, sending a chip of wood directly toward Ben, who managed to remove himself, by deft feint, from this missile's deadly path.

"*Enquire of the printer thereof!*" Wedderburn boomed.

Adams struck an even mightier blow.

"*With his mother, or by himself, as the buyer pleases!*" Wedderburn boomed.

Swinging with a notably elevated level of confidence, Smith sent another chip of jagged wood flying toward Ben, who managed to save himself by a feint in the opposing direction.

"*A breeding Negro woman! Enquire of the printer!*"

Adams swung his axe with such verve as to escape a manly grunt.

"*Nothing but money is sweeter than honey!*" Wedderburn barked.

Smith swung his axe as if to match Adams's resolve, sending, with a manly grunt of his own, an even larger missile hurtling toward Ben, who, in feinting reflexively to rightward, near upon caused his chair, and himself, to topple sideward.

Ben noticed now, to considerable alarm, that he was tethered to his chair, arm and leg, indeed as if unto "an atrocious debasement."

"*£30 per head!—in that article!*" Wedderburn boomed.

Adams swung his axe as if to sever the diminished trunk with a final blow. The great oak quivered, but did not topple.

"*Sell them both, the first good opportunity!*" Wedderburn boomed.

Smith reciprocated with a stroke of such ferocity as to send a missile nearly the size of a cobblestone hurtling toward Ben. In thrusting not only his head but the entirety of his corpus sideward, Ben caused his chair and himself to topple to leftward.

Chair and occupant remained as one, however, the latter being yet bound to the former.

Bartholomew, with assistance from Clarence, righted what in the moment might be construed as a statue reposed upon a pedestal.

"*Why increase the sons of Africa by planting them in America?*" Wedderburn boomed.

Adams swung a blow even mightier than the one preceding, determined utterly, it would appear, not to be outdone by his uncalloused colleague.

"*The wanton and unbridled rage, rapine, and lust of Negroes and Molattoes!*"

Swinging with a savagery that contorted a countenance a'ready become hideous, Smith sent a missile the size of a cannonball toward Ben, who, yet tethered, managed to save his head from grievous injury only by a most-painful strain of neck to rightward.

"*All blood is alike ancient!*" Wedderburn boomed.

Cocking his arms with ferocious intention, Adams let loose the mightiest stroke yet, causing thereby the whole of the tree to quiver like an electrified turkey, as well as the floor in proximity. A low groan grew louder now as the oak began to tilt toward Ben, who, upon apprehending his fate, began to chafe violently, indeed frantically, at his tethers.

"*Need a cannon, malign a Molatto! Need a regiment, demonize a Negro!*"

Ben stared wide-eyed as the great oak tilted directly toward him. He looked to Clarence, but Clarence was disappeared. "Help me!" he begged. He looked to Bartholomew, but Bartholomew was disappeared. "Help me!" he begged.

"Ask Abbe!" someone shouted.

"Ask Peter!" someone shouted.

"Ask King!" someone shouted.

"Ask Jacob!" someone shouted.

"*Enquire the printer thereof!*" Strahan boomed, risen at center of the petitioners' table. Showing no little chagrin, he sat down.

The toppling hulk about to rob man and chair of the dimension necessary to all reality, a bolt of electrical fire shot forth from the crystalline bench, and striking upon the oak as it plummeted, vaporized it unto a residual aether of reddish mist, to a thunderous report.

Ben squealed as might a stuck swine, then quieted, as if drained of all blood, and witnessed the massive stump of the oak sink into a cauldron of roiling reddish liquor.

Adams and Smith approached in the manner of yoked oxen, sans yoke, each holding in hand a sheaf of papers. Adams took station to Ben's left, eyes flashing of reddish fire; Smith to Ben's right, eyes flashing as if of bluish fire. Each man had become transmuted unto ghoulish aspect at least to the extent accumulated unto Wedderburn.

Smith began: "I should like to ask you now, sir, if I might, to summon unto memory a few recollections concerning Miss Polly Stevenson, daughter of Margaret Stevenson, your landlady during your two tenures in London as Pennsylvania agent."

The vitreous circle, Ben noticed, in addition to having become a roiling cauldron, had greatly expanded in diameter.

Smith continued. "Over the fifteen years of your habitation with the Stevensons, sir, you engaged in many an agreeable conversation with Miss Polly, this young lady being in possession of, even at a tender age, a ready and curious mind; am I correct?"

Ben nodded.

"And on the occasions of separation one from the other, these discourses continued in the form of favours writ one to the other; also correct?"

Ben nodded.

"Now, sir, during one such separation, this occurring in Miss Polly's twenty-first year, you wrote to admonish Miss Polly against becoming too much interested in the philosophical arts, at the cost of becoming too little acquainted of the domestic." Smith looked to his papers. "I quote you, sir: 'There is a prudent moderation to be used in studies of this kind. The knowledge of nature may be ornamental, and it may be useful, but if to attain eminence in that we neglect the knowledge and practice of essential duties, we deserve reprehension. For there is no rank in natural knowledge of equal dignity and importance with that of being a good parent, a good child, or good husband or wife.'"

Smith looked to Ben. "Do I give voice to your words as writ, good sir?"

Ben nodded.

"I repeat the last line: 'There is no rank in natural knowledge of equal dignity and importance with that of being a good parent, a good child, or good husband or wife.'" Smith looked to Ben. "Did you subscribe to this sentiment, sir, at the time you counseled it unto Miss Polly, indeed as a father might unto a beloved daughter?"

"I advanced but what I myself embraced."

"And what you expected of yourself no less than you expected of others?"

"No less."

"Very good, sir."

Smith looked to Adams, who, elevating his papers to exaggerated height, sang forth in a voice veritably flushed crimson with High Church rouge.

Ben cringed upon hearing the first words:

> Of their Chloes and Phyllisses poets may prate
> I sing my plain country Joan,
> These twelve years my wife, still the joy of my life;
> Blest day that I made her my own.

> Not a word of her face, or her shape, or her eyes,
> Or of flames or of darts you shall hear;
> Tho' I beauty admire, 'tis virtue I prize,
> That fades not in seventy years.

> *Am I loaded with care, she takes off a large share,*
> *That the burden ne'er makes me to reel;*
> *Does good fortune arrive, the joy of my wife*
> *Quite doubles the pleasure I feel.*

Adams paused, and over-looking his papers, shook his head toward Ben in the manner of an aggrieved schoolmaster. He continued:

> *Some faults have we all, and so has my Joan,*
> *But then they're exceedingly small;*
> *And now I'm grown use to them, so like my own,*
> *I scarcely can see them at all.*

Adams looked to the assembly. "The icing being to cake made fast, is saved for thee to savor last." He continued:

> *Were the fairest young princess, with million in purse*
> *To be had in exchange for my Joan,*
> *She could not be a better Wife, mought be a worse,*
> *So I'd stick to my Joggy alone*
> > *My dear friends*
> *I'd cling to my lovely ould Joan.*

Adams looked to Ben. "Do I see flushed upon pale cheek, sir, a mark of culpability as regards authorship of these humble rhymes?"

Ben looked to his thumbs.

"In fact, sir, you are their very laureate, are you not?"

Ben looked to Adams. "Composed by me, but in close imitation to other such verses of the time."

Adams bowed. "Duly noted. Now, sir, although you name 'Joan' the object of your celebratory exultations—'My Country Joan,' to be precise—you are in truth celebrating a person for whom 'Joan' stands in surrogacy; are you not?"

Ben looked again to this thumbs.

"The court shall take your silence in the affirmative. Now, sir, I wish to make but one query farther as regards this matter. Had the shoe been on the other foot, sir; had Deborah Read Franklin painted *you* in such hues and tones as to suggest shrew and bumpkin, whilst in simultaneity painting herself in such hues and tones as to suggest heroic accommodation and philosophical resignation, what, sir, would have been your response?"

Ben frolicked a thumb by no greater than thinking on it.

"In truth, sir, the reason the shoe was on the one foot and not the other was because you could never quite forgive your Joggy for being the very woman you had taken to wife of little greater cause than necessity, could you, sir? Indeed, the abscess festering upon your domestic bliss at the time you composed your ditty owed not to *you*, sir, not to any choice made by you, not to any expediency advantaged by you, but to your Country Joan, to the person she was, or, more to the point, to the person she was not. Is this not the plain truth of the matter, sir?"

Ben held to silence.

Adams consulted his papers, looked again to Ben. "Do you recollect one Daniel Fisher, sir?"

Ben looked hard upon Adams. "Is there to be no end to this? Am I destined to endure your sour breath and foul insults for all eternity? Am I a'ready whence you would have had me delivered when we were both yet mortal had you been the least able?"

The clerk jumped to his feet. "If 'tis from a pinnacle a man might see to all directions, what does it benefit him to refuse a few more footholds such to attain it?"

The clerk sat down.

Adams continued. "Mr. Fisher, in fact, served a brief tenure as clerk in your Market Street shop, did he not?" Adams paused. "Did he not, sir?"

Ben glanced but fleetingly unto the clerk. "He did."

"Very good. And coincidental to his employment with you, sir, Mr. Fisher roomed at a near neighbor but boarded at your table; am I correct?"

Ben nodded.

Adams looked to his papers. "I quote now, sir, from the journal Mr. Fisher maintained coincident with his three months of employment and boarding with you; to wit: 'I have often seen him'—Mr. Fisher refers here to William, your son—'pass to and from his father's apartment upon business (for he does not eat, drink, or sleep in the house) without the least compliment between Mrs. Franklin and him, or any sort of notice taken of each other, till one day, as I was sitting with her in the passage, when the young gentleman came by, she exclaimed to me (he not hearing): *Mister Fisher, there goes the greatest villain upon earth!* This greatly confounded and perplexed me, but did not hinder her from pursuing her invectives in the foulest terms I ever heard from a gentlewoman.'"

Ben slumped.

Adams looked up from his papers. "If we are to believe Mr. Fisher's account—and there would appear to be no reason for us not to—are we not vexed to inquire, sir, as to what considerable weight of cause, for surely it had to be considerable, could have animated such a confounding and perplexing outburst from your dear Joggy?"

Ben looked to his thumbs.

"Indeed, sir, are you not yourself more vexed than any other in this chamber concerning this curiosity?"

Ben held to silence.

"Allow me then, sir, if I might so indulge myself, to pose, for your philosophic consideration, a theory on the matter. Might it have been the case, sir, that, as you had once abandoned your Country Joan, geographically as well as emotionally, when you ventured to London to acquire the mechanical means to a virtuous fortune, you likewise abandoned her again, geographically by way of pursuing one cause after another"—Adams looked to his papers—"I quote, on this point, Mr. Fisher quoting Mrs. Franklin—'All the world claimed a privilege of troubling my Pappy (so she called her husband) with their calamities and distresses.'" Adams looked to Ben. "And also abandoned her emotionally, sir, by way of focusing the majority of your attentions upon your son, 'the greatest villain on earth,' instead of distributing them more evenly, as well as more demonstrably, such as to fulfill the natural requirements of a dutiful and loving wife?"

Adams held as if spellbound by a pair of frolicking thumbs, then continued. "Jealously, sir! Indeed, have we not here, in your Joggy's pronouncement, manifest even to an eye unschooled in the pathologies of the heart, symptom of this most poisonous, and poisoning of the acid moods? Indeed, sir, does not the orphaned kitten cry out to be reunited with its mother? Does not the abandoned canine cry out to be reunited with its master? Does not the lost sheep cry out to be reunited with its flock? Indeed, sir, might it be the case that a much neglected Joggy would cry out in some fashion toward being reunited with her Pappy?"

Adams leaned forward, delivering thereby a noxious insult upon Ben's a'ready burnt olfactory. "Did you have no ears for such alarms, sir? Were you so afflicted of a deficiency in this regard as to have sense only for the cries and plaints of those who might become your patrons?'"

Ben continued to frolic his thumbs, in the one direction, in the other.

Adams thereupon taking a step backward, Smith, in counterpoint, took a step forward.

"When you embarked for England, sir," Smith began, as if continuing a sentence not yet punctuated, "in company with your son William, your daughter Sally, left behind, was in her fourteenth year, am I correct?"

"As was equally true of Mr. Adams regarding the very point."

"I apologize for being tiresome, sir. There is natural to even essential proceedings a necessity toward tedium. Now, sir, by the time you returned home, five years hence, in the year 1762 to be precise, Sally had blossomed unto a fullness of womanhood; had she not?"

"She had."

"And the responsibility for guiding and measuring Sally's maturation from bud unto bloom had fallen to whom, sir?"

"My good wife."

"Your Country Joan, sir?"

Ben held to silence.

"Even so, must we not assume that the loving father, although absent these five years, made contributions toward his daughter's maturation that, if not essential to it, were surely salutary toward it?"

"I did as would any loving father over the expanse of a separating sea. I urged my daughter toward obedience in her relations with her mother, I encouraged her in music and the domestic arts, and I sent her the occasional gift, including books and references selected toward a proper education."

Smith nodded. "Splendid. Now, sir, during the five years you resided at the Craven Street home of the widow Stevenson, in company with your son William, and your two 'servants,' sir, Peter and King, you established a quality of relationship toward the widow's daughter, Polly, that one might rightly characterize as paternal. A fair statement?"

"I have a'ready confessed to this very point."

"Once again, I apologize, sir, for being so very tiresome. To get at the cream, must we not first eat the cake? In fact, sir, did you not come to regard Miss Polly"—Smith looked to his papers—"she having 'a mind thirsty for knowledge and capable of receiving it,' as more pridefully a daughter unto you than ever had you regarded, or did you regard"— Smith looked to his papers—"'your dutiful and sweet-tempered' Sally, with 'ready hands and feet to do and go and come and get?'"

Ben stiffened. "Your trick, sir, as should be obvious to all present, is to spread cheap ink pretending to tar."

Smith smiled unto hideous effect. "In fact, sir, your dear Sally of 'ready hands and feet to do and go and come and get' was a sequential twin of your dear Joggy, was she not? And for the unrelenting ache this disappointment caused you, sir, you could not quite forgive her, could you? Anymore than you could forgive the block from which this plain chip sprung. And instead of taking responsibility for your part in the matter—for choosing a melding mate of expediency as against compatibility—you faulted and punished her. Is this not the very truth of the matter, sir?"

Ben shook his head, eyes fixed downward.

"Nay, you say?" Smith looked to his papers. "When your dear Sally announced to you, sir, by way of notice carried to your London outpost, of her own choice of a melding mate, the merchant Richard Bache, what was the character of your response, sir? Do you recall it? We have, in fact, but recently touched upon it, as another tine to the same fork.

"Would a disinterested eye adjudge your response celebratory, sir? If not, at least magnanimous? At least respectful? At least civil?" Smith paused, his eyes flashing as if of sapphirous fire, then continued. "In fact, sir, did you not manifest the gravest possible disapproval, firstly by way of holding to a punishing silence, and thereupon by way of hurling haughty insults unto your daughter's betrothed?" Smith looked to his papers. "'Unless you can convince her friends'—*her* friends, sir?— 'of the probability of your being able to maintain her properly, I hope you will not persist in a proceeding that may be attended with ruinous consequences to you both.'"

Smith looked to Ben. "And did you not thereupon add salt to the wound, sir, by way of intimidating your wife toward niggardliness regarding the nuptials?" Smith looked to his papers. "'At present I suppose you would agree with me'—*suppose*, sir?—'that we cannot do more than fit her out handsomely in clothes and furniture'"—Smith looked to Ben—"in the objects, in other words, sir, that most reflect the station of the father?—'not exceeding in the whole five hundred pounds value. I would only advise that you do not make an expensive feasting wedding, but conduct every thing with frugality and economy.'"

Smith shook his head, then continued. "And did you not withhold yourself from standing with your daughter at her wedding rite, sir, the most joyous occasion in her life? Indeed, sir, did you not withhold yourself altogether?" Smith looked to his papers. "'It seems now as if I should stay here another winter.'" Smith looked to Ben. "There being, of course, rites of a higher privilege to attend to, sir?"

Ben drooped.

Smith leaned closer. "You absented yourself from the ceremony joining your only daughter unto a common merchant instead of the prince you had imagined for her. Likewise, you absented yourself from the ceremony joining your only son unto a planter's daughter instead of the fairy princess you had imagined for him. What, however, of the ceremony joining your dear Polly Stevenson unto the notable William Hewson, sir? Did you absent yourself also from this affair, also by way of various 'calamities and distresses' requiring your presence elsewhere? Or did you, in fact, sir, accept not only Mrs. Stevenson's invitation that you attend, at cost of your usual summer travels away from London's fevers, but also Polly's request that you stand with her in the stead of her long-deceased father?"

Ben held to silence.

"One trembles to imagine, sir, what species of paternal regard you might have inflicted upon your dear Sally had you not been absented from her for eight of her first twenty-four years."

Ben held his eyes affixed upon his thumbs.

Smith continued. "When subsequently your daughter gave birth to her first child, sir—not your first grandson, one feels obliged to note, but indeed your first *legitimate* grandson, christened Benjamin Franklin Bache, in your honor—you thereafter referred to him, in subsequent letters to your wife, sir, as 'your grandson,' not *my* grandson, or *our* grandson, but your wife's grandson; correct, sir? Yet, when Polly Stevenson Hewson gave birth to her first child, you immediately began referring to him as '*my* godson.'"

Smith smiled. "A niggling point, you might argue. A little 'cheap ink' pretending toward tar, you might protest. And perhaps you would be correct, sir. Yet, is it not oft the case, sir, that a thing in the small can speak more loudly even than the thing in the large, as indeed in the case of a tradesman wheeling his unoiled cart up a noonday street?"

Smith leaned closer. "Indeed, sir, did you not, inch by inch, measure by measure, abandon your daughter Sally, her mother with her—two Joggys in a jar, as it were—just as you had previously abandoned the woman, one Barbara Johndroe, sir, who had borne you an untimely son, just as you one day would abandon the bastard child himself—in favor of appropriating unto yourself more agreeable, not to mention more complimentary, surrogates?"

Smith looked to his papers. "Item, to Miss Polly: 'This is the best paper I can get at this wretched inn, but it will convey what is entrusted to it as faithfully as the finest. It will tell my Polly how much her friend is afflicted, that he must, perhaps never again, see one for whom he has so sincere an affection, joined to so perfect an esteem; whom he once flattered himself might become his own in the tender relation of a child'—by way of the marriage to William you had so ardently desired; correct, sir?—'but can now entertain such pleasing hopes no more. Will it tell how much he is afflicted? No, it cannot.'

"Item, to Miss Polly: 'My dearest child. I will call you so; why should I not call you so, since I love you with all the tenderness, all the fondness of a father?'

"Item, to Miss Polly: 'I love you more than you can ever imagine.'"

Smith looked to Ben. "Now, sir, labor as we might, we could discover, amongst the several hundreds of papers and favours you so assiduously preserved unto posterity, no such declarations regarding the daughter born unto you and your Joggy, save one, this addressed not to your dear Sally, however, but to the man who would find happiness in her company for two score and four years." Smith looked to his papers. "'I love my daughter perhaps as well as ever parent did a child, but I have told you before that my estate is small, scarce a sufficiency for the support of me and my wife, who are growing old and cannot now bustle for a living as we have done.'"

Ben fixed his eyes hard upon Smith. "You take snippets from here, snippets from there, some from the same rag, some from different such, and stitch of these a counterpane to your own comfort."

Smith looked to the assembly. "Or might it be the case, Dr. Franklin, sir, that we bring to fore, by way of connecting dot unto dot, a constellation heretofore gone unnoticed in a firmament cluttered of glitter?"

Smith took a step backward; Adams a step forward.

Adams looked to his papers. "'I am concerned that so much trouble should be given you by idle reports concerning me. Be satisfied, my dear, that while I have my senses and God vouchsafes me his protection, I shall do nothing unworthy the character of an honest man and one that loves his family.'" Adams looked to Ben. "'I shall do nothing unworthy.' 'One that loves his family.' Pray tell me, sir, were you privileged to be an observer upon these proceedings as opposed to its subject, would you have, at this point, any cause to adjudge either the implicit denial just reminded to you, or the explicit pledge just reminded to you, as beyond all reproach?"

Ben held to silence.

"Was the reverend a little too generous with his needle, sir, toward stitching fast your lips?"

Chortles.

Adams continued. "As should be apparent at this hour, sir, even by those afflicted of limited acuity, as in the example of the unfortunate Daniel Rees, the content and direction of these proceedings have in large measure been determined by the historical record as preserved by no other than yourself. In fact, sir, you took considerable pains to preserve many hundreds of letters either composed by you or addressed to you, not to mention a myriad of other documents either spawned of or associated with your various interests; am I correct as to this point, sir?"

"You are."

"In fact, sir, you made liberal use of this very trove in your project to extend your *Autobiography*—St. Sebastian save us all—unto thirteen volumes; did you not?"

"I consulted the contents of old boxes and chests, not to mention old memories, which my mind caused, by some great mystery, to be restored to me."

"And did you happen to discover upon your rummagings through these old boxes and chests, sir, the particular favour that provoked the denial and pledge just reminded to you?"

"I did not make an accounting of each item."

"In fact, sir, you did not do so because you could not do so. In fact, sir, over the five years of your first tenure in London as Pennsylvania agent, spanning from June 1757 to August 1762, your Deborah sent you a veritable cornucopia of favours, sometimes at the frequency of one per week, including the very one presently at issue. Yet, of all those letters, sir, writ of considerable strain by a woman unschooled in letters, you managed to summon sufficient care and diligence as to preserve unto posterity not a single one—not a sheet, sir—whereas, during this same interval, you were somehow able to summon sufficient care and diligence as to preserve unto history the facile scribblings of a myriad other correspondents, their sheets having accumulated unto several boxes and chests at the time of your return to the colonies."

Adams paused to adjust his wig, thereby drawing attention to a set of horns, in likeness to those of a billy, protruding through his curls. He continued. "In fact, sir, those loving scratchings of your dear Joggy, in holding no substance beyond the mundane, no observation beyond the superficial, no cause for preservation beyond the sentimental, were far more valuable as fuel for your stove than as treasure for your trunk; were they not, sir?"

Adams intruding of a sudden closer, Ben cringed. "Are we close upon pinning the tail to the donkey, sir, or do we stray too far from the ass?"

Chortles.

Adams looked to his papers, then looked again to Ben: "When you embarked on that first mission to London, sir, in the year 1757, you expected—hence your wife and daughter, left behind, expected—that you would be absented no greater than a few months; am I correct?"

"None had cause to think otherwise."

"As it turned out, however, you were separated from your family, they from you, not five months, but five years, as a'ready established; am I correct?"

"We seem ever to be going round and round."

"We can only hope, sir, you shan't become overly giddy of the common thrill of it." Chortles. "Now, sir, at fault for this unexpected interruption of domestic felicity was your conscription into the cause of persuading the heirs of William Penn—Thomas in particular—to pay their fair share of their namesake colony's tax requirements, especially as regards providing for a common defense; am I correct?"

"You are."

"And if you were to fail in this cause, you were to attempt to influence Parliament toward coercing by statute what could not be won by persuasion; also correct?"

Ben noticed now, to no little alarm, that the vitreous circle, yet roiling of a lurid liquor, had grown yet wider such as to encroach yet farther toward where he presently sat.

Adams continued. "Now, sir, by the end of September 1759, two years following your arrival in London, you had brought your business to satisfaction, at least to the extent you judged possible under present or foreseeable circumstances. In fact, although the Penn brothers had not, as expected, proven sympathetic to your petition, the King's Council had"—Adams grinned—"at least on that occasion; correct, sir?"

"As you well know."

"In other words, sir, by the end of September 1759, the balance-pan of civic responsibility had lightened in load to the effect of giving advantage anew to the balance-pan of domestic responsibility; would you tend to agree, sir?"

Ben looked to his thumbs.

"And you being a 'good parent' and 'good husband,' sir, and giving no advice you would not yourself keep, you instructed your servant Peter to pack all your effects, to include, of course, all those letters you had so assiduously preserved, such that you might embark at nearest opportunity for home and hearth; am I correct, sir?"

Ben contrived a steeple of his index fingers, the others remaining clasped.

Adams of a sudden leaned forward, bathing Ben thereby in a sulphurous balm. "In fact, sir, you issued no such instruction, and did not return to home and hearth until three years hence. And the reason you did not, sir? Was it because all the packet ships on the Atlantic had become stricken by Neptunian distempers? Or was it because you had, sir, over the previous two years, subordinated certain interests to certain others, including the very one you would, not a year hence, sir, admonish your Miss Polly against?"

Adams looked to his papers. "'The knowledge of nature may be ornamental, and it may be useful, but if to attain eminence in that we neglect the knowledge and practice of essential duties, we deserve reprehension. For there is no rank in natural knowledge of equal dignity and importance with that of being a good parent, a good child, or good husband or wife.'"

Adams looked hard upon Ben, "Return unto a dull Joggy?—unto a middling Sally?—when there were philosophical adventures to be pursued? Royal appointments to be courted? Land schemes to be conspired? Accolades to be accepted? Country cottages to be visited? Great men to be interviewed? Coffee houses to be frequented? Sojourns to be made?"

Adams straightened. "Oy! Have we run our pen off the sheet, sir?"

Adams taking a step backward, Smith took a step forward.

A string of drool, in likeness to molten glass, was presently elongating from Smith's chin. Smith managing to capture the majority of this with a flourish of hand, he lifted his robe and wiped his hand aside his breeches, these being not plain, as one might expect of a man of the cloth, but brightly blue. Atop Smith's head, Ben noticed, was a pair of billy horns in likeness to those sprouted atop Adams's.

Ungulates of a horn, ever a thorn, Ben mumbled unto himself.

Smith continued as if it were he who had preceded. "On August 24, 1762, sir, three years beyond completion of the business that had compelled you to London, you sailed for Philadelphia, in company with your slave Peter, and him alone, your son having remained behind such that he might attend his nuptials, these to occur eleven days hence. Your other slave, King, had previously severed his shackles that he might seek after the two-fifths of his personhood theretofore denied him; am I correct as to these points, sir?"

Ben looked to the roiling humour in the vitreous circle, drawn to it by an odor that seemed to rival, if not surpass, the noxious emanations from his present examiner.

Smith continued. "Two years hence, sir, you again absented yourself from home and hearth, again to serve the interests of the Pennsylvania Assembly in London, again from your four-room outpost at 7 Craven Street. This tenure, however, instead of incrementing to half a decade, incremented unto a full decade plus one year; am I correct, sir?"

"'Tis difficult not to construe the asking of questions to which the inquisitor must a'ready know the answers with the arranging of a trail of bait unto a snare."

"Or with the giving of a voice unto the two-fifths not yet heard from, sir?"

Ben regarded his thumbs.

Smith continued. "In sum then, sir, betwixt your two tenures in England, you were absent from home and hearth for a total of sixteen years of the eighteen in succession, am I correct?"

Ben held to silence.

"We await your answer, sir, with bated breath."

Hoots.

Smith continued. "As previously established, sir, upon your first removal to England, you took your son William in company with you, he being then twenty-seven years of age, that he might gain the advantages of the experience. I do apologize, sir, for yet another tiresome circling around. Given this magnanimity toward your son, sir, might we assume that, upon your second removal to England, you showed similar magnanimity to your daughter, she being at that time twenty-one years of age?"

Ben glimpsing the clerk staring upon him, he looked to Smith. "She was most desirous toward accompanying me, but her mother forbade it."

"Her mother forbade it, sir?"

Smith uplifted a little his chin and looked to the assembly. "Her mother forbade it!"

Guffaws.

Smith waited upon quiet, then continued. "In fact, sir, Sally not only was greatly desirous toward accompanying you, she expressed sentiments to this effect in the most fervent of terms, did she not?"

"She did."

"And in fact, sir, you held it within your power to use your daughter's desire in league with your own, if not to overcome, certainly to overrule, your dutiful Joan, did you not?"

Ben looked to his thumbs.

"Or would you have us believe, sir, that the greatest negotiator and treaty-maker of his time, perhaps of all time, would not have been able to exercise appropriate flatteries and stratagems to salubrious effect on so fierce an opponent as his Country Joan?"

Ben held to silence.

Smith continued. "Let us try the shoe upon the other foot, sir. Had it been Miss Polly resolving to accompany you—in such case, to Philadelphia—and only her mother's reluctance to stop her, what would have been your resolve in the face of such, not to mention your stratagem?"

Ben contrived his thumbs and fingers unto a symmetry, and looking to the crystalline bench, witnessed the same emerge into being of myriad colorations only then to dissolve away.

Smith continued. "Allow me to supply at least a hint as to the answer that your silence denies us." Smith looked to his papers. "'Dear Polly, I love you more than you can imagine.' 'My dearest child I will call you so; why should I not call you so, since I love you with all the tenderness, all the fondness of a father?'"

Smith looked to Ben. "Indeed, sir, does not all fervor of advocacy derive of such fervor of heart?"

Ben held yet to silence.

Smith continued. "The greater gift to your daughter, however, one might argue, sir, was the one you left behind for her. Do you recall it?" Smith paused, then continued. "You scratched it out, sir, whilst the packet ship taking you to England was stopped at Reedy Island, on November 8, 1764. The circumstances were these: Concerned that enemies you had recently gained might attempt to impugn your reputation in your absence, by holding a glass up to your daughter's every move, you thought it prudent to place Sally on notice concerning such—and thereby flatter her with your deep concern for her welfare. Do you recollect, sir?"

Ben held to silence.

Smith looked to his papers. "'They are enemies and very bitter ones, and you must expect their enmity will extend in some degree to you, so that your slightest indiscretions will be magnified into crimes, in order the more sensibly to wound and afflict me. It is therefore necessary for you to be extreamly circumspect in all your behavior that no advantage may be given to their malevolence.'"

Smith bowed. "It must have been terribly difficult for you, sir, to leave so innocent a child, not yet of a maturity to advantage foreign travels, to fend by her own wits against the perils you so gravely warn her against." Smith stared upon Ben, eyes flashing as if of fired sapphires. Shaking his head, he continued. "You punctuate your general admonition, sir, with a specific measure, to wit: 'Go constantly to church, whoever preaches.'"

Smith leaned forward. "*Go constantly to church*, sir? *Whoever preaches*, sir? Is this an instruction *you* would have received, sir, much less tolerated, in your twenty-second year? In *any* year?"

Gagging to a sulphurous insult, Ben held Bartholomew's pocket linen to mouth and nose.

Smith straightened. "In fact, sir, your daughter had previously expressed to you her intention to end all association with Christ's Church, had she not? And her reason, sir, was it not that the same rector to whom you obliquely refer in your admonishment to her, the 'whoever,' had, on several recent occasions, in impugning your public intentions and private relations, exhibited the same smallness of mind and maliciousness of spirit that had served to turn *you* against dogmatic religion, and at about the same age?"

Ben held to silence, yet holding Bartholomew's linen to mouth and nose.

Smith leaned well forward. "*Dear obedient daughter, I entreat that you sacrifice your daily ease and your Sunday conscience upon the cross of your father's reputation—for without a reputation in America, he can have no influence in England.*"

Ben slumped.

Smith straightened, and upon consulting his papers, continued. "In the spring of 1779, sir, a few months following your appointment as Minister Plenipotentiary to the French Court, you received a favour from your daughter, she now a wife and mother, and into her fourth decade of age, in which she refers to a few items she implores that you send her. Her words, sir." Smith looked to his papers. "'I have taken the liberty of sending a small list to you by Coll Crenis. Mister Bache has sent bills to Jonathan Williams for many things for me and the family, but I have had some other little wants since that time. The minister'— she refers to Monsieur Gèrard, the French envoy in Philadelphia—'was kind enough to offer me some fine white flannel, and has spared me eight yards. I wish to have it in my power to return as good to him, which I beg you will enable me to do. I shall have great pride in wearing any thing you send and shewing it as my Father's taste.'"

Smith looked to Ben. "Now, sir, this request came to you in the wake of General Howe's occupation of Philadelphia and subsequent withdrawal. The Bache home, your home, sir, had been looted and heavily damaged. Shortages continued to worsen, prices to soar." Smith looked to his papers. "'It takes a fortune to feed a family in a very plain way; a pair of gloves 7 dollars, one yard of common gauze 24 dollars.'"

Smith looked to Ben. "But the British were finally gone, and life had begun to return to something akin to normal. Indeed, spirits were elevated." Smith looked to his papers. "'There never was so much dressing and pleasure going on, old friends meeting again, the Whigs in high spirit, and strangers of distinction among us'—the latter being an allusion to General Washington. Do you recollect, sir?"

Ben returned Bartholomew's linen, and amidst doing so glanced upon the clerk. He nodded to Smith.

"And do you recollect your response, sir?"

Ben looked to his thumbs.

"Allow me to refresh your memory." Smith looked to his papers. "'I was charmed with the account you give me of your industry, the tablecloths of your own spinning, etc. but the latter part of the paragraph, that you had sent for linen from France because weaving and flax were grown dear; alas, that dissolved the charm; and your sending for long black pins, and lace, and *feathers*! disgusted me'"—Smith screwed up his face, eliciting chortles from the assembly—"'as much as if you had put salt into my strawberries. The spinning, I see, is laid aside, and you are to be dressed for the ball! You seem not to know, my dear daughter, that of all the dear things in this world, idleness is the dearest, except mischief.'"

Smith intruded close upon. "Salt upon your strawberries, sir? Have we irony here by willful guile or by blind disregard? Indeed, sir, did your daughter have any strawberries about her with which to manufacture a metaphor much less to debauch a sweet cake? Did she have any salt, sir, with which to disappoint the pleasure of a Minister Plenipotentiary afflicted of gout begotten of indulgences knowing no reproof?" Smith looked to his papers. "Here is 'Madam Gout,' sir—or should I say Madam Conscience?—speaking to you by way of your pen: 'Yet, you, instead of gaining an appetite for breakfast, by salutary exercise, you eat an inordinate breakfast, four dishes of tea, with cream, and one or two buttered toasts, with slices of hung beef, which I fancy are not things the most easily digested. Immediately afterwards you sit down to write at your desk.'"

Smith held forward. "Indeed, sir, was it not following one such late-morning repast that you sat your considerable bulk down at your King Louis desk and composed a bitter scold upon your daughter for trans-gressions composed of—of what, sir? Disappointment? A wounded vanity?"

Smith straightened. "Indeed, sir, what might the record suggest upon this point? We have you yet at your King Louis desk, sir, your belly bloated of beef and creamed tea. You break off your scold upon your daughter to bring her news of her son Benny, whom, you mention, you had packed off to Geneva to be made into 'a Presbyterian as well as a Republican,' then, after but a single paragraph of grandfatherly gossip, comes lightning without benefit of an encroaching darkness." Smith looked to his papers. "'When I began to read your account of the high prices of goods—*a pair of gloves 7 dollars, a yard of common gauze 24 dollars, and that it now required a fortune to maintain a family in a very plain way*—I expected you would conclude with telling me that everybody as well as yourself was grown frugal and industrious; and I could scarce believe my eyes in reading forward, that *there never was so much dressing and pleasure going on*; and that you yourself wanted *black pins and feathers from France*, to appear, I suppose in the mode! . . . I therefore send all the articles you desire that are useful and necessary and omit the rest, for as you say you should *have great pride in wearing anything I send and showing it as your father's taste*. I must avoid giving you an opportunity of doing that with either lace or feathers. If you wear your cambric ruffles as I do, and take care not to mend the holes, they will come in time to be lace; and feathers, my girl, may be had in America from every cock's tail.'" Smith looked to Ben. "Including, must one presume, sir, your own?"

Guffaws.

Smith held up a hand as if to implore that the thunder linger a greater interval following upon the flash. "I hold back best for last, as pudding after pork." Smith looked to Ben. "After scolding your 'dear girl' in a manner most demeaning and disrespectful, sir, misrepresenting utterly her desires and intentions, you end your excoriation as follows: 'Write oftener, my dear child, to your loving father.'" Smith leaned for-ward. "'Indeed, sir, would your 'dear child' not be better counseled to fill her belly of broth and chicory and thereupon flog herself unto a righteous purgation?"

A thunder of foot-stomps.

Smith straightened. "We have heard your breakfast, sir, by way of 'Madam Gout.' Here now is your dinner, by way of your maître d'." Smith looked to his papers. "A joint of beef or veal or mutton, followed by fowl or game, with two sweets, two vegetables, pastry, hors d'oeuvres, butter, pickles, radishes, two fruits in winter, four in summer, two compotes, cheese, biscuits, bonbons, and ices twice a week in summer and once in winter."

Smith lifted a sheet that triggered a cascade of other such, these spilling unto the floor and there accumulating. "Your wine cellar, sir, amounting, at the time of your 'loving father' composition unto your 'dear child,' to 1040 bottles—all to be held in store, of course, until such time you might ship them to Philadelphia to fete every patriot who had, by virtue of unflagging Industry and Frugality, survived such deprivation and misery that, although you escaped the teeth and claws of it, held ever constant in mind; am I correct, sir?"

Ben slumped.

Smith looked to his papers. "'If you wear your cambric ruffles as I do, and take care not to mend the holes, they will come in time to be lace; and feathers, my girl, may be had in America from every cock's tail.'"

Ben propped his head in his hands as if to forestall any farther drooping of the former.

Smith continued. "At near the same time, sir, you posted a tease unto your Dear-Polly-I love-you-more-than-you-can-imagine, she in England, you in France, in which you dangled before her the possibility of her becoming adorned of a certain pair of diamond earrings, if a certain lottery ticket, left behind by you, were to turn up a winner. Do you recollect such, sir?"

Ben wiped his face with Bartholomew's linen, and nodded.

"Diamond earrings for your dear Polly, sir, she dwelling in the hum and bustle of London, knowing no material deprivation or discomfort soever, but nary a feather or a pin for your dear Sally, she dwelling in the squalor and despondency of war-ravaged Philadelphia, knowing naught but deprivation and discomfort. Merely an irony of circumstance, sir, or have we here something else altogether?"

Ben again propped his head in his hands.

Smith continued. "In her response to your demeaning judgments of her, sir, your daughter presented to you, point by point, a gentle rebuttal; do you recollect at least the history of this, sir?"

Ben nodded.

"In her rebuttal, sir, your daughter made plain to you what she confessed she had failed to make plain previously, to wit, that she desired no ornamentation beyond what would be fitting for the daughter of Benjamin Franklin, Minister Plenipotentiary, to wear in respect for General Washington, she being summoned unto the latter by formal invitation; and that there had been no cessation of Industry and Frugality in the Bache household soever, neither previous to Howe's sack of the city nor after it; am I correct as to these points, sir?"

Ben nodded.

"And your response, sir?"

"I sent her the remaining items she had previously requested."

"But precisely to *whom*, sir, did you send them—to the girl child you could not, seemingly, other than regard your daughter, or to the thirty-seven-year-old wife and mother your daughter in fact was?" Smith looked to his papers. "'I am glad to hear that weaving work is so hard to get done. 'Tis a sign there is much spinning. All the things you order will be sent, as you continue to be a good girl, and spin and knit your family stockings.'"

Smith looked hard upon Ben. "Indeed, sir, had I not previous knowledge of your daughter being into her thirty-eighth year; and being the mother of three thriving children; and being the mistress of a boldly persevering household; and being servant to your material and social interests in this moment, I could come to no other conclusion, sir, from the extraordinary depths of your condescension, than that you were addressing a child of no greater than seven years."

Smith intruded close upon Ben, eyes flashing as if of blue fire. "Your daughter had no salt with which to smart up the stripes you had inflicted upon her, sir, so you condescended to send her some—*here, my silly little Sally, rub a little of this ready salve into those oozing wounds!*" Smith paused. "Do I err in any regard, *sir*?"

Ben slumped.

Smith straightened. "The bolt of homespun silk; do you recollect it, sir? Your daughter had sent it to you, in company with some squirrel skins, that you might present it, should you approve the gesture, to the French Queen."

Ben nodded.

"Her intention was that it serve as a gift from you, but also—in her words"—Smith looked to his papers—"'to show what can be sent from America to the looms of France,' am I correct, sir?"

Ben nodded.

"Indeed, despite a separation—'estrangement,' sir?—spanning several years, your daughter was well acquainted of your desire for a silk industry for America; am I correct, sir?"

Ben nodded.

"And to forestall any possibility of being overly familiar in this matter, your daughter had gained the blessing of Monsieur Gèrard, the French envoy in Philadelphia, regarding the propriety of making such a gift to the queen; am I correct, sir?"

Ben nodded.

"And your response, sir, as regards your daughter's overture and her etiquette regarding it?"

Ben looked to his thumbs, these showing now a palsy of no one's will indeed but their own.

Smith looked to his papers. "Your words, sir: 'You mention the silk being in a box with squirrel skins, but it is come to hand without them or the box. Perhaps they were spoilt by the salt water and thrown away; for the silk is much damaged and not at all fit to be presented as you propose. Indeed I wonder how having yourself scarce shoes to your feet it would come into your head to give clothes to a queen. I shall see if the stains can be covered by dyeing it and make summer suits of it for myself, Temple and Benny.'"

Leaning closer, Smith well tinted his voice with a mocking sarcasm. "'*Indeed I wonder how having yourself scarce shoes to your feet it would come into your*'—dull, sir?—'*head to give clothes to a queen.*'"

Smith straightened. "How utterly extraordinary. I am one gasp short of swallowing my tongue." Smith again intruded close. "Your daughter makes a magnanimous gesture toward pleasing you, toward winning your approval, by giving you unique means by which to compliment your royal patrons, whilst in simultaneity furthering the interests of the American silk farmer, all in full sympathy to her master's idolatry of Industry and Frugality, and you return the favour, sir, by sending your dull Joggy twin yet another pound of salt by which to inflame the stripes previously etched upon the woman's very soul."

Ben held hands atremble unto his face.

Smith straightened, and upon consulting his papers, continued. "Close upon being chastened for her boldness toward advancing a silk industry in America, sir, your daughter confessed to you her intention to christen her next child, forthcoming, after a French sovereign—the assumption being that you would be most pleased to have a grand-child bearing such a name, you having become, by this date, all but a French sovereign yourself, your face being—as reported by you—'as well-known as that of the moon.' And as icing upon that cake, your daughter invited you to choose a name most pleasing to you." Smith looked to his papers. "Her words, sir: 'The Queen has so many names, one of them will be honour enough. I must beg you to say which will be the most pleasing to you.' Do you recollect this kind and flattering encomium, sir?"

Ben nodded, yet holding tremulous hands unto his face.

Smith intruded yet closer, his exhalations become near as scorching in heat now as in acridity. "And do you recollect your response, sir?"

Ben held to silence.

"Correct, sir! Nary a word, neither of acknowledgment nor of grati-tude. And when, sir, thereafter, your daughter announced that a fifth grandchild had been blessed unto you, a fourth grandson, sir, and had been christened Louis, in honor of your nascent nation's patron saint, what *then* was your response, sir?"

Ben held to silence.

"Correct, sir!" Smith leaned forward. "No cat-o'-nine cuts deeper stripes than that bearing leathers of silence; am I correct, sir?" Straightening, Smith pulled a cat-o'-nine-tails from under his robe, and retiring thereupon two paces, cocked the whip for striking. In the moment of delivery, Bartholomew sprang forth to the effect of taking upon his head and face the full blow of the spiked leathers. Uttering not a sound, Bartholomew crumpled unto his knees.

Smith cocked again his whip.

Lunging from his chair, Ben scrambled upon hands and knees such as to intrude himself betwixt Smith and Bartholomew, and pulling Bartholomew's linen from under the poor man's girding cord, began to minister to his ripped and bleeding face.

"And those stripes delivered upon your daughter, sir?" Smith growled. "Did you fall upon your knees such as to minister to those?"

Ben flinched to discover himself ministering not to Bartholomew but to a young girl, she bearing upon her frock a calligraphy ripped such that the word *Compassion*, in crimson letters, was sundered.

"Thank you, sir," the girl whispered, "for granting me sight with which to see thee, and a voice with which to speak unto thee." The girl held a tremulous hand against Ben's cheek. "The lashes received this day unto yourself, sir, are yet greater than my own. You must endure, sir. You must endure as you have never endured before. All that might have been, all that might yet be, all is in your hands, sir. There is no one else." Withdrawing her hand, the girl bowed her head. When she lifted it, her countenance was returned to that of Bartholomew, it showing a disfigurement of scars now whereat had been oozing stripes.

Clarence helped Bartholomew unto his feet. They together then helped restore Ben to his chair. Smith retiring a step, Adams took a step forward.

The vitreous circle had become so enlarged now, Ben noticed, as to encompass a majority of the area betwixt where he sat and where the crystalline bench stood; and its roiling humour, suggesting of molten glass, was so lurid as to mimic the very embers of hell itself.

Adams, his eyes flashing as if of fired rubies, looked to his papers. "'There is no rank in natural knowledge of equal dignity and importance with that of being a good parent, a good child, or good husband.'" Adams looked to Ben. "A confectionary of sugar plums most sweet, sir, yet held so far aloof, it would seem, as to thwart being brought readily to taste.

"Indeed, sir, are we not faced with a bit of a conundrum here concerning what constitutes a 'good parent?' Your definition by way of your regard toward your daughter Sally would seem at odds with your definition by way of your regard toward your 'daughter' Polly. Perhaps therefore, sir, as regards 'good husband,' you would condescend to move this sugar plum a little closer upon, that we might privilege ourselves to taste of it in the true."

Wedderburn delivered unto Ben in the moment an exemplary rendition, in golden oak, of the mechanical arm Ben had invented for retrieving items, books and the like, from high shelves. Spinning upon his heels, Wedderburn thereupon returned to his seat.

Adams continued. "Now, sir, if you would be so kind as to pluck from upon high, for taste, that sugar plum that is a 'good husband,' we would be most grateful. Be he the husband, sir, who absents himself from his family for five years, returns for two, absents himself for ten more? Be he the husband, sir, who, shall we say, 'misplaces' five years accumulation of his dutiful wife's accounts of domestic relations? Be he the husband, sir, who caricatures his unlettered but headstrong wife in terms of 'bumpkin' and 'shrew?' Or—be he the husband, sir, who orders a grand house to be built and leaves the burden of its furnishment to a spouse judged by him as requiring close scrutiny, lest indeed her taste should supplant his own?"

Ben marveled at the ingenuity of the device presently astride his lap—at the ability indeed of five pounds of raw meat not so much to contrive it, as to conceive it.

Adams consulted his papers and looked again to Ben. "Previous to embarking on your second mission to London, sir, in October of 1764, you contracted with a Mr. Rhodes, a friend to you, to have a house built on the south side of Market Street, betwixt Third and Fourth, to be 34-feet by 34-feet square, red brick, three rooms each floor, three floors, kitchen in the basement; am I correct, sir?"

Ben nodded, his eyes yet affixed upon the mechanical fetching device.

"And the location of this domicile, sir, was but a few steps from the doorway in which Deborah Read, to become your common-law wife, was standing when you first laid eyes upon her, just prior to your purchase of three large buns almost as large as Boston loaves with which to fill an empty stomach; also correct, sir?"

Ben nodded.

"Now, sir, in regard to the construction and furnishment of this three-story domicile, you insisted upon serving, from a distance measured in miles at three thousand, in time at eight weeks, as your wife's overseer, and through her, as Mr. Rhode's director; am I correct?"

"I provided such prudent and essential direction as I was able."

"Indeed." Adams looked to his papers. "Your words, sir: 'I could have wished to have been present at the finishing of the kitchen, as it is a mere machine and, being new to you, I think you will scarce know how to work it, the several contrivances to carry off steam and smell and smoke not being fully explained to you. The oven I suppose was put up by the written instructions in my former letter. You mention nothing of the furnace. If that iron one is not set, let it alone until my return, when I shall bring a more convenient copper one.' 'I am much obliged to my good old friends that did me the honour to remember me in the unfinished kitchin. I hope soon to drink with them in the parlour.'"

Adams looked to Ben. "Now, sir, given that the kitchen you had ordered into your basement was so encumbered with novelty that your Joan would not likely be able to work it without proper instruction, should we not inquire as to what recourse you foresaw for your wife's comfort and convenience until such time as you could give her that instruction? Where might we look for such consideration, sir, amongst your various discourses on domestic husbandry?"

Ben held to silence.

Adams continued. "'The oven I *suppose* was put up by the written instructions.' 'You mention *nothing* of the furnace.' Do we detect here, sir, in your semantical selections and intonations, little hints of pique? Little slaps upon the wrist, sir, for your Joggy having failed to address a more comprehensive inventory of your ever gnawing anxieties?

"'Let it alone until my return.' 'I hope soon to drink with them in the parlour.' "Do we detect here, sir, at least intimations of an imminent return, the very return indeed that had become as essential to your abandoned Joan as sustenance itself? Yet, you allow them these intimations, sir, in June of 1765, when you were deeply embroiled in Stamp Act tumult and well knew you would not be carrying any copper pots unto Philadelphia anytime soon; am I correct as to this point, sir?"

Ben held to silence.

Adams looked to his papers, and then continued. "The blue room, sir. You sent materials to your Joan that were to be fashioned into window dressings, along with instructions on how they were to be cut and hung. Do you recollect, sir?"

Ben nodded.

Adams looked to his papers. "'The blue mohair stuff is for the curtains of the blue chamber. The fashion is to make one curtain only for each window. Hooks are sent to fix the rails at top, so that they may be taken down on occasion.'"

Adams looked to Ben. "In other words, *these* will be the dressings, my Country Joan, and *this* is how you will hang them." Adams stared hard a moment, and then looked to his papers. "'I suppose the blue room is too blue, the wood being of the same colour with the paper, and so looks too dark. I would have you finish it as soon as you can, thus: Paint the wainscot a dead white; paper the walls blue, and tack the gilt border round just above the surbase and under the cornish. If the paper is not equal coloured when pasted on, let it be brushed over again with the same colour, and let the papier machée musical figures be tacked to the middle of the ceiling; when this is done, I think it will look very well.'"

Adams looked to Ben. "Indeed, only *your* taste, only *your* sensibility, only *your* judgment were to serve as compass regarding the ornamentation and furnishment of *your* house, am I correct, sir? Or do I paint with too broad a brush?"

Adams looked to his papers. Smith stepped forth and looked to his.

Adams: "'You mention the payment of the 500 pounds, but do not say that you have got the deeds executed. I suppose however that it was done.'"

Smith: "'I received the two Post Office letters you sent me. It was not letters of that sort alone that I wanted; but all such as were sent to me from anyone whomsoever.'"

Adams: "'The well I expected would have been dug in the winter, or early in the spring; but I hear *nothing* of it.'"

Smith: "'You should never be without tubs sufficient in the area to catch the rain water; for if it overflows there often, it may occasion the foundation to settle, and hurt the wall.'"

Adams: "'I almost wish I had left directions not to paint the house till my return. But I suppose 'tis done before this time.'"

Smith: "'As to oiling the floors, it may be omitted till I return: which will not be till next spring. I need not tell you to take great care of your fires.'"

Smith stepped back.

Adams continued. "In fairness, sir, we must here note that you did indeed bless your Joggy's decision to purchase, without license from London, the property adjacent to your new domicile, whilst it yet lay available." Adams looked to his papers. "'I think you have done very well to buy the lot you mention, though you have indeed given a great price for it.'" Adams leaned forward. "'*Though you have indeed given a great price for it.*' To keep a good servant good, keep her ever agitated; quite so, sir?"

Adams looked to the assembly. "Aye, sir, but to what end? As, for every camel, there is one straw more that will break its back, is there not, for every servant, one reproof more that will break her spirit?" Adams looked to his papers. "'There is great odds between a man's being at home and abroad as everybody is afraid they shall do wrong so everything is left undone.' 'All these things are become quite indifferent to me at this time.'"

Adams leaned forward. "Could you not *hear* the agony in this woman's lament, sir? Could you not *feel* the despair in this woman's capitulation?" Adams looked to the assembly. "Aye, but this was not the agony of Captain Jones watching his beloved *Bonhomme* sink in consequence to gaining a great victory, was it, sir? This was but the ache of a Joggy Joan watching too few tubs overflow of too much drip."

Adams looked to Ben: "And yet, sir, what judgment might the good

Captain himself have passed upon the character of a certain woman under siege, abandoned by all of the masculine sex who might defend her, on the night of September 16, 1765?"

Ben held to silence.

Adams continued. "The circumstances, as you were apprised of them several weeks hence, from afar, were these: In becoming estranged, by an insidious creep of disconnection, from the very interests you had been sent to London to represent, sir, you had so far progressed toward accepting the impositions and coercions of the infamous Stamp Act that you had procured for a personal friend, one John Hughes, the position of collector for Pennsylvania. This news reaching your enemies, rumors began to abound of your being a profiting conspirator in the Act itself. One night of frenzy in this regard, whilst yet you slept in your London bed, a mob was agitated to such a fever in Philadelphia as to threaten the sanctity of your new home on Market Street, and everything in it, including your precious papers and books, your mechanical kitchen, your mohair curtains, your gilt surbase, and your yet un-oiled floors, not to mention the dutiful overseer of tubs herself. Do you recollect, sir?"

Ben nodded, eyes affixed upon the mechanical retrieving arm yet resting across the arms of his chair.

"In fact, sir, the only militia availing itself that night toward confronting this mob was the overseer of tubs herself, assisted by one diffident cousin and one dutiful brother, they present only because your Joan, your uncommissioned Joggy, sir, steadfastly refused, despite ardent urgings to the contrary, to leave *your* house, *your* books, *your* papers, *your* kitchen, *your* mohair, *your* gilt, *your* floors. In fact, sir, your Joan ordered guns into the house, transformed an interior room into a magazine, and made—her words, sir—'some sort of defense upstairs such as I could manage myself.' Indeed, sir, your Joan of Arc made preparation toward, when the moment should come, issuing fusillades of musket fire from a make-shift redoubt, window to window, until King George himself should, quivering in his drawers, suffer to strike his colors."

Adams leaned close upon Ben, his eyes flashing crimson. "A fortress armed, sir, a fortress protected, sir, a fortress preserved, sir, without a single imperative from the lord and master, without a single showing from the ranks of the lord and master's militia"—Adams straightened—"until, that is, the following day, when your allies, being shamed by your Joan's bold defence, made bold declaration that whosoever should pull down *Mrs.* Franklin's house should have his own pulled down in return."

Adams again intruded closer. "Could the brash Captain Jones himself, sir, have fashioned a greater victory of a defeat as imminently certain?" Lifting his robe, exposing thereby a pair of scarlet breeches, Adams produced a carpenter's stick and tossed this article onto Ben's lap. "When taking fair measure, sir, should not the instrument be proper to the task?" Ben about to take the rule into hand, Adams snatched it into his, and sundering it over his knee, tossed the pieces into the cauldron of roiling humour behind, likewise then the mechanical fetching device.

As the pieces of rule and arm began to dissolve, like icicles afloat in a vat of boiling silver, the clerk sprang to his feet. "Double, double toil and trouble; fire burn, and caldron bubble."

The clerk sat down.

Adams took a step backward, to the oblique, such as to avoid befalling the fate of the disappeared rule and fetching arm; in simultaneity, Smith took a step forward.

"On November 25, 1762, sir," Smith began, "you having returned to Philadelphia, your son having remained in London, you wrote a brief letter to your sister Jane in Boston concerning an inquiry made by her regarding recent events in your son's life; to wit: his appointment to the Royal Governorship of New Jersey and his marriage to Elizabeth Downes."

Smith looked to his papers. "'As to the promotion and marriage you mention, I shall now only say that the lady is of so amiable a character that the latter gives me more pleasure than the former, though I have no doubt but that he will make as good a Governor as husband, for he has good principles and good dispositions, and I think is not deficient in good understanding.'" Smith looked to Ben. "Have you recollection, sir?"

Ben nodded.

"Pray tell us, sir, have we in these sentiments the same 'good parent' who had, but three months previous, abandoned London within a fortnight of the very wedding at cause to giving him 'more pleasure than the other,' 'the other' being your son's appointment to high office? Or have we here, sir, the author of one truth for public notice, another for private embrace?"

Ben gazed upon the lurid boil encroaching ever closer to foot and shuddered.

Smith continued. "On August 9, 1765, sir, three years hence, in the heat of the Stamp Act kerfuffle, you sent a set of resolves to your friend

John Hughes at Philadelphia, you at this time being returned to London. Previously, you had procured for Mr. Hughes the profitable position of stamp distributor for Pennsylvania—to end indeed of near costing the man his life. Your remarks to Mr. Hughes on this occasion were stimulated in large measure by the Virginia Resolves of May 29th, which you had recently received in London."

Smith looked to his papers. "'Your acting with coolness and steadiness, and with every circumstance in your power of favour to the people, will by degrees reconcile them. In the meantime, a firm loyalty to the Crown and faithful adherence to the government of this nation, which it is the safety as well as honour of the colonies to be connected with, will always be the wisest course for you and I to take whatever may be the madness of the populace or their blind leaders, who can only bring themselves and country into trouble and draw on greater burdens by acts of rebellious tendency.'"

Smith looked to Ben, his eyes flashing as if of fired sapphires. "'A firm loyalty to the Crown.' A 'faithful adherence to the government of this nation.' The 'honour of the colonies to be connected with.' These are your words, sir, but could they not as readily have been writ by your son, the Royal Governor of New Jersey, not only at present, but equally so a decade hence?"

Ben looked to his thumbs.

Smith continued. "Nine years hence, sir, when your son suggested to you, by favour dated July 3, 1774, that the Bostonians responsible for the Boston Tea Party should make appropriate reparations; that is"— Smith looked to his papers—"'should do justice before they'—'they' being 'the government of this nation'—'ask it'—you scolded him most severely, by way of likening him to a moral chameleon." Smith looked to his papers. "'You who are a thorough courtier, see everything with government eyes.'" Smith looked to Ben. "This was on September 7, 1774. Five months previous, sir, on March 22, 1774, you wrote to your friend Thomas Cushing of Boston as follows." Smith looked to his papers. "'I cannot but hope that the affair of the tea will have been considered in the Assembly before this time, and satisfaction proposed if not made; for such a step will remove much of the prejudice now entertained against us, and put us again on a fair footing in contending for our old privileges as occasion may require.'"

Smith looked to Ben. "In truth, sir, had not your son, in his favour of July 3rd, expressed the very same sentiments as regards just reparations that his father had expressed three months previous, and toward the same end—to wit, preservation of a felicitous bond between the mother hen and her brood of head-strong chicks?"

Ben held to silence.

Smith continued. "Indeed, do we not have something of a conundrum here, sir? If on September 7th, your son, in his advocacy of making *just reparations*, was but a boot-licking government man, 'a thorough courtier,' sir, what then on the previous March, on the 22nd of that month to be precise, were *you*, sir, in your advocacy of offering *satisfactory reparations*?"

Ben slumped.

Smith continued. "On September 14, 1767, sir, upon your first travel to Paris, in company with your good friend Sir John Pringle, the attending physician to the English queen, you wrote to your beloved Polly concerning your experience of commingling with the French king and queen." Smith looked to his papers. "'The king talked a good deal to Sir John, asking many questions about our royal family; and did me too the honour of taking some notice of me; that's saying enough, for I would not have you think me so much pleased with this king and queen as to have a whit less regard than I . . . have for ours. No Frenchman shall go beyond me in thinking my own king and queen the very best in the world and the most amiable.'"

Smith looked to Ben "'*My* own king and queen.' '*The* very best in the world.' '*The* most amiable.' You were here making reference, I feel obliged to remind you, sir, to no other than King George III, the very 'tyrant' indeed whom you and Mr. Jefferson, with no little assistance from my esteemed colleague"—Smith bowed toward Adams, Adams returning the favour—"would vilify but a few years hence, for twenty-eight 'injuries and usurpations, all having in direct object the establishment of an absolute tyranny'—all twenty-eight being either actively unfolding or a'ready unfolded at the very moment you declared *your* king and queen to be '*the* very best in the world and *the* most amiable.'"

Smith looked to his papers. "On May 14, 1768, sir, you wrote to your friend John Ross, in response to an incident occurring in London, in which a mob had been excited into acts of mutiny by a rabble rouser named John Wilkes, whom the king wished to prevent, by any expediency, from sitting in the House of Commons, whereat he might greatly multiply his mischief." Smith looked to his papers. "'Some punishment seems preparing for a people who are ungratefully abusing the best constitution and the best king any nation was ever blessed with.'" Smith looked to Ben. "'The best constitution,' sir? 'The best king any nation was ever blessed with,' sir?"

Ben contrived a prop for his head fashioned of fingers.

Smith continued. "Even as late as September 3, 1774, sir, seven months after my other esteemed colleague here present"—Smith bowed toward Wedderburn, Wedderburn returning the favour—"made certain challenges to your character before the Privy Council, even *then*, sir, you were yet thoroughly 'a government man,' yet holding close the ambition, in consonance with your son, sitting in New Jersey, that the colonies might yet be preserved to the Empire. Indeed, on this very date, sir, in response to learning of the convening of the First Continental Congress, you wrote to your friend Cushing in Boston as follows." Smith looked to his papers. "'All who know well the state of things here agree that if the non-consumption agreement should become general and be firmly adhered to, this ministry must be ruined, and our friends succeed them, from whom we may hope a great constitutional charter to be confirmed by King, Lords, and Commons, whereby our liberties shall be recognized and established as the only sure foundation of that union so necessary for our common welfare.'"

Smith looked to Ben. "'That *union* so *necessary* for our *common* welfare.'" Smith intruded close upon Ben's left ear. "Was not this same sentiment held, sir, in the very moment, by one William Franklin, Royal Governor of New Jersey? And was not this sentiment held by him, sir, of the same 'good understanding,' the same 'good principles,' the same 'good dispositions,' as owing to the author of the words just read you?"

Ben moaned.

Smith leaned closer upon Ben's ear. "Compassion, sir, requires understanding; understanding, sir, knowledge; knowledge, sir, a willingness to look at the whole of a truth, not just those fragments and pieces of such that are expedient to servicing one's petty grievances or false pride. Would you not be inclined to agree, sir?"

Ben nodded, his head yet propped by a scaffolding of fingers.

Smith held close upon Ben's ear. "'Tis a great wonder, is it not, sir, that a man of philosophic inquiry, of reason, sir, could pay so little heed to so fundamental a law? That a leading luminary of the Enlightenment itself could damn his own son, his own flesh and blood, to an agony of eternal estrangement for being true to his own 'good understanding,' his own 'good principles,' his own 'good dispositions?' That a man of liberty, sir, the very one who 'snatched the lightning from heaven and the sceptre from tyrants,' could suffer to wear the mantle of *Pater Patriae* whilst in simultaneity attempting to exercise a prideful will over the sacred sovereignty of his own son?"

Ben groaned.

Smith continued. "As consequence to his disobedience against your will, sir, your son was arrested and imprisoned in a Connecticut jail, leaving thereby his wife Elizabeth, 'so amiable a character,' without, in her words, 'a friend or protector.' Growing ever more frightened concerning her fate, and that of her husband, Elizabeth turned to the one man she knew could save them both." Smith looked to his papers. "'I will not distress you by enumerating all my afflictions, but allow me, Dear Sir, to mention that it is greatly in your power to relieve them. Suppose that Mister Franklin would sign a parole not dishonourable to himself, and satisfactory to Governor Trumbull; why may he not be permitted to return into his province and to his family? Many of the other officers that have been taken during the war have had that indulgence shown them, and why should it be denied him? Consider my dear and honored sir that I am now pleading the cause of your son, and my beloved husband. If I have said or done anything wrong I beg to be forgiven. I am with great respect, honored sir, your dutiful and affectionate daughter.'"

Smith looked to Ben. "And your response, sir, to this pathetic supplication? Was it to seek compassionate means by which to return husband and wife unto a felicitous reunion—perhaps even unto salutary end of keeping the husband quiescent by keeping him domestic?" Smith leaned closer upon Ben's ear. "Or was your response, sir, to lure the Petitioner's stepson, William Temple, away from her, such as to steal him to Paris with you?" Smith looked to his papers. "'Methinks it is rather some merit that I have rescued a valuable young man from the danger of being a Tory.'" Smith looked to Ben. "Who might have conceived, sir, that a West Indian art of no reputation—prick the wife such as to wound the husband—might be so wantonly effective in the hands of someone so utterly unpracticed in it?"

Smith intruded closer upon Ben's ear. "Aye, but the best prick was yet to come, was it not, sir? Indeed, whilst your son languished at Litchfield, was he not apprised that his beloved Elizabeth had taken gravely ill and was slipping rapidly toward an untimely end? And did he not thereupon, sir, petition Congress for a parole of sufficient duration that he might travel to New York to bring what comfort he might to his wife and thereby to himself? And did not General Washington, sir, a man natural to justice, recommend swift approval? And did not your friends in Congress thereupon conspire to allow your son's petition to hold the middle position in a pile of petty concerns until such time its urgency should have expired in concert with its necessity?"

Smith straightened. "And as a result, sir, was not Elizabeth, 'so amiable a character,' condemned to breathe her last in an alien city, in an alien land, 'without a friend or protector' to stand vigil? Was not your son, sir, condemned to witness his wife's death in but his imagination, hence not one time, but a thousand times over, a thousand thousand, with each vision being yet more tormenting of mind, poisoning of soul, sir, than the previous?"

Smith intruded closer upon Ben's ear. "Does it yet remain a mystery to you, sir, as to why your son, once paroled, instead of removing to England, remained in harm's way, indeed that he might sponsor barbarous acts against his enemies? Are you yet so impoverished of imagination, sir, as to be unable to place your son's actions into a context larger than the history of themselves alone? Can it possibly be, sir, that, even now, you are so blinkered in perception as to be unable to see in your son's cruelties the very specter of your own?"

Spinning half-circle around, Smith swept an arm toward the high bench. "Behold, sir, the profit owing to the venging heart!"

In the instant, a scene formed within the crystalline bench in which a woman was lying on a trundle in a room furnished of but few articles—a washstand, a straight chair, a portrait of George II, and little else. Gripped of a paroxysm of ominous violence, the woman, gaunt in cheek, sallow in complexion, rolled to one side, and straining to lift a tremulous head, retched as if a slurry of coal-tar into a washbowl resting upon an uncarpeted floor. Collapsing her head then onto a folded coverlet, serving as pillow, the woman, eyes closed, breathed in labored rasps. A leakage of blood shown below each nostril.

Feeling loosed from his seat, Ben attempted to find purchase on the floor with his heels, and of a sudden discovered himself sitting in the chair next to Elizabeth's bed. The air, insufferably warm, reeked as if of aging cheese.

Her eyes of a sudden opened, Elizabeth struggled to lift her head. "Is that you, Billy?" She choked. "Have you come to me?" She wept. "O, Billy! Billy!" She dropped her head. "O, Billy! O, Billy!"

Ben tried to speak, but his lips would not part. He tried to find Elizabeth's hand, but his own would not move.

Again Elizabeth struggled to lift her head. "O, Billy! Hold me! O, Billy! Please!"

Ben chafed at tethers of no material substance binding him indeed as if to "a little vengeance."

His arms and jaw trembled. His eyes filled.

Elizabeth dropped her head, and drawing in a slow, rasping breath, was still a moment. Drawing in another slow, rasping breath, she was still.

Ben closed his eyes. "O, what have I done?"

"What have you done, sir?"

Ben opened his eyes to discover himself returned to his seat.

Smith leaned close upon him. "Why, you 'have rescued a valuable young man from the danger of being a Tory, have you not, sir?'"

Hoots, guffaws, foot stomps.

Whilst the tumult continued, Smith took a step to side; Adams, in simultaneity, took a step closer. Adams stood silent then, showing a countenance become so hideous as to represent as if a burlesque of itself, until the hum emanant from the three radiances atop the crystalline bench became the only sound.

"In a letter to you dated June 4, 1769," Adams began, "this being in the fifth year of your second tenure as Pennsylvania agent in London, you were apprised that an indisposition suffered by your wife the previous winter had been far graver in both injury and consequence than heretofore you had allowed yourself to conceive. Do you recollect, sir?"

Ben nodded.

"I quote Dr. Bond's words on the matter." Adams looked to his papers. "'Your good Mrs. Franklin was affected with a partial palsy in the tongue and a sudden loss of memory, which alarmed us much, but she soon recovered from them, though her constitution in general appears impaired. These are bad symptoms in advanced life and augur danger of further injury on the nervous system.'" Adams looked to Ben. "'Her constitution in general appears impaired.' 'Bad symptoms in advanced life augur danger of further injury on the nervous system.'" Adams leaned closer. "And your response, sir, to these ominous indications?"

Ben glanced upon the clerk, and finding him slumped in the moment, felt no little alarm, and looked to Adams: "I sought the opinion of Sir John."

"You refer to Dr. Pringle, the queen's physician, am I correct?"

Ben nodded. "I sought his opinion at earliest opportunity, and being delivered of it, forwarded it to my wife at soonest opportunity."

"Toward what purpose, sir? Was Dr. Bond so unpracticed in the medical arts as to require intervention by a counterpart who could have no opportunity to form an opinion upon evidence of his own gathering? Indeed, sir, for what good reason might you forward an untimely and likely redundant opinion to your stricken and imperiled wife in the stead of your beloved self?"

Adams leaned closer. "In truth, sir, in the moment you learned of the gravity of your wife's indisposition, were you not much beguiled by two prospects of equal excitation—the one being the Ohio land purchase you had been scheming in partnership with your yet-to-be-branded 'courtier' son; the other being a government appointment befitting your much-accumulated merit? Hence, were you to remove to Philadelphia at this time, to serve as your wife's friend and protector, would you not have had to abandon all hope of consummating the Ohio land purchase; all hope of securing the appointment to higher office?" Adams leaned yet closer. "Or do we attempt to weave unto whole cloth here too much by way of warp, too little by way of weft?"

Ben held to silence.

Adams continued. "Might indeed it have been the case, sir, that as once you had been too preoccupied with practical matters to ensure that a fragile boy be inoculated, you were now too preoccupied with practical matters to deliver unto a sinking wife the comfort she not only deserved from you, but that represented your solemn duty unto her?"

Ben, bowing his head, moaned as if to a pinch of stone.

Adams continued. "On November 20th of this same year, sir, your wife, having recently received Sir John's opinion, commenced a letter that would require of her a week's struggle to complete, such were the infirmities she now had to overcome in order to greet you by the only means availing to her. She began her favour, sir, by graciously acknowledging Sir John's opinion. She thereupon attempted to apprise you, in pieces and fragments of linguistic torture that seemed to writhe like sundered worms, of her own opinion as to the nature and cause of her indisposition: Close upon the incidence of her affliction, she explained, she had been burdened with the care of two sick women—one being her cousin Debby, the other being the wife of your nephew Benny. These burdens had themselves come close upon her having received from you yet another postponement as regards your return home." Adams looked to his papers. "Her words, sir: 'This added to my distress at your staying so much longer that I lost all my resolution. Both Sally and myself live so very lonely that I got in so very low a strait and got into so unhappy a way that I could not sleep a long time.'"

Adams looked to Ben. "A few lines hence, sir, your wife circles back to trod the same ground, such was her desperation to employ to effect a facility, never strong in her, that seemed now all but lost to her." Adams looked to his papers. "'I am in hopes I shall get better again to see you. I often tell friends I was not sick. I was only unable to bear any more and so I fell down and could not get up. Indeed, it was not any sickness but too much disquiet of mind, but I had taken up a resolution never to make any complaint to you or give you any distress.'" Adams looked to Ben. "'Too much disquiet of mind.' 'I was only unable to bear any more.' 'And so I fell down and could not get up.'" Adams looked to Ben. "And your response, sir?"

Ben shuddered to vision of a woman, eyes wide and uncomprehending, as those of a child awakened from one darkness to discover herself in another, trying to shield herself with striped hands and arms.

Adams continued. "Your wife manages by heroic effort, sir, to squeeze upon paper the few drops of hope yet wetting the pulp of her soul, that you might bear witness and take pity, and you respond, sir, with not a line—not a line of comfort, not a line of solicitude, not a line even of curiosity." Adams looked to his papers. "'My distress at your staying so much longer that I lost all my resolution.' 'I was unable to bear any more and so I fell down and could not get up.'"

Adams intruded yet closer, his eyes flashing as if of fired rubies. "'Where was the manly hand, sir, that would lift this woman up from the depths of despair? Where was the manly heart, sir, that would bring this woman the only happiness ever she hoped after? Where was the 'good husband,' sir, that would meet duty with duty, loyalty with loyalty, grace with grace?" Adams thrust his hideous countenance yet closer, Ben cringing in reflex against the backside of his seat. "*Where*, sir?" Straightening then, Adams took a step to side whilst Smith in simultaneity took a step closer.

"When, sir," Smith began, allowing no accumulation of pause, "you rescued that 'valuable young man from the danger of being a Tory,' this by stealing him off to France with you, at age sixteen, it was your intention that he receive there a proper education, that he might possess both the compass and the means by which to pursue an honorable livelihood; am I correct, sir?"

Ben nodded.

"Might we presume then, sir, that the proper education you intended for your grandson was, in essence, the same as recommended by Richard Saunders in his *Almanack* of 1753, to wit"—Smith looked to his papers—"'Virtue and a trade are a child's best portion?'"

Ben nodded, eyes cast downward.

"Would you be so kind, sir, as to acquaint us with the name of one of the masters under whose tutelage you placed your grandson during the eight years he was under your supervision in France?"

Ben slumped.

"Are we to infer from your wilt, sir, that you were able to discover in all of France, in all of the European continent, sir, not one master suitable for acquainting your grandson with such virtues as were 'necessary or desirable?'"

Ben groaned.

"Are we to infer, sir, that you were able to discover in all of France, in all of the European continent, sir, not one tradesman to whom you might indenture your grandson that he might acquire a practical skill?"

Ben remained well slumped.

"In fact, sir, in lieu of enrolling Temple into the same school or similar into which you enrolled your younger grandson, Benny; in lieu of indenturing Temple to the same or similar master to whom you subsequently indentured Benny; you appointed Temple to serve as your secretary, not of any particular merit or interest on his part, but because he was your grandson, was of sufficient age and facility, and was ready clay in your hands; do I state the truth, sir?"

Ben held to silence, shaking his head.

"Indeed, in lieu of securing unto this 'valuable young man' a 'best portion,' you dandified him in Parisian finery, as might a girl-child her doll; you led him from parlour to parlour in likeness to Madame Helvetius parading her poodle; you encouraged flower and affect in his French; you turned a blind eye to his ever-increasing indiscretions, including impregnation of the wife of a neighbor at Passy; you even had him included in the signing of the Treaty of Paris, when no such honor was due or deserved to so low a functionary. Do I err in any regard, sir?"

Smith intruded closer. "In truth, sir, it was not securing 'a child's best portion' you held foremost in mind for this 'valuable young man,' but molding him into a close likeness of yourself; was it not, sir? Indeed, whereas you had failed, and miserably so, to mold the boy's father into such a likeness, by error of loosing him too freely unto the influence of others, you would succeed with the son, by holding him close, indeed as planet unto sun."

Smith straightened. "Ay, and what better way to *mold* clay into a desired form than to have the clay *imitate* the form. Indeed, sir, was this not the very philosophy that counseled you to require Temple to copy every line of your correspondence in close likeness to your own hand? Indeed, by imitating you in form, sir, would your ward not thereby, through an alchemy perhaps akin to that rendering stone into toad, seaweed into crab, come to imitate the master himself?"

Smith pulled a sheet from his papers and intruded it in front of Ben's downcast eyes. "Identify, if you would be so kind, sir, the author for whom the hand demonstrated on this sheet is uniquely his own."

Ben fixed his eyes on the sheet, then looked to Smith. "The hand, as the substance, is my own." Smith showed Ben a second sheet being in appearance as if the first sheet shown a second time. "And the hand upon this sheet, sir?"

"The same as just shown."

"One sheet bears the template, sir—no pun intended—the other bears the imitation." Smith held both sheets before Ben, side to side, so that Ben might make comparison. "You cannot choose the one from the other?"

Ben looked from sheet to sheet, and shook his head.

"The first sheet shown you, sir, bears the imitation"—Smith removed the second sheet from in front of Ben—"as rendered by your grandson, in his fifth year of service to you. The second sheet, sir"—Smith removed the first sheet, and held forth again the second—"bears the original, as rendered by yourself. It would thus appear, sir, as at least regards the symbols that represent substance, your experiment in transformation by way of imitation was of notable success. But what, sir, of substance—the 'good principles,' the 'good understanding' the 'good dispositions' that are the very pillars of substance?"

Ben held to silence.

"When, sir, my esteemed colleague here present"—Smith bowed toward Adams—"was newly arrived in France to join the commission, he enrolled his eldest son, John Quincy, into the same pension school into which you had previously enrolled Benny. In fact, he did so upon your counsel. Do you recollect, sir?"

Ben nodded.

"Now, sir, even though you subsequently saw fit to remove Benny from this school, such as to enroll him in a similar such in Geneva, to be raised there 'a Presbyterian and a Republican,' you were of the mind, as demonstrated by your counsel to Mr. Adams, that the school in Passy was at least adequate such as to acquaint young minds with the 'necessary or desirable' virtues; am I correct as to this point, sir?"

Ben looked to the clerk, and discovering him as if a schoolmaster gazing upon an obdurate ward, nodded.

"Now, it may be of some interest to you, sir, to learn that John Quincy, in large measure by merit of the schooling he received at the Passy school, as well as at subsequent venues, was appointed to serve as minister to the court of St. Petersburg, indeed by your good friend Jefferson, and subsequently appointed, indeed by the good people you so beneficently helped to enfranchise, to serve as President of the United States. And Benny, whom you arranged to be schooled in Geneva, and thereafter to be apprenticed into the printing trade, subsequently took your place in Philadelphia as both printer and editor." Smith leaned forward. "And Temple, sir? Where might speculation lead you to place your secretary, sir, subsequent to your close influence upon him? Alas, the very question would appear to suggest the answer, would it not?"

Smith looked to his papers, and then continued. "Within the year following your death, sir, your secretary had abandoned the farm you hoped would transform him from the powdered dandy you had made of him unto the gentleman farmer you would have him become. Also within the year, sir, your secretary had sold the entirety of your library, which, along with your manuscripts and papers, you had bequeathed unto him in the stead of your daughter or any of her children. As regards the manuscripts and papers themselves, sir, preserved by you with such care, certain letters from a certain party excepted, your grandson consigned the bulk of these of such careless consideration that many were misused or lost. Even those he kept unto himself he took no pains soever toward preserving unto posterity.

"Being a stranger unto both his family and his country, having had little previous intimacy with either, your secretary removed himself to England, such as to be restored to his father's company, and there fathered a second daughter out of wedlock, unto the sister indeed of his father's second wife, and soon thereafter abandoned both the mother and the child, thereby consigning the child, Ellen, to your son's care, as heretofore mentioned.

"Never to return to America, nor to England, your 'valuable young man' spent the remainder of his life in France, in various states of lassitude and dissipation, causing his father to lament that his son was 'more trouble of mind than I ever before experienced'—this coming in curious emulation to a preceding lament, perhaps of some familiarity to you, sir; to wit: 'Nothing has ever hurt me so much.'"

Smith intruded closer. "In truth, sir, was not Madame Helvetius's pooch better off for having a waist doily in lieu of its dignity than your grandson was for having your likeness of hand in lieu of his own 'best portion?'"

Ben startled to a tumultuous upwelling within the cauldron to front, wherein hideous apparitions appeared, each showing a multitude of tentacle-like arms. Ben gagged to a sickening assault of odor suggesting of slaughterhouse offal. As the boil of humour to center of the cauldron carried these gorgon verisimilitudes toward the perimeter, they of a sudden submerged as if by force of an oppositional flow, their curious appendages flailing about as if for victims to carry unto an unspeakable fate.

Smith took a step to side. Adams stepped closer.

⌒⋎⌒

"On May 1, 1771, sir," Adams began, "two years following your wife's 'indisposition,' seven years following your abandonment of her, you wrote to her in response to discovering she had 'pinched' £30 from your partner David Hall such that she might remit a bill in this amount to you; do you recollect the incident, sir?"

Ben held to silence.

Adams continued. "The circumstances, sir, were as follows. Correct me, kindly, if I err in any regard: Your Country Joan, sir, feeling compelled to send you periodic remittances of £30 in demonstration of her continuing in Industry and Frugality to your favour, but having incurred more debt in the current month than usual, had made a request of £30 from your friends John and Thomas Foxcroft, in whom you had vested the responsibility of meting out your wife's monthly allowance. The £30 requested by her was in addition to her regular allowance of £30. The brothers Foxcroft had refused her request giving no explanation, thereby considerably vexing her, which vexation she confessed to you in the same letter containing a bill for £30.

"In your reply of May 1st, sir, you confessed to your wife that you had instructed the Foxcrofts to limit her allowance to no greater than £30 per month"—Adams looked to his papers—"'for the sake of our more easily settling, and to prevent mistakes.'" Adams looked to Ben. "Which is as specious a statement as was ever uttered by any son of Eve, would you not be inclined to agree, sir?" Adams shook his head, and then continued. "You thereupon added as follows." Adams looked to his papers.

"'I know you were not very attentive to money-matters in your best days, and I apprehend that your memory is too much impaired for the management of unlimited sums without danger of injuring the future fortune of your daughter and grandson.'"

Ben slumped and shook his head.

"'You were not very attentive to money-matters in your best days.'" Adams intruded closer. "Were you not addressing here, sir, the very woman who had served as your loyal servant for near upon forty-one years, uttering over the entirety of these four decades not one word of complaint? Were you not addressing here, sir, the very woman who had tended your shop and kept your accounts in the tender years of your ascendancy, sir, such as to save you the expense of carrying a clerk? Were you not addressing here, sir, the very woman who had assumed to herself the care of *your* bastard son, whilst in return you neglected the son and abused the daughter who were her own maternal fulfill-ment? Were you not addressing here, sir, the very woman you had aban-doned for five years previous, and again now for seven more, leaving her thereby to carry *your* domestic burdens atop her own? Were you not addressing here, sir, the very woman to whom you had delivered promise of imminent return in one season only to abrogate it in the next, season upon season? Were you not addressing here, sir, the very woman who had, two years previous, been 'unable to bear any more and so fell down and could not get up.'"

Adams straightened and looked to his papers. "'Her constitution in general appears impaired'—'these are bad symptoms in advanced life and augur danger of further injury on the nervous system.'"

Ben slumped.

Adams intruded closer. "Is this a woman who deserved to be told, sir, in response to making a desperate attempt toward holding fast upon even a fiber of your ever-fraying attentions toward her that even in her prime she was too limited to be trusted with even the meanest rudi-ments of domestic economy?"

Ben moaned, shaking his head.

"In truth, sir, were you not so scandalized by sight of a dotty wife solic-iting friends of no necessity soever that you had no heart for empathy, no mind for understanding, no soul for compassion?" Adams seemed deliberately to bellow a sulfurous exhalation upon Ben's downcast face. "Is this not the very truth of the matter, sir?" Turning clockwise, Adams swept an arm toward the crystalline bench. "Behold, sir, the wages of a heart chaste of all extravagance lest a promiscuity of solicitude should prevail."

The orderings and disorderings within the crystalline bench coalesced into a scene in which a frail woman, shuffling by aid of a walking stick, entered a room made modestly grand by way of azure in the main, gold in accent. The woman was carrying an envelope, yet showing an unbroken seal, in a tremulous hand.

Ben startled upon recognizing not the round, robust woman last he had seen, but a shadow of this other, with hair whitened as if by the rime of an early winter.

Deborah set the envelope atop a tea table proximate to a standard rocker, the back of this draped with a shawl, blue, and carried a tea service one item at a time from a dumb waiter to the table. Her hand atremble, she poured tea into a cup of delicate china, and upon easing herself into the chair, pulled, with some difficulty, the shawl around her shoulders.

Ben recognized the china, likewise the shawl, as among the many gifts he had had shipped to Philadelphia from London over the years of his absence.

The rocker was positioned close upon a large fireplace, brick in functionality, marble in ornament, such that it faced a glass armonica standing close upon the opposing wall.

Lifting of both hands the delicate cup from its saucer, Deborah took a tremulous sip of tea, and then exchanged the cup for the envelope, which she laid on her lap, seal poised upward. Resting her gnarled fingers atop the envelope, she held her eyes closed a moment, as if in prayer, and taking a deep breath then, as if toward fortifying a flagging resolve, picked up a pearl-handled letter opener from the table, and with considerable effort, the palsy in her hands seeming to worsen of the struggle, managed to sunder the seal.

Deborah again held her eyes closed, and thereupon, hands atremble, slipped a folded sheet from the envelope. She unfolded the sheet slowly, as if against a swelling tide of ambivalence, then raced her dark-brown eyes across the lines of elegant script until her body convulsed as if of a most terrible affliction. Pressing her hands against her chest, one atop the other, the letter clutched betwixt, she wept most pathetically.

Ben jumped to his feet. "I'm here! I've come! I'm here!"

In the instant, Deborah dissipated into a mist of colorations—like a delicate rainbow scattered of a single gust of wind.

Casting himself unto the feet of Adams, Ben looked upward unto a countenance made the more hideous by the severity of the angle. "Let her hear me! I beg of you! Let her hear!"

"And by what manner of magic would you have it so, sir? By rant of Mather? By wand of Mesmer? By bolt of Franklin?"

Ben startled to appearance at center of the roiling cauldron of a hideous head crowned of a papish hat. Bold lettering upon the hat, writ vertically, spelt "Carnegie." Another such head appeared, marked "Vanderbilt." And another such, marked "Madoff." Another head appeared showing no countenance nor hat, but a coiffure of serpentine appendages, these twining and undulating.

Before Ben might make a prudent retreat, he became ensnared of robust tentacles, and being pulled thereupon toward the roiling cauldron, called out to his protectors. Little sooner did Ben hear swords sliding from scabbards than Clarence and Bartholomew were smiting upon the tethers binding him, and sundering these, and others that would replace them, unto a writhing impotence. The ghoulish apparition being shorn bald of its appendages, Clarence and Bartholomew kicked the harvest of their scythes, these yet writhing, into the roiling cauldron, whereupon the shorn head, squealing in the manner of an abused swine, slipped below the surface of the vitreous humour, as if by a downward suction, whilst a tar-like humour poured forth from its grievous wounds.

Upon sheathing their blades, Clarence and Bartholomew retired Ben's chair three yards farther from the expanded circle, and upon restoring Ben to his seat, restored themselves to their stations.

Smith stepped forward, replacing Adams. "In the spring of 1779, sir," he began, as if naught out of the ordinary had only just occurred, "as previously touched upon, you removed your namesake grandson, Benny Bache, to Geneva, at age nine, there to attend the Pension Marignac school, such as to be raised 'a Presbyterian and a Republican;' am I correct, sir?"

Ben shook his head. "No more! Trundle me to what fate you might, but torture me no farther."

Smith stepped closer. "Do *less* unto you, sir, than you have done unto others? Where would be the justice, sir? Apply the sting of truth unto King George, but not unto Doctor Franklin? Where would be the symmetry, sir?"

Ben shook his head. "No more. No more."

Smith looked to the assembly. "Pray tell, is the indomitable *bon homme* striking his colors? Can this possibly be true?"

"No more. No more."

"Is the great *VIR* hoisting his silk in their stead?"

Titters.

Ben startled to a surprise of warming from within, and a small voice from without, the latter as if from a very great distance.

You must endure, sir. You must endure as you have never endured before. All that might have been, all that might yet be, all is in your hands.

"Sir?"

There is no one else.

"Sir?"

Though the hour is late.

"Sir?"

Yet still there is time.

Ben glanced upon the clerk, who nodded ever so slightly. Ben looked to Smith. "Though the ship must sink of trickery and treachery, its colors remain."

"They being of no cheap ink, sir?"

"Dearly so."

Smith looked to the assembly. "Do you refer to the colors carried by you into this chamber, sir, or do you refer to those you might carry from it?"

"I refer but figuratively."

"Toward continuing these proceedings, sir?"

Ben nodded.

Smith looked to Ben. "Your grandson, sir, Benny Bache, whilst under your authority, remained at the Geneva school from his tenth year into his fifteenth, more than four years in total—or one-third the lad's entire history. Do you recollect such, sir?"

Ben nodded.

"And during these four years, sir, Benny sent you many a plea for the comfort of family, he being removed from all such, did he not?" Smith looked to his papers. "'It has been even longer since I have had your news.' 'If you have news of my dear papa, and my dear mama, please let me know.' 'I would like very much to have your news, but I think that business is preventing you from writing to me.' 'I would also like to have news of my papa and mama.' 'I did not have news from you for such a long time, and I was very worried about you.' 'I would love to see my entire family and all my friends again, and have my brother in Geneva with me.' 'I would very much like it if you and my family would take a trip to Geneva.' 'I would very much like my brother to come to Geneva, as well as the son of Mister Adams.'"

Smith looked to Ben. "Please write. Please come. Please write. Please come. Please—please—please." Smith intruded closer. "Did you not hear your grandson, sir? Had you been struck deaf by some errant blow to the head? Or did your negligence owe to some other excuse, sir?

"Three thousand miles distant, sir, the boy's father, Richard, found his son's pleas so viscerally wrenching that he was able to find sufficient courage to attempt to shame you into visiting your despairing grandson; have you recollection, sir?" Smith looked to his papers. "'It would give us pleasure to hear that you had found leisure enough to visit him at Geneva, but I suspect your time has been more importantly employed; [however,] the journey might conduce to your health, and be a means of prolonging a life that is not only of so much consequence to us, but to the world in general. Formerly you used to find a journey absolutely necessary for you, every now and then; surely you must think it equally so now, unless the climate of France should agree with you better than any other climate you have heretofore lived in.'"

Smith looked to Ben. "Please go! Please visit! Please go! Please visit! Please! Please! Please! And your response, sir?"

Ben shuddered.

"A lecture upon the necessities of Industry and Frugality. An exhortation to learn all things 'reputable and useful.' An exhortation to be ever dutiful toward one's masters. A sermon on the high virtue of affixing the date of origin upon one's letters. An exhortation to improve one's penmanship. And the pièce de résistance, sir? None other than a cheap likeness of a visage 'as well-known as that of the moon,' sent in lieu of the solar article itself."

Ben moaned.

Smith continued. "And when, sir, you received notice that your grandson was to be awarded a medallion for transforming Latin grapes into French wine, did you place yourself in attendance, sir, at the Cathédrale St. Pierre, such as to illume upon your dutiful grandson the radiance of a proud parent? No? Did you send your secretary, sir, Benny's cousin, to stand in your stead? No? Did you arrange for some other surrogacy, sir? A friend? A colleague? A thespian for hire? A man off the street? No?"

Smith made a dismissive gesture with his clutch of papers. "Aye, but your time was, in fact, 'more importantly employed,' was it not, sir? There was Madame Helvetius to bemuse in her parlour of bohemians. There was Madame Brillon to console and counsel on matters of domestic distress. There was a wine cellar to provision with notable vintages. There was Meister Mesmer to defrock of delusions toward divinity. There were portrait appointments to keep. There was Temple to shape unto a façade of yourself. There was Voltaire to buss upon one pinked crinkle of crepe and the other." Smith shook his head. "One becomes weighted of exhaustion just in the accounting of it all. If only your grandson had known, sir, the fullness of your responsibilities elsewhere, one would have to speculate, he would have withheld any farther entreaties toward your attentions."

Ben moaned, shaking his head.

Smith looked to his papers, and then continued. "Subsequent to Benny receiving his medallion, sir—this earned by an application of industry and diligence that, obvious to any eye, had to be out of the ordinary—you received assessments from his landlady, the widow Cramer, to effect that her ward appeared to have become infected of indolence. He was taciturn, she reported; he seemed to take no interest in the active pursuits of a boy his age; he even showed no interest in having his allowance increased. 'When reminded of his Latin prize,' she wrote, 'he replied coldly that it had been sheer luck.' Have you recollection, sir?"

Ben slumped.

"Have you recollection, specifically sir, of making a connexion betwixt your grandson falling into indolence under weight of familial neglect, and your wife falling onto the floor under weight also of familial neglect?" Smith made a dismissive gesture with his clutch of papers. "Aye, but I forget. How silly of me. There is but one cause to indolence—hence, but one remedy—quite so, sir? Indeed, no more was necessitated by the widow Cramer's report than for you to stand atop the pedestal of a common-law sainthood and deliver unto this lapsing child a sermon of such flint as might spark an eternity of rectitude; quite so, sir?"

Ben moaned.

Smith looked to his papers. "'You see every where two sorts of people. One who are well dressed, live comfortably in good houses, whose conversation is sensible and instructive, and who are respected for their virtue. The other sort are poor, and dirty, and ragged and ignorant, and vicious, and live in miserable cabins or garrets, on coarse provisions, which they must work hard to obtain, or which if they are idle, they must go without or starve. The first had a good education given them by their friends, and they took pains when at school to improve their time and increase their knowledge. The others either had no friend to pay for their schooling, and so never were taught; or else'"—Smith raised his voice—"'when they were at school, they neglected their studies, were idle, and wicked, and disobedient.'" Smith looked to the assembly. "In short, 'my dear child,' anyone in your circumstance who is indolent in his habits is so affected by no greater cause than being 'wicked and disobedient' in his character." Smith intruded close upon Ben. "The great Mather himself, sir, could not have exceeded you in transforming, by force of a fierce scripture alone, an innocent soul into a spirit so grievously ruined."

Ben moaned.

Smith retreated to side, paused, and returning then, intruded upon Ben's ear. "Have you notion, sir, as to the interest that might compound to paternal neglect year over year?" Smith shifted to Ben's other ear. "Have you notion, sir, as to the interest that might compound to paternal neglect generation over generation?" Smith shifted to Ben's other ear. "A little neglect may indeed breed great mischief, quite so, sir?" Smith shifted to Ben's other ear. "During the four and one-half years your grandson was resident at Geneva, sir, from his tenth year into his fifteenth, did you pay him the honor of a visit, even once?"

Ben moaned.

"Did you arrange for Temple, Benny's cousin and companion, to pay your grandson the honor of a visit, sir; even once?"

Ben moaned.

"Did you arrange for Benny to pay you a visit at Passy, sir; even once?"

Ben moaned.

"Not at Christmastide, sir? Not on the boy's birth anniversary, sir? The eleventh such? The twelfth? The thirteenth? The fourteenth?"

Ben moaned.

Smith looked to his papers. *"There is no rank in natural knowledge of equal dignity and importance with that of being a good parent."* Smith intruded close upon Ben. "'No rank in natural knowledge,' sir. 'Of equal dignity and importance,' sir. 'With that of being a good parent,' sir." Turning half-circle clockwise, Smith swept an arm toward the high bench. "Behold, sir, the interest that compounds to an abiding disinterest!"

In the instant, the colorations within the crystalline bench coalesced into a scene in which a wheeled litter, accompanied by two Negroes—a man and a woman—crashed through a set of metallic doors. The Negro man, wearing a dark-blue uniform, was pushing rhythmically on the chest of a bearded man lying atop the litter. The Negro woman, wearing the same dark uniform, was pushing the litter from behind.

Another woman, wearing a white frock, greeted the litter, and demonstrating considerable agitation, issued a series of commands. A third woman, a Negro of middle complexion, approached from an entryway leftward of the first, and gave over an amber vial to the frocked woman, who, upon studying it, took on a grave aspect of countenance and issued forth yet more commands.

The eyes of the man were fixed into a stare, his beard was much befouled, his nose and mouth were eclipsed of a vitreous mask.

Several other befrocked persons converged upon the litter, and whilst the Negro man in dark uniform continued to pump upon the man's chest, the other functionaries propelled the litter forward and then to leftward; and then past small chambers to either side, some covered over with curtains, some not; and then past litters arranged against the wall of the corridor itself; and then through a wide entryway covered with a heavy curtain. The woman in the white frock thereupon lingered in company with the Negro woman of middle complexion. The latter pulled from pocket then what appeared to be a man's wallet. The other woman nodded as if in assent, then pushed her way through the heavy curtain, leaving behind the Negro woman.

The Negro woman returned to the previous chamber, whereat several people, mostly in frocks of blue or green, were sitting at desks arranged into a circle at about chamber center. Standing near one of these desks, the Negro woman opened the wallet and unfolding it began a hurried examination of the contents, which proved meager—a few bills, and few cards the size of calling cards.

The man and woman in dark-blue uniforms appeared with the litter only recently occupied by the bearded man, the man pulling upon it, the woman pushing.

The Negro woman watched the litter disappear through the metallic doors and slipped from the wallet then a wheel of colorations, twice folded, and then a remnant of newsprint. Unfolding the latter, the woman studied briefly upon it, and then, pulling from pocket a device Ben recognized from previous witness, levered this unto twice its previous size and began to manipulate an array of buttons beneath a luminous pane.

The woman held the device to ear then, and showing thereupon a pique of impatience, struck with particular vigor a key at the bottom of the device, and held the device again to ear. Showing yet another pique of impatience, the woman struck another key, and held the device again to ear. The woman showing yet another pique of impatience—she spoke: "Yes, hello, this is an emergency. My name is Delmyra Jordan and I'm a social worker with the City of Philadelphia. I'm calling concerning a trauma patient at the University of Pennsylvania hospital. His name is Henry Prescott Bahr and I'm trying to reach his next of kin." The woman held silent. "Yes. I believe the father resides in the Washington, DC area, and that his name is Gilbert Bahr. I've tried to locate him, but I think he has an unlisted number." Pause. "Yes, please." Pause. "No, I don't have an address. He might not live right in DC." Pause. "B-A-H-R—Gilbert." Delmyra looked to a small timepiece strapped to her wrist. "Yes, that sounds like the one." Pause. "Thank you." Long pause. "Is this Mr. Gilbert Bahr?" Pause. "Sir, I apologize for the late hour. My name is Delmyra Jordan. I'm a social worker with the City of Philadelphia." Delmyra slipped a card from the wallet that showed a likeness of the bearded man. "I'm trying to reach the next of kin of Henry Prescott Bahr formerly of Cambridge, Massachusetts?" Pause. "Sir?"

Delmyra lowered her device, slowly, as if of some reluctance; was pensive a moment; and then, shaking her head, returned her device to pocket. Refolding the remnant of newsprint, she returned this to the wallet, and also the card.

The woman in the white frock coat, stitched afront *Julia A. Rubin, MD* in red, approached. "We're trying to get him stabilized." Dr. Rubin's voice was anemic, her eyes inflamed, as if the latter facilities were somehow parasitic upon the former. "It's not looking good. He's got a ton of Trazodone in him and unfortunately a lot of alcohol, and who knows what else. Crack, likely. We pumped him, but the damage's already been done."

"He left three pills in the vial. Could that make any difference at all?"

"If the only thing in the mix was the Trazodone, maybe, depending on how many tablets he actually ingested. But with all that alcohol in him?—and the crack?" The woman shook her head. "It's a miracle he's still got a pulse."

"Why keep three back, though. And the vial—why not toss it?"

Dr. Rubin smiled. "I see where you're going. You have a feeling."

"In my business, people tell you more by what they do or don't do than they do by what they say or don't say. This guy wasn't squirreled away in a crack house or holed up in an alley somewhere. I found him under a street lamp, and not just any street lamp, but the one directly in front of my apartment. It just seems to me that if someone really wants to die, he doesn't arrange to be found under a street lamp in front of the house of the local social worker."

Dr. Rubin smiled. "Well, if he really does want to live, his chances are going to be that much better for holding three hits back. Were you able to reach anybody?"

"Yes and no. I think I got hold of his father, but when I told him who I was and why I was calling, he hung up on me."

The doctor stared a moment, then looked to her timepiece. "Might he have thought it was a crank call, given the hour?"

Delmyra shook her head. "I was pretty clear about who I was and why I was calling. And I'm pretty sure he was the right guy." Delmyra took Prescott's wallet into hand. "There's an old clipping in here about a Gilbert Bahr winning a Pulitzer Prize, and your patient's name is Prescott Bahr."

Dr. Rubin smiled. "Not *the* Gilbert Bahr!"

"You know him?"

"He wrote a book back when I was in college called *Ironic Altruism*. It caused quite a stir. Do we know anything else about Prescott?"

Delmyra opened Prescott's wallet and slipped out a card. "Massachusetts license, expired; Cambridge address." She slipped out another card. "Wharton School ID; also expired." She unfolded a small wheel of colorations. "He paints—but not in a studio, it would appear. That's it. Oh—" she smiled—"I didn't see an insurance card."

Dr. Rubin nodded. "Figures." She smiled. "Do we know maybe one other thing?"

Delmyra stared.

"The reason maybe for holding back the three pills? The next two to three hours are critical. If he can hang on that long—if he has something to hang on to—just maybe—"

Delmyra's eyes misted. She nodded.

A crash at the metal doors and a litter appeared bearing a Negro boy no greater than fifteen years, his shirt bearing a dark stain. A man dressed in a dark-blue uniform was pushing rhythmically upon the boy's chest.

A flash—

⁓✐⁓

A boy no greater than ten years, lying abed in a small room illumed of a medium moon, was gazing upon a portrait standing on a bedside table.

Ben winced upon recognizing a face "as well-known as that of the moon."

Adams's hideous countenance intruded close upon. "Where is the 'good father' unto the abandoned child, sir?"

Smith's hideous countenance likewise intruded. "Where is the exemplar unto all posterity, sir?"

A hideous apparition appeared at center of the roiling cauldron.

Adams looked to his papers. "'It wants but a very few days of six years since you left home and then you thought it would be but seven months. My Dear child I hope you will not stay longer than this fall.'"

Smith looked to his papers. "'You ask me when I think I shall return? I purpose it firmly after one winter more here.'"

Adams: "'A little girl came to see him [Kingbird], so after some time he showed her your picture and said *papa*, and then held up his finger and showed to the profile and said is *more papa*, and seemed pleased for her to look at it. I long for you to see him.'"

Smith: "'Your Accounts of your Kingbird please me exceedingly. I hope soon to see him and you.'"

Adams: "'I have not had a letter as yet. I have not allowed myself the liberty to make complaints to you of any sort, but this has been the most melancholy winter that I ever knew in my memory.'"

Smith: "'I must, I find, stay another winter here absent from you and my family, but positively nothing shall prevent, God willing, my returning in the spring.'"

Adams: "'I am very incapable of doing any business as I am not able to walk about and my memory is so poorly and sometimes worse than others.'"

Smith: "Your affectionate husband 'hopes to arrive at home next May. Sends affectionate regards and love to the children.'"

Adams: "'You may see what blunders by the scratching out that I am not capable of writing, so I shall only say that I find myself growing very feeble very fast. I leave Mister Bache and Sally to write as I am very unfit to do.'"

Smith: "'I hoped to have been on the sea in my return by this time, but find I must stay a few weeks longer, perhaps for the summer ships.'"

Adams: "'I was in hopes that would inform when you intend to return again to your own home. I can't write to you, as I am so very unfit to express myself, and not able to do as I used, for that illness I had was a palsy, although I don't shake. My memory fails me; I can't express myself as I used to do.'"

Smith: "'I have had no line from you by several late opportunities: I flatter myself it is owing not to indisposition, but to the opinion of my having left England, which indeed I hope soon to do.'"

Adams: "'I must submit and endeavor to submit to what I am to bear. Sally will write. I can't write any more.'"

Smith: "'It is now nine long months since I received a line from my dear Debby. I have supposed it owing to your continual expectation of my return.'"

Wedderburn arose at table. "'There is no rank in natural knowledge of equal dignity and importance with that of being a good parent, a good child, or good husband.'"

Ben moaned, shaking his head—and then startled to a growl from Adams: "Is not the lash delivered of neglect, sir, equal, in all accounts, to that delivered of malice? And greater still, sir, on the occasion of neglect in the extremity?"

A flash and the scene in the crystalline bench changed to a man in black, his countenance eclipsed by a mask also black, standing close upon a palsied woman knelt before him, her hands clasped in supplication. The man raised a cat-o'-nine overtop one shoulder, and then struck the supplicating old woman about the head and back. "In the fall!" The old woman's body flinched to the blow. "I must submit, and endeavor to submit, to what I am to bear." The masked man struck the old woman again. "In the spring!" The old woman's body flinched. "I must submit, and endeavor to submit, to what I am to bear."

Ben jumped up from his chair. "Stop! Please! Stop! Stop!"

The masked man raised the cat-o'-nine overtop his shoulder.

Ben looked to Adams. "Make him stop! Make him stop!" Sinking unto his knees, Ben clasped his hands into a dome. "Please! Please!"

Adams looked to his papers. "'I did write by Capt. Faulkner to you but he is gone down and when I read it over I did not like it and so if this don't send it I shant like it as I don't send you any news nor I don't go abroad.'" Pause. "'You may see what blunders by the scratching out that I am not capable of writing, so I shall only say that I find myself growing very feeble very fast.'"

Adams cast eyes upon Ben as if the fire of incandesced rubies. "Would you have opinion, good sir, as to how your grievously afflicted wife might have caused in you a keener awareness of the degree to which her faculties of mind and body were diminished than by way of the lines just read you?"

The masked man struck the palsied old woman. "In the fall!"

Ben cried out as if the blow had been inflicted upon himself and looked to the crystalline bench.

"Stop! Stop! Please! Please!"

Adams looked to his papers. "'Sally will write. I can't write any more.'" Adams leaned close upon Ben's ear and lowered his voice to near a whisper. "'I cannot *write* any more.' I cannot *hope* any more. I cannot *endure* any more. I cannot *bear* any more. I cannot *endeavor* to bear any more.'"

Smith leaned close upon Ben's other ear. "Come home."

"In the spring!" Wedderburn bellowed.

"Come home."

"In the fall!" Wedderburn bellowed.

The old woman crumpled to the floor, convulsed, and moved no more.

Resting his head upon the floor, Ben moaned most pathetically, and feeling then as if the sinuous body of a serpent closing around his neck, thrust his head sidelong, and falling in that direction, was mercifully liberated by a blow of Bartholomew's sword.

Clarence kicked a sundered tentacle, yet writhing, into the roiling murk, whereupon it submerged as if pulled from below; likewise the hideous apparition to which it had been attached.

Clarence and Bartholomew restored Ben unto his seat.

Smith continued. "You are familiar, I trust, sir, with the parable of the Prodigal Son."

Ben slumped.

"As you will recall, sir, a father had two sons—let us call the elder one Practical, the younger one Prodigal. They having each come of age, the father bestowed upon them their rightful inheritance, in equal shares. The younger son, Prodigal, thereupon took claim upon his share and traveled unto a distant land, whereat he soon squandered the whole of his inheritance upon riotous living, whilst the elder son held steadfast to Industry and Frugality. Finally realizing the error of his ways, by way of mortal hunger, Prodigal returned to the father and begged for servitude in exchange for bread. In response, the father, and I here quote, sir"—Smith looked to his papers—"'had compassion, and . . . fell on his neck, and kissed him.'" Smith looked to Ben. "Would you concur as to the accuracy of this précis, sir?"

Ben nodded.

Smith continued. "The father thereupon held a banquet to honor his returned son, and when the elder son, Practical, witnessed this, he became very angry, and said to his father"—Smith looked to his papers—"'Lo, these many years I do serve thee, neither transgressed I at any time thy commandment: and yet thou never gavest me a kid, that I might make merry with my friends: But as soon as this thy [younger] son has come, which hath devoured thy living with harlots, thou hast killed for him the fatted calf.'" Smith looked to Ben. "And the father's reply to this lamentation, sir? Do you recollect it?"

Ben nodded.

Smith looked to his papers. "'This my son [thy brother] was dead, and is alive again; he was lost, and is found.'"

The assembly stood in unison. "Hear! Hear!" They sat down.

Smith continued. "Now, sir, being of an analytical bent of mind, would you be inclined to agree that the father in this parable embodies a particular set of virtues, these being Compassion, Generosity, and Forgiveness?"

Ben nodded.

"Would you be farther inclined to agree, sir, that the elder son in this parable embodies a certain counterpoising set of virtues, these being Pride, Spite, and Hatred?"

Ben nodded.

"Now, sir, when last you made amendments to your Will and Testament, had you not therewith opportunity to emulate the father in the parable? Indeed, had you not at this time a prodigal son yet lost to you, indeed yet dead unto you, sir?"

Ben moaned, shaking his head.

"The record on the matter, sir." Smith consulted his papers a moment, and then continued. "On July 17, 1788, sir, twenty-two months previous to your death, precisely such, you amended, by your own hand, your Last Will and Testament to effect of diminishing unto insult the articles of estate bequeathed to your son William, to whom, by previous enumeration, you had bequeathed the majority. In fact, sir, by amendment, you limited your bequest to three assiduously selected items: Firstly, your worthless holdings in Tory Nova Scotia, such as to remind your prodigal son of the failure of his cause; secondly, cancellation of the total of his indebtedness to you, such as to remind him of his pecuniary dependence upon you; and thirdly, only those papers and books of yours a'ready held by him, such as to remind him of his want of 'a good understanding' in relation to your own. In other words, sir, in lieu of embracing the virtues of the loving father in the parable, by way of allowing your original bequest not only to stand but to be enhanced of a fatted calf, you chose to hold fast upon the virtues of the spiteful son. Indeed, in lieu of Compassion, you chose Pride. In lieu of Generosity, you chose Spite. And in lieu of Forgiveness"—Smith leaned well close— "did you choose 'a little revenge, sir?'"

Ben moaned, jaw aquiver.

Smith straightened. "And then, sir, the coup de grace, for all posterity to emulate unto all eternity." Smith looked to his papers. "Your words, sir: 'The part he acted against me in the late war, which is of public notoriety, will account for my leaving him no more of an estate he endeavored to deprive me of.'"

Smith flung his papers overtop Ben's head, and withdrawing Bartholomew's sword from its sheath, flung this article toward the crystalline bench.

In the instant, a scene appeared within the bench in which a man in black was standing near a man prostrate upon the floor, the latter dressed in royal blue and bearing a wig noticeably askew. The man in black deftly caught the sword in hand, and gripping the handle of both hands, plunged the blade into the prostrate man's chest, blood thereupon gushing forth in likeness to wine abounding from a bacchanalian font.

Ben lunged from his chair yelping, holding forth hands dripping of blood, and dropping then unto his knees, at the very edge of the roiling cauldron, plunged his hands into the roiling murk, and whilst he chafed together his hands, a serpentine appendage emerged from the roiling murk, and entwining around Ben's neck, pulled him headlong into the noxious murk.

Scalding as if to a soak in lye, Ben felt a grip upon one ankle, the other—and was soon lying upon the parquet floor, gagging, gasping, vestiges of severed appendage yet twined around his neck. He retched, expelling naught, but loosening the slimy tentacles from around his neck, which thereupon slithered into the roiling murk.

Clarence and Bartholomew helped Ben to his feet, and out of his water-laden jacket, and restored him then to his seat.

Upon wiping his face with Bartholomew's linen, Ben discovered Smith again in possession of Bartholomew's sword, it showing now no stain upon its glittering blade. "Had I not misplaced all memory of what an accomplished swimmer you were, good sir, I would have allowed you to fin for yourself."

Guffaws.

Smith impaled a floor square afront Bartholomew with the latter's sword, and took then a step to side as, in simultaneity, Adams took a step closer.

Bartholomew pulled his sword free, and showing Smith a frown most severe, returned the sword to its sheath.

"If I might, sir," Adams began, "I would like to return to your dear wife's favour of October 29, 1774, specifically to the closing words, the very last your wife would ever write." Adams looked to his papers. "'Sally will write. I can't write any more.'" Adams looked to Ben. "Now, sir, noteworthy here is your wife's use of the term 'any more,' two words, as against 'anymore,' one word. Looking no farther than a literal interpretation of 'any more,' two words, a reader might well conclude that the writer, perhaps from fatigue, perhaps from a poverty of news, could add no farther lines to those a'ready writ. Ah, but naught there is in this world that can be removed from all context; no wall there is can be extended high enough to repel all influence from without; quite so, sir?"

Ben shuddered of chill, then noticed, to a start, that his clothing appeared to be disintegrating—owing, he surmised, to the alkaline nature of the humour of which it was sodden.

Adams continued. "Now, sir, the record would suggest that you interpreted your wife's usage of 'any more' in the literal sense, that is, to mean 'any additional lines in the present letter' as against 'any lines *ever*.' Indeed, sir, in the brief letters you posted to your wife subsequent to your receiving her letter of October 29th, you repeatedly make mention that it had been a long time since you had received the favour of a line from her." Adams looked to his papers. "May 7, 1774: 'My dear child, it is now a very long time indeed since I have had the pleasure of a line from you.' July 22nd: 'My dear child, I have no line from you by several late opportunities: I flatter myself it is owing not to indisposition, but to the opinion of my having left England, which indeed I hope soon to do.'"

Adams looked upon the assembly. "'Which indeed I hope *soon* to do'!"

"In the spring!" leftward sang forth.

"In the fall!" rightward sang forth.

Ben noticed the clerk prostrate, head upon desk, in the manner of a scribe having too long labored over his notes.

Adams continued. "September 10th: 'It is now nine long months since I received a line from my dear Debbie. I have supposed it owing to your continual expectation of my return . . . I have imagined any thing rather than admit a supposition that your kind attention towards me was abated.'" Adams looked to Ben. "Although there is certainly temptation here to address what would appear to be a truly remarkable species of self-pity, let us forbear doing so, for the moment, and return whence we began, that we might place your wife's letter into a proper history, this being of two parts. Let us call the one part 'static;' the other, 'unfolding.'"

Ben noticed that the ambient light within the great hall had become diminished to effect of making the ever-changing colorations within the high bench, as well as the lurid glow of the roiling humour close to front, all the more ominous.

Adams continued. "Now, sir, let us hold in mind the very moment you finished reading your wife's letter of October 29th. In this moment, sir, you had benefit of at least the following facts: Firstly, that your wife had become greatly impaired in her faculties of mind and body, by consequence of her late 'indisposition,' this fact being both confessed by her and demonstrated by her." Adams looked to his papers. "'I can't write to you as I am so very unfit to express myself and not able to do as I used for that illness I had was a palsy although I don't shake my memory fails me I can't express myself as I used to do.'"

Adams looked to Ben. "Secondly, sir, that your wife had become increasingly despairing of your ever returning to her, as manifested by her pitiful lamentations over your continued absence." Adams looked to his papers. "'She has instructed several of the first rank hear if you would let me know if you should return home this fall I heard that Mrs. Write has seen you.'"

Adams looked to Ben. "And thirdly, sir, that your wife had become increasingly embarrassed by the bare poverty of an ever-shrinking life." Adams looked to his papers. "'I did write by Capt. Faulkner to you but he is gone down and when I read it over I did not like it and so if this don't send it I shan't like it as I don't send you any news nor I don't go abroad.'"

Adams looked to Ben. "Now, sir, what say you, upon reflection? Have we here the stuff of 'any more,' no more lines this letter; or have we here, sir, the stuff of 'anymore,' no more lines *ever*?"

Ben shook his head, moaning. Of a fleeting glance, he discovered the clerk's head yet reposed upon his bench. The despair manifest was a gout upon the soul.

Adams continued. "Subsequent events included these: Firstly, yet more months passed without you receiving a line from your wife. Secondly, yet more months passed without you receiving a line from your wife. Thirdly, yet more months passed without you receiving a line from your wife. Quite so, sir?"

Ben noticed, to a start, that his raiment had become so diminished of substance that what little remained was become tinctured of the pallor of celestial flesh.

Adams continued. "Now, sir, were we to place the latter facts in company with the former, what inference would likely spring forth of the combination?" Adams intruded closer. "That 'your kind attention towards me was abated?' That the fallen soldier fails to salute for want of discipline?" Adams straightened. "One struggles to conceive, sir, how the message could have been made more plain: Your wife of forty-three years, fourteen of these being suffered in abandonment, was dying. And whilst desperately she struggled to resign herself to never seeing you again, yet she clung to merest hope that you would miraculously appear at the threshold you had yet to pass over for the very first time." Adams intruded closer. "Your wife was in torment, sir, yet you would not see it, you would not feel it; indeed, you would not be inconvenienced by it." Adams intruded yet closer. "Do I err in any regard, sir, any soever?"

Ben moaned most pathetically.

"In truth, sir, your 'dear Debbie' had been useful in her time—as wet nurse, as governess, as domestic, as shop keep, as secretary—but that time had long passed. Now fuzzy in mind, frail in body, your Country Joan had become no better than a mosquito buzzing about your head." Adams intruded closer. "Alas, could this simple, unlettered, incurious old woman not see that the Great Man had to complete his Great Work before whatever grains might be left in the upper chamber of his fortune could flow unto the lower? How *dare* she interrupt him with her noisome whining? How *dare* she unsettle him with a silence that was, as in the case of the mosquito, the greater vexation?"

Adams straightened. "Your 'dear Debbie' gave you everything in her power to give, sir, and she gave it freely, indeed as a mother unto a child born of her. After forty-three dutiful years of honoring your every expectation, of obeying your every directive, of humouring your every whim, of turning the other cheek to your every abuse, she made of you but one request in return, and only by way of wifely indirection, to wit: to see your face, sir, 'as well-known as that of the moon,' one last time."

Wedderburn jumped to his feet: "'Sally will write. I cannot write any more.'" He sat down.

The clerk, his head yet reposed upon his desk, uttered a most pathetic plaint.

Adams continued. "And Sally did write, did she not, sir?—taking up her pen, in fact, the very next day?" Adams looked to his papers. "'We are all much disappointed at your not coming home this fall. I was in great hopes of seeing and presenting you with two of the finest boys in the world. Do not let any thing, my dear sir, prevent your coming to your family in the spring, for indeed we want you here much.'"

Adams looked to Ben. "Your wife is here pleading through the surrogacy of your daughter, she having no pull upon you of herself. And your daughter is here employing the only attraction available to her, your grandchildren, she having no pull upon you of herself."

The clerk moaned.

Adams shuffled a new sheet to top of his papers. "More indirection, sir, this by surrogacy of your son—though it were not delivered unto you until the bell had sounded to six tolls."

A bell presently sounded as if from a great distance, followed by five peals more.

Adams looked to his papers. "December 24, 1774: 'Her death was no more than might be reasonably expected after the paralytic stroke she received some time ago, which greatly affected her memory and understanding. She told me when I took leave of her, on my removal to Amboy, that she never expected to see you unless you returned this winter, for that she was sure she should not live till next summer. I heartily wish you had happened to have come over in the fall, as I think her disappointment in that respect preyed a good deal on her spirits.'"

From the balcony: "In the spring!"

From the floor: "In the fall!"

From the balcony: "In the spring!"

From the floor: "In the fall!"

Ben shook his head, moaning most pathetically.

"In the spring!" "In the fall!"

"In the spring!" "In the fall!"

Of a sudden, a pulse of brilliant-green light flashed from the high bench, and this striking upon Ben, stripped him of what little raiment remained upon his person.

Within the crystalline bench, an emaciated old woman appeared lying on a Quaker bed, under a plain coverlet. Her eyes were sunken and darkly shadowed, her hair disheveled and starkly white.

Ben swallowed as if against a host of distempered bees stinging at the back of his throat.

The only sound, other than the low hum from the bench, was a slow, rhythmic rasping.

Debbie opened her eyes, and lifting her head from her pillow, it quavering of the effort, peered forth as if of great expectation, one side of her face being so slackened as to be ill suited to the other. As hideous apparitions bobbed to the surface of the roiling murk to front, Debbie held forth her left hand, it trembling, though she had, her life through, favored her right. "Is that you, my child? Are you there?"

Ben jumped to his feet. "I'm here! I'm here!"

Debbie collapsed back onto her pillow.

Ben eluded the sweeping grope of a serpentine tentacle, and another.

Debbie struggled to lift her head from her pillow. "Have you come to me?"

"I'm here! I'm here!"

"Are you there?"

Ben clutched a serpentine appendage, it undulating and squirming, whilst Clarence and Bartholomew sundered it with their swords.

"I'm here! I'm here!"

"Have . . . you—"

Debbie collapsed onto her pillow.

Eluding yet another serpentine appendage, Ben turned to Clarence, and gesturing toward being granted possession of his sword, took this instrument into hand upon merest offer and began to smite upon groping arms and bobbing heads. He struck and slashed until the vitreous humour had become blackened as if of a hundredweight of spilt ink. Thereupon restoring Clarence of his sword, Ben launched headlong into the roiling murk and was no sooner surfaced, minus his spectacles, than was stroking toward the crystalline bench. Progressed no farther than a few strokes, however, he was entwined of muscular tethers, and pulled beneath the surface. His eyes and flesh burning as if to caustic, he was tugged from an ascending current unto a descending such, and thereupon ever deeper—toward a fate well imaginable.

Down, down he went—deeper and deeper.

Yet able to hold dominion over rebelling lungs, Ben fought frantically to free himself—jerking his head, twisting his torso, thrusting arm and leg—but his efforts seemed only to tighten the hold of his tethers. His lungs rebelling the harder, he struggled the harder—until, one last redoubt of will being overrun, he closed his eyes and, about to strike his colors, heard a voice as if from a very great distance.

You must endure, sir. You must endure as you have never endured before. All that might have been, all that might yet be, all is in your hands, sir.

He held fast—

Began to yield—

Held fast—

He was a fool!

Thrusting himself downward, using a stroke he had invented by example of a humble amphibian, Ben had no sooner surged deeper of his own volition than he felt his tethers loosen. Thrusting himself yet deeper, he felt his tethers loosen yet more. Stroking mightily to side then, he entered into the ascending current, and stroking mightily upward then, felt as if Howe's entire fleet attempt to pass in simultaneity through the narrows of his windpipe.

Breaking the surface, gasping, gasping, he stroked mightily toward the crystalline bench, and reaching the edge of the residual floor, pulled himself headlong from the roiling cauldron, and rotating his legs to clockwise, rolled himself, naked, toward the crystalline bench.

Espying a serpentine appendage descending upon him, Ben cringed against the unyielding surface of the bench, and was about to wrestle this Goliathan unto a certain doom, when there appeared another appendage, which, upon twining around the other, pulled the other of such ferocity as to propel it, and the hideous apparition to which it was attached, unto the very ceiling and, by way of a momentary aperture, unto the firmament beyond.

Struggling to his feet, Ben pounded against a surface as unyielding, it seemed, as the great Atlantic was unfathomable. "I'm here! I'm here!"

Debbie lifted her head, haltingly, and attempted to speak but could not, and then collapsed it again onto her pillow.

A heavy exhale gave way to a low arrhythmic humming from the lights atop the bench.

Ben sank onto his knees. "I'm here." He moaned. "I'm here."

"Had you held her equal to yourself, sir, instead of but two-thirds—or was it but three-fifths, sir?—dare we imagine how different this moment might have been?"

Three shrill blares of whistle, a brilliant flash, and Ben was sitting in his chair, spectacles returned to his nose, Clarence and Bartholomew returned to his flanks.

⸰Ψ⸰

Wedderburn, in hideous transfiguration, eyes flashing as if of fired emeralds, was standing atop the examiners' table, betwixt Adams and

Smith, each of whom was holding one of the remaining volumes of the *Autobiography* as if for a public reading, an epistle perhaps from the one, a gospel from the other.

Wedderburn was holding a sheet well to forward as if in accommodation to an impairment upon his sightedness. "'I conceived,'" he read, "'that the great part of the miseries of mankind were brought upon them by the false estimates they had made of the value of things, and by their giving too much for the whistle.'" Wedderburn looked to Ben. "What say you, sir? Are we to include under authority of this scripture the value one places upon a sightedness that allows him to see only what is agreeable to him?"

Wedderburn lifted a pennywhistle unto a mouth oozing of drool and blew a shrill note. In the moment, the crystalline bench began to show a succession of scenes: Negro corpses being thrown over the gunwales of a ship—chained Negroes being sold at auction—a Negro woman being beaten in a rice field—a Negro girl being raped, her mother forced to witness—a Negro boy being lynched—Negroes amidst rural squalor—Negroes amidst urban squalor—

"Or the value one places upon a hearingness that allows him to hear only what is agreeable to him?" Wedderburn blew another shrill note and the scene in the crystalline bench changed to nine-year-old Benny curled unto a fetal mass in his bed—thereupon to Debbie receiving a reprimand for having borrowed £20 with which to demonstrate her Industry and Frugality—thereupon to Sally being reprimanded for having asked for a feather—thereupon to Debbie being whipped by a masked man dressed in black—

"I must submit to what I am to bear."

"Or the value one places upon a sensibility that allows him to feel only what is agreeable to him?" Wedderburn blew another shrill note and the scene in the crystalline bench changed to William Bradford learning of the duplicity of the man he had helped get started in the printing trade—thereupon to a young Negro boy being ripped from his mother's bosom—thereupon to turkey fowl being tortured by electrical shock—thereupon to Elizabeth Franklin convulsing in her deathbed—thereupon to Daniel Rees burning to death of "holy oil"—thereupon to Debbie collapsing unto the floor—

"No? Perchance then the value one places upon certain expediencies such that he might fill his coffers to overflowing?" The crystalline bench showed a sequence of scenes in which a figure in heroic posture, bearing one of the thirteen names Ben had previously witnessed—John D.

Rockefeller, Andrew Carnegie, Jay Gould, Cornelius Vanderbilt, Bernard Madoff—was holding a boot upon a corpse, in the manner of a huntsman dominating his prey. In each scene, the heroic figure quoted, in full basso, a 'moral sentence' from 'Father Abraham': *The sleeping fox catches no poultry—He that hath a calling hath an office of profit and honor—Not to oversee workmen is to leave them your purse open—Get what you can, and what you get hold; 'tis the stone will turn all your lead into gold—God gives all things to Industry.*

At the end of each scene, a gangly figure, white of beard, black of cloak—Father Abraham himself, it had to be presumed—draped a ribbon bearing a pennywhistle around the neck of each figure, and then tapped his shoulders with a golden scepter, declaring in a cadence most solemn, "I anoint thee into the Fraternal Order of the Whistle."

Upon the occasion of each ceremony, Ben groaned to a weight of understanding given him concerning the circumstance and merit of each figure.

The last ceremony completed, the glow of the roiling humour afront grew suddenly more lurid, as if a pyre of embers below had received a robust breath of bellows.

Yet standing atop the examiners' table, Wedderburn tossed an object toward Ben. "Catch it if you can!"

Grasping the object of reflex, Ben discovered himself in possession of the very three-hole whistle he had purchased with all his coppers all those many years ago. He closed his eyes against an upwelling of sensations most keen.

Assaulted thereupon of a bellows of odor most offensive, Ben opened his eyes to discover Wedderburn standing close upon him.

"And so, sir, we return whence we began, as indeed we must, to the thirteen cardinal virtues you advanced unto all posterity as being 'necessary or desirable'—Industry, Frugality, Order, Resolution, and the others. I ask you now, sir, to imagine these virtues as a sort of vegetable stew, and farther, that you imagine boiling this stew into a broth; and the broth then into a distillate. What, sir, would likely be the nature of this ultimate essence?"

Ben shook his head.

"Would you not have, sir, the fundamental humour from which all thirteen virtues commonly derived—as you might, by analogue, have the fundamental humour from which all the cardinal materials of the universe commonly derived?"

Lifting his head, Ben discovered the ambient glow in the great hall to have become so diminished that the correspondence in colorations betwixt the eyes of Wedderburn, Smith, and Adams and the three tongues atop the crystalline bench, was made most striking.

He shuddered to a chill.

Wedderburn continued. "Now, sir, also imagine, if you would, the same reductive technique being applied to the thirteen virtues presented to you in counterpoise to the thirteen of your own advocacy. I refer to Compassion, Empathy, Forgiveness, Sacrifice, and the others. What, sir, would likely be the nature of the distillate in this instance?"

Ben shook his head.

Wedderburn leaned well close. "You have no opinion on the matter, sir? Not so much as a speculation?"

Ben shook his head.

Spinning quarter-circle around, Wedderburn stepped briskly toward the farther side of the examiners' table, as if toward abandoning any further inquiry.

Upon a plaintive lament from afront, most unsettling, Ben looked to source, and discovering the clerk moaning into his hands, whilst rocking to and fro, looked after Wedderburn. "Ambition, the one." His voice was little greater than a whisper. "Sentiment, the other."

The clerk rose at his station, and upon bowing toward Ben unto near a ninety-degree fold, sat down. In near simultaneity, Wedderburn spun half-circle around, and returning to Ben, leaned well close. "*Ambition*, sir? *Sentiment*, sir? Are we speaking of such delicate matters in this chamber that we must resort to the circumspection of the salon? Would not 'desire' stand clothed in less gauze, sir, than 'ambition;' 'love' in less silk, sir, than 'sentiment?'"

Ben nodded, shivering to an ever deepening chill.

"And would you agree farther, sir, as regards desire, that the vector of concern is directed largely, if not wholly, toward one's self—toward the appetites and cravings of one's self—whereas, as regards love, the vector of concern is directed largely, if not wholly, away from self—indeed toward the anguishes and privations of other selves?"

Ben nodded, jaw atremble.

"And so, sir, we have come down to it, have we not—the very reason we are assembled here this. day? Indeed, sir, consider the likely fate of any congregation of mortals encouraged by way of scripture as compass, by way of deeds as template, toward embracing Ambition and Self-Regard, Independence and Industry, Rights and Ownership in lieu of embracing in equal measure Family and Nurture, Charity and Conciliation, Responsibility and Service."

Ben shuddered.

"One last inquiry, sir, and all is done. To which of your various discourses on virtue, sir, as *Pater Patriae*, as *VIR*, sir, might we repair such as to be reminded that only in Compassion, only in Empathy, only in Forgiveness, only in Sacrifice, only in the meek virtues of the heart, sir, might any confederation of mortals thrive as five-fifths each one the other?"

Wedderburn leaned yet closer. "*Which*, sir?"

Ben moaned, shaking his head.

Spinning quarter-circle around, Wedderburn marched to his place at the examiners' table, and remaining upstanding there, looked to the clerk.

Springing thereupon to his feet, the clerk sang forth, in striking falsetto, "All rise," he giving particular height to the latter syllable, and holding it.

The assemblage rose as one, save one.

The clerk bowed unto Ben. "Might the gentleman be persuaded also to be upstanding?"

Shivering near unto infirmity, Ben struggled to rise from his chair, and was no sooner demonstrative in this regard than was assisted by his Intermediaries. Clarence thereupon restoring Ben of his marten cap, and Bartholomew indicating that it would not be improper to put it on, Ben pulled his "wig" onto his head, and accepting his crab-tree cane from Bartholomew, held the golden crown of this in one hand whilst holding his tin whistle fast in the other. Though yet he shivered, he straightened himself unto full stature.

The clerk nodded. "You may take leave of your attendants, sir."

All is done.

Ben bowed unto Bartholomew and Clarence, they bowing in return.

"You may take leave of your petitioners, sir."

Ben bowed unto Collinson, Strahan, and Shipley, they bowing in return.

"You may take leave of your examiners, sir."

Adams, Wedderburn, and Smith bowed in unison. Ben marveled at the sincerity of the gesture, and of his own in return.

It is necessary.

"The petitioner will kindly take a step forward." The clerk bowed.

Closing his eyes, Ben allowed himself to take pleasure in knowing that he had experienced the miracle of life, the awesome improbability of being, and had, despite his errata—alas, his several such—devoted the preponderance of his long tenure upon earth toward farthering the public good in preference to his own. Indeed, no one, not even his examiners, not even Adams himself, could dismiss more than a small fraction of his life to pettiness or venality. Alas, he could not much dispute deserving the fate about to befall him; still, taken as a whole, his life had not been lived in vain; he had 'done good,' in 'silence.' And this knowledge of himself, the comfort of this knowledge, would bear him to endure whatever might await. Indeed, whilst 'hell' might be a venue forced upon one, paradise was surely a province of one's own making.

Looking to the fleeting symmetries within the crystalline bench, Ben marveled at any grammar that could contrive such wondrous sentences, and stopping his breath then, took a forthright step to forward— and was surprised to feel his foot strike upon solid ground.

Strangely, the edge of the vitreous circle had receded by the length of his stride, whilst the level of the humour within the circle had receded by an even greater proportion.

"The petitioner will kindly take a step to forward." The clerk bowed.

Ben took another step to forward, and again the edge of the circle receded by the length of his stride, and again the level of the vitreous murk receded by an even greater proportion—to effect now of the latter being entirely absented from view.

What had been a tap unto a hellish lair, Ben now adjudged, was being transmuted, increment by increment, into a private channel unto such; indeed a birthing channel in reverse.

Ben continued likewise, to like effect, until the circle had receded unto its original breadth, of perhaps six feet. Rising from this now was a plume of lurid vapor, noxious near unto nausea, and a low rumble, harmonic with the low hum from the tongues of light atop the crystalline bench.

"The petitioner will kindly take a step to forward."

Drawing in a breath, Ben recollected something Sally and Richard's servant—nay, their *slave*—Bob—Bob of no name, Bob of no history— had mumbled to no one in particular, or so it had seemed at the time, when Ben was near breathing his last: "You don't know what ya done 'til ya a'ready done it." At the time, Ben had dismissed Bob's lament as a striking example of that species of embarrassment people were wont to inflict upon themselves in moments of keen anxiety. At present, however, Bob's words seemed to unfold like sepals upon a swollen bud. "Forgive him," they seemed to say, "for he knows not what an idle silence hath wrought."

Drawing in another breath, Ben closed his eyes and spoke as if to give voice to words as he writ them: "My Dear Mister Bob: Although my life was conducted with much careful attention as to both action and inaction, were it possible to undertake a second edition, as redactor unto the first, I would make a few corrections. Of these, sir, would be this one in particular: I would refuse to serve as figurehead to any society dedicated to the abolition of slavery whilst yet any man living were being held to three-fifths his sovereign self by my complicity. I would choose in lieu of such hypocrisy, sir, to dedicate myself to your education, such as to restore your sacred honor, sir, such that I might merit emulation unto the seventh generation in the cause of justice."

Opening his eyes, Ben took a forthright step to forward, and discovering himself immersed in a crimson mist, was surprised to sense his entire being suffused of a warmth so overwhelmingly intense, so consummately comforting, that he could not in the moment bear the whole of it.

Sinking unto his knees, Ben caught hearing of what at first sounded like the voices of children frolicking in a distant field, but which grew ever more distinctly into an ethereal chorus of ineffable beauty, emanating, it seemed, from every compass point in simultaneity.

To brilliant flashes now, of red, and green, and blue, the three tongues atop the bench merged into a tongue of purist white, and this descending then into the body of the bench, its radiance grew even brighter until, upon becoming wholly subsumed into the bench, it burst forth toward Ben, he yet kneeling upon the vitreous circle. The tongue of brilliant light coming to rest then just outside the circle, it began to swirl in place, its radiance diminishing as its rotation, in the counterclockwise direction, increased. Gradually at first, then ever more rapidly, a form took shape within the swirling vortex, at center, as distaff unto a swirl of dizening wool.

The vortex having become but a gossamer veil, it was wholly disappeared the next instant, and in its stead stood a woman made luminous as if of the waxing embers of a filling moon. Alabaster of complexion, onyx of eye, ebony of tress, the woman was draped in a gown of white satin, girded at the waist of a cord black as jet, and was cradling in the crook of her left arm an infant so lavishly swaddled in black velvet as to be withheld wholly from view. A strand of pearls, black alternating with white, hung from the woman's neck, and from this hung a medallion in likeness to twin fetuses, indistinct of species, circulating head to tail within a common womb, each twin being in coloration the complement to the other—one black of body, white of eye; the other white of body, black of eye.

Catching a feint of peripheral movement, Ben discovered, rested atop the Madonna's shoulder, a serpent, black of body, white of eye, flicking toward him a ruby tongue. Indeed, the cord girding the woman's gown, Ben now realized, was no cord at all, but the coiled body of the serpent.

"Do you apprehend, good sir, the essential maternity of all being?" The voice came not from the woman but from the serpent.

For a moment, Ben was perplexed as to whether he should address the woman or the serpent, but then realized they were the same. "The one is three; the three, infinity."

"And more?"

"Every beginning an end; every end a beginning."

"And do you apprehend, good sir, the essential truth of all happiness?"

"A scissors of one blade cuts no paper."

"And do you apprehend, good sir, the essential cause of these proceedings?"

"Where the primrose is denied its bloom, the burdock will wield its burr."

"And do you apprehend, good sir, why B. Franklin, printer, was chosen for these proceedings?"

Ben shook his head. "I do not."

The serpent cocked its head such as to peer downward. "The knees, good sir, were contrived for mobility, not for humility, the latter being a posture of character, not of stature. And hierarchy, good sir, has no standing, so to say, in this chamber."

Ben raised himself and was no sooner at full standing than was transported, amidst a brilliant flash, unto a familiar landscape, in which a disheveled lad, three months shy of his eighteenth birthday, his pockets bulging of underwear and stockings, was trudging up High Street in Philadelphia, well before this avenue of commerce had become known as Market Street. The wharf at which he and five other travelers had landed, they together having crossed the Delaware the previous evening, upriver, lay one block to backside.

It was early morning on a Sunday, in a city peopled of pious Quakers, so there was no market this day upon High Street, although the stalls and tables for such stood willing.

Ben felt a tightening around his waist, and sensed movement close upon to rightward.

"You were hungry," the serpent hissed, "having had no supper or breakfast in succession, and having endured, dampened of October dew, a chill night; and so your first order of business was to procure substance by which you might warm and comfort yourself. You had in pocket one Dutch dollar and a few coppers, your only means by which to keep yourself until such time you might gain employment. Hence, when you encountered a young lad bearing fresh bread, you made inquiry as to source, and were directed to a baker on Second Street, whereat you purchased three rolls, these articles being perceived by Boston eyes to be as large as loaves."

Ben witnessed his young self return unto High Street bearing a roll levered under each arm whilst ravenously consuming a third, and encounter thereon several Quakers in Sunday plain converging upon a meetinghouse at the corner of Second and Market. The latter were greeting one the other in a curious argot of thee's and thou's, which manner of speech, upon first hearing, Ben had found eminently enthralling.

Ben witnessed himself venture farther up High Street, and then, nearing upon Fourth Street, espy a teen-aged girl espying him from the doorway of a domicile, to leftward, marked "John Read, Carpenter" on the one side, and "Room to Let" on the other.

His eyes watered.

I'm here! I'm here!

"You turned southward at Fourth Street," the serpent continued, "and walked to Walnut Street, eastward then upon Walnut, across Dock Creek, it reeking of offal, to Front Street, keeping yourself thereby to a close circle, and returning you unto the very location of your disembarkation. The dory that had ferried you being yet tethered at the wharf, you sought of its attendants a draught of water, and whilst this was being prepared, you took notice of the young mother and her child who had been among your fording companions. Inquiring of the mother, you discovered her to be waiting to travel farther down the river, and noticing she had naught to eat, you offered her the whole of the sustenance that could have sustained you the remainder of the day and into the next. Do you recall, sir, what you said to the young mother in giving over to her your remaining rolls?"

"I recall the gesture, not the words."

"Kindly listen and be reminded, good sir, for the words are the man."

Ben witnessed his young self withdraw the rolls from their queer larders and give them over to the haggard mother, whose face thereupon illumed of much more than the orangy orb rising at the moment to eastward.

"Two loaves for thee," Ben heard himself say.

Shuddering as if to sting of Leyden jar, Ben sank unto his knees.

A voice, basso and pure, sang froth from the examiners' table: "'What we have above what we can use is not properly ours, though we possess it'—Benjamin Franklin, 1750."

A second voice, baritone and pure. "'An enormous proportion of property vested in a few individuals is dangerous to the rights, and destructive of the common happiness, of mankind'—Benjamin Franklin, 1776."

A third voice, tenor and pure. "'When, by virtue of the first laws, part of the society accumulated wealth and grew powerful, they enacted others more severe [that] would protect their property at the expense of humanity. This was abusing their powers and commencing a tyranny'—Benjamin Franklin, 1785."

A fourth voice, falsetto and pure, sang forth from the clerk's station. "'A man's story is not told solely by a list of his grand accomplishments, but rather by his smaller, daily goods."

A flash and Ben was transported unto a packet ship bearing toward a froth overtopping a shoal of rocks. Rushing to the wardroom, he discovered the captain drawn unto his comb and looking glass over his sextant and spyglass. Rushing to the forecastle, he discovered the watchmen drawn unto song of siren over whisper of Muse. Rushing to the galley, he discovered the crew drawn unto rum and treacle over fruit and jerky.

A voice sang forth from the petitioners' table, soprano and pure: *All that might have been, all that might yet be, all is in your hands, good sir.*

A second voice, mezzo and pure: *Though the hour is late, yet still there is time.*

A third voice, contralto and pure: *The circle is the only geometry.*

"'I wish it were possible,'" the serpent hissed, "'to invent a method of embalming drowned persons in such a manner that they be recalled to life at any period, however distant; for, having a very ardent desire to see and observe the state of America a hundred years hence, I should prefer, to any ordinary death, the being immersed in a cask of Madeira wine, with a few friends, till the time, to be then recalled to life by the solar warmth of my dear country.'" The serpent flicked its ruby tongue. "The autumn packet is provisioned, sir, her bilge laden of Madeira, her crew waiting upon a shrill note. Would you be aboard her, sir?"

Ben smiled. "I would."

The serpent cocked an eye to downward. "Pray tell us, sir, how one is to bear his trunk unto his cabin from such a posture."

Upon rising to full stature, Ben discovered himself restored to full dress, and laden of a body of received memory of sufficient utility, it would seem, of the heft of it, to render an unwitnessed history, spanning two centuries, at least a little familiar.

Upon stealing a glimpse into this trove of history, Ben smiled most broadly: Adams second; Jefferson third; Madison fourth; Monroe fifth— John Quincy!—*Young* Quincy!—sixth!

And likely the best of the lot!

Aye—until Mister Lincoln.

A veil of colorations began now to swirl around the Madonna, in the counterclockwise direction, to effect of eclipsing her within a spiral of stripes, one green, one red, one blue, which thereupon sundered to form three tongues of fire, one green, one red, one blue, which thereupon spawned yet more tongues of fire, by way of intermingling, until such time Ben was circumscribed by a dozen and one dancing tongues of fire, red unto jade, aqua unto violet.

Spinning in place then, in the counterclockwise direction, each tongue of colored fire transfigured into a woman draped in a gown matching her color, bearing in her hair a lush bloom of *Franklinia alatamaha*, and upon her breast an elegant calligraphy, *Compassion* unto *Contrition*, *Forbearance* unto *Trust*.

Upon clasping hands, the women began to dance around Ben, first in one direction, and then in the other, their collective circumference ever shrinking.

Looking to the examiners' table, Ben was surprised to discover standing there, in the stead of Adams, a figure that could only be that of the Buddha, robed in red; and in the stead of Wedderburn, a figure that could only be that of the Great Sage, robed in green; and in the stead of Smith, a figure that could only be that of the Great Teacher, robed in blue. His eyes meeting theirs, they bowed in unison. Ben bowing in kind, he noticed that whereat had lain the remaining volumes of the *Autobiography*, at either end of the table, lay now two honey-brown rolls, large as loaves, indeed to Boston eyes.

Looking to the petitioners' table, Ben was surprised to discover standing there not sirs Shipley, Strahan, and Collinson, but Margaret Stevenson, draped in red satin; Madame Helvetius, draped in green; and Madame Brillon, draped in blue. His eyes meeting theirs, they smiled in unison, Madame Helvetius adding a wink.

Discovering then the clerk bent near unto a ninety-degree fold, Ben bowed in kind, his head near upon striking upon Forgiveness; and hearing then a din from behind, Ben turned to rearward and was startled to discover not a congregation of wigged and powdered dandies, as at a royal amusement, but a throng of hollow-eyed waifs, as at a public orphanage. His eyes meetings theirs, they extended toward him their arms. "Pater! Pater!"

The dancers elevating of a sudden their clasped hands—

A flash—

Book III

Tribulations

Dear Friend,

We are ever at liberty to choose our comfort by no greater than the least trouble, but I am told by very good authority, in the person of a certain leather apron man, that regret hath the greatest of company.

> *I remain ever—*
> *your humble servant,*
>
> Silence Dogood

One Milk Street, Boston, MA

September 17th, 6:13 a.m.

A brilliant flash illumed to eerie effect a sky held near unto nocturnal darkness by a cloak of sodden clouds. That there should have been a sharp report in near simultaneity, but was not, likely went unnoticed, given the hour.

The red-brick structure directly across the street, being well familiar, was strongly suggesting as to the immediate location, as was the local geometry: the meetinghouse fronting upon a crossing street to his left, and what likely was School Street commencing diagonally askance the crossing street, from the farther side. Slabs of hewn granite underfoot were also of some familiarity, generally so if not specifically so.

Tapping forward a few steps, such as to gain vantage by which to view what stood to his backside, Ben turned half-circle around and discovered himself facing upon a pale yellow building showing a large window revealing naught within but vacancy.

Supposition was progressed unto certainty, however, firstly by way of a bold marquee spanning the full width of a recessed entryway to rightward, reading ONE MILK STREET; secondly by a bust of himself within a roundel centered above a second-level window; and thirdly by lettering raised in relief upon a yellow-stone lintel:

BIRTHPLACE OF FRANKLIN

Not "Birthplace of *Ben* Franklin," he could not help but notice, or "*Benjamin* Franklin," but "Birthplace of Franklin."

He smiled. Indeed, he had been returned to the very site of his birthing, of over three centuries previous. Looking again to the bold marquee, Ben was reminded of the large blue ball that had served a similar function overtop the door to his father's candle shop.

Noticing thereupon a rectangular portico to rightward, extending outward from the building immediately abutting One Milk Street, Ben began to tap his way toward this, that he might take shelter from the rain, which, although yet falling, would soon likely cease, he speculated, given the general temper of thunderstorms.

As he moved slowly up the incline of the walkway, Ben took notice, underfoot, of an arrangement of bricks and stones forming, in concert, resemblance of a pathway leading from the curb unto the recessed entry to One Milk Street. Each of the stones held an inscription, Ben noticed. And a particular one of these, close upon the curb, he could not help but notice, held a precise likeness of the very script John Hancock had famously writ upon the Declaration. Just below this elegant flourish, a sort of subtitle, most curious, read FINANCIAL SERVICES.

Coming thereupon to a curious mechanism to rightward, extending upward from the pavement to the underside of the portico, Ben paused to regard this. It bore a conspicuous label atop, CITIZENS BANK, just below a curious symbol, and was framed by a bright-green border, this bearing to leftward an array of colorated rectangles of the general size of calling cards. A small pane upon the mechanism itself was periodically flashing a brief instruction: Insert Card for Service. Below this pane was an array of buttons, and to the right of this array was a narrow slot marked by a symbol appearing to give instruction, by way of example, as to the proper orientation by which to "Insert Card for Service."

The "Service" being offered, Ben surmised, was that which would be rendered by bank clerk, but requiring no wage, hence, no toleration of ill temperament.

Ben smiled.

There was no limit indeed to the human capacity for invention, Ben mused; the only question was, indeed remained, was there equal capacity for wisdom?

Upon approaching the entry to the building abutting upon One Milk Street, this being also recessed, and even greater in width than the previous, Ben noticed, just beyond it, a small green placard attached to a pillar of sorts at about eye level. Sensing information of interest, Ben tapped his way to the farther end of the portico, and thereupon read, whilst remaining sheltered from the yet-falling rain, the title inscribed upon the placard—BOSTON TRANSCRIPT BUILDING. He continued unto the smaller print, which identified Washington Street—being the crossing street, Ben surmised, immediately beyond—as "Boston's Newspaper Row, home to all the city dailies into the 1950s." The present building, the placard revealed, had itself been the home of Boston's first afternoon daily, the *Boston Evening Transcript.*

Precisely how many newspapers there had been, in serial or in simultaneity, or what the names of these newspapers had been, the modest placard, most parsimoniously, did not reveal. 'Twas a great pleasure to Ben in the moment, however, to learn that an entire community of newspapers, dedicated to the high purpose of maintaining an informed public, had thriven so close upon the very place he had drawn his first breath.

Ben took notice now of an apparent asymmetry betwixt the green-framed instrument of commerce to leftward—its bold size and bright coloration commanding attention—and the instrument of edification here present, its diminutive portions and drab coloration commanding no notice soever.

Ben watched now, enthralled, as a robust vehicle, silver and blue, glistening of wetness, rounded the near corner and stopped directly in front of the entryway to One Milk Street, such that its rightward wheels were encroached upon the walkway, to effect indeed of obscuring Mister Hancock's elegant flourishes. Amber lamps began to flash upon the squarish backside of the vehicle, this bearing the name "Range Rover." Soon thereafter, the black canopy of an umbrella appeared above the roof line of the vehicle. This moving to the front of the vehicle, its bearer soon appeared, a young woman, who thereupon stepped forthrightly onto the walkway. Most curiously, the woman was wearing a man's suit, dark blue, bearing in the vertical a fine silver stripe, and was carrying a bag, dark blue, slung from her right shoulder. Her shoes, somewhat elevated in the heel, matched the coloration of her suit and her bag. Her hair, richly auburn, was closely coiffed, and absent any covering or ornamentation.

Ben was struck in the moment by what appeared, in this young woman's equipage and presentation, to be a deliberate effort toward tempering certain representations of the feminine by way of assuming certain representations of the masculine.

Most curious indeed.

As the woman approached the mechanical clerk, Ben sought to make eye contact, that he might offer polite greeting, his first such toward any mortal in over two centuries. The woman appeared to take no notice of him, however; in fact deliberately so. Unable to comprehend such a rudeness, Ben posited that he might indeed be invisible—a ghost come to witness, not to *be* witnessed.

To test this hypothesis, Ben ventured a greeting: "A good morning to you."

The young woman shifted her umbrella from near hand unto farther, and clutching her slung bag with her freed hand, continued to her destination, whereat, partially collapsing her umbrella, she leaned this instrument against the base of the machine.

Suddenly recollecting, to no little alarm, his previous state of undress, Ben quickly inspected himself, belly to toe, and was relieved to discover himself restored of the very equipage only recently lost to him. Probing his coat pocket, he recognized, by telling aspect, a nail and a tin whistle, but did not recognize a third object, stiff and slender, which he withdrew in concert with the other objects, to discover himself in possession of, besides a three-penny nail and a three-hole whistle, a small card bearing strong likeness to the representations showing in the legend upon the mechanical clerk.

The card was imprinted "Citizens Bank" at bottom, in white upon green, and showed, also at bottom, the same curious symbol—four blunt-tipped arrowheads come together at the diagonals such as to form something of a circle to center—that the mechanical clerk showed at top.

His eyes freshened of a blink, Ben could not help but notice resemblance of this curious symbol to a compass showing the cardinal points. He smiled then, surmising the very destination to which the means presently held in hand might point, indeed as arrow upon compass.

Tucking the whistle and nail into his vest pocket, such as to separate ancient from new, Ben tapped a few steps down street, that he might gain better vantage from which to observe the actions of the woman, that he might then imitate them.

Turning away from pushing buttons upon a paten of such, the woman glared toward Ben, then repositioned herself such as to show him a greater measure of her backside.

Undaunted by this additional rudeness, Ben allowed the bubble and froth of his mood to spill over the vessel of his soul. "'Tis a great day to be alive, is it not?"

Startled thereupon of a screech most alarming, followed by a blare most rude, Ben turned to discover a vehicle stopped behind the woman's, its occupant, male, presenting an uplifted middle finger, apparently in disapproval of an object bearing some authority, owing to mass, intruding upon the narrow roadway, hence unto his inconvenience.

The inconvenienced driver bore sharply to leftward, nearly thereby encountering a vehicle moving in the opposing direction, and uttering thereupon a salutation, "Fucking asshole!" sped onward.

The woman, seemingly oblivious both to Ben's overture and to the histrionics issuing from the roadway, retrieved her card from the mechanical clerk, and snatching up her umbrella, turned toward Ben, her umbrella poised in the manner of a pike. "I don't give money to panhandlers," she snarled, "and I have a whistle"—she touched the top of her bag with her free hand—"so back off."

Ben flinched a step backward.

The woman snatched a chit from one dispenser, and what appeared to be bills of currency from a larger dispenser, and then, pushing the chit and bills into her bag, pulled from the latter, almost in simultaneity, a stubby object, silver. Clenching this object in her teeth, the woman began a measured retreat toward her vehicle, keeping her umbrella partially closed, even though the rain, although abated, had yet to cease altogether.

"You would appear to have a whistle of high efficiency, ma'm," Ben offered. "I do hope, however, you did not too much pay for it."

Turning away, the woman passed in front of her Range Rover, paused to glance left, and then, looking right, trotted across the narrow street and entered a small shop, the Millennium Newsstand, located immediately adjacent to the rear of the red-brick meetinghouse.

Ben affixed his attention now upon the old meetinghouse directly across the wetted street, on the very site of which, in a preceding structure, fashioned of wood well combustible, he had been baptized a Christian and a Presbyterian, on the very morning of his birth, it being a Sunday. Although the present structure was familiar to him—he had in fact attended service within it on more than one occasion, in company with sufficient relatives, including his sister Jane, as to fill the Franklin box—he now regarded it as if for the first time.

Perhaps it was because he held means now by which to draw a contrast where previously he had held no such means, or perhaps it was because his acuity of perception had been freshened by the distance of two centuries. Whatever the cause, Ben noted aspects of this noble old church now that he had not previously noted, and likely would not have, he had to confess, no matter how long he might have gazed upon it.

In addition, these perceptions came not at the end of some empirical progression, one element of discovery leading unto another, unto some ultimate understanding, but in a single flash of insight.

What Ben noticed was that this old church, in its defining architecture, reflected a blending of arc and angle, of round and square, unto a most agreeable balance, this being as natural, as agreeable, as that betwixt the canopy of any tree and its trunk. The effect was made all the more manifest by way of reference to the near structures, which seemed in contrast to be all lines and angles. Most striking in this regard were the windows upon these other structures in contrast to those upon the old church, the latter being arched atop and squared to bottom, the former being squared atop *and* to bottom.

The young woman emerged from the news shop, and carrying a flimsy bag, white, in one hand, her umbrella in the other—no newspaper, Ben noted—hurried across the street. She seemed, as she charged toward her squarish vehicle, all lines and angles. As Ben thereupon watched the backside of her silver-and-blue Range Rover move down Milk Street, he was visited as if by a whisper of Muse:

To behold the geometry within, one need look only to that without.

Turning half-circle around, Ben tapped his way to the mechanical clerk, and leaning his walking stick against it, studied its various aspects. Orienting his card then to match the iconic instruction, Ben urged the card into the Insert Card for Service slot. The card disappearing, the pane displayed a request to "Enter your PIN." Ben pondered upon this mystery for a moment, and then, surmising he was being solicited for a code known only to him, and readily mnemonic to him, and taking notice of where he was at present standing, he pushed the buttons on the paten to the effect of rendering 170106 and pressed Enter. This trial failing to please the clerk—these damnable clerks!—Ben tried 011706. Upon this attempt, the clerk responded by inquiring as to whether Ben wanted to get cash or to make a deposit.

Ben smiled—surely he was much too young, having been born in '06, to be operating so sophisticated a device—and selected $100, the maximum amount indicated, and marveled thereupon when five crisp $20 bills appeared from a dispenser, each so perfectly aligned with the others as to render the whole the feel of a single bill. Taking into hand then a chit appearing from a smaller dispenser, Ben discovered this to be a receipt reflecting his withdrawal and indicating that he yet held in account a balance of $400.

He smiled. A'ready this machine had, by way of a symbol—a diamond being forged that was in simultaneity a circle at center—suggested his ultimate destination. Now it seemed to be suggesting, by way of a limitation upon his means, a proportionate limit upon the amount of time available to him.

Slipping the five bills, together with the bank card and the receipt, into the right-hand pocket on his jacket, Ben probed his vest pocket for his timepiece, and encountering naught but nail and whistle, recalled, to a pinch of chagrin, his oversight.

Turning half-circle around then, Ben looked to the clock upon the belfry of the meetinghouse, this being in likeness to a full moon rising in the east, and took note of its complementing hands, these showing the hour to be 6:29—the very hour, indeed, of his "original" birthing—over three centuries previous!

Smiling, Ben determined he would visit his old Latin School, it being little farther than one block distant, and then visit the old burying ground, it being little farther than that, and perhaps visit then the Common, it being little farther than that. Beyond such, in particular as regards discovering means by which he might progress to farther sites, and ultimately unto his natural destination, he would entrust to knowledge yet to be acquired.

Looking to the Millennium Newsstand, and feeling thereupon a pang of hunger, Ben stepped off the curb, in conformity with the young woman's example, absent the part involving looking to one side and the other, and was nearly struck by a vehicle turning abruptly onto Milk Street from the near crossing street.

Recoiling to a strident blare, Ben stumbled backward over the curbstone close behind, and fell onto the walkway backside down. Although the rain had ceased, the granite slabs of the walkway yet held pools of wetness within the marks consequent to the crude means of their fashioning. As Ben lay prostrate, he could feel a general wetness, owing as if to an affliction of incontinence, insinuate itself against his posteriors.

Upon restoring himself to his feet, he brushed as much wet and grime off his trousers as he could manage, and thereupon took note that, although there was now considerable pedestrian traffic in the vicinity, especially at the intersection immediately above, no man or woman seemed to have taken notice of an old man, bearing a cane, fallen upon his backside. Perhaps, he surmised, given his mode of dress, in particular his curious cap, pulled down nearly upon his spectacles, in context with his incautious launch onto a roadway frequented by vehicles seemingly fashioned to military standards, he had been judged either deranged or inebriated—or both.

In fact, he being not known to anyone, he might as well be the rodent he presently espied scurrying along the walkway afront One Milk Street, desperate, it would appear, to take refuge from vulnerability owing to exposure.

Indeed, it would appear that the Golden Rule derived not from divinity, but from intimacy.

Ben noticed then that he had fallen upon the very stone bearing the distinctive flourishes of Mister Hancock, these seeming to constitute a banner overflying a phalanx of knights constituted of the letters in "Financial Services."

He smiled. *Vanity shall be the undoing of us all—thine, so sorry to say, before mine.*

Making his way then up the incline to the crossing street, Ben was pleased to discover there a street marker bearing the name of his old friend, General Washington, to whom he had, in fact, bequeathed the very crab-tree cane he presently held in hand.

The circle is the only geometry.

Discovering thereupon mechanical means by which to alter the pedestrian lamp to his favor, Ben crossed to the farther side of Milk Street, and tapped his way down street then, toward the Millennium Newsstand. Walking in concert with Newton's gravity, and therefore with less effort, Ben passed by a subterranean stairwell, bordered by a wrought-iron railing, that provided access to Antiquarian Books of Boston, located within the basement of the meetinghouse. Coming upon a plaque attached to the side of the meetinghouse, Ben paused to read this and discovered it to declare, with bronze authority, that Old South Meeting House had been erected in 1729, and that Ben Franklin had been baptized there.

Ben flinched as if to a blow of little consequence of itself, but, in being wholly unexpected, of more consequence than it ought.

He had in fact *not* been baptized in this meetinghouse, which had *not* been erected until twenty-three years following his birth! In truth, he had been baptized in the *previous* structure, called Old Cedar, which had been torn down before it might fall victim to the embers of February, to make way for the present structure.

He had not become acquainted of the present meetinghouse indeed until the fall of 1733, four years following its completion, this being on the occasion of a visit he had made to Boston to reacquaint himself of his family, his sister Jane in particular.

Ben felt an urge now, of some fervor, to leave a corrective note, together with a brief essay on the merits of exactitude, but, alas, he had not pen with which to write, nor sheets upon which to write. In lieu of such, he narrowed his eyes toward the plaque, as if toward its careless author, and shook his head.

Alas, he had been returned to his "dear country" no greater than one quarter-hour's duration and a'ready he had been made wary against accepting as truth anything presented as such by way of public declaration.

Where error is the seep, falsehood is the flood.

It occurring to Ben then that he might be able to procure stationery at the newsstand, he continued onward, and soon came upon a second subterranean stairwell, this one leading also unto a basement shop, The Old South Meeting House Museum Shop. Pausing at the railing fronting this stairwell, Ben glanced upstreet at the previous stairwell, and gazing then upon the meetinghouse proper, noted the erosion, hence the impermanence, of its bricks. It occurred to him then that whereas this venerable old house of worship had once stood upon a foundation of Puritan fervor, that of his sister Jane included, and perhaps in particular, it now stood upon a foundation of commerce.

Smiling, Ben allowed himself a brief imagining of what Reverend Mather might have had to say about this remarkable happenstance. Discovering then an "Open" advertisement close upon the entry to the news shop, Ben noted it to be correct in two regards: The shop was "open" for commerce, and the door was "open" for entry, being presently affixed outward. Several tiers of magazines, Ben noted, all showing faded covers, were displayed in the windows, and affixed upon the panes themselves were several banners, one of these being imprinted "*New York Post* On Sale Here;" another, "*New York Times* On Sale Here;" and a third, larger than the others, "The Lottery—Play Here."

Tapping his way into the shop, Ben discovered there to be but one inmate besides the clerk within, and a good thing this was, he noted, as there was not space in the whole of the shop for more than three or four inmates total at any one instant.

The only patron, a short, frumpish woman whose hair, salted of gray, was only partially contained by a haphazard of amber combs, was selecting from amongst an array of colorated cards hanging on metallic rods extending outward from a partition behind the clerk. To select a card, the woman would name the number of the rod holding it ("a 13 ... and a 17 ..."). The clerk, a short man in perhaps his mid-thirties, tawny of complexion, jet black of hair, would then slip a card from the named rod and add it to a growing stack of such on a small space of countertop close upon the woman.

"What's Megabucks up ta?" the woman demanded, with a cough, her voice hoarse and phlegmatic, as if owing to a recent acquaintance with the consumption.

"Thirty-nine," the man replied, in a lilting species of intonation most agreeable.

"Gimme ten quick-picks," the woman demanded, adding from an open wallet a bill to those a'ready laid upon a small remainder of counter space.

The clerk swept up the bills, and riffling through these, moved sidelong to a device that, in resting upon the counter, took up a goodly portion of this, and which, Ben noticed, was, in form and coloration, reminding of the mechanical clerk at One Milk Street. Reminding also of that other device was the presence atop the present device of a symbol, this one consisting of the term "The Lottery" imprinted upon a puzzle-piece likeness of the Commonwealth of Massachusetts.

Smiling to the pun (common wealth), but also to a wash of nostalgia, Ben recalled his shop on Market Street, perennially scented of his brothers' soap and his mother-in-law's salves, in which he had, on occasion, also dispensed lottery tickets, each one, however, by hand.

Reminding himself as to purpose, Ben began to look about for newspapers, in anticipation of discovering, in short order, rack upon rack of such, in counterpart indeed to rack upon rack of lottery tickets, or so Ben supposed those colorated cards to be; however not a single newspaper did he immediately espy—not a *New York Post*, nor a *New York Times*. What he discovered instead was rack upon rack of dessert victuals, in transparent bags; and rack upon rack of greeting cards, most of these being of a rather prurient nature; and rack upon rack of Zippo devices; and rack upon rack of all manner of confectionaries; plus, upon high, a gallery of likenesses, greatly enlarged, of what Ben presumed to be winning lottery tickets, purchased upon the present premises, of course, and displayed in this manner toward exciting patrons toward incurring yet farther losses in the cause of beating unbeatable odds.

Searching now to rightward, Ben discovered yet more victuals in vitreous bags, plus a glass-fronted cabinet stocked with bottled liquids tinted, it would appear, of every pastel; plus a chart, attached to the near end of the cabinet, showing several rows, 1 through 31, revealing, by script of hand, the most recent "Instant Game Winners."

Reminding himself again as to purpose, Ben scanned more deliberately for what had been strongly implied by way of a public declaration—Newsstand—to be the primary article of commerce therein.
Being now unencumbered of the distraction commanded by all novelty,
Ben soon discovered, on the lee side of a rack of greeting cards, which
articles had previously distracted his attention, a single rack holding
newspapers, on four shelves.

Incredulous that these few items could represent the whole of the
inventory of "news" held by a shop labeled "Newsstand," Ben scanned
the entirety of the shop a third time, with even more deliberation, and
did discover, by such extremity, four small piles of newspapers resting
upon the floor, but quickly judged the lot of these, by the number of
piles, four, and their location, beneath a rack stocked with various other
species of items, to be but farther inventory for the rack of four shelves.

The frumpish woman approached, her eyes reflective of an unrelenting sadness, her gait a bit stiff and asymmetrical. As she took obvious
notice of Ben's sartorial peculiarities—his marten cap in particular—
Ben took circumspect notice of an article in her right hand too small
to be a newspaper, too large to be a magazine, and was surprised to
discover this showing more coloration than newsprint. Smiling, Ben
glanced upon the curious article. "May I inquire, madam, as to which
title you have there in hand?"

The woman regarded Ben in close likeness now to the manner in
which the woman wearing a man's suit had regarded him.

"Might it be one of the New York papers advertised in the window,
madam; or perhaps a local item?"

The woman held the item in hand yet close to side. "The *Enquirer*,"
she said.

Ben lit up. "The *Inquirer*—'tis here?"

The woman stared, eyes slitted as if against a solar glare, then, shaking her head, waddled on.

"Thank you, madam," Ben called after her.

Ben tapped the few steps to the rack of four shelves and was
delighted to find, on the topmost shelf, a few copies of *The Boston
Courant*, its name agreeably consonant with his brother James's *New
England Courant*, in which medium indeed Ben had, under guise of
Silence Dogood, published his first oratories. Smiling now, Ben recalled
the source that had inspired in him this first of many nom de plumes to
follow, this being Reverend Mather's exhortation, "To keep silent one's
own interests such as to be able to attend to those of others."

Ben scanned the bold headline atop the *Courant*—KINNEY CEL-
EBRATES 60TH / PREDICTS 'BIG WIN' IN NOVEMBER—and then
examined a *Boston Globe* from the second shelf, a *USA Today* from the
third, and a *Wall Street Journal* from the fourth.

No *Inquirer*.

Backtracking now, Ben examined the newspapers resting upon the
floor in four piles, but soon discovered, as he had suspicioned he might,
only duplicates of the newspapers a'ready represented in the rack of
four shelves. He thereupon approached the clerk, who was presently sitting upon a stool behind the counter, with his eyes affixed upon a curious device showing moving images upon a squarish pane. This device
was elevated overtop the glass-fronted cabinet, upon a shelf there, and
would seem to be conjuring a separate reality.

Of a sudden a most curious articulation sounded in Ben's mind, as
if called forth from some far recess of memory—"television"—followed
by an essential understanding of the workings of this truly remarkable
device. In the wake of this understanding came another, as if shaken
loose by the first, regarding yet another curious articulation, this one
being "automated teller machine."

Ben smiled. He had surmised the relation, one to the other, indeed
respectably well.

Standing afront the small remainder of countertop, Ben looked
again to the distracted clerk. "Excuse me, sir. Would you be so kind as
to direct me to the *Inquirer*?"

Without moving his eyes from the images showing upon the television pane, the clerk gestured toward a stack of papers resting upon
the counter that, in proportion and appearance, resembled the very
article held by the woman. Ben read the banner—*National Enquirer*—
and understood the woman's perplexity, as well as his own. He read
then the topmost banners:

FIRST DIVA HITS HIGH C OVER B'DAY ORGY ON KINNEY YACHT
Sweet-toothed hubby caught licking double fudge
off bunny's cupcakes.

Ben looked again to the clerk. "So sorry to trouble you again, sir."
Ben waited on a response, but the clerk made no signal toward looking
away from the television. "I am most curious, sir, as to your shop being
declared a newsstand, yet offering no more than four varieties of that
item, with none of these matching the advertisements on your window."
Ben looked to the stack of *Enquirer*s. "Five, if one were to include this

item in common with the four. Am I perhaps misinterpreting the intention of the term 'newsstand,' sir?"

The clerk oriented his head a bit more toward Ben but kept his eyes
affixed upon the television. "All bad news," he said. "Who needs it?
People got enough of their own."

The cultural modulations upon the man's intonations were considerable, requiring close attention.

Ben gestured with the top of his cane toward the stack of *Enquirers*.
"This item would seem not to be of a kind with the others."

The clerk looked to the stack of *Enquirers*. "Which?"

"The one you are presently regarding, sir."

"About the Prez?"

"I am referring to the *Enquirer* as being perhaps a separate kind or
category of newspaper, sir, in relation to the four newspapers in the
rack." Ben pointed to the rack with his walking stick.

The clerk looked to the rack. "All bad news there." He laid a tawny
hand on the stack of *Enquirers*. "All celebrity shit here."

"Toward what satisfaction, sir, is the 'celebrity shit,' as you put it?
Toward what benefit?"

The clerk shrugged. "I got no clue. You'll have to ask my wife. She
makes me bring it home every night." He screwed up his face. "I carry
it in a bag, like a dead fish."

The clerk returning his attention to the television, as if to take a
breath after holding it for as long as he might, Ben looked to the images
imprinted upon the *Enquirer*, the most prominent of which showed a
woman, near upon naked, emerging from a large cake, she being strategically smeared, one might say, of chocolate icing. Ben looked then
to the television pane, upon which a robust woman, scantily clad, was
emerging from a viscous swamp, her golden body near upon covered
over with what appeared to be leeches having engorged upon a bountiful harvest. Ben looked again to the *Enquirer*, again to the clerk. "Have
you stationery for sale, sir?"

After a moment, the man turned his head toward Ben, his eyes yet
holding in view, it would seem, the previous object of their attention.

"Have you any paper or pens, sir?"

Notes of a dramatic timbre emanating from the television, the man
returned his attention to it. He screwed up his face—the woman was
pulling leeches from her forearms with her teeth. Shaking his head, he
looked to Ben. "If you don't see it, I don't got it."

Ben looked to the myriad of items occupying near upon the whole of the countertop, then to the myriad of lottery cards occupying near upon the whole of the wall behind. "Might there be a stationer in the vicinity, sir—a purveyor of writing materials?"

The clerk, yet holding his attention upon the television, gestured in the direction of the near intersection. "Try the bookstore, up at the corner." He glanced to a clock upon the near wall. "They open at 7:00."

"Most grateful, sir."

The robust woman on the television pane, Ben noticed, was holding a fatted leech immediately overtop her uplifted mouth, she being intent, apparently, upon swallowing this serpentine creature in the whole.

Returning thereupon to the rack of newspapers, Ben removed a *Courant* from the top shelf, in simultaneity with an exclamatory noise from the clerk—the leech had apparently been swallowed—and returning to the counter, separated a crisp Jackson from the other four of its species. "If it's not too much trouble, good sir," Ben interrupted, laying the newspaper on the counter, the bill atop, "I am most desirous of purchasing this instrument of general edification."

The clerk slid from his stool and slipped the bill deftly into hand. "Any tickets with that?"

"Tickets?"

The clerk gestured toward the lottery cards displayed on the near wall, and then toward the lottery dispenser resting on the countertop. "Can't win if you don't play."

"And if I were to play, as you put it, sir, would I not sooner draw a lightning strike to my crown than draw a pot of gold from your dispenser?"

The clerk uplifted his eyes toward the gallery of greatly magnified ticket likenesses affixed to the upper wall. "Every lightning bolt's gotta strike somewhere."

Ben noticed that each ticket likeness in the gallery showed a fading from its original purity. "Indeed, sir, but in relation to how many objects that go unstruck?" Ben looked to the *photocopies*—remarkable!—of the lottery tickets. "Should not these representations, sir, if they are to be displayed at all, be counterpoised in fair proportion by those that won their holders naught but penury? If a maiden veils from her suitors all but a few winsome glimpses of her person, sir, and the several aspects hidden do not subsequently match the advertisement of those revealed, has she not deceived most grievously, sir, by way of omission?"

The clerk waved a hand to dismissive effect. "Ah, but it's all for a good cause, so what difference does it make?"

"Cause?"

"The schools."

Ben smiled. "In what proportion, sir, as to the total available?"

The man shrugged.

"What pie passed through many hands, sir, is not but crumbs to the hindmost?"

The clerk regarded Ben's fur cap a moment and then, making change from a cash store, this juxtaposed to the lottery dispenser, delivered to Ben's hand a single Jefferson coin and a few bills—a Hamilton, a Lincoln, and four Washingtons. Thereupon seating himself on the stool, the clerk returned his attention to the television, it showing in the moment a man standing betwixt two all-but-naked females, the three betwixt two glimmering vehicles, the man screaming and gesticulating the while in the manner of a jester.

Ben was most pleased to discover a likeness of Hamilton upon the ten, and of Washington on the one's—both men being so very deserving of such an honor. The bearded man on the five, he—Ah! Mister Lincoln: the man who ended slavery! Obviously Mister Lincoln was most deserving as well!

Taking particular notice now of several tiers of confectionaries, Ben felt anew the pinch of hunger that had visited him previous, and considered making purchase of a few items of these, in particular those bearing names most curious—Snickers, Milky Way, Payday. But then, recalling to himself the distance of his destination, and the unknown potency of his funds, he decided to postpone any indulgence until such time a surfeit of funds should become assured.

Ben looked to the clerk, and following the man's gaze, to the television. The golden woman was bent over, arms propped upon her knees, retching. Ben looked to Washington, and putting the bills and the coin to pocket, looked again to the clerk. "Thank you, sir."

The clerk, pointing a small device toward the television, caused the images on the pane to change, several times over. At the end of his intervention, the pane showed an elegant Negro woman, bountiful of bosom, well adorned of ornamentation, sitting in a chair oriented toward a settee, upon which sat a young man, his shirt unbuttoned from neck near unto belly button. Of a sudden the man jumped up, leapt onto to his seat cushion, and began to scream and gesticulate in the manner of a frighted monkey. The images changed then to two women engaged in fisticuffs, their knuckles being cushioned of fatted gloves.

Lifting the *Courant* into hand, Ben folded it once over and tapped his way from the shop. Pausing just outside, he held the paper up to his nose, breathed in a heady whiff of ink, smiled, then tapped his way upstreet, past the meetinghouse, and across the intersection to the farther side of Washington Street.

The sky had all but cleared and the air had a'ready considerably warmed—as much, Ben surmised, from warm air flooding in from the south, in the wake of the storm, as from influence of a sun not yet visible over the obstructing structures to eastward. Despite the early hour—it being yet shy of 7:00, by the steeple clock on Old South—there were many pedestrians about, most ambulating at a remarkably rapid gait, none taking any particular notice of a fur-capped old man dressed in the style of late 18th-century America.

Ben adjudged the cause of his anonymity—nay, invisibility—to be twofold. Firstly, passersby tended not to make eye contact with him, nor, it would appear, with anyone else. Secondly, the heterogeneity of the fashion presently encountered was so vast—ranging from the neatly trim and circumspect to the clownishly loose and iconoclastic— as to render all modes of dress equally unremarkable.

Ben took comfort presently from his relative unremarkability.

Reaching the intersection of Washington with School Street, Ben noticed that the geometry of the near corner formed a triangle, with the well-windowed façade of a bookshop serving as hypotenuse, and that the majority of this triangle was given over to an arrangement of statuary arranged into two groupings—the nearer consisting of a prostrate family, of three members, in the throes of dire—nay, mor- tal—distress; the farther consisting of a prosperous family, also of three members, in the act of passing by the other family. The mother in the prostrate family was supplicating toward her counterpart, whilst the latter was responding with a frown of disapproval—nay, of contempt. The fathers in the two families were making no eye contact; instead, the prostrate man was covering his face with his hands, as if in shame, whilst the passing man, bearing a symbolic sack upon his back, was holding his eyes to forward. Notably the child in the prostrate family was a girl; that in the passing family, a boy.

There seemed veritably to pulsate from this statuary, from the con- trived drama of it, Ben felt, a palpable throb of anger—nay, of rage.

The statues were surrounded by a brick plaza, this being surrounded in turn by a sitting wall, this being surrounded in turn by beds of low shrubs. There were two entrances, each bordered to side by a pair of plaques affixed atop pedestals of hewn black granite.

Entering now the nearer of the two entrances, Ben began to scan the two plaques there.

The An Gorta Mór memorial, Ben soon learned, had been erected to commemorate the 150th year since onset of "The Great Hunger" in Ireland, brought on by "a virulent fungus" that had devastated the entirety of the potato crop, upon which eight and a half millions had depended for sustenance. From 1845 through 1850, one million Irish had died of starvation, many of this number "on the sides of the road, their mouths stained by grass in a desperate attempt to survive."

The British government had "*callously* allowed tons of grain to be exported from Ireland to pay absentee landlords their rents." Tenant farmers unable to pay their rents, one-half million of these, were "*ruthlessly* evicted from their homes."

Ben paused to ponder the two adverbs encountered, "callously" and "ruthlessly," each writ in italics—why these superfluities had not been struck out by a well-seasoned arbiter. These were not, after all, terms of edification, but of judgment—nay, of condemnation.

Reading farther, Ben learned that the memorial depicted "the Irish exodus from their homeland, their arrival in Boston and ultimate triumph over adversity in America." Perplexed, Ben regarded again the statuary of two parts. Where, he wondered, was the part depicting "the Irish exodus from their homeland?" Where the part depicting "their arrival in Boston?" Where the part depicting their "ultimate triumph over adversity in America?" Had the sponsors of this memorial perhaps failed to raise sufficient funds with which to commission the full breadth of it, or had they perhaps been overruled by interests inclined more toward "a little vengeance" than toward a little history? Or, indeed, had the compositor of the annotation failed to inspect the memorial as it had been wrought before describing it as it had been intended?

Ben tapped his way across the brick plaza to the farther entrance, taking note en route of a bronze basket that lay empty before the supplicating woman. From one of the plaques at the farther entry, Ben learned that two millions of Irish had emigrated to escape starvation, and that "The emigrants boarded vessels so unseaworthy they were called Coffin Ships," and that, "So many passengers died at sea that poet John Boyle O'Reilly called the Atlantic Ocean upon which they journeyed 'a bowl of tears.'"

Ay, but what precisely, Ben wondered, was to be learned from these declarations? That the vessels judged "unseaworthy" had sunk of intrinsic unseaworthiness, to end of drowning all hands—crew and passengers alike? That "many passengers died" owing not to drowning but to conditions incidental to overcrowding, as in the case of the slave ships? Something else altogether? Indeed, in what particular regard had these vessels become deserving of being viewed as coffins?

From the adjacent plaque, Ben learned that the people of Boston had sent 800 tons of aid by way of Capt. Robert Bennet Forbes, who, sailing on March 27, 1847, had reached Cork Harbor in only fifteen days. Looking thereupon for mention of farther such deliveries, Ben found none. Was one to infer then that the only aid sent to Ireland by the people of Boston over the six-year course of The Great Hunger was that carried by Capt. Forbes? And, if this were indeed the case, was not one to infer that the passing family in the statuary represented the people of Boston—indeed the Irish people of Boston?—as much as it did the callous people of England?

And why the mention of Capt. Forbes's rapid delivery? Had this apparently singular accomplishment been to some salutary effect? Had he arrived just in time to save thousands from grass-stained lips? Or was mention of it here but a clumsy braggadocio?

From the next plaque, Ben learned that "the conditions that produced the Irish famine—crop failure, absentee landlordism, colonialism, and weak political leadership—still existed around the world today." Ben shook his head. In truth, was not too much population on too little land at least as relevant a "condition" for famine as "crop failure," or "weak political leadership," not to mention the willful encouragement of unfettered fecundity by certain doctrines?

Ben regarded the statuary now such as to imagine a third grouping of figures—three men in black robes accented of scarlet, each one bearing a basket of fishes toward the starving family.

Bowing toward the starving family, Ben tapped his way to a pair of facing benches close upon the curb along School Street. A street lamp stood just beyond the farther bench, and sitting at the foot of this, his back rested against the post, was a bearded mendicant, desultorily shaking a glassine cup—*plastic*—remarkable!—toward passersby, without noticeable effect.

The man was wearing a drab jacket, threadbare and stained, showing on one shoulder three chevrons and an emblem. Atop the man's head, floating on a haystack of hoared hair, sat a cap, black, imprinted U.S. ARMY / VIETNAM. The visor of this cap was tilted forward such as to shield most of the man's face from ready view. A medallion, heart-shaped and purple, dangled from the breast of the jacket. A pair of wooden crutches lay close upon the man's right side.

Ben was struck by the happenstance of this supplication being in such close proximity to that memorialized a few yards distant.

Seating himself on the near bench, Ben rested his head upon his hands, these folded overtop the Liberty head on his walking stick, and escaped a sigh, aware in the moment of a leaden enervation, owing, he surmised, to a fast spanning greater than two centuries. He thought of the confectionaries at the newsstand, their alluring packaging, and then, unfolding his newspaper, scanned the front page:

> There had been a fatal shooting the previous afternoon outside Boston High. A 17-year-old teenager had been gunned down in a drive-by shooting. According to Police, another teenager, slated to testify in regard to a previous shooting, in Dorchester, had been the intended target.
>
> President Kinney had received a special tercentenary edition of Ben Franklin's *Autobiography* on the occasion of his sixtieth birthday. The President, a Franklinophile, has long claimed to have modeled his own life after the great man's, retiring from a successful business career at a relatively young age in order to devote himself to public service. Although the President declined to identify the source of the gift, his Chief Counsel and long-time friend, Gilbert Bahr, also a Franklinophile, was suspected.
>
> Police had quelled a second night of rioting in Benton Harbor, Michigan, after a black man on a motorcycle was killed while trying to flee from two white officers chasing him at a high rate of speed. Benton Harbor is 92.4 percent black. A dozen buildings and several cars had been burned; several people had been hurt. About 150 state troopers and 100 other police officers had used tear gas and other non-lethal methods to quell the violence. The reason for the chase was not known.
>
> Paul Kenyon, Democratic candidate for President, would be delivering a major policy speech that afternoon at a leadership conference underway at the Waldorf Astoria in New York. The conference was being sponsored by the U.S. Chamber of Commerce, an organization long considered hostile to Democratic candidates. According to the most recent *New York Times*/CBS poll, Kenyon was leading the President by six percentage points: 52 percent to 46 percent.

Of a sudden aware of a presence close upon, Ben lowered his paper to discover the bearded beggar staring at him with all the menace that two rheumy red eyes might muster.

"This is *my* corner, shit breath," the man snarled. "Take a hike."

Ben shifted his eyes from peering overtop his spectacles at the panhandler to peering through them toward the two crutches yet lying upon the pavement nearby the street lamp. "I believe, sir, that in your rush to judgment concerning my intentions, you have inadvertently compromised your credibility, and thereby, by consequence, your immediate prospects in the commerce of pity."

The man's countenance sufficiently attenuated to show perplexity.

"Your crutches, sir," Ben explained. "You have neglected to take them up, apparently by accident of their not being pinned to your person in the manner of your medallion."

The man looked to his crutches, then hung his head as if to a load of shame.

Ben touched the seat to his left. "I suggest you sit yourself, sir, before you should injure your reputation any farther."

The man, yet holding his plastic cup, sat down to Ben's right, infusing the immediate ambiance of an odor most foul.

"Your name, sir, if I may learn it."

The man yet held his eyes cast downward, peered askance toward Ben, revealing a nose pitted and distended, looked again downward, looked askance toward Ben, then held out a hand, well stained, it would appear, of tobacco. "Sergeant Kortright, 75th Infantry, Company E. My friends call me Sarg."

Ben gave a nod as he shook a hand cold and coarse to the touch. "Colonel Franklin, First Pennsylvania Associators. You may call me Ben."

The sergeant flinched. "You a military man?"

Ben smiled. "I am indeed, sir, but not in the sense you imply. Take, for example, the matter of this corner. You discovered me sitting upon this bench and judged me, on the basis of my appearance, a rival to your interests, and your reflex was to accost me with a threat of physical injury. But to what end, sir? Were I a military man in the sense of your inquiry, would I not meet your threat with one yet more menacing, and on and on we should thereupon advance until such time we were alike too deep into pride to withdraw, the only course being to come to blows, unto considerable ruin to one or both? And is this not, sir, the very means by which opposing parties, dominated by our gender, have attempted to settle their opposing interests from the time of Cain and Abel? But where, sir, might we find a body of evidence sufficient to advance this means of resolution as worth anything close to the terrible cost invariably owing to it?"

Sarg drew a wrist across his mustache, this being saturated of nasal discharge, and wiped his wrist upon his soiled breeches. "You one of them nut cases they dump on the streets nowadays?"

"I ask you, good sir, to hear me out, if I might, before you should deliver farther insults."

Sarg shrugged.

"The full record of human history, sir, would seem to advance the theory that if conflicts are to be resolved to any lasting good, they must be resolved not by superior force of arms, but by superior exercise of wits. There is, I submit, sir, no such article as a benign violence, and therefore no lasting resolution to be won of it, nor any true beneficence. In fact, you have witnessed the verity of this fact, first hand, by way of your experience in Vietnam, have you not?"

Sarg averted his eyes and nodded.

"The medallion on your chest, sir; might that article imply that you suffered an injury, most grievous, during the course of your service?"

Sarg touched the purple heart on his chest and nodded.

"You have beside you in the moment, sir, a doubting Thomas, in consequence to his having been rendered wary, within less than one hour's time, by what he has encountered as representing historical truth. Allow him to witness the scar of your wounding, sir, that he might believe."

Sarg regarded Ben most severely.

"Does your delay account to your scar affecting too intimate a location to allow public exhibition, sir, or to some other cause?"

Springing to his feet, Sarg began to stammer, uttering sound but no sense, as if unable to decide which invective he should cock into his bow, all the while gesticulating his arms and legs as if to the heady beat of a vivacious strain of music.

"You are, once again, sir, I feel obliged to make you aware, standing erect absent the service of your crutches."

Sarg threw his cup to the ground, scattering thereby a few coins, and unleashed a volley of invectives, directed upon himself, to the effect of divulging a want of self-regard at once alarming and pathetic. Throwing his cap onto the pavement, Sarg stomped upon this article several times, and collapsing finally onto the opposing bench, held his head downcast, whilst shaking it, yet muttering invectives.

A vehicle passed by on Washington, marked "Police," emitting a most disquieting wail.

"The fault lies not with incompetence, sir, but with the falsehood you embrace. Who amongst mortals can calculate his every action, and deny his every passion, such as to protect his every prevarication? I doubt the angels themselves, one or two of these in particular, their names here to go unmentioned, would be up to the task."

Ben paused. "Have you a home, sir?"

Sarg shook his head.

"Had you one upon a time?"

Ben held silent such that the vacuum force of silence could wield its magic.

⁓

In his growing-up years, Sarg had lived with his mother and a four-years-younger sister, Alice, in a series of "dumps," mostly in Dorchester. His mother had been a "crack head" all this time, so most of what little money they might have at any one time—a welfare check, and whatever his mother could get "banging men at all hours," sometimes two or three at a time—went toward financing her habit. The very morning of Sarg's seventeenth birthday, he had enlisted in the Marine Corps, thinking himself finally and forever escaped. As luck would have it, however, a drill sergeant at Quantico had taken exception to being kneed in the groin—in retribution for having held Sarg's head in a toilet bowl—and so, following six months in the brig, he had been mustered out of the Corps and, with no place else to go, had returned to Dorchester, intending to hole up with his "crazy" mother and his "lunatic" sister only until such time he could find work. With a dishonorable discharge, however, and no high-school diploma, and a record of two felony thefts, he could get not so much as a "no thank you," nor even a "good luck to ya." Then a large real-estate developer had come along and bought up the three-decker Sarg and his mother and his sister were living in, and had evicted all the tenants, "good luck to ya." Sarg had pretty much been on the street ever since, the one exception being, about ten years ago—just after his mother had gotten run over by a taxicab while trying to escape from a giant spider—when he had gotten himself into a "program" and had lived in a shelter for a few weeks. But then he had gotten caught with a bottle of Boone's Farm "fuzzy navel" under his mattress, and that had been the end of that, "good luck to ya."

Sarg had gotten his hopes up a bit recently, though, when a young woman from the Kenyon campaign had approached him, on this very corner, in fact, and had told him that she would get him a place to stay for the winter if he would tell the story about his family being thrown onto the street by Big Jim Kinney. Sarg had done this, at the location of the former three-decker, but nothing had come of it. He had stopped by the Kenyon office on Tremont Street only just yesterday to ask the woman who had promised him "winter digs" when he might get them, but the man he spoke with told him that no one by the name of Courtney St. James was connected with the Kinney campaign. The man gave him twenty bucks and showed him the door, "good luck to ya."

"And what, might I inquire, sir, did you do with the 'twenty bucks?'"

Sarg averted his eyes.

"And your sister, sir, what of her?"

"She run off to New York, thank the good Lord, to get herself into show biz." Sarg shook his head. "She'd 'bout driven me crazy. Every night, the same ol' song, over and over—if I had a hammer, if I had a hammer, if I had a hammer. My mother getting banged in one room, my sister yodelin' in the other. I never hear'd from 'er again, thank the good Lord." Sarg shook his head. "Over and over, Jesus and Mary."

Ben dropped his eyes a moment, then looked again to Sarg. "Might I infer, sir, from your having gotten your hopes up a bit, by way of Miss St. James's promise to you, that you yet value the notion of having a shelter of your own, however modest?"

Sarg shrugged.

"Might I speculate, sir, that you would like to be able to return that 'twenty bucks' given you by the Kenyon campaign, with a generous compounding of interest, 'good luck to ya?'"

Sarg smiled, showing a few absentees in his muster of masticators.

"Might I inquire, sir, whether you might be open to the possibility of kindling, yet one more time, a candle of hope?"

Sarg shrugged, chafing at the brief exposure of cheek betwixt eye and beard.

"Might there be a flower shop in the vicinity, sir?"

Sarg raised his chin and looked overtop Ben. "Jus' up the street there."

Ben rose slowly, leveraging his weight upon his cane. "Which side, sir?"

Sarg gestured toward the farther side.

"Collect your coins, sir, but leave your crutches. You will have no farther need of the latter."

Sarg retrieved what coins he could find, and returning his hat to his head, followed Ben to the near corner, giving his crutches, as he passed them by, not so much as a glance.

Waiting for the pedestrian light to change, Ben took notice of the brick building sited at the opposing corner, marked "Boston Globe Store," which bore some familiarity. He remembered then that a brick domicile had stood upon the very site in the time of his youth, it being one of the very first brick structures to be erected in Boston. Likely, he now surmised, from hint of at least two conjoined architectures, the past structure had been subsumed into the present one.

An apt analogy indeed, he allowed, for all of history.

Taking Sarg by the arm, Ben marched across the narrow street, then tapped up School Street, and soon came upon an eatery, Bruegger's Bagel Bakery, abutting the Globe Store. Feeling another pique of hunger, Ben quickly doused all notion of satisfaction, there being luxury presently neither in time nor in funds for personal indulgence.

Continuing on, Ben led Sarg past a store marked Talbot's, its windows bearing as if crimson eyelashes, and soon arrived at a small flower shop, its frontispiece accented of lavender, bearing the name aBloom. The shop was shut, but upon peering inward through the glass of the doorway, Ben could readily discern the presence of someone within, a woman, standing behind a countertop, her back toward the storefront. A sprightly bouquet of daisies stood to her right.

Instructing Sarg to align himself immediately behind the considerable bulk of himself, Ben knocked gently on the glass with the tip of his cane. The woman, visibly startled, turned from her work. Ben smiled most agreeably, raising his hand in a gesture that was as much a plea as a greeting. The woman approached, wearing an apron.

"We're not open," the woman announced through the thick glass.

"Opportunity knocks but once, ma'm; regret like a child upon his drum." Ben pulled from pocket his bills and splayed these to likeness of a hand of playing cards. "My wallet, ma'm, for a bouquet of your celestial offerings."

The woman, of plain face, looked to her watch, and again to Ben, who bowed as if unto Marie Antoinette, but then straightened abruptly, in recollection of the necessity of yet obscuring what loomed in subterfuge to his backside.

The woman turned a latch amidships on the doorway, and the glass doorway parted into halves.

"We don't normally open until 9:00."

Ben took notice of a golden crucifix hung from the woman's neck by means of a golden chain, and felt temptation to inquire after whether the woman saw any irony in a symbol of deepest humility being forged of finest gold. He placed any gratification to be gained from such a confrontation, however, in the same lockbox with his hunger.

"Thank you, madam," he said, with a nod. "Most kind of you."

Stepping into the aromatic shop, Ben introduced his companion, revealed as if by wave of a conjurer's wand, as Mr. Kortright, lately Solicitor General at School and Washington, now aspiring toward a higher calling.

Sensing the woman unnerved by Sarg's unexpected presence, in conjunction with his own strange appearance, Ben offered the woman his four Jacksons, extending his arm toward her instead of approaching closer. "I have a proposition for you to consider, madam, opportunity here knocking. There would appear to be two modes of retail in your line of trade—the first being passive, waiting for patrons to come unto you; the second being active, venturing forth such as to solicit persons encountered by happenstance. What I am proposing, madam, is very simple: That you add to the first mode of commerce—at which you have obviously attained a high measure of success, or you would not be fast upon your duties at such an early hour—that you add to this mode of commerce some measure of the second mode, by way of selling to Mr. Kortright here, each morning, as many stems as he should have ordered the previous evening, such that he might ply them to pedestrians in need of a little cheer, for themselves or for their acquaintances. To commence this enterprise, Mr. Kortright will now purchase from you, with these bills, as many stems as they should collectively value, along with one modest-sized pot, and a strand of white ribbon, of as many feet in length as there should be stems in his purchase."

Ben smiled overtop his bifocals. "Perhaps you might offer a modest discount for such a purchase, madam, taking into consideration not the present order alone, but the prospect as well of yet greater orders into the future, however remote this prospect might seem to you in the present." He winked, then turned to Sarg. "As for his part, Mr. Kortright, beginning tomorrow, will be attired more manifestly in keeping with the nature of his new trade. Do I speak correctly in your behalf, Mr. Kortright, or do you wish to emend?"

Sarg shrugged, shifting his eyes as if for an object upon which to hold them to some measure of comfort.

Ben continued. "If you please, madam, Mr. Kortright will take delivery this hour of one-half dozen of your splendid daisies, which species you would appear to have available, together with a modest-size pot, and two yards of white ribbon, cut into one-foot lengths. Tomorrow morning, at this hour, Mr. Kortright will take delivery, either at once or in increments, up to the remainder of his total purchase. Or, if you are unable to spare service to this enterprise in the moment"—Ben glanced toward the counter at which the woman had been working—"given the urgency of your current labors—I do apologize for this untimely intrusion, madam—Mr. Kortright will take delivery of the total purchase matching his means in the morning. In either case, the bills are yours to own, even if Mr. Kortright should choose in the interim to return to his former trade, feeling himself not quite up to the new one." Ben nodded to Mr. Kortright, then again offered the four Jacksons toward the woman.

The woman smiled. "I have plenty of daises. I'll be just a minute." Leaving Ben holding the four bills, the woman walked to the rear of the shop, and passing though a set of sliding glass doors, similar to those at the front of the store, entered a room that, in its configuration, replicated the shop proper, with bunches of flowers standing in vases upon shelves to either side. She returned soon thereafter with several daisy stems in hand, and placing these upon the nearer of the two counters, selected two pots from a nearby shelf, one white, one green, and set these also upon the counter. "That about the right size?"

Ben nodded. "Perfect in all regards."

"Green or white?"

Ben turned to Mr. Kortright. Sarg shrugged.

Ben scowled. "Green or white, Mr. Kortright?"

Mr. Kortright pointed to the green pot.

Ben looked to the woman. "Green it is."

The woman measured two yards of white-velvet ribbon from a spool, using a ruler imprinted upon the countertop, measured one additional foot, then cut the whole of the measured length into seven equal lengths.

Ben took notice now of there being seven stems upon the counter as against the six ordered, the former number being consonant with the seven lengths of ribbon just cut. "Thank you, madam, for the good measure."

The woman smiled. "Anything else?"

"Have you any marking pens? I do apologize for being so much trouble."

The woman smiled. "What color?"

Ben turned to Mr. Kortright. "What color, sir, with which to inscribe upon each ribbon a small phrase?"

Sarg shrugged.

"Forgive me, Mr. Kortright, I have neglected to explain my intention. My nearer object is to affix to each stem a ribbon bearing a small phrase. My farther object is for you to follow suit each day hereafter, using phrases gotten perhaps from some compendium of such, or from your own muse. I suggest inscribing each ribbon by hand, as I shall now demonstrate, such as to preserve some modicum of intimacy in a world having become, it would appear, by all evidence, much deprived of such." Ben smiled. "Shall we use yellow, sir, such as to keep in close consonance with the hosting blooms?"

Sarg shrugged, then affixed his eyes upon the ribbons as if to a command heard only by himself. He wrinkled a weather-bronzed brow. "You gonna put words on them?"

"I am."

"Is yeller gonna be dark enough?"

"Ah, so it will not. What color then, say you?"

"How 'bout green?"

Ben looked to the shopkeeper. "A green marker pen, madam, if you please. And should you be well stocked in this article, a black one also."

The woman pulled two marker pens from a squat cup resting on the opposing counter, near a cash store, and gave these over to Ben.

"Thank you, madam." Using the black marker, Ben set about printing the word DONATIONS upon the lip of the flowerpot, then, enlisting the shopkeeper into holding the ends of one of the ribbons, such as to keep the ribbon fully extended, used the green marker to carefully inscribe it, in a flowing hand:

Soft upon the cheek of every child, all hope.

Ben offered the marker to Sarg. "If you would be so kind, Mr. Kortright, as to share the burden. I am more than a little wilted presently of parsimony owing to a lengthy drought."

Sarg shook his head.

"Do you know your letters, Mr. Kortright, sufficiently to write your name?"

Sarg nodded.

"Sufficiently to write Miss St. James a letter of complaint, should ever you be so moved?"

Sarg nodded.

"Mr. Kortright, if we, all of us, were to refuse to participate in any art in which we had not yet a'ready attained a robust level of competency, who then would become apprentice unto master, such as to become master unto apprentice?"

Sarg showed by way of twitch and tic a robust level of agitation.

"Might you perhaps be fearful, sir, of a public humiliation by way of a public failure—a repetition perhaps of some similar agony suffered in years past?"

Sarg began to emit noises as if to provide aural counterpart to his tics and twitches.

"You once held sufficient courage, sir, to undergo the rigor distinctive to becoming a soldier, and, even greater, the courage to bring to the attention of an abusive superior, a bully, sir, at great cost to yourself, the error of his ways. Do you not yet hold within you, sir, in some bastion of your soul, a fair measure of that very mettle?"

Sarg looked to the shopkeeper, whose eyes showed as if a touch of dew.

"You will kindly take this marker into hand, sir," Ben continued, "before I should sag of the burden of holding it yet farther in your stead. I beg of you, sir."

Sarg took the marker into hand.

Ben offered to take the shopkeeper's place, that she might return to her duties, and she accepting, Ben moved to the farther side of the counter, and separating a second ribbon from the others, held it to length upon the countertop. "Tally-ho, Mr. Kortright."

Sarg began to print Ben's phrase upon the second ribbon, his tremulous hand rendering his blockish letters crude and uneven.

Of a sudden Sarg discarded the marker onto the countertop. "Fuck-it-all-t'-hell!" he exclaimed.

Ben immediately saw the problem: Sarg had begun to spell out "child" before pinning a tail on the backside of "ever."

"Ah, very good, Mr. Kortright. You have just given yourself a phrase for tomorrow: 'Soft upon the backside of ever' error, an opportunity.' Most excellent. You are a natural, sir."

Sarg regarded his fortuitous handiwork a moment and then, as if no force upon earth might hold it back, showed a grin, to ultimate effect indeed of releasing a chuckle.

Ben turned to the shopkeeper, she working at the counter close behind. "Our apologies, madam, for the indecorous exuberance. It will not happen again." He looked to Sarg. "Would you be inclined to agree, Mr. Kortright?"

Mr. Kortright looked toward the shopkeeper. "Sorry, ma'm."

The woman smiled.

Taking up the marker, Sarg resumed his handiwork, his face close upon it, using his tongue as instrument, it would seem, as much as his fingers. When finally he had finished, Ben took up the ribbon he had himself inscribed, and tying this to one of the daisy stems, about two-thirds up, formed a bow showing two loops and two tails. He asked Mr. Kortright to follow suit, using the ribbon he had himself inscribed. Sarg hesitated a moment, but then took up the ribbon, and with hands tremulous and uncertain, fumbled and muttered, his frustration rising near unto a boil, but never unto steam, until such time he had formed a bow of more tail than loop.

"Very good, sir. Most excellent. Now to the rest."

Sarg frowned.

"Courage is what is required to take the first step, sir; persistence, the remainder." Ben winked. "Courage is the easy part." Ben ignored a chortle from rearward. "Your task is not one-third completed, sir, and whilst you remain idle, time marches forth, leaving profit unto the coffers of regret."

Muttering more to pretense now, it would seem, than to effect, Sarg set about inscribing the other five ribbons and tying these to the other five stems, his efficiency and skill improving with each iteration. When the last stem had been graced with a bow, equal in loop and tail, Ben asked the shopkeeper for a modest vessel in which to hold the stems in water, this article to be charged against the funds held by her. The woman thereupon produced a white vase of sufficient size to hold a dozen and more stems, it a'ready filled two-thirds with water.

Laying the four Jacksons onto the countertop, Ben was about to take his leave of the shopkeeper when Mr. Kortright stepped forward, with some resolution, and added the coins from his plastic cup to the four bills. Ben nodded to Mr. Kortright, then thanked the shopkeeper for her many kindnesses and reminded her, and thereby Sarg, that Mr. Kortright would be returning in the morning to take delivery of the stems and ribbons yet remaining against his account. Ben thereupon led Sarg through the sliding doors, he carrying the vase of stems, Sarg carrying the flowerpot and, within it, his emptied cup.

⸎

A pair of crutches were yet laying near the lamppost when Ben and Mr. Kortright arrived back at the corner of School and Washington. Ben set the vase of stems onto the pavement close upon these articles, Mr. Kortright following suit with the flowerpot. Ben thereupon asked Mr. Kortright to stand a close watch whilst he made a quick call to the bookshop. Mr. Kortright, shaking his head, advised toward a different venue, the bookshop being notably uncharitable toward public use of its privy. Ben smiled. Tapping his way then around the memorial plaza, Ben entered the cavernous bookshop and, being awed near unto intimidation by the scale of it, removed his cap.

Finally able to orient himself, by way of strategic signage, Ben made his way toward the rear of the present floor, thereafter to the far right corner, whereat an advertisement hanging from a high ceiling—reading "Reference"—directed him to a set of shelves marked "Reference / Public Speaking / Quotations / Genealogy." Looking to rightward, Ben discovered himself peering through a tall window upon the front of the very flower shop he and Mr. Kortright had only recently visited.

He smiled. The circle is the only geometry!

Moving down the left-hand side of an island of shelves, Ben soon came upon three red-jacketed volumes of *Bartlett's Familiar Quotations*. Taking one of these into hand, he scanned a few pages, nodding of approval, chuckling a few times, then, flinching to the price—$50!— gave praise upon himself for having managed not to diminish, through mortal indulgence, what was rapidly proving to be a most meager store of funds.

Holding the volume pressed to his breast, Ben carried it unto one of the counters to front, where the clerk, a cherubic woman of no more than twenty years, complimented him on his costume. The principal at her high school, she offered, wore a similar costume every year on the first day of school, apparently in likeness of John Adams, Ben surmised, the girl's school bearing that name. Ben's costume, however, the young woman allowed, was "a lot more realer."

Ben thanked the clerk for her compliment, then inquired of her what she knew of Mr. Adams.

"He was born in Quincy," she avowed. "Cash or charge?" Ben producing his bank card, the young woman asked him to "swipe" it through the reader, which Ben did, backwards at first, and then, with a little guidance, correctly.

Showing some chagrin, the young woman confessed to knowing naught else about the namesake of her school. She smiled deferentially. "Is he the one who invented electricity?"

Ben smiled. "I knew Mr. Adams to possess something of the sting of the electrical fire, but little of the light." Taking into hand the sale receipt, Ben noted that his $50 purchase had grown—by some black art—to $52.50. Indeed, not all the hands in one's pockets, it would appear, were one's own.

The young woman handed Ben a plastic bag containing his purchase, thanked him, and wished him to "have a nice day."

Once outside, Ben pulled his fur cap back over his head, near unto his spectacles, and tapped his way to whereat he expected to discover Mr. Kortright waiting but, alas, did not. Flowerpot, vase, and man were disappeared; only the crutches remained. Ben bowed his head, and thereupon leaving his purchase upon the bench he had earlier sat upon, began to tap his way up School Street.

"Hey, shit breath? Where ya goin'?"

Ben turned around.

Mr. Kortright, grinning, holding the vase of daises, gestured with his head. "C'mon, I got us a better spot."

Ben retrieved his purchase, and rejoining Mr. Kortright, by way of a sprightly pace, followed him to a lamppost facing upon Washington, a few yards upstreet of the previous post, and thereat gave the bag holding *Bartlett's* over to Mr. Kortright, who, pulling the hefty volume from the bag, looked quizzically upon Ben.

"'Tis a generous tree from which to pluck small fruits," Ben explained. "In time, you may discover such a tree to grow within your own garden."

Ben thereupon instructed Sarg to invert his jacket, and to reverse his cap, "such as," he explained, "to eclipse unto darkness the ugly mask of falsehood." Separating then the four Washingtons from the other two bills, Ben placed these, unfurled, inside the flowerpot. Selecting then one of the daisy stems from the vase, Ben waited for Mr. Kortright to adjust the sleeves on his inverted jacket, and thereupon held the flower before him. "The stem on this daisy, sir, is symbol of the masculine; the tails of the bow, the same. The blossom is symbol of the feminine; the loops of the bow, the same. The two conjoined together, sir, are symbol of complementarity, the essence of all balance, all tranquility, all happiness, indeed all being." Ben paused. "Do you comprehend the meaning of 'complementarity,' sir?"

Sarg shook his head.

"Consider, sir, either half of a pair of scissors in the absence of the other half. Hath the notion of 'cutting' any meaning? Likewise, sir, consider 'good' in the absence of 'evil.' Hath the notion of 'morality' any meaning? We could proceed ever farther likewise: up in the absence of down—hath direction any meaning?—plus in the absence of minus—hath null any meaning?—pleasure in the absence of pain, somethingness in the absence of nothingness, ad infinitum. Methinks, however, you have the notion of it—there can be balance, meaning, well-being, et al., sir, only where there is a complementarity of opposing constituents in equal measure."

Sarg regarded Ben with a sobriety most solemn.

Ben smiled. "I but offer a seed, sir, to the care of your hoe and watering can. Which notion returns us to the business at hand." Ben handed the daisy stem over to Sarg. "Mr. Kortright, sir, you are from this day forward a purveyor of special wares. And with the donations of appreciation you shall receive each day from plying these wares, you will, I do fervently hope, the very day following, purchase yet more of them, minus your expenses, and a modest profit toward your material well-being. And before the end of your days, sir, I do fervently hope you will choose to look after another human being as I today have looked after you, that you will do unto him, or her, similar to what I have today done unto you. Now, sir, one last demonstration and I must take my leave."

Pulling a second daisy from the vase, Ben positioned himself to the right of the flower pot and thereupon offered the daisy toward a passerby, a man in a dark-gray suit straight in line, sharp in angle. Bespectacled and balding, the man was burdened of a satchel distended such as to appear on the verge of foaling.

"A flower for you today, sir?"

The man showed no response, his face as if coiled into an incipient frown awaiting but the pull of a trigger.

"Perhaps tomorrow, sir?—for your son, sir?"

The man stopped, spun around and returned to where Ben was standing. "How did you know I have a son?" His eyes were slitted unto likeness of the tips of arrows. "What kind o' scam you runnin' here?"

"Every man has a son, sir, born unto him of the love of a woman, or delivered unto him of the neglect of others. There is a scam here, sir, I assure you, only by force of a coddled cynicism."

The man took obvious notice of Ben's mode of dress.

Ben offered the flower toward the man. "For your son, sir?"

The man's face became as if grin and grimace in about equal measure. "My son thinks I'm a goddamn Nazi, OK? Because my views don't happen to coincide with his far more enlightened views, OK? So the last thing—oh, Jesus Christ, I don't need this." The man turned away, and shaking his head, began forthrightly to remove himself.

"And if your son were to die this day, sir?—struck down while crossing a busy street, chased perhaps by a giant spider?—by a very important man impatient to get to his office?—upon which he depended for every ember of his happiness? A flower for him upon *that* occasion, sir?"

The man stopped and returning to Ben lowered his briefcase to the pavement. Slipping a twenty-dollar bill from his wallet, he dropped this into the flowerpot, and took the daisy stem into hand. Thereupon regarding Mr. Kortright, he shook his head. "I'm a goddamn idiot."

"And your son, sir? Will he regard you as such upon presentation of your gift?"

The man stared a moment, looked to Mr. Kortright, then continued up Washington Street, a fatted briefcase in one hand, a sprightly daisy in the other.

"Complementies," Mr. Kortright said, looking after the receding balance scale.

"Very good, Mr. Kortright. Most excellent."

Stepping to one side, Ben gestured for Mr. Kortright to take his place. "Solicit interest in your own way, Mr. Kortright, but—if I may suggest—persist in it only with the greatest of respect. Many will see today only to accept tomorrow, or the day following. Patience, sir." Ben removed himself a few more steps down street, toward a set of curious stations marked "Verizon"—a most curious name, it having, it would appear, no intrinsic meaning.

Mr. Kortright, looking no little ill at ease, thereupon offered a daisy stem toward a young woman in company with a small girl child. A generous surfeit of roundedness upon the woman's essential person was rendered all too plain by the woman's careless manner of dress. The girl child in this regard was her mother in miniature—indeed, her sequential twin.

"A flower for you today, ma'm?"

The woman looked to the offered item and shaking her head, rather sharply, looked away.

"For your little girl, ma'm?"

The little girl began to pull against her mother's grasp, whilst issuing shrill demands toward the flower. The mother jerked the child with a sharp pull, and threatening corporal consequence to any farther disobedience, continued to pull the child against the girl's manifestly superior will. The girl beginning to wail, the woman looked to the flower as if for an excuse to take an interest in it of her own accord, such as thereupon to indulge her child whilst yet preserving her personal dignity, not to mention her parental authority.

"Is there something written on that ribbon?" the mother asked, her voice hoarse and phlegmy, not unlike Sarg's.

Sarg nodded.

The woman smiled. "Like in a fortune cookie?"

Sarg nodded.

Releasing hold of the girl, the woman pulled a bill from a bag slung from her shoulder, and dropping this into the flowerpot, took the daisy into hand, thereupon passing it on to her daughter, who held the exuberant bloom up to her nose.

"It don't smell," the little girl declared, her face contorted as if of an astringency most sour. She thereupon discarded the flower onto the pavement.

"Pick that up!" the mother demanded.

The little girl showed little inclination toward obeisance.

"I paid a whole dollar for that flower, 'cause you said you wanted it. Now pick it up!"

No response.

"You pick that up right now, young lady, you hear me!"

Mr. Kortright stooped low, and picking the flower up from the pavement, held it toward the mother. "A flower for you, ma'm." His voice, though in the declarative, was close upon a whisper.

Taking the stem into hand, the woman pulled her daughter to the sitting wall surrounding the memorial plaza and planted the girl upon this with such violence as to precipitate a farther peal of wails. The mother thereupon seated herself and, as her daughter slid away, as if by force of opposing magnetism, laid the flower upon her lap. Upon pulling the ribbon free of the stem, the mother held her eyes closed a moment, as if to recite a private prayer, and then drew the ribbon through one hand by pull of the other, such that she might read the inscription. Of a sudden the woman placed her hands upon her face and began to weep. Her daughter edging closer, the woman pulled the little girl into her arms. "I'm sorry," she wept. "I'm so sorry."

Sarg, appearing not a little bewildered, looked to Ben. "What you have done here today, Mr. Kortright," Ben offered, "cannot now, I dare say, easily be undone."

Sarg looked no less bewildered.

The woman and girl removing from the wall, Ben bowed to them. The woman smiled to Ben, and then to Sarg. She led her daughter then toward the near corner, the girl holding the daisy stem in one hand, her mother's hand in the other.

"Complementarity," Sarg said.

"And all your doing, Mr. Kortright."

Sarg grinned.

Ben thereupon noticed a young Negro man approaching from the same corner, suggesting in dress and in gait a hostility only barely restrained. He was wearing a purple stocking over his head, this partially obscuring a tidy encampment of close braids, and upon his ears a curious device. He seemed to be agitating himself in rhythm to a compelling beat. "Mr. Kortright, there comes, methinks, a gentleman truly in need of your wares."

Sarg looked in the direction of Ben's attention, and thereupon, at Ben's command—"Make yourself ready, Mr. Kortright!"—pulled a daisy stem from the vase and took station close upon the flowerpot. When the Negro man was a step away, Sarg extended the stem toward him. "A flower for you today, young feller?"

In a motion little slower than a flick of a serpent's tongue, the Negro man had hold of the flowerpot. In near simultaneity, Sergeant Kortright was flat upon his back, undressed of his baseball cap. Beside him, the flowerpot was emptied and broken, the vase toppled and spilt.

Sarg held his right hand upon the opposing side of his mouth.

Ben leaned forward such that his face overhung Sarg's. "Have we something of a setback here, Mr. Kortright?"

Extending a hand, Ben helped Sarg to his feet, and held his arm tightly then whilst Sarg, a bit wobbly in the knees, dabbed blood from his lower lip.

Noticing the broken flowerpot, Sarg hissed an invective in the general direction of the disappeared thief, and punctuated this with a solemn pledge to exact retribution upon "that mother-fuckin' sonuvabitch" at first opportunity. Wiping his blood-stained hand upon his indelibly soiled breeches, Sarg restored his cap to his head, visor forward.

"Are you quite purged of your pique, sir," Ben inquired, "if not quite your humiliation?"

Sarg frowned upon Ben as he might indeed, at first opportunity, upon "that mother-fuckin' sonuvabitch" himself.

"If I may, sir," Ben continued, "I would propose to you that, were a reasonable man to take a step backward into a tranquility of mind, he would come to identify two possible ways of viewing this incident: Firstly, and instinctively, as yet one more opportunity to exact an eye for an eye, toward ultimate effect of universal blindness; or, secondly, as an opportunity to gain benefit of a practical wisdom, this being, to wit, sir, that any street merchant being intimate of both the niceties and the not-so-niceties of human nature would show no greater number of bills in his cash store, at any one time, than would be sufficient to prime the spigot of public generosity. Would you be inclined to agree with this proposition, sir?"

Sarg nodded, yet frowning.

Ben looked to the spilt vase. "You have four stems left, sir, plus one in hand, and several more to your account, held in escrow by your provisioner, she now also, methinks, your ally. In addition, you have strong indication of your wares being of appeal, and you have all else you require presently to continue in your new trade, at this location." Ben paused. "Kindly remove your jacket, sir."

Sarg removed his jacket and handed it over to Ben, who pulled one sleeve through, and the other through, then returned the jacket to Sarg, and asked him to restore himself to full uniform, if he would be so kind.

Sarg pulled on his jacket, restoring thereby his medallion and stripes to full visibility.

"You will kindly come to attention, Sergeant."

Sarg stiffened.

"I, Benjamin Franklin, duly elected Colonel of the First Philadelphia Volunteers, do hereby promote—your given name, sir."

"Robbie."

"I do hereby promote Robert Kortright to the rank of First Sergeant, 75th Infantry, Company E, billeted at Washington and School. And, in recognition of his recent injury in the cause of complementarity, and his subsequent restraint from seeking retribution in kind, such restraint requiring equal if not greater courage than a willful pursuit of the cause occasioning the injury, I hereby award him the medallion of the Purple Heart." Ben saluted, Sarg responding in kind, and grasped Sarg's hand. "I congratulate you, Sergeant. You have well earned these honors."

Sarg's eyes filled as he shook Ben's hand, as if indeed the handle of the very pump watering him.

"No blubbering, Sergeant, till you have more cause for such than I might give you."

Sarg wiped his eyes, and turning from his benefactor, set about collecting the spilt vase and stems, muttering the while.

Ben bowed unto Sarg's back and tapped his way then to the near corner. As he passed by a pair of abandoned crutches, he smiled to a sweet refrain emanating from behind: "A flower for you today, sir? For your sweetie perhaps?"

Tapping his way then up School Street, Ben soon came upon a marquee marked "The Freedom Trail" and discovered upon one side of this a map showing the Old Burying Ground and the Common in relation to School Street.

Continuing on, Ben espied askance, fronted upon the next crossing street, a structure long forgot but bearing familiarity, this being King's Chapel. In orientation, Ben noticed, this old church stood in relation to School Street exactly as Old South Church stood in relation to Milk Street, indeed as if each structure, although in service to a radically different orientation in philosophy, the one Anglican, the other Puritan, had been physically orientated in accordance with some underlying principle of commonality. Reinforcing this notion was the fact that each structure had been wrought of wood in the original but replaced thereafter of red brick, in the case of Old South, and red stone, in the case of King's Chapel.

At the rear of the Chapel, Ben noticed, an empty lot, circumscribed by shrubs and a wrought-iron fence, occupied at least part of the site whereat had stood the grammar school into which Josiah Franklin had enrolled his tithing son toward eventual ordination into the ministry.

Ben chuckled out loud now to notion of what species of injuries might have been inflicted upon the good name of religion by a Most Reverend Benjamin Franklin.

South Grammar had been torn down, Ben recollected, to accommodate an addition to King's Chapel, and a replacement structure had been erected directly across the street, on the very side he was presently traversing. Not long thereafter, he farther recollected, King's Chapel had itself been replaced, by the present structure, the very one bearing familiarity from the experience of his visit to Boston in the summer of 1763, in company with Sally.

Ben again chuckled out loud, recollecting now having fallen from his horse on that occasion not once but two times over!

An ache, or memory of such, began to throb deep into his right shoulder, in likeness indeed to a visitation by Madam Gout, and was soon followed by an ache of a different sort, in conjunction with recollecting that he had not seen his sister Jane since that very visit, so very long ago now.

Coming upon the bookshop window through which he had earlier peered, Ben became captivated by a white-marble, palace-like structure on the opposing side of the street, standing betwixt a narrow alley to rightward and the empty lot to leftward. Although a filigree of intervening twigs and leaves partially obscured his view, Ben could discern four stories of striking windows, robustly arched atop, and remarkably reminding, by way of orthogonal muntins, of a heraldic shield bearing the cross of St. George.

The central section of this singular structure was pronounced forward, to effect of defining a wing to either side, and bore atop as if a large, four-sided crown. The overall impression was toward the French style.

As Ben advanced into closer proximity to this unexpected apparition, he discerned a shallow courtyard afront it, and standing within this, biased toward the nearer wing, a large statue, the present asymmetry of which seemed to compel a counterpart toward the farther wing.

The forward perimeter of the courtyard was lined of wrought iron to modest height, and a hedgerow of trees, the foliage of which was largely the cause of his impaired view.

Tapping his way several yards farther, Ben came upon a striped pathway leading unto three entrances to the courtyard—a carriage entrance to center, and a smaller pedestrian entrance to either side. From this vantage point, Ben could discern, on a lintel overtop the carriage entry, the words OLD CITY HALL, spelt in gold lettering, and at front of the farther wing of the palace, a second statue, as anticipated, standing as if in looking-glass imitation of the first. And whilst the likeness of the first statue, decidedly heroic in demeanor, was not immediately familiar to him, the likeness of the second statue, standing at about where at least a portion of his old grammar school had once stood, was indeed familiar—it being a likeness of himself!

The two pedestrian entrances unto the courtyard, Ben noticed, although closely guarded by imposing stone sentinels, were unencumbered, thereby inviting entry. Also inviting entry was a marker on one of the sentinels, announcing the presence of *maison robert Restaurants Français*, as also were the names of the *restaurants* themselves, one being *Ben's café and terrace*, the other being *Bonhomme Richard.*

Ben could not help but succumb to a transient smile.

A vehicle stopping at the striping, Ben tapped his way across the narrow street, and passing through the pedestrian entrance to rightward, tapped his way past a curious bronze jackass, and made his way to the first statue he had espied, whereat he was struck by the close juxtaposition of a bronze jackass to a heroically poised bronze figure draped in Greek robes. Looking to the engraving on the front of the pedestal, Ben was pleased to discover the man being elevated to be JOSIAH QUINCY, 1772–1864.

Although Ben had not known this Josiah Quincy, the third such, to his knowledge, to hold this honorable name, he had known the previous two, to some intimacy, they being father and grandfather to the present namesake.

The father, Ben recollected, had served with him in London, for a brief period, whilst he was yet laboring to hold the chafing colonies fast to the imperial bosom. A brilliant young man, educated in the law, Quincy No. 2 had been a most nimble and efficacious colleague, amidst the intrigues of the hour, and a most agreeable companion as well, this latter role having extended even unto the young Quincy helping to console his elder by four decades on the occasion of the latter's attaining his 70th birth anniversary, indeed at a most festive congregation of intimates at 7 Craven Street. Sadly, young Quincy had contracted the consumption during his brief stay, of an unfortunate penchant, Ben suspicioned, for the conviviality of the English tavern, and had perished during his voyage home, leaving a young son, the subject of the present statue, without a father, and a young wife without a provider.

Gazing presently upon the heroic rendering of the fatherless son, Ben saw not an honorable Mayor of Boston, 1823–1828, nor an esteemed President of Harvard, 1829–1845, but an eternally aggrieved boy who had known the pleasure of his father's company only by way of forever attempting to become, in reputation and achievement, the man lost to him.

Ben could not help now but recollect the grandfather, who had become a dear friend on the very occasion of their first acquaintance, during the time of the French and Indian War. Josiah had traveled from Boston to Philadelphia to petition the Pennsylvania Assembly for funds with which to finance a campaign against Crown Point, it to be waged in parallel with General Braddock's campaign against Fort Duquesne. In cunning service to this cause, Josiah had thought to petition Ben Franklin first, over a bottle of fine Madeira, as well as a goodly store of news of those in Boston for whom Mister Franklin held no little affection, including his much beloved sister Jane. Indeed, Quincy's shrewd exercise of flattery on that occasion was the very sort Ben would have himself used had the situation been in reverse.

Gazing again upon the iconified figure before him, and taking note of the near-comical excess of heroic posturing, Ben was visited by notion of how the Greek pantheon itself might have come into being. To wit, likely indeed the heroes of ancient Greece, both military and civic, had been iconified in the very manner Josiah Quincy had been; that is, in the form of oversized statuary of idealized aspect. However, for mere mortals to be elevated upon pedestals of stone was inevitably for them to be elevated unto the thrones of Olympus itself, as, in similitude, 'twas the habit of mere legend told around the hearth to be elevated unto the parchment of scripture itself.

Ben smiled. Alas, that old O.T. peacemaker Isaiah had (be)gotten it only two-thirds correct—

They shall beat their swords into ploughshares, and their spears into pruning hooks—and they shall hew their pedestals into millstones.

Ben bowed unto Josiah Quincy No. 3, and tapping his way then to the farther side of the courtyard, stood before the iconified likeness of himself.

Although this likeness was not draped in heroic robery, it was nonetheless presented in larger-than-life aspect, both physically—his modest five-foot, nine-inch frame being transposed unto a nine-foot, five-inch such—and symbolically, by way of showing him holding a tri-corner hat (symbol of patriotism), and wearing a frock coat fringed to front of fur (symbol of commercial success). In truth, rarely had he ever worn any such hat, and near upon as rarely had he ever worn any such garment.

Ben was pleased, however, to discover himself holding a walking stick the very likeness, or so it would appear, of the stick he presently held. The intent of including this quaint artifact, he surmised, was to suggest unto the holder of it the reputation of a humble and well-traveled philosopher, but also the mortality of a mere mortal. Indeed, no marbled Olympian was this!

The pedestal upon which the statue stood, Ben noticed, consisted of two blocks, the upper block being taller and variegated in green and gold, the lower block being wider and unremarkably grayish. A tableau attached to the upper block commemorated "The Declaration of Independence / 4 July 1776." By implication, Ben noted, the commemoration seemed specific to the *signing* of the Declaration, which, in fact, had not occurred until near upon a full month subsequent, on August 2nd.

Ben leaned forward such as to examine the tableau more closely.

Five upstanding men, including, obviously, himself—the rightmost of these figures—were facing generally rightward, toward a seated man, obviously Hancock, President of the Congress at the time and hence the only figure wearing a wig. One of the five upstanding men, the middle of these, was offering a parchment toward Hancock, whilst four other men, standing at the far right, were facing generally to leftward, as if compelled into such an unexpected pose by necessity of an artful symmetry.

The particulars were obvious. The leftmost group of men constituted the Committee of Five, which had been charged with writing the Declaration, and whose principal member, the one presenting the parchment, had been Jefferson. The depiction was not, therefore, of the signing of the parchment Declaration on August 2nd, but of the presentation of the final draft to Hancock, such that he might put it to the assembly for a vote, which vote, although begun on July 4th, had not been completed until July 9th.

Noticing then that he was shown holding a pair of spectacles, the only person in the tableau to be associated with this symbol of fragility, Ben found himself as pleased by this inclusion as by the inclusion, in the statuary above, of his walking stick.

Tapping his way counterclockwise, toward the rear of the pedestal, Ben found himself staring upon the entrance to the *bon homme restaurant*, which, to his surprise (he had assumed it to be located within the palace proper), appeared to be subterranean. Fortunately, it was shut, such as to put a quick end to any notion toward squandering his remaining ready money upon a gastronomical indulgence.

Ben thereupon noticed that a yellow canopy overtop the restaurant entrance corresponded to a similar canopy overtop a sort of counter, or bar, standing at the far end of the courtyard. This coincidence,

together with the presence of several round tables on the street side of
the statue, and the nearby presence to these of several stacks of simple
white chairs, gave strong implication as to the location of *Ben's café*—
which also was shut.

Turning his attention to the tableau attached to the rear of the upper
pedestal block, Ben discovered it to depict his Philadelphia experiment.
In the rendering, Ben was shown standing within a wooden shelter,
itself standing in an open field, with William crouched behind him and
to his right, holding at the ready a bolt of string. Striking a stiff, near-
upon imperial pose, Ben was shown holding a string in one hand whilst
extending a knuckle of the other hand toward a key tethered to the
string. The string itself was ascending through the shelter entrance,
and upward then unto, by implication, an unseen kite. Visible in the
upper left of the tableau was a bolt of lightning, and to the right of this,
a row of tall trees extending toward the shed. Beneath one of these
trees, two horses were nuzzling as if of an abiding affection, and in utter
innocence, it would appear, of the impending danger represented by
the lightning and the proximate trees.

Ben could not help but notice that William was depicted not as the
adult of twenty-one years he had been at the time—indeed, the official
clerk of the Pennsylvania Assembly he had been at the time—but as a
lad of no greater than sixteen years. Indeed, William was diminished
here not only in the temporal dimension, Ben noticed, but also in stature, by being shown crouched, and also in courage, by being shown
retreated, and also in dignity, by being shown subservient.

Looking again to himself, Ben saw a man too occupied of his own
interest to sense, much less to see, the imminent peril of the two horses,
indeed the peril of all of nature; nor the profound needfulness of the
man-child crouched behind, indeed the profound needfulness of all
of youth.

Ben held his head bowed a moment, then tapped his way yet farther
to counterclockwise, hoping to discover upon the next tableau bold
mention concerning the true significance of the present site, it being
the location of the first public grammar school in America versus the
school Benjamin Franklin had attended at the age of eight years for but
for three months.

The third tableau, however, commemorated not the first public
grammar school in America, nor even the school Benjamin Franklin
had attended at the age of eight years for three months, but Ben's participation in the signing of the "Treaty of Peace and Independence /

3 September 1783." In this rendering, Ben was depicted, somewhat accurately he had to confess, standing whilst everyone else was seated, holding a quill whilst everyone else was empty-handed, and confessing a bald pate whilst everyone else was wearing a wig.

Ben thereupon tapped his way to the last façade of pedestal, certain he would find upon these a proper commemoration of the grammar school, this side of the statuary being primary by way of facing upon the street. What he discovered instead, however, was a depiction of young Ben Franklin industriously setting type in his brother James's print shop in Boston, learning the trade that would fate him to Philadelphia, seat him upon the Committee of Five, allow him his electrical experiments, sail him to Paris, and launch a thousand other ships unto a thousand other parts.

Acquiring a trade was indeed of great importance, Ben had to agree, but what was the merit of a trade, of whatever prospect, in the absence of a proper nobility of character by which to direct its ends? And how was such a character to be acquired other than by a careful instruction in all the arts, not just those in service to achievement and acquisition?

Taking a few steps backward now, toward the white tables and chairs constituting *Ben's café*, Ben imagined a replacement monument, to wit: Where presently there was a pedestal of grayish stone, squared unto four mutually separated façades, there would be a large flowerpot, hewn of white marble. And where presently there was a bronze statue of himself, there would be a bouquet of seven stems of bloom, of seven different species, each stem wrought of bronze and burnished unto a distinctive hue. And in the stead of the four tableaus, there would be three bronze figures, of no particular identity, separate from the flowerpot but stooped toward it, each holding a watering vessel, one vessel bearing the label KNOWLEDGE; the second, VIRTUE; the third, WISDOM. And upon the body of the flowerpot itself would be engraved a label reading, SITE OF THE FIRST PUBLIC GRAMMAR SCHOOL IN AMERICA—A.K.A., THE GARDEN OF READIN'.

Ben tapped his way from the courtyard, and passing through the nearer of the two pedestrian entrances, headed upstreet toward King's Chapel. Reaching a point about even with the facing direction of the statue of himself recently abandoned, which object Ben could discern through the feathery foliage of shrubs lining the courtyard perimeter, Ben discovered at his feet the very commemorative he had so fruitlessly been searching for within the courtyard.

Bordered by red bricks, a mosaic mimicking the shape of the

windows on Old City Hall—being rounded on one end, squared on the other—spanned perhaps eight feet, and was nearly as wide as the walkway. Directly within the brick border was a second, constituted of a child's blocks which alternated betwixt letters of the alphabet and depictions of everyday objects—squirrel, apple, the like—except upon the bottom, whereat the border was constituted of the numerals 1 through 10. No zero, Ben noted.

The bottom two-thirds of the mosaic was divided into scenes of children engaged in various forms of play, which scenes, the overall constellation of these, constituted a child's hopscotch. The upper third of the mosaic held a school building topped with a bell and surrounded by words, including, at bottom, in large letters, the name LATIN SCHOOL. Ben was at pains in the moment to reconcile "Latin School" with the "Children at Play" theme that seemed to inform the mosaic in general, from skip rope unto hopscotch. Indeed, the only play he had himself engaged in on School Street consisted of sledding upon it, from atop Beacon Hill, in the dead of winter.

Ben noticed a quotation, attributed to himself, arranged directly below the word *School*: EXPERIENCE KEEPS A DEAR SCHOOL, BUT FOOLS WILL LEARN IN NO OTHER. He smiled, but then imagined a line in substitution: *Where learning is not its own reward, schooling is all water and no wheel.*

Continuing on, Ben tapped his way past King's Chapel—its two tiers of windows also arched atop, squared at bottom, as upon Old South—and then, upon a favorable light, scuttled across the intersection in near pace with a herd of other hurrieds, to the farther side of Tremont Street. Pausing there, on the back shore of a stream of perambulators, Ben looked upon the front of King's Chapel, and noting the curious lack of a spire, and the array of pillars supporting the portico—six to front, three at either side—it occurred to him that in any symmetry, of whatever species, there could never be an eminence, hence never a domination. Indeed, for every element, or member, there could be naught else but a perfect counterpart, sometimes opposing, but always to equal measure.

Indeed: *In all symmetry, balance; in all balance, equality.*

What conflicts amongst peoples, Ben wondered, could not be diminished unto naught, or avoided altogether, were the essence of this simple truth to be honored with humble obeisance?

Ben tapped his way across School Street, up Tremont, and soon came upon a wrought-iron fence bordering what, in his day, had been named Middle Burying Ground. A stone marker being close upon the fence, Ben paused to regard this. Modest of height but robust in girth, this marker was larger than any other in the immediate vicinity, and bore upon its façade, this being crudely hewn, a plaque reading, SAMUEL ADAMS . . . / BORN 1722 / DIED 1803. A small flag posted rightward of the marker bore a constellation of stars upon its canton numbering several times the thirteen Samuel had helped gather unto the original constellations.

Ben smiled to fond recollection now of the ever-fevered man who had hosted perhaps the most memorable soirée of all time, an event especially memorable to Ben, it having served as cause for his public whipping before the lords of the Privy Council. Noticing now that the size and location of Samuel's marker, in relation to the other markers in the vicinity, suggested an eminence to the former, Ben shifted his attention, with some reluctance, not to mention dread, to the center of the burying ground, whereat he espied a towering pyramid of such eminence and shape as to suggest the very spire missing from King's Chapel. Although beheld but fleetingly in the moment, this grand, white-stone monument seemed even more disproportionate in scale than as remembered.

Making his way to the entry to the burying ground, Ben passed betwixt two pillars shouldering a large lintel, and looked to a bronze tablet attached upon the entry gate, the latter affixed open to rightward: GRANARY BURYING GROUND / 1660 / WITHIN THIS GROUND ARE BURIED / THE VICTIMS OF THE BOSTON MASSACRE, / MARCH 5, 1770. / JOSIAH FRANKLIN AND WIFE. / (PARENTS OF BENJAMIN FRANKLIN).

As if to avoid an infliction of grit into his eyes, by way of swirls and eddies, Ben held his eyes cast downward, and tapped his way upon a cobbled pathway, lined at either side by gently festooning chains, to whereat a set of placards invited perusal. Scanning these in succession, Ben recognized most of the names—Samuel Adams, Crispus Attucks, John Hancock, James Otis, Robert Treat Paine, Paul Revere, and, of course, his own: STATESMAN, AUTHOR AND INVENTOR BENJAMIN FRANKLIN WAS BURIED IN PHILADELPHIA IN 1790. HERE LIE HIS PARENTS, HIS 16 SIBLINGS, AND A RELATIVE OF THE SAME NAME.

Relieved to find a (another!) small error upon which to dwell, Ben relished in its correction: He had indeed had sixteen siblings, but his eldest brother, Josiah, named after their sire in common, had been lost at sea, and could not, therefore, except by way of a most remarkable happenstance, be one of the sixteen siblings alluded to as "here lying."

But for a correction, the fact was lost; but for the fact, the truth was lost; but for the truth, the lesson was lost; but for the lesson. . . .

Tapping farther toward the center of the burying ground, it being at the cross-point of orthogonally intersecting pathways, Ben allowed himself to gaze forward upon the monument he had commissioned following the death of his mother. The commemoration, and thereby the commemorator, was unmistakable, FRANKLIN being imprinted in bold, raised letters upon the middle of the five trapezoidal segments constituting the monument. Also bold, even if recessed, was the tablet bearing the tribute Ben had composed to honor his dutiful parents, as well as, he had now to confess, their dutiful son. Although the text of the tribute was itself not yet discernible to him, by impairment of distance, its concluding lines rose unto mind's eye in the moment like a specter from a disturbed crypt: HE WAS A PIOUS AND PRUDENT MAN; SHE A DISCREET AND VIRTUOUS WOMAN. THEIR YOUNGEST SON, IN FILIAL REGARD TO THEIR MEMORY, PLACES THIS STONE.

Yet seeing through mind's eye, Ben placed a star after "stone" and writ below, preceded by a matching star: *What tribute naming its author is not more a vanity than a charity?*

As Ben advanced yet closer upon the Franklin obelisk, he noticed that the modest monuments to either side of the pathway he trod, being mostly top-rounded slabs of slate, arranged in rows, gave appearance of a garden of mushrooms a'ready sliced.

Stopped at the platform upon which the Franklin monument stood, Ben began to speak aloud, his voice tremulous: "Honored Mother, Honored Father, I am tortured, here standing, of a burden of regret equal in measure to the pride I once carried onto this very ground, near two and one half centuries previous. In truth, the exhibition of this centric spire, and the public tribute it bears, were conceived as much to enhance the reputation of their sponsor, and to assuage an abiding discomfort owing to an abiding neglect of you both, as to 'honor thy father and thy mother.' Indeed, the sentiments I commissioned to be displayed here, upon this tablet, as if upon the golden door of a tabernacle, I should have confessed to you in private, in plain speech, within the temple of your warm and loving home. I deeply regret my negligence, and my vanity, as I deeply honor your forbearance."

Ben held to silence a moment, head bowed, then, clearing his throat, continued. "I honor also your abiding apprehension of family as worthy above all else. Although you were indeed at liberty, as much as any other of your time, to become affixed upon lower interests seeming higher, you remained ever faithful to the primacy of your family, its care and well-being, at cost of all else that might have captured your interest or your esteem.

"Regrettably, your youngest son was unable, for whatever reason, it matters not, to attend to the lesson of your example, indeed to the degree he would now command of himself, at whatever sacrifice to himself, such as to forestall inflicting upon the innocents fated unto his sacred care the agonies he did indeed inflict upon them, these being now accumulated unto himself as a burden of regret he cannot other than bear throughout all eternity. Alas, a man affixes his attention whereat he vests his interest, the former being the metal, the latter being the magnet. Indeed, as a man attending upon prosperity cannot be more than a pretense at husbandry, so a man attending upon philosophy cannot be more than a sophist at paternity. 'Tis this sentiment, if any such at all, that I should have graven upon a tablet placed not at *your* monument but at my own."

Beginning to weep, Ben heard as if a whisper from behind: *What forgiveness in the seeking of it, is not ever the gaining of it?*

Turning such as to look over one shoulder, Ben discovered no one behind. Turning such as to look over the other shoulder, Ben discovered no one behind. In returning his attention to forward then, Ben discovered a man, standing a few yards distant, looking his way. The man smiled, and thereupon approached. He was perhaps in his middle fifties, was wearing a light jacket, medium green, imprinted "Gnu Age Networks" upon the left breast, and was holding in hand a maroon umbrella, folded. His russet hair was tinged of hoarfrost upon temple and mustache. His eyes, azure, seemed as if windows unto a great depth.

"Are you OK, sir?" the man inquired, his face manifest with concern.

"Some things there are, I fear," Ben replied, his voice phlegmatic, "which can never be made so, neither by petition nor by deed." He smiled. "Yet, I feel appreciably better for your inquiry, kind sir, and I do thank you for it."

"No problem. Are you a docent here?"

"I am under no employ here, sir, though I must confess to wishing for a tenure of sufficient duration as to allow me to disassemble"—he looked to the Franklin monument—"this centric axis around which all else herein would seem imposed to turn."

"And why would you be wanting to do that, if I may ask?"

"Do you not find this monument, sir, in this plot of humble souls, as if a figwort amongst parsnips?"

The man smiled and looked past Ben to westward. "No more so than that one over there."

Following the man's aim of eye, Ben beheld a monument he had not previously noticed, likely because of its location, it standing against a backdrop of drab brick. In contrast to the pyramidal form of the Franklin monument, with its four canted sides converging unto a point, this monument, noticeably taller, was uniformly squared to a height of perhaps twenty feet, and thereupon rounded.

Ben caught himself drawing solace from the presence of what would appear to be cause for an embarrassment even greater than his own.

What embarrassment owing to a stranger is not a balm to one a'ready intimate of it?

Ben looked again to the russet-haired man. "I thank you again, sir, for the kindness of your concern. I feel very much better for it, thank you."

Ben bowed; the man bowed in return.

"Have a nice day," the man said.

"Thank you, sir, and likewise to you."

"Thank you."

Stricken now of curiosity, Ben turned to westward, and tapping his way to the taller monument, a distance of perhaps fifty yards, discovered, none to his surprise, a bust of John Hancock embossed upon its primary façade, this oriented not upon the burying ground proper, but toward Tremont Street. He then perceived, to surprise encroaching upon shock, an unmistakable resemblance betwixt this twenty-foot shaft of stone and a male member at full muster.

At first doubting his perception, Ben conceived the possibility of the name "Hancock" being masqueraded here by suggestive symbol, but found himself incredulous, doubting that such a joke would have been perpetrated upon such hallowed ground.

Peering upon the monument's crown piece, this being of a shape, and having a cornice, startlingly evocative of phallic counterparts, Ben noticed it to be covered over of engravings to effect of rendering it in the whole a darker tint of gray relative to the shaft. Three of the engravings were central relative to the others. The bottommost of these showed a human hand, the right member, with the palm forward, fingers elevated; the second, centered just above the hand, showed three cocks arrayed in an arc; and the third, and topmost, showed a winged dragon in profile. Underlying these engravings was a Latin phrase, which Ben recognized: OBSTA PRINCIPIIS—Oppose First Encroachments.

There appeared now to be a profundity of meaning, Ben allowed, whereat previously there seemed little but scatological mischief. Indeed, the single hand (resonate to Han) would appear to represent the resistance of individuals acting independently—*Halt! Encroach no closer upon my person or my property!*—whereas the three cocks would appear to represent the resistance of men, normally of an independent bent of mind, acting in concert. And the dragon, by force of logical extension, as much as by force of symbol, would appear to represent the resistance of the colonies unified into a single, indomitable ferocity.

And, of course, in all three forms of resistance, John Hancock, native son, had not only had a "hand," but also—to continue the symbology— a larger part altogether. Indeed, the phallic representation of the whole seemed now, under stronger light, to be a tribute to a particular species of manly power, the same required indeed of David in opposing Goliath.

Taking notice now of the inscription graven upon the shaft—THIS MEMORIAL ERECTED A.D. MDCCCXCV BY THE COMMONWEALTH OF MASSACHUSETTS TO MARK THE GRAVE OF JOHN HANCOCK—Ben discovered himself intrigued both by the date, 1895, it being over a century subsequent to Hancock's death, and by the benefactor, it being not any member of the Hancock family, but the Commonwealth at large. Ben smiled then, perceiving the pretentiously oversized Franklin monument as the strutting cocks of the Commonwealth must have perceived it—a full century subsequent to any practical need to keep parochial jealousies any longer at bay—as an encroachment indeed upon the historical significance of *true* native heroes, those who not only had lived their lives to fullness upon native soil, but had died thereon, and been buried therein.

These same cocks, Ben surmised, whilst they could never have enjoyed sufficient license by which to remove outright Franklin's overbearing encroachments upon their historical sovereignty, could indeed have enjoyed sufficient license by which to erect an artifact of sufficient stature and symbology to rival it.

And so, there it was, yet again—one cock's bold act of pride provoking yet the bolder in a rival, back and forth, bolder and bolder—alas, unto what end?

Feeling as if freighted of a great weight now, this appended not upon his back but upon his soul, Ben turned a quarter circle rightward and

returned to the Franklin monument. Pausing thereat, his eyes watering, he imagined in the place of this massive pyramid a simple marker,
rounded atop, squared to bottom, inscribed with the names of all who
lay there, the dates of their earthly tenure, and naught else.

*'Tis not sweet Charity nor fair Temperance that most wantonly fails at
winning our favour, but shrinking Humility.*

Tapping to the exit pathway, Ben noticed a hideous gnarl protruding from the lower trunk of a large maple tree standing immediately
rightward of the Franklin plot. Sensing by this manifestation a malady
deeper within, as in the case of a similar growth discovered upon a
human trunk, Ben lifted his eyes until he espied, at a height just shy of
that of the Franklin monument, a gaping abscess of decay. This poor
tree was doomed, Ben knew, of an insidious rotting from within, the
kind indeed that tended to confess itself only after all opportunity at
remedy has expired.

Turning southward, Ben tapped his way down the cobbled pathway
on which he had entered, and upon passing through the gate pillars,
realized he had forgotten to carry with him from the flower shop the
newspaper he had only just begun to study. He considered returning
for it, the shop being but two blocks distant, but then, raising his eyes,
discovered a clock atop a steeple tower in the direction of the Common
and was reminded by this that he had no luxury of time for redressing
small errors.

Tapping toward the Common, Ben soon discovered himself standing at the intersection of Tremont and Park Streets, with the church
bearing the clock steeple standing close upon his right, the Common
lying directly to front.

Peering up Park Street, Ben espied an imposing golden-domed
structure, showing pediments and columns to front, that was reminding of Jefferson's Monticello, which mansion Ben had seen in sketches
wrought in Jefferson's own hand. By way of its location, atop Beacon
Hill, and its grand architecture, Ben surmised the present structure
likely to be the working quarters of the Massachusetts Assembly, the
interests of which body, in a distant era, Ben had represented to the
nincompoops of the English Parliament.

Looking to the Common, Ben discovered it to bear little resemblance
to the ungulate-fouled field of his youth. What he had known indeed
as an egalitarian pasture exploited by everyone, kept by no one, had
obviously been transformed into a public park, groomed and shaded, it
would appear, to accommodate, even encourage, individual repose and

reflection, and also, if one were to judge from the number of persons ambulating its pathways, to accommodate willful afflictions of exercise.

Tapping his way across Park Street, Ben stood near upon a marquee of four sides, similar to the marquee he had encountered on School Street. This one showed the same "Freedom Trail" map, but also a map of the Common area itself, marked BOSTON / COMMON / FOUNDED 1634. Ben was uncertain as to how mere purchase of fifty acres for common use could be regarded as a "founding," but decided to withhold judgment on the matter, at least for the interim. If he had learned anything from his brief tenure as a civil jurist in Philadelphia, it was the necessity of withholding all judgment on a matter at issue until such time as one had heard from all sides, indeed unto exhaustion. Still, the apparent lack of precision suggested here seemed to be of a piece with previous incidents of such, and disquietingly so.

Looking presently to two identical shed-like structures, one close upon to rightward, the other farther to leftward, the pair seeming to stand as if portals unto the Common itself, Ben noticed that each structure bore the same markings: "MBTA—Park St / red—Park St / green—All Trains." By gift now of received memory, he apprehended the purpose of these curious structures, but not the reason there were two such, their precise duplication of appearance implying a precise duplication of function. Ben looked from one to the other, and over again, for any hint of difference betwixt them, but perceived no such.

Beyond these two entries to the underground, Ben noticed, were several carts from which vendors were plying various wares, mostly gastronomical in nature, and mostly, it would appear, to patrons either newly emerged from one of the underground entries or imminently to enter into one. Ben was reminded of Market Street in Philadelphia, whereat various vendors, mostly Quakers and Germans from beyond the confines of the city, had plied similar wares.

Scanning to rightward, Ben noticed that although the hour was yet early, and the grounds likely yet damp from the recent rainstorm, several persons were reposed upon the green to likely effect that they might encounter the growing warmth of the rising sun, and were sitting upon wraps previously worn against the very same wetness, or, in a few cases, upon newspapers folded to that purpose. The distribution of those so reposed was in likeness to points of light held in correspondence one to the other only by way of the lineaments of an ancient myth long forgot.

Searching for a possible source of the newspapers, Ben soon

discovered to leftward, close upon Tremont Street, at least a dozen dispersers, of various colorations, including one dispenser, he was pleased to discover, upon tapping a few steps closer, for the *Courant*. Continuing to tap toward the *Courant* dispenser, Ben noted several pigeons scavenging the nearby walkway, apparently for crumbs dropped by humans attempting to partake of their pastries or biscuits while remaining in motion and yet burdened of their bags and devices.

Noting a coin slot on the dispenser, and the price advertised for the items within, Ben pulled from pocket the two remaining bills, and the lone Jefferson coin, yet left to his discretion. Looking to a pastry cart, he was visited by a most rational expediency by which indeed a stomach might be sated by way of a newspaper being replaced. About then to tap his way unto the cart, Ben noticed, to rightward, a pigeon pecking at a large crumb, consuming this by the bit, and losing but a few of such to competitors. The crumb becoming consumed, the pigeon, its remarkably iridescent head bobbing to and fro, began to search for another accidental morsel, manna indeed from heaven.

From the predator, all strategy; from the scavenger, all economy.

Imitating now his teacher, by way of undulating his own head to and fro, grinning the while, Ben tapped his way betwixt the duplicate entries to the underground trains, and following then a generous pathway leading diagonally into the Common, soon came upon a plaza, octagonal in geometry, whereon a bench was stationed at each of the eight sides of perimeter, poised to face inward upon a singular sculpture at center.

Surrounding this sculpture was a raised platform, also octagonal, of three levels, and standing on the top level of this platform were benches having no backs arranged in counterpart to the eight benches at the perimeter of the plaza. The benches having no backs were juxtaposed to an octagonal garden, which itself was juxtaposed to what appeared to be the bottommost of three round basins of graduating diameter, smallest at top, largest at bottom.

The bench immediately to rightward, Ben noticed, was about half the length of the other benches circumscribing the plaza—the other half having apparently been sacrificed toward an unencumbered entry onto the plaza—and was presently occupied by a young woman dining on a smallish loaf sliced into halves, each half being slathered with a milk-white spread. The loaf halves, one partially consumed, were resting atop a wrapper itself resting upon the woman's lap, whilst a tall cup of what Ben presumed to be coffee, given the hour, was resting upon the bench to her right. The next bench in succession, to counterclockwise, was occupied on its farther end by a man of angular features reading a newspaper, or, more precisely, one of several sections of this, the other sections being rested upon the bench seat to the man's left. Ben tapped his way to this bench, and was about to seat himself such as to be within hailing distance of the man, but not so close as to be adjudged encroaching upon any claim he might have on the proximate territory, when he discovered himself wondering whether this man's claim ended at the farther boundary of the additional sections of newspaper, or whether it lay yet farther on. Alas, there were but two ways to make discovery: Inquire of the man directly as to the reach of his sovereignty, or give it a go!

Let the experiment be made!

Seating himself close upon the newspaper sections resting upon the bench, Ben straightened his back, his cane in parallel, both hands atop the liberty head top, and looked to the fountain sculpture, which showed no water.

Four children, cherubic in aspect, were depicted standing underneath the top basin, upon a narrow ledge just above the middle basin, and were matched in counterpoint by four adults, mythic in aspect, reposed underneath the middle basin.

Ben sensed his fellow occupant glance in his direction. The man thereupon snapped his paper such as to collapse it into half, and shook it then toward straightening the seam, the latter effect being reminding of a rattlesnake, newly coiled, shaking its tail.

Ben looked to the man, noting him to be reading the "Business" section of the *Courant*. "'Tis a great day to be alive, is it not, sir?"

The man folded his paper outwardly top to bottom, then inwardly side to side. He then stood up from the bench, and retrieving a tote from below the far end of the bench, stepped briskly into the direction from which Ben had recently arrived.

Ben looked to a pigeon, whiter of feather than its fellows, that was scavenging the plaza a few feet to front of the woman dining on the round loaf. "How'd I do?" Ben asked of the bird, smiling. The pigeon regarded him with a beady yellow eye, and then continued its scavenging, its head undulating to and fro.

Turning to the sections of the *Courant* abandoned by their previous claimant, Ben discovered the main section, marked A—which he had begun to peruse when interrupted by Sergeant Robert (Robbie) Kortright—just under the section marked "Sports." He thereupon resumed his perusal from the point he had left off:

> A man had been arrested in Atlanta, Ga., for sending an explosive device disguised as a cell phone to the CEO of Global Tel. The device had failed to go off when the package was opened. The man claimed he had not intended for the device to go off; he simply wanted to get someone in authority at the company to pay attention to his complaints, which he had registered several times, by various means, including certified mail, to no effect. The CEO of Global Tel, D. Sanger Bornstein, recently received a performance bonus valued at $35.5 million.
>
> A Catholic bishop had resigned from office after being charged with leaving the scene of a fatal accident. The same bishop had recently struck a deal with prosecutors to avoid indictment for protecting priests accused of child molestation. The bishop had admitted to having allowed priests to work with minors after allegations of sexual misconduct were made against them, and to transferring accused priests to new ministries without informing their new supervisors. The elderly woman struck by the bishop had died at the scene.
>
> A thirty-year-old mother of two daughters, ages twelve and nine, had died two days following being knocked out during a boxing match with another woman. The match was part of a "Toughman" competition staged for a TV reality show.
>
> A man in Springfield, Illinois, had gone on a shooting spree, wounding five people, two seriously, in what police characterized as "a total freak out" following the man's unsuccessful attempts to assemble an anemometer sold by Northwest Scientific, an American company, but made in China. The man's wife told police her husband, a "weather nut," had been unable to make sense of the instructions that had accompanied the device.
>
> Ashlea Skiles of Somerset, N.J., had gotten her first credit card during her freshman year in college, when she was 18 years old. Now 23, Ashlea had run up a total debt load of over $43,000, on 19 different cards.
>
> A Rhode Island mother was looking to "cash in" by auctioning the advertising rights to her two sons, a 3-year-old and a 2 ½-months-old, on eBay. Bidding was set to start at $1500. The

winning bidder would supply logo T-shirts or bibs for the children to wear whenever they were outside their home.

A man who had filed a claim with the Transportation Safety Agency for the loss of his favorite belt from his luggage had been waiting for four years for a resolution to his claim. The belt disappeared sometime during the time the man checked his baggage at Boston and picked it up at San Diego. To date, he had been unable to get a response of any kind either from the TSA or from American Airlines, despite repeated letters, faxes, and phone calls. A plea to his local Congressman resulted in an invitation for the man to become a member of the Congressman's "Round Table" for a donation of $1000 or more.

The Coca-Cola Co. had admitted to rigging a marketing test for a new product, Frozen Coke, at Burger King restaurants. The soft drink maker made the admission after a former employee had made public allegations. The former employee has since received several death threats.

A woman had been charged with child endangerment for breastfeeding her baby while driving on an interstate highway from Detroit to Pittsburgh. The woman said she had fed her baby before leaving Detroit but the child had become hungry again. She usually stopped to nurse, but was "forced to nurse while driving" due to her busy schedule.

A severe shortage of qualified math and science teachers in public schools nationwide had become a crisis. U.S. schools needed to fill nearly 200,000 vacant positions in secondary math and science; however out of 288 recently certified teachers trained at one college, only 12 were certified in science. Low pay, unruly students, a lack of parental support, and large class sizes were being given as primary reasons.

A girls' rugby coach had been beaten unconscious during a weekend match. Police were seeking criminal charges against several adults. "I never saw them coming," said Craig Stewart, 55, who was kicked in the head and face by parents and another coach, according to witnesses and police.

Paul Kenyon, Democratic candidate for President, currently leading in all the major polls, would be speaking at an international leadership conference being held at the Waldorf Astoria in New York. Sponsored by the U.S. and Canadian Chambers of

Commerce, the high-profile conference was being attended by the CEOs of several of America's and Canada's largest corporations.

A reporter at the *Courant*, Brian Lynch, had recently uncovered widespread cheating in the Boston Public School system perpetrated not by students but by teachers and administrators. According to Lynch, teachers and principals at several schools had been changing the answers on MCAS examinations in order to make their classes and school "pass muster" under President Kinney's Kids First education reform program.

The board of directors of Wall Street firm Harris Upshaw & Co. had decided to retain its chief executive officer, Paul A. Johnson, despite suggestions by the New York State attorney general's office and other critics that Mr. Johnson bore ultimate responsibility for misrepresentations made by several of the firm's employees concerning the investment quality of certain firms with which Harris Upshaw had a special relationship. The decision came after Harris Upshaw agreed to pay a $50 million penalty. Mr. Johnson was described as "an exemplary leader" by Kathryn G. Norquist, chairwoman of the Harris Upshaw board.

Turning to another sheet, Ben was startled by an advertisement filling the whole of it, in which a young woman, wearing breeches seemingly one size too small, was sitting upon a bench, knees apart, holding a slender device in close proximity to her crotch. She was looking coyly, even alluringly, into the eyes of the reader. Her blouse, its cuffs shortened by enfoldment, was affixed at front by but two of four buttons, to effect of revealing an impermanent seam at front of her breeches, and exposing her upper chest to near midway betwixt the symmetrical distensions of her bosom. The color of the bench, magenta, was matched by the color of the first two words of a declaration atop the sheet, to rightward: "*Get more* with a Global Tel 3-Day Weekend." The overall appeal seemed, paradoxically, to be oriented more toward the intimate contact suggested than toward the more prosaic contact represented by the communication device.

Although curious as to how an association betwixt a communication service and new heights of carnal delight might contribute to the civic good, Ben could not imagine how, in a world of such estrangement as he had so far witnessed, one might go about discovering the proper party to which to issue an inquiry. He recollected now the unfortunate gentleman who had attempted to gain the attention of Mr. Bornstein, the executive officer of the very company sponsoring the present adver-tisement, such that he might register to him his complaint.

When the grease of commerce is falsehood, how long before the wheels fall off the wagon?

Looking up from the newspaper, Ben made a survey of the plaza. Most of the benches were occupied, he noted, but none was occupied by more than two persons, and several by only one person. In each instance of two people occupying the same bench, the occupants were sitting as if bookends on an empty shelf; and in almost every instance of only one person occupying a bench, a personal item of some kind—a tote, a bag, a jacket—was occupying the space immediately adjacent. Perhaps a third of the occupants, Ben noticed, were talking on devices such as the one shown in the advertisement just examined.

Looking to the fountain, Ben noticed that the four cherubs standing beneath the topmost of the three basins were arranged such as to be evenly separated and at the same time to be held in close communion by way of holding hands. The corresponding adults, reposed beneath the middle basin, were similarly arranged, but were rendered into com-munion not by way of physical contact, as in the case of the cherubs, but by way of neighboring pairs turning unto each other and, in the case fully visible, offering a gift of grapes.

Both arrangements, it would appear, were in service to the same truth, to wit, that human beings were naturally inclined toward separa-tion and self interest and that in order to become conjoined in mind, body, and spirit toward mutual benefit they had to make a deliberate effort toward this end. They had deliberately to hold each other's hand, they had deliberately to turn their eyes one to the other, they had delib-erately to offer each other a portion of their bounty.

The water one would expect to be communicating from basin to basin, Ben posited, served as a source of cleansing and renewal, and although the children had their baptismal, and the adults had theirs, the water, of its endless cycling, rendered the two as if one.

Yet there no water. Why? Ben now wondered.

Setting the newspaper to side, Ben noticed the woman to leftward wrapping a remnant of her roundish loaf. The woman tucked the rem-nant into her tote, and rising from her seat, tossed her coffee container into a barrel standing betwixt the woman's bench and Ben's.

Their eyes meeting, Ben smiled, and then nodded. The woman smiled in return, but with a starchy cast of reserve. "If I may inquire, ma'm," Ben ventured, "as to that loaf you were recently partaking of, what one might call it in a shop trafficking in such?"

"It's a bagel," the woman replied, her tone and brevity seeming to add sinew to her reserve.

"It appeared to have a sort of icing."

The woman postured as if to take imminent leave. "Cream cheese."

Ben nodded. "I'm wondering if the bread might have been unleavened."

The woman shrugged. "I don't bake."

Recollecting the aroma of golden-brown loaves newly removed from his mother's oven, Ben felt in the moment as if swaddled in a warm embrace.

The woman gestured in the direction of Tremont Street. "There's a café just across the street. I highly recommend it."

Ben bowed. "I thank you, ma'm, for benefit of your opinion."

Looking in the direction of the woman's gesture, Ben espied a marker on the farther side of Tremont Street, "Bagel Plus Café," and felt a pull as from a leash. The woman passing across his line of vision, tote in one hand, umbrella in other, Ben affixed his eyes upon her, such as to follow her course, this taking her close to the rightward side of the sculpture. As the woman navigated past a pediment there, betwixt octagonal sides of the sculpture platform, a disheveled man, sitting on a step proximate to this pediment, held a hand out to her. The woman veered to starboard, as if struck by a sudden gale, and continued onward.

A flutter of wings drew Ben's attention to an assemblage of pigeons, numbering perhaps a dozen, sitting upon the rim of the top basin on the sculpture. Each bird was facing outward. Of the alighted number, all were essentially indistinguishable save one, which, being almost wholly white, was likely the same bird Ben had observed scavenging the plaza in front of the neighboring bench.

Returning his attention to the disheveled panhandler, Ben watched the man ambulate as if on enfeebled limbs and then claim a seat on the leftward side of the sculpture, proximate to another pediment. Ben was surprised to discover then, approaching from streetward, the russet-haired man he had encountered only recently in the burying ground. The man was holding, in addition to his umbrella, a small white bag similar to the one that had lain on the bagel woman's lap.

Taking notice of Ben, the man showed recognition, but was there-upon distracted by the disheveled man who was presently extending a quavering hand toward him. The red-haired man began to unroll his white bag, but then gave the whole of it over to the quavering suppli-cant, and thereupon steered a course toward Ben.

"We meet again," the man said, upon approaching.

"We do indeed, sir. Would you care to have a seat?"

"Yes, thank you." The man sat down in the place of Ben's previous bench mate, and passing his hand then through a cord attached to the handle of his umbrella, smiled toward Ben. "If I don't do this, I'll forget it for sure. Half the world is provisioned by the things I've left behind."

"As in the case of your breakfast?"

The man leaned against the bench back and patted his stomach. "All to the good."

Ben eyed the russet-haired man's midriff. "You imply a surfeit I do not observe, sir." He patted his own stomach. "Now here, sir; here is surfeit, and, as happenstance would have it, also in the paradoxical. If you care to replenish your stores, sir, I should be only too happy to look after your storm shelter, if such would unencumber you."

The man flipped his free hand open. "Not a problem. I'll just pick something up on the way"—he chortled—"to my office, I was going to say." He held a smile toward the general direction of the sculpture, and then continued. "I got laid off a couple of weeks ago. The only office I've got now is a desk and a phone at an outplacement firm up the street"—he gestured with his head—"and I only have that when some-body else isn't using it." He glanced at his watch. "Which is why I try to be the early bird."

Several pigeons had gathered to front of his bench mate, Ben noticed, and some of these, heads bobbing, were venturing almost to within pecking distance of the man's feet. "I'm very sorry to learn of your mis-fortune, sir."

The man nodded.

"This outplacement firm, sir, of what practicality is this to you?"

Leaning toward a pigeon nearing his feet, the russet-haired man showed the undulating bird open palms, the gesture causing it to retreat a brief staccato of steps. "I don't have anything for you today. Sorry." He looked toward the leftward side of the sculpture. "Go ask that guy over there. He's flush." The man looked to Ben. "Mainly it's just a place to go every day to keep up appearances. You don't have a job to go to anymore, but everybody thinks you do—the neighbors, the mailman, your dog—and you don't want them to think otherwise, so you sort of make believe."

"Is this the only service rendered, sir, or should I infer from 'outplacement' that some measure of service is offered toward helping you gain a new situation—a new place to go to, as you put it?"

The man nodded. "That's actually the real purpose. I'm just giving you the pity-party part."

"What was your trade, sir, if I might inquire, at your previous situation?" Ben offered his hand. "Since we are, it would appear, to engage to some degree of intimacy here, sir, might I have your name? Mine is Ben—though it has, at different times, been also Richard, Silence, Molly, Mehemet, and a few others." He smiled. "In the main, it has been, and remains, Ben."

The man grasped Ben's hand. "Henry. Henry Ditweiller."

"'Tis a pleasure, Mr. Ditweiller."

"Henry."

"'Tis a pleasure, Henry."

"Likewise, whoever you are." Henry looked to a covey of pigeons milling and cooing in front of him. "C'mon, guys, you're making me guilty." He showed the gathering both palms. "See? Nada." He looked to Ben. "I was a technical writer."

"I am not familiar with that term, and naught of the intelligence recently settled upon me is of any compensatory assistance in the moment. What was the object of your service, sir?"

"Essentially, I wrote 'how to' manuals—that kind of thing."

"Instructionals?"

Henry nodded. "And 'expositionals.' Sometimes you need to know how things work in order to be able to use them properly."

"Ah, yes. When first I invented the lightning rod, most thought it attracted the lightning, and were wary of its use, whilst in actuality it did the very opposite. Had they understood the workings of the instrument, they would not have feared it, and likely would have more prolifically, as well as properly, installed it."

Henry smiled. "Who did you say you were?"

Ben smiled in return. "Concerning what particular instrument or such, sir, if I might inquire, did you provide instruction?"

Henry looked again to the pigeons cooing close upon his feet. "The company I was working for was developing a suite of nano-based products for a next-gen global communications network. I was in charge of writing the configuration guide for a satellite-borne nanoswitch."

"And this company, sir, it was perchance Gnu Age Networks?"

Henry showed surprised.

"Your jacket, sir."

Henry glanced upon the left breast of his jacket. "I was number fifteen." He looked again to Ben. "By the time they hired number 150, I was supposed to be filthy rich."

"The best made plans, sir?"

Henry smiled. "About two months ago our CEO called a company-wide meeting to tell us the company was being sold to a Chinese firm, and that all the commodity functions, like technical writing, were going to be outsourced to China and India. Everyone affected would be getting three months severance plus medical, plus outplacement services. Have a nice day."

"Good luck to ya?"

Henry grinned, nodding.

"Might I assume, sir, that you had immigrated to this company from one previous?"

"And one before that, and one before that, and one before that. If you want to make money in my line of work, you have to sort of sleep around. If you stay with the same company, you'll get a bump of maybe three to four percent a year, but if you jump ship, you can easily get as much as fifteen to twenty-five percent. I once got almost forty. And if you were lucky enough to be able to jump ship to a start-up, you were all but guaranteed to be filthy rich within five years." He smiled. "Or so some of us allowed ourselves to believe."

"This 'configuration guide' you mentioned, sir, toward what end was this directed, if I might inquire?"

Henry held his eyes as if fixed upon an inward puzzle, and then began: "Say you have a telescope. One night you want to look into deep space. Another night you want to take infrared photos of Betelgeuse. Another night you want to set up a series of time-lapse photos of the Big Dipper. For each of these purposes, you would need to use a particular combination of lens, timers, stabilizers, and the like, in a particular way. And to do this, you would need a certain amount of instruction. The switch I was writing about can accommodate a variety of end states relative to voice and data traffic. My manual explained how to configure the various components of the switch in order to accomplish each end state."

"A most facile description, sir. You were as if a master unto the indenture—his teacher—am I correct, sir?"

Henry held pensive a moment, then nodded. "I hadn't thought of it that way before, but, yes, I did provide instruction, so, technically at least"—he smiled—"a little pun there—I guess you could say I was a teacher, although the reality hardly seems to befit the term."

"Do I detect a note of negativity? Was your trade lacking in satisfaction, sir?"

"It was a paycheck. And medical insurance. It was very little else."

"Yet were you not drawn to it?"

"Yeah, like someone with a toothache is drawn to a dentist. It was the solution to a problem."

Ben shivered. "A most instructive analogy, sir."

Henry revealed now, by way of a certain comportment of countenance, a perhaps chronic inclination toward shyness. "Thank you."

"Do I detect, sir, from your analogy, that some measure of urgency was involved?"

Henry breathed a sigh. "When I was in my third year of graduate school, Lucy, my wife, became pregnant. We had not planned it, but there it was, the product of a bottle of Peruvian malbec, and so a daughter, as well as a PhD, was to be delivered to us on or about the same day the following May. But then Lucy got very ill and had to leave her job, which left us without medical coverage, which we badly needed. I had a master's degree at that point, but what the hell can you do with a master's degree in particle physics? I checked into teaching high school, but I couldn't get hired, other than as a substitute, until I was certified, and I couldn't get certified until I had taken a bunch of required education courses, which would have taken me years and cost thousands." Henry paused a moment. "Then I saw an ad for a technical writer on Craigslist, and a week later I had a job that paid over twice what I would have gotten as a full-time sub, and gave us full bennies t'boot."

"You have a child, then?"

Henry looked away.

"Forgive me, sir. I make too many inquiries. I shall make no other."

The white pigeon previously espied joined the flock a'ready alighted close upon Henry's feet.

Ben looked to the disheveled man to whom Henry had given over his breakfast. Whilst yet the man ate, a wrapper lay loose close upon his feet.

Looking to the sculpture, Henry cleared his throat. "My wife miscarried in her third month. The very next day she was diagnosed with nephrites. She spent the next nine and a half years in dialysis. She wouldn't give up; I wouldn't let her. We died together."

Ben winced to a sting at the back of his throat. "I'm deeply sorry, sir."

Henry brushed his cheeks and looked to his watch. "Oh, shit, there goes the worm!" He poised to rise but Ben held him fast by quick imposition of another inquiry.

"One last inquiry, Mr. Ditweiller, if I might. If one were to allow the water of his grief to fall upon proper ground, might not the full promise of himself yet spring forth?"

Whilst Henry regarded Ben with no little perplexity, Ben retrieved the front section of the *Courant*, and holding this toward Henry, pointed to a headline: BRAZEN DRIVE-BY AT BOSTON HIGH LEAVES TEEN DEAD. "How might one make his way to the ground, sir, of this most grievous tragedy?"

Henry turned from the newspaper to generally southwestward. "I think Boston High's up on Arlington, near the pike. You could take the T up to Arlington and then walk over—it's three or four blocks maybe. Or you could grab a cab. At this time of day, the T'd probably be faster, not to mention a helluva lot cheaper."

"Might I presume, sir, that in missing the worm at one 'place to go to,' you have liberated yourself to seek the worm at another 'place to go to?'" Ben arose forthrightly, thereby affrighting the entire congregation of close-upon pigeons into a common retreat. "T for two, sir?"

Henry shook his head and then rose to his feet, umbrella securely in hand. "Why do I get the feeling I'm going to regret this?"

"Regret's throne, sir, is an empty palm. Seize the moment, sir! Lead on!"

Noticing the disheveled man flick a wad of paper toward a pigeon, as if this article were a biscuit enlisted into the artillery, Ben was reminded of Henry's given-up breakfast: "Forgive me, sir. I am too intent upon other concerns. We must replenish your stores. Few are the journeys expected to be brief that do not extend considerably longer. I have indeed intimate knowledge in this regard."

"Not a problem. Really, I'm good."

"You are certain, sir?"

"I am."

"A moment's delay then, sir, and we shall hoist sail."

Ben tapped his way to where the disheveled man yet sat, and bowed to him. "A good morning to you, sir. May I have a word?"

The man appeared quizzical and hostile in about equal measure.

"Complementarity?" Ben could hear Sergeant Kortright inquire, in a rhetorical stance.

"There comes with every kindness received, sir, a like measure of obligation." Ben pointed his cane toward Henry. "The gentleman there—as well as the one presently standing before you, and yet many others in absentia—would be most appreciative if you would retrieve the refuse you recently cast forth to no good end, it being neither biscuit nor bomb." Ben pointed his cane toward a ball of white paper resting upon the pavement, and then toward the barrel into which the bagel woman had earlier deposited her refuse—"and place that article into that repository, for which purpose it perhaps too humbly advertises itself."

The man contorted his face as of affrontment, and looked askance.

"The choice is entirely yours, sir. I make but a request, one gentleman to another." Ben bowed, and turning away, began to tap toward Henry.

"Oh, all right!" The man shuffled the few steps to the ball of paper, and taking this article into hand, with some difficulty, shook his head. "Don't know why people can't be mindin' they own business."

Ben bowed. "I do sincerely thank you, sir."

The man shuffled toward the barrel, mumbling.

"Sir?"

The man continued on as if unhearing, the volume of his mumbling noticeably elevated. "Don't know why people can't be mindin' they own business."

Ben followed the man to the barrel. "Your demonstration of civic pride, good sir, stimulates an idea. This area requires policing on a regular basis, such as to protect it from desecrations owing to the practices of people who mind their own business only. I am unable, of myself alone, sir, to meet this need. I require a deputy. Might you be willing, sir, in continuation of your present attentions, to serve in this capacity? You would be charged with ensuring that all visitors to this area properly dispose of their castaways, and otherwise honor the right of all citizens to enjoy in common the aesthetic and contemplative pleasures offered here. You would need to use some measure of diplomacy in this regard, sir, as all people require respect, even when they do not quite deserve it. Would you be willing to serve in this official capacity, sir?"

The man looked askance.

"Your supervisory services are sorely needed here, sir."

The man held his eyes askance.

"I am sorry to have troubled you, sir." Ben bowed, and turning away, began to tap toward Henry.

"Oh, all right. Don't know why people can't be minding they own business."

Ben returned to the barrel. "Excellent. May I have your name, good sir?"

"Ernie."

"May I have also your surname, sir? Your family name."

"Siderski."

"Please place your left hand on the barrel, sir, and raise your other."

Ernie placed his left hand on the rim of the barrel and raised his right hand, the latter quaking as if of a palsy.

Ben raised his left hand. "Ernest Siderski, I hereby deputize you Sheriff of this plaza, granting you all the powers and responsibilities pertaining thereto, including the power to enlist others into the cause of keeping these premises ever worthy of a queen's smile." Ben bowed. "Serve well and honorably, sir."

Ernie jerked his head into a nod.

Turning away then, Ben tapped his way toward Henry, who, upon Ben's approach, began to shake his head.

"Who the hell *are* you anyway?"

"The question of the moment, good sir, is not who the hell *I* am—I'm just an old man—but who the hell *you* are. This question being most deserving of an answer, let us hoist our canvas to full mast and discover what we might." Ben looked to the clock gazing out from the Park Street Church steeple: 8:05. "The hour grows dear."

Whilst following Henry up the path earlier traversed, Ben made inquiries concerning "particle physics." Henry providing a brief education on this topic, Ben lapsed into exaltation: "O, what marvels of understanding were to be had! O, would that I could have preserved myself forward a full two centuries!"

At the mutually duplicating MBTA entries, Ben followed Henry to the one leftward, and passing through a set of doors there, descended a long flight of steps divided by a handrail. As Ben attempted to keep pace with his guide, wincing to pangs of gout, several people brushed past, some of these descending two steps at a time, one of a sudden striking him with such force as to cause him nearly to lose balance, no apology offered. At the bottom of the steps, Henry led Ben to a row of devices reminding in aspect of the teller and lottery devices previously encountered. "You being Ben Franklin and all"—Henry grinned—"I take it you've never been on the T before."

"You take it correctly, sir."

"OK, you're going to need a ticket." Pulling a bank card from his wallet, Henry was about to insert this into a slot on the closest-upon device when Ben, pulling his own bank card from pocket, made objection.

Henry ignored Ben's card by way of inserting his own. "My pleasure," he said, manipulating the screen by no greater than touching it. Henry slipped a ticket from one slot, a receipt from another, and giving the ticket over to Ben, slipped a ticket in likeness from his shirt pocket. "OK, we're good to go. Just do what I do."

Following Henry to a gate constituted of a horizontal bar, Ben imitated Henry's use of his ticket and soon discovered himself entered into as if a catacomb. In the moment, a metallic screeching excited a herd of denizens into a stampede toward a slowing train of cars. Ben followed Henry into the herd, and thereupon past several cars, tapping himself along as fast as he might, and thereupon into a funnel as if of sheep queuing into a pen. Propelled forward then by a steady press from behind, Ben soon discovered himself inside the pen, and so compressed into close company as to feel obliged to offer apology for an intrusion of intimacy he could not diminish, to effect then of feeling obliged to offer yet farther apologies.

The door sliding closed to a heavy exhale, the train lurched into motion, hurtling Ben against his neighbors, whose proximate presence saved him from becoming as if an untethered pipe of Madeira loosed in a bilge. Offering yet more apologies, Ben looked to Henry, separated from him by a frizzled pile of magenta-hued hair, and seeing that Henry was holding onto an overhead support, discovered a similar support and grasped this with his free hand, and none too soon, for the train abruptly slowed, pressing Ben into the young woman with the magenta hair. No sooner had Ben offered his apologies, which apparently went unheard, they being obstructed by a listening apparatus pressed over the woman's ears, than the train lurched again into motion, hurtling Ben into his neighbors in the opposing direction, and causing him thereby nearly to lose grip upon the overhead support. The train bore sharply to rightward then, to a screech reminding of a ravenous blade ripping through a log of oak, causing Ben nearly to tumble upon the passengers sitting proximate.

Ben judged his present situation to exceed in peril even that of casting about in an Atlantic tempest. In the latter case, at least there was some measure of predictability, of rhythm. Here, there was none such.

Indeed, one dare not loosen one's hold, or limber one's stance, even for an instant.

After a few farther such hurtlings and pressings, lurchings and lean-ings, a disembodied voice mumbled in what seemed to be a foreign tongue salted with a word or two of English. Soon thereafter the train came to a stop, whereupon the door slid open and people began to disembark, nay, to disgorge, from the stifling car. Ben looked to Henry, who managed to convey, by way of gesture, that their stop was the very next. Ben could not but wonder what might have been his fate had he not had readily available to him the expert services of a native pilot.

As a bead of perspiration scudded down his spine, Ben made study of the local demographics, noting there to be nearly as many "tawnies" present as "milk-and-roses," and thereupon made study of the local etiquette, noting that several women, including a stout Negro matron, her brow and cheeks glistening, were being caused to stand by way of young men remaining comfortably seated.

The train once again lurched into motion, the disembodied voice once again mumbled unintelligibly, and the train once again swayed and screeched. When again it came to a stop, Henry gestured to effect that Ben should bear with haste toward an exit to leftward.

Ben shuffled to close proximity of this, and pausing to allow several passengers to precede him through the doorway, their need being man-ifestly so very much greater than his own, stepped through the doorway himself onto a platform, whereat he noticed "Arlington" imprinted upon the wall immediately forward. Looking to rightward, Ben glimpsed dis-embarked passengers hurrying toward a flight of steps. Looking to left-ward, he glimpsed a young Negro man, newly emerged from a car, who bore striking familiarity—firstly by way of the purple head-stocking he was wearing, secondly by way of his braided hair, and thirdly by way of the listening device he was wearing over his ears. Indeed, he was the very same gentleman who had robbed Sergeant Kortright!

The young man now disappeared amidst several other disembarked passengers into an exit marked "Escalator to Arlington Street."

Henry appeared, and suggesting they use the escalator as against the stairs, led Ben toward the very exit into which the young Negro man had disappeared, and then onto a flight of stairs moving up a tunnel barely sufficient in width to accommodate a moderate girth, to say nothing of worse.

At the conveyor's summit, an equally narrow passageway led unto

an open area, whereat Henry entered into a turnstile of three compart-
ments and attempted to push his way counterclockwise through. The
rotator, however, recalcitrant at first, soon became immovable, and
Henry discovered himself unable to move either farther forward or in
reverse.

Espying to rightward a row of gates similar to those at Park Street,
Ben tapped his way to one of these, and bearing his bulk against the
horizontal bar, in imitation of the person preceding him, tapped his
way in haste to where Henry was yet entrapped. By way of Ben pulling upon the rotator whilst Henry pushed upon it, Henry was soon
liberated.

"How is it," Ben inquired, "that a mechanism of such obvious importance can be allowed to deteriorate to such an advanced state of corruption and remain so?"

"That's an easy one. Nobody gives a shit."

Ben looked to another hapless victim's efforts to rotate the turnstile,
then tapped his way to a glass-fronted booth standing close upon the
line of gates. The Negro woman sitting inside the booth, which showed
no obvious aperture for communication, took no immediate notice of
him. She appeared indeed to be reading something held below Ben's
line of sight. "A good day to you, madam," Ben greeted, his voice commanding, as if delivered from atop a saddle. The woman looked up.

Ben showed a smile of at least seven candles in radiance. "The round-
about exit over there, by my colleague"—he pointed his cane toward
Henry—"is not functioning properly—it will not rotate full around—
and because there is no notice to that effect presently proximate to it,
people are being greatly inconvenienced, if not endangered. Is there an
authority we might contact toward seeking a proper redress?"

The woman looked to the turnstile, to Ben, then smiled. "I'll take
care of it. Thank you."

Ben nodded. "And thank you, madam, for—as my colleague would
phrase it—giving a shit."

The woman grinned.

Ben returned to Henry. "Might it be the case, Mr. Ditweiller, that in
order for people to give a shit in such instances, they must first be led
to the privy?"

Henry's eyes sparkled as he laughed, in likeness indeed to an emerging sun jewelling drops of rain. He thereupon led Ben toward a set of
steps.

Espying a flower vendor to rightward, Ben noted a bouquet of daises, smiled, and followed Henry onto the steps. Climbing slowly, whilst gripping the railing with his free hand, Ben paused at the first landing, pangs of gout exacerbating those of hunger, and chided himself for having not fortified himself with at least one roundish loaf called a bagel. He was, after all, he reminded himself, returned to flesh, and thereby to all the dependencies and infirmities inescapable thereof.

Emerging into an ambiance immediately restorative, Ben paused to relish a few measured breaths, and discovered himself peering across a well-trafficked street—Arlington, he presumed—at yet another heroic figure elevated upon yet another robust pedestal. Struck by lack of any notable distinction betwixt this figure and the likeness of Josiah Quincy at Old City Hall—each figure bearing the same aspects of pose, it seemed, toward the same effect—Ben could not but wonder if he were bearing witness to a truth heretofore gone by him wholly unnoticed: That all mortals elevated toward a common divinity must converge upon a common perjury.

Henry led Ben to the near crossing street, whereat Ben noted a street marker imprinted "Boylston" crosswise to one imprinted "Arlington," and recollected the likely honoree, the physician Zabdiel Boylston, who had, with Cotton Mather, advocated for public inoculation against the smallpox—and recollected then also his collusion with his brother James toward opposing inoculation, as a subterfuge toward opposing Mather himself, the insufferable righteousness of the man. What he had done, of course, he had now to confess, was to allow the fervor of his contempt toward dogma to impugn the whole of a man who, in truth, was constituted of as many positive aspects as negative, instead of confining his judgments to those aspects that deserved it. Alas, how many more children might Reverend Mather and Dr. Boylston have saved had a smug Benjamin Franklin been able to recognize the excess of his own righteousness?

The more solar the faults of others, the more shadowed one's own.

Ben looked to Henry, who seemed a bit shadowed in spirit. "Concerning our brief discourse on natural philosophy, sir, I meant to inquire whether your interest tended toward the empirical or toward the speculative."

Henry brightened. "Actually, both. I love the intellectual athleticism of pure speculation, but I also love the creativity that goes into empirical attempts to confirm theory, especially when the theory involved is thought to be all but impossible to confirm, as in the case of string theory." The *Walk* signal illuminated and Henry launched forth as if by a little push from behind.

Ben winced, attempting to keep up, as if to the stings of one bee here and another there, each then residually an ache. Henry grasped him by the arm. When they had arrived at the farther side of Boylston, Henry suggested they get a taxi.

"A visit from Madam Gout, sir—ever commanding of one's attention, ever reminding of one's transgressions. Lead on! I shall give her but what she deserves in kindness returned."

"You sure?"

"I am."

With Henry allowing Ben to set their pace—generally to southward, by arc of the sun—Ben resumed the discourse he had commenced: "I have some understanding of this theory you mention, sir, but entirely by way of, let us say, indirect means. I have made no personal study upon it. I would be most appreciative, therefore, if you would apprise me of the essentials."

"According to string theory," Henry began, "all the fundamental building blocks of the universe—those that make up matter as well as those that carry force—quarks and photons, for example—are themselves made up of even smaller building blocks, billions of times smaller, that exist in either one or two dimensions, and are always vibrating. Some of these objects are open ended, like tiny pieces of string, hence the name, while others are closed into loops. Different strings have different vibrations, or notes, just as the different strings on a guitar have different vibrations, or notes; and it is these different vibrations that determine whether a particular combination of strings manifests as a quark or as a photon—or, one might say, as a folk ballad or a street rap."

"Remarkable. Truly remarkable."

"It gets better. According to the theory, there aren't four dimensions to reality, three of space and one of time, but eleven—ten of space and one of time—with the seven extra spatial dimensions being folded up on themselves like the petals of a flower bud. Some versions of string theory call for even more dimensions.

"That's it in a nutshell. The beauty of it, for me, is that it neatly resolves a fundamental conflict between quantum theory and general relativity. General relativity explains gravity in terms of space-time curvature, whereas quantum theory can't explain gravity at all. As far as quantum theory is concerned, gravity doesn't even exist! In string theory on the other hand, gravity is simply another force, like electromagnetism, that's carried by particles made up of strings—photons in the case of electromagnetism, gravitons in the case of gravity. No separate, made-up construct is necessary to accommodate gravity. Are you familiar with Occum's Razor?"

"Yes, I believe I am, by grace of gift. The simplest explanation for any phenomenon is most likely to be the correct one. Am I within proximity?"

"You are. And that, to me, is what string theory is—the simplest explanation. No round pegs being pounded in square holes."

They had arrived at another crossing street, this one marked "St. James Avenue." There was a hotel, the Park Plaza, on the corner at the diagonal. Dark-red awnings, like rouged eyelids, were drooped over the second-level windows.

"I thank you, sir, for an elucidation most lucid indeed. I do have one consternation, however, concerning the objects you described as being of only one or two dimensions. Indeed, the term 'object' would seem a bit grand for something to which is attributed vibration but insufficient structure, it would seem, with which to manifest any movement soever, much less a staccato of such. Would I be correct, sir, to assume, from your description, that these small objects are constituted of a substance that itself has no constituent substance?"

Henry led Ben at a moderate pace across St. James Avenue.

"That's what most string theorists believe, yes."

"'Tis the innermost then of the Matryoshka dolls?"

"That's the idea."

"And what have these theorists to say, sir, as regards the nature of this innermost essence? In other words, sir, to be direct, what is it of these string objects that is vibrating? Surely we are not to believe that a vibration, like a smile, exists disembodied of all means necessary for its being."

"Well, as a matter of fact, yes. They would say it was meaningless to even ask the question. A paragraph is made up of sentences, they would say, by way of analogy, sentences are made up of words, words of letters, but letters are made up only of themselves. Letters are just letters. Strings are just strings."

"And tautologies just tautologies, sir?"

Henry smiled. "Well, I pretty much had that same reaction at first. The more I got into the math of it, though, the more everything seemed to make sense."

"Sense as regards the mind, sir, or scents as regards the olfactory? Indeed, is there not whiff here of a red herring being tossed to rightward such as to distract the hounds from the quail cowering to leftward?"

Henry grinned. "I take it you're not buying 'strings are just strings.'"

"I grew up under the thumb of received Calvinism, sir. I learned early in my years to be wary against wholesale purchase of anything rendered substance by mere air of authority."

"Little did I know when I got up this morning—"

"Do I overbear, sir?"

"No, no, not at all. Please continue."

"Might I infer then, sir, on the basis of a confession just made by you, that you have at least some familiarly with mathematical formulae and the ciphering of these."

"I do."

"Consider then, sir, a circle ten feet in diameter generated by its Euclidian relation, C equals pi times ten. Does this circle actually exist, sir?"

"It does, and it doesn't. It doesn't exist physically, if that's what you mean. It only exists conceptually, as an abstraction."

"Writ upon the tablet of the mind?"

"Yes."

"Now, this abstraction implies two other such, does it not, sir?— indeed, a precise point to serve as center, and a precise line to serve as boundary?"

"It does."

"And these abstractions, sir, as in the case of your vibrating string, are of but one dimension; are they not?"

"They are."

"And necessarily so, such as to define a particular circle to absolute uniqueness; am I correct?"

"You are."

"Now, these same abstractions, sir—circle center and circle circumference—even though they have no physical reality, they do have practical utility—and have, in fact, I presume you will agree, proven most useful toward advancing material and intellectual progress over millennia. Watchmakers, for example, have used these very abstractions for centuries to imagine the intricate relations of gear works, yes?"

"Yes. Without a design or blueprint it'd be difficult for anybody to implement *anything* of any real complexity."

"A design being a sort of map, or approximation, of something to be built or constructed; correct?"

"Correct."

They arrived at an intersection formed not of one crossing street but two, these intersecting each other as well as Arlington. The crossing walkway, instead of being straight on, was located several yards rightward, and was of two parts—the first leading to a median betwixt the intersecting crossing streets; the second leading diagonally from the median to the farther side of the crossing streets. Directly ahead, on the opposing side of the two crossing streets, stood a strange, castle-suggesting structure, fronted with a tower and parapet, that appeared to be listing forward, in the manner of the notorious tower at Pisa.

"A highway engineer, therefore," Ben continued, "in similitude to our watchmaker, might use lines and curves of one dimension to imagine a complex arrangement of roadways and crosswalks, such as that presently before us."

"Absolutely."

"Or an architect might use them to imagine a most curious structure, such as the one presently before us."

Henry looked to the parapeted castle. "To be sure."

"Now, sir, in addition to facilitating conception of complex models of what *might* be made real—watches, highways, castles, parapets, and such—might such abstractions be employed also toward conceiving complex models of what already *is* real?"

"The relationship is entirely symmetrical. It goes both ways." Henry led Ben toward the crosswalk to rightward.

"Now, sir, can any physical object, including a line drawn upon paper, which has at least some height and breadth in addition to length, exist in the absence of a volume of space sufficient to accommodate it?"

"I can think of no exception."

"We might say, then, with some measure of confidence, that space, the existence of space, is necessary to the existence of the objects that strings, as fundamental building blocks, build of themselves, and by inference then, is necessary to the existence of the strings themselves. In other words, sir, we would be hard-pressed to have something physical exist within a context that is unable to accommodate it, would we not?"

"We would." Henry led Ben onto the crosswalk, and then toward the median separating Stuart Street from Columbus.

"And the inverse; is it also true? Are strings, the existence of strings, necessary to the existence of the space that is necessary to accommodate the existence of strings?"

"If they are, we've got a problem."

"Yet strings are fundamental to all else—in fact, are the building blocks of all else—are they not, sir?"

"They are."

"So strings must be the building blocks of all space as well as of all mass and force, there being naught else of which space might be rendered into being."

"Oops."

Henry led Ben onto the second crosswalk, and then to the corner of Columbus and Arlington. There Ben paused to study upon the castle-suggesting building directly before him, his gaze rising gradually to the parapet atop the tower. "To what purpose is this curious structure, sir?"

"Originally, it was an armory. It's now an office building, I believe."

"A sword rendered into ploughshares?"

"Perhaps, but the new armory is even larger."

Ben shook his head and continued onward. "I would like to return, sir, if I might, to these singular objects you call strings."

"The bait befits the prey."

"There is no entrapment here, sir. There is but an abiding concern after truth. So consider, sir, if you would, kindly, the consequence to human progress of declaiming as truth the model of the earth as a flat object; or the model of the universe as a concentricity of crystalline spheres; or the model of the divine as tribal benefactor; or the model of disease as demonic possession; or the model of Negro as three-fifths person; or the model of happiness as satiation of appetite; or the model of nature as inexhaustible resource; or the model of 'me' being perennially preeminent over 'thee.' Indeed, sir, whenever a map is regarded as the very territory it represents, or a myth is regarded as fact, or a mathematical abstraction is regarded as physical reality, should we not trouble ourselves to burden the conceiving theorists with a bald challenge?"

"I see your point."

"Shall I press on?"

"Curiosity killed the cat."

"Consider the alternative, sir—the living cat dead to all curiosity." Ben paused, and then continued. "Allow me to pose an interrogatory, sir, concerning the scents of flowers within the same species. Are these

likely to be weakly variant within their kind—scent of jonquil in relation to scent of daffodil, for example—or are they likely to be strongly
variant within their kind?"

"Weakly variant, I would have to say."

"And the scent of these curious string objects, sir. Does your intellectual olfactory suggest to you a stronger kinship with the scent of
mathematical abstraction—point and line—or with the scent of manifest reality—fire and dew?"

"With the former, I would have to say."

Henry paused at the entrance to a paved lot marked "Park Here," then
led Ben across the street to the farther side of Arlington, where a narrow street, Winchester, abutted. "We're almost there," Henry assured.

Ben continued. "Are you familiar, sir, with a symbol having appearance of two fetuses, indistinct of species, circulating within the same
womb, each being in coloration the complement of the other; each
holding of its eye the essence or idea of the other?"

"The Yin-Yang symbol, yes."

"Now imagine yourself, sir, if you would, facing northward, holding
a likeness of the symbol aforementioned in your right hand, as if onto
an electrode of positive charge, and a representation of those curious
string objects in your left hand, as if onto an electrode of negative
charge."

Henry paused, and turning nearly a half-circle around, held his arms
straight outward from his sides, fists clenched. "Like this?"

"You are most accommodating, sir."

"What I am is Scarecrow, and what you are is Dorothy, and when we
get to the end of the Yellow Brick Road, I'm finally going to get a brain,
right?"

"I believe the character to which you allude, sir, already had a brain.
What he lacked, I believe, was understanding. And it was toward this
end, we must suppose, that the Great Oz granted him a degree in
Thinkology. Yet the scarecrow's first exhibition of understanding, we
should note, was thus, or close akin: 'The sum of the square roots of
any two sides of an isosceles triangle is equal to the square root of the
remaining side.' Now, sir, besides being comically erroneous, this declaration betrays an orientation not toward 'Thinkology'—or rationality,
we must assume, in the broadest and deepest sense—but toward thinking constrained to mathematical formulization. What the scarecrow
required for true understanding, sir, you now hold in your right hand,
in equal measure to what you hold in your left."

Henry turned half-circle around, in reverse direction, still holding his arms orthogonal to his sides.

Ben smiled. "You make a fine scarecrow, sir."

"Thank you. It's been my life's ambition."

The pair passed a stopped car, black as tar, windows darkly tinted, in which a Negro man was sitting in the driver's seat, window unrolled, moving in rhythm to a ponderous, repetitive thumping. The very ground seemed to be vibrating in resonance.

"This should be it," Henry thereafter announced, looking rightward to a red-brick building of four stories, each story showing a profligacy of tall windows. A narrow stopping lot adjacent was well filled with cars; a modest entrance, likely for accommodating the stopping lot, appeared to be of secondary utility. Ben thereupon followed Henry to the farther side of the building, whereat three cars marked "Police" were stopped along the street fronting the school. Ben noticed a uniformed officer standing afront an entry unto the near section of the building. This section projected leftward of a larger and higher middle section, whilst a mirror image of the near section projected to rightward. A pole bearing the national banner angled outward, at about forty-five degrees, from just below a second-story window at the very center of the middle section. The ground-level windows, as well as those in the entry doors, were covered over with robust grates, as in a dungeon.

Ben followed Henry down a set of concrete steps to the near end of a small stopping lot filled with vehicles. A Negro girl, youthful of countenance but well abloom in other respects, was just emerging from a car emitting metallic noises of an alarming nature. "Fuck you!" the girl now exclaimed, in the general direction of the driver, an adult Negro woman with hair the color of Henry's. The girl now slammed the car door shut, using considerable force. "Fuck you!" she repeated, as if to provide a reminding echo in the absence of natural means.

The car was oriented such that it could neither proceed forward, for lack of space ahead in which to turn about, nor regress to rearward, there being now two cars paused behind, the second of these presently being absent its driver.

Henry and Ben paused at the bottom of the steps such that the Negro girl, showing indications of self-eminence, might precede them. As the girl climbed the steps, Ben noticed that her ebony midriff was exposed fully around, and that her breeches fit upon her limbs like the skin of a serpent much overdue for a molt. She was bearing no books. A lintel embedded above the entry doors bore an inscription: ABRAHAM LINCOLN SCHOOL.

The uniformed officer standing afront of the rightward member of two doors regarded Henry and Ben from behind spectacles fashioned, it would seem, of looking-glass panes as opposed to spectacle lenses.

"A very good morning to you, sir," Ben chimed.

The officer rendered a nod that was more an involuntary tic, it would seem, than a greeting.

The girl passed through the leftward door without minding whether someone might be following close upon. Henry caught the door before it could shut, and held it open for Ben.

The foyer was vacant but for a set of white marble steps leading to another set of doors, these bearing no iron grates over their glass. Ben noted three bundles of newspapers resting haphazardly against the wall to leftward, each bundle yet to be liberated from its bindings.

Another uniformed officer, a woman, was standing close upon the top of the steps.

"A very good morning to you, ma'm," Ben chimed, upon reaching the top of the marble steps, a tad out of breath.

"Good morning," the woman replied, showing a smile of palpable warmth.

Passing through the second set of doors, Ben discovered himself in the foyer of a stairwell wainscoted with yellow bricks to a height of about six feet. Two large women, the farther one Negro, the nearer one tawny, were sitting at a small table to rightward. Two uniformed officers, one male, one female, were standing leftward of the table, each holding an instrument that, although not manifestly a firearm, was of menacing aspect. The Negro girl scribbled an entry, as if in defiance of all standards of penmanship, upon a sheet containing several preceding such. The sheet was attached to a board topped by a robust clip.

The Negro woman chided the girl, calling her by name—Shaunta—for yet another infraction of tardiness.

"So, like, one asshole of a mother isn't enough? I gotta have two?"

"Excuse me, miss," Ben interjected from behind, following a sharp tap of his cane against the floor.

Turning, the girl showed Ben a countenance well seasoned, it would seem, to hosting hostility.

"Tardiness," Ben continued, "when chronic, not to mention rudeness when chronic, is suggestive of a certain bent of attitude, if you don't mind my saying, that is itself suggestive of a certain agitation of the spirit. I do not wish to intrude upon ground to which I have not been invited, but I would like to suggest, miss, if I may, that she who is not master over that which agitates her spirit is necessarily subservient to it."

"Who the fuck are you?"

The tawny woman, seeming to take notice of Ben for the first time, opened her eyes as if her arms to him. "Oh, sir, we are so glad you are here. Assistant Principal was just looking for you." The woman held a device to her mouth now as if indeed to take a bite of it. "He's here!"

A reply, not only audible but loudly so, came almost immediately. "Oh good! I'll be right down. Have him sign in and I'll take him right up."

The tawny woman moved a clip-bearing board closer upon Ben. "Sign in, if you would, sir, and Assistant Principal will take you right up to your room."

Ben gestured toward Henry, who was obscured in part behind. "We are together."

The woman looked perplexed.

"Two for the price of one," Ben added, with a bow. "Mr. Ditweiller here is credentialed in the science of physics; myself, in the art of philosophy. Together, we are as flour and yeast."

The woman beamed.

Ben noticed that Shaunta was standing in a posture similar to Henry's of a few minutes previous, her arms extended out from her sides in the manner of a scarecrow. The female officer was moving an intrusive device up and down Shaunta's legs, front and back, inside and out. In the moment, a woman all but sprang from the bottommost step of a flight of stairs ascending from leftward, and showing Ben a radiant smile, introduced herself as Renee Corvallis, the assistant principal. "It was so very nice of you to come in costume. The kids will love it." She looked to Henry, who looked to Ben. The tawny woman interceded to explain that the two gentlemen were together—"two for the price of one."

Renee beamed. "Oh, splendid, splendid." She looked to Ben. "You're all signed in?"

There hadn't been time, the tawny woman interceded.

"Not a problem, you can do that later." Renee looked between Ben and Henry. "Either one of you. I assume you have an agreement between you."

"The gentleman here will oblige, I am sure," Ben said.

Henry rendered unto Ben a small blow of punishment from behind.

Renee looked to Henry. "Just stop by the office after school." She looked to Ben. "I'll take you up to your class. I just *love* that costume."

About thereupon to enter the stairwell, Renee was paused by an authoritative intercession. "*Everybody* gets wanded," the male officer growled.

"The horse is just a wee bit out of the barn, wouldn't you say, officer?"

"I'm just doing my job here, lady. If I don't wand these people, you're not the one who gets to explain why."

Ben stepped closer to the male officer, and giving his cane over to the female officer, held his arms elevated to either side whilst the male officer applied his device to body and limb. The officer soon discovered therewith a nail and a pennywhistle in Ben's vest pocket, and a single coin in his coat pocket. When the male officer had restored Ben to his pocket possessions, the female officer restored him to his cane, and brought his attention to the presence of several longitudinal fissures in the shaft.

Ben nodded. "Yes, thank you. 'Tis very old, but remains serviceable, for 'tis not the longitudinal crack, the fissure of aging, that ends all serviceability, but the latitudinal crack, the fissure of violence."

Upon Henry being discovered to harbor naught but a small pocket knife and three coins, Renee led the two accidental tutors into the stairwell.

"They send us this boy from Dorchester," Renee muttered, as they climbed, "to get him out of harm's way, they tell us, because he's the only witness against a gangbanger who's about to go on trial for murder, and what do they provide us in the way of protection—for *everybody* concerned, not just this kid? Zero. Zilch. Not a single officer. They don't have the manpower, they tell us. I protest, but I get nowhere. Principal protests; she gets nowhere. We call Super, and she tells us we've got to be good citizens. So, of course, this gangbanger finds out where the only witness against him is being kept out of harm's way and sends a couple of his homeboys over to take him out, but they hit Ricky Jimenez instead, who happens to be in the wrong place at the wrong time, and one of the nicest boys you'd ever want to meet"—Renee's voice cracked—"and now here they are, out in force, hassling everybody half t' death, after it's too damn late." Renee slumped—they had just reached the landing between the two flights of stairs—and covering her face with both hands, leaned against the near wall.

Henry placed his hand on Renee's shoulder. "I'm so very sorry." He stood in silent witness.

We died together.

Ben looked to his shoes.

Renee struggled for composure. "I'm sorry." She pulled a tissue from under a sleeve. "I didn't mean to embarrass you."

"Not a problem," Henry assured.

Renee dabbed her eyes and cheeks. "I'm *so* glad you're here. We had six teachers call in this morning, two of them—including, Mr. Ellis, the teacher you'll be subbing for—to announce their resignations." Renee shook her head. "I can't say I blame them, but still." She sighed. "Anyway, two of the subs we were supposed to get from District were no-shows— three we thought, until you arrived—so Principal is covering one class, and I'm covering another—which I've got to get back to. Thank God, you're here to cover the third. Tomorrow it'll be easier. Today, we've just got to survive. Anyway, thank you for coming."

Ben caught Henry's eye. Henry smiled.

Renee led Henry and Ben to a second landing, and then through a set of windowed doors into a corridor illuminated from above by banks of tubular lanterns. A uniformed officer was standing at a doorway to rightward about halfway up the corridor. Banks of metallic cabinets, some marked with swirls of coloration, stood against the wall to left-ward. A shorter corridor to the immediate left led crosswise.

"Our students were traumatized by what happened, as you can imagine," Renee continued, as Ben tapped a steady rhythm on the floor, "but we decided to go ahead with classes today anyway, feeling it important to keep our kids together, so they could deal with their shock and grief as a community. We also thought it was important to maintain a semblance of order and stability. Chaos is the norm for most of our kids. Chaos they didn't need any more of."

Renee glanced at her watch. "We had a general assembly during first period, so we're actually now in the first class-period of the day, abbreviated to thirty-five minutes. All class periods today will be shortened to thirty-five minutes, and then we'll end the day with another assembly. Your first-period class is American History, mostly seniors, with three or four juniors mixed in, including TJ, our witness friend—hence the officer at the door—belatedly. We didn't expect TJ to come in today, after what happened yesterday, but he was almost the first student to arrive this morning. Apparently the police were supposed to bring him in, but he came by T instead, by himself. TJ is an unusual young man. I have a great deal of respect for him. I just wish he was somebody else's responsibility."

A tall Negro boy approached, having just emerged from the room being guarded by the officer. Renee eyed him. "OK, off with the doo-thingy, Quint darling. You know the deal." Quint was wearing a black head stocking similar to the purple article of this species that Ben had seen on the young man who had robbed Sergeant Kortright.

Quint grimaced as if stricken by a fit of gastric distemper, then passed to rightward, swaying back and forth in the manner of a shallop caught in a crossing sea. The bilge of his oversized breeches was all but scraping bottom. Indeed, should it catch on a snag there, the poor lad might well be deprived of all modesty.

Renee stopped and turned. "Quinton!"

Quinton righted himself, and reaching up, pulled the stocking from his head, this covered over of tight braids in curls.

"Thank you, love."

Once again swaying to and fro, Quinton banged his way through the double doors at the end of the corridor. The cavernous corridor reverberated of the report.

Realizing he had forgotten to remove his own cap, Ben lifted it into hand and stuffed it into the pocket opposite that holding what remained of his ready money.

Renee continued. "Where was I? OK, the class can tell you what they've been working on, but please don't worry about trying to accomplish anything more today than just keeping the kids as engaged as possible. All we really want to do today is just try to assure everybody that normalcy is going to prevail at this school come hell or high water. Whatever it takes. If anybody needs to talk about the shooting, you should refer them to the counselors down in the assembly hall. Everybody who attended the assembly this morning was told they could leave class at any time to meet with a counselor. I'll reiterate this to your class, to make sure your late arrivals all know this."

The uniformed officer was wearing a pistol on one side of a wide belt, a cudgel on the other. Both instruments seemed to Ben to be rudely out of place, like a spittoon and chamber pot set upon a tea table.

Curiously, the classroom door was marked "205" upon the window glass, in black numerals, and "14" upon the door proper, in gold numerals. Ignoring the officer, Renee opened the door and forthrightly led Ben and Henry into the classroom.

The door opened close upon one end of a rectangular room in which several rectangular tables were arranged into a larger rectangle. At least two dozen students, all but two or three of dark or dusky complexion, were sitting at the tables, several with their head rested upon the immediate tabletop. A covey of girls, one of whom Ben recognized—Shaunta herself—was raucously conversing at a table well to leftward. Four students, sitting in relative isolation, were intent upon small devices being held and manipulated by the same hand, the latter action by way of thumb. At the very rear of the room, beneath one of four tall windows, a group of boys was engaged in a card game. A similar group was similarly engaged at the next table over.

Leftward of the latter table, a dark-skinned Negro boy was sitting in relative isolation. His feet were propped against the near edge of a table, and were rhythmically in motion, now in synchrony, now in counterpoint. He was wearing a cherry-red blouse, seamless and generous of fit, and a gauzy, tightly-fitting head stocking, stark white. Two long tails, as if escaped from the rear of the head stocking, were draped over one shoulder. The boy was holding a device against his leftward ear.

Something about this young man was immediately compelling. Ben had noticed the same allure in the young Paul Jones the moment he had met him. How had Voltaire put it? Ah, yes—*His face was the true index of his mind.*

Wondering now if this young man might be the witness from Dorchester, Ben soon had his answer. "OK, TJ, just because you've got permission to have it doesn't mean you have to use it. Put it away, please." The young man in the cherry-red blouse responded with an expansive salute. "Thank you, love. I wish you were not sitting so close to that window, love. OK, now listen up, everybody, especially those of you who came in late this morning. You know who you are." Renee was looking directly at Shaunta. "Counselors will be down in the assembly hall all day today. If you need to talk to somebody about what happened yesterday, go see somebody. Please don't sit on your feelings. Grief, anger, fear, whatever you're feeling, go talk about it. You have open permission to go at any time. Also, we're shortening classes today to thirty-five minutes, so we can hold a second assembly last period. Mandatory. OK? Got that? Man-da-tory."

Most of the students who had been in full repose had uplifted their heads. A few, however, remained prostrate.

"OK, we have a special treat for you today"—Renee turned to Ben—"Benjamin Franklin himself." She looked to Henry. "And his partner. Mr. Adams perhaps?"

Ben shuddered. "Mr. Newton," he offered, "as a young man."

Henry showed a grin leavened of amusement.

Renee looked again to the class. "And Isaac Newton, the famous scientist . . . who discovered gravity." She looked to Ben and Henry. "If you gentlemen need anything, I'll be in 313, or in my office, 309." She smiled. "Good luck. And again, thank you for coming." She looked to the class. "OK, now be the ladies and gentlemen that I have caught each and every one of you being at least once." As she approached upon the door, a Negro girl, her belly distinctively distended, was just entering.

Renee glanced at her watch with deliberate attention. "Glad you could make it, Sabrina, love."

Sabrina showed as if a load of stress added unto a residual of such, indeed near unto a faltering point.

"You OK?"

Sabrina shook her head.

"Come see me right after class. I'm in 313. Ben and Isaac here will take good care of you in the meantime." Renee smiled toward Ben and Henry, and then left. Sabrina flopped into a chair at one of the near tables. The boy next to her, manipulating a hand-held device with his thumb, did not look up.

Ben looked to Henry.

"Shall I begin, Sir Isaac, sir?"

"Oh, by all means, Dr. Franklin, sir."

A white and shiny writing board, being obvious by being incomplete in covering over a previous generation of such, spanned almost the full length of the interior wall of the room. Above the top of the writing board, running nearly its full length, was a blue-and-yellow banner imprinted, "You never know what you can do until you try."

Ben tapped his way to about the midpoint of the writing board, and depositing his cane on a tray affixed to the board, selected a marker, brown, from the tray. The only other colors available were green and purple. Ben thereupon drew a large half-circle on the board. "This is representation of a large knoll," he explained. "A hill." Using the two other markers, Ben drew a figure atop the knoll. "This is a tree," he explained. He drew a second figure at the bottom of the knoll, to rightward. "This is another tree," he explained. The tree on the top of the knoll—purple trunk, green foliage—was rendered meager in relation to the tree at bottom of the knoll—green trunk, purple foliage.

Ben turned to face upon the class. More students were in full repose now, he noted, than had been in that posture only a few moments previous.

"We have a very important task before us, for which we require the services of two volunteers—one of the male gender, to oversee the orderly disposition of the tables at either end of the room; the other to be of the female gender, to oversee the orderly arrangement of the chairs into a circle. Might we a have a volunteer concerning the stacking of the tables?"

There being no immediate declarations, Ben began a measured survey of the room, allowing his attention to hesitate upon each boy, and affixing his gaze finally upon the witness from Dorchester. "Mister TJ, your tongue denies what your eyes appear to assent. From which organ, sir, should I take your notice concerning the matter at hand?"

TJ shrugged. "Yeah, OK, I'll do it. Not by m'self, though." Removing his feet from the table edge, TJ poised to rise.

"I beg one moment, Mister TJ. Let us first discover our other overseer. Our task is equally of two parts."

TJ shrugged. "You the man."

Ben looked to the class. "Might we a have a volunteer to oversee the arrangement of the chairs?"

There being no immediate response, Ben again surveyed the room, allowing his attention to hesitate upon each girl. Noting fewer heads rested upon tabletops, he affixed his eyes finally on one of the occupants at the conversation table. "Miss Shaunta, is that yet more arsonous fire I see in those exotic eyes, or am I witness to the unbridled passions of a helping heart?"

Shaunta contorted her face as if in response to a wedge of ancient cheese being placed close upon her olfactory. "You talk kinda funny, Mista." She swelled up her eyes, and showing these to those sitting close upon her, elicited a brief eruption of giggles.

"Indeed I do, young miss, as do you. 'Tis a big world, of many voices, each striving to be heard in the only way it knows—citizens striving to be heard by their leaders, workers striving to be heard by their employers, spouses striving to be heard by their mates, students striving to be heard by their teachers, customers striving to be heard by their suppliers, sons striving to be heard by their fathers, daughters striving to be heard by their mothers—indeed the very mothers who, in their own time of youth, strove to be heard by their mothers; and they by their mothers; and they by their own."

Ben held his eyes fixed upon Shaunta. "Be that as it may, you know precisely what it is I am asking of you, to wit: Are you of an inclination toward overseeing the arrangement of these chairs into a circle, or are you not? In other words, young miss, are you of an inclination toward continuing upon a path of 'fuck you'—'fuck you,' indeed, unto a mortal wounding of your own essential self—or are you of an inclination toward leading yourself, and perhaps a few others here present or not, upon an entirely different path?"

Shaunta averted her eyes.

Ben looked to a clock affixed upon the rightward wall, and noticing adjacent to this a curious doll bearing a skirt fashioned of the business end of a floor mop, looked again to Shaunta. "I'm sorry to be unable to exercise endless patience concerning your answer, young miss. There is much to be done, and very little time in which to do it."

Shaunta banged a fist on the table. "Oh, all right!" She sprung to her feet.

Ben looked to TJ, who thereupon rose to his feet.

Noting no heads reposed now upon the tabletops, Ben looked to Henry, who was sitting at a desk, presumably Mr. Ellis's, located in the far rightward corner of the room. "I see you have found your bench, Sir Isaac."

Henry grinned and waved, obviously enjoying the fortuitous entertainment.

Ben looked again to TJ. "Well, Mister TJ, are you going to just stand there, awaiting a stroke of inspirational fire from the fourth dimension, or are you going to enlist a brigade of hardy young souls and charge them with the task at hand?"

TJ surveyed the room. "You want all the tables stacked up, that it?"

"Exactly so, at either end of the room, sir. The object is to replace a geometry inviting separation and repose with a geometry inviting the very opposite. The present geometry cannot be replaced, however, until it is removed from encumbering that which it should have accommodated long previous. The means to the desired effect are now wholly within the province of your authority, sir."

TJ looked to his classmates. "OK, you heard the man."

A minimal response now was mostly toward cross-purpose.

"Mister TJ," Ben called forth. "Are you the master of the ship to which you have assumed command, or are you its cook? These tables are not likely to yield their ground, methinks, to a mere clang of ladle against a pot."

Stepping forth, TJ began to appoint specific individuals to specific tables, and specific tables to specific locations. Tables began to move.

Ben looked to Shaunta. "We have need, Miss Shaunta, to fashion a circle of sufficient circumference to accommodate, by my count, twenty-six persons. There would appear, however, to be an obstacle of sufficient magnitude to frustrate this design. Do you perceive it?"

Shaunta took a step to rear to allow two boys—both former somnolents, Ben noted—to remove the table from directly in front of her. "There isn't enough room," she said.

"Precisely so. And what might be the way around this obstacle, given that 'tis not so much a circle in the full we are after as it is a replacement of repose by upright."

Shaunta pondered a moment. "Make the circle sort o' squished."

Ben drew an oval on the writing board. "Like this?"

Shaunta nodded.

"Why so?"

"It would fit the room better."

Ben drew a rectangle that, in fully encompassing the oval drawn previous, touched it amidships top and bottom, end and end. "Like this?"

Shaunta nodded.

Ben drew a circle centered within the oval—to overall effect indeed of rendering likeness of a large eyeball filling a horizontal window. "As opposed to this?"

Shaunta nodded.

"Excellent, dear girl! Excellent!"

Shaunta showed as if a hint of dawn against backdrop of a long night of darkness.

Ben looked to the class. "And what do we name such an accommodation, it representing not the whole of what we desired or intended but a portion sufficient to purpose?"

"A compromise."

Ben looked to the boy who had been sitting next to Sabrina, his attention presently no longer affixed upon his device.

Ben looked to Henry. "Did you hear that, Sir Isaac?"

Henry uplifted a thumb.

Ben looked to the boy. "What is your name, young sir, if I may have it?"

"Rafael."

"Excellent, Mister Rafael! Excellent!"

Rafael smiled.

Ben looked to Shaunta, and finding her a'ready engaged in overseeing formation of a "squished circle," looked to TJ. "I thank you, Mister

TJ, and your brigade of hardy lads, for a job well done. You were most expeditious."

TJ shrugged. "Hey, no problem."

Looking now to one of the former conversants at Shaunta's table, Angelina she now gave as her name, Ben inquired of her whether she would be amenable to imprinting the letter C upon three separate sheets of paper, to effect of each C being of a different color and oriented to face a longwise edge. Upon receiving affirmation in the form of a shrug, Ben handed Angelina the three markers from the writing-board tray.

Laying the markers on the floor, Angelina pulled a wire-bound folio from a flaccid pack, and kneeling upon the floor, tore three sheets from the folio, and used the floor surface to accommodate her task. When she had finished, she handed the sheets and markers to Ben, who, upon thanking her most profusely, surveyed the completed "squished circle" of chairs. "I thank you, Shaunta, and your troop, for a job well done. You were most expeditious."

Ben looked to the class. "If you would be so kind, please seat yourselves around the circle such as to alternate the genders." He looked to Henry, yet sitting at Mr. Ellis' desk. "There are twenty-six chairs, Sir Isaac, sufficient to accommodate all present."

Henry joined the circle, maintaining the alternation of gender, as did Ben, cane in one hand, Angelina's sheets in the other.

"I have in hand three sheets," Ben began, "each imprinted of the third letter of the alphabet." Ben held forth the sheet bearing the letter C in brown, rotating it then in the counterclockwise direction. "Now, how might these sheets be arranged such as to form a symmetry at the center of our oval?"

Ben was sitting such as to be facing upon Mr. Ellis's desk; TJ, such as to be facing upon the door. TJ rose, and taking the sheets from Ben, arranged them on the floor, at about oval center, such as to form of them an interior triangle, with the bowl of each letter C facing outward. He sat down then, and placing one ankle atop the other, began to jiggle his legs.

Sabrina began the applause, which thereupon erupted around the circle.

TJ appeared as if desperate for a place, a burrow perhaps, in which to shield his face from farther burn.

"Most Excellent," Ben declared, as if in way of striking a mark of punctuation. "I ask you now, if you would be so kind, to reacquaint yourselves with the crude representations I have drawn upon the writing board. As you will recall, I named the first of these representations a large knoll; the second, a tree rooted at top of the knoll; and the third, a tree rooted at bottom. I now adjust these hasty renderings such as to accommodate them to present purpose. The top of the knoll is not smooth and benign, as might be inferred from my simple arc, but is instead rocky and windswept, and often made harsh of bitter cold; hence the misshapenness of the trunk and limbs of the tree rooted there, and the paucity of its fruit and foliage.

"The bottom of the knoll, to the contrary, is a fertile valley, holding to bosom a meandering stream. Rooted upon the bank of this stream is our second tree, straight and true of trunk and limb, plump and lush in fruit and foliage. Now, it so happens that the tree rooted atop the knoll, and the tree rooted at bottom, were derived of seeds issued from the same parent tree, and came to their contrasting locations wholly by whim of fate—the one by gale of wind, the other by meander of stream." Ben scanned around the circle, meeting each pair of eyes. "Have you the picture in mind?"

Heads nodded in assent.

"When both trees were but seedlings," Ben continued, "they were equal in robustness and stature, there having been insufficient time and opportunity for contrasting forces and conditions to render any significant differentiation. As time passed, however, the tree atop the hill, buffeted by harsh winds, pelted by sleet and hail, denied a richness of soil, watered by cold rains soon run off, became increasingly stunted and misshapen, until it lost all opportunity to realize the full promise of itself. The tree in the valley, meanwhile, grew ever more robust until such time every bough erupted of bloom, and thereafter of fruit, there being no conditions or circumstances to conspire to the contrary."

Ben noticed that the students to rightward had oriented themselves in their chairs such as to be able to look alternately betwixt him and the writing board. "Alas," Ben continued, "the tree rooted atop the knoll aspired most keenly, of its very nature, to be as robust of trunk, lush of foliage, and fecund of fruit as the tree rooted in the valley. 'Twas indeed only for want of conditions salutary to its essential needs that it was not able to do so."

Ben glanced upon the wall clock, noticing again, with a smile, the mop-skirted doll hanging adjacent. "Our allegory, however, takes us only so far. Indeed, whilst trees have roots that fix them to circumstance, people have legs that enable them to remove themselves from any such—legs indeed not only of body but also of mind. And 'tis these latter legs that we are to be concerned with today, for 'tis these legs that can take us to where our physical limbs can but follow. In this regard, I ask you to cast your eyes to the center of this circle, upon the appearance there of the letter C, as rendered one in brown, one in purple, and one in green."

Ben watched as eyes around the circle affixed upon the sheets TJ had arranged into a symmetry. "As there are three essential elements to our physical legs," he continued, "these being Bone, Muscle, and Ligament, there are three essential elements to our psychic legs, these being Comprehension, Collaboration, and Connection. The first of these, Comprehension—being knowledge, awareness, and understanding—is represented in this symmetry by the letter tinted of brown. The meaning is this: If we are to remove ourselves from atop the windswept knoll, we must make ourselves knowledgeable in at least one practical art or trade; and we must make ourselves keenly aware of what is required to be a good friend, a good neighbor, a good spouse, and a good citizen; and we must gain an understanding of the general working of things. In short, we must make of ourselves a person who is both useful to others and agreeable to others. Or, to flip the cake, there are no useful legs to be fashioned of ignorance in any form." Ben paused. "Does this hold sensible?"

Several nods.

"As to the second element, Collaboration," Ben continued, "being membership, alliance, and cooperation, here represented by the purple letter, there is an old saying, 'Two heads are better than one,' with which I trust you are familiar." Several nods. "When I was little advanced in years over yours, I asked myself a simple question: If two heads were indeed better than one, what might seven deliver? Soon thereafter, I organized a small group of fellow tradesmen into a meeting club, which I named the Junto, toward encouraging all manner of collaborations, not only amongst ourselves, but also in association with others. We educated each other, we funded each other, we encouraged each other, we promoted each other, we even censured each other, when such was warranted. In sum, we helped each other realize far more prosperity and well-being than any of us could have attained as individuals operating in isolation. In my own case, but for a generous loan of funds from my fellow Junto members, and their interventions into the community of prospective clients, my print business, my newspaper business, and my *Almanack* business, and all else ensuing, would likely never have been, and I would not likely be here with you in this circle at this moment, having accumulated no legitimate standing to justify such an honor." Ben pulled the three-penny nail from his vest pocket and held it forth. "But for a nail, the shoe was lost, but for the shoe, the horse was lost, but for the horse the rider was lost, but for the rider the battle was lost."

Returning the nail to pocket, Ben looked to the banner running atop the writing board and read aloud: "You never know what you can do until you try." He looked around the circle. "Does this declaration fit upon you as might a suit of clothing tailored to your physicalities?" Nods. "Would it yet still were I to take the liberty of emending it to read, You never know what you can do together until you try together?"

Nods, smiles.

Ben glanced upon the wall clock, and then continued. "Now, as to the third essential element, Connection, being relation, inclusion, and intimacy, there is within us, I submit, an abiding tendency to place all persons beyond ourselves into one of two categories: Us, or Them. Us being all persons with whom we hold a personal relation, and who are thereby a source of some comfort to us; Them being all persons with whom we hold no personal relation, and who are thereby a source of some anxiety to us. Would you tend to agree?" Several nods.

Ben looked to TJ's legs, which, ankle upon ankle, were twitching and flexing as if of a palsy. "Consider the example of Mister TJ's legs. Does the agitation manifest there owe to an excess of youthful energy, do you think, or to an abiding anxiety concerning the intentions of strangers?"

TJ sat himself upright, and folding his legs beneath the seat of his chair, looked once again as if desperate for a place to hide himself.

"I apologize, Mister TJ," Ben added, "if I forced unwanted attention upon you. My intention was to associate apparent anxiety with likely cause, toward farthering the point at hand. With your permission, I shall see my purpose to end."

TJ shrugged whilst his fingers, interlaced upon his lap, pulsated, they having taken up, it would appear, what his legs had been denied.

"I thank you, sir." Ben looked around the circle. "Given Mister TJ's recent experiences, what would you speculate as to the content of his current Them list, in relation to the content of his current Us list?"

"Lotta Thems," came an answer. The speaker, a dark-skinned Negro boy, slight of build, hair trussed into scalp-hugging curls, was sitting to leftward of Henry.

"May I have your name, young sir?"

"Daryl," the boy replied, avoiding Ben's gaze.

"And what, Mister Daryl, if I may inquire of your opinion, might be the effect on Mister TJ of having in the moment 'a lotta Thems?'"

Daryl glanced to TJ, and extending his legs outward, began to agitate these, one ankle upon other, his hands as well, and thereupon the whole of his arms, also his head.

Giggles and chuckles.

Ben smiled. "Exactly so." He looked to TJ, who, grinning, was shaking his head. "Mister TJ, it would be most instructive, I think, if you would give us an account of the present content of your Us list, not in names, but in categories and numbers—for example, three brothers and sisters, two parents, twelve good friends, and perhaps even the party to whom you were speaking on your talking device a few minutes previous. Would you be so willing, sir?"

TJ shrugged. "My homeys, my mom, and my aunt."

"Homeys to what number, if I may farther inquire?"

"'Nough."

"'Nough toward what end, Mister TJ? 'Nough to make it through another day unscathed by the Thems on your list? 'Nough to be escaped from the top of a windswept knoll, should ever you discover yourself marooned upon such?"

TJ shrugged.

"Although I must confess it far easier said than done, I suggest it of tantamount importance that, despite any counter lesson taught you by way of experience, you acquaint yourself with as many of the Thems on your list as you possibly can, such that you might render as many of these as possible into Us's; and farther, that, whatever rebuffs you might suffer in this cause, you"—Ben tapped his cane against the wood floor—"persist! persist! persist!"

Ben paused a moment, and then continued. "There are indeed men and women of ill will in this world, but also great numbers of potential friends, partners, mentors, teachers, clients, customers, colleagues, boosters, and, yes, potential mates. I suggest farther, therefore, that, should you wish your last gesture upon this earth to be formation of a smile, you make it your business to get to know as many of these people as you can—*everything* about them. How they think. What they believe. What they aspire to. What they hold dear.

"Do not wait for Mohammad to come to the mountain. Take the mountain to Mohammad. And should you be unable to bear the load alone, for whatever reason, enlist the help of others. Form a Junto!" Ben looked upon each face around the circle. "Am I being sensible, or am I just a silly old man telling fairy tales toward his own amusement?"

Smiles. Murmurs.

Ben glanced again upon the wall clock. "With your permission, I should like to share with you one additional thought, then I must, of pressing necessity, leave you in the good hands of my most capable colleague, Sir Isaac, who will explain how his Third Law of Motion, to wit, 'For every action there is an equal and opposing reaction,' applies to everyday life, and most especially, to what we call 'progress.' Am I accurate on this point, Sir Isaac?"

Henry checked his watch and grinned. "Seven minutes to go. No problem."

Chuckles.

Ben looked again from face to face. "There is no happiness to be had, I submit, in the absence of meaning, and no meaning to be had in the absence of relation." He held his gaze upon Shaunta, and then continued. "Should you doubt the fullness of this truth, consider yourself in possession of all the wealth in all the world—all the gold, all the ready money, all the gemstones, all the castles, *everything*—but, alas, there is not another living soul to envy you. You are, in fact, the only living creature upon earth." Ben held his gaze upon Daryl, and then continued. "Of what value, of what meaning, are all those rubies, all those emeralds, all those sapphires, all that gold, all that ready money?" Ben held his gaze upon TJ. "Indeed, what portion of your trove would you not sacrifice for the company of even your worst enemy?"

Sabrina nodded.

Ben rose, and sliding his chair backward, removed himself from the circle, and slid his chair back into place. "I thank you all for your gracious toleration of my philosophizing." He nodded toward Henry. "Sir Isaac here is a scientist, but also a humanitarian. If you are in want, he will discover a satisfaction. If you are in pain, he will comfort you. If you are dying, he will die with you—such is the nature of this man."

Henry's eyes filled.

"He is here this day to be your teacher for this day at least. I cannot speak for him concerning tomorrow, but perhaps you, working in concert, can discover a way to hold him close." Ben looked to his empty chair. "It may appear, by my removal from the circle, that I have broken the symmetry. I have not, for I leave in my stead not a vacancy but an invitation. Indeed, as every inn holds a place at table for the unannounced wayfarer, so every circle should hold a chair open to the same purpose. 'Tis not good manners alone, but good policy also. I shall leave it to you to discover the ways."

Ben tapped his way to the door, and turning there, looked to Henry, who appeared as if stricken. "Consider the universe, Sir Isaac, as a diptych—no strings attached." He smiled. "On the rightward panel is the symbol we discussed previous; on the leftward panel is a trinity composed of three numerals: One, its negative, and null."

Ben looked to TJ. "Mister TJ, I greatly admire your courage, for 'tis of the rarest sort, being innocent of all corruption owing to zealotry. Though humility is the hardest lesson to keep, no virtue exceeds courage in the cost exacted by it."

Turning to the doorway, Ben encountered Quinton, returning from whence he had recently traveled, likely to one of the counselors referred to by Vice Principal. His "doo-thingy," Ben noticed, was restored to his head. "Your chair at table awaits," Ben said, by way of greeting.

Quinton showed Ben a curious commingling of suspicion and perplexity—indeed the two faces of estrangement. Ben thereupon tapped his way through the doorway, and closing the door behind, nodded to the officer standing sentinel. Tapping his way then to the purple doors at the end of the corridor, he slowly descended the stairs to the foyer, whereat the two officers were yet stationed, the two ladies yet seated. Ben inquired of the ladies the location of the offices of *The Boston Courant*, and was pleased to learn that these were not far distant: "Go outside, turn left, go two or three blocks to Harrison, and you'll see the *Courant* building on your right. You can't miss it." The ladies in turn inquired of Ben the reason for his early departure, and were pleased to learn that Sir Isaac was an expert on the relevance of the Third Law to practical life, and required no assistance.

Taking his leave, Ben made his way to the outer foyer, and in descending the marble steps, noticed that the three bundles of newspapers espied previous were yet to be liberated from their tethers. Outside, Ben nodded to the officer standing sentinel, made his way to street level, and bearing to leftward then, close upon where the three police vehicles were stopped, tapped his way up Marginal Road.

As he walked, an unrelenting roar from a depressed roadway to rightward engendered notion of a sort of invisible hedgerow constituted of naught but sound. Closer at hand, an accumulation of careless leavings alongside the curb—paper of various sorts, plastic of various sorts, bottles of various sorts, odd pieces of wood, shards of broken glass, the carcass of a long-deceased cat, other such—constituted a different species of hedgerow.

Arriving at the corner of Marginal and Washington, Ben realized he was presently standing on the very street he had trod but a few hours earlier, on which indeed Sergeant Kortright was likely standing at the very moment hawking his wares.

The circle is the only geometry.

Tapping his way to the intersection of Marginal with Harrison, Ben discovered, catty-corner across, a rectangular building of two stories, yellowish, imprinted on its north face THE BOSTON COURANT, in blue lettering. About to step off the curb, such as to cross over Harrison, Ben recoiled as a vehicle, yellow, marquee atop, bore perilously close upon him.

Considering the fate of the cat whose carcass he had recently encountered, Ben concluded that inattention, once a largely surviv-able erratum, was no longer such. The scale of contextual peril—in size, speed, and density—had grown so disproportionately large, it would seem, as to render inattention tantamount to pointing a pistol at one's head.

Embracing such vigilance now as might be expected of a chastened sentinel, Ben made his way across Harrison, across Marginal, and onto the over-bridge spanning the depressed roadway. Pausing to peer downward, Ben noticed that the roadway below was accompanied to one side by two sets of tracks, these leading generally to eastward in the one direction, and in the other, by logical inference, generally toward New York and Philadelphia.

Ben crossed over Herald Street, and tapping his way a short distance down street, arrived at the *Courant* building. Approaching the portal, he came upon a bronze relief, circular, incorporated into the walkway. The relief bore at top a banner, THE BOSTON COURANT, in an arc, and below this, a tableau showing a boy hawking newspapers. The boy was holding an issue bearing a bold headline: NEW ENGLAND'S GREATEST NEWSPAPER.

Greatest? In which particular regards? Ben burned to inquire—or was it *en*quire? To what particular ends?

Was there anything emptier than the empty boast? The boaster perhaps?

Entering into a cavernous foyer, Ben discovered close upon the entryway a sentinel sitting behind a three-sided station. There was little else in the room toward justifying its cathedral volume. To rightward, a row of simple chairs, very like those at the Lincoln School, stood against a wall. To leftward, an open stairway ascended unto the ensuing floor. To immediate leftward, a small, spindly tree, its leaves brown of desiccation, stood in a plastic pot.

As Ben approached the desk, the man, advanced well past middle age, it would appear, regarded Ben with eyes like windows illumed of waning embers within. He was clothed in an ensemble of dark green.

"A good morning to you, sir." Reaching to remove his cap and not finding it, Ben discovered it yet stuffed in pocket. "I have come to interview with Mr. Brian Lynch, author of an article in this day's issue of your newspaper"—Ben pointed his cane toward a stack of newspapers resting atop the count—"should he be disposed to receive me."

The man's eyes seemed indecisive betwixt suspicion and hostility as a watchdog might betwixt bark and snarl. "Do you have an appointment?"

A hedgerow of noise, a hedgerow of litter, and now, as if by necessity toward completing the trinity, a hedgerow of inhospitality.

"I have a proposal for Mr. Lynch with which he might become intrigued were he to hear at least the nub of it. It relates to Mr. Lynch's article this day concerning certain unseemly failings within the area of public education. Should, however, Mr. Lynch, or this newspaper, be inhospitable toward notions and ideas conceived by mere citizens, by force of an abiding disdain for such, pray tell me so, that I might solicit interest from a more accommodating keeper of the public interest."

The man stared upon Ben as if upon the Tower of Babel, and then looked to a rectangular device setting on the countertop close upon where he sat. He manipulated a small device by one hand, and picking an instrument up then from a sort of cradle, held this to ear and mouth.

"Your name, sir?"

"Franklin. Benjamin Franklin."

The man punched four buttons in succession upon the cradle device. After a pause, he spoke, "This is Jimmy. There's a Mr. Franklin here to see you. Something about your article in the paper today." Pause. "He didn't say. Just a moment."

Jimmy looked to Ben. "Who are you?"

"A printer and a newspaperman, lately of Philadelphia, but here present as a private citizen wishing to advance the public good."

"Says he's a newspaper guy." Pause. "Yes, Benjamin. That's what he said." Jimmy shifted his eyes toward Ben. "Kinda old-fashioned like." Pause. "Yes, sir."

Returning the communication device to its station, Jimmy directed his eyes toward the row of chairs. "Have a seat. He'll be right down."

Ben smiled. "And if I do not have a seat, sir, will Mr. Lynch remain up until such time as I sit down? Thank you, sir." Tapping his way toward the row of chairs, Ben wobbled to a fit of vertigo, but managed to seat himself before he might collapse. Bowing his head then well to forward, he drew in a few measured breaths, then looked to the potted tree near the entry.

"Excuse me, sir," he spoke forth to Jimmy, "but do you think it possible that a few pints of water might be delivered unto that unfortunate tree." Ben pointed his cane toward the benighted tree adjacent to the entry. "Or is the patient beyond all remedy?"

Jimmy looked to the tree, and upon a perfunctory nod, returned his attention to his previous concern.

Ben sat for perhaps five minutes that were fifteen; ten minutes that were an hour; fifteen minutes that were an eternity. Afflicted increasingly of an unsettling sense of déjà vu, as if he were yet waiting levee in Lord Hillsborough's parlour, denied all courtesy for having dared to imply, by his presence, an equality betwixt a mere tradesman and a lord of the realm, Ben stood, such as to expend not another minute in the cause of futility, but thereupon espied a man descending, with thunderous celerity, the stairway located against the opposing wall.

The man, of perhaps early middle age, was woolly of hair, black as coal, upon head and face alike, it showing not a hint of hoarfrost. Black Irish, Ben surmised. The man approached Ben bearing a smile as if in reflex to a private amusement. His wire-rim spectacles, Ben noticed, were reminding of his own.

"OK," the man said, unaware, apparently, of several small crumbs caught in the wire of his beard, "who put you up to this? It was Barnigle, the sonuvabitch, wasn't it?" The man regarded Ben head to belly. "Jesus, you look just like him. There's a guy in Philly who does this. Archbold, I think his name is—no *i*, I remember. He was the entertainment at a convention I attended—like Holbrook doing Twain. He didn't have the resemblance you do, though. It *was* Barnigle, wasn't it?"

Ben smiled. "I assure you, sir, that I am here in behalf of no one's interest but yours, and that of unnumbered children for whom you might, in turn, serve as champion. Indeed, if you have a moment, sir, I would like to submit to your consideration an idea derived of certain events and experiences of this day, including the occasion of my happening upon a fine newspaper article—expertly wrought, in my opinion—concerning a certain insult upon the public trust. Should I continue in my assumption, sir, that you are indeed the same Mr. Lynch who wrote this most provocative piece?"

The man smiled. "The MCAS piece. Yes, sorry." He held out his hand. "Brian Lynch."

Ben clasped Brian's hand and leaned into a bow. "Ben Franklin."

Brian grinned. "A great pleasure." He looked to his watch. "I can only give you a few minutes—I'm on deadline—but, yeah, c'mon up and tell me what's on your mind."

"I thank you, sir, but I must decline your kind hospitality. I have but little time left at my disposal, as I calculate it, and much ground yet to cover. Might we remain here for a few moments that I might at least, as they say, put a bug in your ear?" Ben grimaced. "A most unsavory analogue, that one."

Brian removed a chair from the row of such and turning it half-circle around pointed to his right ear. "I've already got one." He made a buzzing sound. "Tinnitus." He smiled. "Too many trips to the mosh pit in my stupid days, or should I say stupider days?"

Whilst Ben sat down upon the same chair as previous, Brian reposed upon the facing chair, and slipped a diminutive tablet and a pen from his shirt pocket. "Shoot."

Ben nodded. "By way of introduction," he began, "I offer the following conjectures as facts, to be confirmed or corrected by you. I assume as fact, sir, a shortage of teachers throughout the nation, not only teachers highly qualified in their averred art, but teachers of any qualification soever. Am I correct in this conjecture?"

Lynch nodded. "Especially in the inner cities. It's so bad in some places—Baltimore and Chicago, for example—that they're offering bribes just to get warm bodies into classrooms. Make it till Christmas and we'll reimburse you for your bulletproof vest. Make it till the end of the school year and we'll pay for your funeral."

Ben smiled. "I have long held a particular affection for the acerbic wit."

Brian smiled.

"I assume also as fact, sir, that there is a particular shortage of teachers qualified to instruct in the realms of mathematics and science."

Brian nodded. "Huge. Anybody with a math or science degree today can make a helluva lot more money in the private sector today than in the public sector. There are some structural reasons for this—most teachers only work ten months a year, for example—but the main reason is that the teacher unions make it virtually impossible for school districts to compete on the open market. They can't offer a physics teacher, for example, any more money than they're paying their dime-a-dozen English teachers. It's one size fits all, baby, take it or leave it. Most choose to leave it."

"There is, then, a certain lack of civic interest within the education community."

Brian chuckled. "That's one way to put it."

"It has long been my experience, sir, that where a poverty of civic interest hinders the public good, such a poverty might be overcome by no greater than putting a bug, so to say, into a few, well-chosen ears. If this were not the case, there could never have been any such as militias, nor fire brigades, nor lending libraries, nor hospitals, nor insurance companies. Which truth compels me, sir, to pose the following question: What if, in regard to this teacher shortage and its attendant conundrums, certain persons holding degrees in mathematics or science were to be shared betwixt the private sector, as you name it, and the public?"

Brian narrowed his eyes as if toward sharpening their perception. "I'm listening."

"Every problem suggests of its own particulars at least one solution. In the case of a disparity in electrical charge betwixt two points, which disparity might result in a discharge to ill effect, the solution is to draw charge from the point of surfeit unto the point of poverty before such time the surfeit builds too large to be tamed."

"We wouldn't by any chance be talking lightning rod here, would we?"

Ben smiled. "There is within the education community, I believe, sir, a tradition of renewal called the sabbatical, derived, in name, of the same root as Sabbath."

"Also a tradition of the opposite, called tenure, derived of the same root as dead wood."

Ben smiled. "You are most acerbic, sir."

"Comes with the territory."

"Or might the territory come with the acerbity, sir? Indeed, which comes first, the play or the platform?"

Brian smiled. "We wouldn't be talking 'The play's the thing' here would we?"

Ben smiled. "An academic sabbatical involves, I believe, liberating a master from his duties for one full year, every seventh, that he might renew himself in mind and spirit through activities having some relation to his area of scholarship; am I correct?"

"That's the idea."

"Consider now, if you would, this same concept transferred from the public sector to the private. What if mathematicians and scientists were to be granted a sabbatical every seventh year or so, by their employers, such that they might renew themselves by way of providing instruction, well tempered of practical wisdom, to children in the public schools?"

"It *was* Barnigle who sent you!" Brian slapped his knee. "I knew it!"

"I am glad for your amusement, sir, but it is not my intention to deliver such. I am here under supposition, perhaps foolishly drawn, that you, as a journalist of high civic sensibility, would receive my testament as might a judge at bench."

Brian held his dark eyes upon Ben as if in anticipation of the inevitable confession, then smiled. "You're serious."

"I am, sir."

Brian shook his head. "Jesus Christ, man, do you have *any* idea what the teachers unions would do with this? I mean, how long do you think it'd take them to start rolling out thirty-second 'public service' spots along the lines of, say, a bunch of fat cats slurping raw oysters at a sushi bar, in slo-mo, while a voiceover insinuates a conspiracy by corporate America to take over the public schools? 'Good-bye football team, not cost effective.' 'Good-bye Special Ed, not cost effective.'" Brian shook his head. "I know these people. They'll stoop to any means to protect their turf."

"Even so, sir, have we not obligation to join against all such, at whatever cost? Is not this, in fact, the message, at core, of all Scripture?"

"Four of the Ten Commandments are all about kissing God's ass."

"They are indeed, sir, but what about the other six? What about the Sermon on the Mount?"

"When's the last time you heard any politician, of any stripe, refer to the Sermon on the Mount? 'Turn the other cheek?' Forgetaboudit. Bring it on, baby!"

"Be that as it may, sir, would it not seem, in the present case, that the behavior you allege to these unions, being such as to bring harm unto innocents by way of denying them the best possible instruction, naturally invites a public shaming? And would not such a measure be especially effectual if it were to be rendered by one skillful in the art of acerbic wit?"

Brian smiled. "Are you stooping to any means here, Mr. Franklin?"

"Can praise lavished deservedly be also flattery?"

Brian hung his head and shook it.

"Now, sir, as regards employing shame in the cause of justice, I must refer you to your own imagination, of which, I am confident, you are more than adequately equipped. However, if I may, I would like to suggest there to be no greater means by which to embarrass the devil than to stand him next to an angel. And toward this end, sir, I would like to refer you, if I may, to a man visiting Boston High School this day in the role of surrogate. His name is Henry Ditweiller." Ben smiled. "Illuminate the character of this man, sir, and others like it, and they shall, of a common radiance, expose the moral poverty of any man or institution that might be so foolhardy as to attempt to misrepresent or impugn them." Ben winked. "Bring it on, Mr. Lynch."

Brian hung his head and shook it.

"In fact, sir, you might wish to consider requesting of your own employer a parole of one year's duration so that you might exemplify the very virtues you are soon, I am certain, to advocate." Ben smiled. "Indeed, who better to teach young people the power of language, sir, than one who has a'ready wielded such power, with no little courage, in behalf of the innocent?"

Ben attempted to rise from his chair, but fell back directly, and slumped his head well to forward.

"You OK?"

Brian moved to the chair adjacent to Ben and placed a hand on Ben's shoulder.

Ben lifted his head. "I am, sir, thank you. A spell of vertigo, now dissipated. I perhaps raised myself too quickly."

"Where you headed?"

Ben took a measured breath. "My intention is to follow to source the tracks paralleling the recessed highway nearby, that I might discover transport to New York. Would it be far?"

Brian rose. "Not far, but too far." Brian called to Jimmy and asked him to call a cab. "On us," he said to Ben.

"Most kind of you, sir."

"It won't take but a minute to get here; they like to keep us happy. Let me help you."

"Most kind of you."

Brian helped Ben to his feet, and clutching Ben's arm, escorted him toward the entrance. En route, Ben mentioned the meeting he hoped to attend in New York, on the subject of leadership, there being no topic of greater import.

"Strange, isn't it," Brian said, "that the one thing the world needs more of than anything else, on every level, it's getting the least of, and less all the time."

"Might it be, sir, that the true leader, of his very nature, is reluctant toward office, whereas those who seek after it are anything but?"

Brian grinned. "It's called ego."

They arriving at the entry, Ben directed his cane toward the potted tree standing to rightward. "Might you be willing, good sir, to extend your kindness to include this poor benighted plant? A little water, methinks, might yet transform this accidental symbol of one condition into its opposite."

Brian regarded the desiccated tree and then, turning to the desk, asked Jimmy if he would mind watering the fig tree. Jimmy said he couldn't leave his station unattended, but if somebody would "hold down the fort a minute" he would attend to it.

Brian looked to Ben. "I'll take care of it."

"This day forward?"

Brian grinned. "This day forward."

"Most excellent, sir. Most excellent."

A yellow vehicle, marquee atop, stopped at the end of the pathway leading unto Herald Street. "Told you," Brian bragged. "Power of the press."

"Thank goodness. One might otherwise assume no better than the scent of money."

Brian chuckled. Escorting Ben then to the taxicab, Brian helped him into the rear seat whilst the driver, resembling in feature and complexion the man Ben had encountered at the Millennium Newsstand, held open the door. Thereupon slipping a bill from his wallet, Brian gave this over to the driver. "South Station," he said. Crouching then, Brian peered inward upon Ben. "OK, now who are you, really?"

Ben smiled, pulling on his marten cap. "Shut the door, good sir, that you might discover for yourself."

His eyes becoming as if small cakes of perplexity iced of curiosity, Brian closed the door and crouching then that he might peer upon Ben, through the glass, shrugged. Of a sudden he flinched as if struck by a bolt. He smiled.

The taxicab moved forward.

Despite as if a hundredweight of fatigue accumulated upon each eyelid, Ben felt obliged to engage the driver, it seeming impolite to do otherwise in such an intimate space. "Are you a native of this land, sir, or of another, if I may be permitted to inquire?"

The driver bore the taxicab to rightward. "Pakistan."

"Ah, yes, formerly a part of India, I believe."

The driver nodded into a rear-facing looking-glass.

"How long since your immigration, sir?"

Pausing the taxicab at the near intersection, the driver peered again upon the rear-facing mirror.

"How long have you been in America, sir?"

The driver smiled, holding up three fingers.

"Three years?"

The driver nodded. Moving the taxicab into the intersection, the driver of a sudden braked so abruptly, upon imminent peril of being struck by an intruding vehicle appearing from leftward, as to agitate, it did seem, an entire hive of bees into stinging both of Ben's kidneys in simultaneity. Ben yelped aloud.

The intruding vehicle, black as tar, windows darkly tinted, resembled, Ben noted, the very one he and Henry had encountered behind the Lincoln School stopped at the curb.

Whilst the taxicab driver issued complaint, by way of issuing a lingering blast of horn, the object of his wrath disappeared at the ensuing intersection.

Muttering, the driver moved the taxicab through the intersection, and pausing at the next intersection, turned leftward onto Marginal, and then rightward onto Washington. Almost immediately, the taxicab entered into as if a far-distant land, the shops showing Chinese pictographs; the pedestrians, Oriental features.

Resting his head against the back of his seat, Ben allowed his eyes to submit to the burdens weighing so heavily upon them—

⌒⅏⌒

Upon opening his eyes, Ben discovered the taxicab stopped, and the driver turned in his seat, offering him a few bills and some coinage.

Declining the offer, Ben made gesture toward removing from the taxi, but being unfamiliar with the procedure, could progress no farther.

Soon rescued by his driver, Ben was reminded of it being far easier to enter unto some venues than to escape them. Thanking the driver for his kind attentions, Ben bowed, and turning away, discovered himself gazing upon a robust structure close upon to front. Squat and round, like a grandmotherly queen, it was fashioned of large reddish-brown stones, perfectly cut and joined. Above, a colonnade in the Ionic style stood over the top two tiers of modest windows, the lower of these bearing as if rouged eyelids—the third such resemblance he had encountered.

Rightward, a series of red banners, the nearest bearing "South Station," seemed to direct one's attention toward an entrance constituted of glass doors, these hospitably recessed toward providing a portico against inclemency.

In the opposing direction, Ben noticed, stood a structure of a rather different sort, a giant monolith set as if upon a pair of stubby legs, betwixt which spanned a curious appendage in likeness to an infant's napkin sagging of a night's accumulation. The front side of the monolith showed tier upon tier of windows, all lines and angles, whilst the near side showed but a single window, behind which stood a small tree, reminding, in both aspect and condition, of the one in the lobby at the *Courant* building. An imprimatur upon the front side of the nearer of the two "legs" read FEDERAL RESERVE BANK OF BOSTON.

Tapping toward the set of recessed doors, Ben discovered a curious shed standing at the near corner, pyramidal in architecture, but not symmetrically so, and fashioned entirely of transparent panes. An open front, triangular, was marked "Silver Line / Red Line / South Station."

Noticing a second set of recessed doors, rightward of the first, opening by no greater than one's presence, Ben tapped his way to these, and they opening indeed as if by celestial spell, he entered into the stationhouse. Thereupon passing by a flower shop to leftward, and several ATM devices to rightward, he soon arrived at an open entryway unto a great room. A red marker atop the entryway bore "Tickets" in juxtaposition to an arrow pointing to leftward.

Stepping into the great room, Ben took inventory counterclockwise around: A Bestsellers shop; several stations purveying victuals of various sorts; a few clusters of small tables; a large marquee hanging from a skeletal ceiling, flanked by two smaller such; a shop appearing to purvey many of the same items Ben had observed at the Millennium Newsstand; and, well to leftward, an entryway bearing atop a red marker in consonance with the previous: "Tickets."

Navigating his way unto this beacon, Ben entered into a room floored and paneled of marble, and joined a serpentine queue afront four clerk stations attended and three not. To bide his time, he caught the eye of random persons as opportunity permitted and attempted to elicit a smile by showing one. By the time he had arrived at one of the four windows open to patronage, the accountancy of his experiment had amounted to five warm smiles, three tepid half-smiles, and two cold avoidances.

Ben smiled now upon a young woman of no greater than thirty years. "'Tis a great day to be alive, is it not, young miss?"

The woman smiled in return, taking discreet notice of Ben's manner of dress; his fur cap in particular.

"I would like to inquire, miss, as to when I might secure passage to New York."

The young woman looked immediately to her watch. "In about two minutes. You can still make it. Track 4. One way or round?"

"Though line is but illusion, I shall require no greater than such for the present."

The young woman smiled. "One way, I take it."

Ben bowed.

"That'll be ninety-nine dollars."

Ben pulled his bank card from pocket. "Would this be sufficient?"

"Debit or credit?"

Ben could no better than show perplexity.

"Do you need a pass code?"

Ben smiled. "O, yes. Seventeen"—the woman covered her ears—"aught one, aught six."

Removing her hands from ears, the woman took Ben's card, and passing it through a device resting upon the countertop, asked Ben to punch in his code. Ben pushed buttons as he had done on Milk Street. The woman returned Ben's card and soon thereafter gave him a receipt to sign, a receipt to keep, and a ticket to—"Go!"

Ben went.

Entering again into the great room, Ben discovered, to leftward, a row of exits numbered for Tracks 13 to 10. Navigating to rightward, that he might take hypotenuse as against two sides, he passed a large wooden bench populated to some intimacy, and thereupon past a shop marked "Martin's News Stands," whereat he could not help but notice a cornucopia of confectionaries arranged overtop a few stacks of newspapers.

No sooner had Ben slowed his pace, that he might ogle the confectionaries, than he heard a voice, female, announce the immediate departure of Amtrak 2163 for Washington, DC, with stops at New York and Philadelphia. "Track 4."

"All aboard!"

Restoring himself to full charge, Ben passed through the exit marked

"Track 9," the door there accommodating his passage of its own volition, and entered into a yard of several berths, "13" descending to rightward. Four of the berths were presently occupied by great silvery vessels— including the one marked "Track 4."

Hurrying toward Track 4, as fast as he might, each step a willing embrace of torture, Ben noticed a woman wearing a round cap standing close upon an entry unto a silvery car. Her station and demeanor suggested official function. As the woman turned to ascend into the car, Ben heard a rapid pattering of footfalls from behind, and supposing the source to be a passenger rushing to catch the same train, was surprised to be passed by a Negro boy wearing a cherry-red blouse, a snow-white head stocking, and a pair of oversized shoes.

Upon TJ disappearing into the same entry into which the woman had disappeared, Ben heard a pattering of footfalls emanant from close behind, and pressing his eyes to leftward, such as to maximize his acuity in that direction, of a sudden lurched to leftward.

A Negro man, wearing a purple head stocking, caromed from the considerable mass thrust into his path, and tumbled into the empty cavity of the near berth.

Continuing unto the same silvery car into which TJ had disappeared, Ben extended a hand toward the woman in the round cap, she standing close within, and lunged forward then to an unexpectedly strong pull. The woman struck a large button, causing the entry door to slide shut.

The woman smiled. "You always cut it that close?"

Ben bowed, being too occupied in breath to speak. The woman showing no excitement, Ben assumed her to be unacquainted with the small drama that had but recently transpired without. "A young lad wearing a cherry-red blouse," Ben managed.

The woman grinned. "Fell in a heap right about where you're standing. Got a bit more bruised than he let on, too, I think."

Ben smiled. "Two articles there are that never show a limp: a man fleeing his humiliation; an army, its capitulation."

The woman smiled and looked uptrain. "He went thataway."

Ben bowed, and entering into the car alluded to, studied the head dressings and faces to either side as he progressed.

The train lurching into motion, Ben steadied himself by clutching a seatback, and glimpsing thereupon movement to leftward, discovered a young Negro man, wearing a purple head stocking—the very man who had robbed Sergeant Kortright!—moving on the platform without, peering inward. The man pointed a finger at Ben, thumb elevated, and then, stopping himself in place, levered his thumb downward. The Negro man thereupon disappeared, the train moving past him.

Ben shuddered as if to a chill, and then tapped his way into the succeeding car, and failing to discover TJ therein, entered into the next car. No TJ. Entering thereupon into a car in which victuals of a modest sort were available from a man standing behind a small counter, Ben tapped his way through an invisible haze of alluring aromas into a succeeding car, and another, and into a seventh and last car. No TJ.

Having to ponder now the possibility that TJ had departed the train by way of one of the other exits before the train had started into motion, Ben quickly discarded this possibility, by merit that all the exits had faced upon the platform, whereon TJ would have once again been made available to his assailant.

There was indeed a more likely possibility.

Retracing his steps, Ben checked the occupancy status of the first door he encountered marked "Men," and finding it to be "Vacant," searched onward until he came upon one showing "Occupied." Continuing on, he checked the remaining doors marked "Men," and discovering none showing "Occupied," returned to the one yet advertising this status. Tarrying close by a sufficient duration for any business of nature to be completed, Ben tapped upon the door with the head of his cane. "Master TJ, your pursuer failed to advance onto this conveyance. You may emerge with all confidence as to your safety."

After a moment, the latch sounded a mechanical note and the door opened inward. TJ, his face set hard, brushed past Ben, and loped to the other end of the car. Encountering there a man wearing a round hat entering from the succeeding car, he flopped into a seat to leftward.

Ben waited for the man to pass him by and tapping his way then to where TJ was seated, stood close upon TJ's legs, these being fashioned into a barrier by way of purchase upon the opposing seat. "May I join you, Master TJ, or do you seek such solitude as to forbid all society?"

TJ made no response, his face being steadfastly poised toward the window. Of a sudden then, he removed himself to the adjacent position, proximate to the window, to end of vacating the seat claimed by his feet.

Ben sat down on this seat and after a few moments of silence ventured a query: "Would I be correct to assume, Master TJ, that there has been yet another attempt to thwart the noble intentions of an exceptional young man?"

TJ continued to hold his face toward the window, arms intertwined across his chest, feet purchased upon the opposing seat, legs jiggling, then looked sharply toward Ben. "Them muthafuckas let them bangers come right in there at me. Just give me right up, like I's nothin'." He looked again to the window, then pulled his legs from the opposing seat and leaned toward Ben, in the manner indeed of a cobra taking measure. "How else they get in, huh? How else?" He stared hard a moment, eyes narrowed unto dagger points, then looked again to the window, arms folded across his chest, legs jiggling.

After a moment, he spoke as if to himself. "Nobody was guardin' the back door. I checked when I come in. Not to worry, they, say. We gotcha covered, they say." He looked again to Ben. "You tryin' t' get at somebody, which door ya gonna come in, huh? The one they 'gotcha covered,' or the one they *say* they 'gotcha covered?'" TJ struck the near bulkhead with a sidelong blow.

Ben flinched.

TJ struck the bulkhead twice more, then glowered toward Ben as if upon the very object of his rage itself. "They know'd right where t' find me—right where I's gonna be, 'zactly what time. What the fuck that tell ya, huh? Principal changed all the period times. How'd they know? Huh?"

Ben felt a cold breath of dread insinuate deep into his soul. He barely dared to ask: "You have managed to escape grievous injury, young sir, and for that I am most grateful. Might I assume the same of all the others?"

TJ looked to the window, was silent a moment, then spoke: "Them bangers come in when ever'body out in the halls, includin' your friend. Your friend see'd 'em comin' up the hall before I do and jumps in front of me and yells for everbody to run. My guard shoulda been there t' take care o' things, but he not." TJ looked again to the window. "Your friend never had no chance; run right at 'em. Sounded like fuckin' cannons goin' off—.38 mags for sure."

No!

TJ leaned to Ben to such extremity now as to near upon require him to lift himself from his seat. "Where the cops? Where my bodyguard? Where 'gotcha covered?'" TJ narrowed his eyes. "Get to know 'em, he say. What they thinks, he say. What they believes, he say." TJ rose from his seat. "All I gotta know about what white folks thinks is jus' one thing: White be right, black be jack." Passing to front of Ben, TJ pulled Ben's cap lower upon his head to effect of shedding Ben of his spectacles.

"What the fuck you know? You don't know nothin'."

A heightened level of clatter was followed by rapid abatement.

Ben bowed his head, yet covered over with his cap, and wept.

Hearing again a heightened level of clatter, followed by rapid abatement, Ben fumbled for his spectacles, and heard a voice, familiar: "Ticket."

Discovering his spectacles upon his lap, Ben lifted his cap above his eyes, and managing thereupon to get his spectacles affixed into place, found himself peering up at the woman encountered previous, she wearing a round hat.

The woman showed, as if by reflex, a look of concern. "Are you all right, sir?"

Ben nodded. "I've had a bit of a shock—two or three in succession, in truth—but I require no special assistance, thank you." Ben searched his coat pocket, and finding his ticket in company with two receipts, two bills, a Charlie Ticket, and a green-and-white bank card, separated the ticket from the other items and handed it to the woman.

"New York?"

Ben smiled. "As regards an ultimate destination, this would be yet uncertain. As regards a more immediate destination, this would be New York."

The woman scored the ticket by way of a squeeze device, returned the stub to Ben, and affixed a chit to the rack overhead. "Unfortunately, your young friend doesn't have a ticket, sir, so, unless you have one for him, I'm afraid we're going to have to put him off the train at the next stop." The woman looked apologetic. "Policy."

Slipping his bank card from pocket, Ben offered it toward the woman. "Would this be sufficient toward keeping my friend unmolested of policy?"

The woman shook her head. "We can't do that anymore." She again looked apologetic. "Policy."

"Cannot do what exactly, if I might inquire?"

"Issue tickets on board."

"What rule is there, ma'm, that does not invite a challenge by force of common sense, if not of common decency? Pray tell, do you possess a personal communication device?"

"I do." The woman touched a small holster tethered unto her belt.

"Might you be able to use this device to request of a clerk at the next stop that a ticket be issued to my young friend, against my account, and that this article be passed to you upon the occasion of this train next stopping?"

The woman smiled. "I see no problem with that."

Ben handed the woman his card. "If my account should hold sufficient funds, you may make whatever charge you must. What else beyond sufficient funds you might need, you must obtain from the young man directly. I know him only as TJ, and I know not his destination."

"That's very kind of you."

"There is kindness, and there is conscience. Where the one might end, the other begin, I know not. In truth, I 'don't know nothin'."

The woman smiled with maternal warmth. "I think you know a great deal."

The woman continued up the aisle, her office of responsibility ending, Ben presumed, at the victuals car, whereat likely began the office of the man encountered wearing also a round hat.

Looking to the window, Ben peered upon what soon held appearance of an endless stream of flotsam—decaying buildings, rusting vehicles, careless leavings, garish advertisements, blackened timbers, snares of wire—and thought of the unattended tree in the lobby at the *Courant* building, and the similar article in the window at the Federal Reserve building.

He thought of the stunted tree atop the windswept knoll.

What seed holds not the whole of the tree; what symbol, not the whole of the truth?

He thought of Henry.

We died together.

He wept.

West Philadelphia

September 17th, 1:09 p.m.

Delmyra parked at the curb opposite 4968 W. Thompson. Slipping her cell phone into her tote, she scanned the area behind, using all three mirrors.

No one was sitting in the other parked vehicles, which were few, and there were no pedestrians within striking distance.

On Ellie Mae's side of the street, a white man was standing behind a van parked a few doors down. The rear door was open. A few doors upstreet, three black men were loitering in front of the convenience store there.

Delmyra climbed from her baby-blue Focus, locked the door, and walked across the street, tote in hand. The rot along the eave on Ellie Mae's porch was as she had feared—worse. A few loose tails of tarpaper, and a jury-rigged prop next to a rotted support post appeared to be the extent of the landlord's response to the maintenance request Delmyra had helped Ellie Mae fill out on Delmyra's last visit, several months ago now.

Section 8 housing—just more carrion for the vultures.

The door, already ajar, opened a little farther to Delmyra's knock. Audible from within were those canned shrieks and screams distinctive to reality shows.

Gotcha!, Delmyra guessed.

"Yo!"

Delmyra pushed the door open. A white plastic chair stood just inside, to the left; the stairway to the second floor ascended from almost directly ahead.

Entering a smallish room, dimly lit, overly warm, Delmyra was greeted by a little girl, about three years old, holding a Juicy Juice incautiously in one hand. Her hair was woven into tight braids, most of which were tied at the end with bright-green bows.

"You're Emerald, aren't you?"

Emerald nodded, smiling.

"You're getting to be a big girl. Do you remember me?"

Emerald shook her head, the whites of her eyes seemingly made larger and whiter by the daylight streaming through the open doorway.

Delmyra lowered herself onto one knee, and extended a hand toward Emerald. "I'm Miss Jordan." She spoke just loud enough to compete with the television. "I'm here to visit you and your brothers and sisters and your mama."

Emerald slapped at Delmyra's hand, screeched, and ran toward her mother, who was sitting on the near end of a floral-print couch that faced toward the far end of the room, where a television, disproportionate in size, stood encased in a large, funereally dark media center. The media center itself took up most of the area between the entry to the kitchen, to the right, and a partially covered window to the left. "Mama! Mama! Miss Jo-en! Miss Jo-en!"

"Hush now! You wake you brother!"

Emerald jumped up and down, sloshing Juicy Juice onto the floor, then ran toward an upholstered chair to the right of the couch, near where Delmyra was standing, and encountering the front of it without benefit of hitting the brakes, pressed her face against the seat cushion as if this would somehow hide the entirety of her from view.

Two other upholstered chairs, neither matching the first, or each other, were aligned with the first to form a row of three, perpendicular to the floral-print couch. Beyond this row of chairs was the open entry to the kitchen, and directly across the room, also perpendicular to the floral-print couch, was a facing row of three chairs, two of these matching, the third missing its seat cushion. The effect of this arrangement was to form a sort of theater in the rectangular, with the big-screen television set serving as the stage.

The television, and the media center housing it, were new since Delmyra's last visit.

Mama Pratt, Ellie Mae's mother, was sitting in the middle of the three chairs to the left of the couch, and holding a second girl child, younger, on her lap—Ruby, Delmyra knew. Mama was braiding Ruby's hair without so much as a glance at it, in the manner of an accomplished instrumentalist playing a score from memory.

To Delmyra's far left, a third child, a toddler, wearing only a diaper—Keeshaun, Delmyra knew—was asleep, thumb in mouth, on a mattress lying on the floor.

The room architecture there—the exterior wall to the left, a narrow span of interior wall straight on, and the left side of the gas fireplace—formed a little alcove.

This same place had served as a fourth bedroom, Delmyra recalled, for D'Juan, because of the three small bedrooms upstairs being filled to capacity: Ellie Mae and Mama Pratt in one; Ebony, Emerald, and Ruby in another; and Jamal and Keeshaun in a room little larger than the closet-sized bathroom they all shared.

The same gangsta poster, showing a menacing Al Pacino holding a machine gun, was tacked onto the wall space between the exterior wall and the fireplace. A second poster, below the other, showing a menacing 50 Cent holding a pistol, was new since Delmyra's last visit. Also new was a memorial arranged on the mantle over the gas fireplace, where previously, Delmyra recalled, there had been an arrangement of family photos. A large picture frame, black, containing a photo of D'Juan lying in a casket, was flanked by a smaller frame, also black, holding a newspaper clipping, and by a single angel, white, seven or eight inches tall. A small coil of black hair was meticulously attached to each item; in the case of the angel, on top of its head.

The news clipping, Delmyra knew—she had, in fact, a copy with her—chronicled, in three short paragraphs, yet another shooting death of a black teen in West Philly, the victim in this instance being D'Juan Samuel Fremont, age twelve, thought by police to have been responsible for the shooting deaths of two other black youths a few days earlier, on a local playground.

"May I come in?"

"You in, ain't ya?"

Delmyra pushed the door closed—it did not latch—and approached Ellie Mae from behind. Ellie Mae was just crunching on a potato chip selected from several resting on her lap. The source, a large bag of "B-B-Q Flavored" chips, was lying open on the couch beside her, next to a remote control.

Ellie Mae was wearing a velour sweat suit, plum with pink accents.

Her mother was wearing a plain, light-colored housedress, and, although the room was very warm, a pale-blue sweater.

A table fan was emitting an intermittent grinding sound as it labored in front of the blind-covered window to the left of the media center. Several of the slats in the blind were broken or missing.

Ellie Mae's right foot was propped up on a white plastic chair matching the one stationed near the front door. The toenails on this foot, from their luster, appeared to have been freshly lacquered, the color matching in tone the pink accents in her sweat suit.

"The door wouldn't latch. Is that OK?"

Ellie Mae cocked an ear slightly toward Delmyra.

Delmyra repeated her question.

Ellie Mae nodded, then frowned toward Emerald, who was sitting on the chair to the right, a Barbie doll, missing one eye, sitting on her lap, in apparent imitation of Ruby sitting on Mama Pratt's lap. The carton of Juicy Juice was resting on its side next to her. "You let Miss Jordan sit there. Where's your manners, girl?"

Delmyra winked at Emerald, then looked to Ellie Mae. "If you don't mind Mrs. Fremont, I'll use the chair from the door. That'll work better for me."

Ellie Mae shrugged. "Suit you self."

Emerald slid off the chair, doll in hand, and leaving a wet spot behind, where the remainder of her Juicy Juice had drained onto the seat cushion, carried her Barbie, held close to breast, toward the kitchen.

Delmyra set her tote down on the floor, and fetching the plastic chair from near the door, positioned it slightly forward of, and facing, the floral couch. Noticing a slice of bread on the floor, peanut-butter-side down, near where she would need to place her feet, Delmyra adjusted the position of her chair accordingly, and sat down.

"I noticed the porch roof. Are they going to fix that for you?"

Ellie Mae cocked an ear toward Delmyra.

Delmyra leaned closer. "The porch roof—are they going to fix that?"

Ellie Mae shrugged.

"Have you called?"

Ellie Mae cocked an ear toward Delmyra.

"Would it be OK to turn the volume down a little, do you think?"

Ellie Mae picked up the remote from near the bag of chips, and pointing it toward the television, clicked once. The volume indicator appeared on the screen. "Mama don't hear so good." The volume indicator disappeared.

"Have you called the Section 8 office—about fixing the porch roof?"

Ellie Mae cocked an ear toward Delmyra.

Delmyra leaned closer. "Do you think we could talk in the kitchen? I won't be long."

Ellie Mae kept her eyes on the television. "This is me 'n Mama's favorite show. We watch it ever day, right at this time. Don't we, Mama?"

Mama Pratt nodded, tying a crimson bow on the end of a newly woven braid.

"Would it be better if I came back another time?"

"You was supposed be here at 12:30, wasn't ya?"

"I'm very sorry, Mrs. Fremont. As I explained to you on the phone, if somebody's having a bad time of it, I can't just pick up and leave. I have to do what I think *you* would do in the same situation."

As Delmyra moved toward getting to her feet, Ellie Mae, shaking her head, pulled her foot from the plastic chair, brushed the debris from her lap, and lunging herself forward, slipped her feet into a pair of pink slippers, and heaved to her feet.

Delmyra picked up her tote, and following Ellie Mae toward the kitchen, noticed a gallery of photos arranged on top of the media center. If these had been in the room on her previous visit, she hadn't noticed them. The largest was a collage of Ellie Mae's three older children— Ebony, D'Juan, and Jamal—peering through the face holes in cartoon cutouts. Ebony was peering through a cutout of Snow White; Jamal, through a cutout of Daffy Duck; and D'Juan, through a cutout of Robin Hood. There were also a few school portraits.

An older photo, showing Mama Pratt in her perhaps mid-teens, the only photo in a metal frame, reminded Delmyra that she still hadn't called Ms. Tolman about her genealogy project.

The media center was straddled by towers holding music media from top to about the extent of Keeshaun's reach. The components of the implied music system were presumably hidden behind a pair of closed doors directly under the television.

These icons of relative luxury, Delmyra knew, had not come from the paternal largess of Mr. Fremont, who had long since abandoned domestic interests for others, nor from the institutional largess of the Department of Human Services, which had cut its budget the past three years in a row.

Delmyra followed Ellie Mae into the kitchen.

Emerald was standing on the seat of a white-plastic chair at a round patio table, and was reaching into a large container of peanut butter. Barbie was sitting on the table to her right, propped against a package of white bread.

A washing machine stood to the immediate left, a refrigerator to the immediate right. A sink counter spanned from the refrigerator to a gas stove. The only cupboards were attached to the wall over the sink counter. There was no pantry. The only adornment was a plastic, rose-pink tablecloth covering the table.

Barbie's mouth, Delmyra noticed, was smeared with peanut butter, as was Emerald's own, not to mention her cheeks, the end of her nose, and the front of her T-shirt.

"Sit down, girl, 'fore you hurt you self! Look it you! You supposed to eat it, girl, not wear it!"

Emerald lowered herself to a squat.

The only other chair, standing a few feet back from the table, was occupied by a pile of clothes.

Ellie Mae grasped the back of Emerald's chair. "We gotta have that chair, honey."

Delmyra looked toward the back door. "Would it be better to go outside, do you think?"

Ellie Mae shrugged. "Hot out there."

"We won't be long."

"Suit you self."

Delmyra followed Ellie Mae into a grassless backyard little larger than the living room, bordered on the sides by rusty chain link fencing and at the rear by a concrete-block wall. The windows on the backsides of the abutting row houses were covered over with iron grates.

Two taut clotheslines, holding several articles of clothing, mostly children's, spanned the width of the yard.

Looking for a place to sit, Delmyra found two white plastic chairs just to the right of the doorway, one standing, the other tipped forward. Setting her tote down, she righted the tipped-over chair, and positioning it at about a 45-degree angle relative to the other chair, waited for Ellie Mae to sit down, and then sat down herself.

"Feels like gonna rain again," Ellie Mae said, glancing skyward, a luster of perspiration showing on her creamy chocolate-brown face.

"They were predicting thunderstorms on the radio this morning," Delmyra said, lifting her own eyes. "For late."

Ellie Mae nodded.

"Is Jamal in school today?"

Ellie Mae shrugged, eyes averted toward a small pink pail with a white handle, standing forlornly toward the rear of the yard, next to a shallow depression in the grayish soil.

Pulling a folder from her tote, Delmyra opened it onto her lap, lifted out a few sheets, and closing the folder, laid the sheets on top of it. "As you know, Mrs. Fremont, Jamal's school recently reported him to DHS for writing what they considered—or thought *might* be considered—a threat against his teacher."

Ellie Mae lifted her chin and narrowed her eyes.

"I think it's important to keep in mind here, Mrs. Fremont, that"— Delmyra touched a finger—"one, this came out of an assignment given out by Jamal's teacher—it wasn't something Jamal came up with on his own; and"—Delmyra touched another finger—"two, Jamal was reported more as a precaution than for any other reason. Jamal's principal goes out of her way to make this very point in her report.

"In fact, no one is sure at this point, Mrs. Fremont, just what Jamal's intentions really were when he wrote what he did. He claims he was just doing what the teacher asked. It could be just that simple. We have to be sure, though. Everybody wants to give Jamal the benefit of the doubt, but the language he used was of a sort that warranted at least some kind of inquiry. Which is why I'm here. I'm the inquiry. I'm here to try to find out if anything's going on with Jamal, and if it is, to try to figure out what we might do to help him resolve his issues. I'll want to speak with Jamal in person about all this, of course, but I wanted to speak with you first, because you know him best. OK?"

Ellie Mae lifted her chin without taking her eyes off the pink pail. "You do what you gotta do, honey."

Delmyra noticed that the handle on the pail was unattached on one side, in perfect harmony, it seemed, with the support post on the porch being unattached on one end.

"I grew up in this neighborhood, Mrs. Fremont, just three blocks from here, and along the way I needed a little help, too. I took this job, ten years ago now, because I felt an obligation to return the favor. I thought that if I could help a few young people get themselves on the straight and narrow, the way I had been helped, perhaps some of them would choose to do the same thing when they grew up, and so on. I was young and very naïve. I didn't allow for the fact you can't give anyone something they don't really want."

Ellie Mae held her head bowed a moment, then looked again toward the pail.

"As I mentioned, Mrs. Fremont, what Jamal wrote was in response to a writing assignment given out by his teacher. It wasn't something he came up with on his own. What happened was that Ms. Chambers gave out an assignment—this was a few weeks ago, right around the beginning of school—that asked each student to write a short poem using"—Delmyra looked toward the sheets on her lap—"'I wish I *blank*, so I could *blank*,' as a model for each line. Each student was to write as much, or as little, as they wanted, and whatever they wanted. There were no constraints in other words concerning what a child might say."

Delmyra looked again to the sheets on her lap. "Here's what Jamal wrote: 'I wish I had me a gun / Sos I could have me sum fun / Id jam it up that bitches fat ass / And put an end t'all her black ass sass.'"

Ellie Mae held her head, elbows propped on her knees.

"Ms. Chambers was a bit concerned about this, understandably, but she decided not to report it, because she'd given permission for everyone to write whatever they wanted. After learning about the circumstances surrounding D'Juan's death, however, she decided she had to report it. She makes clear, though, Mrs. Fremont, that she very much likes Jamal, thinks he has a tremendous amount of potential, and does not see him as being in any way a 'bad boy.'"

Ellie Mae straightened but kept her eyes averted from Delmyra. "It me, ain't it? It my fat ass Jamal write about."

Emerald appeared and half-ran, half-skipped toward the pink pail.

"Jamal's certainly angry, Mrs. Fremont, but let's find out exactly why before we jump to any conclusions. Let's get him hooked up with a counselor over at Community Health and see if we can get him talking."

Ellie Mae shook her head. "That what the lady 'fore you said about D'Juan. Better get him into Community Health, she say, 'fore he hurt somebody. But they tell me over at Community they can't take 'im for 'nother three months." Her eyes flashed. "That the way it always be."

Delmyra returned the loose sheets to the folder on her lap and closed it. "I'm not a mental-health worker, Mrs. Fremont. I'm trying to become one—I'm back in school—but I'm not there yet. What I do, as a caseworker, is I make assessments about what folks need and then I try to get them hooked up with the right services. To do this, I ask a lot of questions, as you know. If I may, Mrs. Fremont, I'd like to ask you a few more? Would this be OK? You don't have to answer, of course."

Ellie Mae nodded.

"Since D'Juan's death, Jamal is your oldest male child, is this right?"

"Em-heh."

"And he's sleeping in D'Juan's old bed, downstairs, right?"

"Em-heh."

"Even though he still has a place upstairs."

"Em-heh."

Emerald carried the pink pail toward some dead leaves that had accumulated between the back wall and the chain link fence to the right.

"Given the condition of the front door, Mrs. Fremont, and Jamal's new standing in the family as man of the house, I'm wondering if he might be holding himself responsible for protecting the whole family from external threats, especially at night."

Ellie Mae pursed her lips.

"I don't know if this is the case, but if it is, it would seem a lot of responsibility for a twelve-year-old boy to take on, would you agree?"

Ellie Mae shrugged. "Ain't got nobody else."

Emerald was squatted on her haunches, pink pail at her side, gazing at something of particular interest, it would appear, in the nest of accumulated leaves.

"I'm wondering, Mrs. Fremont, if getting that door fixed might ease Jamal's mind a little. What do you think?"

"And who gonna do that?"

"We'll work on that, Mrs. Fremont. But let's first try to figure out what might be going on inside Jamal's mind. When he wishes in his poem, for example, that he had a gun, I'm wondering if he might be telling us that he needs to feel powerful in proportion to the responsibility he now feels he has toward the family, with D'Juan being gone."

Ellie Mae narrowed her eyes and jutted her lips.

"I didn't have any brothers, Mrs. Fremont, only one sister, but I've learned over the years, from working very closely with boys, that causing them to feel powerless is to shame them. Shame a girl and she's likely to blame herself, even punish herself—cut herself, for example. Shame a boy, though—make him feel powerless—and look out. He's going to get even. He's going to get his pride back, whatever it takes.

"As I said, though, I'm no expert. The people at Community Health are, however, so let's get him in over there. If it takes us three months, at least we're moving in the right direction. In the meantime, let's get that door fixed, Mrs. Fremont—and the roof. Do you still have the Section 8 phone number?"

Ellie Mae shook her head. "Won't do no good be callin' *them* people. I called 'em a hundert times since you was last here, and nobody ever call back. James down the street done what he can, but said come the first snow t' amount to anything this winter and the whole damn thing's gonna come down, for sure."

"I'll call 'em." Mama Pratt was standing in the doorway.

Ellie Mae cocked her head in the direction of her mother. "Hey, Mama, you missin' the program being out here. Who gonna tell me what happen?"

"Ain't gonna hurt nobody to call them folks one more time, now, is it?" Mama turned away and disappeared into the kitchen.

Ellie Mae screwed up her face as if to a foul odor. "Ain't gonna hurt nobody to call them folks one more time, now, is it?"

Emerald appeared in front of her mother and held the pink pail such as to invite a look inside.

"Whacha got there, girl?"

Leaning forward, Ellie Mae peered into the pail—flinched, shrieked, and batting the pail out of Emerald's hands, recoiled against the back of her chair with such force as to nearly topple the chair and herself over backward.

A dead bird, a starling, crawling with maggots, was left on the ground near where the pail struck the ground.

Emerald, shrieking, ran into the house.

Ellie Mae shuddered, jumped up from her chair, and fled into the house.

Delmyra stared at the dead starling a moment, then got up from her chair, and gathering up her tote, entered the house.

Ellie Mae was sitting on the couch, staring at the television. Keeshaun, awake now, was sitting on Mama Pratt's lap. Ruby was sitting on the couch next to Ellie Mae, eating potato chips. Emerald was not in the room.

Delmyra stood in front of the white plastic chair she had sat in earlier. "I'll call you, Mrs. Fremont, when I've arranged an appointment for Jamal at Community Health. I'll try to schedule it for right after school. Would that be OK?"

Ellie Mae cocked an ear toward Delmyra.

Delmyra repeated herself, in a raised voice.

Ellie Mae shrugged.

"When would be a good time for me to speak with Jamal, do you think?"

Ellie Mae cocked an ear toward Delmyra.

Delmyra raised her voice.

Ellie Mae shrugged. "I got no sway over that boy. You gonna hafta ax 'im you self."

Delmyra leaned closer. "Does he have a cell phone?"

Ellie Mae nodded.

"May I contact him directly?"

"Suit you self."

"Do you have his number?"

"Two-zero-zero, still waitin' for my hero. Twenty-three and twenty, make forty-three already."

Delmyra slipped her appointment book from her tote. "Two zero zero, two-three, four-three," she confirmed. She smiled. "Jamal's not the only poet in the family, it would appear."

Ellie Mae showed no response.

Delmyra slipped her appointment book back into her tote, and moving the plastic chair back to its previous location by the door, returned to retrieve her tote.

"I'll be in touch in a day or two, Mrs. Fremont. Sorry again about being late."

Ellie Mae peered toward her mother. "What'd she say?"

"Said she had an abortion when she was seventeen."

"I know'd it!" Ellie Mae whooped. "Gotcha!"

Returning to the door, Delmyra found Emerald making her way down the stairs, Barbie clutched to her breast. Delmyra winked. Emerald winked in return, both eyes, more or less, at the same time. Delmyra pulled the door closed behind her. It did not latch. She would send Prescott over to fix it. Prescott and Rosie.

The three men were still loitering upstreet, near the corner. The van had left from down the street. The opposite side looked clear.

Delmyra waited for a car to pass by, hurried across the street, and climbing into her car, set her tote onto the passenger seat, next to a hefty volume titled *Foundations of Family Therapy*. Locking the doors, she pulled slowly away from the curb, passed the three men standing on the corner at St. Bernard, and turned left onto North 50th Street. About a third of the way up the short block, she pulled to the curb, and dropping her head onto the steering wheel, wept.

New York City

September 17th, 2:43 p.m.

Ben opened his eyes to discover a Negro boy, well familiar in the articles of a cherry-red blouse and a gauzy white head stocking, seated obliquely to rightward, his feet propped against the opposing seat, his legs jiggling in an erratic rhythm.

Looking to the window, Ben could see in the distance, veiled in a sepia haze—reminding of London in February—the kingly towers of a great city. In the foreground, a stream of more modest structures, the hovels in the field, as it were, showed backsides of jaded brick, yellow here, red there. Betwixt foreground and after, a body of water, a moat, as it were, was over-spanned by a colossus bridge, the platform of which was held suspended from graceful festoons of what appeared to be pliable piping.

TJ held a green-and-white card toward Ben. "The conductor tol' me t' tell ya she couldn't use your card 'cause she didn't have your code, and didn't wanna wake you, but not to worry, 'cause everthin's been taken care of." TJ smiled. "Thanks. They was gonna put me off at Back Bay."

Ben slipped the card into his coat pocket. "You are most welcome."

"You gettin' off here?"

"If this is New York we are presently approaching, then, yes, I will be disembarking here."

TJ nodded.

"And you?"

"Philly." TJ looked to the window, then again to Ben. "I'm sorry 'bout what I said."

Ben smiled. "You were distempered of a sting no hive of hornets could match. What takes you to Philadelphia, if I might inquire? Have you refuge there?"

Ben cast a private smile upon the accidental juxtaposing of "Philadelphia" and "inquire."

Not quite a pun, but close.

The best of wit, hence the rarest, is innocent of all contrivance.

"I'm gonna hang out at my aunt's for a while, till I get things figured out. What's happnin' in New York?"

"I hope to attend a discourse on a topic of keen interest to me, at a meetinghouse called the Waldorf Astoria. Have you any familiarity with it perchance?"

TJ shook his head, was silent a moment. "Want me t' help ya find it?"

Ben leaned into a bow. "Most kind of you, sir, but you need not inconvenience yourself. You have travails enough. I am certain I will be able to find a driver for hire who might deliver me by no greater guidance than I might presently give him."

TJ shrugged. "I got nothin' else t' do. You been t' New York before?"

"I have, in truth, on several occasions, but not, as it were, in recent times."

"The subway's a lot cheaper. Ya gotta know how t' use it, though. You know how?"

"I have had but one brief experience, and that in Boston. Your aunt, sir. Is she not waiting in some agitation upon your arrival?"

TJ shook his head. "I called 'er when I was on the train and left a message sayin' I was comin' down for a visit but didn't know 'zactly when I'd be gettin' there. Then I called my mom t' tell 'er not t' be callin' my aunt an' makin' 'er all worried. She tol' me the man'd jus' called there lookin' for me, which, o' course, had made her all worried." He smiled. "She had a few words for 'im."

Ben straightened his back. "Well, in truth, Mister TJ, I would be most grateful, most grateful indeed, to have your company, not to mention your assistance."

TJ smiled.

The ambient light dimmed near unto darkness, the train having entered, Ben presumed, a passageway beneath the moat surrounding the kingdom of towers. The train slowed, and jostled and creaked, as small orange lights, close upon the window, appeared to move past a stilled train, the rate of their passing slowly diminishing. The tunnel thereupon began to widen into a cavern that revealed, by way of tubular lanterns affixed overhead, first a concrete abutment, then several platforms in parallel, these similar to those Ben had seen at the Boston station.

Passengers began to rise from their seats, and upon lifting their burdens from the overhead rack, to gravitate toward either end of the car. The train slowed unto barely the crawl of a 'possum, then stopped. Immediately thereupon, an inward rush of unfamiliar sounds seemed to compel, by Newtonian imperative, an outward flow of passengers.

TJ poising to rise, Ben preceded him into the aisle, and thereupon followed him onto the platform without, this lined at the near edge by a wide yellow strip. Encountering there the woman attendant, Ben bowed to her. "I thank you, madam, for your kindness to the lad, and thereby to me."

The woman smiled. "You're most welcome, both of you. Our little secret, though." She winked. "Policy."

Ben bowed. "Regarding which, ma'm, I have a small curiosity. By disembarking at this intermediary point, as opposed to his ultimate destination, will the lad here be able to embark upon another train, at a later time, such that he might suffer no farther excitements this day?"

The woman smiled. "He's booked on a later train to Philadelphia. When he found out you were getting off at New York, he asked to do the same, to make sure you got to wherever it was you were going." She looked to TJ, and then smiled to Ben. "He said you were real smart about some things, but didn't have a clue about others."

Ben looked to TJ, who, peering fast upon his oversized shoes, was tapping his toes whilst working his fingers in the manner of kneading bread.

"I am in your good hands, Mister TJ—lead on!"

Ben bowed to the attendant, then followed TJ to an enclosure marked "Exit Amtrak—NJ Transit," located in the middle of the platform, and then to an enclosed escalator marked "Exit LIRR—Subway," also located in the middle of the platform. Following TJ onto the moving steps, Ben grasped the railing with his free hand and spoke forth from behind: "I could not be more appreciative in the moment, young sir, to have benefit of your guidance, as 'tis abundantly clear to me that were I abandoned in this cavern with naught but my own wits to guide me, I would not, as it were, have a clue."

TJ turned and showed a grin at once endearing and reassuring.

At the top of the moving stairs, Ben followed TJ through an open entryway into a wide, brightly illuminated corridor low of ceiling, busy in traffic. To rightward, a marker advertised tracks 7–8; to leftward, a marker advertised tracks 11–12. From these clues, Ben deduced that their train had arrived upon track 9.

Bearing to leftward, they soon passed under a marker showing "LIRR—Subway," this intelligence miming that encountered in the cavern below, and soon thereafter came upon a marker, near Track 17, bearing the curious phrase "Exit Subway," followed, on the same marker, by two sets of three circles: a leftward set, red, holding numerals 1, 2, 3; and a rightward set, blue, holding letters A, C, E.

A little farther on, near Track 19, they came upon an overhead marker identical to the previous in all respects save one—the addition of a fourth red circle holding the numeral 9.

Ben could not but wonder why the previous marker had not also shown this fourth red circle; and, too, whether "Exit Subway" constituted a single term or two separate.

Ben felt much the better presently for being in the company of a guide.

The present corridor terminated at a crossing corridor of equal width and height. A red-and-blue ATM beacon, Ben noticed, was affixed upon a shop window directly to front.

Ben could not readily discover at this juncture any manifest indication as to which direction, leftward or rightward, one should travel such as to resolve the "Exit Subway" mystery; nor could he discover any indication as to what the red circles containing numerals represented, nor what the blue circles containing letters represented; nor could he discover any indication concerning which direction one should choose such as to farther pursue one color or the other.

Fortunately, his guide needed no such indication, for he led Ben to leftward with such boldness now as to wholly reassure. "I must repeat," Ben managed, struggling to keep pace, "how appreciative I am, young sir, to have benefit of your guidance. In want of it, I should surely be afflicted of the panic of a child missing its mother."

They soon came to a marker overtop a set of ascending steps reading, "8th Av & Subway C E," with the letters C and E each contained in a blue circle. Beyond the stairs, another marker, overtop a set of gates similar to those Ben had encountered in the Boston underground stations, read, "Entry C E Uptown & Queens Local." As previous, the letters C and E were each contained within a blue circle.

Comprehending now the meaning of "Exit Subway," it parsing into two separate meanings—"Exit" applying to 8th Avenue, "Subway" to itself—Ben wondered why this cryptic rendering had not been made plain by simple addition of a separator betwixt the two terms, in the manner of a fence betwixt two properties. It was also clear now that the blue circles encompassing individual letters referred to separate trains servicing separate routes.

The only mystery yet remaining was why the set of blue circles on the markers in the previous corridor had been placed to rightward of the set of red circles, thereby implying that to attain the blue subway trains one should bear rightward at the corridor juncture, as opposed to leftward, when the very opposite was the very truth!

But for a modicum of empathy...

TJ led Ben up the steps, and obliquely leftward, to a squarish booth enclosed by glass panels. A subway train was stopped rearward of the booth and a throng of passengers having exited from it was presently queuing through the gates to rightward, as well as through a second set of gates to leftward. The latter passengers were thereupon hurrying toward an "escalator," if his gift of received memory correctly served, directly beyond a set of gates marked "33 St & 8 Av."

TJ addressed a buxom Negro woman seated within the booth. "How do we get to the Waldo"—he looked to Ben—

Ben bowed. "To the Waldorf Astoria, ma'm."

"Take the E train to Lexington, go one block west to Park, then one block south." The woman pushed a map through a small aperture engineered, it would seem, by a domestic rodent.

TJ gave the map over to Ben, and thereupon led him to leftward, to a row of devices similar in appearance—and likely in function, Ben adjudged—to the device from which Henry Ditweiller had procured him a Charlie Ticket.

"How many stops, you think?"

Ben stood dumb.

"Where we goin' after the Waldo?"

"Ah, I see your quandary. My ambition is perhaps a bit high in this regard. I wish to stop upon two persons long neglected, though I have not 'a clue' as to where we might discover them in relation to where the Waldorf Astoria stands."

TJ shrugged. "I'll get a bunch."

Ben pulled his bank card from pocket and gave it over to TJ, who, slipping it into a slot, manipulated the screen by no greater than touching it, as had Henry at the Boston station. TJ moved a little to one side. "Enter your code, but stand close so's nobody can rip it."

Ben stood close upon the device and pressed "170106" upon a pad of buttons showing on the screen.

TJ returned Ben's card, delivered a receipt, and thereupon took into hand a ticket similar to a Charlie Ticket. "Six for the price of five," he boasted. "If we need more, we can add jus' what we need."

"Most frugal of you, sir! I am in very good hands indeed!"

TJ led Ben to the gates to leftward of the booth, and stepping into the maw of one of these, held the ticket toward a slot affixed upon a sort of shoulder. This arrangement differed from that at the Boston station. "Watch me," TJ instructed. Slipping the ticket though the slot, TJ pushed his way through the barrier and reaching across the barrier gave the card over to Ben.

"Now you do it."

Ben moved the ticket through the slot and weighed against the barrier, but the barrier would not yield.

"Do it again," TJ instructed.

Ben made a second attempt, but still the barrier would not yield. "It would appear this device has judged me unworthy, sir. How might one win its favor?"

"Hold it like this." TJ held the ticket with his thumb, on one side, held against the tips of his fingers on the other side.

Holding the card thusly, Ben slid it through the slot a third time. The barrier thereupon yielding, Ben pushed through it with barely an effort, as if, in having made the proper sign, he were accommodated into a Masonic chamber. "I must confess a third time, young sir, as to how grateful I am to have you as my guide. One has to wonder why so much of what should be hospitable toward the innocent is instead so very much to the contrary."

TJ grinned. "Once ya got a clue, dude, you good." TJ led Ben onto the platform close upon which a train had recently been stopped. Several people had a'ready accumulated in anticipation of a subsequent train, they being governed in arrangement by some principle, it would seem, requiring greatest density at middle and ever less outward from either side.

Being allured by a most agreeable percussion, Ben discovered a Negro man, to rightward, slapping a set of small drums with his palms. He was sitting Indian style upon the floor, knees pointed to either side, with his back close upon the wall behind. A small basket was positioned directly to front. His face was hideously disfigured, as if by a ravage of flames.

Being reminded of the pennywhistle players he had so frequently encountered in London, Ben pulled his remaining Hamilton from pocket, and folding it twice over, tapped his way to the basket and made a modest investment in one man's music. The Negro man nodded.

An ominous rumbling was soon followed by a terrible squealing.

"E train!" TJ announced.

The train stopping, Ben stationed himself close upon TJ, and following him then into the near car, was surprised to discover the seating to consist of facing benches, one bench to side. There being a few seats yet unclaimed, TJ picked an adjoining pair of these.

The train thereupon lurching into motion, a disembodied voice delivered an unintelligible drone toward no greater purpose, it seemed, than to provide a bass line for the squealing and clanging of the moving train.

Ben leaned closer upon TJ. "Might I inquire, young sir, whether you are apprised of the meaning of the term 'empathy,' as derived from the Greek?"

TJ pulled his device from pocket, and upon pushing a few buttons, spelt aloud whilst pushing yet more keys. "E-M-P-A-T-H-Y. That right?"

"Exactly so."

TJ advanced the text upon the screen of his device by no greater than drawing a finger over it, then gave his device over to Ben. "Empathy," he said.

Ben read aloud. "'One: the imaginative projection of a subjective state into an object so that the object appears to be infused with it. Two: the action of understanding, being aware of, being sensitive to, and vicariously experiencing the feelings, thoughts, and experience of another of either the past or present without having the feelings, thoughts, and experience fully communicated in an objectively explicit manner; also: the capacity for this.'"

Ben hung his head, shook it, then looked to TJ. "You will conclude from this experience, I do hope, young sir, that the miracle you have employed to provide answer to my inquiry is only as useful as is the sense it should grasp. In demonstration to point, I ask you now, if I might, to relate in your own words what meaning you were able to derive from the intelligence just delivered unto you."

TJ shrugged.

"Might I have a brief loan of your shoes, sir?"

His shoes being a'ready unlaced, TJ pulled them from his oversize feet and gave them over to Ben, who, removing his own shoes, slipped his stocking'd feet into TJ's, with considerable ease. Ben thereupon handed his marten cap over to TJ. "If you would be so kind as to place this upon your head, sir."

TJ pulled the cap over his head stocking, and grinned. "Cool."

"Each of us is now in a state of empathy relative to the other. I am standing in *your* shoes, this condition being symbolic for seeing the world though *your* eyes. You are sitting under *my* cap, this condition being symbolic for seeing the world through *my* eyes. In entering into these conditions, each of us gains an understanding of the other, in particular as regards what the other requires of natural or acquired need, and each of us derives thereby a generosity of spirit toward the other. Have you now the meaning?"

TJ nodded.

"Now, if I might take advantage of the moment, sir, I ask that you instruct me concerning the procedure by which you manipulated your device toward plucking two lemons, very sour indeed, from the Tree of Knowledge?"

TJ shrugged. "Sure. Simple." Taking his device from Ben, TJ cleared the screen, then gave Ben careful instruction on how to access the "Internet," how to access the Merriam-Webster Online site, and how to enter a term.

Ben thereupon entered H-Y-B-R-I-S; then selected "hubris" from a list of possible alternatives; then read aloud from the screen, "'Exaggerated pride.'" He looked to TJ. "'Hybris' is the warning, 'empathy,' the heeding. If a certain king had heeded such, he would have kept an empire. If a certain father had, he would have kept a son."

The train coming to a stop, TJ looked to a map imprinted upon the opposing side of the car and held up two fingers.

Ben nodded, and restored TJ of his device. "Many years ago," he added, "I devised a mechanism that served also to extend the human grasp, but 'twas of no greater reach than to the highest shelf. The reach of your device would appear to be of no bound soever."

TJ smiled. "Pick sumthin'."

"Another word?"

"Anythin'. Don't matter."

Ben smiled. "Madeira. M-A-D-E-I-R-A."

TJ entered "m-a-d-e-i-r-a" into a box preceded by the curious term "Google," writ in colorated letters, and displayed then a list of "hits," as he called them, the second of which read, "Madeira wine—Wikipedia, the free encyclopedia."

Ben pointed. "That one."

TJ thereupon caused a body of text to appear that subsequently included, upon TJ drawing a finger over the screen, representation of

a dark bottle labeled in white lettering, also a tulip-shaped glass holding a modest portion of humour so darkly red as to be near upon black.

Ben smiled. "O would that your device might deliver in the material
that which it is so readily able to deliver in representation."

The train coming again to a stop, TJ looked again to the map
imprinted upon the opposing side of the car, and again to his device.
"Watch this." Causing thereupon a list of segmented numbers to appear
on the screen of his device, TJ magically replicated the topmost of these
in the Google box, and pressed a button. An address appeared on the
screen: "D. Willis, (617) 782-2797, 123 Bowdoin St #4, Dorchester, MA
02122."

TJ beamed. "My mom."

Ben shook his head. "Your device is of such power, it would appear,
as to liberate one from all need to rely upon his own faculty of memory,
except in the case of the most mundane." He held pensive a moment.
"One has to wonder, however, what effect such lassitude allowed to one
faculty of mind might have upon its neighbors, lassitude being, as in
the case of the yawn, of some contagion."

Ben pointed to the sequence of numerals. "This number of three segments, sir; might this be the address by which you were able to direct
your device to grasp the ear of your mother as against that of any other?"

TJ smiled, nodding.

"And might I deduce from the listing from which you selected this
calling number that your device keeps a temporal accounting of the
numbers you employ, the topmost of these being the most recently
employed?"

TJ smiled. "You got it."

Ben shook his head. "One staggers of wonderment."

The train beginning to slow, TJ arose from his seat, and looking to his
unshod feet, quickly slipped his forefeet into Ben's silver-buckle shoes,
to end of his heels overhanging to rearward. As the train doors slid
open, TJ grasped Ben by the arm, and pulling him from his seat, led
him forthrightly from the train, all the while scuffing his feet such as to
forestall leaving Ben's shoes behind, whilst Ben did similarly as regards
TJ's oversized shoes.

No sooner had they exited onto the platform than the doors slid
closed behind.

Scuffing their way then to the near wall, laughing the way, they
restored each other of the proper footwear, TJ rendering assistance
unto Ben in this regard, there being no bench upon which Ben might sit.

His smallish feet once again secure in their casings, Ben bowed unto TJ. "I thank you, young sir, for yet another rescue, but mostly for making no sport regarding my failure at filling your shoes."

TJ grinned, and then led Ben in the direction into which a stream of disembarked passengers had recently as if drained—the tunnel at this stop being as if a large conduit—and thereupon onto an extraordinarily long escalator. Whilst rising as if unto the very gates of heaven itself, Ben basked in a cooling breeze descending from above, and noticed that TJ was yet wearing his marten cap, apparently unawares.

At top, TJ led Ben to a set of turnstiles, hardly the gates to heaven, and thereupon up a set of steps to leftward, and another set orthogonal to the first, and thereupon into a glare of daylight undiminished by a vitreous shield affixed overhead.

Matching the intensity of their glare, it seemed, was a din of roars and honks and reports like no other Ben had ever experienced.

TJ led Ben to the near intersection, across a much-trafficked road-way marked "Lexington," and generally then to westward along a street marked "53rd."

They progressing now at a slower pace, abreast, Ben managed to catch his breath.

"Might I inquire, Mister TJ, regarding your family? You have a mother for whom you have a high regard, as betrayed by your attentiveness upon her. Have you also such a father?"

TJ shook his head. "My daddy was killed when I was little. I never really know'd 'im."

"I'm so very sorry. How, if I may inquire, was your daddy killed?"

"By a roadside bomb."

"Your daddy was a military man?"

"He was in the Guard. 'Cordin' to my mama, the only reason he sign up was for the extra paycheck. He wasn't lookin' for no fightin' 'er t' be a hero 'er enathin' like that. They made 'im an MP 'cause o' him bein' a parole officer 'n all, and the MPs was 'mong the first units t' be called up back when the war began. He was over there almost a year, and was supposed to be comin' home in a few days, but they made 'im stay, and that's when he got blowed up. I was only seven back then, but I can still see them uniforms standin' at the door, and my mom startin' to wail even before they gets t' say anythin'. I never hear'd her wail like that before. And never again."

"I'm so very sorry." Ben held silent a few taps. "You have the good fortune, however, Mister TJ, it would seem, of having the kind of father a son can look up to even if he never really knew him."

TJ chuckled. "T' hear my mama tell it, though, it sure didn't start out that way."

"Did your father require a little burnishing around the edges?"

"My mama should be the one t' tell it—she'd have ya on the floor—but I can give ya the bes' parts, if ya want."

"Please do!"

"My mama grow'd up in Philly, and she 'n my aunt used t' go t' Phillies games all the time, 'cause they was both big fans. They got that way 'cause my grandpa Willis used t' take 'em with 'im when they was little girls. He didn't have no sons. Anyway, one day, some asshole—that the word my mama use—some asshole sittin' right behind 'er gets int' the beer and keeps gettin' louder 'n louder—more 'n more 'noxious, my mama would tell it—until she's had all she gonna take. So she stand up, ever'body else still sittin', and lay int' this asshole in no uncertain terms, right there in front o' everbody in the 'ho' park. She tell 'im t' use 'is sorry-assed manhood for sumthin' beside makin' a goddamn fool o' his sorry-assed self. That the way she tell it. A couple o' innin's later she get a note writ on a hot dog wrapper all covered with mustard: 'I real sorry. Will you mary me'—M-A-R-Y."

Ben laughed aloud. "This is your father to be, of course."

TJ grinned. "He tol' my mama later on he know'd a good thing when he see'd it and no way in God's earth was he gonna let 'er get away. He had t' come t' six more games, though, before she give 'im her phone number. And the Phillies lost all six. The way my mom tell it, the only reason she give in t' 'im was t' break the jinx he'd put on 'er team."

"And did it?"

"They won the next game—then lost the next three."

Ben laughed aloud. "And this series of events ultimately led, I presume, to your father using his manhood for something besides making a fool of himself."

"My mama tol' my daddy she ain't takin' no courtin' from 'im until he go t' school and get his sorry ass a real job. She tol' 'im she ain't supportin' no puffed-up, diamond-studded, sorry-assed nigger. So my daddy, he goes t' school and gets hisself a GED, 'n then he gets hisself a real job makin' sure ex-gangbangers stays on the straight 'n narrow. So my mom marry 'im"—he grinned—"two r's—and they have me, and my daddy gets a better job up in Boston, so we move up there." TJ smiled. "My mama still a Phillies fan, though."

Nearing the intersection of 53rd Street with Park Avenue, Ben espied a running lintel atop a low wall to leftward that was reminding, in variegation, of the marble pedestal holding the oversized image of himself afront Old City Hall in Boston. The variegation here, however, was more pronounced, such as to cause the course of the lintel to resemble a stream of dark water frothing white by way of agitation within. Closer upon the corner, a curious brass roundel embedded into the walkway was suggesting of a compass absent an arrow.

The walkway itself was constituted of large squares of pink-and-black granite, a material that, being dear, would seem extravagant relative to the immediate purpose, but well consonant with the grandeur of the avenue, and the temples of commerce flanking it.

Turning to leftward, with TJ stationed upon his right, Ben continued. "It was in Boston then where your father joined the militia?"

TJ shook his head. "Actually, he signed up when we was still livin' in Philly, jus' after I was born. He tol' my mama no son o' his gonna hafta go through what he did—gettin' all cat-scratched in front o' half o' Philadelphia an' all—t' get hisself on the straight 'n narrow, so he gonna join the Guard so he can start a college fund for me. And when he got the gig up in Boston, he got hisself transferred to a unit up there so's he can keep the fund goin'. Two years later he got called up, 'n a year after that he was dead."

"It would seem your mother also knew a good thing when she saw it."

TJ smiled.

They came upon 52nd Street, where, to leftward, a line of food carts reminded Ben of those he had encountered at the Common in Boston. To rightward, across the wide avenue, a marker upon a marble-faced building, reading GLOBAL TEL, reminded Ben of the piece he had discovered in *The Boston Courant* concerning an aggrieved patron who had sent the master of this very company a symbolic representation of his unredressed grievances.

As they crossed to the farther side of 52nd, Ben inquired of TJ if he had any siblings. "Negative," TJ reported—but almost. His mother, he explained, was pregnant at the time his father shipped out, but miscarried two months later, and almost bled to death. TJ had called 911, but nobody came. He called three times. Finally, out of desperation, he called his aunt in Philly, and she got help from there, she being a city worker and all.

"A lad of six years sounds the alarm, his mother being in grave extremity, and no one comes at the run to lend assistance?"

"Dorchester."

Ben held silent a few taps. "Your mother did not remarry?"

"Too much work, she tell it. No one woman got more in 'er than it take t' d'mesticate jus' one man."

Ben chuckled. "A wise woman, your mother."

They had arrived at 51st street, whereat, to leftward, a bearded man, swaddled in a soiled blanket, was quivering as if to a chill, although the ambient temperature, Ben adjudged, could be no less in the moment than 75 degrees. A box wrought of heavy paper stock, brown, was positioned directly to front of the man, and upon the face of this box was imprinted, in letters evenly wrought, "Thank you for your help."

Begging TJ's indulgence for a moment, Ben diverted himself to whereat the bearded man was pathetically hovelled. Upon Ben's approach, the man regarded Ben with eyes seemingly afflicted of resentments long accumulated, to indelible effect, as in the case of the stains upon his blanket. A white residue, owing as if to a recent frothing of distemper, marked each extremity of the man's purplish lips.

"Concerning the message upon your alms box, sir, I must congratulate you. You are a most clever fellow. Indeed, extend words of gratitude unto a generous soul not yet deserving of them and watch him pick his own pocket toward assuaging the nettle of guilt you have so subtly planted in him. Most clever indeed."

The man shifted his eyes as if for evidence of the regiment to which Ben was the vanguard, then sprang forth, like a cornered cougar, and was upon Ben before Ben might mount any defense soever. Sent stumbling backward, Ben was saved from falling onto the pavement by virtue of a capture from behind, TJ having apparently anticipated, he "having a clue," what Ben had not.

Ben urged TJ from any farther advance, such as to save the bearded man from a thorough pummeling.

"The fault was entirely my own," Ben declared. "One should choose his battles with great care, as in the example of General Washington, so as not to squander his forces." He smiled, whilst urging TJ toward a retreat. "I must thank you yet again, noble sir. You have saved me from a most grievous injury, not to mention from a humiliation most keen."

The bearded man yet maintaining a menacing posture, TJ directed an insult toward him concerning the man's relations with his mother. The man returned the favor by way of a digital gesture, whilst jutting his jaw, in lieu of, it would seem, articulating the last word.

Yet holding fast upon TJ's arm, Ben urged his young guide and protector toward the near curb. "You have a keen sense of justice, Mister TJ, not to mention loyalty. This is both a good thing and a bad thing, in simultaneity, as I trust you will agree."

TJ nodded.

Ben espied near underfoot now a roundel similar to the one discovered two blocks previous, it also being suggesting of a compass absent its arrow. The entire neighborhood, Ben now adjudged, appeared to be denied ready means by which to gain a proper direction.

Woe to the denizens of Park Avenue!

Looking to the farther side of 51st Street, Ben was surprised to discover there, extending well eastward, a curious structure reminding of an Eastern temple. Upon leading TJ to the farther side of 51st Street, Ben was surprised to discover this curious structure to be not a temple, nor even Eastern, but indeed a Christian church, bearing in honor, as chance would have it, the very name of his beloved Intermediary, Bartholomew.

Also curious were two large banners projected streetward from atop the vestibule, each being colorated in red, white, and blue; each bearing a constellation in the upper-left quadrant. The nearer banner, its constellation composed of stars, its body of horizontal stripes, red and white alternating, was the official emblem of the nation, Ben well knew, whilst the farther banner, its constellation composed of crosslets, its body of St. George's cross, was, Ben presumed, the emblem of the sect there worshipping.

Ben looked to TJ. "Until discovering these emblems in close company, each being as if the complementary side to the same coin, I had rather been under the impression that God was Italian. How very gratifying to discover Him American."

TJ grinned.

"Pray tell, Mister TJ, whether or not you are familiar with a small prayer, complete in three words, that reads, 'God bless America?' 'Tis invoked in particular, I believe, as a sort of a-men by public persons keenly concerned with the public perception of their piety, not to mention their patriotism."

TJ nodded. "Ya, ya hear it all the time."

"Pray tell also, Mister TJ, whether or not, were you to be blessed of seventeen children, you would be inclined, upon hearing a petition for special favour from one of them, to grant such favour to him to the neglect of granting the same unto the sixteen others?"

TJ shook his head. "Everbody get the same."

"Because justice demands such?"

TJ nodded.

"And were you the petitioning child, sir, would you not suffer at least some small measurement of embarrassment for having made such a request?" Ben of a sudden raised one hand as if to signal a halt. "Yet again I climb into the pulpit unbidden!" He looked to the palm of his hand, his fingers being now separated. "Why must Humility be ever elusive to a grasping hand?"

TJ chuckled. "Who let you outa yer cage enaway?"

Ben smiled. "That, young sir, is a very long story."

Ben took notice of a curbside queue of overlong vehicles, most of these black and gleaming, a few white and gleaming. Several men, mostly Negro, mostly dressed in ensembles of black alike, were standing in proximity—a few in isolation, most in small groups.

The queue extended to southward beyond the 50th Street intersection, as well as eastward upon the farther side of 50th Street itself. Affixed to each vehicle, Ben noticed, was a number composed of three digits, presumably to establish a unique marking of identity.

"Hey! Ya comin'?"

TJ was partway across 50th. Catching up, Ben followed TJ to the farther side of the roadway, which seemed, in relative width, more a lane than a street. One of the few white overlong vehicles was stopped at the corner there, along the Park Avenue curb, but such as to partially intrude headlong into 50th Street. The number 373 was affixed to a window too opaque to penetrate of sight. Two men standing close upon the vehicle did not share the complexion of the other men noted previous, nor the uniform—nor the sociability.

Ben smiled, and then, looking ahead, discovered a gilt portico extending to the curb, and beneath this, people ambulating in one direction or the other betwixt the near building and several taxicabs, all of them yellow, haphazardly stopped at or close upon the Park Avenue curb. Above the portico, two poles at the oblique were reminding of those in front of St. Bartholomew's, with the nearer of the present pair bearing, as in the case of St. Bartholomew's, the emblem of the nation, the farther one bearing a banner showing the likeness of a single red maple leaf against a snow-white background.

A Negro footman, bedecked in equipage generally ornate and maroon, was lending assistance to two people removing from a taxicab stopped well into the avenue relative to the curb.

Entering under the shelter of the portico, Ben took notice of uniformed officers standing one to side at each of a pair of rotating doors. Not far beyond these doors, other uniformed officers were standing at either side of a second pair of doors, these not rotating. Betwixt the two rotating doors, affixed to the wall there, was likeness of a laurel wreath holding two gilt letters: W A.

Noticing one of the officers take particular notice of TJ, Ben grasped his guide and protector by the arm, and urging him toward the nearer rotating door, waited for him to push his way through, and then pushed himself through.

Standing then as if in the anteroom of a grand palace, upon an emerald carpet, Ben reached up to doff his cap, and discovering it absent, was reminded that TJ yet retained this ancient artifact upon his own head.

The emerald carpeting led unto a stairway a few paces to front, which thereupon led unto the majority of the anteroom. A Negro man to leftward, wearing a uniform absent any ornament, was rolling a device over the carpeting, apparently to forestall accidental debris from accumulating unto unsightliness. Standing atop the stairway stood, at either side, were yet more uniformed officers.

The stairway also was carpeted in emerald, overtop white marble, and was divided into halves by a railing of polished brass at center, to effect of suggesting an upward avenue to rightward, a downward avenue to leftward.

Ascending now the upward avenue, Ben held himself well to rightward, such as to be well removed from traffic, and emerged ultimately, strained for breath, unto the main level of the foyer, and thereupon discovered himself standing atop a large mural in the round, wrought predominantly in tones of amber and sepia, these tones of color being consonant with the honey glow of a large overhanging chandelier. Directly ahead, an open entry unto an inward-leading corridor was flanked at either side by a squarish column, ivory, and to front of each column stood a large vase, metallic, in likeness to a conical vial tapering in the manner of a flute unto a foot.

The entry corridor itself was encumbered at center by a squat bullfrog of a table, the primary utility of which, it would appear, was to draw the eye unto the means of deeper ingress, this attention being effected not so much by signal of the table itself, as by beacon of a spherical spray of flowers atop it, these spouting from a magnificent vase of intricate design and coloration.

The generally white-and-gold motif of the anteroom was yet

enhanced within the corridor, with the floor holding a preponderance of the gold, and phalanxes of squarish columns at either side holding a preponderance of the white. Ben paused at the table, and encountering there a man spraying a fine mist upon the remarkable bouquet, inquired of the man if he might have permission to pluck one bloom from the many, such that he might adorn his lapel with its favor.

The man providing no encouragement in this regard, Ben moved on, espying then, upon exiting the corridor, obliquely to rightward, a marquee in likeness to the tablets of Moses, with the text thereon being illumed in red letters by artificial as opposed to graven by celestial chisel. The second commandment, upon the leftward tablet, rendered the guidance sought: International Leadership Conference / Grand Ballroom.

Feeling a tap upon his shoulder, Ben turned to discover TJ holding by a short stem a fulsome bloom wanton in lavender and cream. "I see you have paid a visit to Eden," Ben said, with a wink. "Even better than the bounty, the bloom. I thank you."

Ben affixed the orchid to his lapel, using for a pin a three-penny nail pulled from pocket. Resuming thereupon the previous course, Ben led TJ into a large room, dimly lit, that, upon first impression, seemed the sanctorum of a singular idol, strikingly golden, standing at room center. A large head, although squarish, showed a round face, stark-white, as well as small horns sprouted from either temple—John Adams himself! A golden plume rose from atop. The torso, showing no limbs, was ornate in aspect, octagonal in geometry, and well elevated upon a pedestal, also octagonal, fashioned of vertical panels of, it would appear, burnished walnut.

Four large columns, consonant in shape and aspect with the columns in the anteroom and entry corridor, ebony here, however, as opposed to ivory there, served to emphasize the centrality of the idol. The surrounding walls, only slightly less dark than the ebony columns, served to give particular notice to an ivory ceiling discreetly illumed as if of celestial candlelight.

Upon closer inspection, the golden idol revealed itself to be no idol at all, but a remarkable sculpture of three parts: two octagonal pedestals—the lower, plain and wooden; the upper, ornate and golden—bearing a squarish clockwork, also ornate and golden.

In the moment, the clockwork began a peal of chimes, these suffusing the dim ambience with a most agreeable aether of sound.

The carpeting, grayish blue in the main, with accents of royal blue and gold, was consonant in tone and intensity with the ceiling above. Several chairs and settees, softly salmon, were arranged such as to center upon the clockwork. A suffusion of tranquil music, in concert with the modest lighting, seemed to instruct the denizens to maintain their voices, as well as their activity, at a restrained level of volume as well as cadence.

Approaching the sculpture, Ben noticed that the clockworks comprised not one timepiece but four, in a square, and that each of the vertical façades upon the upper pedestal bore a tableau in bronze relief. The ornament atop the clockworks, Ben could now discern, was not a plume at all, as first sight would have it, but a separate statuary, of a woman, robed and crowned, holding aloft a torch serving as either beacon or lantern.

Distance had been the progenitor of his misimpressions. *Alas, what little estrangement is not the very mischief from which all misapprehension is wrought?*

Standing directly afront the sculpture, Ben noticed that a shelf betwixt the two pedestals, it extending such as to form a modest overhang, was wrought of the same variegated marble as the lintels upon the low wall leading unto the corner of 53rd Street and Park Avenue. He noticed also that a cameo close upon the top of the nearmost façade was marked "Jackson"—the very Jackson, he surmised, as was imprinted upon the bills delivered to him on Milk Street; and that a similar cameo to rightward of the first was marked "Lincoln"—the very Lincoln, he surmised, as was associated with the Boston High School; and that a cameo to leftward of the first was marked—

"Franklin!"

Smiling in reflex to a small revelation of vanity, Ben turned that he might gather TJ's attention—to what good is vanity, after all, in the absence of an audience—and discovered his audience slouched in a chair close upon one of the ebony columns. The column itself, Ben noticed, was constituted of the same variegated marble, black and white, as the shelf upon the sculpture.

No color, all color—no possibility, all possibility—but for the one, not the other—ever it was, ever it would be.

The circle was the only geometry.

He had given the key to Henry.

Henry was lost.

Ben choked.

TJ was speaking into his device, legs a-jiggle one ankle atop the other, and wearing yet Ben's marten cap.

Looking again to the sculpture, Ben discovered the tableau directly beneath the cameo of himself to depict male figures leaping over obstacles of daunting elevation. What relation this sport had to him, however, he could not in the moment grasp, he having participated in not one steeplechase over the span of eighty-four years. Perhaps the manly sport depicted here was intended more toward the symbolic than the literal, such as to implicate the honoree as a man of action equal to any challenge—or so a generous revelation of vanity might be drawn to speculate.

Looking thereupon to the tableau beneath the cameo of Jackson, Ben was surprised to discover it to depict male figures engaged in swimming.

Indeed, if his own history had been sufficiently known for him to be judged worthy of inclusion in this Pantheon, would it not follow, as a matter of course, that he be associated with, if any manly sport at all, that of swimming? He who had been an avid swimmer over most of his eighty-four years? He who had contrived several novel swimming strokes, not to mention a propulsion device in likeness to a fin? He who had swum in the Thames to a distance of six miles, on a dare? He who had swum in the Seine despite impediments of stone and gout, not to mention a general infirmity owing to age?

Indeed, it would appear that, for having insufficiently consulted the charts of history, the author of this sculpture had steered his rendering off course by one-eighth of a compass round, and imparted thereby, even if inadvertently, a most important lesson, to wit: The less a man should consult history, the more off the mark his best efforts were likely to be.

Ben took notice now of a girl standing close upon the sculpture in company with an older woman of noticeable resemblance. The girl was wearing a top, bearing no sleeves, so undersized as to bring bulges and folds of worldly indulgence unto bold relief, and a pair of breeches, tinted of indigo, so spare as to appear to be the girl's very skin. The net effect was that of one corset squeezing from above whilst a second squeezed from below, to end of producing a superfluity of flesh amidships strikingly in likeness to dough oozing over the rim of a leavening bowl.

Ben tapped his way to where TJ was yet speaking on his device, yet jiggling his legs, yet wearing Ben's cap.

Upon noticing Ben's presence, TJ began a secondary communication by way of hand gestures toward Ben, whilst yet continuing the primary. He thereupon broke off the secondary communication such as to interrupt the primary, such that he might thereupon continue the secondary as if it were the primary. "Talkin' t' m' homies," TJ explained. "Ever'body lookin' for me. Ya gonna be long?"

"If circumstance should prove favorable, but a few minutes. If unfavorable, but a few moments. Will they find you?"

"Nota chance. Meetcha here." TJ grinned. "Try not t' get y'self lost, OK?"

Ben bowed and tapped his way to a counter marked, upon the wall behind, Bell Captain. A Negro man, wearing a blue uniform and a bluer cravat, was standing behind the counter at either end of which sat a small lamp, brass, warmly aglow.

No "bell" was readily visible.

The Negro man, Lester by way of a lapel marker, made a discreet survey of Ben's anachronistic costume, which was absent, blessedly, his marten cap. "May I help you, sir?"

"If you would direct me, kindly, to the Grand Ballroom, I would be most obliged."

The man gestured to Ben's left, whereat a corridor extended yet farther inward, indeed as if in continuation of the previous. "Go up the corridor and bear to your right. You'll see the elevators on your left."

"And the level, sir?"

The man smiled. "There's only one stop."

Ben bowed. "Thank you, sir."

Tapping his way up the corridor, Ben passed a few shops and curio closets, the latter illumed such as to give allure to the wares on display. Bearing right then, into a crossing corridor, soon espied to leftward three shallow recessions, each framing a large silver-and-gold door embossed with a fluid design. Noticing a button upon the wall betwixt the second and third door, Ben surmised its function, and tapping his way to close proximity, pushed it with the end of his cane. A set of doors slid open. Stepping into the chamber revealed, Ben espied a button labeled Up, and pressing this with the tip of his cane, felt a slight compression, and a few moments subsequent, a slight extension.

The doors opening of their own accord, Ben stepped into as if a vaulted corridor at Versailles. Overhead and to rightward, a line of globular chandeliers, each showing concentric petticoats of crystalline jewels, were suggesting of jellyfish suspended in a celestial sea. Underfoot, a pattern of checkerboard squares, black alternating with white, was reminding of the arrays upon which Ben had composed his magic squares whilst bound by duty to his clerk's chair in the Pennsylvania Assembly.

Passing by a series of closed doorways, these intermittent along the opposing side of the corridor, all of them shut, Ben soon came upon an open such, and passing through this, entered into a large room—the very anteroom, he surmised, associated with the Grand Ballroom. A large chandelier, suggestive of an inverted torch, was suspended from a recessed roundel within the ceiling. Beyond this practical ornament, a set of doors was overtopped by a pair of mirrors, paned in the manner of windows, to effect of appearing to give visibility to a chandelier, within a subsequent room, in exact likeness to the one being, in fact, reflected.

To leftward, at the far end of an open expanse of crimson carpeting, a table draped of white linen spanned the full width of the room, and behind this table presently stood three people. A marker affixed to the linen read "Registration."

Flanking the twin doors directly to front were two sentinels reminding of the officers encountered at the front entrance to the hotel. Approaching these potential obstacles, Ben recalled the tableau under his name upon the clock sculpture, and felt now some affinity to it. A marquee was rested upon an easel close upon the sentinel to rightward:

1:30–3:00	Panel Discussion: "Where have all the Washingtons, Adamses and Jeffersons gone?"
3:15–4:30	"Why leadership *must* be moral" Paul Kenyon, PhD, DD
5:00–6:00	Open discussion

The rightward sentinel regarded Ben now as the bell captain had recently regarded him, but with less discretion. "Can I see your pass, please?"

Ben touched the tip of his cane against the marquee and winked, using his left eye, such that both sentinels might witness. "I have come," he declared, "such as to bring a little surprise unto these somber proceedings."

The leftward sentinel smiled. "Showtime?"

Ben bowed. "Though the hour is dear, sir, yet still there is time."

The leftward sentinel looked to the rightward sentinel, who

thereupon employed upon Ben a device similar to the one employed upon him at the Boston school, apparently to the same purpose. After an effort more perfunctory, it would seem, than exacting, the rightward sentinel told Ben he might proceed.

The leftward sentinel held open the nearer door. "Knock 'em dead," he said.

"I would rather hope for the opposite," Ben replied, with a wink and a nod. Tapping his way then unto the periphery of what held aspect of a most remarkable common area, Ben beheld a regiment of several hundreds of persons assembled into ranks and files perfectly aligned, each person being attentive upon a large dais to rightward.

Someone was speaking, the volume of his voice greatly amplified: "...left the pulpit at Emmanuel to assume the position of Executive Director at the Charles B. & Marion C. Godfrey Foundation. Over the course of the next five years, Dr. Kenyon was to lead—to quote this city's leading newspaper—'a crusade against malfeasance in America'—"

Moving from under a low ceiling, this partially obstructing his view, Ben was astonished to behold not a common area for general assembly, but indeed as if a royal opera house, the general seating being upon the present level, the private apartments elevating unto two tiers to rear and to side.

Showtime indeed!

"I see we have a visitor."

Several hundreds of faces turning upon him, Ben felt a churn of unease, this being greatly amplified by sight of his image grotesquely enlarged upon a monstrous picture frame in the corner of the chamber leftward of the dais.

"I'm sure Dr. Kenyon wouldn't mind if we were to precede his remarks by a few from Dr. Franklin, or Poor Richard, as the case may be." Pause. "Yes, thank you. Dr. Kenyon agrees. Would the gentleman please come forward."

Thereupon making his way toward the farther end of the platform, whereat the man speaking was standing behind a lectern, Ben nodded to each of several persons seated on the dais directly above him, at a long table preceding the lectern. Each person smiled in return, seemingly of amusement, or the expectation of same, in the manner of courtiers waiting upon the antics of the jester.

Ben assumed these persons to be the panelists involved in the discussion that had only just ended. A placard afront each one bore his or her identity and association: six men and three women. These were followed by Ian McGillivray / Chamber of Commerce of Canada, and Paul Kenyon / Democratic Candidate for President, and by an empty chair, whereat sat, when not serving as master of the proceedings, Ben surmised, the man presently standing at the lectern, his own placard reading, "George A. Dunleavy / U. S. Chamber of Commerce."

"Let's hear it for the good doctor," Mr. Dunleavy commanded, "who apparently still makes house calls!"

Laughter followed by applause.

Discovering his toleration of public attention to be no greater now than two centuries previous, Ben climbed the steps unto the dais—three, and three more—with his eyes held averted. Upon attaining the dais, he bowed to Mr. Dunleavy, who invited him, by way of gesture, to take his place at the lectern. Stepping back then, Mr. Dunleavy joined in the applause.

Casting his eyes now upward, as if for a venue of escape, Ben beheld, suspended from the ceiling, a chandelier of seven globes, six surrounding one lower, the collection being interlaced of golden filaments. Directly above this ornament, upon the face of the ceiling, an intricate mosaic was framed within a geometry of squares. The mosaic itself, being hued in tones of honey and amber, was reminding of the mosaic embedded into the floor of the anteroom.

Ben turned to Mr. Dunleavy, who had reclaimed his seat at the table. "If it should not be too much trouble," Ben said, startled by the amplification of his voice, "I would prefer the screen to my right"—he gestured—"to display any object other than my image. The agonies of history would suggest it generally unwise to represent any man in a form ten times greater than his natural stature." Ben bowed.

Mr. Dunleavy gestured toward a small window in likeness to a peep hole, hardly noticeable above the upper tier of private apartments. After a moment, the large picture frame to Ben's right went dark.

Ben bowed toward the peep hole and noticed that several of the private apartments below it held banners affixed to their fronts, and that some of the names borne upon these banners were familiar to him: AIG, Tyco International, Exxon, Global Tel, Google. Several others, on the other hand, were unfamiliar: Microsoft, Citigroup, Altria, Halliburton, Lockheed-Martin.

He noticed also, suspended above each of the upper apartments, a crystal chandelier in likeness to a teardrop, to overall effect, it did seem, of forming an encirclement of lamentation. And whereas the upper apartments were rounded unto the general shape of inkwells, the lower were steadfastly squarish, to effect, it did seem, of reflecting a principle in common with windows arched to top, squared to bottom. The main assembly, Ben noticed, was arranged as if into three battalions, of at least two hundreds each.

Taking a deep breath, Ben began: "Though the hour is dear, yet still there is time."

Ben held silent a moment, and then continued. "Many years ago now, during the course of a leisurely chess match, my opponent, the sister of a notable admiral and an equally notable general, told me a story that, at the time, I surmised a ploy toward distraction. It had been told her, she avowed, showing a certain affect of eye, whilst holding her queen's rook betwixt two fingers, by a serpent in her garden. It bears, I hope you might agree, repeating."

Nary a sound.

"Not so very long ago, a great seafarer, greatly troubled by the course of events in his native world, this being called by us Mars, after the Roman god of war—'god of *war*,' good people—set out in his brigantine to sail the great seas of Mars, in company with himself alone, in search of a great leader. His earnest intention was to prevail upon this leader to save his people from a fate most dire, they having abandoned their sextants and compasses, of their own free will, such as to follow a sundry of pipers and sirens unto a ready fulfillment of every desire. He first sought out a great leader of state, he ensconced in a great white castle, and asked of him, 'Good sir, for whom would you forfeit your office and all your powers such that they, each one, might have opportunity sufficient?' Whereupon the great leader of state consulted his timepiece and declared himself tardy for a ceremony of high importance. Next, our seafarer sought out a great leader of commerce, he ensconced in a castle of glass and steel, and asked of him, 'Good sir, for whom would you forfeit your office and all your riches such that they, each one, might have means enough?' Whereupon the great leader of commerce consulted his timepiece and declared himself tardy for a meeting of high importance. Next, our seafarer sought out a great leader of religion, he ensconced in a great castle of fresco and gilt, and asked of him: 'Good sir, for whom would you forfeit your office and place in heaven such that they, each one, might have hope enough?' Whereupon the great leader of religion looked to his timepiece and declared himself tardy for a ritual of high importance. And so it went, from sea to sea, continent to continent, isle to isle, until our seafarer had exhausted all possibility."

Nary a sound.

"Discouraged but undiminished of resolve, our seafarer fitted his brigantine for navigating the great aether, and embarked then, to a fair solar wind, for a nearby world, the one known to us as Venus. At no greater than halfway to this other world, however, our intrepid seafarer happened into a great cosmic storm and, blown off course by unrelenting gales of negative seeking after positive, positive seeking after negative, was carried instead to the world we know as Earth, there coming to rest upon a great shoal of rock. Dropping his anchor into a rocky crag, in caution against tides unknown, our seafarer took to his glass and soon espied a man, very strange in appearance, sitting upon a nearby ledge, his face uplifted toward the sun. This strange apparition had very long hair, purely white, an even longer beard, also white, and was wearing a robe as purely white as his beard and hair. Even stranger still, this man appeared to have only two eyes as against three, and only two arms as against six, and he showed no purple of complexion soever."

Nary a sound.

"Buoyed now by a flood-tide of hope, our seafarer launched his pinnace and rowed through gentle currents of air—whilst a great winged creature, white of crown and wingtip, yellow of beak and eye, soared in proximity—to whereat the bearded man was seated. Tethering his pinnace to a gnarled shrub rooted in a small fissure, our seafarer approached the bearded man, and clearing his throat, such as to gain the strange man's attention, said unto him, 'Take me unto your leader, good sir, if you would be so kind.'"

Murmurs of amusement.

"The bearded man stared at his curious visitor, purple of complexion, bearing not two eyes but three, not two arms but six, and gave the only reply he might: 'I cannot, sir, for there is none such to be found here, whether I should pilot you to north or to south, to east or to west.'

"To this declaration, our seafarer slumped as if to loose a burden he could no longer bear.

"'If it were an Egoist you sought, sir,' the bearded man continued, 'or a Narcissist, or a Self Aggrandizer, there are bazaars innumerable, north and south, east and west, to which I might direct you.

"'If it were a Demagogue you desired, sir, or a Chauvinist, or a Populist, there are flesh houses inexhaustible, north and south, east and west, to which I might direct you.

"'If it were an Ideologue you required, sir, or a Zealot, or a Dogmatist, there are carnivals aplenty, north and south, east and west, to which I might direct you.

"'But a leader?' He shook his head most severely. 'I fear, sir, you have traveled a very long way to no avail soever.'

"One great weight compounded by another, the latter being fatigue, our seafarer inquired of the bearded man if he might tarry with him for a spell in repose, sufficient that he might recover his strength, thereby his resolve, before resuming his journey.

"'Rest for as long as you require,' the bearded man replied, 'or longer still. You are most welcome here. Be cautioned, however, that this small shelf is affixed to an earthly bowel much disposed toward fits of colic.'

"Our seafarer sat down, releasing a deep sigh, and inquired of his host by what name he should be addressed.

"'I have no name,' the bearded man replied. 'In one time and place, I was called The Awakened; in another, The Wise; in another, The Prophet. Now, I am called by no name at all, by no man at all.'

"'Should I not call you Teacher then, in keeping with what your very nature would seem to name you?'

"Thereupon the man of no name directed toward our seafarer a scowl most severe. 'You should not. What I was by natural inclination of heart and spirit, I did *not*, to my eternal regret, become by will and resolve.'

"Our seafarer looked away for a moment, marveling at the aerial grace of the great winged creature he had earlier espied, it gliding nearby, then looked again to the man of no name. 'Should I infer then, sir, that if you were to be granted means to travel backward in time, and have opportunity thereby to correct all your errata, or any selection thereof, you would invite Will and Resolve to power your wagon?'

"'I would do precisely that.'

"'Leading it thereupon to where, sir, if I might inquire?'

"'Aught else but to this airy prison.'

"'And just how was it, if I might inquire, sir, that you came to take residence here?'

"The man of no name looked down upon his crossed legs—he being seated in the Indian manner—then, taking a deep breath, cleared his throat. 'I was banished to this igneous shelf for having committed the most egregious of all earthly sins: to wit, speaking that which is not to be heard, challenging that which is not to be questioned, accusing those who are not to be reproached. I had become much alarmed, you see, too alarmed to remain passive, thereby acquiescent, over a prolif-eration of penny pipers playing false anthems throughout the land, to effect indeed of equating pleasure with happiness, desire with need, acquisition with success, satiation with fulfillment, self with center. By inclination of heart—certainly not that of good sense—I made attempt toward some measure of dissent. I carried a small box onto a public Common, and standing upon this pulpit, sang out, 'The true leader promotes, by example, not appetite but need; not acquisition but contribution, not satiation but fulfillment; not profit but succor.' Before I might draw a breath such as to continue, I was removed from my trespass by bludgeons of scorn and derision. Bruised of feeling, but undaunted of spirit, I carried my box to a second Common and there sang out: 'The true leader does not crave power, but is embarrassed by it, does not run for office, but from it.' Before I might repeat myself, however, in the cause of reinforcement, I was removed from my trespass by fusillades of brick and stone. Bruised of body but undaunted still, I carried my box to a third Common and there sang out: 'The true leader dwells not in a great domed palace, serviced by eunuchs, but with his flock, bearing in tempest and peril all that they must bear.' I was thereupon set upon by a mob of Knights of the One True Way, pummeled to the very threshold of a blessed death, and brought before the Supreme Directorate for the Propagation of Proper Thinking, which body declared me, prima facie, a minion of the Unholy One and banished me to wherefrom no man might call me forth. I was carried here by the very raptor you see soaring and gliding about this lonely platform, keeping always one yellow eye upon me.'

"Animated now as if by stroke of electrical flux, our seafarer cried out, "Tis you! 'Tis you I seek!' He thereupon explained, in a single semantic unit, unbroken by any mark soever, the purpose of his mission, and the cause of its urgency. When finally he had finished, the man of no name, who had listened in a grudging silence, replied, most vehemently: 'I am no such thing!' He pulled at his beard as if at a cord to summon the sergeant-at-arms. 'Besides which,' he added, 'we are of wholly different worlds, you and I.'

"Our seafarer smiled in a knowing sort of way, being cautious, however, not to tread unto smugness. 'I am a great seafarer, sir. I have been to most every place there is to go, and I can tell you, sir, with a confidence rivaling your resistance, that there is no such thing as *separate worlds*. The line of demarcation with which mortal beings separate one thing from another, one self from another, one world from another, is but a construct of convenience, with no basis in fact. We declare separation but where expediency invites, such as to accommodate ownership, hence avarice; such as to accommodate hierarchy, hence dominion; such as to accommodate boundary, hence difference. True, you are not purplish, as I; but is it coloration that marks the true leader, sir, or is it something deeper? True, you have only two eyes as against three, as I; but is it acuity of sight that marks the true leader, sir, or is it something far keener? True, you have but two arms as against six, as I; but is it agility of limb that marks the true leader, sir, or is it something far more facile?'

"Feeling in the moment a violent quaking of the earth, and hearing a deep rumbling, our seafarer looked up to discover a large boulder hurtling down the declination of the mount, directly toward the ledge upon which he and the man of no name were seated; and in that instant, he sprang to upright, as if indeed of mere reflex, and grasping the man of no name by facility of six arms in simultaneity, tossed him, without benefit of ceremony, into the safety of the pinnace, taking thereupon the falling rock fully onto himself.

"On the world known to us as Mars, named after the Roman god of war—'god of *war*,' good people—a man named Argaa opened his eyes, all three in the instant, and discovered himself in his comfortable bed, within his humble abode, which stood at the edge of the great sea Lauraa, within the shadow of the great volcano Tomaasio. In the moment, Argaa knew what it was he must needs do, could no longer decline from doing, to whatever excuse. And in this moment he felt most keenly not that blessed relief that attends upon escaping an imagined horror, but a most profound sense of grief, for his very life, he knew, was forfeit.

"'Check, and mate,' my wily opponent said unto me, in way of concluding her story.

"'Ah, I see I am beaten,' I lamented.

"'Is not such a condition known but to Pride?' she replied.

"'Ah, so it is,' I said. 'So it is.'"

Ben peered up at the chandelier of six globes surrounding one lower, and thereupon looked upon the three battalions of militia arrayed before him. "Several are the measures of the true leader. Three such, however, I submit, should precede all others. In the form of interrogatives, asked of one's own self, they are thus:

"For what causes would I, without benefit of forethought, forfeit my very life, that these causes might succeed?

"For what principles would I, without benefit of forethought, forfeit my very life, that these principles might prevail?

"For what persons would I, without benefit of forethought, forfeit my very life, that these persons might continue in theirs?"

Ben counted as if six tolls of bell, and then looked to Mr. Dunleavy. "I do hope my remarks were appropriate to the occasion, sir. I yield to the speaker who would be the president of your nation, such that he might commerce remarks too long delayed by a foolish old man."

Dr. Kenyon, turning to Mr. McGillivray, struck the fingertips of one hand against the open palm of the other. Mr. McGillivray, showing considerable agitation, as if caught betwixt call of wife and lure of mistress, made the same gesture toward Mr. Dunleavy.

As Ben thereupon tapped his way across the dais, behind the table of panelists, the only sound was the tap of his cane, this muted by way of a veneer of crimson carpeting. Nearing upon a brass railing, he heard, emanant from the rear of the chamber, a rhythmic percussioning. Looking to source, he espied a Negro man, by manner of dress a wait servant, clapping his hands. In the manner then of a single wave bobbing all boats, soon the chamber was filled of a thunderous din.

Descending the six steps to the floor, these in mirror image to those at the other end of the dais, Ben made his way toward the doorway through which he had entered. Nearing upon a pillar, squat and squarish, bearing, in concert with several like it, the tiers of private apartments above, Ben encountered a young woman standing immediately afront the pillar, she wearing upon her breast a conspicuous label bearing, in blue lettering: Courtney St. James / Kenyon Campaign. Inscribed thereunder was a number, 179. Ms. St. James was herself applauding, and in the very moment of Ben's eyes meeting hers, she directed toward Ben a most cordial smile.

Pausing to bow, Ben unpinned the lush bloom of lavender and cream from his lapel, and returning the three-penny pin to pocket, extended the delicate bloom toward Miss St. James. "A flower for you today, Miss St. James?"

The young woman, of no greater than her twenty-fifth or twenty-sixth year, took the flower into hand, yet smiling most cordially.

Ben turned away, and then turned back.

"By the bye, Miss St. James, you will find Mr. Kortright, Sergeant by preference, at the corner of Washington and School Streets in Boston. He has for you there, I have reason to believe, also a flower, but of a species far greater in worth than my own."

Courtney's eyes seemed to swell unto near double their native size.

Mr. Dunleavy announced a brief intermission.

Bowing again to Miss St. James, Ben tapped his way to the doorway through which he had earlier entered, and nodding to the two sentinels upon passing through, was visited by a thought most disquieting. Thereupon hurrying unto the vaulted corridor and into the elevator alcove, Ben struck the wall button with his cane, and entering the middle of the three elevators, soon thereafter exited unto the corresponding alcove on the main floor.

How could he not have anticipated?

Striding unto the main corridor, Ben tapped his way toward the clockworks room, making attempt as he progressed toward peering ahead, but being thwarted in this regard by intervening perambulators, some of whom were emerging from, or entering into, a corridor to rightward, this soon revealing itself to be another alcove of elevators, likely in service to the floors above the ballroom. Amongst those presently emerging was a young couple, the young man of which held some familiarity. Ben's immediate concern, however, hence his attention, lay elsewhere, freighted by a deepening sense that it had been a terrible mistake to leave TJ abandoned in a chamber in which he could not other than be rendered conspicuous by way of certain anomalies.

As he entered into the clockworks room, Ben felt his stomach invert such as to begin to digest his liver. Two men in uniform were standing immediately afront TJ, the latter yet enthroned in a salmon-and-silver chair faced upon the clock sculpture.

Ben was about to cry out to effect of laying claim to the young gentleman when TJ delivered unto the two officers an uplifted middle finger. Subsequent events thereupon followed in rapid succession: The uniformed man to leftward lunged toward TJ, but was met by an uprising TJ with such force as to be felled upon a low table directly behind. Almost in the same motion, TJ pushed the other officer of such force as to send him stumbling backward unto the clockworks. Launching forth then, into Ben's general direction, TJ encountered, before he might accumulate any opportunity soever toward avoidance, the young couple Ben had witnessed emerge from the elevator alcove. Striking fully upon the young woman, TJ managed to embrace her for some fraction of a moment, whilst rotating himself away from her, these acts in concert serving to diminish the overall force of his blow, but at cost of TJ losing possession of his device, this hurtling beyond ready reach, and also his balance, he hurtling thereupon unto the floor, rolling full circle, in the manner of an acrobat, and restoring himself to his feet of his own momentum.

The second officer, having righted himself, launched into an eager pursuit, and would likely have apprehended his quarry, by advantage of the delay accumulated to the latter in saving the young woman from harm, but for Ben navigating himself, as if unawares of the immediate drama, directly into the pursuer's path.

The impact sent Ben onto his backside with such violence as to cause his head to strike upon the marble floor. When, following some interval absent any awareness soever, Ben was sufficiently restored of sentience, he discovered poised above him the countenance previously recognized, but starched presently unto a grave solemnity.

"You OK?"

Mr. Kinney's companion—Anne, she must needs be—was standing immediately adjacent, her fair cheeks bearing such inflammation as is oft attendant upon a winter venture or a vigorous exercise. Another face appeared, also familiar, it being that of Lester, the bell captain. Other faces followed—all starched, it would appear, of the same wash.

Upon offering assurances concerning his condition, Ben was helped to his feet by Mr. Kinney and the bell captain.

"That was a nasty fall," Kevin said, restoring Ben of his cane.

"I thank you, sir. Most kind of you." Ben could not help but take notice of the singular facing upon Kevin's timepiece, it being of the coloration of fledging shrubbery at springtime.

Kevin smiled. "You look just like him." He looked to Anne. "We should send him down to Cratchit. He'd love it."

Anne smiled.

The bell captain touched Ben's arm. "Shall I call the hotel physician for you, sir?"

"O, most kind of you, sir, but I'm quite all right."

Several grotesque apparitions, brandishing weapons of sinister aspect, trudged unto the direction in which TJ had made his escape. They were wearing black vests, black boots, and black head armor, which, in sum, gave suggestion of an alien species burdened unto excess.

Ben thought of Braddock's redcoats, burdened of their own excesses— he grinned—trudging after fleet-footed quarries also long since fled.

"Are you sure you're all right, sir?" Anne inquired.

High in cheekbone, delicate in clavicle, this woman, Ben adjudged, effused an air of nobility, though it was her eyes, like windows unto Eden, that most arrested his attention. He bowed. "I am certain, madam, thank you. As to body, I have padding strategically gathered. As to head, little sense left to forfeit."

Bowing then unto Kevin, Kevin nodding in return, Ben turned away and began to tap his way toward the bell captain's desk. He stopped after but a few paces and turned back. "O, Mr. Kinney?"

Kevin turned from an opposing advance as if to hail from Banquo himself.

Ben slipped hand from pocket. "I have something I believe might be of service." Ben tossed a slender object toward Kevin, who, of reflex, grasped it.

"The nail being no longer lost, sir, can there be yet need of one penny more?" Bowing unto a countenance become as pallid as his companion's was ruddy, Ben turned half-circle around, and resuming his advance toward the bell captain's desk, noticed a man to rightward lift an object from the floor. "Ah, *there* it is! I feared it lost. Thank goodness, thank goodness." The man was wearing the same uniform as the bell captain, and bore one of the pleasant countenances that had recently shown upon Ben in his repose.

The man held TJ's device forth, an interrogative writ upon his face. Ben nodding, the man gave the device over.

"I thank you, sir. You have saved me from an injury avoidable by no other means." Ben bowed. The man nodding in return, Ben made his way to the bell captain's desk, whereat Lester greeted him with a demeanor of countenance gravitating toward amusement, and a demeanor of eye gravitating toward accusation.

Slipping his map from pocket, Ben unfolded it upon the bell captain's desk. "Might I impose on your kindness yet farther, sir, and ask direction to St. Paul's Chapel, or its remains? If either should exist, I would expect it to stand rather far to southward, close upon the Sound."

Lester smiled. "St. Paul's still stands, sir." Orienting the map toward himself, Lester laid a finger upon it. "Take the Green Line down to Fulton Street. The Chapel is on the corner of Fulton and Broadway." Reorienting the map toward Ben, Lester touched upon Fulton Street, then upon another spot, upon Park Avenue. "You're here—and the closest station to the Chapel is here, at John Street, I believe." He pointed to the map. "About one block up from Fulton."

Lester thereupon gestured toward the same corridor to which he had earlier directed Ben. "Go almost to the end of the corridor and follow the exit signs. You'll be on Lexington; bear left. There's a Green Line entrance about two blocks up. Take any train to Grand Central, that's the first stop, and walk across the platform. Get on the first train you see."

Ben nodded. "Thank you, sir. Most kind of you."

Lester refolded the map and handed it to Ben. He smiled. "You stepped in front of that officer on purpose."

Ben slipped the map to pocket. "I did indeed."

"Are you a terrorist?"

"I am."

"And the young man?"

"A journeyman in that trade, under the understanding that nothing terrorizes the affrightable greater than one in whom truth is betrothed to courage."

Lester stared at Ben as if in anticipation of a few words in beneficent opposition, and then, becoming sensible to a ringing to rightward, attended to it.

Ben took his leave, and following Lester's instructions, soon discovered himself standing in close company aboard a No. 6 train bound southward.

On the occasion of the first stop—42nd Street—Ben followed a small herd of fellow travelers onto a No. 4 train stopped across the platform, upon which, it being less populous, he was able to claim a bench seat, directly adjacent to a woman of plain appearance and generous proportion. The bench itself faced upon a looking-glass image across the aisle. Upon this latter bench sat a Negro man, of dark complexion, marking upon a tablet clipped to a thin board laying upon his knees. He was holding a yellow drawing stick in his left hand, his right hand being wholly absented. His dark face showed disfigurements, the largest of these running from the left temple, over the eye—rendering this half closed—and ending at the lower lip. As he worked, the man kept lifting his eyes toward the large woman sitting to leftward of Ben, apparently such as to take, so to say, the measure of her.

A disembodied voice, female, offered admonishment concerning "the closing doors." The doors thereupon closing, the train started into motion.

Noticing a small marquee close upon the ceiling of the car announce, in red lettering, the next stop—14th St Union Sq—Ben turned to the woman sitting to leftward. "Excuse me, madam."

The woman, clutching a handbag set upon her lap, was scowling toward the Negro man sitting opposite. Turning now toward Ben, she showed him a pair of eyes seemingly fixed into a permanent squint, and a nose, disproportionately small, modestly upturned. Her hair, medium brown, was long and in need, it would appear, of a hundred strokes. Resting upon the swells of her bosom were a few crumbs fallen, apparently, from a recent indulgence.

"I am a stranger here," Ben continued, "and subject therefore to all manner of errata owing to ignorance. In this regard, might I trouble you with a question concerning the habits of this train?"

The woman showed Ben an expression akin to that with which she had been regarding the Negro artist, to effect of causing Ben to regret his choice of a Good Samaritan.

"I apologize for my intrusion," he said.

Even though there was hint now of a thawing, a fair amount of frozen ground remained around the eyes. "What's your question?"

"How many stops might there be to Fulton Street?"

Unclenching her handbag, the woman counted to the third finger of her right hand. "Third stop," she said. "Union Square, City Hall, Fulton Street."

Ben nodded. "Thank you, ma'm. Most kind of you."

The woman looked away, and discovering the Negro man peer upon her from across the aisle, shook her head, and once again affixed her eyes upon her handbag.

The Negro man, wearing a dark-blue cap, "NY" imprinted at front, slid his drawing instrument into that crevice betwixt head and ear seemingly made for such, and substituting for this instrument his index finger, used the latter in the manner of a pen. The purpose of such, Ben surmised, was not to dispense yet more residue but to smear, unto artistic ends, some measure of the residue previously dispensed.

The Negro man regarded his work, made a few emendations by way of the yellow stick and his finger, and regarded his work again. Thereupon unclipping the sheet bearing his work from the board holding it, the man abandoned his seat and presented toward the woman sitting to leftward of Ben a black-and-white likeness of herself. "For you, ma'm," he said. "There is no charge." A most-pleasant coloration of tones hinted toward a foreign origin.

Ben adjudged the rendering of the woman a most agreeable verisimilitude, it serving neither to flatter overly nor to judge severely, but to, so to say, bring the subject into best light. Indeed, despite the plainness of the subject, and therefore of the likeness, there was to the latter a palpable sensuality, this seeming neither coerced upon nor inappropriate to the subject.

The woman shifted her head to leftward, whilst holding her eyes cast downward, such as to represent, it would appear, a rejection.

"For you, ma'm," the man repeated.

Of a sudden, the woman snatched the offering from the Negro man and sundering it into two pieces, loosed these to the floor.

Ben winced.

The Negro man nodded, in the manner of a footman comprehending an instruction communicated by gesture alone, and returned to his seat, leaving his artistry where it lay.

"The nerve," the woman mumbled.

"Indeed," Ben said, as if in reply to a direct address. "More nerve than I could summon myself with which to wage the daily struggle of that gentleman." Leaning forward, Ben retrieved, with some difficulty, the two pieces of the sundered portrait from the floor, and held them together, above his lap, as best he might. After a moment, he moved the portrait, as held together, to leftward. "'Tis interesting, is it not," he said, "that the disfigurement to the portrait would appear to match rather closely that upon the face of the artist. Of course, the one was voluntary; the other, presumably, was not."

"He should have asked," the woman snapped, shifting her eyes fleetingly toward the Negro man. "I would have told him I didn't want it."

"You are quite right, madam. Yet, if you and I were to remove ourselves of our present skin, such as to take on that of the gentleman, I suspect we would rather quickly come to the understanding that it is sometimes a worthy risk to create likenesses without commission, it being far more facile for people to turn down items not yet rendered appealing to their senses than it is for them to turn down wholly completed renderings in the presence of a needful artist."

The woman looked from the sundered portrait to the Negro man, and back then to the sundered portrait.

The train slowed, an illuminated platform came into view, and the train squealed to a stop. The doors sliding open, people egressed, people ingressed, and a gentleman assumed the seat to rightward of Ben. A disembodied voice thereupon warned about the closing door, the train started again into motion, and the marquee silently announced City Hall to be the next stop.

Ben noticed that the Negro man had not begun another sketch. Instead, he was poised, a cloth bag pressed with one hand against his abdomen, as if to launch forth upon occasion of the next stop.

Ben held the sundered portrait toward the man to rightward, who seemed to be in a state of some distress, as evidenced by a firmly grasped chin and a pensive stare downward. A newspaper resting on his lap showed an article titled, HARRIS UPSHAW STANDS BY ITS MAN / BOARD DECLARES FULL CONFIDENCE IN PAUL JOHNSON, RECENTLY ACCUSED OF OVERSEEING $300M FRAUD. Ben was reminded of a similar piece he had earlier encountered in *The Boston Courant.*

The man, being perhaps in the latter half of his sixth decade, but showing no more than a tinge of hoarfrost upon his temple, was wearing a medium-blue suit bearing a thin stripe, and was clutching a leather satchel betwixt his ankles. His spectacles were fashioned of lenses particularly large. "Excuse me for intruding, sir," Ben interrupted, "but might I have your opinion on this rendering?"

Seeming at first uncomprehending, the man thereupon looked to the portrait, held his eyes fixed upon it a moment, and then nodded. "Well done. He's captured the essence of her, I should think."

"Would you like to have it, sir? There is no charge."

The man regarding Ben with some consternation, Ben met the man's eyes with an earnest gaze. The man nodded. "Yes, I would. Thank you." Looking again to the portrait, the man took it into hand. "I have a place for this in my office," he added. "And I know a very good restorer."

The woman to leftward of Ben uttered a most pathetic plaint: "I'm sorry! I'm sorry! Please, let me keep it!" Pulling forth a wallet from her handbag, the woman opened this article, giving opportunity thereby for Ben to espy within a card, in collection with her likeness: Cynthia A. Sibbowicz / 52 Bond Street #4 / Brooklyn, NY 11217.

Cynthia slipped a Hamilton from her wallet, hesitated, added a Jackson, and heaving forth, held the two bills toward the Negro man across the aisle. "Here, please take this. I'm so sorry."

The Negro man shook his head. "I cannot take your money, ma'm, because the sketch is ruined. And I cannot make you another, because I need very badly to pee." He grinned. "But if you will delay your trip at the next stop, I will sketch you again." The train beginning to slow, Cynthia looked to her watch and then to the sundered portrait yet held by the man sitting next to Ben. The man offered the portrait toward Cynthia.

Showing in response a yet greater agitation, Cynthia uttered a groan and presented the bills again to the Negro man, who again shook his head. The train squealing to a stop, the Negro man, rising from his seat, bowed toward Cynthia, and hurried toward the open doorway. Cynthia uttered a most plaintive squeal, and retrieving a squarish bag from under her seat, followed the Negro man off the train.

Ben watched through the car windows as the Negro man indicated to Cynthia where she should wait on him. The man thereupon gave over to her his cloth bag, apparently in escrow until he should return relieved of a burden declared most forthrightly.

The train started again into motion, the marquee announced "Fulton Street" to be the next stop.

"Rwandan," the man next to Ben announced. "I can tell by the accent. Probably Tutsi, given the missing hand and the scar." The man looked to the sundered portrait lying atop his folded newspaper. "So, what do I do with this?"

Ben shuddered to a heady tide of received memory regarding the Zimbabwe genocide, the Rwandan genocide, the Darfur genocide, the Bosnian genocide, the Cambodian genocide, the Ugandan genocide, the Holocaust genocide, the Stalinist genocide, the Armenian genocide—

For one terrible moment, he was denied all breath.

He forced an inhalation. "May I suggest, sir," he thereupon managed, "that you do with it as you indicated to the woman. She would like to believe, I think, that you in fact hold in your breast the measure of respect for her likeness, and hence for her self, that you implied by way of your declarations. I fear, however that she does not. A perhaps unjust portioning of life's trials has made her, methinks, more than a little wary concerning the honor and trust of others." The train began to slow. "May I suggest, sir," Ben continued, "that after you have done as you have indicated, that you invite the woman to your office to bear witness." He paused. "I have her name and location. Do you have means by which to record it, sir? This is my stop."

The man slipped a wallet from inside his suitcoat, and pulling forth two cards, gave one over to Ben: Paul A. Johnson / Chief Executive Officer / Harris Upshaw & Co. / 17 Wall Street / New York, NY 10005.

Whilst Ben slipped the card to pocket, Mr. Johnson produced a golden pen, and turning the card yet held by him unto its blank side, poised the pen upon it.

Ben rose from his seat. "Cynthia A. Sibbowicz," he said, spelling out the surname. The train coming to a stop, Ben added the address, and tapping his way toward the open doorway, turned back.

"Madame Norquist had cause to support you, sir, at risk of her own reputation, did she not?"

Paul Johnson showed consternation presently unto the very cusp of shock. He nodded.

"Very good, sir."

Ben turned, and tapping toward the doorway, held his cane betwixt the closing doors, causing them thereby to reopen.

"You look just like him," Mr. Johnson called from behind.

Ben raised his free hand such that it might be seen from behind, and was no sooner on the other side of the doors than these were closed. Turning half-circle around, Ben bowed unto Mr. Johnson, who held up the card upon which he had captured Cynthia Sibbowicz's address. The car thereupon moving onward, Ben began to tap his way in the direction of the flow of the recently disembarked passengers. Progressing forth on complaining legs, he encountered markings reading, "Exit Dey St. & Broadway," but no mention of Fulton Street, or John Street.

Upon weighing through an exit gate, Ben bore left, slowly climbed a set of grimy stairs, and emerged into daylight at a small newsstand incorporated into the side of the near building, to leftward. A panhandler was sitting on the pavement directly ahead, facing toward Ben, his back rested against a low partition betwixt the present stairway and a second, to forward. The man's only effort toward engagement was to shake a plastic cup toward persons emerging from below ground, whilst in simultaneity asking for "loose change." The man's long beard, white in the main, so to say, bore a yellowish stain that seemed to invite analogy to the "ink" of male canines suffering recurrent fits of jealousy over encroachments upon their territory.

Ben paused, laboring for breath, then peered upon eyes pinked and rheumy. "I have little of value to give you, sir," he confessed, "and what I have I must husband toward a purpose I do not yet fully apprehend, knowing to fullness only the destination toward which I must progress. However, if I might sway you toward a more enterprising bent of mind than you presently manifest, I have reason to believe that you might fill your cup well toward overflowing this very day."

The man regarded Ben with a frown well suffused with suspicion.

"Have you means of transport unto a meetinghouse called the Waldorf Astoria, sir?" Ben looked to the plastic cup. "Have you coinage enough for the underground?"

The man scowled. "Them a-holes is tighter 'n bark to a tree."

"Have you experience, sir, concerning the shagbark hickory?"

The man gestured for Ben to remove himself from his line of sight. "If you don't mind."

"I do not." Turning away, Ben tapped his way to the near corner and discovered it marked Broadway / Canyon of Heroes at the crosswise, Dey Street at the parallel. He could discover no mention of John Street, or Fulton Street, nor any marker he might use as compass unto these.

Returning to the newsstand, this showing, as in the case of the Millennium Newsstand on Milk Street, confectionaries in the large, newspapers in the small, Ben inquired of the clerk, a man being in close resemblance to the tawny at the Millennium Newsstand, where he might encounter Fulton Street. The man gestured with his head. "One block."

"And St. Paul's Chapel?"

"On the corner."

"Thank you, sir." Ben turned to leave, and then turned back. "Pray tell, sir, am I the very first traveler to have made this inquiry of you?"

The man grinned and shook his head. "Many, many."

Ben bowed. "Thank you, sir, for supplying a service that might well be expected to be provided by others."

Passing again by the white-bearded panhandler, he showing no recognition, Ben returned to the near corner, and crossing over Dey Street, soon espied the portico of St. Paul's Chapel, the same that had sheltered the pious Tories of New York whilst they disembarked their carriages.

Having not beheld this Georgian extravagance since the spring of 1776, whilst en route to Quebec, whereat he had procured his marten cap, Ben had forgotten the surprisingly reddish coloration of the pillars, they matching the quoins and cornice upon the church proper.

Coming upon Fulton Street, Ben espied a Metro entry upon the farther side to leftward, and beyond this, demarking the church grounds, a grayish wrought-iron fence, and beyond this, upon the grounds themselves, an obelisk much reminding of the one standing to center at the Old Burying Ground in Boston. Forward of the obelisk, toward Broadway, stood two flagpoles, one bearing the national banner, the other bearing the same banner as at St. Bartholomew's.

At the near corner of the grounds, anchoring the fence, stood a large stone monument, taller than the fence. Sitting with his back against the base of this monument, was yet another panhandler, he being oriented such as to take best advantage regarding foot traffic on the near walkways, in particular the walkway leading unto the Metro entry.

Crossing over Fulton Street, Ben gazed upon the panhandler, a Negro man whose eyes were jaundiced and protruding, and whose head was quaking as if of a palsy. "I have little of value to give you, sir," Ben confessed, "and what I have I must husband toward a purpose I do not yet fully apprehend, knowing to fullness only the destination toward which I must progress. However, if I might sway you toward a more enterprising bent of mind than you presently manifest, I have reason to believe that you might fill your cup well toward overflowing this very day."

The man chuckled. "Where I be hearin' that b'fore?"

"'Tis the wise dog, sir, who judges every opportunity upon present merits as against past betrayals." Ben bowed. "A good day to you, sir." Ben continued toward the entrance to the church.

"Hey, man, wuz yer scam? I only got me one good ear."

Ben returned. "And which ear might that be?"

The man pointed to his left ear.

"May I suggest, sir," Ben directed toward the man's left ear, "that not every opportunity to advance one's condition must necessarily be a scam, as you put it." He looked to the man's cup. "Have you sufficient coinage, sir, for transport, by way of the underground, unto the meetinghouse called the Waldorf Astoria?"

"Ha!" The man spat to one side. "Them people's tighter 'n bark to a tree—f'gitaboudit."

"Have you any experience, sir, concerning the shagbark hickory?"

The man smiled, orienting his left ear toward Ben. "Talk t' me."

"Somewhere close upon the corner of Park Avenue and 50th Street, sir, nearby the front entrance to the meetinghouse there, you will discover an overlong livery—what you would call a limousine, I do believe—bearing the numerals 1-7-9 upon a placard affixed to a window. Sometime within the next hour, I calculate, a young lady of about twenty-five years, bearing upon her breast these same numerals, writ small upon a card bearing her name, this being Courtney St. James, will claim the service of this livery, likely in league with an overly groomed man of about fifty years. If you approach this young lady and call her by name, Miss St. James, and explain to her that a portly old gentleman, by the name of Franklin, has suggested that you should test the measure of the lady's charity toward her fellow man, I suspect the lady will well pass the test, to your immediate benefit. Of course, you would thereupon be burdened with making a choice as to how best to leverage this benefit, there accompanying this benefit no chart nor compass."

The man narrowed his eyes. "How do I know this's legit?"

"As in all such cases, sir, you must make an assessment by way of your own wits and vest your trust accordingly." Ben bowed. "A good day to you, sir."

Ben turned away, and then turned back. "Might I make one small request, sir?"

The man showed Ben his left ear.

"Should you choose to engage my suggestion, I ask you to consider placing a coin or two from your cup into the same of the gentleman currently laying claim to the territory proximate to the Dey Street Metro entry. None of us is immune to benefit of a baptismal of humility now and again." Ben bowed, and tapping his way then toward the entrance to the church, took notice of a surprisingly tall steeple at the farther end of the church building, the spire portion of which was unfamiliar to him. In his own time, there had existed only the pedestal portion of the steeple, a four-square structure that strongly resembled the truncated tower on King's Chapel in Boston.

The architecture of the spire portion of the steeple seemed at odds with the generally Georgian theme of the church proper, as if indeed this crowning ornament had been kidnapped from a tribe of Eastern heathens and pressed into service here, all in the good name of frugality.

Passing through an open gate, Ben climbed three modest steps mounting to the portico, and entered into a narrow vestibule, whereat paraphernalia to leftward seemed to hint more toward museum than worship hall, as did also two men in uniform, as did also displays upon easels and pedestals within the church proper.

The nave, to rightward, was made modestly grand by way of barrel vaults, and grandly modest by way of crystalline chandeliers. A celestial sensibility was encouraged by way of a blue-green firmament. The walls, pinkish, were interrupted by floor-to-ceiling windows constituted mostly of clear glass as opposed to stained, the former having been favored, one might speculate, to minimize the initial demand upon capital funds whilst maximizing a continuing hospitality toward natural light.

The floor immediately underfoot was similar in pattern to that of the hallway outside the Grand Ballroom at the Waldorf Astoria, it being composed of checkerboard squares, dark alternating with light.

There were perhaps a dozen persons in residence, most of whom were presently attentive toward the exhibits arranged beneath a gallery circumventing the nave upon two sides and one end. Only two people were sitting in the brown-and-ivory pews—a woman, middle age, at the near side; another woman, also middle age, at the farther side. A man, older than the women, was kneeling at a bank of flickering votives close upon the chancery.

Ben made his way now to the rear of the nave, whereat a central aisle led rearward unto a vestibule, a burying ground beyond, and in the other direction unto the altar and chancery. Looking to the altar, Ben was surprised to discover a sculpture at center to resemble a golden idol, as in the case of his first impression regarding the clock sculpture at the Waldorf Astoria. The present sculpture, being of ivory and gold, was fashioned such as to suggest an Egyptian sun god straddling an ebony throne constituted of the twin tablets of Moses. The idol's countenance, a burst of gold surrounded by a nimbus of ivory, was suggesting of a daisy bloom.

The man kneeling at the votive bank seemed as if in supplication to the idol, he being knelt but a few paces from it, outside a low balustrade running the width of the chancery.

As Ben tapped his way up the aisle, he noticed, toward the leftward side of the chancery, an elevated pulpit, ivory and gilt, overtopped by a robust coronet, also ivory and gilt. The pulpit box was hexagonal and upon its frontmost panel a radiant sunburst was consonant with the countenance of the idol. Steps leftward of the pulpit gave access.

Looking to the rightward side of the chancery, Ben espied, affixed upon the wall there, three memorials—the two nearer being elongated; the one farther, being squarish. He shuddered although no chill could be at cause.

Tapping his way now past the votive bank, and the abject supplicant there, Ben let himself through a gate in the low balustrade, and bowing to the idol, made his way to the memorials to rightward. Upon close approach, he affixed his eyes upon a name included in a lengthy inscription upon the middle memorial: ELIZABETH FRANKLIN.

His throat aching as of an upwelling of bile, Ben made attempt to swallow away the discomfort, but to no avail.

The memorial was of three parts: A squarish tablet holding the lengthy inscription; a marble urn centered upon a mantel overtopping the tablet; and an ebony backplane to the whole, in the form of an obelisk. The third article, the backplane, seemed in the moment a diminutive of a much larger obelisk, indeed the very one that stood at center of the Old Burying Ground in Boston. In fact, the present article, in opposing the other in both coloration and stature, seemed to anticipate not only this very moment, but also these very eyes, the only such that might discern a private inscription as if writ in the shadow of the public such, to wit: By *a cast of shadow, a daughter is included wherein she ought to have been by loving embrace.* From *a cast of shadow, a son is liberated to whence he ought to have been by loving grace.*

Ben held his eyes closed, and then read the public inscription aloud, in a whisper:

Beneath the Altar of this Church are deposited the Remains of
MRS. ELIZABETH FRANKLIN, Wife of his Excellency WILLIAM FRANKLIN Esq.
late Governor under His Britannick Majesty, of the Province of New-Jersey
Compelled, by the adverse Circumstances of the Times to
part from the Husband she loved, and at length deprived
of the soothing Hope of his speedy Return,
She sunk under accumulated Distresses, and departed this
Life on the 28th Day of July 1778, in the 49th Year of her Age.
SINCERITY and SENSIBILITY
POLITENESS and AFFABILITY
GODLINESS and CHARITY
Were, with Sense refined and Person elegant, in her UNITED!
From a grateful Remembrance of her affectionate Tenderness,
and constant Performance of all the Duties of a GOOD WIFE,
this Monument is erected in the Year 1787,
By Him who knew her Worth, and still laments her Loss.

In the 49th Year of her Age.
She sunk under accumulated Distresses.
By Him who knew her Worth.

Sinking unto his knees, Ben bowed his head. "I'm so sorry," he whispered. "So very sorry."

"I'm sorry, sir, but no one is allowed up here."

Ben startled, and rising to his feet with all the celerity he could manage, turned to discover a young woman smiling upon him. "Not even Benjamin Franklin," she added.

"O, my apologies, ma'm." Ben bowed. "I should have thought to make inquiry. How easy it is to become absorbed in one's own travails."

The woman's face took on an aspect of concern. "Are you all right?"

"As well as to be expected, I should think—thank you."

Following the young woman to the gate, Ben preceded her through it.

"Nice costume," the young woman said, smiling, closing the gate.

"Thank you," Ben replied, with a small bow. "'Tis my best, although missing its crown, which I hope yet to retrieve, its current host also."

"Was there something in particular you were looking for up here?"

"There was indeed, but I have managed to discover it, absent the assistance for which I should have thought to make inquiry." Ben bowed.

The woman smiled, and then, taking her leave, proceeded up the aisle.

Tapping his way past the votive bank, Ben noticed that the gentleman who had been in supplication there had removed himself to one of the pews, to leftward, whereat his distress seemed only to have compounded.

Ben paused.

The man was slumped well to forward, his arms tightly clutched across his chest. Although he was likely past his seventy-fifth year, there was yet hint of russet unto hair otherwise gray, in particular at the lower extremity of this, whereat it was yet prosperous. He was wearing a suitcoat, dark blue, that suggested, by way of wear and soiling, that it had no partner with which to alternate. His breeches did not match the coloration of his coat.

"Might I join you, sir?" Ben said, his voice hushed.

The man showing no response, Ben invited himself into the pew, propping his cane thereupon against the seat front, betwixt himself and the gentleman.

"I do not wish to intrude upon your privacy, sir, nor to add to your travails, but might I inquire as to the cause of your distress, which would appear to be considerable?"

The man made no response.

Ben looked toward the golden idol to front. "I am myself here," he continued, "of an agony of regret. I very poorly treated a daughter-in-law who deserved naught less from me than my fullest compassion; likewise a son, her husband, who deserved naught less from me than my fullest understanding. And although I come here this day to offer apology, the remains of my daughter-in-law being interred here, I find the act wholly unsatisfactory, as in the case of loading a table with the finest fare but having no company with whom to enjoy it."

The man stirred, and slowly lifting his head, turned to Ben, wafting into Ben's direction thereby an odor reminding of moldering cheese. The man's face, pink as a sow's, bore a nose bloated and veined, and a chin bristling of stubble. Strikingly, the man's eyes, though rimmed of inflammation, held as if in timeless purity the coloration of sapphires.

The man's lower jaw trembled as he attempted to speak. "My boy's dead," he managed, beginning thereupon to weep.

Ben held his eyes closed a moment. "I'm so very sorry," he whispered.

The man shook his head whilst yet he wept.

Contorting himself now to clockwise, Ben rested a hand upon the man's back, betwixt the shoulders, and felt a most pathetic quaking. When the man had exhausted himself, Ben removed his hand. "Might I inquire, sir, as to cause?"

The man yet held his head bowed, and then, upon clearing his throat, transferred unto one hand a string of mucous festooning from his chin. He wiped his hand upon his breeches, and then his nose upon a sleeve of his soiled coat. "Somebody shot him," he managed, his voice so weak and tremulous as to be near inaudible. "Why?" He shook his head. "Why?"

Ben beheld within his mind's eye a kindly face, bearded of russet and gray, bearing eyes resembling sapphires of purest quality. He shivered. "Perchance, sir, did this tragedy occur at Boston, in a schoolhouse there?"

The man nodded. "I don't know what he was doing there," he mumbled, shaking his head. "I don't understand." Hunching to forward, his arms again clutched across his chest, the man appeared desperate to forestall a violent rupture of what pulsed within.

Ben held his eyes closed for a moment. "Were you perchance estranged from your son, sir, such that the details of his life were not regularly communicated to you?"

Mr. Ditweiller held himself to silence, and then nodded.

"As was I, sir, from my own son, this condition being indeed the source of my own unhappiness. And the fault, of course, owed entirely to myself. I thoroughly encouraged my son to become a loyal servant to the crown, and then thoroughly condemned him when he became exactly that. And because his dear wife was of a piece with what my son had become—of what I had encouraged him to become—I condemned her also. I allowed a foolish pride to darken my heart, and a childish compulsion toward revenge to taint my soul. And the reward, sir, has been a seat upon a pyre of eternal regret." Ben wept, bowing his head.

After a moment, he felt a touch upon his back, betwixt his shoulders.

"I'm sorry," Mr. Ditweiller said.

Ben nodded. "As am I, sir, as regards your own misery."

"You wouldn't, though," Mr. Ditweiller said, his voice halting, "if you knew what kind of person you were sitting next to."

"Put me to the test, sir."

Mr. Ditweiller held silent a moment, and then began his story, haltingly at first, then more evenly, as in the case of a siphon, once primed, flowing of its own accord.

"In another lifetime," Mr. Ditweiller confessed, he had been a stockbroker at Bache & Company on Broad Street, just a few blocks from where they now sat. He had interned there, he explained, over the two summers preceding his graduation from NYU with a degree in finance, summa cum laude, and was invited to join the firm as a trainee even before he had received his diploma. Over the twelve years he was licensed as a broker there—"or financial advisor, as they call them now"—he did very well, rapidly advancing his income into "six figures." He did not do well enough, however, he confessed, to satisfy an unfortunate appetite for wagering. As his debts in this regard mounted, mostly from betting on sporting events, so did the threats against his person, these issuing from his "creditors." One night, on his way home, he was accosted by two men who beat him severely with batons, permanently damaging the hearing in one ear. (He pointed to his right ear.) The very next day, he said, he began to "borrow" funds from some of his clients, the older ones, especially the widows. Of course, nothing was settled by this measure, because the gambling continued, as did the losses, as did the borrowings.

On many an occasion during this troubled time, he promised himself that if he made just one big score, just one, he would quit gambling forever. He would not wager a single dime ever again. Not one, not ever. Of course, the big score never came. What did come, of course, was the inevitable audit, followed by the inevitable arrest.

Unable thereafter to find aught but menial work—he was currently janitor-dishwasher at the same sports bar he had long patronized—he took to drink, substituting thereby one addiction for another. Spiraling into despair, he become increasingly belligerent toward his family, his son in particular. One day, in a fit of rage, in attempting to kick his son in the "rear end," he caught him on the wrist instead and badly fractured it. The following day, while anesthetizing himself at his "watering hole," his wife escaped to Saginaw, Michigan with their two children, Saginaw being where she had grown up.

Jenny, his wife, had subsequently passed away of cancer, but their daughter, Mary, still lived in Saginaw, judging anyway from the post-mark on the Christmas card she sent every year to Joey's Sports Bar, with no return address. It was through his daughter, in fact, that he had learned of his son living in the Boston area, then of the death of his son's wife, and now, as of little more than two hours ago, of his son's death. Mary had left word—at Joey's.

Mr. Ditweiller wept so violently now as to capture the attention of persons in the aisle to rightward. The woman Ben had met earlier approached and asked if everything was all right.

"The man has lost a son," Ben explained.

The woman's eyes filled. "Oh, I'm so sorry." She looked toward the aggrieved father. "Please let us know if there is anything we can do, sir; anything at all."

Ben nodded, surmising the woman a parent herself, sympathy coming most readily to those made vulnerable by similar circumstance.

Mr. Ditweiller held quiet for a moment, then transferred yet more mucous from his chin to his breeches by convenience of hand.

"How is it," Ben asked, "if I may inquire, that you have come to this church, at this particular time?"

Mr. Ditweiller cleared his throat. "This is where I made all those promises—one big score and I was done." Lifting his eyes now, Mr. Ditweiller looked to front, toward the sun god. "I'd pop over here sometimes after market close." He chortled. "Never on a down day, though. Even so, I never made the one promise I needed to make—to quit altogether, no quid pro quo, no big score." He shook his head. "I just didn't have it in me. I was too weak." His voice faltered. "Always was." He shook his head and began again to weep.

"Weakness, sir, if I may sermonize for a moment, is not an absence of strength, but simply its usurper. 'Tis a choice that we allow of a certain species of passivity, for whatever reason. What measure of strength we require we always have within us, as a hibernating bear always has within her a beating heart. We choose to continue in slumber, or we choose to awaken."

Ben pulled a small card from pocket, the one given him by Paul A. Johnson / Chief Executive Officer / Harris Upshaw & Co. "By the bye, sir," Ben continued, "I am well familiar with the name Bache, as 'twas the family name of my son-in-law, Richard, given by him unto my daughter, Sarah, called Sally, whose fair self, I must confess, I treated with far less respect than she deserved." He paused. "The name Bache is of Scottish origin, as you may know."

Mr. Ditweiller, clearing his throat, shook his head.

"I mention this more to myself than to you, as my 'previous life' was well represented in Scotsmen, for reasons of chance likely, but perhaps of something else." Ben offered Mr. Johnson's card toward the man. "Take this card, sir, if you would, and seek out the one declared upon it. Tell him that a portly old gentleman riding the underground in his company recommended you to him. Tell him all you have told me, and ask him to show you to his mop, that you might bring a renewal to the floor upon which you both in that moment commonly stand."

At first hesitant, the man took the card into a tremulous possession.

Ben patted the man upon his knee, it skeletal to the touch. "Regret has the greatest of company, sir. Find others bearing your species of torment and strip naked your soul to them, that they might be encouraged to do the same." Ben took up his cane, and rising to his feet, added, "Thank you for listening to my confession, sir. I feel much relieved."

Mr. Ditweiller met Ben's eyes and made attempt toward a smile but could not complete it.

"Good luck to you," Ben added.

The man appearing as might an orphan suffering yet another abandonment, Ben bowed and began to tap his way down the aisle. After a few steps, he turned back. "Mister Ditweiller?"

The man turned swiftly half-circle and regarded Ben with eyes so much expanded as to suggest a sudden increase of cranial pressure.

"Never mind how, sir. 'Tis of no concern. As regards promises, sir, you might wish to view those also as no better than usurpers. Action, sir! Action is the thing! To *vow* action is veritably to invite failure; to *take* action, veritably to forestall failure. Indeed, what action earnestly directed can be deemed a failure in itself, sir, or the cause of such? Action, sir!" Ben lifted his cane. "The card, sir! Follow the card! Though the hour is late, yet still there is time!"

Ben continued to tap his way down the aisle. "Action!" he exclaimed, "is its own promise!"

Having drawn the attention of two uniformed men standing at the entry to the vestibule, Ben smiled unto one of these, and unto the other. "I apologize for my bayings," he said, bowing to the latter, looking then to the former. "I allow myself sometimes a bit too much excitement of the spirit." He bowed. "Might I inquire if there is someone upon premises who might direct me to the last resting place of the first printer of this realm, he being one William Bradford, formerly of Pearl Street, and a communicant, I believe, of Trinity Church?"

The uniformed man to leftward, the shorter of the two, tawny in complexion, spoke in reply whilst gesturing one hand to leftward, but Ben was unable to parse the meaning, for the thickness of the accent.

The other man offered interpretation. "Trinity's four blocks down," he said.

"And do you know if the gentleman, Mr. Bradford, is buried there?"

The taller man shrugged, the shorter man having become distracted by another inquirer. "Just a sec," the taller man said, disappearing then into the vestibule. After a moment, the man returned in company with the same young woman Ben had encountered on two previous occasions, she smiling now upon occasion of their third encounter.

Ben bowed, and repeated then his inquiry.

"Oh, yes," the woman exclaimed in a whisper. "I'll show you." The woman led Ben into a small office off the vestibule and sat down at a desk, afront a viewing device holding as if a broadside. On the same desk, to rightward, a picture held in a silver frame showed the young woman in company with a man of her age, wholesome in appearance, and two children, a lad and a lass, the former resembling the woman in fundamental aspects of feature.

The woman made a click with a small device held in hand, and another, and in the instant a colorated broadside appeared showing likeness of a burying ground marked "Trinity Churchyard / Explore Three Centuries / of New York History." Yet another click brought forth a brief list of names, the first being "Hamilton, Alexander;" the second, "Bradford, William." The woman clicked yet again and the broadside changed to show two maps in company with a small likeness of, presumably, the same burying ground. One of the maps, marked "Section N6," appeared to be a fuller rendition of a green-tinted portion of the smaller map.

The woman thereupon pointed a slender finger toward a small red circle near the bottom of the larger map. "That's it," she said, and peering up at Ben then, pointed to rightward. "Go down Broadway about four blocks, maybe five, they're short, and you'll see Trinity on your right. Follow the nearer side of the church to a gate, which should be open."

The woman thereupon pointed toward the smaller map on the screen. "You'll see Bradford's gravesite right there, just inside the gate." She smiled. "May I ask why the costume?"

Ben smiled. "An old habit, so to say."

"You look just like him."

Ben looked to the picture resting upon the woman's desk. "And your son, madam, just like you. He has your eyes—gentle and kind."

The woman brightened. "Thank you."

"And thank you, madam, for your gracious assistance." Bowing then, Ben took his leave, and tapping his way into the church proper, discovered Mr. Ditweiller to be disappeared from his pew. Smiling, he tapped his way to the portico, and descending the three steps unto the walkway, bore rightward and tapped his way to the near corner.

Discovering the Negro panhandler to be disappeared from his post, Ben smiled anew, taking note thereupon that the Metro entry was marked by, amongst a host of colorated balls, two that were blue, the first bearing the letter A, the second, the letter C. Trains bearing either of these markers would, he surmised, return him unto Penn Station, he having witnessed there, when yet in the company of TJ, the same markers.

Ah, TJ, how do you fare? Ben smiled. *If yet in your own hands—well I trust!*

Soon arriving at Dey Street, Ben espied, the white-bearded panhandler yet sitting betwixt the juxtaposed stairwells, yet holding forth his cup. He smiled near unto a grin now imagining the encounter he had contrived betwixt this obdurant mendicant and the one not.

⁓⁓

Tapping onward, Ben was soon gazing upon a Gothic-reminding structure of dark, reddish-brown stones and sleek, serrated spires. The Trinity Church of his own time had been far more modest a structure, he recalled, indeed, but a simple rectangle of fieldstone overtopped by a gambrel roof. It had been largely destroyed in the great conflagration of 1776, he recalled, and rightly so, all the clergy there, to a man, having sided with the Crown!

Walking aside a fence wrought of iron spikes, Ben noticed that although the church and its grounds were surrounded by buildings taller even than those bordering the Old Burying Ground at Boston, the church itself did not seem at all diminished by these towering structures. In fact, if anything, the reverse seemed to be the case.

Ben followed the iron fence to the near side of the church, and this then unto an open gate leading into a burying ground. The memorials here, mostly slabs of stone squared at bottom, arched at top, were reminding of those in the Boston burying ground, but were, on the whole, more substantial, this reflecting perhaps a greater degree of means, or a lesser degree of modesty, or—the local census being far more weighted toward Anglican than Puritan—both!

Bradford's monument, a squarish slab of gray-white stone, bearing atop near upon a half circle such as to create shoulders to side, stood as the map showing upon the woman's viewing device had indicated, being just inside the gate and the rightwardmost of three memorials close upon a pathway leading unto a great obelisk. Although relatively modest in stature, Bradford's memorial was the largest within the immediate area. A small tree to front of the middle memorial lent a degree of shade unto all three. A diminutive American flag, attached to a round stick bearing also a five-pointed star, stood at the leftward end of the pedestal supporting the memorial.

The flag and the star, Ben surmised, were in honor of William Bradford, Patriot. Indeed, unlike the clergy of his chosen church, William Bradford had been steadfastly loyal to the land he had adopted and that had allowed him, as its first printer and newspaper publisher, to earn a handsome livelihood.

Moving closer, stooping a little, Ben read the words graven upon the face of the memorial, these being somewhat attenuated in legibility by way of a greenish patina:

> Here lies the Body of Mister William Bradford
> Printer, who departed this Life May 23
> 1752, aged 92 Years. He was born in
> Leicestershire, in Old England, in 1660:
> and came over to America in 1682, before
> the City of Philadelphia was laid out: He
> was Printer to this Government for upwards
> of 50 years and being quite worn out
> with old age and labour he left this
> mortal State in the lively Hopes of a
> blessed Immortality.

Thereupon sinking unto his knees, Ben addressed the monument, whispering aloud: "Whilst yet you lived, good sir, I failed to honor you, even to respect you, as you so well deserved. Indeed, I sent into this city, in my stead, one David Hall, to enter into a competition against you, to the end of forcing upon you an ignominious retirement. I placed opportunity before justice, profit before gratitude, self-interest before rectitude. And for these transgressions, sir—against you in the specific, against common decency in the large—I deeply apologize. But for the succor you allowed the seed of it, sir, one particular oak could not have rooted as it did, whereat it did, to the height it did. We are all the cause of many an effect, but also the effect of many a cause. Little is the credit, hence, that any one man might allow unto himself as owing entirely of himself."

Bowing his head to forward, Ben wept, his body quaking, but then stilled himself to a voice, feminine, as if from behind: *What forgiveness in the seeking of it is not ever the gaining of it?* Turning his head over one shoulder as far as he might, and then the other, Ben could discover no one within proximity. Arising then, with no little difficulty, he turned half-circle around. No one was to be discovered anywhere near.

Suffering now a fit of vertigo, Ben held fast to the small tree a moment, and then, bowing unto Bradford's memorial, tapped his way from the burying ground, and turning to leftward, retraced his steps unto Fulton Street. Crossing this, he entered into the Metro stairwell to leftward, this being littered of refuse and wanting of care, and found his way, guided by the blue circles bearing A and C, unto the leftward side of a platform marked, albeit not at all conspicuously, "Uptown."

Several people were standing upon the platform, dispersed to either side with decreasing density. One of this company, a girl of perhaps nine or ten years, standing a few paces to rightward, was presently paying Ben particular attention. Upon a smile and a nod from Ben, the girl approached and looked up at Ben with eyes held wide as much of a latent innocence, one might presume, as a curious wonderment. "Are you Benjamin Franklin?"

Ben smiled. "I am indeed."

Upon the girl holding out her hand, a woman close upon issued a stern command. "Jennifer, get over here!"

Ben grasped the girl's hand and squeezed it, sufficient to leave an imprint of a sort. "Pleased to meet you, Jennifer."

"Jennifer!"

Upon the girl retreating, a great rumbling sound, building rapidly unto fortissimo, soon produced a train bearing the letter A within a blue circle, in proximity to a marker reading, "8 Av Exp." Whilst wait-ing thereupon for passengers to emerge through a doorway to leftward, Ben noticed Jennifer, and presumably her mother, moving toward a doorway to rightward. The girl looking his way, Ben bowed, and then watched the girl disappear through the doorway whilst yet waving toward him the hand not held by her mother.

Thereupon entering the car to leftward, Ben sat down on the first seat to leftward, and had no sooner taken a deep breath, and expelled this, than the train lurched into motion.

Although several seats remained unoccupied, at either side of the car, a wantonly-thin woman, wearing a bright-blue coat reaching unto her ankles, remained standing betwixt the opposing doorways, holding onto a pole. Her face, like that of a Roman sculpture, bore an expression of such alabaster neutrality as to reveal naught of either the substrate or the surface of the figure.

The car was twice the length of any previous car Ben had occupied; was colorated of hues previously unencountered—orange in seat, tan in else—and was absent any marquee device, overhead or elsewhere, toward announcing the next stop.

In keeping with the general architecture encountered above ground, the general architecture below ground would seem also to be a hodge-podge of whimsy and taste.

An older Negro woman, sitting across the aisle, was slumbering with her chin in her hand, her head being tilted to side such as to rest against the window. There were several other somnolents in residence, totaling perhaps to five.

By cry of what watchman, Ben now wondered, would these passengers know when to awaken, such as not to miss their stop? Indeed, might it be that human kind were subject to entering into spontaneous cooperatives, absent either signal or discussion, such that at least one 'goose' was always standing vigil?

Looking the length of the car now, Ben could not help but notice that his complexion of "milk and rose" was well into the minority.

He was sitting in his reading chair, his writing desk easy upon his lap, surrounded by shelf upon shelf of books, unto the very ceiling.

To a light tapping upon the door, he called forth, "One minute, kindly," and proceeded to capture the thought yet held in mind—"your persons, fortunes, wives, and daughters shall be subject to the wanton and unbridled rage, rapine, and lust of *Negroes, Molattoes*, and others, the vilest and most abandoned of mankind."

He nodded of satisfaction, and then called forth, "Enter!"

The door opening, albeit slowly, Peter stepped inward a sufficient extent to open the door to fullness, but no greater. He was yet wearing his smithy's apron, smeared of blood, he having spent the day in the shed of Jeremiah Perkins, to whom he had been lent for the day, as butcher. Peter's brow glistened of perspiration. He bowed. "Sorrah t' dahstub y', sah, but mistress say ah sho'd come up heah an' not be wahst'n ah singah min't."

Ben smiled "I have a surprise for you."

"Yessah."

"I'm sending you home."

Peter's eyes swelled as if to specter of Armageddon itself. "Home, sah? T' Charst'n, sah?"

Ben shook his head. "*Home*. I'm sending you *home*, Peter. To Africa!"

"O lordy, sah! *Dis* m' home! *Dis* m' home!"

Ben shook his head. "I fear you fail to apprehend my meaning. I'm emancipating you, Peter. I'm making you a free man!"

"Dis m' home, sah! Dis m' home!"

"Consider your scripture, Peter! Should what is wrongly carried off remain with the thief, or should it be returned to whence it was taken?"

"O lordy!" Tears now. "Dis m' home, sah! Ah beg o' you! Dis m' home!"

"A bluebird is a bluebird, a blackbird a blackbird, not so?"

Peter sank unto his knees. "Please, sah! Ah beg o' you!"

"'Tis all for the best, I ascertain, for all concerned."

"O lordy! 'av mercah, sah! Ah beg o' you! Dis m' home! Dis m' home, sah!"

"*Africa* is your home."

Peter slumped, weeping, straightened himself, and drawing his butcher's knife from the scabbard belted to his waist, held the handle by way of both hands, and plunged the blade into his breast.

"And blood, sah," he whispered, "be blood—"

◦───

Startled by a disembodied voice, distinctively Negroid in timbre, Ben opened his eyes to discover the train slowing aside a platform lined of people, and looked to the wantonly-thin woman yet standing at the pole betwixt the opposing doorways. "May I inquire, madam, as to this stop?"

"Penn Station," she replied, showing nary a hint of an abiding humanity.

The train stopping, the doors to leftward slid open and Ben, launching forth from his seat, tapped his way to the doorway as briskly as he might, and onto the platform. Feeling of a sudden a disquieting lightness of being, and beginning to falter in knee, he managed only just to get himself to a bench at the near wall before becoming too infirm of knee to remain upstanding. Thereupon bowing his head well to forward, he remained in this posture, taking measured breaths, until of a sudden visited by the specter of Peter, impaled of his butcher's knife, slumping forward of gravity's inexorable pull, his knife thereby piercing through to his backside. Shuddering then as if to a violent chill, Ben launched forth from the bench and soon thereafter came upon an overhead marker reading:

   ↓ Exit 34 Street & 8 Avenue
      Penn Station, Madison Square Garden / C E Local

Finding some comfort in this compass, Ben tapped his way to a set of stairs, down these, and thereupon forward to another marker, this one bearing "↓ Exit 34 St & 8 Av C E."

The substance on this marker being sufficiently consonant with the one previous, Ben hitched his wagon onto it, and climbed a set of stairs, bore to rightward, climbed another set of stairs, bore to rightward, pushed though a gate, bore to rightward, climbed a set of stairs, and emerged into daylight soon proving to be as good as darkness, there being naught of familiarity or promise upon which to affix his eyes.

Indeed, whereas he had well expected to emerge into the station house, he was emerged instead into a hellish assault of rude noise and wind-driven grit.

O, TJ, where art thou when thy comfort and thy knowledge are so desperately required?

Ah—yet they are present!

Reaching to pocket, Ben felt the bulk of TJ's communication device, and also the flat of TJ's map. Pulling the latter article from pocket, Ben tapped to the near corner and by way of the markers there determined the street to leftward to be 34th Street, and that to front to be 8th Avenue. Holding his cane then betwixt upper arm and side, Ben made attempt to orient the map in consonance with the geometry of the intersection, but discovered there to be no ready reference by which to match compass to territory, the sun being wholly obstructed.

His cane of a sudden slipping from place, Ben attempted to regain possession before it might escape him, but in so doing loosened his grip upon TJ's map, which, snatched from him as if by Aeolian hand, was thrust aloft. Thereupon floating out over 8th Avenue, the map was sported with by various vehicles passing underneath, and was delivered a coup de grace, not easy to witness, by a large, fume-belching livery in the shape of a caterpillar.

No sooner had Ben slumped as if to a load of lead upon his soul than he felt as if a feather touch upon one shoulder. Turning half-circle around, he discovered peering kindly upon him the alabaster statue from the train. "Lose something?"

Ben smiled. "My guide left me means by which to conduct my own navigation, but, alas, it has been snatched away from me. I had preferred he had left himself instead, he being more withstanding to tricksters, and far better company."

"Where ya headed?"

"Pennsylvania Station."

The woman pointed her eyes across 34th Street. "One block down. You can't miss it."

Ben aligned his eyes with the woman's, and then bowed toward her. "Most kind of you."

"Not a problem. You look just like him."

"Thank you. I do my best."

The woman smiled, and was about to take her leave when a gust of wind, well salted of grit, caused her to raise a hand whilst bowing her head. She turning then to leeward, the whole of her hair flew from her head, as if snatched by the same hand that had recently robbed Ben of his map. The hairpiece thereupon landed upon the walkway like a shot bird, a few paces to leeward.

Three quick steps and a deft flip of his cane and Ben held in hand the woman's hair piece. A moment hence, he had returned it unto its owner.

"Thank you," the woman said, showing naught of the chagrin that might be expected to attend so public a humiliation. The woman restored her wig unto its perch. "Chemo."

"Chemo?"

"I have cancer."

"O I'm so very sorry." Ben regarded to discreet measure the woman's obvious frailty. "You were standing when you might have sat."

"And you were sitting when you might have stood."

"I am an old man."

"I'm a dying woman."

Ben nodded. "I take your point."

The woman smiled.

Ben bowed. "I thank you again, madam, for your kind assistance. I wish you—indeed what should I wish for you?"

"Less wind, more gentlemen."

Ben chuckled. "The two would seem to come in the same box, such that I might need make but one wish unto you!"

The woman grinned. "So they would."

Taking her leave then, the woman walked up 8th Avenue.

Ben looked after her a moment and then, turning half-circle around, tapped his way across 34th Street, and southward along 8th Avenue. At the succeeding intersection, he espied upon the farther side of 33rd Street a glass-walled edifice, rounded at the near corner, of promising aspect. Upon crossing over the street, Ben discovered a Metro stairwell, to leftward, marked with the letters C and E, as well as A.

How was it he had not, despite following like markers bearing C and E, emerged from *this* stairwell instead of the one from which he had in fact emerged, Ben could not in the moment explain to himself, nor imagine.

Indeed, when the compass maker takes ill care, what is to be the fate of the wayfarer?

A standard marked "Taxi" stood at the curb to rightward, whilst beyond, alongside the curb, a queue of yellow carriages extended downstreet. A second queue, constituted of people bearing or drawing various articles of luggage, stood in rough parallel upon the walkway. A sergeant-at-arms equipped with no greater than a whistle was exercising a fierce despotism over both queues, toward, it would appear, a mutual accommodation betwixt.

To leftward, past the MTA stairwell, a plaza fronted an entryway of many doors, it being overtopped by a large portico bearing, in gold letters, PENNSYLVANIA STATION.

Steering a course toward the many-door entryway, Ben soon came upon a green barrel being attended by a Negro man shabbily dressed. A squarish bag bearing two thin loops atop was reposed at the man's feet. As Ben passed amidships, the man pulled a metallic container from the barrel and dropped it into the squarish bag, indeed with nary a glance toward ensuring a proper aim.

In obedience to some principle of relative opportunity, it seemed, several pigeons were as attendant upon the squarish bag as the man was upon the roundish barrel.

Another Negro man, his back being rested against a pillar supporting the portico, was attendant upon a pushcart wrought of a metallic mesh the color of quicksilver. The cart was well filled with various containers so expertly fitted together, in the manner indeed of puzzle pieces, as to render not a cubic inch wasted. A small dowel, elevated from a rearward corner of the basket, bore a greenish bag containing what appeared to be salvaged leavings similar to those the Negro man was at present mining from the green barrel.

Meeting the eyes of the cart's attendant, these being as if so contaminated of soot as to show no light, Ben bowed and noticed two other Negro men, standing within a shallow recession a few yards to rightward of the pushcart, whereat three glass doors, obviously not in use, stood in a row. A large metallic cylinder standing afront these doors, rising perhaps to 15 feet, and supporting naught but itself, bore the marking, MADISON / SQUARE / GARDEN.

On the farther side of the cylinder, Ben noticed, several more doors, at least six in number, were arranged at a bias to the nearer set, and being also recessed, also offered some measure of shelter. Spanning the two sets, well overtop, a large advertisement seemed calculated to draw one's eye, like a moth, unto a candle flame marked "Levitra."

Looking again to the two men in the nearer recession, Ben surmised the reason they were favoring this one over the one more commodious was the greater anonymity afforded the smaller recession by way of the fifteen-foot cylinder standing directly afront it.

Noticing now as if a shadow or menace darken upon the countenance of the cart attendant, Ben proceeded briskly to the station entryway, and pulling his way through one of the several glass doors, slowly descended a long flight of steps, keeping well to rightward such that he not encumber overtakers being as if nipped at the heels by jackals.

Nearing the bottom of the steps, Ben noticed to leftward a flower cart marked "The Petal Pusher" at top and holding bouquets of a handful of species. All but two of the bouquets were standing in dark-green buckets to which were affixed conspicuous pricings. The two exceptions, gatherings not of flowers but of inflated bladders, were floating above the flower bouquets, and were being held from farther ascendance by string tethers pretending at being stems.

Following the flow of traffic to rightward, Ben entered into a great room dominated at center by a large marquee marked "Departures." The ceiling from which this marquee was suspended was relatively low, and of unremarkable aspect. The marquee itself, if not remarkable, was at least commanding, as evidenced by a goodly portion of the people presently standing on the near side of it, numbering perhaps to four score, gazing upon it.

A Negro man close upon to rightward was foraging within a metallic barrel, and was holding a bag similar to the one serving as a repository for the findings of the forager encountered above.

No pigeons, however, were here attendant.

Ben tapped his way toward the Departures marquee that he might examine the intelligence thereon. As he neared his range of discernment, a disembodied voice, female, announced the delay of the Washington Express, amounting to forty-five minutes.

The voice was monochromatic—indeed a medium gray.

Another voice, immediately following, was anything but—

> *If I had a hammer*
> *I'd hammer in the morning*
> *I'd hammer in the evening*
> *All over this land...*

Turning half-circle around, Ben espied a woman, more an apparition than an embodiment, it seemed, standing betwixt a modest marker reading, "Women," and a like marker reading, "Men."

> *I'd hammer out danger*
> *I'd hammer out a warning*
> *I'd hammer out love between my brothers and my sisters*
> *All over this land...*

Ben recalled to memory now a verse, near an echo, from Sergeant Kortright's recent lament—

"Every night, the same ol' song, over and over—if I had a hammer, if I had a hammer, if I had a hammer. My mother getting banged in one room, my sister yodelin' in the other. I never heard from 'er again, thank the good Lord."

Many of those persons recently looking to the marquee were now, Ben noticed, looking toward this singular nightingale—blue of breast, owing to a too-large sweater of this coloration; white in the majority, owing to a skirt fringed of ruffles; black of feet, owing to shoes overly large in relation to her stature; and crimson of cheek, owing to roundish smears of rouge only recently applied, it would appear, given their intensity.

As if frosting upon cake, Alice was wearing not one but two flaxen pigtails, one at each ear, bound by bright-green ribbons. In one hand, she bore a carpetbag imprinted of a riotous pattern.

> *If I had a bell*
> *I'd ring it in the morning*
> *I'd ring it in the evening*
> *All over this land . . .*

As Alice continued her song, there seemed to develop of it a sort of magnetism, to effect of drawing yet closer upon her those dozens of individuals bearing witness to her recital, to ultimate effect then of transforming an archipelago of islets into a single continent.

> *I'd ring out danger*
> *I'd ring out a warning*
> *I'd ring out love between my brothers and my sisters*
> *All over this land . . .*

Approached now by two men in dark-blue ensembles, each bearing a baton at one side, a pistol at the other, Alice responded by adding a measure of urgency to her tempo, as if indeed the guillotine awaited:

> *If I had a song*
> *I'd sing it in the morning*
> *I'd sing it in the evening*
> *All over this land*
>
> *I'd sing out danger*
> *I'd sing out a warning*
> *I'd sing out love between my brothers and my sisters*
> *All over this land . . .*

Upon being seized by the officers, one at either arm, Alice began a lively protest: "No! Don't make me! No! No! Don't make me!" Throwing back her head, she screamed most pathetically. "Stop! You're hurting me! You're hurting me! Make 'im stop! Make 'im stop! Robbie! Robbie! Where are you? Where? Where?" Of a sudden slumping, as if upon escape of one last mote of hope, Alice wept most profusely.

Launching forth now toward the tumultuous scene, Ben called ahead whilst tapping out ringing punctuations: "Excuse me! Excuse me! One moment, please, one moment!"

Upon reaching Alice and her captors, Ben continued his bold

intervention: "If you gentlemen would forbear for one moment, please, one moment, kindly, I will attempt to bring a more peaceable end unto this unhappy affair."

The taller officer showing presently a starchiness of eye not likely to be softened, Ben looked to the shorter officer: "Sir?"

The officer took notice of Ben's manner of dress. "You with Public Affairs?"

"I am as I appear, sir, and no else."

"She knows the rules."

"There is knowing, sir, and there is *knowing*. Bear with me, kindly."

The officer looked to Alice, she whimpering at the moment, and then to his watch. "One minute."

"Thank you, sir." Ben laid a hand upon Alice's shoulder. "'Tis intermission, Madam Diva. Rest here, if you would be so kind, and I will return with alacrity."

Thereupon hurrying to the Petal Pusher cart, Ben made a quick inventory of his funds—one Lincoln, one Jefferson—and thereupon purchased, by way of the whole of his treasury—a tax of fifty-two cents being forgiven—a bouquet of seven blooms, the lot of these being in likeness to daisy flowers colorated pink, lavender, or red, as opposed to separately white.

A minute's time having apparently been closely counted, Alice began her song anew:

> *If I had a hammer*
> *I'd hammer in the morning . . .*

Thereupon hurrying back to the point of his bargain, Ben offered the bouquet toward Alice, who, desisting of her song, indeed as if by flick of a baton, brightened in countenance, and taking the bouquet into hand, cradled it against her breast as a mother might a naked newborn babe.

Ben retreated a pace, and calling forth, "Bravo! Bravo!" began to clap his hands. Almost in simultaneity, the gathered assembly, accumulated perhaps unto seven dozens of persons, joined in.

Whilst Alice curtsied—forward, leftward, rightward—Ben relieved the taller officer of Alice's carpetbag, though naught of his starch, and offered to Alice then an unencumbered arm. Alice joining Ben's arm with her own, Ben paraded Alice toward the stairwell recently descended by him. The applause continuing, Ben paused after a few paces, that Alice might make one last curtsy, and leading her thereupon into the foyer preceding the stairwell, released her arm.

Ben bowed. "You are Alice Kortright, sister to Robert Kortright, called Sergeant by preference, am I correct, Madam Diva?"

Alice stepped onto the escalator and began to ascend. "Gotta get t' my wagon. A body can't trust *nobody* these days." She shook her head. "A body can't even take a minute t' do 'er business."

Ben watched Alice ascend, she mumbling the way, then realized, to no little chagrin, that he yet held her bag! Stepping forthrightly onto the escalator, Ben called after Alice, but she showed no hearing. Upon reaching the summit, Ben continued to call after Alice, but she continued to show no hearing.

Upon following Alice through one of the glass doors, Ben espied the same Negro man at the same green barrel, he bearing now, betwixt thumb and near finger, a smoldering wick. The same squarish bag, yet attended by likely the same pigeons, yet rested at the man's feet.

Ben noticed now, missed previously, upon the farther side of 8th Avenue, a grand edifice of white stone, and columns suggesting of the great Parthenon of Greece. Toward its rightward end, a modest marker satisfied his curiosity: UNITED STATES POST OFFICE.

Ben smiled, recalling his closet-sized post office at Philadelphia. From mere seed unto great oak indeed!

Passing overtop a grate, this emitting ponderous rumbles and grating screeches, emanant, it would seem, from Hades itself, Ben followed Alice unto the portico pillar to leftward, whereat the pushcart attendant, removed now to the other end of the cart, was slumped over that end, face downward, arms dangling, as if he had expired at his station, perhaps, as would appear, of starvation.

The man was bearing upon his back a pack similar to those Ben had witnessed at the Lincoln school in Boston. A bald spot atop the man's head seemed to gather particular emphasis unto itself from a frizz of overlong hair at the fringes.

Upon a bellow from Alice—"Whadja sell on me, eh?"—the man startled, as if to an electrical insult, and noticing Ben, regarded him with narrowed eyes, one of these, Ben noticed, being fixed in place.

Ben retreated a step.

The man looked to the bouquet Alice yet held to breast and smiled in that flaccid manner distinctive to those being near upon wholly untoothed. "Pretty," he said.

Alice deposited her bouquet into a separate basket at the rear of her cart. "Don't you try t' sweet talk me, Clementine o' Mine. I know what you been up to." Pulling a much-tattered sheet from her bosom, and unfolding this, Alice began to take inventory of the contents of her cart, each container therein bearing a number that corresponded to, or so one would have to assume, a numbered listing upon Alice's sheet. Alice's efforts toward a full accounting soon appeared more ritualistic, however, than exacting.

Hearing a raspy chuckle from behind, Ben turned half-circle around and discovered the Negro man nearby the trash barrel looking upon him. "Better watch out there, m'man. The lady's wacko." He circumscribed one side of his head with a finger.

"Sir?"

The man again chuckled, triggering a fit of coughing. Upon quelling himself, he spat upon the pavement, giving fright thereby to a pigeon narrowly spared a most unsavory indignity. "She one o' them procession-repulsive types. Do 'er list like that ever' goddamn day t' see if ol' Clem been naughty 'r nice." The man shook his head. "Course, ol' Clem always been naughty." Raising his wick to his lips, the man squinted, and, upon expelling a misty plume, shook his head. "Dunno how he take it like that all the time."

"And yet, sir, the lady here has a full cart of inventory, and her attendant would appear to be as willing as able to serve as sentinel, whilst you, sir, I see, have but a modest load of inventory, and but a pigeon or two willing to attend upon it. Perhaps there is some advantage to this condition to which you apply the term 'wacko.'"

The man stared a moment, then showed Ben his tongue, and then his backside. As he walked in the direction of 33rd Street, bag in hand, his gait was greatly inclined toward a swagger.

Finished with her accounting, Alice pulled from her overly large blue sweater a round loaf similar to the one the young woman had partaken of at Boston Common, and offered this to Clem, who took it eagerly into hand. Moving with a pathetic limp, the right knee being unbending, Clem removed himself to the three-door recession, whereat, facing away from the only denizen remaining there, he began to partake of the loaf.

Ben looked to Alice. "Your system of accountancy, Miss Alice, would be of great advantage to your brother in his new trade, I do believe, having witnessed it."

Alice frowned with such ferocity as to fissure a crust of white paste circumscribing her eyes. "What you talkin' about?"

"Your brother has taken to purveying stems in close resemblance to those presently in your cart, with each stem being affixed of a ribbon in the manner of the gatherings of your braids, with each ribbon bearing upon it a message of some small beneficence."

"My ass. That boy ain't no good for *nothin'*."

"No good for nothin' in all regards, Miss Alice, or no good as regards serving in the stead of an absented father when but a child himself, in need of the same care and protection as yourself? Or do I stray upon forbidden ground?"

Alice pushed her face well toward Ben's, there presently coming to Ben the scent of an eau de cologne oversubscribed in gardenia. "Who are you, anyway?"

Ben smiled. "Your brother's banker, one might fairly claim."

"You lent him money?"

"I did."

"You're a goddamn fool."

Ben smiled. "That I am—many times over, to be sure; and perhaps even yet again. However, I judged your brother worthy of my trust, as you might one day judge him worthy of your forgiveness."

Yanking her cart to forward, Alice pushed it toward the 8th Avenue walkway. "Gotta go get my supper."

Ben looked after Alice pushing her cart, and then realized, to no little chagrin, that he was *yet* in custody of her bag! Launching forth, Ben pursued Alice onto the 8th Avenue walkway, and thereupon southward. "We are all cowards in one way or another," Ben called forth. "Your mother was a coward in her way, your brother in his. I am a coward in my way, I do confess, and I suspect you are in your way, Miss Alice—otherwise you would not be running from me with so muscular a determination. Would you at least pause long enough, Miss Alice, to take possession of your bag?"

Alice broke into song: "If I had a hammer / I'd hammer in the morning..."

"Ah, but you *do* have a hammer, Miss Alice, do you not?"

"If I had a bell / I'd ring it in the morning..."

"Ah, but you *do* have a bell, Miss Alice, do you not?"

"If I had a song / I'd sing it in the morning..."

"Ah, but you *do* have a song, Miss Alice, do you not?"

Of a sudden, Alice snatched the bouquet from the forebasket on her cart and turning half-circle around threw it toward Ben. It landed well short of the mark. She wheeled onward then, toward the near crossing street.

Ben paused to gather up Alice's bouquet. Thereupon placing all seven stems into Alice's carpetbag, he labored to close the gap that had widened betwixt himself and his quarry. "Indeed, Miss Alice," he called forth after several brisk steps, "is not the hammer of which you sing but a symbol for particular tools or facilities of mind, to include, in your case, a particular facility for accountancy, as manifested by your system of inventory?"

Ben held silent a moment, such as to restore his breath, and then again called forth: "And the bell of which you sing, Miss Alice, is this not but a symbol for particular sentiments of heart, to include, in your case, a particular sentiment toward generosity, as manifested by your gift of sustenance to your friend Clementine o' Mine?"

Ben paused at the crossing street, this being 31st, whereat the station house ended to leftward, the Post Office building to rightward. A Negro man was foraging through a barrel here similar to the one at the other end of the station house. He was wearing long strands of braided hair, shoes like TJ's, untethered, and a long black scarf.

No pigeons were here attendant as there was no bag upon which to attend.

Ben crossed over 31st Street, paused sufficiently to catch his breath, and continued onward. Upon closing the distance to his quarry a few paces, he again called forth: "And the song of which you sing, Miss Alice, is this not but a symbol for particular inclinations of the soul, to include, in your case, a particular inclination toward making the world a safer place, as manifested by your choice of this particular ballad?"

Alice began her song anew: "If I had a hammer / I'd hammer in the morning / I'd hammer in the evening / All over this land . . ."

The distance betwixt himself and his quarry become now increased, Ben began to doubt the wisdom of his pursuit. How far should he allow himself to be drawn? What if he could not get himself back to the station house? Was he risking too much for the sake of one half-witted old woman, intransigent as regards both distrust and resentment?

Pausing now to catch his breath, Ben looked after Alice's backside as, head down, arms outstretched, the Diva of the Pennsylvania Station ever increased the gap betwixt them.

Ben advanced a step farther, then stopped.

He had tried. No one could reasonably expect more.

Abandoning Alice's bag to one side, whereat she might discover it upon her return, Ben began to retrace his steps, free of all burden. Having advanced no farther than seven taps, he paused.

Two turned backs do not an embrace invite.

Turning half-circle around, Ben retrieved Alice's bag and continued onward, free of all burden.

Beyond 30th Street, Ben took notice of a change in the faces encountered, they tending now more generally toward the swarthy; and also in the surrounding architecture, this tending now toward two parts perpendicular, as in the case of a cross. The principle underlying this arrangement, Ben surmised, was likely maximization of external exposure at the expense of internal volume, the very principle indeed that would be expected of residential interest over commercial.

Also noticeable was a commonplace of calling stations. Ben could not recall having encountered a single instance of these stations within the environs of the Waldorf Astoria or the Pennsylvania Station. Apparently, Ben surmised, the swarthy denizens of the present environ were generally less able to avail themselves of the convenience of private communication devices, such as the one he yet held to pocket.

Ben crossed now to the farther side of 29th Street, whereat an advertisement read, "Italian Deli," and then crossed to the farther side of 8th Avenue, whereat stood another calling station. Looking ahead to Alice, she having progressed well to westward, Ben pressed on, committed, he suspicioned, to his own doom.

To leftward, a fence wrought of interwoven wire was reminding of the fence that surrounded the common area whereat Ben had witnessed one child take the lives of two others. As in the case of that other fence, a sundry of careless leavings was accumulated at the foot of the present one, as well as along the curb to rightward.

Beyond the fence to leftward, a modest common area held no visitors, nor any perceptible entry unto it. Farther to leftward, the street subsequent to 29th showed itself to be well concaved toward the present street.

Following by eye the curvature of this street generally to westward, Ben espied a spire above tree and roof, and allowed himself to suspicion—indeed to hope—that the destination of a particular empty stomach inclined toward practical piety was close at hand!

Two women approaching, in serial, Ben held well to rightward. The first woman, red-haired, was holding at leash three small dogs also red-haired. The second woman was holding at leash one dog as stubbed and pugged as herself.

Were the owners sensible of the imitation, Ben wondered? Or were just the dogs? He grinned.

Upon reaching the corner of 29th Street and 9th Avenue, Ben looked to southward and glimpsed Alice turning leftward, indeed not far past the intersection of the concave street with 9th Avenue. At the nearer corner of this intersection, several Negro men appeared to be engaged in a lively frolic, derived, Ben most fervently hoped, by that species of euphoria commonly attendant upon a sated stomach.

To rightward of the present corner, a blue-sided shop marked "Billymark's West" held garish advertisements in two windows upon its near side. One such advertisement, "Bud Light" spelt inside a blue oval, reminded Ben of the garish ATM advertisement within the Pennsylvania Station that had served as a sort of beacon.

Each moth to its flame.

At the curb of the present corner, a barrel was overflowing of leavings, and immediately adjacent to it, a yellow bag was spilling leavings from a grievous wound.

Thereupon tapping his way southward, Ben passed yet more iron fencing to leftward, and then two call stations to rightward, each showing to center as if a perched canary, and arrived then at the corner whereat the Negro men, numbering to three, were sporting with each other whilst passing amongst them, Ben now noticed, a stubby-necked bottle sheathed in a brown wrapper. Upon Ben greeting each man in turn, each responded in turn—firstly, "Hey what up;" secondly, "Wazzup;" and thirdly, "Heyup."

Not certain at first whether he was being interrogated as to his immediate intentions, or whether he was being greeted by the same idiom in three flavours, Ben decided upon the latter.

Each man was bearing upon his back a pack similar to the one borne by Clementine o' Mine, it containing, Ben surmised, the majority of each man's worldly possessions.

Looking to the farther side of 28th Street, Ben could see in fullness now the church building implied by the spire he had espied from 29th Street. In aspect and architecture, this church was rather different from St. Paul's, it being smaller, wrought of brick as opposed to stone, and fashioned in the cruciform style, by virtue of a rearward chamber being crosswise to a central chamber. The near end of the crosswise chamber held within its upper third a large roundel of stained glass, this being divided as if by spokes into parts, and was matched in geometry as well as aspect by a diminutive roundel upon the spire tower, indeed whereat one might expect presence of a clock. The majority of the windows upon the central chamber were similar to those upon Old South Meeting House in Boston, being squared to bottom, arched atop.

The church grounds were circumscribed by a stockade of iron spikes, as in the case of both St. Paul's and Trinity, but they harbored no memorials, nor poles bearing banners.

The purpose of circumscribing a church ground with an iron stockade was not immediately clear to Ben, he being unable to imagine even the most inept of sprites being unable to breach such a barrier by mere wiggle of its nose.

Upon crossing over 28th Street, Ben paused to blot an accumulation of perspiration from his forehead and upper lip, using as linen the sleeve of his jacket.

By what humour he might produce such dew, he could not imagine.

A commodious vehicle to rightward, stopped at the curb there, was revelatory by way of an appellation upon the forward door, HOLY APOSTLES / CHURCH, with the first two words forming a sheltering arc overtop the third.

Tapping a few steps southward, Ben discovered the same appellation inscribed at top of two marquees in likeness to tablets, one of which was affixed at either side of the main entry to the church.

Was this not indeed the third occasion, Ben inquired of recent memory, he had encountered the tablets of Moses?

An iron gate afront the main entry was shut, but a second gate, ten taps to southward, was open, and men similar in dress and appearance to Heywhatup, Wazzup, Heyup were entering into this and being greeted thereupon by men—Negroes and tawnies—wearing bright orange vests.

Entering into this same gate, Ben discovered Alice's pushcart stopped almost directly forward, betwixt sections of movable fencing to leftward and, to rightward, a ramp bearing a hand railing. The persons newly arrived, Ben noticed, were being given a ticket by the men in orange, and were thereupon moving up the ramp and disappearing through a reddish door, to rightward, that entered upon a squarish structure abutting the crosswise chamber of the church.

The number of authorities present being sufficient, Ben adjudged, to ensure against any claim upon Alice's inventory, he deposited Alice's carpetbag onto the forebasket on her "wagon," and retrieved from this article then the seven stems of bloom, wilted though they were.

Upon a Negro man emerging from a wooden door adjacent to the main entry to the church building, followed by a woman, Caucasian, thereafter by another man, tawny, Ben surmised this entry to be the present egress unto the church, and the red door to rightward to be the ingress. Tapping his way now to the wooden door, Ben caught it in hand upon it next opening, nodded to the gentleman egressing, and entered into the church.

Passing through a brief vestibule of low ceiling, Ben entered into a modest nave vaulted at center as well as, to a lesser height, at either side. At front, another nave ran crosswise to the main nave, in accommodation to the cruciform style.

In the main nave, two rows of ivory-colored pillars, they delimiting the central vault, served to divide the main nave into three sections. In the central section, whereat normally a central aisle would be expected, several circular tables were arranged into two rows, with each table accommodating up to eight diners. In the leftward section, whereat pews would be expected, three tables were arranged also into row, whilst a fourth table, to front, stood close upon a pipe organ.

The tables were occupied mostly by men, with the great majority of these being of shabby dress and ill groom. Despite the intimacy encouraged by the geometry of the tables, there appeared to be little converse amongst the diners at any table, including the only table, located in the farther section, to be occupied by women, these to include the Diva of Pennsylvania Station. Indeed, those diners whose attentions were not fixed hard upon their plates tended to hold a gaze at some undeterminable object beyond the perimeter of their immediate circle, in the manner indeed of an invalid gazing beyond the boundary of his infirmity. The preponderance of what interaction was noticeable was betwixt certain of the attendants servicing the tables, most of these being women of milk and rose, and particular of the guests with whom these attendants seemed to have some history of familiarity.

Directly ahead of whereat Ben presently stood, this being in the rightward section of the main nave, guests were converging upon a line of barrels and tables such as to unburden themselves of their leavings and dining equipage. Offsetting this outward stream was a steady flow of newly arrived guests bearing full plates from the direction of the immediately abutting building.

The object here, one might conclude, was not to bask in the warm glow of agreeable society, whilst ruminating upon the remains of the day, but to fill one's stomach as quickly as possible, with whatever sustenance hand and ladle might allot, and thereupon return one's self as quickly as possible to the comfort and safety of one's agreeable anonymity.

Tapping his way now to leftward, Ben passed a marble baptismal and stopped soon thereafter at the table at which Alice was presently seated, her back poised toward him. Pulling a lavender bloom from the bouquet held in hand, Ben placed this close upon Alice's plate.

"A flower for you today, Miss Alice?"

Alice flinched as if to a fright, and upon regarding the flower as if it were an intruding insect, attempted to shoo it away with gestures of hand and fork. The intruder yet remaining, Alice turned her head from it as far as she might, and there held it.

Circling the table, counterclockwise, Ben placed a stem close upon each plate, there being seven diners, and leaned close then upon Alice's ear, from rearward: "It has been a great honor to meet the Diva of Pennsylvania Station, however briefly."

Reviewing thereupon the contents of Alice's plate, Ben decided against wishing her *bon appétit*. Instead, he wished her the possibility of one day being reunited with her brother, as no one in this world, not even a failed hero, should be left abandoned to his regrets. Tapping his way then toward the chancel, Ben took notice of the simple altar directly to front, it being constituted in the main of a platform holding at center a low table draped in purple. A brass lectern in likeness of an eagle stood to rightward, whilst to leftward a pulpit of golden filigree, hexagonal in geometry, as at St. Paul's, stood upon a wooden pedestal. Behind the table stood a row of seven chairs, the middle member of which showed a higher back to conspicuous effect.

In which of these chairs, Ben presently wished mightily to inquire, would the Humble Carpenter Himself have sat in?

Behind the row of chairs, a plain white cross, elegant of its very simplicity, was centered upon a wall bearing no other ornament. To leftward, close to the far wall of the chancel, stood several queues of folded chairs, these likely used, Ben surmised, in place of pews on the occasion of regular services. To leftward of the chairs, the pipe organ noted previous, in soaring to a lofty height, obstructed the wheel of stained glass Ben had espied from without. The sacrifice here of one aesthetic for another was necessitated, it would appear, by some immutable law of ecclesiastical economy.

Looking in the opposing direction, in anticipation of symmetry, Ben discovered a roundel of stained glass in mirror image indeed to the one obstructed.

Climbing now onto the raised platform, this showing the same checkerboard pattern, black squares alternating with white, as encountered in the corridor at the Waldorf Astoria, Ben turned half-circle around, such as to face upon the archipelago of tables.

"It would appear to be a general law of nature," he began, his voice only slightly elevated, for lack of strength to raise it farther, "that in every group of at least seven persons, there is at least one leader." He paused, allowing a modest clattering emanant from the ancillary building to become the only fissure upon an eggshell of silence. In the interim, he noticed a Negro man, light of skin, peering upon him from nearby the entry to the ancillary building. The man's dress and deportment suggested authority; his phrenology, Jamaica; his eyes, equanimity.

The man nodding, Ben returned the gesture in kind, and then continued. "It would appear to be a general law of nature, good friends, that in every accidental assemblage of at least seven persons, there is included amongst them at least one natural leader—as indeed was the case in ancient China, in the year 4004 BC, when, according to Chu Fung Ming, the great chronicler, seven wayfarers discovered themselves one moonless night fallen into the same pit, at the bottom of which was a well filled to brim. Their prison being absent any purchase for ascendance, their fate would appear to be absent all hope.

"At first, there was much despairing amongst the seven, and not a little self-pitying, but then, come morning, one of the seven, ciphering by eye the height of the pit, and gaining the attention thereupon of his six companions, this by way of breaking into song— *If I had a hammer / I'd hammer in the morning / I'd hammer in the evening...*'—said unto his comrades: 'Fellow travelers, if we are to stand here as individuals, alone in our despair, passive in our helplessness, dispirited in our sorrow, here we shall remain; here we shall perish, none of us having yet fully lived. If, however, we were to agree to decide, by simple lottery, who amongst us should be escaped by the other six, we might then construct a ladder of ourselves, each man, save the bottommost, sitting upon the shoulders of another, such that the highestmost might then stand to full height upon the shoulders of the second-highest man, and thereupon pull himself unto liberation.'

"All agreeing to this scheme, our seven accidental victims proceeded to draw lots, each knowing that only one of their number would be escaped, but that, even so, the six left behind would have helped a fellow traveler gain a second chance at living his life to fullest. Now, as fate would farther have it for our seven star-crossed travelers, the leader of this scheme, although drawing lastly, drew the numeral 1, thereby entitling him, by assumption of the six others, to first choice regarding claiming a position upon the human ladder. Immediately thereupon, there was much grumbling and dissension amongst the six losers, this devolving unto accusation and recrimination, our unhappy six having previously learnt, by way of much travail, to suspicion the intentions of any but themselves alone. Our leader, however, being in fact a *true* leader, responded in the only way such a one might, saying unto his companions: 'O no, no, you misunderstand. I thought I had been clear: The person drawing the numeral 1 is to stand in the *first* position, that is, at bottom, whilst the person drawing the numeral 7 is to stand in the seventh position, that is, at top.' And with this declaration, the other six travelers freely assented to their chosen lots.

"And so a human ladder was constructed of our seven travelers, the sixth bearing upward the seventh upon his shoulders; the fifth bearing upward these two upon his shoulders; and so on and so on until the first man, our leader, was bearing upon his shoulders, at bottom, more weight than any man should ever be expected or allowed.

"Steadied then by the uplifted arms of the sixth man, our seventh traveler raised himself to full height and, reaching upward, managed to grasp sufficient purchase beyond the rim of the pit as to be able to pull himself unto freedom, leaving thereby his fellow travelers behind— which condition, our escaped traveler at once realized, he simply could not abide. Indeed, the six fellows left behind, only recently but strangers to him, were now his brethren. Either all seven were to thrive together, or all seven were to perish together—and that was an end on it!

"In this moment of realization, something very strange occurred: Where, in the far recesses of this traveler's imagination, there heretofore had been little evidence of natural cunning or creative facility, there now emerged, like a genie from a lantern long unattended, a most vivid image, which image our escaped traveler immediately strove to imitate. Firstly, he implored his comrades to bear yet a little longer the burden the draw of lots had fated upon each one. He then set about renting his shirt and breeches into ribbons, and weaving these into a strand of sturdy cord. Upon finishing his work, he lowered one end to this cord to the sixth traveler, such as to be able to pull his brother also unto liberation.

"Now, as you might have anticipated, upon his being escaped by this collaborative means, our sixth traveler converted his own clothing into a strand of cord, which article he added to the first, such so that he and his comrade could thereupon pull the fifth traveler unto freedom.

And so it went until all seven comrades were escaped, and standing in each other's company, as starkly and joyfully naked, except for the last comrade, as babes new born."

Looking to Alice, Ben discovered her partly obstructed from view by an attendant, who, removing something from pocket, gave this over to Alice. Looking to the Jamaican gentleman, who nodded, Ben nodded in return, and then continued. "As most of you can well affirm, I suspicion, pain tends to shorten the range of one's vision. The greater the agony, the shorter the range. Consider the miller whose hand has become entrapped under a grinding stone. How far beyond the wall of his agony might this poor fellow, in the moment, cast his eyes?

"Indeed, the more pain we suffer, of whatever species, emanant of whatever source, the more likely we are to miss observing that, no matter how wretched might be our present circumstance, no matter how deep might be the pit into which we have tumbled, we are never alone. Always there are like-others in close proximity, indeed not more than an arm's length away. In this regard, you might wish to take notice in the moment that you are presently in company with, in most cases, at least six like-others; and farther, that the lot of you are arranged as you would be were you sitting at the bottom of a pit containing a well; and farther, that there is no immediate cause for you to leave the company of your tablemates until such time as one amongst you has ventured to stand and sing a few notes of a worthy ode."

Ben held now to silence, the only sound being a muted clattering emanant from the ancillary building. The Jamaican gentleman appeared as if not breathing. The milk and rose attendants among the tables were wholly hesitated from rendering farther service.

Of a sudden Alice Kortright upstood at her table: "If I had a hammer / I'd hammer in the morning / I'd hammer in the evening—"

A gentleman rose at a table just forward and rightward of where Ben was standing—"I'd hammer out danger / I'd hammer out a warning—"

A gentleman rose at a third table—"I'd hammer out love between my brothers and my sisters / all over this land."

Another woman rose at Alice's table.

And so on—and so on—

Upon nodding unto the Jamaican gentleman, the gentleman nodding in return, Ben descended from the altar. Making his way then toward the baptismal, he came upon Alice, she yet upstanding, and discovered her holding in hand a lavender bloom, upright, like a candle. Affixed to the stem was a bright-green ribbon upon which something had been writ, there being two letters visible toward the terminus of one tail: V-E.

The other of Alice's hair ribbons, Ben noticed, was affixed upon the stem of bloom in the hand of the woman to rightward, she being also upstanding, and also singing.

"I'd ring it in the evening / all over this land / I'd ring out danger / I'd ring out a warning / I'd ring out love between my brothers and my sisters / all over this land . . ."

Thereupon tapping his way into the vestibule, Ben paused there, and turning half-circle around, faced upon the chancel.

> *Well we've got a hammer*
> *And we've got a bell*
> *And we've got a song to sing*
> *All over this land*
>
> *It's the hammer of justice*
> *It's the bell of freedom*
> *It's the song about love between my brothers and my sisters*
> *All over this land*

Taking his leave with a bow, Ben tapped his way from the church, and thereupon to the near intersection, whereat he discovered Heywhatup, Wazzup, and Heyup yet on the farther corner, yet engaged in amiable repartee. Shivering of a sudden, as if to an insinuation of late-afternoon chill, Ben was reminded that he had no hat, and thereupon turning his thoughts to TJ, reached to pocket and felt therein the lump that was TJ's communication device. He smiled.

Partway across 28th Street, Ben was as if assaulted by a swarm of winged insects, their collective drone filling his ears, their collective veil clouding his vision. His knees losing all strength, he staggered to leftward and, to his great fortune, directly into the arms of one of the corner men, the shortest of these, Heywhatup.

A robust odor tinctured of perspiration presently served as a smelling salt.

"You OK, man?"

Heyup, coming to the assistance of his friend, grinned. "Hey man, I know'd the food in there was bad, but, Jesus Lord, I di'n't know'd it was *this* bad!"

The two men helped Ben to the curb and eased him into a sitting posture, such that his legs extended onto the street pavement.

The Jamaican gentlemen appeared in company with Wazzup, and lowering himself onto bended knee, was gently solicitous toward Ben's symptoms, the lilt of his voice being as soothing as a Gulf breeze.

"I was overtaken by a spell of faint-headedness," Ben assured, "but suffered no injury, to the credit of these kind gentlemen. I should have taken a little rest. I was too much in a hurry." Ben made gesture toward rising. "If you would be so kind as to assist me to my feet, I would be on my way. I have yet far to travel."

The Jamaican gentlemen gripped one of Ben's arms, Heyup the other, and the two men pulled Ben to his feet. Wazzup thereupon restored Ben of his cane.

"Where you headed, if I may ask?" the Jamaican gentleman inquired.

"The Pennsylvania Station."

"We'll take you. It will be no trouble." The Jamaican gentleman turned to Heyup and asked him to summon Hakeem. Heyup thereupon loped across 28th Street, his gait reminding of a land surveyor taking liberal measure.

Ben thanked the Jamaican gentleman and the corner men for their kind assistance, and had only begun to protest any farther intervention on his behalf, when a Negro man in an orange vest appeared, showing a fulsome set of teeth and a nest of braids in likeness to Medusa's serpents. The man's smile lingering, Ben thought it perhaps a permanent posture in consonance with a like-humored temperament.

"The gentleman needs a ride to Penn Station," the Jamaican said to Hakeem.

"He got it," Hakeem replied, with a punctuating snap of his head.

Hakeem and Heywhatup thereupon helped Ben across the street and to the rearward door of the commodious box of a vehicle marked "Holy Apostles/ Church."

Whilst Hakeem opened the door, the Jamaican extended a diminutive hand toward Ben. "I very much appreciate what you did in there today."

Ben bowed, grasping the gentleman's hand. "And I very much appreciate what you do in there every day, sir. 'Tis one thing to fire the embers upon occasion to much notice; quite another to maintain those embers day to day to no notice soever."

The gentleman smiled, and grasping Ben by the arm, helped him onto his seat, whilst Hakeem assumed the helm to front.

Once tethered, at the Jamaican's insistence, Ben bowed toward the three corner men, they bobbing in return.

"You be careful o' y'self," Wazzup said. "Hakkey drive that thing like Spidahman here walk"—"Spidahman" being, apparently, a reference to Heyup and his disproportionately long legs. The three laughed at this, slapping hands high and low.

The Jamaican gentleman wished Ben Godspeed, closed the door, and turning to the three corner men, was soon in possession of a small paper-sheathed package.

Hakeem looked to a rightward mirror, and thereupon launching forth into the near lane of traffic, wove his way down 9th Avenue, lane to lane, such as, apparently, to pass traffic deemed too slow for even a moment's toleration. For particular offenders, Hakeem drew from a a greatly abridged lexicon of compliments. Indeed, Ben was not long in appreciating the Jamaican's insistence upon Ben being tethered to his seat.

Hakeem turned leftward at 26th Street, leftward again at 8th Avenue, and wove his way then to the Pennsylvania Station, whereat he came to a stop behind a queue of yellow taxi vehicles. Opening the rearward door, Hakeem helped Ben out of his seat, and whilst shielding him from approaching traffic, onto the walkway.

Ben bowed. "You are most kind, sir." He bowed again. "Might I request a delay of one minute to your return, sir?"

Hakeem looked upstreet to the sergeant-at-arms with the whistle, then to Ben. "*You* the man"—he gestured with his head—"'til *he* be."

"Thank you, sir." Tapping his way then as briskly as he might to the three-door recession behind the large cylinder, Ben discovered Clementine o' Mine yet standing in the corner into which he had earlier retreated. His head, being bowed, was rested against the conjoining planes of granite that formed the inward corner of the recession. His was trembling. "Mister Clementine o' Mine," Ben called forth, "come hither! A hot meal, and a most agreeable delivery thereto, presently await!"

Clementine o' Mine turned his head such as to peer over one shoulder. There being no expression of countenance, there was no conveyance of sentience.

"Come! Come!" Ben commanded. "There are those who would foil this scheme of no greater than a lack of patience!"

Clementine showing no obedience, Ben added Sergeant Kortright's stripes to his sleeve. "Give me your arm, sir! The livery might wait but little longer! Food, sir, food! Heat, sir, heat!"

Hooking Clementine's near arm with his own, Ben pulled Clementine from the recession, and thereupon urging him toward overcoming his infirmity of leg, led him to whereat Hakeem was presently paying his compliments to a taxi driver parked close upon to rearward, the latter personage showing his appreciation with robust notes of horn.

"If you would be so kind, Mr. Hakeem," Ben said, "as to deliver Mr. Clementine to his supper, and return him hither, if such should be his wish, I would be most grateful, as would be, I am quite certain, his ancestors unto the seventh generation."

Hakeem looked to his watch, near upon the size of an astrolabe, and grinned. "No probleemo. Got us a whole ten minutes yet." He looked to Clementine. "All aboard, Bro! Kitchen closes in ten!"

Clementine began to show agitation, indeed as if a fair measure of trepidation left in the shelter of the recession had only just now caught up with him.

"Alice is there," Ben assured. "Alice has a chair waiting for you. Methinks, however, you might be required to sing for your supper."

Clementine smiled.

The taxi driver who had only just played a hardy score of horn, was replaced now by another such musician, who thereupon began to take up the very melody left off by his predecessor.

Whilst Hakeem led Clementine to the compartment at rear of the vehicle, wherein his unbending leg might better be accommodated, Ben tapped his way to the street-side window of the standing taxi to rearward and addressed the driver: "Have you your inoculation, sir?" The man showing consternation, Ben continued, gesturing toward Clementine: "The gentleman is stricken of leprosy, sir, the reach of which, unfortunately, amounts to some forty paces to leeward. If only you had not paused here, sir, such as to lay claim, but had simply continued on to our windward, a more salutary outcome could have been assured you." Ben shook his head. "My condolences to your family, sir. I am so very sorry."

Clementine having again become agitated, Ben hurried to dampen the ember before it might burn down the house, and holding Hakeem from closing the compartment doors, smiled upon Clementine. "'Tis likely to your favor, sir, that you not witness the process of your delivery, only its completion." Of no forethought then, Ben grasped Clementine's near hand, cold as the fate it betrayed, and squeezed it firmly. Thereupon retreating to the walkway, Ben stood at the curb until Hakeem had sped around the near corner. Bowing his head then, Ben made attempt to swallow as if an ill-ripened cherry, and thereupon tapped his way to the station entry. Bearing himself to rightward, as previous, he descended slowly to the bottom, whereat, visited by another fit of faint, he gripped the near railing until such time he felt sufficiently restored to continue. Tapping his way then into the great room, Ben approached upon the marquee suspended from the low ceiling.

Being as fatigued of mind now as of corpus, Ben discovered himself unable to parse the intelligence attached upon the marquee. After several ebbs and flows of lucidity, he was finally able to determine, to a fair degree of certainty, that a departure to Washington—hence, by implication, to Philadelphia—was imminent, it being marked "boarding." Upon a moment of farther study, Ben was able to determine, to some certainty, that the earliest subsequent departure to Philadelphia would be no sooner than two hours hence.

Animated now by a sense of urgency, Ben searched for a ticket area consonant with the one he had patronized in the Boston station, and soon espied such, although it were but feebly advertised, well to rightward, beyond the farther of two rows of portly pillars. Upon approaching this area, Ben was crestfallen to discover that, although there were several stations for accommodating patrons, only a few of these were presently attended by a clerk, and the queue of patrons waiting upon these numbered at least unto a score.

By happenstance then, Ben espied a young lady manipulating a device, intriguingly marked "Quik-Trak," that bore strong resemblance to an ATM device. It was one of several such devices clustered around a portly pillar, and there were several other such clusters.

No clerks required!

Upon closer approach, Ben confirmed the Quik-Trak device to be usurping of the ticket clerk in the very way the ATM device was usurping of the bank clerk. Much encouraged, he inserted his bank card into a slot marked for such, but soon discovered himself as if caught in a maze of invisible turns and twists—retreating from one apparent dead end only to discover himself in another. He could summon naught but gratitude, however, when the object of a growing desperation, passage to Philadelphia for one, was finally delivered unto him for two. And although frugality demanded immediate redress of this unintended superfluity, Ben discovered himself well disposed toward exception on this one occasion, even Frugality being subject to tempering by a larger logic.

Returning to the marquee as briskly as he might, Ben determined the track number for his departure, and made way then to whereat a downward escalator was marked "9W." His ticket receiving attention by a man in authority, Ben proceeded onto the escalator, and riding this to the bottom, was attended by another man in authority, who, upon inquiring of Ben's destination, directed him unto a third man in authority, who thereupon directed him onto a car that, upon his entering into it, seemed a'ready filled to capacity.

About three-quarters the distance to the farther end, Ben came upon a seat claimed by no greater than a large bag, dark blue, bearing a long strap. Proximate to this article sat a young woman who bore some familiarity, however unlikely such a happenstance might be. She was wearing a man's suit, dark-blue, bearing a fine silver stripe. Her hair, richly auburn, was closely coiffed, and absent any covering or ornament.

"Sorry to trouble you, madam, but might I inquire as to the status of this seat?"

The train eased gently into motion.

Turning her attention from several papers rested upon a tray, this drawn from the back of the forward seat, the woman removed the bag from the adjacent seat, and depositing this to the floor, to leftward, returned her attention to her papers.

Ben eased himself onto the seat made vacant, and closing his eyes, allowed himself to savor that species of euphoria that attends upon being safely arrived whereat, not one minute farther, one would be denied.

He remembered! The young lady in blue was the very one he had encountered at the ATM device on Milk Street—the very one indeed who had taken him for a creature of predation!

Peering askance upon the woman's papers, Ben discovered the typescript to be well legible to him, owing to the intimate arrangement of the seating, and adjudged it to be public fare, for lack of any discernible effort by the owner toward holding it private.

A line of text close upon the very top of the sheet presently exposed was in three parts: "Blue Team" to leftward; "TGL Campaign—Phase II" amidships; and "13" to rightward. Below this line, after a void, several other lines were arranged into paragraphs, and amongst these, as well as in the margins to side, were several scribblings, writ in ink tinctured unto a robust blue.

At bottom, a phrase reading, "Company Confidential," sat centered atop another such, reading, "Ambrose & Augustine." Barely visible in the background of the whole was a watermark: A & A.

"Would I be venturing far into error, madam," Ben ventured, "were I to suggest that all hues of blue, the bolder in particular, were favored by you?"

The woman looked to Ben as if upon a spouse newly confessed of more than ten but fewer than twenty-five infidelities. "Excuse me?"

"Your vehicle is blue, your suit is blue, the ink of your pen is blue, and your 'Team' is 'Blue.'" In the instant, the woman turned twelve pages upon the thirteenth such as to veil the whole. "Every truth being scribe to a pattern that reveals itself," Ben continued, "might we have uncovered one such betwixt us?"

"How"—the woman took notice of Ben's manner of dress—"I remember you!" She cocked eyes become pistols. "Are you stalking me?"

"That is a possibility, I do suppose, at least in base concept, so to say, given my presence here. As a practical matter, though, given that I had but a cane rent of fissures, and two legs crippled of gout, with which to compete with the speed and range of a wagon pulled by a thousand horses, I think it quite improbable. Would you not agree?"

The woman showed a luminosity of eye now as if from a breaking dawn within. "Did Barnigle put you up to this?"

Ben chuckled. "You are the second person this day to pose that very question to me."

"The first being?"

"A newspaperman—a Mr. Lynch."

"Brian?"

"The very one."

"You have got to be kidding. Brian's my S-O!"

"S-O?"

"Significant other."

"I do apologize, madam, but I have no familiarity, received or derived, with that term."

"Well, you wouldn't, would you, being Ben Franklin and all. Brian's my partner. We live together."

"In the common-law sense, should I assume?"

"Technically, I guess; but it's really a lot looser than that."

"Looser?"

The woman regarded Ben a moment as if in appraisal of how intimate she should be revealing toward him. "Neither of us is committed to anything—you know, long term. If things work out, maybe we tighten things up a bit. If not, neither of us gets saddled with any complications."

"Might I assume there are no children betwixt you, they being rather keen upon bringing complications into the home, not to mention frogs and mud pies?"

"No children. Maybe later, if, as I said, things work out."

"Might I inquire, madam, by what means you and your partner determine what is to be accommodated in the other and what is not? For example, in the event of an infirmity suffered by one of you, what is the expectation of the other?"

"What is this, a—?" The woman stared hard upon Ben. "It *was* Barnigle, wasn't it?"

Ben smiled. "I assure you, madam, that I have had no commerce with anyone named Barnigle, either in my present travels or in any previous. Perhaps you would be so kind as to apprise me as regards how this gentleman's motives and my own might become so readily aligned in the opinion of both you and Mr. Lynch."

Softening now in eye and brow, apparently of trust accumulated to a sufficient level, the woman offered her hand. "I'm Lucy Myers."

Ben grasped Lucy's hand and offered no pressure receiving none. "My pleasure," he said, with a small bow.

Lucy smiled. "You look just like him. Who are you *really*?"

"We are all *really*, I do suppose, as we clothe, shoe, and hat ourselves, Mr. Barnigle included."

Lucy chuckled. "Interesting that you should say that. I hadn't really thought about it before but I can't imagine Barnigle wearing anything but a shirt-and-tie with a pair of grungy old jeans." Lucy smiled. "Barnigle—surprise, surprise—does not much like to follow convention. I think he likes to give people the impression he's a team player—the shirt and tie part—but at the end of the day, he's going to do it *his* way—the grungy jeans part."

Ben smiled. "You would appear to know Mr. Barnigle very well."

"Not all that well. Mainly just through Brian, who's known him since college, although I'd read his column a few times before Brian and I got together. It was quite good, actually. *Was*, because a few years ago—and this ties in with what I just said about him—he got caught making up some of the material he used in his columns and was fired. This was at the *Globe*, where he was one of their lead columnists. Since then, he seems to have become, of all things, a sort o' professional prankster—the Alan Funt of the practical joke, you might say—hence the alignment of motives you alluded to.

"He'd always shown an inclination in that direction, pulling little pranks here and there, on April Fool's, people's birthdays, that sort of thing, but since losing his job, he's been upping the ante a bit. A few months ago, for example, he hired a guy to impersonate that Publishers Clearinghouse guy who makes house calls, and had him deliver a six-foot check for ten million dollars to a family in South Boston. Everybody got sucked in, including the *Globe*, his former employer, which did an exclusive on the 'Big Winners.'"

"Might the embarrassment to the latter party have represented the majority of his intention?"

"Could be. According to Brian, though, what he's really up to is he's trying get enough media attention to interest a producer in doing a reality show based on the concept of springing elaborate ruses on unsuspecting victims. *Jokers Wild*, he wants to call it." Lucy shook her head. "Personally, I think the guy let his enthusiasm for stunts get carried over into his journalism, and that this is the reason he ended up blowing his career."

"'Tis sometimes a delicate membrane that holds one humour from insinuating into another."

Lucy smiled. "No pun intended?"

Ben bowed. "By happenstance alone."

Lucy took note again of Ben's manner of dress. "So, what are you doing traveling around the entire Eastern Seaboard, it would appear, dressed up like Ben Franklin?" She smiled. "Drumming up a little interest in your own reality show, are you?"

Ben squinted to a sudden bounty of light, the train having emerged, he surmised, from beneath the Hudson River. "Actually—and it occurs to me you might be of some assistance in the matter, should you be willing—I am on my way to Philadelphia to make a delivery." Ben pulled TJ's device from pocket. "I must deliver this device to its rightful owner. I know not the proper address; however, Master TJ, the owner, made a call to this very address by means of this device, which, as was demonstrated to me by him, holds a facility for keeping an accounting of all calls made of it, for the sake of subsequent expediencies; and which also has, as was also demonstrated to me, a facility for matching a calling number against the physical address to which that number is bound."

Lucy smiled. "Need a little assistance from the Help Desk, do we?"

"I hesitate to interrupt your labors yet farther, Miss Myers, but I must confess to being too old a dog to learn a new trick upon a single demonstration, however well presented."

"Not a problem." Taking TJ's device into hand, Lucy set about pressing buttons and touching the 'screen,' as TJ called it. "OK," she said showing Ben a listing of numbers, the first several of which showed 617 to front. "His most recent calls were all to the 617 area code, which is Boston."

"One such was directed to his mother, I know, whilst the others, I presume, were directed to friends called by him 'homies.'"

Lucy smiled. "Your friend is black."

"Should he be yet hiding under the costume of my bonnet, as I anticipate, considering recent events, he might well be regarded as something else altogether."

Lucy showed a moment of perplexity, and then looked again to TJ's device. "The next number has a 215 area code, which is Philadelphia. Shall we go with that one?"

"Let the experiment begin."

Lucy pressed a few more buttons, touched upon the screen, and singing forth then—"Ta-da!"—held the device toward Ben:

D Jordan—(215) 535-5876—217 South 47th Street, Philadelphia, PA 19139.

"Shall I write it down for you?"

"I would be most appreciative."

Slipping a small card from the bag she had earlier consigned to the floor, Lucy scribbled upon the blank side of this, in cerulean ink, and handed the card over to Ben, who, upon thanking her, looked to the script writ upon the one side, and then read the lettering imprinted upon the other side: Lucy A. Myers, Director / Team Blue / Strategic Marketing Division.

Ben slipped the card into pocket.

"Are you familiar with Philadelphia?"

"Of a time long past."

"Would you like to see a map?"

Ben looked to TJ's device. "It has facility also for map making?"

Lucy smiled. "It does, but I've got a better way."

Returning TJ's device to Ben, Lucy exchanged the place of her manuscript for that of a squarish object of little thickness, blue in coloration, that had been largely hidden by several sheets atop it.

Ben peered upon TJ's device as if upon the long-sought Grail itself. "There would appear to be as many heads to this Hydra," he said, "as legs upon a centipede." He returned the device to pocket.

Lucy levered the blue object into two parts, the top part showing as if a darkened window, the bottom part holding a regiment of squarish buttons, each showing a letter or a numeral—the whole being in close similitude to the device that the woman at St. Paul's Chapel had used to discover the location of William Bradford's gravesite.

Upon Lucy pressing a round button close upon the hinge, the window shone as if of celestial embers and soon thereupon held a host of curious symbols against a cerulean firmament. "This way you'll be able to see the whole thing at once," Lucy said, manipulating a small arrowhead over the screen.

A broadside appeared bearing "EarthMap" at top.

"I hesitate to inquire, in fear of appearing 'clueless' beyond all toleration, but by what name is this curious device known?"

Lucy smiled. "You're good. Barnigle did well. It's a laptop."

Ben sensed a window open upon a chamber of received knowledge. "Also called 'a computer,' am I correct?"

"You are." Lucy pressed three numeral buttons: "Two, one, seven." She paused.

Ben retrieved Lucy's card from pocket and read aloud the remainder of the address: "South 47th Street / Philadelphia, PA 19139."

"Shit!" Lucy as if punctuated. Upon transposing then "71" unto "17," Lucy pressed a larger button whilst the arrowhead rested overtop "Get Map." She thereupon biased the screen toward Ben, that he might gain benefit of a frontal view of a colorated map showing a red star to center, this marking, Ben surmised, the location of Auntie D's domicile.

Surrounding the red star, an intricate network of filaments, of helter-skelter design, gave appearance of a web spun by a spider habitually taken to drink.

Although little showed in the way of reference markings, this poverty was soon addressed by way of Lucy manipulating the map unto a smaller aspect and shifting the whole of it rightward, such as to include representation, in blue, of what Ben assumed to be the Schuylkill.

A few greenish areas, most of these close upon the river, marked, Ben surmised, areas of vegetation yet preserved.

Lucy moved a symbol in likeness to a finger such as to point at "N 30th St."

"This is the 30th Street Station," she said, "where we'll be arriving." She moved the finger over a large area tinted of purple, marked "University of Pennsylvania," and rested it then upon the red star, from which emerged a small box showing, "217 South 47th Street."

"And this is where you'll be going."

Lingering his attention upon the purple area, Ben recalled a modest meetinghouse, seed to this very oak, whereat any idea, however offensive to orthodoxy, might enjoy a fair hearing. "But for a close tending of it, no flame long endures," he whispered.

Lucy showing perplexity, Ben bowed. "My deepest appreciation, Miss Myers, for your kind assistance. I have my mission, and now my compass."

"You're most welcome."

Lucy darkened her computer device, and bringing her manuscript again to fore, moved the thirteenth page to bottom, thereby revealing an advertisement, claiming near upon half the fourteenth page, that bore strong resemblance to the advertisement Ben had encountered in the *Courant* showing a coquette poised in an alluring posture upon a magenta bench.

Get more!

The present advertisement showed the same young lady, clad in two wisps of magenta silk, one high, one low, lying upon the bow of a sleek watercraft. She was wearing darkly tinted spectacles and was speaking upon a device whilst her golden hair streamed overtop a shield of glass upon which her head was propped. Directly behind her, at the helm, stood Adonis himself, also wearing darkly tinted spectacles, also speaking upon a cell phone.

Get more!

Ben hung his head. As Poor Richard says, *Get what you can, and what you get hold.*

University of Pennsylvania Hospital

September 17th, 5:32 p.m.

P rescott opened his eyes to a nurse directing a man and a woman to the row of chairs to his right, which was perpendicular to his own row of three chairs. The man looked to be in his fifties; the woman, four or five years younger. The row of blue and plum chairs there, and the row where Prescott was sitting, formed a small alcove of two sides, a table and a lamp in between. A larger alcove, of three sides, was located farther to the right, on the lee side of a low wooden barrier, while a third alcove, essentially a mirror image of Prescott's, was located across the room, to the left.

The man sat down in the middle chair, the woman, in the chair to the man's right.

The man was wearing high-top shoes, brown; the woman, calf-high boots, black. The woman's complexion, a bit swarthy—naturally so, it seemed, versus solarly so—and her facial features, which tended a bit toward the exotic, suggested a non-Anglo ethnicity, possibly Eastern European. The man, gray-haired, was wearing dark jeans and a gray zip-neck sweater. He was holding a large radiology envelope and a magazine.

Upon the nurse leaving, the man set the envelope on the empty chair to his left and opened the magazine. The woman, wearing a long dark skirt, shed her pocketbook to the floor, but remained poised well forward in her chair.

Upon the nurse reappearing, the woman popped up from her chair and followed the nurse toward the same inner sanctum in which Prescott had had, about five hours ago now, it seemed, his vitals taken. The man looked toward his departing companion, then resumed reading his magazine.

Prescott rested his head against the wall behind his chair.

The reason it was taking so long, he tried again to make himself believe, was because they had worked him in.

And the reason they had worked him in, he tried again to make himself believe, was not because the news was bad, but because it was good and they wanted to let him know ASAP so he wouldn't worry himself into an acute case of armpit BO.

What in God's name was the evolutionary benefit to armpits stinking of fear?

Prescott rested his eyes on a painting hanging on the opposite wall, to left of a wall clock, which he avoided. Obviously a print, the painting showed a jaded farmhouse set between a gauzy sky and a yellow field. A single tree in the background held a few residual leaves on arthritic limbs.

It was still *spring*!

All of summer lay ahead.

All of autumn lay ahead.

A middle-aged man approached a woman sitting in the mirror-image alcove to the left of the painting. The woman, immediately attentive, engaged the man in conversation even before the man had sat down in the blue and plum chair next to her. They chatted back and forth in that easy manner of intimates discussing the remains of the day.

They had not a worry between them.

At least half of summer, and all of autumn, lay ahead.

A female doctor appeared—white coat, red stitching above the breast pocket—and greeting the couple with a smile, led them away.

The swarthy woman in black boots reappeared, holding a clipboard. Reclaiming her seat, she began to fill out a form affixed to the clipboard, using a pen tethered to the clip.

She was either being referred, Prescott surmised, or getting a second opinion.

The couple began to converse in a language that sounded like Russian, not about illness or urgency or fear, but about something the man had discovered in his magazine. As they spoke, the man held the magazine toward the woman. The demeanor of both as they continued to converse was much like that of the couple across the room—casual, relaxed, routine. They could as well have been sitting poolside on a cruise ship.

After a moment, the man returned to his magazine, the woman to her clipboard.

After a few moments more, a young male doctor—white coat, red stitching—approached.

"Mrs. Resnick?"

The woman looked up from her clipboard.

The doctor nodded toward the man, and looked again to the woman. "Come on back."

The woman stood up; her companion after her. The man gave the large envelope over to the doctor, nodded with a smile, and returned to his seat. As the woman followed the doctor, the man returned to his magazine.

Normalcy.

They had at least half of summer ahead of them, and all of autumn.

Prescott rubbed his palms on his knees, which felt not just bony but skeletal.

It took two people to pretend.

A pact.

A subterfuge.

"Mr. Bahr."

Prescott looked up at the same nurse who had taken his vitals—Valerie. "You can come back now. Dr. Rosen is getting your films. He apologizes. He's running a little late."

Prescott felt his stomach flinch as if to a swallowed ice cube.

Barely able to breathe, he rose as if his pockets were full of lead, and managed to follow Valerie up a short corridor to a door at the end labeled "Exam Room 7." An acrylic clip affixed to the door held a folder showing a color-coded number on the tab.

A windowed door a few feet to the left was labeled "Staff Only." A corridor extending to the right presumably led to other exam rooms.

Valerie waited for Prescott to precede her into the room.

A red-topped table stood against the wall to the left; a small white-topped desk against the wall to the right. A chair on rollers was parked in front of the desk; an auxiliary chair stood to the right of it, facing inward. The blue and plum upholstery on both chairs matched the upholstery in the waiting room. A light box was attached to the wall above the desk; various other instruments were attached to the other walls. A large window, spanning most of the exterior wall, looked out onto what had to be 34th Street.

"The doctor will be right with you." Valerie closed the door.

He had brought this on himself.

He was a goddamn idiot.

Sitting down in the chair beside the desk, Prescott took a deep breath, and wiping his hands on his knees, stared at a pattern of alternating white tiles and black tiles on the floor—each tile a square if you looked at it one way, a diamond if you looked at it another way.

A glass half empty if you looked at it one way; a glass half full if you looked at it another way. A mean-spirited sonuvabitch of a God if you looked at the sonuvabitch one way; a laissez-faire sonuvabitch of a God if you looked at the sonuvabitch another way.

Two raps. Before Prescott could respond, a slight man, mid-forties, dark kindly eyes and hints of gray at the temples, entered the room. He was wearing a white coat embroidered with *Alvin B. Rosen,* MD above the breast pocket, in red stitching. A riotous tie featuring lilac and fuchsia was loosely knotted at his neck; a lavender stethoscope was draped around his neck. The folder from the door, and a large radiology envelope, were clutched in one hand.

Dr. Rosen closed the door. "I'm sorry to keep you waiting, Mr. Bahr. It's been a hectic day. Did anyone come with you today?"

Prescott felt his stomach try to wriggle itself under a rock.

He shook his head.

Why hadn't he asked her to come?

Why?

He was a goddamn idiot.

Dr. Rosen laid the folder and large envelope on top of the desk and pulled several shadowy films from the envelope.

"It's too soon to make a diagnosis, Mr. Bahr, but the preliminary indication is that you have an abnormality on your brain stem."

It wasn't even summer yet!

Dr. Rosen held up a film, set it aside; held up another, set it aside, held up another, and switching on the light box, slipped the film under the pinch on the viewing panel toward Prescott.

Prescott stopped breathing.

Slipping a tuning fork from his breast pocket, Dr. Rosen pointed it toward the light box. "See this area here?"

He was trapped inside one dream being forced to witness a second—

He'd wake up any second now and find himself—

"Can you see this, Mr. Bahr?"

Rising from his chair, Prescott found himself staring at a—

᷍

—bird, high overhead, so utterly suffused with sunlight as to appear pure white, like an angel. The bird disappearing, as if absorbed into an azure infinity, Prescott moved on, and soon came to a modest headstone of speckled granite. The inscription on the polished face was new to him—

KATHARINE FRALEY BAHR

It had been added since that day, eight years ago now, to the day, he had stood on this same ground, trying ever so hard not to ask Rev. Perkins, a well-meaning sort, to make sense of a fucking asshole of a God, who would call one of his children to his bosom with such urgency as to compel her to grease the skids with nineteen hits of Trazodone.

Sinking to his knees, Prescott held his head to the ground, sobbing, shuddering, drooling, until his throat felt half burned away by vomitous upwellings. Getting to his feet then, he lifted his face into a coolish breeze and looked again overhead.

A bird, so utterly suffused with sunlight as to appear pure white, like an angel, was as if writing, in sweeping strokes of cursive—

There is always hope.

⌒♏⌒

Prescott dropped into his chair and slumped.

"Are you all right?"

Prescott nodded, holding his eyes on a white square underfoot. Or was it a diamond?

Dr. Rosen switched off the light box, and rolling the desk chair backward, positioned it to face Prescott. He sat down. "As I mentioned, Mr. Bahr, it's too early to make a diagnosis. We know there's an abnormality, we know it's on your brain stem, and that's all we know. We're going to take things one step at a time. There are several possibilities, each one subject to various recourses. OK?"

Prescott looked at a whitish splotch lingering on the light box. "Worst case."

Dr. Rosen straightened himself and took a deep breath. "Worst case is you have what we call a glioblastoma multiforme, or glioma. But, as I said—"

"Which is what, exactly?"

"It's a cancer."

"A death sentence."

"There are several treatments, and many people respond to at least one of them."

"How long?"

Dr. Rosen patted Prescott on the knee as if to deliver a gentle reprimand. "Mr. Bahr, all we know at this point is—"

"How long, please? Worse case."

The doctor sagged. "Following diagnosis, usually eight to twelve months. With treatment, sometimes up to several months longer. But, once again, Mr. Bahr, we don't know at this point exactly what you have. All we know is you have an abnormality. To find out exactly what you have, and what the ramifications are, we're going to have to get a biopsy done." He smiled. "This is a very simple procedure. A surgeon makes a small hole in your skull and extracts a small sample from the area of abnormality. That's it. Usually you're in the day before and out the day after." He smiled. "I assumed you'd want to go ahead with this so I arranged for you to see Dr. Chatterjee early next week. He's the guy I'd send my daughters to in a similar situation. He'll go into all this further with you, and set up an appointment for the procedure. Of course, the sooner you get it done, the sooner we'll know exactly what we're dealing with."

Prescott liked the "we." We, we, we . . . all the way home!

"They'll have an appointment slip for you out at the desk. I believe they have you scheduled for next Tuesday morning. They'll also have a number for you to call if you have any questions or concerns in the meantime, or if you just need to talk to somebody. We all know how anxiety-provoking this kind of thing can be, so, please, Mr. Bahr, as questions or concerns arise, don't hesitate to call us."

Prescott nodded—a sort of scissors stroke for ending the interview. He was done.

"Do you have any questions for me now?"

Prescott shook his head.

Dr. Rosen lifted the color-coded folder from the desktop, and opening it on his lap, thumbed to the second sheet. He lingered for a moment, then looked toward Prescott. "Any change in the headaches?"

Prescott shook his head.

The doctor looked at him.

"No change in intensity?"

Prescott shook his head.

"Any change in the weakness you've been experiencing?"

Prescott shook his head.

The doctor paged to the third sheet, lingered for a moment, then, setting the folder back on the desktop, pulled a prescription pad from the desk, made a few scribbles, and handed a sheet to Prescott. "This'll help with both the headaches and the generalized weakness. You've got some swelling in there and it's pressure from this that's causing your symptoms. Start with what I've ordered and let's see how you do. Have you noticed any other problems at all? Any problems with speech, any difficulty swallowing, anything like that?"

Prescott shook his head.

"Any tunnel vision?"

Prescott shook his head.

"Good." Dr. Rosen patted Prescott on the knee. "You've got one of the best neurological teams in the world in your corner, Mr. Bahr." The doctor smiled. "Keep the faith." Rising quickly from his chair, the doctor snapped the film from the light box, and slipping it and the other films back into the large envelope, took both the envelope and folder into the same hand.

Prescott peered up at the doctor. "You know what it is, don't you?"

"Other than what I've already mentioned, Mr. Bahr, the only other thing I know for sure is what my mother used to tell me every time I got another Dear Alvin letter, which was about once a month: 'There's always hope.'" He smiled. "If that weren't the case, Mr. Bahr, I wouldn't have three wonderful daughters today, and I most certainly wouldn't be in the line of work I'm in." He moved to the door and held it open.

Prescott rose slowly from his chair.

"We'll give you a call just as soon as we have the results from your biopsy. Again, if you have *any* questions or concerns in the meantime, please do not hesitate to call us. OK?"

The doctor disappeared through the Staff Only door, leaving Prescott more alone than he had ever been before in his complete disaster of a life.

Delmyra was in class.

His mother was dead.

Did anyone come with you today?

⁓

"Constance—Marie—Augsbury."

Prescott climbed the next step, keeping a firm hold on the back of Jeremy's robe, as Connie strode self-confidently across the platform toward Dr. Bromley.

Except for the medallion, Dr. Bromley's costume was exactly the same as the regalia Prescott's father used to wear at Harvard ceremonies, the doctors Bahr and Bromley having both received their PhDs from Princeton, both from the same department, both on the same day, and back to back—or was it back to front?

It was this fortuitous circumstance, in fact, that had led to those two Frankliana figurines becoming fixtures in his father's library, and to Dr. Bahr's beloved son being only a few steps away from *finally* being certified respectable.

"English Literature. Summa Cum Laude."

Watching Connie's father follow his daughter with his video camera, Prescott tried to reconcile the Connie Augsbury headed to New York to write ad copy, of all things, with the Connie Augsbury who had written such lines as:

> *What mystery named light*
> *allowed beyond shutter and shade*
> *Fires not the prism*
> *mother miracle has made?*

Prescott squirmed to a trickle of sweat down his spine.

Anticipating the next announcement, he gave Jeremy a goose.

Jeremy jumped.

"Jeremy—"

Jeremy stepped toward Dr. Bromley.

"Matthew—"

Prescott ascended to the platform.

"Averdesian."

Prescott felt as if he had just stood up in a canoe.

"Philosophy—"

Prescott tried to will himself to steadiness.

"Magna Cum Laude."

Prescott watched Jeremy's father follow his son with his camera and tried to reconcile the Jeremy Averdesian headed to Harvard Law, of all places, with the Jeremy Averdesian who had written *Time to Say Goodbye: A Manifesto for Dissolution of the Union.*

"Henry—"

Prescott lurched into motion.

"Prescott—"

He aimed at Bromley.

"Bahr."

He drifted left.
"Art History."
He overcorrected.
Gasps.
He plummeted.

⸙

Prescott took the stairs down to G level and found his way to the main lobby. About to step into the revolving door, he deferred to a black man pushing an elderly white woman in a wheelchair. Stepping then into the next compartment, Prescott emerged into a maelstrom of sound and fury. Several black valets wearing blue baseball caps were attending cars arriving and departing. A car alarm was sounding. People were coming and going. The wind was whipping up grit. An elderly black man, wearing a Phillies cap, was attempting to transfer from a four-legged walker to a wheelchair. An elderly black woman, presumably the man's wife, was holding onto the chair, but was obviously unable to lend any greater assistance.

Prescott grasped the man's arm, to prevent a fall, but was dismissed by a black man wearing a HUP badge. "I got it."

Arriving soon thereafter at the near corner of Spruce and 37th, Prescott paused to a burst of wind-blown grit—just long enough, it seemed, for 'fright' to catch up to 'flight.'

Just when he was finally *beginning to get his life together—*
Tears.

Hurrying up Spruce, head down, Prescott crossed over where the 39th Street walkway began and strode up the walkway as if he were late for an appointment. Feeling suddenly nauseous, he veered to a bench near the Locust Walk intersection, and dropping down on this, his back to the walkway, leaned forward and retched.

Finally purged, Prescott spat out a few bits of debris, wiped a sticky wetness from his beard, blew debris from his nose, and holding his head in both hands, closed his eyes.

Did anyone come with you today?

Springing to his feet, Prescott staggered to a sudden stab of agony deep in his brain, faltered, fell. Scrambling to his feet, he winced to another stab of agony, staggered—and willed himself forward.

The pain began to ebb.

Arriving at the intersection with Walnut, where the 39th Street walkway became a street, Prescott crossed Walnut against the light, and a few yards further, arrived at the easily overlooked entrance to the Treatment Research Center.

Buzzing himself in, Prescott found the waiting area illuminated but empty. Entering his office, he locked the door, and logging on to his computer, typed "white house switchboard" into the Search field on the tool bar. He scanned the top hit:

> Contacting the White House
> The White House 1600 Pennsylvania Avenue NW Washington, DC 20500. Phone Numbers Comments: 202-456-1111 Switchboard: 202-456-1414 FAX: 202-456-2461, TTY/TDD ...
> www.whitehouse.gov/contact/—14k—Cached—Similar pages—Filter

He blew a nugget of debris into a tissue, cleared his throat, dialed 202-456-1414, and cleared his throat.

A voice—distinctively black, matronly—answered after one ring: "The White House."

Prescott cleared his throat: "I'd like to speak with Gilbert Bahr, please."

"Who's calling, please?"

"Prescott Bahr. Henry Prescott Bahr. I'm his son."

"Do you have his direct number?"

"No, I'm sorry, I don't. I need"—his voice quavered—"I need to speak to him." He swallowed. "It's very important."

"Just a moment."

Prescott started to hang up, retreated; started to hang up, retreated—

The woman came back on the line. "Sir?"

"Yes."

"Mr. Bahr says he doesn't have a son."

He was crawling on his hands and knees. He passed his mother's room, breath bated, and then his father's room, heart stopped. He felt a rush of relief then at arriving at his own room. Finding the doorknob, he unlatched the door with as much control as he could muster, crawled inside, and turning the knob with as much control as he could muster, got slowly to his feet, using the knob and the near wall to steady himself.

Turning around, he flinched to a strange apparition not three feet distant.

Marley?

A blow to the side of the head was followed by a choke hold around the throat—

Down the hallway he went—

Thump, thump, thump down the stairs—

Thump, thump, thump down the stoop—

Down the walkway he went—

"Worthless piece o' shit."

Twinkle, twinkle little star—

✣

"Sir?"

"Sorry to have troubled you. My mistake."

Prescott stared at a smudge on Frank Peoples's intake form, where he had tried to correct an error by writing over it, thereby making it worse. Snatching the form into hand, Prescott tore it into shreds, and jumping to his feet, bludgeoned his computer monitor with his telephone handset, and then, all but blinded by stabs of agony in return, flung the handset against the wall.

Worthless piece o' shit.

Falling backward into his chair, Prescott lunged to his feet, as if in recoil, and yanking "Lifeboat against Dark Sky" from the near wall, slammed it broadside over the back of his chair, to another stab of agony, and tore the ruptured canvas to shreds—

Worthless piece o' shit.

Likewise "Solitary Swan"—*worthless piece o' shit*—likewise "Moon over 63rd Street"—*worthless piece o' shit*—likewise "Seven Pigeons in a Row"—*worthless piece o' shit*—until, holding "Delmyra's Wicker Rocker" overhead, he began to tremble— and then to sob. Sinking to his knees, Prescott lowered "Wicker Rocker" onto the floor, and collapsing atop it, drew himself into a ball.

Did anyone come with you today?

30th Street Station, Philadelphia

September 17th, 8:09 p.m.

Ben awakened with a start to discover Lucy Myers well poised toward abandoning her seat. "We're in Philly," she announced. Several passengers in proximity, Ben noticed, were a'ready upstanding in the aisle, some pulling parcels and articles of luggage from the overhead rack, others queuing toward the near exit.

"O, my apologies." Ben stirred himself toward rising from his seat. "I must have dozed off, though the images yet lingering in mind seem of a kind rare to the furnishings of mere fantasy."

The train, moving slowly through a dimly lighted catacomb, came now to a gentle stop.

Ben arose from his seat, against his druthers—he would rather have sat until the aisle had cleared—and insinuated himself into the queue, with apologies, whereupon Lucy rose and insinuated herself, a bag, and a tote also into the queue, to the general inconvenience of all in the immediate vicinity.

Pulling a third bag from the overhead rack, this one larger than the two other, Lucy added the bulk of this article to the a'ready compressed queue of flesh and freight, causing Ben thereby to backstep onto someone's foot. Not having sufficient room in which to turn around, Ben issued an apology as if to all the denizens of the car at large.

Lucy drew a handle from the top of her bag and affixed her tote to it.

The queue surging forward, Ben followed Lucy onto a platform lined at the near perimeter by a wide yellow stripe, in the manner of the platform in the New York catacomb. A marker on a post to rightward read "Track 6 / Location C." To leftward, a brass plaque, attached to a pillar at about eye level, read "Elevator / Escalator." A second plaque, directly beneath the first, bore a forward-pointing arrow.

"Good luck," Lucy called, in simultaneity with a backward glance, she

493

marching forth then, in the direction of the forward-pointing arrow, before Ben might reply.

"My gratitude for your kind assistance," he called after her. "And regards to Mr. Lynch—and to Barnigle!"

Lucy waved a hand, adjusted the strap on her shoulder, and was soon wholly disappeared.

Near alone abandoned on the dimly lit platform, Ben became sensible to low rumblings in likeness of those that had emanated from the ground grate at Pennsylvania Station. As then, it was not difficult for the imagination to ascribe such growls to a primordial creature newly sensible of an empty stomach.

Tapping his way now past the pillar bearing the forward-pointing arrow, Ben soon arrived at an entryway unto a stairway juxtaposed to an escalator. An overhead marker read "Amtrak Welcomes You to Philadelphia."

As Ben ascended upon the escalator, a firmament of honeycomb, in maroon and gold, came into view, ever increasing in expanse and grandeur until the whole of a great room, of wondrous proportion and appointment, became wholly revealed. A disembodied voice, seeming to speak directly to him, but from no particular direction, commanded his attention by way of warning: "You are nearing the end of the escalator. Please stay forward and be prepared to jump off."

Making a little jump, Ben found himself standing as if within a great temple, at either end of which stood a phalanx of massive pillars, in the Corinthian style, serving to frame floor-to-ceiling windows composed of tier upon tier of translucent panes.

A sculpture afront the leftward pillars showed an angel, wings at the vertical, holding the slumped body of a man. Surprisingly, the pose of the wings suggested descent, by command of gravity, as opposed to ascent, by triumph of wing.

Was there an irony here, inadvertent or no?

In similitude to the station at New York, the stairwells to the subterranean platforms were arranged at either side of the room, each marked by a number, and a large marquee stood at about room center, attached upon an Information Center, however, as opposed to hung from the ceiling.

Disembodied voices, of either gender, made intermittent broadcasts, these amplified, and slightly distorted, it seemed, by way of echo.

Espying a vertical banner directly across the room reading "Food Court," Ben felt a bold ache, followed by a bolder rumble.

Apparently, at least some of the denizens recently heard were in fact resident in a nearer catacomb!

Bringing to mind the map Lucy had shown him, Ben looked to rightward, and espying a modest marker, "30th Street," affixed above the centermost of several entryways, tapped his way past the Information Center and made his way up the central aisle of the great temple—alas, a temple unto which god? Industry perhaps? Approaching a revolving doorway, as at the Waldorf Astoria, Ben spied a flower shop to leftward, occupying the whole of the corner there, and smiled—

> *If I had a hammer*
> *I'd hammer in the morning*
> *I'd hammer in the evening*
> *All over this land—*

Passing through the doorway, Ben discovered himself under a portico fronted by massive pillars, these mirroring those within the temple proper. The underside of the roof, honeycombed in consonance with the temple ceiling, was illumed to eerie effect.

Beyond the portico, night had descended, but the ambient light was such that, although the house-lights had been extinguished, the theatre proper was yet illumed by a myriad of lime lights.

To leftward, Ben could see perambulators moving in parallel to what had to be, given a cacophony of roar and blare, now familiar, Market Street.

Passing around a pillar to leftward, Ben tapped his way to a crosswalk biased to rightward, and looking to leftward there, discovered in the background, both far and closer upon, several great towers standing like dark sentinels at the portal of hell itself. Each tower was distinguishable from the others by way a distinctive matrix of illuminated windows, as well as a distinctive crown atop. In the foreground, whereat the Schuylkill surely lay, a span fording it was suggested in outline by lamps in likeness to bunches of grapes held bottom end up.

Ben passed over the crosswalk, and over another such, and thereupon over a narrow roadway marked "30th Street." A modest structure here, showing a cornice of blue over green, was marked "30th Street Station." There being no ready indication concerning how this naming might associate to the grand structure at his back, the latter bearing the same name, Ben was left to his consternation.

The near end of the present 30th Street Station, by way of being open, such as to accommodate traffic, revealed within naught but a single bench spanning the length of the farther wall. Although people were entering and exiting both the near entryway and another such facing upon Market Street, not one person sought repose upon the bench.

Moving on to eastward, yet deeper into what, two centuries previous, had been mostly wilderness, Ben wondered what preservation had been extended unto the native tenants, from insect unto fowl. Likely, he dreaded, the same that had been extended unto the Canastota Indian.

Marking the roadway at either side here, Ben noticed, were poles each bearing a blue-and-yellow banner imprinted of the likeness of a dragon, in yellow, above the term "Drexel," also in yellow. Below, writ in blue upon yellow, was the term "University." The object here, Ben surmised, was likely to associate the symbology of the dragon with the term "Drexel" such that the latter might become, by sly equation, the former.

To rightward, past a modest plaza of small trees standing in squarish planters, was a modest structure bearing the same blue over green striping upon its cornice as Ben had observed upon the similar structure at 30th Street. The present structure being marked "Septa," Ben surmised Septa to be in counterpart to MTA and MBTA, and both this and the previous structure to be an entry unto an underground station.

Bringing to memory now Lucy's map, Ben crossed over 31st Street, and over Market Street, and encountered thereupon a red-brick building, marked BENNETT S. LEBOW / ENGINEERING CENTER / DREXEL UNIVERSITY, that showed naught of ornament, neither roundel nor arch, every aspect of its architecture being, it would appear, in service to practicality alone.

The following crossing street, Ben soon discovered, intersected Market only at the farther side. At the near side, in the stead of a continuation of the crossing street, the latter necessarily being 32nd Street, a commodious pathway led obliquely to southwestward—indeed, unto the very area, Ben surmised, that had been tinted purple upon Lucy's map.

Close upon the entry to this pathway, to rightward, was a statuary showing a man sitting upon a chair, the latter and its occupier being elevated upon a squarish pedestal variegated as if by some intrinsic phosphorescence. The man, hunched well forward, appeared to be brooding over some perplexity yet elusive to his understanding. A building immediately behind, plain and squarish, was marked MATHESON HALL / DREXEL UNIVERSITY.

Upon entering a few steps onto the oblique pathway, Ben, yet look-ing to the statuary, discovered an inscription graven upon the pedes-tal, and paused to regard it. Able to perceive no more than Science & Industry, he approached a low barrier of black granite bordering the pathway, but still he could perceive no more of the inscription.

Giving a little bow now, in honor, he assumed, of the namesake either of the building marked Matheson or of Drexel University itself, Ben turned away. The pathway ahead, being marked at either side by lamps of modest stature, seemed to draw him forward of a sort of luminous magnetism.

Tapping his way toward the first of these lamps, Ben encountered a young man, presumably a matriculate of Drexel University, speaking into a device held in hand, and soon after him, another such, a young woman. A third student, a young man, was holding in hand a small device from which a wire led unto one ear. In each case, the eyes of the young person were cast downward, such that, as he or she passed by, in close proximity, there was no meeting of eyes, nor opportunity for such.

The pathway was agreeably wide, such as to accommodate a fair volume of traffic, and was wrought, it would appear, of that substance called "concrete," in consonance with the plain practicality previously noted. In the middle of the pathway, Ben noticed, a trail of paw prints, rendered in blue, suggested a mortal presence of the very dragon emblazoned as symbol upon the banners marking Market Street.

Crossing over a modest plaza, within a common area circumvented by more plain buildings, Ben continued upon the pathway, and soon came upon a small plaza, adjacent to a busy street, whereat the here-tofore monopoly of plainness in service to practicality was loosed a bit, by way of a mostly concrete pavement including now a few accents of brick.

Looking askance across the intersection of 33rd and Chestnut, Ben could discern, whereat indeed expectation would have it, a continua-tion of two rows of lamps at the oblique. Thereupon crossing over 33rd Street, and then over Chestnut, Ben discovered himself traversing upon a pathway composed entirely of brick, arranged in the herringbone style, and lined to side by ebony curbstones. The lamps here, taller than those previous, were in likeness of swans bowing their heads, and were arranged such that each illumed a slab bench wrought of the same ebony stone, it would appear, as were the curbstones.

Although the pathway here, as previous, was well populated of young persons in transit, some propelling velocipedes—called "bicycles," he seemed to recall—many bearing a device, or a wire to ear, not one was to be discovered reposed upon a bench, chin upon fist, such as to contemplate some perplexity yet elusive to the understanding.

Close upon to rightward, a small marker showed "Woodland Walk" as well as, below, a diminutive escutcheon divided into two parts—an upper part, red, and a larger part, white. The lower part held within it an inverted V, blue, and upon this were imprinted three white dots, the middle of which was elevated above the other two. Although there was indeed a hint of ascendancy in the present environs, relative to the previous, there was hardly a stick of wood with which to justify "Woodland."

Nearing upon another intersection, Ben espied, at the farther side of 34th Street, green markings and accents reminding of those associated with the ATM device on Milk Street in Boston. Crossing over 34th Street, Ben tapped his way to a set of glass doors under a green awning, and peering through the nearer door, discovered several ATM devices arranged along an interior wall. He pulled on the handle of the immediate door, and then the other, but neither would yield.

This inhospitality was indeed most perplexing, as the alcove was illuminated such as not simply to accommodate entry therein but to invite it.

In the moment, a young man arrived upon a bicycle, and tethering this modest conveyance to a small station fashioned in the shape of an inverted U, nearby the curb, approached the glass door, and slipping a card from a wallet taken from a pack tethered to his waist, slid the card though a small device to rightward of the doors. Upon a mechanical click, the young man pulled the near door open and entered into the alcove.

Removing from pocket now his own card, Ben slid this through the card device, in imitation of the young man, and pulled upon the near handle, but the door was yet unyielding. Feeling of a sudden lightheaded, Ben slumped forward, hands upon knees, and took a measured breath. Whilst so postured, he noticed upon the card device an icon demonstrating as to the proper orientation of the card. Upon another measured breath, Ben imitated the icon, and to a mechanical click, was permitted into the alcove.

Thereupon stepping to the ATM device at the farther side of the one presently claimed by the young man, Ben discovered it, to his relief, to be similar to the one he had mastered at Milk Street. Great was his surprise then, when, upon inserting his card into the slot accommodating it, and entering his code by way of the pad of buttons, the device spoke to him: "Say or select your transaction," the device said, in a monotone reminding of a disembodied voice in a stationhouse.

"Good evening," Ben replied.

"Good evening," the young man said, smiling toward Ben. "You look just like him."

"Please repeat your request," the machine said.

"Thank you, sir. Most kind of you. I do try my best."

"Please repeat your request," the machine repeated.

"Ready money," Ben said.

"Please repeat your request."

"Paper currency," Ben tried.

"Get cash," the young man said.

"Thank you," the machine said.

"Thank you," Ben said.

"You can just use the screen," the young man said. "You don't have to speak."

"Thank you," Ben said.

The young man left.

Following the young man's counsel, Ben was soon in possession of five crisp Jacksons. Returning then to the near corner, he crossed over Walnut Street, in the wake of several young people crossing against the permission signal, to whereat the oblique pathway continued. To leftward here, a curious pole of totems confirmed by way of direct advertisement—University of Pennsylvania—what had heretofore been but hinted at, that Ben had indeed entered upon the purple area on Lucy's map.

To rightward, a large marquee, larger even than the one Ben had encountered at the corner of Washington and School Streets in Boston, bore the same advertisement as the totem, and below this, a map showing in spectral differentiation what Lucy's map had shown collectively in purple—open space in yellow, structures in orange, pathways in white.

Locating his present position upon the map, Ben determined that by continuing at the oblique he would soon arrive at Locust Walk, which pathway, he knew from Lucy's map, would lead him westward unto South 47th Street.

Sensing imminence of another faint spell, Ben rested his head against the vitreous shield over the map, and gripping the near end of the marquee, took comfort in being in possession of five Jacksons with which he might hire a livery, should he encounter such. Taking now a measured breath, and feeling sufficiently restored, he continued onward.

The pathway here was changed in constituency, Ben noticed, from brick to cobblestone, and the number of young people traversing it was increased, the latter likely owing, Ben surmised, to an increased proximity unto the heart of things.

Some of these young people smiled upon him, or commented regarding his manner of dress: "Cool," one said. "It must be after midnight," another said.

Shortly past a marker bearing "Locust Walk" and a forward-pointing arrow, Ben came upon a building showing upon its near side naught but window glass, to effect of revealing several denizens within engaged in wanton acts of study. The intent here, it would appear, was to remind wayfarers without, engaged with their communication devices, as to a higher calling.

Entering now into a common area holding a few trees, sparsely distributed, Ben winked unto himself. Perhaps this was the "Woodland" alluded to earlier.

To rightward here, directly afront of the "fish bowl," a curious sculpture was reminding of a large button swooning to a mysterious source of heating. Behind this, several bicycles were tethered to stations manifestly fashioned for such.

To leftward, an elevated sculpture, silhouetted by a celestial glow emanant from behind, was reminding of the one encountered earlier, the present such being also of a figure reposed. Looking to the celestial glow behind, Ben discovered it to be emanating from the vestibule of a grand edifice reminding indeed of the very manor house of that most ignominious of scoundrels, Lord Hillsborough himself!

Drawn forth now of curiosity, Ben entered onto the pathway leading to the sculpture, and upon approaching the reposed figure, recognized, with a start, the distinctive aspects, although these were greatly outsized, of his own head!

Alas, north was here become south, east become west.

If any figure should be here reposed, Ben adjudged, it should be the one previously encountered, or the like. Indeed, if anything soever in this world should be elevated unto highest honor, upon this ground or the like, it should be the very facility for thought itself, naked of all vanity.

Ben hung his head a moment, and then, turning his back upon

himself, noticed a bronze relief embedded in the pathway close upon
his feet. Being circular, it was reminding of the bronze encountered
afront the *Courant* building in Boston, and bore, in a peripheral arc,
BLANCHE P. LEVY PARK—toward conferring upon the named, one
might suspicion, in exchange for a sufficient number of Jacksons, one
might suspicion, affectionate remembrance unto all eternity.

Ben recalled a verse he had penned in counterpoint to such commerce, to wit: If you would not be forgotten / as soon as you are dead
and rotten / either write things worth reading / or do things worth
the writing. He imagined now a kindred verse, to wit: If you would not
be pinched of regret / over an eternity of fit and fret / bake thee three
loaves each day / the better two to give away.

Returning to the main path, Ben paused to bear witness to a young
man yodeling atop the melting button, under supervision, it would
appear, of an overseer, and tapped his way then to southwestward,
which direction, he did fervently hope, had not become, by some
alchemy of wrongheadedness, northeastward.

Arriving at an intersection whereat the present pathway continued
on at the oblique, to southwestward, whilst a crossing pathway led
directly westward, Ben looked for a marker complementary to the one
pointing toward Locust Walk, but discovered instead, ahead and to the
right, a curious sculpture fashioned such as to compose LOVE in scarlet
blocks, with the first two of these being seated atop the latter two. Ben
smiled, the symbology here being as clever as unmistakable, it capturing both sunderment and conjoinment in simultaneity.

The location of the westward pathway relative to the present pathway seemed congruent with what Ben had observed on the marquee
map recently studied. In addition, the westward pathway seemed wider
and more trafficked than the present pathway, as might be expected of
a main artery leading unto the very heart of things.

Bearing rightward, Ben tapped his way onto the westward pathway.

The pavement here seemed more ancient than any previous, with
many of the bricks showing fractures or discolorations or both. Inlaid
at the center of the pathway was a curious pattern, fashioned of small
cobbles, suggesting a wave being propagated in a jagged line as opposed
to a rounded such.

As if riding the energy of this wave, Ben soon entered into a sort of
tunnel formed of small trees to side and their overspreading branches
above. A leafy filigree held a myriad of jeweled lights like stars. As Ben
moved under this magical firmament, he began to feel as if mesmerized

unto levitation. This airy illusion was soon deflated, however, by a broadcast of blare and percussion from an open window to rightward, near to which a banner bearing a skull-and-crossbones was displayed with palpable boldness.

Reminded of the role of this very symbol in the rites of freemasonry, Ben was visited by image of the young Daniel Rees, aflame of spilt oil, screaming of an agony beyond the ability of any chronicler to relate, or the facility of any ear to endure. He shuddered—and was startled by a bicycle passing precariously proximate, the rider being engaged upon a device held to ear. A mechanical throbbing from overhead began to rival the broadcast of blare and percussion, then began to yield, ever more rapidly, by way of recession.

There was no starry firmament here, Ben noticed, illusory or otherwise.

Picking up his pace, such as to hasten his removal from proximity to the broadcast window, Ben soon came upon a crossing pathway marked as a street, 37th *Street*, despite being in width and constituency identical to the present pathway, marked as a walk. This violation in symmetry, Ben surmised, likely owed to the incongruity of "37th Walk."

Indeed, shorn of their wool, all men were poets.

Espying a young man standing at a call station to leftward, Ben could not but surmise, given recent experience, that the poor fellow must have lost use of his communication device, and was presently engaged in making a desperate plea for rescue.

Espying then a bold mosaic at center of the intersection, Ben approached upon this, and discovering it to be a rendering of a compass, surmised he had arrived at the very *le coeur*—or was it *les coeurs*?—to which various hints and clues had consistently been conspiring.

Resembling a wheel upon a Roman chariot, this remarkable rendering was constituted of a reddish hub at center, a gray-white rim at perimeter, and eight reddish spokes, like balusters, betwixt. Four ebony spires pointed from the hub unto the four cardinal directions, the latter denoted upon the rim by letters of gold: W, opposite; S, leftward; E, near to foot; and N, rightward. The W was slightly biased to leftward relative to the line of Locust Walk, implying thereby that Locust Walk did not run quite true to westward. It was not clear, however, whether the orientation of the compass was in reference to geologic north or to magnetic north. Whatever the case, this remarkable symbol, Ben adjudged, was entirely fitting to location, this being the center of a universe of learning, the purpose of which was, one would ardently hope, to provide an appropriate bearing of direction unto the wayfarers being indentured there, that they might thereupon steer not only the vessel of their lives unto a proper destination, but also, with others in concert, and in humility, the great ship of state.

Continuing toward South 47th Street, still ten intersections distant, Ben had progressed perhaps three-quarters the expanse of the mosaic when he sensed an imminent encroachment from leftward. Looking to this direction of reflex, Ben discovered a rider, upstanding upon a strange conveyance—a mere stalk betwixt two large wheels—bearing down upon him whilst holding a device to ear, eyes askance. And even though the rider espied Ben in the very next moment, and made desperate attempt to amend his trajectory to westward, whilst Ben made equal attempt to retreat to eastward, both actions came a fraction of a moment too tardy.

The one party now came into intimate contact with the other, in a glancing blow, but with sufficient force as to cause Ben to fall backward onto the pavement.

Although immediately aware of an agony in his right shoulder, Ben was distracted by a potentially far graver affliction, and upon confirming his spectacles missing, sat up and was about to conduct a search, fearing the worst, when he received his spectacles by hand of the young rider. "I'm *so* sorry," the young man said. "Are you all right? Is anything broken? Should I call 9-1-1?"

"If I can stand, sir, and take a step, I am intact."

Making effort to get to his feet, Ben was assisted toward this end with great solicitude by the young man, who thereupon restored Ben also of his cane. No sooner had Ben taken this instrument in hand, however, than he began to wobble.

Grasping Ben by the arm, and thereupon clasping him around the waist, the young man urged Ben toward a bench he assured was located very close by. "You probably know it," he added.

Before Ben might query into this curious speculation, the young man offered to summon someone toward gathering him home.

"You are most kind," Ben replied, "but I require but a few moments of repose to collect myself." He sighed. "It's been a most strenuous day."

Noticing the young man's vehicle to be yet upstanding on but two points of contact, seemingly in defiance of a certain Newtonian imperative, Ben deduced the only truth possible—wizardry had kept apace with invention, the broomstick thereby with the horse.

As they passed close upon the call stations, Ben discovered the same young man to be yet standing at one of these, he having apparently taken no notice of the calamity that had recently transpired almost at his very feet. Espying then a bench set back a few feet from the walkway, Ben could discern a figure reposed upon the leftward end of this, biased as if toward someone a'ready occupying the other end. As they drew closer, Ben recognized a bronze likeness of himself, holding a broadsheet in one hand, a walking stick in the other. A bronze bird was alighted upon the back of the bench, toward what symbology Ben could not immediately speculate.

The young man eased Ben onto the rightward end of the bench, and upon excusing himself, departed to retrieve his "Segway," as he named it.

Ben closed his eyes, and judging himself ill fit to perambulate more than modestly farther, determined to inquire of the young man as to where, close upon, he might hire a hackney.

Returning upon his broomstick, the young wizard dismounted, and pressing something upon the gripping arms, these crosswise to the stalk, eased the stalk forward until it rested upon the pavement. He looked then from Ben to his bronze likeness, and back. In the moment, Ben was holding his cane in his left hand, his right shoulder being yet bothersome—in mirror image indeed to his likeness, which was holding its cane in its right hand. "Great shot," the young man apprised, pulling his device from pocket.

Aiming his device then toward the sculpture, at about eye level, the young man took a few steps backward, requiring thereby a passing perambulator to issue a polite warning and to veer to rightward, such as to avoid a collision.

"That device, good sir," Ben admonished, "is likely to be the instrument of an untimely demise—your own, or that of some unfortunate innocent."

The young man extended an apology toward the perambulator, a young lady showing Oriental aspects of countenance and stature, and then again held the likely means of an untimely demise at about eye level. A flash left Ben temporarily unseeing, and sensible of a circle tinted to reddish. The young man thereupon held his device such that Ben might see himself poised in symmetry with his likeness. "You're a dead ringer," the young man declared.

Ben smiled. "Indeed."

Returning his device to pocket, the young man elevated his wrist to sufficient height that he might read his timepiece. He was a tall lad, perhaps near unto six feet, although likely rendered taller than in actuality by way of a slender stature. His hair, closely coiffed, was dark and curly. His eyes, deeply set, were reminding of buttons recessed upon a settee cushion. Perhaps most distinctive about this young man, however, was that aspect of presence one experienced as a sort of magnetism.

Ben thought of TJ.

"Mind if I hang with you a bit? I can't stay long, but I'm not going to be able to rest easy unless I'm certain you're going to be OK. You took quite a hit back there. I'm really sorry."

Ben lifted a hand. "You need not attend upon me any farther, good sir. I feel quite hale if not quite hardy. I'm sure you have other matters to attend to. You have been most kind."

The young man offered his hand. "David Bornstein."

Changing his cane to his other hand, Ben gripped David's hand to the firmness felt. "Benjamin Franklin."

David grinned. "I had an inkling."

"I would invite you to take a seat, Mr. Bornstein, toward your own comfort, but there would appear to be no such available."

David crossed his right ankle behind his left ankle, and biasing himself slightly forward, lowered himself directly into a sitting position, knees akimbo.

Even at the height of his prowess as a lissome swimmer, Ben surmised, he would not have been able to master such a skill. He looked to this supple wizard's curious means of transport. "Your broomstick, sir, is a relatively uncommon means of transport, is it not? I have encountered no other such in the course of sojourns through three great cities."

David smiled. "Yeah, they're a bit pricey, and the logistics can be a bit of a pain. Mainly they're just a novelty. The only reason I've got this one is because my father sent it to me. He thought it'd be perfect for getting around on campus. He told me he was going to send me his, which had probably been sitting in his garage since the day he bought it, but then decided I should have the latest version, with all the latest bells and whistles, so he had this one shipped instead."

Ben recalled the tableau in Boston that showed William behind a mechanics-enamored father in a posture of genuflection. "Do I sense a father being perhaps a little too encouraging toward his son becoming a likeness of himself?"

David smiled. "I hate gadgets—always have. After twenty-four years, you'd think he'd finally get the message!"

Looking to the oversized wheels on David's broomstick, Ben was reminded of the wheels on a Roman chariot, indeed of one such "wheel" at the near intersection! "I harbor a curiosity, sir, as to whether, in standing upon this relatively uncommon device, you perhaps stand upon something of a center of things, by way of the notice, if not the envy, thereby drawn unto you." Ben smiled, holding his cane to front, one hand atop the other. "Feel free to scold me, sir, if I am too forward in inviting myself into your parlour."

"No problem." David moved his head side-to-side. "I'd have to agree with what you suggest, in principle—don't all novelties draw attention? But, as I said, the only reason I've got this particular novelty is because my father sent it to me, with the expectation I would use it."

"Should I infer then that you employ this particular novelty, even against the cumbersome logistics to which you allude, not for the utility it renders you, nor for the notice it draws unto you, but alone toward meeting an obligation received apiece with the novelty itself?"

David smiled. "OK, it *does* separate me from the crowd a bit; and, *yes*, there is some degree of satisfaction in that."

"I am in the presence of an honest man." Ben bowed.

David smiled.

"Now, sir, if I might remain in your parlour a moment longer, might it likewise be the case that you enjoy some measure of satisfaction in being a matriculate at this institution, it being also a center of things? I take liberty to assume you are indeed a matriculate at this institution."

David smiled. "You're tough." He nodded. "Yes, I am a matriculate here. I'm at the Wharton School. And, yes, I have to agree with what you suggest"—he grinned—"being an honest man and all."

Ben thought of his old friend Samuel Wharton, and, his cheeks warming, the scheme he and Samuel had advanced, in league with certain other gentlemen "at the center of things," toward realizing the Grand Ohio Company, to which 20 million acres were to be granted by the Crown in exchange for little greater than £10,000.

What saint is not subject to greed's contagion? What angel is not susceptible?

"Might one infer, sir, from your confession, that esteem is of some importance to you, and, by inference, you being representative of the larger whole, to the majority of your race?"

David smiled. "A basic requirement, I think."

Ben bowed. "Now, sir, before your kind hospitality should discover its limit, might I have your opinion regarding whether there should be as much consideration attended upon the means by which one gathers his esteem as upon the object itself?"

"More, I would have to say."

"And the reason?"

"Machiavelli to the contrary, the ends don't always justify the means."

Ben smiled. "I'm in the presence of a philosopher—which no honest man can other be."

David smiled. "Whatever you're selling, I'll take a dozen."

"I have no intention toward flattery, sir."

David nodded. "Thank you."

"Now, young sir, begging your hospitality yet a moment longer, might I have your opinion as regards the nature of esteem itself? Is there but one flavour of this aether that varies in degree, or might there be a variety of flavours each one varying in degree? For example, sir, is the esteem one might derive from attaining a high office of a flavour with the esteem one might derive from denying oneself the same office such as to serve his family with closer attention?"

"A variety, I would have to say."

"And which of the two flavours just mentioned, sir, if I might linger in your parlour one moment longer, would hold its sweetness to tongue unto one's last breath?"

David smiled, nodded.

Ben leaned a little forward. "If, by way of lingering too long in your parlour, sir, I should press you to consult your timepiece that you might beg your leave with grace, I would take no offence, please be assured."

David held forth his hands and grinned. "I'm not going anywhere until I find out where all this is going. Who the hell are you anyway?"

Ben slouched against the back of the bench. "I'm a simple traveler, sir, in search of truth that I might live it; live it that I might tell it. As to where all this is going, as you say, 'tis likely to go wherever we should, in concert, steer it. In this regard, sir, might I inquire of you as to whether, in your opinion, the very place of our chance meeting might also be something of a center of things?"

"It's the physical center of the campus, if that's what you mean."

"And the symbol embedded thereat, sir; what do you make of it?"

"It's a compass."

"Such as used by seafarers to ensure a proper course?"

"Minus the needle."

"And the message intended of this symbol, sir, being at this particular location—supposing of all symbology an intention toward communicating a particular body of truth—have you opinion on this?"

David smiled. "I don't, but I suspect *you* do."

Ben bowed. "I apologize. I am too eager, time being too short. Might it be reasonable to infer of this symbol, sir, that it is as important to be concerned with the direction of one's life as it is to be concerned with its position?"

"Are you referring to career choice?"

"Career is itself a choice, is it not, sir? Whether to embrace such a thing or not?"

"It is, but it's a given in the culture. You *will* go to college. You *will* have a career."

"You *will* conform. You *will* not question."

David smiled.

"Are you an author, sir? Do you scribe various essays and such toward meeting the requirements imposed by your masters?"

"Lots and lots."

"And do you ever undertake such projects without benefit of the guidance, call it direction, that an explicit statement of purpose provides?"

"'Compare and contrast the theories of John Maynard Keynes and Leo Strauss in one hundred words or less'—that what you mean?"

"Precisely so."

"No."

"The content of every essay then, every coherent piece, is a function of a particular purpose, would you be inclined to agree, sir."

"I would."

"By way of analogy, sir, might we apply this same truth to the contents of every life? Indeed then, are we not all the scribes of the essential contents of our lives, line by line, paragraph by paragraph, such that he who adopts as his central purpose an amassment of gadgetry—the prestige deriving of novelty—shall author a very different history than he who adopts as his central purpose the rendering of aid and comfort to the ill fated?"

David smiled. "I take your point."

"In fact, sir, human beings make no choice, whether such be a whimsical winking of one's eye or the posting of a lethal device to the chief officer of a large company, without there being a purpose behind it, such purpose providing the very direction toward which the choice is aimed, would you agree?"

David held his eyes upon Ben as if upon an object thought to be one thing but suggesting itself in the moment to be quite another. Thereupon relaxing his gaze, having apparently reassured himself against all suspicion, he gave answer: "As long as you're not requiring the kind of purpose you're talking about to be always consciously held. I think a lot of people do a lot of things without really thinking about it or knowing why they're doing them."

"Yet, every choice is still made to purpose, is it not? In fact, is not the unconscious mind every bit as willful—call it purposeful—as the conscious mind? Is it not as likely as not, in fact, that Archimedes was asleep in his bathtub at the very moment of his famous 'awakening?'"

"Who *are* you anyway?"

"A *dead* ringer, I have been led to believe."

David shook his head. "From now on I'm going to be *very* careful about looking where I'm going."

Ben smiled. "I expect you shall. Now, sir, considering again the compass embedded at the near intersection, would you be inclined to agree that one cannot stand at center of this rendering without assuming a particular bearing of direction, the two states—standing at center of a directional, and assuming a particular bearing—being as inseparable as two faces upon the same coin?"

"I would."

"Might you be inclined to agree also, sir, by way of analogy, that one cannot stand at center of a particular purpose without assuming a particular bearing of direction?"

"Do I have a choice?"

Ben bowed. "In fact, sir, is not the compass at the physical center of this university a representation of the university itself, the latter being, in effect, a kind of center upon which young men and women are invited to stand, and thereon to be asked in a myriad of forms, by innumerable interlocutors, the greatest of all questions, to wit: *What is to be the purpose of the life with which you have been uniquely blest*? And is not the answer each individual renders to this inquiry, sir, by way of his faculties of reason and reflection, the very arrow by which the vessel of his life is given direction? And does not this direction thereupon determine, in large measure, sir, the flavour of the esteem he shall gather, indeed whether it shall be of a kind to turn unto sour or of a kind to hold steadfastly unto sweet?"

David shook his head. "Am I dreaming this? Am I going to wake up now?"

Ben smiled. "One can be awake and asleep in simultaneity, sir, just as one can be riding his broomstick and talking on his device in simultaneity, no?"

David dropped his head and shook it.

"Although I have tarried you in your parlour too long a'ready, sir, by way of my meddlesome inquiries, if I might be indulged one last curiosity, I would like to inquire of you the particular purpose you presently hold for your own life, the very one, presumably, that has directed you unto this campus."

David looked to his watch. "Another time." He smiled. "I'm meeting my dad in a bit. He's taking the train down from New York."

"A special visit?" Ben held image of Benny lying in his bed, weighted of emptiness so crushing as almost to stop all vital function.

"He's giving the keynote at a convention tomorrow." David smiled. "'The Next Big Thing in Telecom.'"

"Your father must be a man of considerable stature."

"He's the man at Global Tel."

Ben smiled. "Might I infer from the nimbus I presently witness about you, sir, that this fact about your father, that he bears golden epaulettes upon his shoulders, is a source of some pride to you? That it places you perhaps in a kind of center of things?"

David grinned. "You'd be great in a courtroom."

Ben bowed. "Thank you, sir. I do indeed have some experience in that arena—rather more, however, as the bull than as the matador. Now, as to your answer, sir?"

"Yes, my father's position is in fact a source of some pride to me, as you put it; and, yes, it does, I suppose, place me in a kind of center of things, as you put it."

"And your father's present course, sir—his own bearing of compass—is this, or similar, to become yours, as gosling after goose?"

"That's sort of why I'm here, I suppose."

"At the Wharton School."

David nodded.

"Well then, fair winds to you, sir!" Ben poised to rise. "Might you direct me, kindly, to where I might enlist the services of a hackney cab. I have a delivery to make, a destiny to keep."

By way of reversing the wizardry by which he had assumed a sitting position, David returned himself to a standing position. Ben rose then also, but by way of a lesser magic.

David glanced at his watch. "This time of night—" He looked northward, southward, eastward, westward—back to Ben. "Tell you what." He looked to his broomstick. "Take my Segway. It's real easy to operate and it'll get you around this time of night a lot faster, and a helluva lot cheaper, than anything else."

"Most generous of you, sir! Most generous indeed! But do you not require service of your device yourself, sir, such as to greet your father?"

David's countenance took on a a sheepish demeanor. "That was my father I was talking to when I bumped into you. He called to tell me he'd be taking an early train down in the morning instead of the late train tonight. Paul Kenyon had invited him to a private dinner. There were intimations of an ambassadorship."

"I'm so very sorry. You must be greatly disappointed."

David shrugged. "No big deal. I was only going to get to see him for a few minutes anyway."

"You must be greatly disappointed."

David dropped his eyes.

"I'm grateful."

"For what?"

"Being in the presence of an honest man."

"I lied to you."

"To protect yourself, at no injury to me." Ben looked to David's Segway. "If I were indeed to accept your kind offer, sir, how might I return your device to your good hands once it had delivered me unto my fate?" He smiled. "Or does it return itself upon a proper incantation?"

David smiled. "Close."

Levering the stalk to vertical, David slipped something from a pack attached toward the top of the stalk, and inserting this into a receptacle at the top, in the manner of a key into a lock, pushed a red button leftward of the receptacle. The stalk thereupon stood upright of its own accord. Stepping onto the riding platform, David demonstrated how to move the device to forward, to backward, to leftward, to rightward by no greater than leaning in the direction of intention, and thereupon demonstrated how to turn the device in place by no greater than rotating clockwise or counterclockwise a rotation device on the leftward hand grip.

"Your speed," David continued, "depends on how much you lean in the direction you're moving in. To stop, you simply stand upright—like this." David straightened himself.

Ben shook his head. "This object, sir, presumably as numb to sense as that brazen sculpture sitting upon the bench, would appear nonetheless to be as sentient as yourself."

David smiled. "Funny you should say that. I had that very discussion with a classmate back when I first got this thing. Actually, he pretty much had the discussion all by himself: 'Can it keep itself upright of its own accord?' he asked 'Yep,' he answered. 'Can it detect external stimuli—changes in the rider's center of gravity, for example?' 'Yep,' he answered. 'Can it translate these stimuli into specific actions?' 'Yep.' 'Can *you* do these things?' 'Yep.' 'Can your bicycle do them?' 'Nope.' 'QED.'"

Ben smiled. "Your colleague would appear to be well practiced in the methods of the venerable Sage."

"He's a dropout from the philosophy program at Chicago. He said he didn't want to spend the rest of his life driving a cab."

"And you are being schooled in what area of knowledge yourself, sir, if I might inquire?"

"Business. I'm in my second year at Wharton."

"Such being the flavour of the topping you have chosen for your cake, sir?"

David smiled. "One way of putting it."

"And as to the flavour of the cake itself, sir?"

"Both. White and chocolate. Psychology and English lit. I couldn't decide between them, so I did both of them."

"Might one infer then, sir, that you abide an ardent curiosity concerning the mysteries of human nature."

"One might."

"Most interesting. Your colleague is enamored of the mysteries of fundamental reality; you, of the mysteries of human behavior; and yet here you are, the pair of you, matriculated at a school of commerce. Most interesting indeed." Ben leaned forward as if to examine the Segway more closely and then straightened. "If I might indulge my curiosity yet one measure farther, sir, might I inquire as to the means by which this device receives instructions from its helmsman and thereupon translates these into a proper course?"

"Well, as I said, my dad's the gadget guy. I'm just a button pusher. All I know is it uses a gyro to keep itself upright and something called a tilt sensor to detect changes in the rider's center of gravity, and a microprocessor to turn various inputs into various actions. How it all works, I haven't got a clue."

"You are clueless then, sir?"

David smiled. "I am."

"You are truly an honest man, sir." Ben mused a moment. "Now, sir, viewing your curious device in light of this new intelligence, might we liken the gyro to an inner ear, regarding stability; the tilt sensor to a nerve ending, regarding sensing; and the microprocessor to a brain, regarding computation?"

"I think you just did."

Ben bowed. "Have you a name for your device, sir, such as one customarily attaches to a house pet?"

David grinned. "Sloan."

"And do you likewise have a name for your communication device?"

David shook his head.

"You have a term of endearment for a device which has, by your own account, ear, nerve, and brain; you have no such term for a device which has no such instruments. Quite so?"

David threw up his arms. "QED!"

Ben bowed. "'Tis at least interesting, would you not agree, sir, how readily one can be led by the reins of a carefully managed line of logic?" He winked. "Ah, but we have become distracted from the original inquiry. I had inquired, I do believe, sir, as to how I might return Mr. Sloan to your good hands once he had delivered me unto my fate?"

"No problem."

David stepped off the platform, the stalk remaining erect, and demonstrated how to tether the right wheel hub to a stationary object, such as a light pole or bike rack. He then explained how he could locate his Segway at any time by way of a "GPS" device. "When you're done with it," David concluded, "just lock it to a light pole, and I'll find it." He smiled. "How about a test run?"

"You are certain, sir, you wish to commit the fate of your broomstick to an old man of no familiarity soever with such wizardry?"

"No problem." David helped Ben stow his cane betwixt the stalk and the pack attached to it, and then helped him mount the platform. Ben stood unmoving a moment, as if frozen into a statuary, then leaned forward, causing thereby the device to launch forth, and he, straightening himself of reflex, nearly to topple over.

"Oops." David placed himself to front of the Segway. "I forgot to mention that there're three modes. Right now you're in the highest mode, so the responses to your leans are going to be a bit more sensitive than they'd be in either of the other modes. If you want, I can lower the mode, but you won't be able to go as fast—five to ten miles an hour versus about twelve. If you stay a little tentative at first, you should be fine. Like anything else, it takes a little getting used to."

"I shall place my trust entirely in your counsel, sir."

"Let's keep it in high. You'll be fine."

"Thank you, sir. It would appear you have a clue after all. Now, if I might indulge my curiosity one measure farther, sir—by what principle does your mechanism propel itself? I note no chamber sufficient to lodge a slavish gnome, nor sail with which to capture an airy current."

David grinned. "That's about the umpteenth 'one measure farther' I've heard in the last twenty minutes."

"Curiosity kills the cat, sir, but not the man. The man it makes useful."

"That's about the umpteenth epigram I've heard in the last twenty minutes!"

"What specie given in the small, sir, is not soon a pocket filled?"

David groaned, shook his head, and then looked to the platform upon which Ben was standing. "There's an electric motor and battery pack right under your feet. The pack's good for about twenty-four miles. I keep it well charged, so you should be fine. Did I show you how to turn it off?"

"I did observe you lay your device to ease, but I do not think I could replicate the effect without specific instruction."

David helped Ben from the platform, and pressing the red button upon the grip handle, held the stalk from collapsing. "That's all there is to it. Don't turn it off, though, unless you're absolutely sure you won't be needing it anymore. I've got to keep the key with me, so once it's off, dude, it's off. OK?"

"I stand forewarned."

David restarted the Segway, and after helping Ben back onto the platform, remained close upon a few steps as Ben eased the device into motion.

Navigating his way then to the compass mosaic, Ben steered full circle around the perimeter in the counterclockwise direction, and then in the clockwise direction, and then eased to a stop upon the hub, by way of straightening himself to upright.

Ben smiled toward David. "No problem."

David grinned. "Fair winds to you, sir!"

Ben bowed, shifting his balance in simultaneity such as to deny the tilt sensor false notice. "I wish toward you, young sir, not that there be no storms in your life, for such would be a disservice, but that there be no storms but that end in a glorious rainbow." Rotating the left grip, Ben turned the broomstick upon its wheels, and leaning forward, ever so slightly, eased the device into motion—to westward.

Once a post rider, always a post rider!

"Good luck!" he heard from behind.

"Tally ho!" he replied.

Staying well to rightward, such as to avoid colliding with perambulators and fellow riders, Ben soon came upon an archway overtopping a roadway, which, by logical extension, had to be 38th Street. The archway was bordered at either side by a high fence, as well as, close upon the pavement, by ground lamps in the stead of pole lamps. A cacophonous roar rose from below.

Continuing on, Ben soon came upon a singular sculpture rising from either side of the pathway. Fashioned as if of large red cylinders, it suggested two arteries, the higher spanning the pathway in the form of a ninety-degree arch, pointed upward; the lower being denied fully spanning the pathway by way of being sundered of a vital section of itself. What intelligence or admonishment was intended by this singular configuration was not immediately apparent.

Ben recalled now the LOVE sculpture, discovered near the intersection of Woodland and Locust, that captured, most cleverly, both sunderment and conjoinment in simultaneity.

Beyond the sculpture, pole lamps continued at either side of the pathway whilst the pathway itself was changed from all-brick to an admixture of brick and concrete, as if indeed to signal a transition from the one to the other, as proved to be the case regarding the previous incidence of the same admixture.

More than a few bumps now were unavoidable.

Upon passing a stone church marked ST. MARY'S EPISCOPAL, Ben espied, to northwestward, a row of shops of like size and aspect featuring awnings that were colorated such as to constitute a most agreeable collage. Implicit in this artistry, it would seem, was a restraint of individual taste and preference toward encouragement of a common aesthetic, at least for a few hundreds of yards.

Soon arriving at 40th Street, whereat the agreeable row of shops with awnings began their commonality, Ben noticed that the lamps lining Locust Walk ended at the near curb, whilst the pathway itself, become all concrete, continued westward in the width and aspect of a roadway.

Steering Sloan over the curb, Ben took a disquieting shock, and upon stuttering over a train track embedded into the roadway, he took another shock in surmounting the farther curb.

Remaining saddled, he pressed onward.

Tally ho!

⌇

Approaching the intersection of Locust and 47th Streets, Ben espied upon the farther side of 47th two buildings of four stories each, on opposing corners, each building showing tall windows in distinct groupings, as in the case of the Lincoln School in Boston. In fact, there seemed little cause to speculate these buildings other than schools, one hosting perhaps the lower grades, the other the upper grades.

Whilst the leftward building appeared to face upon Locust Street, its rightward counterpart appeared to face upon 47th Street, and to present thereto two towers terminating in turrets, as might be expected to mark the grand entry unto a castle.

Looking to the street marker, Ben determined No. 217 to be found rightward within the block, and visited presently by a most agreeable sensation, as in espying land for the first time in eight perilous weeks, turned Sloan in place and proceeded northward.

Only a few vehicles were stopped at the near curb; none at all at the opposing curb. Upon the roadway itself, there was no traffic soever. Searching ahead, Ben could discern little of distinction, the ambient light being but dim.

Keeping his attention affixed to rightward, Ben soon came upon a pair of juxtaposed domiciles arranged such that the nearer stood in mirror image to the farther. Four brick columns afront the pair bore a common balcony overtop a common porch—the latter being so far elevated above the walkway as to require a stoop in common to extend outward onto the walkway. This arrangement, together with a high brick bulkhead fronting the porch at either side of the stoop, seemed encouraging toward notions of ramparts and drawbridges.

Towers and turrets at one side of the street; ramparts and drawbridges at the other!

Two doorways were hosted within a recession at center of the domiciles, and affixed to either side of this recession was a modest numeral of metallic aspect: 229 to rightward, 227 to leftward—and, by implication, 217 close at hand!

Looking ahead, Ben espied a lone figure approaching from the farther crossing street, and allowed himself to speculate that he might well be witnessing TJ arriving at his aunt's address close upon the same moment as himself!

A second figure, Ben now noticed, to some startlement, was reposed upon one of the stoops extended onto the walkway, indeed at about where one would expect to discover No. 217. And upon the head of this reposed figure, Ben soon could discern, was a head dressing of no little familiarity!

Presently a pair of headlamps, in likeness to luminous eyes, entered upon 47th Street from the father crossing street, and progressing southward, soon took on strong semblance of the very vehicle Ben and Henry had passed on their way to the Lincoln School in Boston, the very one indeed that had near riven the taxicab Ben had embarked at the *Courant* building.

Espying now something long and slender, like a walking stick, extend from the rear window, followed by a head bearing a stocking, Ben pulled his whistle from pocket and blew a shrill note. Gaining thereby the attention of the reposed figure upon the stoop, he blew another note, and pointing forth, called out, "Assassins! Take cover!"

Springing to his feet, TJ looked to the approaching vehicle and lunging at a man passing the stoop, sent the man sprawling onto the pavement.

A fusillade of flashes now was accompanied by a staccato of reports.

The vehicle accelerating, Ben turned sharply to rightward, and lunging to side, impacted most painfully upon the pavement. A staccato of reports was accompanied by a stinging spray of bits of brick.

Allowing no indulgence in caution, Ben struggled to his feet as quickly as he might and thereupon hobbled, his heart stricken of dread, to where TJ lay face down upon the pavement. The man who had been saved, getting to his feet, hesitated a moment, and then fled.

Discovering TJ's blouse to be darkened proximate to several perforations, Ben rolled TJ onto his back, revealing thereby an ominous stain upon the pavement. Fountains of blood were upwelling in rhythmic surges through several rents in TJ's blouse.

Fixing his eyes upon Ben, jaw aquiver, TJ raised his arms.

Pater! Pater!

Ben pulled TJ into an embrace and began to rock him side to side.

TJ gagged—shuddered.

"I would have been most honored," Ben whispered, "to have had you as a son, as I am indeed most grateful to have had you as a friend."

TJ shuddered—slumped.

Uttering a most pathetic moan, in likeness indeed to a ewe robbed of her lamb, Ben raised wetted eyes unto a sullied firmament. "Why? Why? To what end?"

The circle is the only geometry.

In that moment, every agony ever suffered by a "likely Negro"—every lash, every prod, every kick, every jab, every slap, every pummel, every slash, every poke, every abuse, every tether, every shackle, every slight,

every negligence, every insult, every sunderment, every rape, every
abuse, every incarceration, every degradation, every disparagement,
every diminishment, every deprivation, every exploitation, every
abasement, every humiliation—became as if a smolder of molten tar
upon the soft tissue of Ben's soul.

Incineration of the corpus in the whole seemed the only mercy.

"He saved my life."

Ben startled, and gasping for breath, shook his head as if to wrest
sentience from that which would douse it of all light. His chest heaving, throat rasping, he turned to discover a Negro man standing close
upon, his gaunt visage of some familiarity, it seeming as if an apparition
escaped from a dreamscape only recently visited.

"I shouldn't o' run off like that," the man said, his voice little more
than a whisper.

Ben eased TJ's limp body onto the pavement, and bunching the
marten cap under TJ's head, such as to fashion a pillow, drew TJ's lids
overtop his eyes. Getting to his feet then, Ben turned unto the man. "It
matters not, sir," he said, his own voice barely a whisper, "that you fled,
only that you returned. Obviously this young man regarded your life
worth the sacrifice of his own. I can see, by your witness here, that he
was entirely correct in his judgment."

The man's eyes flooded in the instant. He began to sob with such
violence then as would seem must fracture a frame too fragile to bear
more than its own weight.

Pulling the man into an embrace, Ben rocked him to and fro, whilst
denying all reflex against the stench of a rotting soul.

There coming to ear then a distant wailing, emanant as if from
several directions in simultaneity, Ben released the man, and bowed.
"Might I beg of you, sir, that you remain fast upon this hallowed ground,
that you might explain to fullness what has occurred here? I cannot do
so myself, for reasons I must ask you to trust unheard."

The man's eyes swelled as if to sight of Satan himself. "Hey, man, they
be thinking *I* done it! You white. They believe you."

Ben looked from the man's terror unto splotches of blood showing
upon the man's face and shirt, and again unto the man's terror. "Are you
guilty of this crime, sir?"

"You knows I ain't. Tha's wha' I's sayin'."

"*I* knows you ain't, and *you* knows you ain't, so look them muthafuckas right in the eye, my good man, and let your courage be both your
savior and your solace. I could do no better."

The man showed a deportment of countenance now well trodden

onto the fore acreage of dumbfoundedness. Grinning, he nodded as if to render a proper mark of punctuation unto what yet held writ upon the aether to front.

Ben nodded in return. "Good man."

Reaching to pocket, the man produced a small vial showing a tint of blue at the top, and gave this over to Ben. "I can't be lookin' them muthafuckas in the eye and be thinkin' 'bout this bein' in m' pocket."

Ben smiled. "I take your point." He winked. "Pure of pocket, clean of conscience."

Frank shook his head. "'Bout ever'thin' that come outa you got two heads on it. One hardly know which one to look at."

"A conundrum suffered only by those, Mr. Peoples, who happen to be blessed with such eyes as are able to perceive the one as well as the other."

Frank showed a dumbfoundedness yet greater than the one previous. "How you know my name?"

The wailing having greatly encroached, Ben slipped Frank's vial into his coat pocket and bowed. "I must leave you, sir. Courage, sir!" Sinking onto one knee, Ben spoke aloud, "I had regarded humility the hardest lesson, young sir, until you taught me the one harder. I thank you." Raising himself, Ben wobbled to an onset of dizziness, steadied himself, and then, nodding to Frank—"Courage!"—hobbled to whereat Sloan awaited in the manner of a loyal horse. Crossing to the farther side of 47th Street, Ben noticed WEST PHILADELPHIA HIGH SCHOOL graven overtop the entry to the building he had previous speculated a school. A tower with turret atop stood at either side, whilst a generous expanse of steps lay to front.

As Ben bumped Sloan over the farther curb, a blue vehicle stopped close upon where TJ lay. A Negro woman emerged and rushing unto TJ's prostrate body, issued such wails as to cause Ben to moan as if to a thousand pinches of stone. A thousand thousand.

"Oh my God! No! Oh my God! No! No!"

Several wailing vehicles approached from ahead, lights flashing, whilst several others announced proximity from behind.

Feeling a sharp urgency to rush unto Delmyra's side, Ben paused Sloan in place, but then, upon discovering Frank ministering to the bereaved woman, directed Sloan onward.

Police vehicles stopped mid-street from above and below.

Moving soundlessly northward, Ben could discern furtive presences standing at unlighted windows to either side.

Towers and turrets at one side; ramparts and drawbridges at the other.

Upon arriving at Sansom Street, better to be called a lane than a street, Ben glimpsed in the distance, moving over an elevated platform, the lights of a train passing to westward. Given the circuitous geometry of his navigation, Ben surmised he was witnessing a track line presently running above ground that ran below ground from and to the 30th Street Station. He was witnessing, in other words, he assured himself, a beacon unto Market Street.

At Chestnut Street, Ben waited for a wailing ambulance to commit itself unto 47th, and then, eyes wetting anew, directed Sloan across the street, thereupon discovering two encumbrances—a car stopped such as to block ready access unto the walkway, and a stopping lot squatting whereat 47th Street should continue toward Market Street.

A wailing police car approaching from westward turned onto 47th Street. Ben watched the flashing lights progress rapidly toward whence he had only just escaped, wept anew, and then proceeded along the curb unto the entrance to the stopping lot. Continuing eastward upon the walkway, he soon arrived at Farragut Street, which name he recalled having encountered whilst progressing up Locust Street.

Turning onto Farragut, such as to arrive upon Market Street at earliest opportunity, Ben proceeded up a narrow walkway littered of careless leavings and lined of sickly vehicles. The abutting domiciles to side showed a level of disrepair likely from which there was no redemption.

Distracted by a jarring bumpiness, Ben was startled by appearance of a scrawny feline moving into his path and only barely escaping with its inventory of lives undiminished. Ben paused such as to recover his breath, and then continued on, encountering thereupon a Negro woman, who, bearing herself well to leftward, showed him no eyes, though he offered his own.

Approaching a curious advertisement overhanging the walkway— "New York Fried Chicken"—Ben suspected that, had he encountered similar in New York, it would have read "Philadelphia Fried Chicken," foreign goods always being better than domestic.

Almost directly beneath the advertisement, a lanky Negro man, of unkempt appearance, was standing at a call station and speaking with such animation as to require Ben to bear as far as possible to rightward that he might not be struck by the man's flailing arms.

An advertisement, "Checks Cashed," affixed to a window of the chicken shop, was made perplexing by way of the host showing no evidence soever toward being a counting house, nor, for that matter, a purveyor of fried chicken.

A thunderous rumbling drew Ben's attention to an elevated platform overtopping the near crossing street. Upon arriving at the curb of this street, it being marked Market Street, as surmised, Ben espied a stairway rising unto the near side of the platform. A few Negroes, eyes affixed downward, were presently descending it. A second stairway rose unto the farther side of the elevated platform, and a few Negroes were presently descending it also. A Negro man, wearing a bright-red cap, was standing close upon the farther stairway, beyond the pavement of Market Street. As in the case of Mr. Peoples, this man seemed as if an apparition escaped from a dreamscape only recently visited.

A dark-blue car, approaching on Farragut, swerved from the roadway of a sudden and stopped close upon where Uncle Tom was standing. After a moment, Tom hobbled unto the car and delivered something from pocket unto an open window, and something from the same window unto pocket.

Ben watched the car turn eastward onto Market, and southward then onto what likely was 46th Street, whereat the elevated platform seemed to terminate.

Thereupon looking to Uncle Tom, Ben discovered him holding a device to his ear whilst scanning about as if for glints of sword. Their eyes meeting, Ben averted his own, and was about to direct Sloan eastward when he noticed a second car, this one black, stop close upon where Uncle Tom was standing. Returning his device to pocket, Tom held still a moment, and then hobbled unto the black car. Leaning forward, he had only just put hand to pocket when the door of the car, being thrust open, struck him of such force as to deliver him onto his backside. Two Negro men thereupon emerged from the car, one at front, one at rear, and setting upon Tom, began to beat upon him with fists and truncheons, whilst Tom attempted to deflect their blows by no better than holding his forearms betwixt body and injury.

Whistle a'ready pulled from pocket, Ben blew a shrill note upon this instrument, and crying out then, "Unhand that man or bear the consequence," charged forth, yet blowing shrill notes. Upon crossing over the roadway, it showing no traffic, Ben slipped his cane from its makeshift scabbard, and raising it overhead, cried forth, "Tally ho!"

Whether 'twas by way of "the consequence" promised and delivered unto head and backside, or by way of the specter of an eighteenth-century knight charging about on a twenty-first century Rocinante, the two Negro men were soon returned to their safety, their safety returned unto its motion.

Dismounting Sloan now, close upon Tom's unmoving body, Ben lowered himself to bended knee, and reaching toward Tom's neck, that he might discover a pulse or no, was heartened by a groan, and presently by a parting of eyelids.

"Are you badly injured, sir? Should I summon assistance?"

Giving no answer, Tom attempted to raise himself onto his knees, and upon uttering a most terrible plaint, faltered. Lying again upon the ground, Tom wept, indeed most pathetically.

Inviting Tom's hand unto his own, Ben planted his cane at a bias, and served as counterweight then as Tom pulled himself to upright.

Tom nodded toward Ben, one eye being half closed. Upon wiping blood from nose and mouth, he stooped to retrieve his cap, but desisted upon a sharp plaint.

Ben deftly caught the errant cap upon the tip of his cane and delivered it forthwith unto Tom, who restored it to its station. Plumbing then, with considerable urgency, the pocket into which he had sheathed his device, Tom came up empty.

"Muthafuckas!"

Tom searched his other pockets.

"Muthafucka's got m' phone! Got ever'thin!'" Beginning to cough, Tom winced to each paroxysm. Upon quieting, he spat, and then looked to Ben as if having become aware of his presence only in the moment.

"You a knocker?"

"I am no greater than I appear, sir." Thereupon hooking his cane in his waistband, Ben slipped a blue-topped vial from one pocket, TJ's device from another, and held these articles toward Tom in opposing palms. Ben raised a little the hand holding the vial. "In this hand, sir, solace in the present at the cost of torment in the future." Ben raised a little the hand holding TJ's device. "In this hand, sir, torment in the present to the gain of solace in the future." He looked Tom in the eyes. "You yet hold upon your person, I do believe, sir, where indeed you keep 'the port'n stuff,' the number to call."

Tom's eyes swelled as if to a terrible fright.

"It matters not, sir," Ben continued, "by what means I have a little intelligence regarding your circumstances; nor by what means I come by this vial, recently shopped, I do believe, at this humble marketplace. Nor does it matter by what means I came by this device. It matters only that you make a choice, sir." Ben lifted the vial a little higher; the device a little higher. "Of course, there is a third choice, of which, I suspicion, you are at the moment contemplating, such being the oft tragical nature of desperation. Indeed, you can rob me of my offer altogether, in company with what few other items I might hold upon my person. Of course, to do so would be to consign your soul unto the very ring of ignominy unto which those who recently robbed and abused you have long since consigned theirs. Have you the allusion, sir?"

"Dante," Tom whispered.

Ben bowed. "You are a most literate man, sir."

Tom's eyes filled. "I ain't nuthin'."

Ben smiled. "The trap of the double negative. In truth, is it not they who hoard of greed, sir, they who betray of ambition, they who injure of hate, they who defame of envy, they who demean of arrogance—is it not truly *they*, sir, who 'ain't nuthin'?'"

Tom wiped his mouth and nose with his hand, his hand upon his shirt. He spat, wiped again his mouth, wiped again his hand.

Ben lifted a little the vial; lifted a little the device.

Tom shifted his eyes betwixt the two articles, and reaching forth then toward the vial, jaw aquiver, began to weep. Slumping well to forward, Tom braced his arms upon his knees, and shook his head. "It ain't no good, no good."

"We are, sir, as we choose, our first breath unto our last."

Tom shook his head. "No good." He spat, wiped his nose, straightened, wiped his hand on his shirt, regarded again the two articles yet offered him. Beginning again to weep, he reached forth, hand shaking; retreated; reached forth, hand shaking; retreated; reached forth, and snatching the vial into hand, turned half-circle around and hobbled at quick time toward the near stairway. He stopped as if shot through the heart and, doubling over sobbed most pathetically.

Ben approached from behind. "Possession is not necessarily choice, sir. A Puritan born into Puritanism is not really a Puritan, a Papist born into Papism is not really a Papist, until such time they choose to be." Ben moved to front. "I know your possession, sir. What is your choice?"

A ponderous rumble overhead rapidly transmuted into a noisome screech.

Tom yet making no response, Ben bowed unto him. "I pray thee peace, sir."

Returning to Sloan, Ben mounted the platform and was about to sheath his cane when he heard a plea most vehement. "No!"

Ben returned to where Tom was yet slumped. "'No' as regards what, sir?"

Tom straightened himself and held the blue-tipped vial toward Ben.

Taking the vial into hand, Ben assumed a grave comportment of countenance. "By your choice, sir, you have consigned to yourself an interim of agony of such magnitude as to be beyond the ability of most human beings to endure. Does not the logic of happiness compel, therefore, that you should bargain for the vial to hold in company with the device, such that they together might assure you of at least some measure of comfort?" Ben looked to Tom's cap. "Your cap, sir, for the vial. I have, in fact, only recently become deprived of my own. Have we a bargain?"

Tom peered upon the vial now as if upon Blackbeard's treasure, and beginning again to weep, took TJ's device into hand and thereupon repelled the other article.

"You are certain? 'Tis only one, after all."

Tom shook his head with some violence.

"Bargain for the vial now and you could assure yourself of a firm resolve on the morrow. The morrow, after all, is another day; is it not, sir? Have you the allusion?" Ben held the vial yet closer unto Tom. Upon Tom again repelling it, Ben slipped it to pocket. "As you have chosen, sir, so you must abide."

Ben bowed, turned to Sloan, and turned back. "That boy, sir, sitting upon that two-wheel conveyance called a motorcycle, the very lad waiting for his father to take notice of him—he is yourself, is he not, sir?"

Appearing in the instant as if struck by a blow, Tom stumbled backward a few steps and falling onto the ground, upon his back, folded his arms across his chest, as if to hold together something fractured there, and issued from his throat, nay, from some deeper chamber, a sound beyond the facility of any word, or any concoction of such, to capture. It was a cry not of woundedness, nor of abandonment, nor of grief, nor of betrayal—but of all of these.

Sinking unto his knees, Ben took a coarse, quivering hand into both of his. "I'm so sorry. So very sorry."

Tom thereupon wept as if not for himself alone, but for a thousand others. A thousand thousand.

"No greater privilege is afforded any man," Ben whispered, "than to be the progenitor and protector of new life. Yet, no privilege on this earth is more keenly abused. The reasons for this great tragedy are of some complexity, but they are not, can never be, exculpatory." Ben cleared his throat. "A great injury has been inflicted upon you, Thomas Mayback, but no salve or poultice toward its healing can be presently applied other than by your own hand. Your forebears were slaves, sir, and you imitate them in legacy. For them, force of will could only compound their misery. For you, such is the only means by which you might free yourself. Make the call, sir. Make the call. The number was given you of no less, sir, than deepest respect."

Upon Tom quieting, Ben got to his feet and helped Tom unto his. Reaching to pocket, he drew forth one of the Jacksons recently deposited there, and offered it toward Tom. "Would you be so kind, good sir, as to hold twenty for me?" Ben winked.

Tom smiled, and shook his head. "Don't knows I can ever repays ya."

"Well, sir, as a cat might be deprived of its liberty in more ways than one, unto a count of nine, might not a debt be settled also in more ways than one, perhaps to a count of ten times ten? If a man borrows a hundredweight of wheat from a farmer, for instance, but restores it, long after the farmer has succumbed to the inevitable infirmities of age, by way of delivering a hundredweight each unto the farmer's five heirs, is not the debt paid in full?"

Ben looked to Tom's cap. "Your cap, sir, if I might."

Tom hesitated, then delivered his cap to Ben, who, in turning it bottom-side up, exposed various artifacts protruding from under the sweatband. "If I may, sir."

Tom nodded.

Pulling a card from the sweatband, Ben folded the Jackson around it. Pulling a second Jackson from pocket, Ben added this one to the previous, and so forth unto a fourth Jackson. Slipping the fattened card under the sweatband, Ben returned the cap to Tom.

Eyes glistening, Tom restored his cap to its station, although not to its previous fit.

Turning to Sloan, he yet patiently at wait, Ben mounted the platform. "You look just like 'im," Tom declared, grinning. "Quixote, I mean."

Ben bowed. "Most kind of you, sir." Turning Sloan half-circle around, Ben extended his cane overhead, and waving it to and fro, spurred Sloan across Market Street. "Make the call!" he shouted. "Action is its own promise!"

"Yo!" he heard from behind.

Returning his sword unto its makeshift scabbard, Ben resumed his previous course, to eastward, and upon looking ahead, considered the forty-odd blocks yet separating him from his destiny. He could only hope that Sloan held sufficient charge in his Leyden jar as to carry him so great a distance.

⌐⁄ℓ∽

A warmish breeze being briskly upon his back, Ben accelerated rapidly unto full sail, and continued without abatement then, except upon incidence of a few bumps, there being no encumbrance of pedestrians soever. Indeed, outside the two campuses he had traversed, he had encountered but few pedestrians, this owing not only to the lateness of the hour, he suspicioned, but also to the darkness of it.

At 42nd Street, Ben encountered a most remarkable sight. Upon the near corner here, a car had impacted upon a metal pole, head on, indeed as if by willful intention. The pole remained upstanding, but the car was most severely deformed. No one was about, neither attending unto the wreckage nor ministering unto any injured parties. Ben brought Sloan to a pause that he might peer inside. Discovering naught to warrant concern, he continued on.

As he sailed straight upon eastward, Market Street took on aspect of a compass arrow pointing toward the very spot upon which a like symbol had, near upon three centuries previous, pointed westward, indeed from the very point of his landing at the Market Street wharf, unto Fifth Street, the upper limit of settlement at that time.

At 40th Street, Ben encountered a stairwell marked "Market-Frankford" that led below ground and thereupon, Ben assumed, to the very Septa trains that were elevated over Market Street from 46th Street westward. Several loiterers here, mostly Negroes, were standing about in idle postures. As Ben passed them by, he peered upon each one such that he might wonder upon the history to which each was witness, and whether, in likeness to the conundrum concerning the falling tree, there could be any history at all in absence of eyes to see it, ears to hear it, flesh to sense it.

Ben recalled to memory now a story told him long ago by one of his post riders, who, coming upon a butterfly alighted in a wagon rut, dismounted his horse that he might urge the splendorous creature from harm's way, only thereafter to encounter another such, and another, and another. Ultimately, he had ridden with his eyes held such that he might take no farther notice of butterflies alighted in harm's way.

At 39th Street, Ben espied a building ahead that bore a marquee across which was flowing a sequence of letters. Although Ben held close attention upon this curious broadside, he found it difficult, nay, impossible, to make sense of the messages being constructed, letter by letter, owing to the speed by which the letters moved to leftward, and their quick disappearance. It occurred to him then that should the pilots of vessels in the roadway make a similar effort toward capturing unto sense these kinetic compositions, to sacrifice of minding port and starboard, they might well meet with calamity. He wondered if the proprietors of this commanding mode of advertisement had taken such possibility into consideration.

Upon approaching the next crossing street, whilst he still strived to parse the messages flowing across the marquee, Ben held his course and speed steady and upon a jarring bump found himself sprawled upon the 38th Street pavement, Sloan idling in proximity. Dazed—owing more to surprise, it would seem, than to injury—Ben looked after cause, and discovered he had anticipated a pedestrian ramp to front that was arranged instead at the oblique, such as to serve the two crosswise directions in common. He had, therefore, in progressing forward without minding the watch, dropped off the curb onto the roadway, and suffered the consequence.

There being no one to render assistance, Ben got himself onto hands and knees, and then onto his feet, and then onto Sloan. Vowing to exercise a greater caution, he sailed onward.

Upon arriving in proximity to whereat he should encounter 37th Street, Ben discovered this expected roadway to extend northward at the farther side of Market Street, but not to southward on the present side, unto the very intersection indeed upon which he had encountered the likeness of a compass and the kindness of Mr. Bornstein. In lieu of a roadway to southward, Ben noticed, was a most curious sculpture in similitude to a creature bearing a long neck but no head, the latter having apparently been cleaven. Also missing was a significant segment of the creature's torso, whereat indeed a mortal counterpart would be expected to hold a pulsating heart.

Steering now such as to avoid passing under the creature's cleaven neck, Ben conjured to mind the two sculptures previously encountered, and was struck in the moment by a bolt of understanding of such enormity as to cause him nearly to steer off the curb.

He bowed his head and wept.

It was too late.

The breeze freshened from behind.

Sloan rolled onward.

⁓ϖⵒ

At 34th Street, Ben passed a small shelter, marked "Septa," showing a stripe of blue over green at the cornice. Why one underground station should be marked in one manner, whilst another station, but a few blocks hence, should be marked in a wholly different manner, presently escaped all attempts by Ben toward a practical understanding.

Espying now, atop the near light poles, blue-and-yellow banners emblazoned of a dragon, Ben surmised he had returned unto the realm of "Science & Industry." Upon passing 34th Street, he encountered a building to rightward that, in being walled to front almost entirely of glass, was reminding of the "fish bowl" he had encountered upon the previous campus, in which several students seemed conspicuously engaged in study, perhaps in stratagem toward reminding those without, blinkered by their communication devices, of a higher calling, so to say. In the present "fish bowl," however, only one person was conspicuous, a young lady, she being reposed such as to face upon the glass wall whilst holding a device close upon one ear.

Approaching 33rd Street, Ben discovered, at the farther side of this, upon a small plaza there, a sculpture of the very dragon, it would appear, that was emblazoned upon the blue-and-yellow banners aloft. Instead of being colorated, however, in consonance with the emblem upon the banners, this wholly dark, and illuminated by way of subterranean sources unto sinister effect.

Approaching whereat 32nd Street extended to leftward, Ben recognized, to rightward, reposed upon a chair having no back, the man of "Science & Industry," yet pondering upon some mystery elusive to his understanding. Perhaps, Ben allowed, this thinker's task was like that of Sisyphus, perhaps in recompense for having failed to turn his attentions half-circle around when yet there was opportunity as well as need, such as to embrace a diminutive supplicant there, knelt upon one knee.

At 31st Street, Ben discovered another shelter bearing the marker "Septa," as well as blue-over-green striping at the cornice, in consonance with the shelter encountered at 34th Street. At 30th Street, he discovered a similar shelter, this one standing near opposite the shelter marked "30th Street Station," which, although it bore on its cornice the first incidence of blue-over-green striping Ben had encountered, did not bear, anywhere upon it, the marker "Septa." Nor, in reverse, did any of the shelters marked "Septa" bear a location marker such as to be in consonance with the shelter marked "30th Street Station." Nor did any of the shelters marked of blue-over-green stripes stand in consonance with the roofless stairwell encountered at 40th Street. Yet, all these structures served in common the same function.

Alas, what noisome little inconsistency is not but the fever of a larger ill?

There being no pedestrian ramp at the present intersection, Ben urged Sloan off the curb, this precipice being no greater than a few inches in height, and steered Sloan smoothly onto the walkway at the farther side, there being no curbing there to serve as barrier. To leftward, the Amtrak station, with its grand columns to front, shown like a Parthenon illumed of holy pyres, whilst to forward, a host of dark towers seemed as if stalagmites in the den of Evil itself.

To rightward, a large building spanning nearly a block seemed an attempt to establish a symmetry of form and scale in relation to the grand station house standing at the opposing side of the street. Indeed, one might see it as the temple of a companion deity, of a bit lesser rank—a queen perhaps unto an opposing, alas, imposing, king.

Of a sudden jarred by several bumps in succession, Ben near upon collided with a light pole standing amidst the walkway. Steering of reflex to rightward, onto several shards of glass, he maneuvered around more such perils, and ultimately unto a Stop sign. The crosswise roadway here, to front, though well trafficked of vehicles, showed no obvious marker to name it. By logical inference, however, it would seem to warrant being known as 29th Street.

On the farther side of this street, a stone monument, bearing atop the likeness of an eagle, its wings poised toward flight, marked entry onto the span Ben had previously surmised to overtop the Schuylkill. Just beyond this likeness stood a candelabra suggesting an upside-down bunch of grapes. Another such stood at span center, and another at the far end. Counterparts stood on the opposing side of the span.

The crossing light giving license, Ben rolled Sloan across 29th Street and onto a walkway, flanked to leftward by vehicles stopped at the curb, and to rightward by a robust balustrade. The balustrade, being about four feet high, was composed of large stone pilasters upholding a running lintel of stone slabs. The stone itself, ashen in pallor, appeared to be the very same as composing the majority of the two "temples" to rearward.

Upon rolling near halfway to the center of the span, Ben dismounted Sloan, and stepping onto a raised ledge paralleling the balustrade, leaned well forward. Below, a languid flow of turbid water, at about twenty feet, was illumed in the foreground as if from some mysterious source on the underside of the span. Watching now various articles of flotsam drift by, Ben recalled the first span erected over the Schuylkill, a structure of such modesty in relation to the one present as to be regarded "primitive," although the imagination conceiving it must needs have been as keen or greater.

Peering downriver, Ben discovered a span paralleling the one present, about a block distant, to be underlain by two arches outlined by small lights—as was likely the case, Ben surmised, regarding the present span, hence the mysterious illumination of the fore water.

Peering yet farther downstream, Ben recalled his old friend John Bartram and the botanicals kept by him at his riverside plantation, not a mile farther downriver—alas, one species in particular. Feeling a warming now in his cheeks, Ben shook his head. Indeed, no mortal, of whatever station or reputation, should be honored at cost of forcing upon botanists unto all eternity such a puzzlement of articulation as *Franklinia alatamaha*.

Ben flinched as if to a surprise visitation. It being September, the *Franklinia* would be in its season! Indeed, were the breeze presently in a southerly cast instead of a westerly such, he might well catch scent of his own embarrassment!

About to remount Sloan, Ben caught glimpse of what appeared to be a figure standing atop the balustrade proximate to the mid-span candelabrum. Because however the ambient light was so very diffuse, and the apparent apparition so close upon the candelabrum, it was difficult to distinguish the one thing from the other, such as to be able to arrive at certitude.

Mounting in haste unto Sloan, Ben slipped his whistle from pocket, and upon progressing a few yards farther, blew a shrill note, such as to gather the attention of, it was now clear, a man swaying perilously atop the balustrade. The effect was near unto the opposite, however, by causing the man a fright, to end of causing him to lose hold upon what facility of balance was left to him. Only by way of a desperate flailing of his arms did the man succeed in regaining a fair measure of equilibrium.

Ben paused several feet distant such as to cause Mr. Bahr no farther alarm.

The man's beard, and his agony, had given him away.

"Where is it written, Mr. Bahr," Ben boomed, in a volume rivaling that of the Reverend Whitefield himself, "that in ending all hope regarding one's own interests, one thereby derives the right to end all hope regarding the interests of others? Did you not, sir, recently give your private number to a person in great need? And did you not in doing this, sir, oblige yourself unto a contract most solemn, in likeness indeed to that of a parent in relation to his child, which he has brought into the world in a state of utter dependency?"

Though not naturally of strong voice, Ben commanded unto himself now a thunder heretofore not likely known upon Olympus itself. "Or are you in fact, sir, precisely the kind of man your father believes you to be?"

Upon receipt of this rhetorical challenge, Prescott uttered a plaint most pathetic, and began to weep.

"The answer you render, sir, this moment or next, by one action or the other, must needs stand for all time, as regards not only *your* happiness, sir, but that of others as well. We are not individuals alone, sir, as you well know, who might ever do whatever they will, but members of larger groups who must ever restrain private interest for the sake of the larger need.

"As regards your father, sir, your untimely demise cannot punish him. It can only punish those who remain innocent of any abuse toward you." Ben held silent, and then continued. "Will you not come down, sir, such as to spare me prospect of flailing in waters made inhospitable by too many individuals regarding themselves as individuals alone?"

Prescott slumped now, as if to a usurping resignation and made gesture toward quitting his perch.

Ben was about to ease forward to render assistance when a rude call from the roadway—"Jump, asshole!"—in near simultaneity with a missile shattering upon the pedestal holding the candelabrum, a second striking upon a softer target, caused Prescott to lose hold upon an equilibrium a'ready in a perilous state.

In an instant he disappeared!

Shedding shoes and waistcoat, Ben pressed the red button upon Sloan, and hobbling to whereat Prescott had disappeared, mounted the ledge paralleling the balustrade. He elevated himself, of no little effort, onto the lintel, and rolling forth then, plunged the twenty feet unto the water below, impacting this, upon his backside, of such force as to relieve him of what little air he held yet to lung, and deliver him unto a perilous depth.

Stroking of arm and leg, Ben managed to hold his airways sufficiently long above water to draw a breath, though not a second. Indeed, his beloved woolens, which so often had filled his heart with resolve, now promised to fill his lungs with sewage.

Feeling a grip upon his collar, Ben was soon gasping for breath, and thereupon was being drawn, in the manner of a barge by mule, toward the easterly embankment.

Restraining himself from all direct participation in his rescue, Ben looked to the span from which he had recently plunged, and was struck by the grace of the underlying arcs as illumed in outline, as set in contrast by the line of the balustrade above.

Looking to see if anyone had been drawn to the balustrade, Ben squinted toward effecting a clearer focus, and realized, to a sharp chill of dread, that he had lost his spectacles in the plunge.

He shuddered.

Becoming aware then of the labored breaths of his rescuer, these audible even above the ambient roar, Ben closed his eyes—

Gagging unto awareness, Ben discovered his rescuer afront him clinging to a ladder. "I'll go up first. Can you hang on here ok?"

Ben tried to make reply, but managed only to aspirate yet more water, to effect of another fit of gagging. Prescott maneuvered Ben to leftward, and directed him to hook his arm around one leg of a ladder. Whilst Prescott thereupon ascended, Ben tried to restore his lungs of air, it occurring to him that he should have asked his rescuer to relieve him of his sodden woolens.

"You've going to have to climb a few rungs before I can reach you. Can you do that?"

Making no reply, Ben maneuvered himself to the front of the ladder, and discovering a submerged rung by way of his stocking feet, hooked his arms around the tubular legs of the ladder and ascended to the next rung. He then ascended to the subsequent rung, but with considerably more effort, in consequence to a loss of buoyancy most embarrassing.

His legs beginning to quaver, Ben peered upward, and discovering an extended hand as if fading into the ambient dusk, was reminded of the unfortunate loss of his bifocals. Unhooking one arm, Ben struggled to climb a rung higher, such that he might grasp the extended hand, but his legs faltered, and he fell backward into the fetid water, and sank.

A silent percussion was followed by a grip upon his collar. Soon thereafter, he was once again gagging and coughing, and gasping for breath. Maneuvered unto the ladder, Ben clutched it of both hands, and restoring himself to breath, declared, in barely a whisper: "You must go, sir. You have, I have reason to be certain, yet greater interests to attend to. I shall ascend of my own accord, when I am able. I thank you."

Prescott pressed Ben closer upon the ladder. "Hold on as best you can."

Ben could hear Prescott charging his lungs. A moment later, he could feel his feet being fitted upon Prescott's shoulders. Surmising what was to come, Ben grasped the ladder at either side, and upon a powerful boost, Ben adjusted his grasp upward. Soon elevated by this means close unto the top of the ladder, Ben encountered a large pipe, of no obvious purpose beyond obstruction, running upon the bulkhead to which the ladder was attached.

Leaning precariously forward, Ben grasped the pipe as best he might, it being too great in girth to grasp to any certainty. Upon another boost from below, he lunged overtop the rude pipe, and rolling sidelong down the sloped backside of the bulkhead, struck upon the ground below. Robbed of all breath, he lay upon his backside breathing in desperate gasps.

Become aware of a like rhythm close by, Ben rolled himself onto hands and knees, and managing to get himself to upright, subverted a fit of giddiness by way of leaning well to forward, hands upon knees, derrière rested against the rounded backside of the bulkhead. Rising after a moment to full stature, Ben encouraged Prescott toward like status by way of inquiry—"Your communication device, sir; might you have it yet upon your person?"

Prescott getting himself to a sitting posture, Ben offered him a hand, and held fast whilst Prescott got himself to full stature.

"Who *are* you?"

"Not as good a swimmer as once I was, I cannot other than confess. I thank you, sir, for rescuing me to your peril."

Prescott pulled his device from pocket and offered it toward Ben.

Ben shook his head. "No, 'tis not for my use I inquire after your device, sir, but for yours. Might submersion have drowned it, you think?"

"You've been talking to Tom."

"He who yet awaits to be noticed."

"Who the hell *are* you?"

"Who I am, sir, is of no consequence. Who you are, however, is all to the point. Your device, sir, does it yet breathe?"

Showing a fair measure of consternation, Prescott opened his device, it gleaming to the glow of nearby pole lamps, and pushed a button. A soft toll sounded in simultaneity with the appearance of an eerie cast of greenish light. "Seems OK."

Prescott manipulated his device by thumb. "Two calls." Pause. "Strange." He looked to Ben. "You knew about these. What the hell's going on here?"

"Whilst you make demands, sir, to no good end, precious time passes."

Prescott manipulated his device yet farther and held it to ear. "It's me." In a blink Prescott's comportment transformed in likeness to a glass filled of overly chilled water receiving a shock to the rim. "Omigod! How?—Omigod! I'll be right there." He paused. "I'm"—his voice faltered—"I'll be right there. Oh, Del—Jesus—I'm so sorry. I'll be right there. I love you."

His hand trembling, Prescott again manipulated his device by thumb, and again held it to ear. Pause. "Who is this?" Pause. "Tom? Jesus Christ! How did you get my nephew's cell phone? What the hell's going on here?" Prescott looked to Ben. "He's here. Right next to me! He"—Prescott shook his head—"I don't understand any of this." Prescott looked to Ben. "What the hell's going on?" He continued to Tom. "Meet me at the HUP E-R. I'll be there in ten minutes. I can't explain." His voice faltered. "Just be there, OK?" Pause. "Thank you."

Prescott looked to Ben.

Ben preempted. "An explanation would serve no good purpose, sir."

Prescott stared.

Ben gestured with his head. "Be gone."

"You going to be OK?"

"I am. You are a strong swimmer, sir—as much in the figurative sense, I have every reason to trust, as in the literal. Now be gone!"

Of a sudden grasping Ben by the arm, Prescott all but pulled Ben up an embankment of onerous inclination, Ben protesting the way. Upon their reaching level ground, whereat the pole lamps illumed a wide pathway paralleling the river, Ben slouched well forward, hands upon knees, such as to recover his breath.

"Are you sure you're going be OK? Can I call somebody?"

Ben shook his head.

In the moment, a man clad as if in undergarments alone trotted past, showing a wire extending from one ear unto a holster of a sort tethered unto his waist. Although the man was, at closest separation, no greater than four yards, he took no notice soever of two persons close upon him who appeared odd in more ways than being half drowned.

Taking his leave, Prescott ran unto a stairway of daunting height, and ascending this with remarkable celerity, unto an elevated walkway which spanned betwixt Market Street and Chestnut Street, continued toward Chestnut.

Remembering now, to a deep chill of dread, he had abandoned Sloan upon the Market Street span, Ben hobbled his way toward the stairway as swiftly as he might, issuing a plaint upon each step, his gout having become a hive of bothered bees, his unshod feet being vulnerable to every nettle.

He paused at the bottom of the stairway such as to collect himself, then ascended the metallic steps one foot up and then the other. Finally attaining the elevated walkway, Ben rested his head upon the near railing of this, such as to quell a fit of giddiness, and continued then toward the Market Street bridge, whilst a warmish breeze, scented of inclemency, struck him to port.

Although the angle of incline was slight, Ben found himself near upon collapse by the time he attained the easterly end of the bridge. Pausing of necessity, he rested his head upon the balustrade, close upon a likeness of the very eagle he had encountered at the westerly end of the span, and began to weep, of no greater cause indeed than an exhaustion too great farther to bear.

Hearing voices then, as if of children at play, Ben straightened himself, and squinting into the dusk to westward, glimpsed movement at about mid span. The voices continuing, Ben launched forth, and hobbling at the double, called forth: "Mercy to an old man! Mercy! Mercy!"

Several figures retreating, in the manner indeed of discovered wolves, Ben hobbled yet faster, wincing ever more keenly.

Upon attaining the mid-span candelabrum, Ben of a sudden screamed to an agony rendered unto one foot and then the other. Halting in the instant, he made attempt to pull shards of glass from the bottoms of his feet. Discovering however that he could do no better than lose his balance, unto an even greater calamity, he advanced to leftward over yet more shards of glass, and thereupon lunged forth onto the ledge paralleling the balustrade. Crawling then, upon hands and knees, he made his way to whereat he should encounter Sloan—his shoes and waistcoat as well—but could discover naught of what he had left behind. He crawled yet farther, propelled by a cold dread distilled unto a chill desperation, but still could discover naught of what he had left behind.

Lowering his head onto the concrete ledge, Ben no sooner had begun to weep than he heard a voice, a whisper, as if carried upon the wind—

You must endure, sir.

You must endure as you have never endured before.

All that might have been—all that might yet be—all is in your hands, sir.

Ben wept the harder.

There is no one else.

Ben shook his head.

Though the hour is late—yet still there is time.

He wept.

Finally depleted of all moisture, Ben rolled onto his back, and getting himself to a sitting posture, pulled one foot toward him, and then the other, such as to extricate shards of glass from the bottom of each. Brushing thereupon the bottom of each foot with extended fingers, he extricated yet finer shards whereat his fingers were pricked.

Removing his vest and shirt, Ben tore his shirt into shreds, and used these to bind his feet as best he might. Upon restoring himself of his vest, he was visited by an irony most poignant. Indeed, the only possession yet remaining to him, showing at the moment from the watch pouch of his vest, was the very whistle for which he had paid too much.

Getting himself to his feet, of no little trouble, Ben continued westward, remaining close upon the balustrade such that he might use this to brace himself. Upon arriving at the westerly end of the span, he discovered the crossing street he had deduced to be 29th Street to be marked "Schuylkill Expressway." Upon a favoring light, he crossed over the roadway, and passing the lamp pole he had nearly bumped into earlier, stopped whereat a hash of yellow strips extended to the farther side of Market Street. Glancing behind himself, such as to apprise what notice the spectacle of himself might be gathering, he was alarmed to discover a trail of bright red stains leading to whereat he presently stood.

Feeling of a sudden as if being drained of all vitality by way of open bilge cocks, Ben embraced a near lamp pole, and held fast to this until such time the crossing signal favored him. Staggering then across the roadway, as if burdened of one draught too many, he hobbled the short distance to the Septa shelter marked "30th Street Station" but not "Septa."

Entering the shelter by way of the entry facing upon 30th Street, Ben discovered but one denizen, an overly-fleshed Negro woman sitting upon a bench at the rear. The woman's breeches, Ben could not help but notice, appeared to be on the verge of ripping asunder at the thighs, so desperate was the press of flesh there. She was coughing as if to a mortal fit of the consumption, whilst holding betwixt two fingers a smoldering wick.

Straight on, a shut entry suggested access to an elevator. To leftward of this, an open entry was as if taking in and expelling people in the same breath. Through this now came a familiar rumbling, followed by a familiar screeching.

Various leavings were strewn over a floor so perfectly despoiled, it seemed, as to have taken on the very stain of neglect itself. Upon attempting to harvest a castaway tumbler, by reaching to it, Ben discovered himself lying upon the floor, face pressed upon a sticky wetness. Managing thereupon to raise himself unto hands and knees, he begged assistance from the woman yet sitting upon the bench, but received from her no countenance soever. Looking then toward the entry to the trains, Ben begged assistance toward a succession of persons emerging there, but could elicit no greater than a firefly flash of pity.

Crawling unto the bench, the tumbler clutched in his teeth, Ben managed to leverage himself onto the seat, and thereupon to raise himself to upright. Staggering then unto the entryway to the trains, Ben discovered himself standing at a railing afront a stairwell of two parts: an upper part, to rightward, descending unto a lower part, directly below whereat he stood.

Espying a floor mat close upon the top of the stairway, to rightward, Ben hobbled to this, and kneeling upon it, poised his feet toward the wall behind, such as to protect passersby from the offense of a profligate hemorrhaging. Leaning forward then, Ben used the heels of his hands to smear the bloodstains to front such as to disassociate the compass line of these from their source.

Holding forth his cup then, hand atremble, Ben addressed the first person to mount the stairs, a man of middle age: "One fare, sir. That is all I require. Please, sir."

The man continued onward.

In like manner, he addressed the next person encountered, a heavy, limping woman approaching the stair head: "One fare, ma'm. That is all I require. Please, ma'm."

The woman limped onward.

In like manner, Ben addressed the next person encountered—and the next—and the next—until such time he discovered himself affronted by two men in uniform, each showing a pistol affixed to one side, a truncheon to the other.

"Get your ass out o' here, flapjack," the younger officer commanded. "Can't see you're in the way?"

Ben could not help but notice that the only obstacles to free passage to and from the stairwell at the moment were the two people standing before him.

Of a sudden gripping Ben by the arms, one to side, the officers pulled him to upright, and led him from the shelter to whereat a police vehicle was stopped at the curb, blue and red lights flashing atop.

Upon the officers releasing their grip, Ben began to sink, but managed to summon sufficient strength as to remain upstanding.

The younger officer took notice of Ben's feet. "Haven't seen that one before." He looked to the walkway near where Ben was standing. "You're making one helluva mess, flapjack."

Gripping Ben by the arm, the younger officer forced Ben to turn half-circle around. "See? See what you're doing here, flapjack?" The officer intruded a starched face close upon Ben's. "We'll be back in fifteen minutes. If you're still here, or anywhere near here, we're gonna take you for a little ride."

"Yeah, up to Mickey D's," the older officer added, "so you can work off all that ketchup you stole." He laughed.

"'Tis naught, sir, but my own—"

"Are we clear, flapjack?"

Ben nodded.

No sooner had the officers departed than Ben sank unto his knees, unable to hold himself upright a moment longer. Clutching his cup in his teeth, as previous, Ben crawled unto the 30th Street end of the Septa shelter, to epitaphs of disgust, and poised himself upon chafed knees. The volume of passersby would be lesser here, by consequence of location Ben knew, but to set himself closer upon Market Street would be to present himself as advertisement unto the constabulary.

Holding his cup in two hands now, they trembling as one, Ben addressed the first person encountered, a youth burdened of a pack upon his back: "One fare, young sir. That is all I require. Please, sir."

The youth hurried onward.

In like manner, Ben addressed the next person encountered, a man of graying hair and perspiring brow: "One fare, sir. That is all I require. Please, sir."

The man hurried onward.

In like manner, Ben addressed the next person encountered—and the next—and the next—until such time he lowered his cup of neither strength nor will sufficient to keep it elevated. Lowering his head then, he began to weep—but was soon stirred from this indulgence of pity by an alert from that sense sometimes called the Sixth. Lifting his head, Ben discovered standing before him a Negro girl dressed in little more than rags.

The girl curtsied. Ben nodded.

"In the absence of charity, sir, whence hope? In the absence of hope, sir, whence resolution?"

Ben bowed his head well to forward and began to weep. "I'm so very sorry," he whispered. "So very, very sorry."

Catching whiff thereupon of a scent most sweet, Ben lifted his eyes to discover the Negro girl gone, and whereat she had stood, a large bloom of five oblate petals radiant around a golden orb. Discovering thereupon a remnant of newsprint in close proximity, Ben crawled unto this, and taking it into trembling hands, managed to sunder from it a narrow strip. Getting himself then into a sitting position, legs akimbo, Ben released the bandage to one foot of sufficient duration as to accumulate a puddle of blood. Slipping his whistle from pocket, he sucked blood into the whistle chamber, and by tremulous hand, writ a line upon the newsprint as best he might, he being half-failed of eye at close proximity.

By way of charity, hope; by way of hope, action!

Binding the tatter of newsprint unto the sprig of *Franklinia*, Ben rendered the tails of the tatter into a bow, and turning his attention then toward the crossing over 30th Street, held the bouquet of ribbon and bloom toward the next person to approach, this being a well-groomed man of perhaps five and fifty bearing a portfolio in one hand whilst drawing a larger article of luggage upon wheels with the other: "A flower for you today, sir?"

The man looked to Ben but continued onward, entering the Septa shelter by way of the near entry. No sooner then had Ben returned his attention unto the crossing over 30th Street than the well-groomed man had returned. He stuffed a Lincoln into the cup held betwixt Ben's knees.

"O, good sir, I thank you!" Ben gave the bouquet over to his benefactor. "Your kindness is no less than the sweetness of this rare bloom."

The man took particular notice of the tatter. "What the hell is this?"

"'Tis a ribbon, sir."

"It's a piece of newspaper!"

"'Tis more than the medium, sir, if you would care to have a look."

"Crap." The man pulled the makeshift bow from the stem with some violence, and upon discarding the remnants onto the pavement, stuffed the blossom into his portfolio. Replacing the Lincoln in Ben's cup with three Washingtons, the man disappeared into the Septa shelter.

Ben watched three pieces of newsprint swirl in an eddy and then lay moribund.

Ah, but no time there was for despondency!

By way of charity, hope; by way of hope, action!

Though the hour is late, yet still there is time!

Slipping the three Washingtons into pocket, Ben was about to return his whistle also to pocket when he glimpsed of motion close upon—

His head striking against the newsstand behind, Ben felt his brain erupt into a conflagration of cold fire—

Felt his pockets rudely probed—

Glimpsed a gleaming blade—

Heard a terrible cry—and more such—

Glimpsed a silhouette close upon—

"My God, what's happened to you?"

The voice was familiar. That indeed of Sloan's master!

O! O! What of Sloan?

"Hang in there. I'm getting help." David had his device in hand.

"O, I beg of you, good sir"—Ben strained to lift his head—"to summon no assistance beyond your own. Please, sir."

"You're bleeding to death for god's sake! Look at you!"

Ben tasted of blood owing to the recent violence. "You would interrupt, sir, what must be held whole to any cost. I can tell you no more, because I know no more. Will you help me?"

"I'm *trying* to help you! What are you talking about anyway?"

"You must trust to the urgency, sir. You must. All is in your hands."

A wailing now, from westward.

"You've gotta crawl back into your crypt before midnight, right?"

"There is no one else, sir."

David shook his head. "This is nuts." He began to punch at his device.

Ben began to weep. "Please, sir. *Please.*"

David hesitated, then shook his head and raised himself to upright. "OK, where we going?" David slipped his device to pocket. "I'm going to regret this for the rest of my life."

"Christ Church, sir."

"Now why didn't I think of that? That's where you're buried, right?"

"You must trust, sir. I beg of you."

David shook his head. "I can't believe I'm doing this." Embracing Ben from behind, arms under Ben's armpits, David lifted such as to bring Ben forthrightly to upright.

Noting thereupon that he yet held his whistle, Ben slipped it into pocket.

David pulled a card from his wallet, and slipping this into the rightward pocket of his breeches, took Ben onto shoulder and back as he might a bound sheep, and hunching forward then, such as to effect an even distribution of load, grasped Ben by the leg to one side, by the arm to the other.

"You are a man of considerable strength, sir."

"I'm an idiot is what I am. Can you sing?"

"Sir?"

"You're drunk. I'm carrying you home."

"I have a song to sing, sir."

"This is nuts."

"It is not quite ordinary, sir, to be sure; but neither, I have come to believe, are you."

As David trudged toward the near entry unto the Septa shelter, Ben broke into song, though in a voice afflicted in no small measure of anemia—

> *If I had a hammer*
> *I'd hammer in the morning*

He continued through the shelter—

> *I'd hammer in the evening*
> *All over this land*

He continued unto the stairwell—

> *I'd hammer out danger,*
> *I'd hammer out a warning,*
> *I'd hammer out love betwixt my brothers and my sisters,*
> *All over this land*

He continued down the first set of stairs—

> *If I had a bell*
> *I'd ring it in the morning*
> *I'd ring it in the evening*
> *All over this land*

I'd ring out danger,
I'd ring out a warning
I'd ring out love betwixt my brothers and my sisters
All over this land

He continued down the second set of stairs—

If I had a song
I'd sing it in the morning
I'd sing it in the evening
All over this land

I'd sing out danger,
I'd sing out a warning
I'd sing out love betwixt my brothers and my sisters
All over this land

He continued to leftward—

Well I've got a hammer
And I've got a bell

He continued to leftward—

And I've got a song to sing
All over this land

He continued to rightward—

It's the hammer of justice
It's the bell of freedom

He continued unto a gate—

It's the song about love betwixt my brothers and my sisters

David deftly slipped his card through a slot to rightward.
Ben continued unto the farther side of the gate—

All over this land

There rapidly building now a crescendo of heavy rumbling, David broke into a ponderous trot, and descending a set of stairs, to a terrible screeching, approached a stopped train to rightward, and intruding a foot betwixt closing doors such as to cause the doors to recede, advanced into the car. The doors closing behind, David lowered himself onto one knee and, in demonstration of as much skill as strength, manipulated Ben into a seat, to the immediate and fastidious disapproval of the woman sitting opposite, who forthwith removed herself to a seat at the opposing side of the car.

The train thereupon easing into motion, as if in the backward direction, David collapsed into the seat to leftward of Ben, and breathing as if under mortal duress, hung his head well to forward.

Absent sufficient resolve with which to hold them open, Ben closed his eyes—

And could feel the sun warm upon his brow—

Hear the voices of children joyous upon his ears—

Smell the scent of honeysuckle sweet upon his olfactory—

Feel the radiance of a loving presence close upon his side—

". . . doors are opening . . . Frankford train, making all stops. . . ."

"You OK?"

Ben looked to David, whose brow was wetted of perspiration. "Well enough, thank you." The train eased again into motion. "Thank you, good sir, for discovering me at a most salutary moment."

David smiled. "You left quite a trail. How in God's name did you end up in the river?"

"A man in a despairing temper of mind required a little reminding as to the precedence of one's duty over one's pity. An external event intruded and, in short, one event led unto another."

The train coming again to a stop, the doors on the near side of the car slid open. A marker upon the wall beyond the platform read, though in some diffusion, "13th Street." "Those skills of intimate combat, sir, employed so deftly in service to my protection, under what circumstance did you acquire those, if I might inquire?"

The train eased into motion: ". . . next stop, 11th Street . . ."

David held silent a moment, then spoke as if with some hesitancy. "I failed someone once, about as much as one person can fail another, and vowed I'd never allow that to happen again, whatever it took."

Ben shuddered to a chill reaching into the marrow of his soul. "Might a young lady have been the object of your failure, sir, if I might inquire?"

David breathed a sigh. "We were in the park one evening having a picnic to commemorate the first anniversary of our first meeting in that same park. We were both runners and we'd finished a 10k there together the year before. It hadn't gotten dark yet, but the spot where we were, near a duck pond, was a bit remote, so I should have known better. Suddenly there was a knife at my throat." David paused. "There were three of them." He paused. "They took turns with her while making me watch."

Ben closed his eyes.

"About six months later, I got a note in the mail from Miriam's father. There was only one word: COWARD. All in caps—underlined."

The train again stopping, the doors on the near side slid open. A marker on the wall beyond the near platform read "11th Street," if Ben squinted just enough. The woman who previously had removed herself from near proximity now removed herself from the train.

Ben patted David's arm. "Never in my life, sir, have I witnessed the equal of the personal courage and martial prowess you exercised in the cause of my rescue from those ruffians. Indeed, your legs were as if transformed into four sets of arms. Lord Shiva himself, sir, you had become. You saved my life."

Turning from a catch in his throat, David looked to the window.

In the moment, Ben's stomach felt as if it were being swallowed whole by a viper.

Standing on the platform, close upon the wall, was Lucy Myers, the very woman who had sat in David's relative position upon the train from New York, and moving forthrightly toward her in the moment was the very man Ben had recently encountered bearing a portfolio in one hand whilst drawing a larger article of luggage on wheels with the other.

Lucy and the man embraced with unabashed familiarity.

The man thereupon opened his portfolio, and removing from this a single bloom of *Franklinia*, offered it toward Lucy, who accepted it with such effusion as to leave her countenance as if glossed of honey butter.

David slumped, and clutching his chest with both arms, folded forward upon himself as if to a pinch of colic. He moaned a terrible plaint despite an obvious attempt not to.

"I'm so very sorry," Ben whispered. "So very sorry."

David wept.

Ben laid a hand on David's shoulder. "He proves himself not the man you are, sir; nor to be of such potential as to become what you would make of him were you able. Forgive him, sir, and as this train moves on toward a proper destination, forgive yourself for what you perceive to be your own failures. You deserve no less."

When the train next stopped, David, yet damp from the previous inclemency, cleared his throat and looked to Ben. "Next stop."

Ben shuddered, indeed as if of an incipient rigor mortis.

"You OK?"

"Well enough, sir. Thank you."

"Do you think you could make it to the gates? It's not far."

"I shall make every effort."

Rising from his seat, David stepped over Ben's hemorrhaging feet, and pulling Ben to upright, led him, firmly clutched, close unto the exit. Upon the doors sliding open, David helped Ben onto the platform, and rightward then unto a turnstile. Easing Ben into the near chamber, David pushed him through, himself in the succeeding chamber, and managed to grasp Ben on the farther side before he might sink of faltering knees. By deft maneuver then, David took Ben again onto his back.

"If I say 'sing,' *sing!* OK?"

"I shall make every effort."

Upon settling his load, David trudged unto a set of steps, and as he made a laborious ascent, one step at a time, Ben—

Could feel the sun warm upon his brow—

Hear the voices of children joyous upon his ears—

Smell the scent of honeysuckle sweet upon his olfactory—

Feel the radiance of a loving presence close upon his side—

He ached to lay his hand upon hers, to feel the abiding warmth of it, the diminutive femininity of it, the agreeable complement of it, but his own would not obey the command of his will, and though he mounted this unto tremble and tears, yet his hand would not obey. Hearing then a tenor voice, agreeable in tone, but as if under considerable strain—

Ben discovered himself rested upon David's back, close upon a high brick wall—

> *Well, I've* got *a hammer*
> *And I've* got *a bell*
> *And I've* got *a song to sing*
> *All over this land*

"My apologies, sir. I seem to have abandoned all duty."

"No problem."

They turned rightward whereat the wall cornered. Upon a few steps farther, the brick wall was interrupted by a wrought-iron fence, the latter like a gate, and was spanned near at top as if by a sail stowed in a reddish cover. On the farther side of the fence, a slab of darkish stone lay a few inches above ground, it being otherwise about "six feet long, four feet wide, plain, with only a small moulding round the upper edge"—indeed precisely as he had specified in his final instructions.

The brick wall resuming, Ben caught glimpse of his image graven upon a bronze plaque.

Upon one step farther, David lowered himself onto one knee, and by deft maneuver then, unburdened himself to effect of reposing Ben on the pavement such that his back was a'ready rested against the wall. Upon reposing himself likewise, David rested his head against the wall and breathed in a ponderous rhythm whilst holding shut his eyes.

Peering across the near street, toward whereat he had owned a parcel of land, tenants upon it, Ben could discern a marker affixed upon the near end of a robust building: UNITED STATES MINT. He smiled. What small commerce in tenancy did not ever beget its larger?

"You're about to tell me you need to be on the other side of this wall, aren't you?"

"You would appear to possess that rare facility of mystery by which one person might freely grasp the thoughts of another, sir."

A low rumble from northwestward.

Ben made gesture toward rising. "The hour is late, sir. Might I impose upon your kindness yet one more time?"

David rolled his head back and forth against the wall. "This is nuts. Absolutely insane." He looked to Ben. "Instead of helping you over this wall—which I believe is there to keep people *out*—I should be getting you to a hospital." He looked to dark pools forming whereat Ben's heels rested upon the pavement. "What's this all about anyway? Why should I be helping you bleed to death?"

"I have intelligence, sir, only as to the urgency; naught else. If you would continue your trust but a few moments longer—" A fit of coughing caused Ben to desist. Upon managing to quell himself, he continued. "All is in your hands, sir. There is no one else."

David struck his head against the wall as if in symbolic gesture toward knocking himself sensible, or perhaps insensible, and looked to Ben. "OK, let's say we can get you up there, then what? How're you going to get down the other side without breaking both legs?" He shook his head. "This is nuts."

"I shall make every attempt toward minimizing the extent of my fall, sir, by way of extending my legs over the farther side as far as possible before committing myself to my fate."

"And land on *what* below? Do you know?"

"All is risk, sir." Afflicted of another fit of coughing, Ben winced to each paroxysm. Afflicted of another fit of light-headedness, he—

Could feel the sun warm upon his brow—

Hear the voices of children joyous upon his ears—

Smell the scent of honeysuckle sweet upon his olfactory—

Feel the radiance of a loving presence close upon his side—

He ached to lay his hand upon hers, to feel the abiding warmth of it, the diminutive femininity of it, the agreeable complement of it, but his own would not obey the command of his will, and though he mounted this unto tremble and tears, yet his hand would not obey. Hearing then a low growl—

He discovered David, shed of his blouse, tying shreds of cloth into a length of such. "My vest, sir—would it not be better to purpose?"

David shook his head. "You're going to need it." Getting himself to upright, David returned a small knife to pocket, and pulling Ben to upright, tied the makeshift cord tightly around Ben's chest, just below his arms, such that the knot was located to back. He thereupon positioned Ben such as to face upon the wall, legs slightly apart.

"You ready?"

"I am, sir."

Intruding himself betwixt Ben's legs, David lifted Ben onto his shoulders and then unsteadily but inexorably upward, to effect of Ben being able, with some additional assistance from below, to crawl onto the top of the brick wall.

Lying upon his belly now, this protected against rude chafing by service of his vest, Ben peered downward upon David, who was holding the untethered end of the makeshift cord. "By any chance," Ben inquired, "were you a sojourner in China in the year 4004 BC?"

David showed consternation.

Another rumble from northwestward.

"Of no importance, sir."

David instructed Ben to pull the cord unto himself, wind it half around his chest, clockwise, and return it unto him. He thereupon pulled the cord taut. "OK, when you're ready, just roll off the edge—all at once. The idea is to end up facing outward, with me holding you in place. Got it?"

"I do."

"And just so you know, if I don't hear from you within five seconds, I'm calling 911. You ready?"

"I am."

Ben closed his eyes, and holding his breath, rolled boldly forth, whereupon—his stomach feeling as if ripped from its comfort—he felt a sharp constriction across his upper chest, a rude chafing near upon his armpits, and a modest blow to his backside.

Upon opening his eyes, Ben discovered himself suspended such as to be faced upon the burying ground, just as David had prescribed. Directly below, there appeared to be naught but grassy ground, whilst, a few feet to front, a gravel pathway, lined of cobblestone, led unto whereat, to rightward, lay not one but two stone slabs—one close upon the wrought-iron fence; the other, whitish, juxtaposed to the first. Both slabs appeared luminescent by way of the glow from a street lamp standing close upon the wall along 5th Street. Surrounding both slabs, unto a perimeter of sufficient extent as to include Frankie's marker, which caused Ben to choke, was a squarish plaza of brick.

Upon surmising the lighter slab to be the covering stone for Sally and Richard's resting place, Ben choked anew.

"You OK over there?"

Ben swallowed as best he might the torture at the back of his throat. "I am, sir—as well as can be expected, given circumstance."

Descending now by increment, Ben felt his feet touch upon the ground, at which point the shards of glass recently removed therefrom seemed as if cruelly returned. Collapsing unto his knees, such as to remove the burden of himself from his lacerated feet, Ben heard another distinctive rumble from northwestward.

David called from the farther side: "The rope's free. You can pull it over."

Gathering the makeshift cord unto himself, Ben stuffed it under his vest, and crawled then, upon hands and knees, toward the two stone slabs, keeping to the grassy ground. Nearing the plaza of brick, he discovered David standing at the farther side of the wrought-iron fence.

"Need any help sliding the cover off?"

"Your wit, sir, shall carry you far; your kindness, yet farther." The object resembling a stowed sail, Ben noticed, was actually a tarpaulin affixed from unrolling by way of a few girds bearing hooks at either end. "I apologize for the demise of Sloan, sir. I was careless in my naïveté. If I could make restitution, I would do so, and more, but I have naught to my person now but this"—Ben produced his pennywhistle from pocket—"for which I paid too much. Would you care to own it, sir?"

David showed his calling device. "Whistle enough, thank you."

Another rumble.

Ben returned his whistle to pocket. "There is one favor more you might extend unto me, sir, should your willingness to accommodate a strange old man be yet abiding."

"Do I have a choice?"

"Is there a coin of any realm of one side only, sir?"

David grinned.

"The stays upholding that covering, sir. If you would rotate each sufficiently toward yourself, you might unfasten each one in turn. This solemn chamber needs be, for an interim, if I might be allowed so presumptuous a notion, a private confessional, as against a public monument. Extend unto me this one last kindness, sir, and be gone." His voice faltering, Ben hesitated. "I am sorry, sir, to be so precipitously inhospitable. The hour has grown perilously late."

"And *then* I get to call 911, right?"

"You are of an unrelenting temper of mind, sir."

"I had a great teacher."

"As others might, upon a time, say of you, I do heartily believe."

As David unhooked the stays, an increasing portion of the tarpaulin unfolded unto the ground. He hesitated at the last stay. "Are you still bleeding?"

"I am sufficiently preserved, good sir, for whatever might ensue, with thanks owing entirely to yourself."

David shook his head. "This is nuts."

Ben bowed. "Steer ever true as thine compass should direct, sir."

David bowed in return. "I shall make every effort."

The last portion of the tarpaulin dropped unto the ground, to effect of covering the whole of the interlude of wrought-iron fence in the manner of a window dressing.

Another rumble, closer upon.

Crawling onto the brick plaza, his knees issuing bitter complaint against being used as unshod feet, Ben approached the stone slab surrounded by "a small moulding." In stronger light, the moulding showed to be black whilst the slab itself showed to be a variegated marble of light and dark aspect. The top of the slab was well sprinkled over of coins: some of these silver, most copper.

Ben smiled. *A penny tossed is a penny lost.*

Espying an inscription graven upon the slab, Ben, being near blind at close proximity, used his fingers to decipher it: BENJAMIN / AND / DEBORAH to leftward, FRANKLIN to rightward, 1790 beneath. There appeared to be no mention of the year of Deborah's death, it having come sixteen years previous, in 1774.

I must submit, and endeavor to submit, to what I am to bear.

Ben bowed his head.

In the fall!
In the spring!
In the fall!
In the spring!

"I am so very sorry," he whispered. "So very, very sorry."

Slipping his whistle from pocket, Ben laid it upon the marble slab. "I paid too much for whistle," he whispered, "too little for song." Thereupon resting his head upon the marble slab, he began to weep, but was soon interrupted by a voice close upon—

"Though the hour is late, sir, yet still there is time."

Raising his head as if of reflex, Ben discovered standing close upon him a luminous woman in close likeness to the previous such he had witnessed. As to difference, whereas the previous Madonna had borne a striking medallion in likeness to two fetuses, indistinct of species, circulating head to tail within the same womb, each being, in coloration, the complement of the other, the present Madonna bore a pendant in likeness to a caduceus, one serpent being black in body, white of eye, twining to clockwise; the other being white in body, black of eye, twining to counterclockwise. And whereas the previous Madonna had cradled her infant in the crook of her left arm, the present Madonna was cradling her infant in the crook of her right arm.

The Madonna's countenance transfigured now, such as to increase in familiarity, until Ben discovered himself peering upon the countenance of the young mother who had crossed the Delaware with him, from the New Jersey shore unto the Market Street wharf, on that chill autumn night so many, many years ago.

The woman smiled. "Your kindness of that day, good sir, was never forgot, and was passed on in the manner of pollen upon the feet of bees. It returns now to whence it began, as every act, whether to good or to ill, needs must."

Sensing a second presence, Ben turned to rightward to discover close upon him a Negro boy of familiarity, holding a silver tray upon which rested two honey-brown loaves, these yet perspiring of oven heat, and a crystalline goblet filled to the majority of a ruddy liquor. The boy bowed.

Recognizing the boy now with a start, Ben bowed in return. "You are Jacob, the lad who took bludgeons of boot and truncheon onto himself such that his mother's life might be spared, she being newly delivered of child, your sister, named Jericho."

Ben gasped as Jacob's countenance of a sudden transfigured such as to show swellings and disfigurements so boldly offensive to sensibility as would seem to require a reflex of revulsion. Ben pulled Jacob into his arms, thereby spilling loaf and goblet onto brick, and held the boy close upon his bosom. "I am so very sorry," he whispered. "So very, very sorry."

Upon the boy returning to original countenance, Ben stooped toward retrieving the items spilt, and was startled to witness the goblet restore itself unto wholeness, the wine restore itself unto the goblet, the goblet and loaves restore themselves unto the tray, the tray restore itself unto Jacob, indeed as if time itself had taken four steps in reverse.

Jacob extended the tray toward Ben. "Two loaves for thee, sir."

Ben peered upon the richly redolent offerings as if upon a cruel tease. Jacob bowing, Ben took a loaf tentatively into hand. Jacob bowing again, Ben laid the first loaf upon the marble slab, and taking the second into hand, claimed unto an ineffably joyous palate a goodly morsel.

"The Madeira," the Madonna whispered, "is drawn from a cask carried by the tardiest barque ever to ply waters of sufficient breadth as to fate spoilage unto all savors save one."

Tears having begun to scud down his cheeks, Ben lifted the crystalline goblet of both hands, these trembling, and drew unto an ineffably joyous palate a generous measure of heady liquor.

"As the rarest is sweetest," the Madonna whispered, "so the sweetest is rarest."

Ben indulged himself of another morsel of bread, and another draw of wine—and another and another—and another and another. Upon savoring the last morsel, the last drop, Ben returned the goblet unto the tray, and bowed. "I am at a loss for an expression of gratitude sufficient to the occasion."

Jacob bowed in return. "The words shall come, sir, as they must, if not toward gratitude then toward an end far greater. There is no one else."

In the moment, a bolt of fire, brilliantly blue, struck upon the slab of marble with such a hammer blow of violence as to cause Ben's whistle to leap upward the equivalent of its length and more, the second loaf to do likewise. A second bolt, brilliantly green, thereupon followed, to equal effect; likewise a third, brilliantly red.

Whilst flames of blue and green and red sizzled overtop the marble slab, the slab itself grew ever more vitreous in aspect, ever greater in height. Of a sudden then all went quiet and in place of the slab of variegated marble stood now a crystalline bench four feet by six as previous, but now two feet in height. Clearly visible within, indeed as if preserved in a block of ice, two persons were reposed such that the right hand of one, she glorious in a gown of cerulean blue, was rested upon the left hand of the other, he resplendent in a suit of pastoral green.

"What forgiveness in the seeking of it," the Madonna whispered, "is not ever the gaining of it?"

His head collapsing onto the bench, betwixt loaf and whistle, Ben had no sooner been stricken of a paroxysm of wrenching sobs than a hammer blow was delivered onto the crystalline tomb of such violence as to shock Ben near upon insensible, and of such fire as to ignite the entire bench into a sizzling conflagration. The whistle and loaf thereupon becoming engulfed of hissing flames, they each erupted of a sudden into flashes of purest light, to end that whereat had lain the loaf lay now a sheet of parchment, and whereat had lain the whistle lay now a feather pen.

"I do believe, sir," the Madonna whispered, "that you have a song to sing."

Ben held unto perplexity a moment, and then heard as if an echo come full circle—

We have now been reminded, sir, of the thirteen virtues you espoused as being 'necessary or desirable.' Likewise, we have been reminded that you espoused these virtues in your Almanacks, *under guise of Poor Richard; and in your* The Way to Wealth, *under guise of Father Abraham; and most especially within the pages of your* Autobiography, *which volume you long struggled to bring to term, against much adversity, in lieu of, we should here mention, the volume you had promised several times over to your friend Lord Kames, as well as others, to be called* The Art of Virtue; *quite so?*

"You allude, I do believe, to those verses promised by me to Lord Kames but never delivered unto him."

The Madonna bowed. "The last that might have been first, sir; but in being last, might now be best."

Ben bowed in return, and looking to the parchment, was surprised to discover his eyesight to have been relieved of all infirmity, by effect, it would appear, of the recent shock unto his senses. Discovering thereupon no ready source of ink, Ben returned his attention unto the Madonna, that he might make inquiry, but discovered her disappeared; Jacob also.

Thereupon taking the quill into trembling hand, Ben twisted himself sufficient that he might hold the nib in a crimson pool accumulated whereat his left foot rested. Upon the quill stem taking on, as if by force of magic, a crimson cast, Ben turned unto the crystalline bench and began to write, at top-center of the parchment, in as careful a hand as he could manage:

The Art of Virtue
or
Two Loaves for Thee

Happiness is the practice of virtue unencumbered of all doctrine; virtue, the practice of love unencumbered of all desire.

If you would be happy, my friend—

Ben moved the quill pen into the first quadrant, and continued—

1

Recognize the difference betwixt craving and yearning; gratification and fulfillment. A dog barks, we reach for a bone. A cat rubs against our leg, do we reach also for a bone?

2

Strive to love, accept, and sacrifice without expectation or condition. In committing ourselves to a life of spontaneous generosity and compassion, we assure ourselves of everything we will ever really need.

Thusly did Ben versify until his script became as if stricken of anemia, whereupon he replenished his pen by way of the previous magic. Suffering thereupon a fit of faintheadedness of such severity as to near upon deny him all sentience, he lowered his head onto the parchment and closed his eyes. After a moment, he heard a voice as if from a very great distance.

You must endure, sir.

Though the hour is late, yet still there is time.

Hearing another rumble, Ben lifted his head, and laying again the nib of his pen upon parchment, continued on—

5

Discover early in your uncertain tenure upon this earth the blessings with which you were uniquely graced. Tarry not till the hour of regret.

6

Dream not with your desires, but with your gifts. When craving is
compass, disappointment is destination.

Thusly did Ben continue until, having filled the first quadrant, he
advanced into the second—

14

Risk making mistakes. Error is the flour of all true success; the
yeast of all true wisdom.

15

Choose the company of upbeat friends and let the whiners and
naysayers go their own miserable way. Leave the dirge to the
already dead.

Thusly did Ben continue until, having filled the second quadrant, he
advanced into the third—

27

Be swift to voice complaints, as swift to apologize for errors.
Leave no wound to fester, no grievance to sunder.

28

Do unto your community as you would have your community do
unto you.

Thusly did Ben continue until, having filled the third quadrant, he
advanced into the fourth—

40

Recognize the difference betwixt religion and spirituality.
Religion is a room with a door and a window. Spirituality is the
window.

41

Live within your means. The quality of life depends not on the
quality of what you possess, but on the quality of you.

Desisting now to another fit of coughing, Ben rested his head upon
the parchment until he was quieted. Thereupon replenishing his pen,
to another distinctive rumble, he continued on—

50

Remind yourself during those inescapable moments of
powerlessness and despair that you possess, always and

undiminished, the greatest power any human being can ever possess: the power to see the unseen, the power to abet the unabetted, the power to embrace the unembraced.

51

Wait not for happiness to be delivered unto you; not parent, not polity, not deity owes us the gift of joy. If we are to receive happiness in this life, we must deliver it unto ourselves.

52

Play not to win, but for the struggle. The sweat is the victory.

Ben lifted his eyes unto a tumultuous firmament, and buffeted by a burst of breeze, held the parchment to place. The wind abating, he overturned the parchment and continued on, by tremulous hand, close upon the top—

Happiness

Of a sudden drawn to the last two letters writ, Ben was reminded, by way of imagining "s" bounded within a circle, of the medallion worn by the first Madonna; and, by way of reversing the second "s," and imagining this reversal partially imposed upon the first "s," of the pendant worn by the second Madonna.

Bowing now as if to the one, and to the other, he whispered, "More ways there are to be blind in this world than to suffer an infirmity to one's eyes."

He continued on—

Happiness is the practice of virtue unencumbered of all doctrine; virtue, the practice of love unencumbered of all desire.

Upon a robust clap of thunder, Ben replenished his pen to partial capacity, there being no time for greater, and thereupon continued on, having now to hold his pen of both hands—

If you would be happy, my friend—
Bake thee three loaves each day
Place the one smaller in thy larder
Leave the two larger in hunger's way

From close upon now came a splitting-tree crack of thunder, and from equally close, as if in counterpoint, a pealing of bell.

Laying aside his quill pen, drained of all ink, Ben got himself to upright, to a second pealing, and upon a third, thought of the Diva of the Pennsylvania Station.

> *Well, I've got a hammer*
> *And I've got a bell*
> *And I've got a song to sing*
> *All over this land*

"Blessed are the song makers," Ben whispered, "for they shall bring hope unto all yet impoverished of it."

Upon a fourth pealing, Ben felt his flesh tingle as if to a sudden flood tide of the electrical fluid.

Upon a fifth pealing, he became sensible of a wailing most urgent, and smiling near unto a grin, looked whereat last he had glimpsed of the likely agent of a noble treason.

"Bless you, my son."

Upon a sixth pealing—

West Wing, the White House

September 22nd, 6:23 a.m.

Gilbert looked at his watch, and again toward the guard station.

Any second now.

He was *really* looking forward to this.

Never was he more on top of his game than when he was the only voice of reason in the room.

Bingo! A gleamy black Town Car appeared in the driveway, a red-white-and-blue banner showing ostentatiously at one side of a highly polished grille, an all-blue banner at the other.

When the limo had stopped, George opened the rear door, holding an umbrella. Tom emerged, waved off George's offer to carry his valise—it was handcuffed to his wrist after all—and hurried toward the foyer entrance. George and Malcolm seemed to compete for the privilege of holding an outsized umbrella overtop the CIA Director's outsized head.

A cold rain had been falling now since at least 3:46 a.m., when Gilbert's bedside phone had interrupted a dream in which Gilbert was inside a labyrinthine building and couldn't find the men's room. He was about to wet his pants.

Returning to his desk, Gilbert took a sip of tepid Costa Rican Tarrazu, no cream no sugar, and leaning back in his chair, mug in hand, awaited Teresa's call.

Any second now.

He was *really, really* looking forward to this.

Bingo!

Gilbert waited for the third ring. "Gilbert."

"Good morning, Mr. Bahr."

"Good morning, Teresa."

"Director Fiske has just arrived, and the President's already in the Oval."

"I'll be right over."

Gilbert took another sip of coffee, straightened his tie, and exiting his office through his private entrance, headed down the corridor toward the southwest corner of the wing. Walking briskly, he responded to eye contacts with perfunctory grunts and nods. Bearing left at Morrie Stern's office, he headed for the southeast corner of the wing, and entering the open door to Teresa's office, could see Tom already standing in the Oval.

"You can go right in," Teresa said.

Gilbert nodded.

The President was standing behind his desk talking on one of his phones, the white one—to Bertie Chambers it soon became clear.

Gilbert had never once seen the President sit while talking on the telephone; always he stood like Patton in his tent.

Tom was standing in front of the desk, looking twitchy and sweaty, and as if he hadn't slept in three days. His valise was resting on the floor, the chain having been removed by Teresa, she being the keeper of the only key on the near end. Lily was lying near the Presidential Seal, per usual, chewing on one of her indestructible spheroids, per usual.

Gilbert listened in on the President's side of the conversation long enough to be assured the President was not in any way compromising, or straying toward compromising, the absolute secrecy to which the three men had sworn, at Gilbert's insistence, at the end of each of their conference calls over the past four days.

Gilbert looked toward Tom and marveled anew at this man's truly remarkable set of indelicate features—a protuberant brow and generally oversized head that made one think of Mary Shelley's creation; a pair of fleshy, elongated ears that bore knobs like tree knots; a highly arched nose that appeared to have been broken at some point and repaired to the effect of adding a speed bump; and large, meaty hands with knuckles like walnuts.

As frosting on this remarkable cake, Tom bore the wages of four decades of chain-smoking in the form of a sallow, death-warmed-over complexion. Although he had gone cold turkey almost four years ago now—one of the conditions of his appointment—the damage done over the previous forty-plus years was manifestly not to be undone.

As Gilbert and Tom made eye contact—Gilbert showing Tom an easy smile, Tom showing Gilbert an anxious counterpart—Gilbert was reminded of the four cardinal reasons he had recommended Tom for the critical position this former linguistics chair at MIT had held now—with the unflagging (little pun there) competence Gilbert had expected of him—for nearly four smoke-free years: (1) the man had an IQ of 184 (how many "public servants" could claim even half that?); (2) the man could speak nine languages, including Mandarin and Farsi; (3) the man had an abiding weakness for bondage pornography; and of course, (4) this documentable fact was known by only two people on the planet—Tom Fiske, and Tom Fiske's beneficent patron.

The President peered at Gilbert and signaled "one more minute."

Gilbert nodded and then looked toward the seating area, where coffee and fat pills had already been delivered. He considered suggesting to Tom that they sit down and pour themselves a cup of coffee, but the President hadn't indicated permission to precede him. If they remained standing, however, Gilbert well knew, he was going to have to deal with Lily, who sooner or later was going to try to slime him into a game of tug-and-pull.

Gilbert tried to catch the President's eye, but the President was turned too far toward the French doors to notice.

"Sox lost again last night," Gilbert announced toward Tom, knowing full well Tom held no interest whatsoever in baseball.

"Lost a pair myself," Gilbert imagined the response.

"Sorry," the President said, emerging from the other side of the desk. "OK, let's get right to it. Tom, what've you got for us?"

Lily looked up from her ball.

Tom looked toward the open door to Teresa's office.

The President gazed toward Gilbert, and then looked to Lily. "Stay, girl."

Gilbert closed the door to Teresa's office and then sat down in his usual place, opposite the President. The gas fireplace, likely lit by Roy Peoples when he delivered the coffee and donut holes, was radiating a welcome aura of heat.

Gilbert offered to pour a cup of coffee for the President, who accepted. He then offered to pour a cup for Tom, still standing, who declined. He then poured one for himself.

Tom lifted his valise onto the table, and removing an aluminum tube, capped at one end, placed the tube near the platter of donut holes. He then removed a clear plastic bag, containing a slender object, silver, and placed this on the table.

The President picked up the bag. "This the whistle?"

Tom nodded.

"OK to take it out?"

Tom nodded.

Removing the silvery object from the bag, the President examined it a moment, and then raised one end to his mouth.

"We traced it to London, late 1600s to early 1700s," Tom said. "It has the manufacturer's mark on it."

The President grinned to a squeak he managed to elicit. Gilbert and Tom grinned with him.

Tom pulled a red folder from his valise, and laying this on the table, removed a few paperclipped sheets from it. "Before I proceed," he said, "I'd like to read you something." He looked to the President. The President signaling permission, Tom continued. "Keep in mind, please, that these two artifacts were found just after midnight, four days ago, after an electrical storm of particular intensity. They were laying on the marble slab that covers Franklin's grave. More on this in a moment."

Gilbert lifted his eyes as if in response to a shaken sheet of tin, and found himself gazing at the plaster relief on the ceiling.

Tom cleared his throat and began to read: "'In my opinion, we might all draw more good from this world than we do, and suffer less evil, if we would take care not to give too much for whistles. For, to me, it seems that most of the unhappy people we meet with have become so by neglect of that caution. You ask what I mean?'"

"Tom," Gilbert interrupted, "the President and I both know what he means. We know the piece very well. I don't think we need to go through the whole thing." Gilbert looked to the President. Tom looked to the President. The President nodded.

"Sorry," Tom said, a twitch toward a smile betraying a pinch of cha-grin. "It's important to keep this piece in mind, though, I think, as we proceed." Tom set the paperclipped sheets down on the red folder. "It serves as a sort of attractor, I think."

"A who?" The President was poised to pluck a fat pill from the platter.

"An attractor," Gilbert took control. "Tom is invoking chaos theory. In chaos theory, an attractor is a point around which order—or design, as I think he intends here—organizes itself."

Tom nodded toward Gilbert, and then looked to the President. "May I sit?"

The President, his mouth full of donut, gestured toward Gilbert's couch.

Tom sat down and poising himself forward on the cushion, took a deep breath. "As I mentioned on the phone—sorry again about the ungodly hour—recent events have taken a bit of a turn." He laid a hand on the red folder. "I've got complete contact information in here for all our sources, if you'd like to hear directly from the horses' mouths."

"How many horses?" Gilbert asked.

Tom looked caught off guard and, for a fleeting moment, resentful. "Well, I'm not sure exactly. We've conducted several analyses, involving several people. I'd have to add them up." He looked to the red folder. "It's all in there."

"Five? Twenty-five? A hundred and five?"

Tom again looked resentful. "More than five; less than twenty-five."

"Fewer."

Tom looked as if he had been addressed in Songhai.

"*Fewer* than twenty-five. *Less* filling; *fewer* calories."

"Oh—yes, sorry." Resentment, repressed elsewhere, seemed to creep now into the puffy flesh around Tom's eyes. He looked to the President and continued. "Before I go on, just let me say here that I led with the whistle bit because I've become convinced, especially over the past twenty-four hours, that this thing, as I mentioned"—he held up the pennywhistle—"is key to understanding what's going on. You may well disagree. I'm not going to argue the point." Tom returned the whistle to the table. "All I'm going to do here this morning is just give you the facts as these have developed over the past twenty-four hours, and leave you with this folder, so you can hear directly from the horses' mouths, if you wish to do so. Then I'm going to go home and go to bed. I haven't slept more than five hours in the past four days."

Tom shifted his eyes back and forth between Gilbert and the President as if in anticipation of a challenge. He continued. "There are three new developments. The first"—he touched the index finger on his right hand—"concerns those handwriting analyses we had done. As you know, we did those to see if we could get some idea of who wrote the text on the parchment. We weren't sure this would get us much, because of the obvious attempt toward imitating Franklin's handwriting, but we decided to give it a shot anyway. Any clues, we felt, would be better than none. So, as you know, we sent samples to five experts—three in the U.S., including one at the CIA; and two in Britain—one at Scotland Yard, the other at Oxford.

"Now, as it turns out, the profiler we contacted at Oxford had once been an authenticator for the Franklin Papers at Yale. When he saw the sample we sent him—he had no information, by the way, concerning its origin, or anything else about it—he thought he recognized the style and took it upon himself to do a comparative analysis. When we got his results, we immediately asked four other authenticators to conduct a similar analysis." Tom paused to clear his throat. He continued. "All four came in with exactly the same result. The handwriting on that parchment"—Tom looked toward the aluminum tube—"is *not* a clever imitation of Franklin's handwriting after all. It's the real deal." Tom shifted his eyes between Gilbert and the President. He continued. "Remember, I'm just giving you the facts here as these have developed over the past twenty-four hours. All four authenticators also agreed that the writer—Franklin himself, they would say—appeared to have been under considerable stress at the time of the writing. As you know, we believe the writer was bleeding profusely at the time, and was, in fact, using his own blood as ink."

Gilbert lifted his eyes as if to another rumble of tin.

The President looked toward Gilbert. "What've we got here, Gil?"

Gilbert looked toward Tom. "What've we got here, Tom?"

"There's more."

Gilbert looked to the President. "There's more."

The President smiled, and leaning forward, picked up the whistle. "You're not going to tell me this's Franklin's actual whistle, are you?"

Tom appeared as if stricken by sciatica. "The facts, sir, the facts as we have been able to determine them to date, allow for that possibility."

The President looked to Gilbert, who, hands clasped on his lap, was fluttering his thumbs in a sort of syncopated dance. The President smiled, and returning the whistle to the table, sat back in his seat. "The others?"

"OK, the second development concerns the missing cane. As you know, Franklin's famous crab-tree cane was discovered missing from the Smithsonian on the same day that these two artifacts"—Tom nodded toward the aluminum tube and whistle—"were discovered at the Franklin gravesite. And, as you also know, a person fitting the description of the Franklin look-alike who apparently left these artifacts at Franklin's grave was seen earlier that day in three different cities—Boston, New York, and Philadelphia—in possession of a silver-tipped cane fitting the description of the very one that went missing from the Smithsonian."

"How does something go missing, Tom?"

A shadow passed over Tom's face.

Gilbert flipped a hand. "Never mind. Keep going."

Tom looked to the President. "Late yesterday afternoon, we got word that a groundskeeper at Bertram Gardens, located on the west bank of the Schuylkill, not far from the Penn campus, found Franklin's cane washed ashore there. John Bertram, as I'm sure you both know, was a close friend of Franklin's. And, as you also know, the blood found at Franklin's gravesite precisely matches the blood found on the Market Street Bridge, which is located just upriver from Bertram Gardens."

Gilbert again lifted his eyes toward the relief on the ceiling.

"The third development concerns the parchment itself. When we got the last of those handwriting analyses in, we decided to do an analysis of the parchment itself, to see if we could determine how old it was and where it came from, that sort of thing. Our thinking was that if the parchment proved to be only ten years old, or even a hundred and ten years old, we'd have some pretty good evidence countervailing against the handwriting analyses. So we arranged for an analysis at the Archives. This was last night. In fact, it's there I called you from this morning."

Tom opened the red folder, and removing two photographs, handed one to the President, the other to Gilbert. "You will note," he continued, "that the top of the parchment found on Franklin's grave is positioned to abut the bottom of the parchment that bears the *Bill of Rights*. That parchment is an exact photocopy, by the way, because the actual document can't be removed from its case. You will note also that the two parchments have exactly the same width, the same tone, the same texture, and the same general appearance, and they fit together, top to bottom, like two pieces of a puzzle."

The President looked to Gilbert, who was rhythmically touching his thumbs together, hands clasped. The President looked to Tom. "Can we see it?"

"Certainly." Tom unscrewed the cap from the aluminum tube, and turning the tube upside down, caught a scroll wrapped in a sheath of clear plastic. Removing the sheath, Tom nudged the platter of donut holes toward the silver tray holding the coffee paraphernalia, and unrolling the scroll onto the table, oriented it so the script faced toward the President. To hold the parchment flat, he set the coffee creamer on one end, the sugar bowl on the other. He peered toward Gilbert. "As I said, I'm just reporting the facts here. I'm not drawing any conclusions."

The President leaned toward the parchment and read aloud, "'*The*

Art of Virtue or *Two Loaves for Thee.*'" He peered at Tom. "You're thinking the 'Loaves' mentioned here are a reference to the loaves Franklin
purchased on his first morning in Philadelphia, am I right?"

"I am, but if *Two Loaves* were the title by itself, I probably wouldn't.
Paired with *The Art of Virtue*, however—which, as you know, is the title
of a volume Franklin intended to write but never did—it's hard *not*
to. Just as it's hard not to view the document itself as a sort of *Bill of
Responsibilities* in counterpart to the *Bill of Rights*. It wasn't given the
latter as a title, though, one could argue, because who's going to pay any
attention to a screed titled the *Bill of Responsibilities*?"

"Oh—my—gawd!" Gilbert was peering up at the ceiling, arms
stretched over his head. "Moses has returned! Smash all the graven
images!"

"Let me guess, Gil," the President said. "You have a different view on
the matter."

Gilbert surged forward. "We take *one more step* down this path"—he
hammered the tabletop with a fist, sloshing coffee from his cup—"and
we're going to end up at the bottom of a goddamn cliff." He pushed his
bifocals back on his nose, finger to bridge, and picking up the whistle,
waved it: "Child's whistle, or piper's pipe?" He tossed the whistle onto
the table, and looked to Tom. "You geniuses at Langley invent a sophisticated speech replicator, one that can inflect nuances of every possible
sort, and some other geniuses, on the other side of the river, can't do
the same goddamn thing to replicate handwriting? That it?"

Gilbert looked to the President. "OK, here's what's going to happen
here if we don't get our goddamn shit together. Our Franklin look-alike
friend is going to turn up again, very soon"—he glanced to Tom—"you
can bet the farm on it—and when he does, it's going to be in conjunction with some other goddamn miraculous event. This time it was the
miraculous appearance of The Four-Score and Twelve Commandments
on Franklin's gravesite"—he glanced again to Tom—"during an electrical storm of particular intensity." He threw up his arms. "Hallelujah!
Next time, it'll be the miraculous cure of some limp-wristed Nancy
boy with AIDS on Good-Bye America!" Gilbert threw up his arms.
"Hallelujah! Then it'll be something else, and something else. And the
average bozo out there is just going to eat it up. Then, at some point, our
mysterious friend will declare for Kenyon. The message will be clear:
God wants Kenyon to be President. And once this genie is out of the
bottle, boys and girls, there's no putting the sonuvabitch back. We try
to counter with our three Eves crying 'rape' and there isn't a Country

Joan in the entire goddamn universe who won't see it as a desperate attempt by a desperate man"—he looked to Tom—"pulling his lever behind the curtain."

Gilbert looked to the President. "As to Ben's cane going missing, not to mention disappearing, when's the last time a lock was invented by human hands that could not be broken by human hands? To paraphrase Bahr's Corollary to Gödel's theorem: It is physically impossible, because it is *logically* impossible, for human beings to invent any lock that other human beings cannot break." Gilbert looked at Tom. "Remember *Mission Impossible*? What was the message?"

Gilbert looked to the parchment, and then to the President. "As to our mysterious parchment being of a piece with the *Bill of Rights*, what school kid today, equipped with an $800 laptop, can't make one piece of parchment, or anything else, fit together with some other piece of parchment, or anything else, in less than five minutes?"

Gilbert paused as if to give Tom sufficient time to take the bait.

Tom held his counsel.

Gilbert continued. "The psychological underpinning here is worthy of Machiavelli himself: Give gravitas to a few pieces of questionable evidence by juxtaposing them with one piece that, on the surface of it, seems incontrovertible, while letting the multiplicity of the pieces distract close attention away from any one piece. Brilliant. My suspicion is that this is the brainchild of His Righteous Reverend His Own Fucking Self. The man is a goddamn snake. Unfortunately, he's also a goddamn genius."

The President smiled. "I just love it when you get your knickers in a knot, Gil." He looked to Tom. "What do you think, Tom?"

Tom glanced to Gilbert, and then looked to the President. "If the premise is correct, our response would seem obvious."

"Strike now?"

Tom nodded.

"And is the premise correct, do you think?"

Tom held his eyes on the President. "I'm not sure it matters. Our primary reason for holding off until October was to minimize the amount of time Kenyon would have to make a recovery. It's unlikely he'd be able to do much of anything, however, no matter how much time he had, so I don't see much of a downside to our moving the timetable up a little."

The President looked to Gilbert. "You agree, Gil?"

Gilbert nodded. "If we make our move now, any additional magic shows from the Kenyon camp will play to an empty house. They could have George Washington himself descend from a cloud and place a crown on Kenyon's head and it wouldn't matter. If a tree falls in the forest and there's no one there to hear it, it's just another dead tree."

The President smiled, and leaning forward, moved a hand toward the parchment, as if to touch it, but then withdrew it. "That really blood? It looks kind o' dark."

Tom nodded. "Type A positive. It matches the blood we found on the bridge, at two Septa stations, on a subway car, and, of course, at the cemetery itself. And if it all came from the same bleeder, he effectively bled out."

The President shook his head. "These people will stop at nothing."

"Absolutely nothing," Gilbert agreed.

The President grinned. "Well, seeing these people like to bleed, whataya say we accommodate them?" He looked at Tom. "You got everything ready to go?"

Tom nodded.

"Then, go!" The President popped a chocolate donut hole into his mouth.

"Yes, sir."

"There is, however," Gilbert said, glancing to Tom, looking to the President, "one small problem. A certain virus has been introduced into several persons outside the walls of the castle"—he looked to Tom—"more than five, fewer than twenty-five"—he looked to the President—"and if we don't take certain preemptive measures, and very soon, we're going to have a very large problem on our hands. The trouble with viruses is they tend to leave a trail of dots that trace back to source." He looked again to Tom. "Would you agree, Tom?"

Tom, looking as if he had recently bled out, nodded.

"Sometimes," Gilbert continued, looking to the President, "the only way to stop such a virus, one that could do irreparable harm, is to ensure that the carriers are no longer dots. Sometimes it's the only way." Gilbert looked to Tom, who averted his eyes, and then to the President. "Are we all in agreement on this?"

The President looked pensive, and then shook his head. "These people'll stop at nothing."

"Absolutely nothing," Gilbert agreed.

Gilbert picked the empty tube up from the table, screwed the cap on, and handing the tube and empty evidence bag over to Tom, rose from his seat. Picking the pennywhistle up from the table, he slipped it into his coat pocket. Picking up the parchment, he carried this and the plastic sheath to the fireplace, and standing before the Duplessis rendering of Franklin, pulled the screen a few inches forward and dropped both items into the fire.

The parchment browned, blackened, and then burst into flames. The plastic sheath writhed, withered, and then melted.

Gilbert returned to his seat.

The President offered the platter toward Gilbert. "Gil, have yourself a fat pill. You deserve it."

Gilbert smiled. "Well, I think I will." He picked out a Boston cream and popped it into his mouth. "Thank you, sir."

The President offered the platter toward Tom. "Tom, have yourself a fat pill. You deserve it."

Tom selected a honey glazed. He said nothing.

Returning the platter to the table, the President looked to Gilbert and shifted his eyes toward the opposite end of Gilbert's couch.

Gilbert gave a furtive nod.

The President looked to Tom. "Gil was right about you, Tom. You were absolutely the best man for the job. You've worked tirelessly, and you've been more effective, in my opinion, than anyone who's ever held your position."

Tom brightened.

"Most of all, though, you've been absolutely loyal. And as you know, there is nothing I value more in this world than loyalty—and nothing I reward more." The President smiled. "Come next term, Tom, how about an ambassadorship? China, India, anyplace you want—hopefully, though, someplace where we can take advantage of those language skills of yours. Or, you can stay right where you are. You decide. Whatever you want. Tom, carte blanche."

Tom looked like a game-show contestant who had just opened the right door. "I don't know what to say," he managed.

"You don't have to say anything, Tom. Think about it, and let me know what you want to do. Whatever it is, consider it done."

"Thank you, sir."

The President picked up the platter and held it toward Tom. "Have yourself another fat pill, Tom. You deserve it."

"Well, I think I will!" Tom picked out a Boston cream. "Thank you, sir."

The President held the platter toward Gilbert. "Gil?"

"What the hell." Gilbert picked out a honey glazed.

Returning the platter to the table, the President selected a chocolate pill for himself, and looked to Gilbert. "So, Gil, what the hell's the matter with our Sox?"

Gilbert shrugged, deadpan. "Darned if I know."

The President hooted.

Apparently activated by the sudden injection of conviviality, Lily rose from the floor, and standing at the end of the table, red ball held fast in her jaws, fixed her eyes on her master. Gaining no notice, she shifted her eyes to Tom. Gaining no notice, she shifted her eyes to Gilbert. Gaining no notice, she pled the circle around again. Turning away then, she flopped down atop the Great Seal, and releasing the red ball from her mouth, rested her chin upon one paw, yet holding her eyes upon her master, as though, by keeping vigil, she might yet gain his notice.

Celestial Chamber of B. Franklin

17 January 1706–17 April 1790

Ben bolted upright, sick with dread, as if only barely escaped from a dreamscape most horrific.

No solace was there to be summoned, however, nor quarter to be sought.

There is no one else.

He wept.

When finally he was quieted, Ben eased himself from his bed, and upon dressing himself in his brown suit, let himself into the adjoining chamber, which, although never visited by him, was well familiar. Oval in geometry, accented of blue and gold, it held upon the floor an embroidery of the Great Seal, and upon the ceiling above, a pale imitation of same. To leftward, a pair of blue-and-gold sofas faced one upon the other, whilst directly forward, a wooden desk stood robustly afront three floor-to-ceiling windows. Directly opposing the desk, upon the wall, a most familiar image, old *VIR* himself, framed in rococo superfluity, hung above a mantelpiece of white marble.

Upon the floor near to foot lay a red ball, in company of itself alone.

Hobbling to the fireplace, Ben lowered himself onto both knees, and reaching forth into the fire pit, cupped ashes into his hands, and levering his hands then overhead, spilt the ashes upon his head and brow. He repeated this gesture until, a residual dew of grief and dread serving as adherent, he was wholly transformed.

Rising then, with no little difficulty, Ben looked again to the image upon the wall. "Farewell, old friend," he whispered. Bowing then, he hobbled unto a doorway to rightward of the one through which he had entered, and letting himself into the adjoining chamber, discovered himself standing in his library at the "good house," Bob, his old servant, waiting upon him.

Bob smiled unto a grin. "Most fetching, sir. Ashes to ashes?"

Ben smiled unto the comic effect of a minstrel. *"The circle is the only geometry."*

Bob bowed. "I thank you, sir, for the kind words at court."

Ben bowed in return. "I am more sorry than I can say."

"You treated me well."

"Not as well as you deserved, sir." Ben looked to the shelves holding the residual 4036 of the volumes he had gathered unto himself over four score and four years. "In truth, I indulged upon little more than half these, although I did at least nibble at most."

"Truth is a boon like no other."

"The very foundation of all else."

"Do you think there could be more of it, sir?"

"I cannot allow myself to believe otherwise."

"You have decided then?"

"I have."

The old Negro's eyes glistened. "Alas, there is no one else."

"You test, methinks, a vanity only recently chastened."

"Can you name another?"

"If I knew all who were knowable, sir, I might name a thousand. A thousand thousand."

"Your desk awaits."

Ben bowed. "Most kind of you."

Bob turned at the door. "As truth is the only salvation, sir, so the truth teller is the only savior. A thousand such? A thousand thousand?" Bob shook his head, and closed the door behind.

Ben slumped, and wept.

When finally he was quieted, he wiped a paste of soot from one cheek and the other, and discovering himself peering upon the very "French *Pamela*" he had sent to Sally so many, many years ago now, wept anew.

When finally he was quieted, he wiped one cheek and the other, and smearing his trousers of wetted soot, seated himself at his writing desk, on which burned three candles—one red, one blue, one green. Taking into hand then a white-feathered quill, he dipped the nib into a bottle of—he grinned—"cheap ink," and began to scratch upon the sheet Bob had anticipated for him:

"Petitioner: B. Franklin, January 17, 1706—April 17, 1790.

"If it should please the court—"

Book IV

Circles

The circle is the only geometry.

Celestial Chamber of B. Franklin

17 January 1706–17 April 1790

Ben awakened with a start to discover himself sitting in the very chair that had served as tub to many an air bath. Interestingly, the only other feature in the chamber at present, other than the door, to rightward, was the very window that had served as spigot unto his baths.

He smiled.

Another rap at the door and of habit Ben listened for welcoming notes from Margaret. Recalling then, to a chuckle, the present state and status of his fate, he made immediate effort toward rising. Realizing thereupon, with a chuckle, the present state and status of his modesty, he called forth, "Enter!"

The door opening, Clarence appeared, draped in a plain white gown girded with a simple black cord, and bearing upon his head a simple garland. Bartholomew followed, wearing the same gown and garland, but with the girding cord knotted upon the opposing hip. Clarence was holding a shroud, black as coal, draped over one forearm. Bartholomew was holding a garland of red roses.

They bowed in unison. "'Tis time, sir," Clarence announced.

Ben bowed in return, and in the instant of his rising, both tub and spigot disappeared, indeed as if by wave of conjurer's wand, leaving the chamber in the very state of his first occupancy.

"Will this chamber be occupied by another?" Ben inquired, to no greater end than toward satisfaction of an abiding curiosity.

"We are informed, sir," Bartholomew replied, "of a tenant waiting upon your leave. A pretender to holiness, we are told, who placed the reputation of his dogma above the responsibility of his trust."

Ben nodded, and looked then to the items held by his Intermediaries. "Are these adornments I see before me?"

"Of a sort," Clarence replied, with a small bow.

"Toward modesty or toward flattery?"

"Toward a fitting majesty," Bartholomew replied, showing a twinkle of eye.

Draping Ben of the shroud, Clarence girded it with a plain white cord, taken from around his neck.

Ben regarded himself as newly cloaked. "*Must* I wear a shroud?"

"Shroud, sir?"

Ben smiled. "Ah, yes, quite so. 'Tis, in fact, not the gown that vexes but the coloration, the lack thereof, which state I have long held in disfavor for being ever reminding of the Puritan habit of mind."

Bartholomew made attempt toward placing the garland of roses upon Ben's head, but was foiled by a deft feint to one side.

"I should prefer," Ben said, firmly, "to bear no crown. Indeed, what crown borne upon one's head does not render the bearer into a statuary of his own making?"

Bartholomew bowed, and withdrawing from the chamber, soon returned in possession of a cap fashioned of the pelt of an unfortunate marten.

"O joy!" Ben erupted. "I had assumed that old rag and this old soul forever lost one to the other, likewise all memory of its previous tenant, like a son to me." Thereupon pulling Bartholomew into an embrace, Ben danced him full circle around, and pulling then the cap onto his own head, danced Clarence full circle around.

Upon Ben completing his enfevered demonstration of gratitude, Bartholomew lifted from his own neck a cord composed of one black strand intertwined with one white such. "There is one thing more," he said, showing Ben a striking pendant in likeness to a caduceus, one serpent being black of body, white in eye; the other serpent being white of body, black in eye. Bartholomew held the pendant toward Ben. "If you would be so kind, sir," he continued, "as to remove your dear pet from your head, a lady asks that I place this ornament around your neck, it only recently taken from her own, as a token of the regard in which she shall always hold you."

Ben shook his head. "I honor the gesture, sir, but I should prefer to bear no ornament. Indeed, what ornament is not a perilous weighting toward a slide unto vanity?"

"And what gift spurned of a stubborn righteousness, sir, is not the greater vanity?" Bartholomew held the pendant yet toward Ben.

Ben peered from Bartholomew to Clarence and back. "There is no besting either of you this day. I can only capitulate." Removing his cap, bowing his head, Ben allowed Bartholomew to lay the splendid pendant upon his neck.

Bartholomew thereupon took a step to backward. "Absolutely splendid," he declared.

"Most fitting," Clarence agreed.

Ben pulled his dear pet back onto his head.

Bartholomew, disappearing now through the doorway, soon reappeared holding in hand the garland of roses only recently removed by him, and placing this atop Ben's marten cap, took a step backward. "Absolutely perfect," he declared.

"Ineffably majestic," Clarence chimed.

Ben shook his head.

Bowing in unison now, Bartholomew and Clarence led Ben to the doorway, and stood at either side, betwixt a transom strikingly ebony, whilst Ben surveyed a chamber showing neither hue nor hint of either him or his history.

"What wiped slate," Clarence sang, "begs not to be writ upon anew?"

Ben held his eyes closed a moment, swallowed a small astringency from the back of his throat, and then followed Clarence and Bartholomew into a most remarkable corridor, which, oval in geometry, seemed a passageway through a vast ocean of ink. Underfoot, a checkerboard pavement was fashioned of white squares alternating with black, whilst to either side, and overtop, an infinitude of colorations flashed in and out of being in likeness indeed to a kaleidoscope showing yet no pattern but ever the possibility of such.

With Clarence leading, Bartholomew trailing, they soon arrived at a plain door, emerald green, before which stood a lone figure—indeed Alexander Wedderburn himself! Wedderburn bowing, Ben returned the gesture in kind, and discovered himself peering upon the kindly visage of the Great Sage, who spake thusly: "There is an awareness of self, good sir, I am required to remind you, only by facility of memory. Render one's memory to oblivion, render one's self to oblivion. The death you freely embrace, good sir, must of necessity be both total and irreversible. All knowledge of you by you shall be forever lost. Do you yet willingly proceed?"

Ben straightened. "I do."

The Sage bowed unto a generous declination.

Bowing unto equal measure, Ben discovered himself peering at the kindly countenance of Henry Ditweiller, and pulling his beloved friend

into a robust embrace, wept upon him most profusely. Unable thereupon to discover words appropriate to the occasion, Ben removed the
garland of roses from atop his cap and placed this crown upon Henry's
head.

"The circle is the only geometry," Henry said.

"No end, no beginning, no one point greater than any other," Ben
added.

"Forever has it been so, forever shall it be."

Henry bowing unto a generous declination, Ben bowed in equal
measure, and upon straightening himself, discovered Henry disappeared—indeed lost to him forever more.

Ben slumped.

Taking Ben by either arm, Clarence and Bartholomew led him
through the green door and into a large rectangular room, strikingly
emerald, the walls being wholly of this coloration, the carpet and
upholstery being agreeably accented of it. At the very middle of the
room lay a single green ball. At the very end stood a lone figure before
a plain door, sapphire blue—indeed the reverend William Smith himself! Smith bowing, Ben returned the gesture in kind, and thereupon
discovered himself peering at the kindly visage of the Great Teacher,
who spake thusly: "There is an awareness of self, good sir, I am required
to remind you, only by facility of memory. Render one's memory to
oblivion, render one's self to oblivion. The death you freely embrace,
good sir, must of necessity be both total and irreversible. All knowledge
of you by you shall be forever lost to you. Do you yet willingly proceed?"

Ben straightened. "I do."

The Great Teacher bowed unto a generous declination.

Bowing unto equal measure, Ben discovered himself peering at the
kindly countenance of Prescott Bahr, and pulling his beloved friend
into a robust embrace, wept upon him most profusely. Unable to discover words appropriate to the occasion, Ben removed the pendant
from his neck and placed this ornament upon Prescott's.

"The circle is the only geometry," Prescott said.

"No end, no beginning, no one point greater than any other," Ben
added.

"Forever has it been so, forever shall it be."

Prescott bowing unto a generous declination, Ben bowed unto equal
measure, and upon straightening himself, discovered Prescott disappeared—indeed lost to him forever more.

Ben slumped.

Taking Ben by either arm, Clarence and Bartholomew led him through the blue door and into a large oval room, strikingly sapphire, the walls being wholly of this coloration, the carpet and upholstery being agreeably accented of it. At the very middle of the room lay a single blue ball. At the very end stood a lone figure before a plain door, ruby red—indeed John Adams himself! Adams bowing, Ben returned the gesture in kind, and discovered himself peering upon the kindly visage of the Great Buddha, who spake thusly: "There is an awareness of self, good sir, I am required to remind you, only by facility of memory. Render one's memory to oblivion, render one's self to oblivion. The death you freely embrace, good sir, must of necessity be both total and irreversible. All knowledge of you by you shall be forever lost to you. Do you yet willingly proceed?"

Ben straightened. "I do."

The Buddha bowed unto a generous declination.

Bowing unto equal measure, Ben discovered himself peering upon the kindly countenance of TJ, and pulling his beloved friend into a robust embrace, wept upon him most profusely. Unable to discover words appropriate to the occasion, Ben removed the marten cap from his head and pulled this crown over TJ's head stocking.

"The circle is the only geometry," TJ said.

"No end, no beginning, no one point greater than any other," Ben added.

"Forever has it been so, forever shall it be."

TJ bowing unto a generous declination, Ben bowed unto equal measure, and upon straightening himself, discovered TJ disappeared— indeed lost to him forever more.

Ben slumped.

Taking Ben by either arm, Clarence and Bartholomew led him through the red door and into a large rectangular room, strikingly ruby, the walls being wholly of this coloration, the carpet and upholstery being agreeably accented of it. At the very middle of the room lay a single red ball. At the very end stood a plain door, strikingly white, whereat Clarence and Bartholomew turned unto Ben in simultaneity, one moving to clockwise, the other to counterclockwise, and revealed unto him wetted eyes, each one.

"No greater love," Clarence declared, bowing unto a perilous declination.

"The perfect gift," Bartholomew declared, bowing unto a perilous declination.

Ben bowed unto equal peril and discovered himself peering not upon his two beloved Intermediaries, but upon his beloved daughter Sally to one side, his beloved son William to the other. Ben embraced the one, the other, the one, the other, all the while hooting in similitude to an aborigine become newly acquainted with the magical powers of yeast.

Thereupon lowering himself unto both knees, Ben lifted his eyes unto Sally, she handsome in fancy ribbons and a homespun gown. "I am so very sorry," he declared.

Sally bowed. "What forgiveness in the seeking of it, dear father, is not ever the gaining of it?"

Ben looked upon William, he handsome in his royal finery. "I am so very sorry," he declared.

William bowed. "What forgiveness in the seeking of it, dear father, is not ever the gaining of it?"

Ben slumped well to forward, and closing his eyes—

Could hear the voices of children joyous upon his ears—

Smell the scent of honeysuckle sweet upon his olfactory—

Feel the radiance of a loving presence close upon his side—

Thereupon lifting his hand, it being wholly unencumbered, Ben rested it upon a diminutive other, warm to the touch, and heard a voice as if from close upon—

All that might have been, all that might yet be, all is in your hands, dear husband, there is no one else.

He wept.

Do you willingly proceed, sir?

He wept.

Do you willingly proceed, sir?

He wept.

Do you willingly proceed, sir?

Ben squeezed upon Deborah's hand, and feeling equal in return, answered: "I do."

Thereupon rising to his feet, Ben bowed toward whereat his beloved daughter had stood, and whereat his beloved son had stood. Turning half-circle around then, he entered into the very chamber of his examination, and approaching the vitreous circle, noticed, with a start, a familiar figure reposed upon the elevated seat to rightward. He called forth, "Are you left alone in this chamber, friend?"

"I am, sir."

"Is this your destiny?"

"It has been so."

"Of your own choosing?"

"Of necessity, sir."

"I am sorry to hear this."

"'Tis little trouble, sir, but I thank you for your concern."

"And I thank you, friend, for your wise counsel during the course of my examination. Though 'twas ever communicated in gesture, 'twas ever stentorian in effect."

"You are most welcome, sir."

"Fare thee well, friend."

"Fare thee well, sir." The clerk stood, and bowing near unto the horizontal plane, held fast unto that posture.

Ben bowed in return, and upon stepping onto the vitreous circle, was engulfed in a column of purist light, and beginning then to spin, in the clockwise direction, was soon regressed unto merest infancy—

Hospital of the University of Pennsylvania

June 17, 7:32 a.m.

Another thunderclap like a tossed bowling ball.

"Almost there," the doctor reported. "Just a few more pushes."

Uncle Tom grimaced to the exhaustion showing on D's face. How much could one person bear? Prescott dead. Her sister dead. Her nephew dead.

"You're doin' great," he said. He was about to wipe the perspiration from D's brow when another thunderclap, very close upon the heels of the previous one, seemed to shake the entire building. Unattached objects, particularly those on trays, rattled.

"That was close," the nurse said, her brown eyes made all the browner, it seemed, by the whiteness of her mask and the immediacy of her concern.

Something was different.

"Real close," Tom agreed, having no more stomach for thunder than he did for that goddamn overhead mirror that would reveal more than it ought if he were to allow it to.

"OK—push!" the doctor commanded.

Delmyra groaned as if against a bout of constipation nine months in the making.

"Here he comes!" the nurse exclaimed. "Can you see?"

Delmyra, looking now into the overhead mirror, nodded as she groaned, the exhaustion seeming to have all but evaporated from her face.

"One more," the doctor said. "Ready?—Push!"

Delmyra grimaced, groaned—

"Here he comes! Here he comes!" Tom exclaimed, looking up at the goddamn mirror. "Can you see? Holy"—

A flash—

᠊ᴥ᠊

581

He was sitting on the back of a motorcycle black as tar, his arms wrapped around the driver's studded belt.

They half-rode, half-slid down a slope of white-as-bone sand, and splashing into a curling, foaming surf, sputtered to a stop.

The driver rose in his seat such as to straddle it, stared for a moment toward a featureless horizon, and then turned around.

It was *him*!

Father to no son!

Son to no father!

Recoiling, he plunged into the water.

Sinking, he flailed—

His lungs about to burst, he looked up—

A light—

Soft—

A woman was peering down at him.

Something was tethered to his nose.

The woman was wearing a white coat embroidered on one side with red stitching.

"There was a terrible accident," she said. "We don't know for sure what happened. A lightning strike, we think." She paused. "We were able to save the baby—and you."

Tom closed his eyes. Swallowed.

Wept.

"Are you a relative?"

He could feel the snake stir deep within, like a worm in a fallen apple—

I need you to be there, Tom. For her. For me.
There's nobody else.

Tom peered up at a brownish stain on the ceiling, and turned his head toward the doctor. "Uncle," he whispered.

"Uncle Tom."

Supreme Celestial Court of Petitions

The clerk descended from his station, and stepping onto the vitreous circle, was engulfed in a column of purist white light. He beginning thereupon to spin, in the counterclockwise direction, he was soon transfigured into the form of a frail woman, one side of her face slackened—and thereupon, unto merest infancy.

Children's Hospital

3959 Broadway, New York, June 17th, 8:19 a.m.

Another thunderclap like a tossed bowling ball.

Annie—panting like an overheated border collie—looked to Margaret. "Where's Kevin?" Her voice was hoarse, barely a whisper. She resumed panting.

"He'll be here," Margaret whispered. "Try to stay focused."

"Your baby's about to crown," the doctor reported. "I'm going to ask you to push and then to hold. OK?"

Annie nodded.

"OK—push."

Annie grimaced, grunted.

"Here she comes!" Margaret exclaimed. "Can you see?"

Anne nodded toward the mirror.

"Hold!"

Annie—panting again—looked to Margaret. "How close?"

"Just another push or two."

"Where's Kevin?"

"He can't be more than minutes away. If there was a problem, I'm sure we would have heard from him again."

About to wipe perspiration from Anne's brow, Margaret jumped to a near-simultaneous flash of lightning and crack of thunder. A succession of ponderous booms immediately followed, the whole of Children's Hospital, down to its very foundation, seeming to shake to each boom. Unattached objects, particularly those on trays, rattled.

"That was real close," Cynthia, one of the nurses, said, her eyes like eggs simmering in a skillet.

"Real close," Bgurdee, the other nurse, agreed, in a lyrical accent.

Something was different.

"OK," the doctor said, "ready . . . push!"

Annie groaned as if against a bout of constipation nine months in the making.

"Here she comes!" Margaret exclaimed. "Can you see?"

"Kevin! Oh, Kevin!"

A figure—in the doorway—

A flash—

Three giant balls—one blue, one green, one red—were rolling directly toward him.

He turned.

Three giant balls—one blue-banded, one green-banded, one red-banded—were rolling directly at him.

He turned.

Three giant white balls were rolling directly toward him.

He turned.

Three giant black balls were rolling directly at him.

He turned—and turned.

All my pennies for a horse!

"Kevin! Oh, Kevin!"—

Too late! Too late!

"Mr. Kinney."

Kevin lifted his head. He was slumped on a couch, his neck stiff.

A woman, tiny, Indian, was standing next to him; someone larger, darker, was looming behind.

In the instant he was so filled with dread as not to be able to breathe. He remembered.

"We don't know what happened. A lightning strike, we think." The woman paused, her eyes anxious. "Your baby's fine." She paused, eyes reluctant. "Unfortunately, we were not able to save your wife. I'm so very sorry, sir. We did everything we could." She turned to the black woman, who was wearing a greenish frock, and upon taking a compact bundle into her tiny hands, offered it toward Kevin. "Your daughter, sir. She's perfectly fine. Whatever took the life of your wife had no apparent affect on her. We can't explain it." Her eyes filled. "I'm so very sorry, sir. We tried everything."

Kevin denied himself any response, even a twitch. Even the slightest hint of a reaction on his part would be to reify a horror he simply would not be able to bear. "Denial is our first line of defense," he could recall Dr. Pasternak, his shrink, telling him, "and very often, our only defense."

Looking now to a puckered, scowling face, like that of a shrunken old man, all but lost in the tight folds of a pink-and-blue blanket, Kevin reached up, and taking the offered bundle carefully into hands nearly as large as what they were about to accept, for all time, bowed his head—and sobbed.

"I'm so very sorry, sir."

A light touch was followed by a sensed retreat. When finally Kevin had exhausted himself, he kissed Bridget's—no, Annie's—wrinkled brow, and sensed a return of the previous presence.

He peered up at a kindly face and two soulful eyes. Rose.

"When can I take her home?"

"They'll want to keep her a day or two for observation." Rose winked. "I won't be lettin' 'em keep her any longer than that, though, OK? Shall I take her now?"

Kevin kissed Annie's wrinkled brow, and then gave her over to Rose.

"Can I call anyone for you, Mr. Kinney?"

Kevin shook his head.

Rose—swaying in an easy rhythm—smiled on the puckered face. "What's her name?"

"Annie. It was going to be Bridget, but now it's going to be Annie."

"Your wife's name?"

Kevin nodded, and beginning to weep, choked himself silent.

"Y'know, sir—none o' my business—but now that I get a good look at your beautiful daughter, she looks a lot more like a Bridget to me. Y'know how that is?"

Kevin peered up at Rose, and nodded. "You're right. Thank you."

"I'm so very sorry, sir."

Beginning again to weep, Kevin choked himself silent. "Was anyone else—?"

"Your doula was pretty bad struck. They took her to the ICU. I'm not sure o' her condition. They was able to resuscitate her, though—all to the good."

Kevin nodded.

"I can check on her for ya if y'd like."

Kevin nodded. "Please."

"I'll come right back down, OK?"

Kevin nodded.

"You sure there's no one I can call for you, Mr. Kinney?"

Kevin nodded.

"God bless you, sir."

"Thank you. And thank you for 'none o' my business.'"

Rose smiled. "I'll be right back."

Rose carried Bridget to the farther side of the room, and entering the middle elevator there, smiled toward Kevin as the doors closed—

Leaving him alone.

More alone than he had ever been before in his—

Beginning to moan, Kevin shook his head, and reaching for his cell phone, found it missing from its marsupial pouch. Surging to his feet, he searched his pockets, and found himself holding that strange artifact he had come into possession of exactly nine months ago, to the day, and had been carrying around with him ever since—why, he had no idea.

Denied his phone, which he had left in the limo, he was sure, Kevin made his way to one of two Verizon stations attached to the wall to his right. Laying the old three-penny nail on the tray, he placed a call, from memory, using his credit card.

Gilbert's voice came on the line almost immediately, absent the usual familiarity, he having no way of telling, by the usual means, who was calling him on a private number known only to a handful of people.

"The Boston trip was a complete success."	Gilbert was sitting at his desk, a mug of coffee close at hand. "Tiny Tim?"
"God bless us everyone."	"Good boy. Where you calling from?"
"A pay phone." Kevin switched the receiver to his other hand and picked up the three-penny nail from the tray.	"Is that wise?" Gilbert switched his cell phone to his other hand and picked up a silver pennywhistle from his desk.
"Probably not. Nothing I've done in the past ten years has been particularly wise."	Gilbert stiffened. "What are you saying?"
"I'm done. I'm out. Things have changed. *Everything* has changed."	Gilbert jabbed his desk with one end of the pennywhistle. "*What's* changed? What are you talking about?"
"Annie's dead."	"What? My God—what happened?"

"They don't know what happened. She's dead."

"Where are you?"

"I'm in fucking hell. Can't you fucking tell?"

"Look, Kevin—Tim—you've had a shock. These things happen. You've got to be strong. This is a test. It's no time to be making any decisions."

"She's fine."

"What? *Who's* fine?"

"My daughter. My life." He hung up.

"Kevin!" Gilbert jumped to his feet, and pitching the pennywhistle against the wall, smashed his desk with both fists, spilling his coffee.

Kevin was about to sit back down when one of the elevators opened and Rose stepped out, smiling. "Good news, Mr. Kinney." Each approached the other. "Ms. Caffry is conscious. She's still listed as critical, but that's routine in cases like hers. I told the charge nurse to let Ms. Caffry know you was asking for her. Now, as to you, sir, you should *not* be alone. I want to know who I can call for you."

Kevin held the three-penny nail up, pinched between two fingers. "Do you think it'd be OK if I left this somewhere near Bridget?"

Rose smiled. "I'll ask the tooth fairy." She winked. "I'm sure there's something she can do." Kevin gave the nail over to Rose, who slipped it into a side pocket on her frock. "Now, who can I call for you?"

Kevin averted his eyes, and shaking his head, began to weep.

Rose pulled him into arms like a fortress.

The White House

September 17th, 5:35 a.m.

Gilbert reached for his portfolio, and not encountering it, realized he had left it at his condo. In his rush, and fog—there had been no time for coffee—he had slipped out of his routine. Climbing from his seat, he scowled toward George, who was holding an umbrella in one hand, the car door with the other. He shivered.

He had also forgotten his coat.

A cold rain had been falling since at least 4:36 a.m., when Gilbert's bedside phone had interrupted a dream in which Gilbert was wearing only a T-shirt, out in the open, and there was no place to hide.

"The President wants you in the Oval ASAP," Teresa had said, her voice uncharacteristically clipped.

Gilbert hurried toward the foyer entrance, head down, accompanied by Malcolm holding an umbrella over his head. Shedding his minder at the guard station, Gilbert passed through the hall gallery and found the main lobby empty, as would be expected at such an ungodly hour. The day's newspapers, however, had already been distributed among the tables.

Instead of bearing right, toward his office, Gilbert bore left, passed though the doorway opposite the one he would normally take, and walking briskly past the Roosevelt Room, turned right, and hurried down the crimson-carpeted corridor to Teresa's office. Finding the door open, he entered.

Teresa looked up without pausing from her typing and greeted Gilbert with a look both unexpected and disquieting; it reminded him of the look on his mother's face the morning after she received an anonymous call concerning a certain Brookline address being frequented by her husband.

Noticing that the door to the Oval Office was closed, Gilbert felt an unfamiliar disquietude turn into a more familiar, and comfortable indignation. Not once in the past five years had the door to the Oval been closed upon his arriving for a meeting with the President.

Not once!

Teresa got up from her desk, and upon rapping twice on the closed door, cracked it open. Gilbert could see the President, talking on one of his phones, hold a finger up to Teresa.

Teresa closed the door and turned to Gilbert. "He'll be just a minute."

What the hell's going on? Gilbert wanted to ask, but, of course, did not.

Teresa returned to her desk. "You may take a seat if you wish, Mr. Bahr."

Take a seat? Why the hell would he want to do that?

Teresa fixed her eyes to the left of her screen and resumed typing.

"Extra-early start this morning, eh?"

Teresa lifted her eyes toward Gilbert, and showing him a smile that had not yet had its morning coffee, looked back to her work.

You wouldn't have that job without me; you know that?

Suddenly aware of the absence of his portfolio, the gravitas of it, Gilbert folded his arms across his chest, then unfolded them, then folded them, then unfolded them, then sat down in one of the chairs arranged between the door and the desk occupied, during "normal" hours, by Stephanie Blanchard, the President's personal assistant.

Several newspapers were neatly arranged on a table to Gilbert's left. Shuffling through these now, Gilbert found the sports section of the *Post*, and turning to the box scores, winced.

The Sox had lost to the Indians, 4–3 in thirteen innings.

Gilbert startled to Teresa's phone ringing.

Teresa answered and then looked to Gilbert. "You may go in now, Mr. Bahr."

Gilbert waited for Teresa to open the door. Striding briskly then into the Oval, he was surprised to find not the President waiting for him, but Director McGonagall, alone.

"Morning, Gil."

Teresa closed the door.

"Morning, Stan."

Where's the President? Gilbert wanted to ask, but of course did not.

"What's up?" Gilbert asked, in a voice innocent of all anxiety.

Director McGonagall gestured toward the fireplace, which was casting a homey glow. Seeing nothing noteworthy about this—Roy Peoples almost always lit the fireplace on chilly mornings—Gilbert lifted his eyes, and flinched to discover the Duplessis portrait of Franklin replaced by an odd landscape, gloomily dark, that seemed to feature a luminously white basketball net attached to a bent and broken hoop.

"You will find the artist's signature in the lower left-hand corner."

Gilbert navigated around the sitting area to the fireplace, and pushing his bifocals back on his nose, finger to bridge, uplifted his head to find the inscription.

A modest script was so dark in tone as to be almost indistinguishable from the background.

Gilbert moved closer.

H. Prescott Bahr.

"Do you have a son, sir?"

217 South 47th Street, Philadelphia, PA

September 22nd, 5:44 a.m.

He was in a field of tall grass, every direction like every other. Although the moon was full, it was directly overhead, and therefore no compass. Although a breeze was blowing, it was ever shifting, and therefore no compass.

The cry had come from his left—

Searching in that direction, he heard it from behind—

Searching in this direction, he heard it from his left—

Searching in that direction, he heard it from behind—

Searching in this direction, he heard it from his left—

Growing ever more desperate, he searched ever more frantically, until, exhausted, he found himself peering up at a luminous wafer encircled as if of a diffusion of itself.

Awakening with a start, to an indignant squalling—where the hell are you?—Tom jerked his head up from his pillow, and peeling back the covers, swung his legs over the side of the bed. Retrieving his flashlight from the floor, he shined it on the bedstand clock.

It had been less than three hours since Richard's last feeding.

A bottomless pit, this one.

Heaving himself to his feet, Tom shuffled to Richard's crib, and insinuating one hand under the infant's head, the other hand under his padded bottom, lifted thirteen pounds of total dependency into the cradle of his arms.

The squalling ceased.

Kissing Richard's forehead, as if of reflex, Tom pulled a bottle of formula from the mini-fridge, and while this was warming in the microwave, changed Richard's diaper. Carrying infant and bottle then to D's wicker rocker, poised at the ready by the window, Tom eased himself into it, and touching Richard's lips with the nipple, rocked gently as Richard tugged a few times on the nipple, stopped, tugged a few times, stopped—tugged a few times—

The shade being bordered now with the heralding glow of a new day, Tom paused to raise it, and peering across the street, saw not a school building but an Arthurian castle in which young men were blessed into a beneficent knighthood.

Resuming rocking, Tom closed his eyes to a gentle tug-tug on Richard's bottle—opened them—then closed them—

—and was trudging through a field of tall grass, an infant clutched to his chest. He was lost—but where was he going? He was late—but for what occasion? Suddenly coming upon a sheer cliff, and nearly plunging over this, he managed to regain balance. Taking a step backward, he could see a valley below and meandering through this, a river, like a giant serpent, and nestled into a fold of this serpent, a village, each house like every other house.

Rising from below came now the sound of bells, as if from a carillon, and thereupon, from the opposite direction, the voices of children.

Turning into the latter direction, he shouted a warning—"Stop! Stop!"—but the breeze swept his voice away like dust from a fallow field.

What to do? What to do?

If he unburdened himself of his ward, he might catch a child or two, but at what cost?

If he kept his ward clutched to his chest—

What to do? What to do?

The near grass now beginning to move, Tom held Richard fast to his chest, and dropping onto his knees—

Heard a thunderous pounding of hooves, the very ground quaking of it—

Heard a booming chorus of voices—"Halt!"—the very air stilling of it.

Opening his eyes, he found himself peering—

—at sunlight glinting off a window on the school building across the street.

A car door slammed. He looked toward the street directly below and saw a bright-green car double-parked. The car started to move and soon disappeared up the street.

Feeling Rosie rubbing against his leg, her "motor" running at "high rev," as Prescott would put it, Tom lunged from the rocker, and returning Richard to his crib, bunched blankets at either side of him. Following Rosie downstairs, her tail at full periscope, Tom found a large envelope laying on the floor under the mail slot.

Setting the envelope on the stairs, he went into the kitchen and fixed Rosie's breakfast. He fixed himself a mug of java and then carried mug in one hand, envelope in the other, up to the bedroom. He looked in on Richard, fast asleep, and then set the mug down on the windowsill and eased himself into D's rocker. He rested his head against the high back, and closing his eyes, took a deep breath.

He was exhausted.

After a moment, he unfastened the large envelope and slipped out a handwritten note clipped to several other sheets, and then slipped out a smaller envelope. The note was written on UPenn letterhead. Opening the smaller envelope, Tom slipped out several photographs, the identifying surnames on the backsides being mostly Jordans and Thompsons.

Setting the two envelopes on the floor, Tom took a cautious sip of coffee, and then began to read the handwritten note:

Dear Mr. Mayback,

I'm sending you the enclosed materials not knowing who else to send them to. They concern a study I'm doing that Delmyra volunteered to participate in. I wrote the attached letter to her in June to report some of my findings, but then did not send it when I learned of her untimely death. I'm so very sorry I did not get in touch with her sooner. Anyway, if you don't mind, I'm going to leave it up to you to decide what to do with these materials. I tried to contact Delmyra's sister in Boston, but learned, sadly, that she also had died. Some gang members, I'm told, tortured her in trying to make her give up her son. This is truly a troubled world we live in.

Please contact me if you have any questions, or if you'd like to get in touch with Ms. Olivia Pruitt (see attached letter).

Sincerely,
Denise Tolman

Tom unbound the clipped sheets, and slipping the top sheet to the bottom, took another sip of coffee. He began then to read Denise's careful script.

Dear Delmyra,

I'm sorry it's taken me so long to get back in touch with you. Thank you again for entrusting me with your family photos. Those, together with the family tree you put together (thank you for going to all the trouble of doing that) have been a big help.

As you know, my study involves tracing AA lineages as far back as circumstances will allow. It's been a hard slog! In your case, it was particularly hard on your father's side. In general, though, once I got down to the time of the Civil War (if I was lucky enough to get that far) I'd pretty much hit a wall. This was true whether I was tracking a 'high yellow' line or a 'dark skin' line. Of course, this wasn't unexpected. In fact, it was the exceptions I was after. If a line traced farther back than the Civil War, then there had to be a reason for this. Skin tone? Geography? Demographics? Dumb luck? What?

I'm still compiling my findings, but I wanted to give you a preliminary report because of a discovery I recently made that I thought you would be particularly interested in, especially in light of recent events in your life (Givvy has been keeping me posted. I'm so very sorry about Prescott).

I also wanted to get your personal items back to you. I apologize for keeping them so long. Having never before engaged in anything like what I've gotten myself into with this project, I simply had no idea just how much time would be involved. Wow!

Anyway, I was hitting dead end after dead end in your case, as I had in the cases of several others (the risk of a small sampling), and was about to throw in the towel (my meager travel budget was about shot) when I decided, on a hunch, to follow a distant cousin of yours, Jacob Blackburn, and his wife Abigail, from Charleston down to Montgomery. The Blackburns, both schoolteachers, moved to Montgomery in the spring of 1873, with their seven children, to run a post-Reconstruction school down there. (The school they ran, by the way, was twice burned to the ground, the second time with Abigail inside. I was able to locate the exact place where it last stood. There's a liquor store there now.)

In Montgomery, the trail got complicated in a hurry, of course, with the one line dividing into seven, but one of these secondary lines (Henry, the eldest son's line) ultimately led me to a little white house on Burton Street, not far from the Alabama State University campus, where I found a 91-year-old retired 4th-grade teacher named Olivia Blackburn Pruitt, and in her possession—

Rosie jumped into Tom's lap, turned three-quarters around, lay down with her head toward Tom, and began to purr.

Holding Denise's note a little higher, Tom continued—

. . . and in her possession, a leather-bound diary kept in the late 18th century by a woman named Jane, who just happens to be Olivia's great-great-great grandmother, and therefore, as it turns out, your great-great-great-great-great grandmother!

Tears erupted. From nowhere. A gush.

Rosie lifted her head and placing a paw on Tom's chest peered up at him.

"Where the hell did that come from, girl, eh? Jesus Christ."

Tom wiped his eyes, and then continued on. Rosie resettled herself.

Olivia's diary is apparently one of seven kept by Jane over a span of thirteen years (she died in childbirth at age 26). All seven were kept together through succeeding generations, according to Olivia, until they passed into the possession of Jacob Blackburn, who divided them among his seven children. Olivia's diary, the oldest of the seven, came to her through Jacob's eldest son, Henry. Lore has it, according to Olivia, that Jacob distributed the diaries to his children after his wife was burned to death in the school they ran together. One can imagine he wanted to increase the likelihood of at least one of Jane's diaries surviving into perpetuity. (By the way, Olivia claims to know where two of the other diaries are, including the very last one kept. I have not had time to track these down, but perhaps you will want to do this yourself.)

Interestingly, the first entry in Jane's first diary, made on February 4, 1793, Jane's 13th birthday, goes on for several pages. One might suppose this young lady was just a-bustin' to get things down on paper! (I never appreciated just how important permanent family records were until I got into this study.) Jane begins by expressing her gratitude toward "Miss Elizabeth" (daughter of her mistress) for the gift of the diary, goes on to mention the current weather conditions ("uncomon chil"), and then, to our very good fortune, launches into bringing us up to date as regards her family history, to the extent she knew it. You'll be able to read all this for yourself, of course (Olivia has invited you down to tea!), but I thought you might like a quick summary. Anyway, I'm just a-bustin' to give it to you!

Tom listened toward Richard's crib, took a sip of tepid coffee, massaged Rosie's ears, and continued—

According to Jane, her maternal grandfather, Justus (don't you just love it!), was purchased in Philadelphia sometime in the mid 1700s, when he was very young, and taken to South Carolina to work in the rice fields on a large plantation near Charleston. There is no mention of a mother or a father. Subsequently Justus had two sons and a daughter, by a woman named Sarah: Jacob, Justus, and Jericho. Just a few days after giving birth to Jericho, according to Jane, Sarah became ill while working in a field with Justus and her boys (apparently, judging from the details given, from a postpartum hemorrhage). She began to wander off, was judged insubordinate by her overseers, and brutally beaten. Her life was saved, according to Jane, by intervention of her elder son, Jacob, who rushed to her aid and took to himself the fatal blows that otherwise would have been inflicted on his mother. He was nine years old.

A few years later, when Jericho was not yet thirteen, according to Jane, one of the sons of the plantation owner forced Sarah to procure her daughter for him, and then made Sarah watch while he raped and impregnated her. When Sarah's remaining son, Justus, found out about the rape, he and two other young slaves tried to kill the son, but failed, and were hanged. The elder Justus subsequently went mad, Jane tells, and was pushed out to sea in a small skiff. Shortly thereafter Sarah swallowed a lethal dose of lye.

The plantation owner, Obadiah Barr, had two daughters and three sons, the eldest son, Nathan, being the one who raped Jericho. Nathan was eventually disowned by his father, according to Jane, following a series of other embarrassments, and was forced to change his name from Barr to Bahr (the "h" being, according to Jane, for "hell," as in "burn in"). Nathan Barr-become-Bahr went on to have other issue, but apparently under more conventional circumstances.

Although Nathan was essentially banished from the family fold, the issue from his rape, this being, of course, Jane herself, was given a privileged position within the household, was taught letters, and was eventually freed (on the very day, by the way, that Thomas Jefferson took his first oath of office). Shortly after her emancipation, Jane took on the name Barr as her own, as indeed it was.

Of course, at this point in my investigation, I had no choice but to follow up on the other spelling of the name, to see where it might lead, given your association with it. So I returned to Charleston (after begging a small supplement to my travel budget) and was able to trace there, in short order, through public records, a direct line from Nathan Barr-become-Bahr to his great-great-great-great-great-great-great grandson, Henry Prescott Bahr, through the lineage of one Samuel Bahr, and to Nathan's great-great-great-great-great-great-great granddaughter, Delmyra (Barr) Jordan, through the lineage of one Jane Barr!

If ever a star-crossed child were to be born into this crazy, mixed-up world of ours, he has to be the one about to be born to Delmyra Barr Jordan Bahr and Henry Prescott Barr-become-Bahr!

Feeling his skin tingle his body over, Tom looked to Prescott's painting of the white wicker rocker, hanging over Richard's crib, the very rocker he was sitting in, the very one Delmyra had been rocked in, the very one Delmyra's mother had been rocked in.

A flash—

One of the windows above the school entrance had become mirror to the rising sun, and was so intensely incandescent in the moment as to render WEST PHILADELPHIA HIGH SCHOOL invisible on the lintel over the massive entryway.

On the sidewalk below, nearby the steps converging on the grand entryway, two boys were bullying a third with taunts and jabs that could be resisted, Tom well knew, only at great personal risk.

Heaving himself from the rocker, Tom lifted the window sash to maximum height, and protruding his torso through the void, shouted in a clarion baritone: "Yo! You two chickenshits . . ."

The two bullies looked up at Tom.

"Get yo muthfuckin' asses inta that building—*now!*"

One bully and then the other saluted Tom with an uplifted middle finger.

Tom withdrew from the window, and gathering his flashlight from the floor near the bedstand, again protruded himself through the window. He aimed the flashlight toward the two bullies.

A flash, and another, and the two bullies ran up the steps and disappeared into the school.

The third boy gestured now as if to high-five a phantom counterpart.

Tom returned the gesture in kind, and then pointed toward the school entrance. "You get your ass in there, too. I'm gonna be watchin' from now on, got it?"

The boy stiffened, saluted, and running up the steps, disappeared into King Arthur's castle.

Two hours and thirteen minutes later, Uncle Tom was on the phone with Olivia Blackburn Pruitt.

Corner of Washington & School Streets

Boston, MA, January 17th, 9:13 a.m.

Sergeant Kortright paused from shifting foot to foot long enough to offer a daisy tied with a bright green ribbon to an approaching gentleman wearing a heavy coat and carrying a valise. The gentleman passed by without making eye contact, shaking his head.

Shuddering to another assault of what felt like needles of ice on his bare hands and face, Sarg heard what sounded like the warble of some shitbreath ratcheting up his story for maximum effect.

Or was what he was hearing in fact the wind carrying full circle his own yodels of woe?

Lord knew he had cause. His business had been falling off even before the prez's impeachment and had reached the point now where he was moving less than half his peak volume.

So far today he'd moved only three stems. Normally he would have moved three times that.

He'd thought long and hard about trying to find a better corner—but where?

The recession wasn't just here and there; it was everywhere.

He'd thought long and hard about trying to find a better line of work—but what?

He didn't have this or that to offer; he had *nothing* to offer.

Shuddering to another assault of ice needles, Sarg pictured himself collapsing to the pavement and hitting his head just hard enough on the curb to produce a puddle of blood.

They'd have to take him in and keep him overnight.

But then what?

The warbling being closer now, Sarg was able to make out some of the words—and by God fill in the rest!

I'd sing it in the morning
I'd sing it in the evening
All over this land

The warbler was standing conspicuous as a dandelion in December, cattycorner at the top of Milk Street, waiting to cross over Washington. She was wearing a flaxen pigtail on either side of her head, one tied with a bright red ribbon, the other tied with a bright blue ribbon, and was holding in both hands a carpet bag showing every color of the rainbow and then some.

His eyes flooding, Sarg joined in—

I'd sing out danger
I'd sing out a warning
I'd sing out love between my brothers and my sisters—

AND THERE'S AN END ON IT.

Acknowledgments

THE AUTHOR WISHES TO THANK the following Barkis-be-willings for their generous contributions to *Poor Richard's Lament*:

Claude-Anne Lopez, author of *The Private Franklin* and *Mon Chér Papa*; Roy E. Goodman, Curator of Printed Materials, the American Philosophical Society; Michael Zuckerman, PhD, Department of History, the University of Pennsylvania; Ralph Archbold, "Ben Franklin"; Nancy Mullen, Steve Grabbert, Michael Malardo, Sandy Hamlin, and the students of Hope High School, Providence, RI; Nicole Bahnan, Pamela Hilton, Samantha Dawson, Mister François, Candice Anderson, Dinora Walcott, and the students of Boston Community Leadership Academy, Boston, MA; Kate Ohno, Assistant Editor, *The Papers of Ben Franklin*, Yale University; Anna Rose Childress and Donna Simpson, the Addiction Treatment Research Center, Philadelphia; Sindha Ramchandren, MD, Myrna R. Rosenfeld, MD, PhD, and Nathalie Maulin, MD, Department of Neurology, the Hospital of the University of Pennsylvania; Rebecca Harmon and Olivia Fermano, Department of Public Affairs, the Hospital of the University of Pennsylvania; Stephanie Abbuhl, MD, Department of Emergency Medicine, the Hospital of the University of Pennsylvania.

Also Meghan Dubyak, Department of Homeless Services, New York; Neville Hughes and Clyde Kuemmerle, Holy Apostles soup kitchen, New York; Sonia, Paula, and "Poor Richard," the streets of New York; Ella Jenness, St. Paul's Chapel, New York; Joan M. Reid, "Ben Franklin's House," 36 Craven Street, London; Alex Kotlowitz, author of *There Are No Children Here*; Gary B. Nash, the University of California at Los Angeles; Bob Travis and Andrew Gully, *The Boston Herald*; Evan Shu and Julia Johnston, Old South Meeting House Museum, Boston; Shelly Clark, the Waldorf Astoria; "Librarian 1," the New York Public Library; Melanie Bower, the Museum of the City of New York; Reuben Jackson, the National Museum of American History; Joan Vanhammond; and Carmelita Kingsley.

Also Karen King, Nancy Gordon, Janel Leacock, and Sylvia Witherspoon, Children's Services, Inc., West Philadelphia; Pat DiDomenic, West Philadelphia; Harry Rubenstein, the National Museum of American History; Michael Gullison, Pease & Curren, Inc., Warwick, RI; Corrie Hobin, Carleton University, Ottawa; Jessie Kahn Duve; Donald U. Smith, Christ Church Preservation Trust; Bernard A. Wolf, MD; Abby Holcolm, Columbia Medical Center; Diane Cappelletti, Labor and Delivery Unit, the Hospital of the University of Pennsylvania; Betty Vohr, MD, Brown University; Jennifer Silva and JoAnn Tillinghast, Women and Infants Hospital, RI; Katherine Marusin, Senator Lincoln Chaffee's Office; and Abby Holcolm and Francilla Thomas, Morgan Stanley Children's Hospital of New York.

To my reviewers (Joshua Sandeman; Matt, Sean, and Laurie Fitzgerald; Linda Watts Jackim; Tom Gidley; Sam McGregor; Marcia Goodnow; the Walnut Creek Book Club; Jeremy Katz; Dori Hale; and Lew Treistman), and to my copyeditors (Tiffany Shiebler Mottet, Susan Hunziker, and Gregory Teague), a special thank you.

To Sid Hall and Amy Wood at Hobblebush Books, who not only took me in but gave me a place by the fire, an extra special thank you.

To Laurie, the goddess from whom I derive what divinity I might, an extra-extra special thank you.

To Michael Zuckerman, who charged over the hill, bugle blaring, just when all seemed lost, an extra-extra-extra special thank you.

Kiss-kiss.

Mon Chér Papa:

You combine the kindest heart with the soundest moral teaching, a lively imagination, and that droll roguishness which shows that the wisest of men allows his wisdom to be perpetually broken against the rocks of femininity.

MADAME BRILLON TO B. FRANKLIN
December 15, 1779

Mars Ascendant ♀, Venus in Conjunction ♂:
The wisdom of men, the rocks of femininity

Industry
Uninformed by imagination, industry follows but recipe;
Uninstructed by soul, it serves but appetite.

Frugality
'Tis one of the great ironies of understanding that frugality should reward so profligately.

Resolution
Better a back without spine than a promise without resolution.

Order
Whilst order is the genie of all efficiency, 'tis the hobgoblin of all creativity.

Cleanliness
As bee is lured by scentliness, butterfly by bloom,
so patron is lured by cleanliness, companion by groom.

Silence
No great idea was ever divined but in a cathedral of silence.

Chastity
Chaste in creed; pure in deed.

Sincerity
Naught fills a shop so readily as sincerity, empties it so utterly as falsity.

Temperance
Temperance is a cake cut into eighths, partaken in half as much.

Justice
Justice and heaven are whatever in circumstance we need them to be.

Tranquility
Calm seas without, tranquility of bowel; calm seas within, tranquility of soul.

Moderation
Moderation and a dampened stove give heat the winter through.

Humility
Humility is the last lesson learnt, the first forgot.

All that might have been,
all that might yet be,
all is in your hands, dear reader;
there is no one else.

Venus Ascendant ♀, Mars in Conjunction ♂:
The wisdom of women, the rocks of masculinity

Compassion
Commandment is the rule without the gold; compassion, the gold without the rule.

Empathy
Empathy is that facility of character by which we might become worthy of the miracle of our existence.

Forgiveness
To begin to understand the injurer is to begin to forgive the injury.

Sacrifice
Charity is what we can afford to give; sacrifice, what we cannot.

Reverence
True reverence is kneeling before the divinity of a cockroach.

Generosity
Generosity is your wallet a'ready in hand whilst your companion yet fumbles for his.

Contrition
Contrition is regret leavened of humility.

Forbearance
To smile upon one's own faults is to wink upon those of others.

Nurturance
Nurturance is what parents do in imitation of what was done to them, or in spite of it.

Fairness
Fairness is the vaccine against that which justice can only pretend to be the cure.

Loyalty
There are a thousand shades of loyalty; but one of betrayal.

Tolerance
Tolerance is allowing our eyes sufficient time in which to adjust to the dark.

Trust
Trust reaps good fruit or bad in accordance with the good sense or bad with which it is cultivated.

Though the hour is late, yet still there is time.

No problem.

Last Word

O, ye so certain—
mute thy self!

O, ye so reticent—
speak up!—
insist!

O, ye so mighty—
sit thy self!

O, ye so demure—
stand up!—
persist!

F. W. PEOPLES,
W. Phil., PA

Cast of Characters

Dunleavy, Carrie   President Kinney's appointments secretary.

Dunleavy, George A.   President of the U.S. Chamber of Commerce.

Ellis, Mister   The absent history teacher at Boston High School for whom Ben and Henry Ditweiller serve as substitute.

Fiske, Thomas Edward   Director of the CIA.

Fremont, Ellie Mae   Single mother of eight children in West Philadelphia.

Fremont, Jamal   Twelve-year-old son of Ellie Mae Fremont.

Gutierrez, Teresa   President Kinney's secretary.

Hakeem   Livery driver for Holy Apostles Church.

Jacob   Nine-year-old son of Justus and Sarah. Seven-year-old son is named Justus. Daughter is named Jericho.

Jimmy   Guard at *The Boston Courant*.

Justus (senior)   Slave of Obadiah Barr. Father of Jacob, Justus junior, and Jericho.

Jamaican gentleman   Meals director at Holy Apostles soup kitchen.

Johnson, Paul A.   CEO, Harris Upshaw & Co., New York.

Jordan, Delmyra   African-American social worker in West Philadelphia; Gilbert Bahr's significant other.

Jordan, Tyrone (TJ)   Delmyra Jordan's seventeen-year-old nephew; student at Boston High School; witness to a gang murder.

Katharine Fraley Bahr   Prescott Bahr's mother.

Kenyon, Paul   Democratic candidate for President. Ordained UCC minister and former pastoral counselor at a church in Eugene, Oregon.

Kinney, Anne   Kevin Kinney's wife.

Kinney, James Michael   Republican President of the U.S.

Kinney, Kevin   President Kinney's thirty-year-old son. Member of a New York law firm.

Kinney, Maggie   President Kinney's wife. A mezzo-soprano; studied music at Eastman School.

Kinney, Tess and Tonya   President Kinney's daughters. See Kevin Kinney.

Kortright, Sarg (Sergeant)   A panhandler (Vietnam vet) who works the corner of Washington and School Streets in Boston.

Lewis, Mary Ellen   Prescott Bahr's boss at the UPenn Treatment Research Center (TRC).

Lily   President Kinney's golden retriever.

Lynch, Brian   Reporter at *The Boston Courant*. See Lucy Myers.

Mayback, Thomas Drummond (Uncle Tom)	West Philadelphia drug dealer; was Prescott Bahr's supplier.
McGonagall, Stanley	Director of the CIA (Tom Fiske's replacement).
Medwick, Kimberly-Ann	College classmate of Prescott Bahr (a closet poet).
Myers, Lucy	Director, Team Blue, Strategic Marketing Division, Ambrose Augustine & Co., Brian Lynch's "partner."
Peoples, Frank	West Philadelphia drug addict; brother of Roy Peoples.
Peoples, Roy	Oval Office morning steward.
Popkin, Barry	Research assistant at the UPenn Treatment Research Center (TRC).
Rankin, Ken	White House Secret Service agent.
Rose	Nurse at Morgan Stanley Children's Hospital.
Rosen, Dr. Alvin B.	A neurologist at the Hospital of the University of Pennsylvania (HUP).
Rubin, Dr. Julia A.	Attending physician in the ER at the Hospital of the University of Pennsylvania.
Scheetz, Rodney (Roddy)	Former crack addict; currently in a treatment program at the UPenn Treatment Research Center (TRC).
Shaunta, Quinton, Sabrina, Rafael, Daryl	Students in Mr. Ellis's history class at Boston High.
Sibbowicz, Cynthia A.	Passenger on the #4 train to Brooklyn from Manhattan.
Sibley, J. Fredrick	Dean of Students at Prescott's college.
Spidahman	Long-legged "corner man" who frequents Holy Apostles soup kitchen.
St. James, Courtney	A worker for the Paul Kenyon presidential campaign.
Steinfels, Callie	Kevin Kinney's assistant.
Stern, Morrie	President Kinney's chief of staff.
Thompson, Avery	Director of 47th Street Shelter in West Philadelphia.
Tingly, Bernice (Bernie)	Gilbert Bahr's secretary.
Tolman, Denise	A graduate student in sociology at UPenn; conducting an ethnological study regarding skin tone.
Vander Jagt, Jeremy	College classmate of Prescott Bahr (a closet philosopher).